Further praise for *Pinkerton's Sister*

'Unforgettable' A.S. Byatt

'A treasure trove of a novel, complex, rich and satisfying' Susan Hill

'A wonderfully weird and enjoyable novel . . . Funny and original, disturbing beneath its witty surface' *Spectator*, Books of the Year

'A magnificent achievement . . . Alice's sad life story makes a subtle, polished novel, a monument to Peter Rushforth's perseverance and well worth the long wait' *Sunday Telegraph*

'The prose is as light as thistledown and gives you that priceless impression of being read to, rather than having to expend any effort in reading . . . Rushforth perfectly captures Alice's knowing madness' *Daily Express*

From the very first paragraph of this richly textured, highly literary and musical novel I found myself absorbed into a bizarre and unsettling world, utterly unlike anything I have read' *Independent*

'Quite exceptional, a fine rendering of the confusions and flippancies, the idiocies, the desires and disgusts and self-loathings that a life of reading can produce . . . a book as enthralling and as curious in its many extraordinary jaunts as, say, Tess memorably walking through the fields with the cuckoo-spittle on her skirt, crunching the snails underfoot' *Guardian*

Peter Rushforth was brought up and went to school in Leeds. His first novel, *Kindergarten*, won the Hawthornden Prize. His second novel, *Pinkerton's Sister*, twenty-five years in the writing, was published to huge critical acclaim. Peter Rushforth died in September 2005, just after finishing *A Dead Language*.

A DEAD LANGUAGE

Peter Rushforth

**POCKET
BOOKS**

LONDON • SYDNEY • NEW YORK • TORONTO

First published in Great Britain by Simon & Schuster UK Ltd, 2006
First published by Pocket Books, 2007
An imprint of Simon & Schuster UK Ltd
A CBS COMPANY

A CIP catalogue record for this book is available from the British Library

This book is a work of fiction. Names, characters, places and incidents are
either a product of the author's imagination or are used fictitiously. Any resemblence
to actual people living or dead, events and locales is entirely coincidental.

ISBN: 978-1-4165-2626-1

Typeset in Fournier by M Rules
Printed and bound in Great Britain by
Cox & Wyman Ltd, Reading, Berks

This is for
Paul Barton

1. *Quis amat?*   Who loves?
   Pater.   The father.

2. *Quem amat?*   Who does he love?
   Filium.   (His) son.

3. *Quid agit pater?*   What is it the father does?
   Amat filium.   He loves his son.

Short Exercises in Latin Prose Composition
and Examination Papers in Latin Grammar
Revd Henry Belcher
(1874)

His name was Sorrow.

His mother killed herself when he was two years old, but that was not why he had been given this name. It was the name he had always had, the name she had given him, and she had called him this because his father had gone away and left her before he was born. His father was a foreigner who did not know that his son existed, and he had gone back home to America three years previously. When he returned to Japan he had a new bride, a real American wife, and that was when Sorrow's mother had committed suicide, as if unable to bear the shame of abandonment. Her name had been Butterfly, an oddly embarrassing, doll-like name, and when Sorrow remembered her – he did, for a little while, glimpses from the corner of his eye when he was thinking of other things – he thought of her in terms of this brightly colored insect: the fluttering hands and fans blurring with an animatedly wings-like susurration, a pale powdered face with the faint luminosity of a moth at twilight, the lazy swirl of drifting gorgeous kimonos. You had to hold a butterfly very carefully, your two hands hollowed around it to create a little space that would not crush it. You would feel the ticklish wings, hear the faint frantic beating like something struggling for breath. If you touched it the dust would come away upon you – pollen-like powder in the whorls and ridges of your fingertips (the tainted hands disquietingly like the evidence of a crime) – and the butterfly would die. So might you – he had been told – because such dust was poisonous, blinding you if it was rubbed into your eyes, suffocating you if it was inhaled.

Great Uncle Eugene had collected butterflies, just as he had later hunted for big game and Red Indians, generally employing the same vocabulary when he described a particular triumph over one or the other. Whether it was butterflies, or big game, or Red Indians, the real pleasure had come with the killing. On the dark walls of his house, amongst the stuffed heads of the big game, and the photographs of the Red Indians (Great Uncle Eugene didn't bother to conceal his sense of grievance at not being allowed to display stuffed Red Indian heads), there were the glass-covered cases of butterflies, laid out in rows with pins stuck through their abdomens, each species identified in bad-tempered crabbed handwriting on the backs of old *cartes-de-visite*. He probably killed two birds with one stone (here was an expression that would have appealed to Great Uncle Eugene) by making sure that the points of the pins, after satisfactorily crunching through the insect corpses, went right through the heads of the chosen people in the photographs. There'd be nothing random about the way he would do it. He would strike home like Mrs. Albert Comstock pinning a vast brooch to her landscape of a bosom, and the pins would penetrate eyes, mouths, and ears with surgical precision. He would listen eagerly for news of inexplicable crippling pains assailing recent visitors to the house (visitors who had failed to charm the watchful, restless, discontented child), hysterical maids screaming of masters and mistresses struck blind, struck dumb, struck deaf, like ill-fated witnesses to some fearful biblical excess. He was fully alert to the powers of the black arts. Mrs. Alexander Diddecott – though, at that time, still a Miss Barton – had developed her interest in the occult early, and had sought disciples with a missionary zeal that would have done credit to Dr. Vaniah Odom.

Sorrow (though this, by now, was no longer his name) visualized Great Uncle Eugene as a small boy (his beard shrunk to child-size to maintain the correct scale) in a white sailor-suit – like the one he himself possessed – in implacable pursuit of rare butterflies through Verbrugge or Heneacher Woods. (Most butterflies would be rare by the time *he'd* finished.) The net he bore aloft like some frantically signaling flag of surrender (a concept entirely alien to

Great Uncle Eugene) – pallid against the intense green of the trees – was as huge as a trawler's cramming in the fish off Cape Cod, and he was eager to capture vast swarms, emptying the air of all its color. This would be the prelude to the real pleasure: the killing bottles (the fluttering of the wings increasing desperately, then slowing, slowing, stopping, the little neatly combed beard reflected in the glass as he watched hungrily, missing nothing), and the – this was his favorite bit – insertion of the pins. He'd bend his little knees and bring his full weight to bear upon his applied and flat-squashed thumb, a lady of fashion inserting her best hatpin prior to venturing out for a walk in her biggest hat as the wind blew its fiercest, or a miniature strongman about to balance his whole body upon that single digit, slowly revolving like a muscled compass needle seeking magnetic north. What he would really like to have done – he'd decided was to insert the pins without making use of the killing bottle, to feel the doomed butterflies' attempts to escape, though there was a worrying risk of torn wings, damaged specimens. He'd need to do it really carefully. His observant parents – made pensive and anxious by his gleeful malevolence (a slightly protruding tongue, distinct symptoms of an increased pulse-rate) – had discreetly attempted to steer his interest toward what they naïvely imagined to be more innocent and boy-like pleasures: model boats, toy soldiers, that sort of thing, "Won't this be *fun*, Eugene?" they enthused. Eugene did not enthuse. Where was the *fun* in sailing model boats, even when you were so appropriately dressed for it? He'd destroyed all his boats in the Hudson, their sails ablaze, cramming them with his toy soldiers, their lead limbs melting and dripping into tortured postures before they sank. Well, yes – come to think of it – perhaps there had been some pleasure to be found in sailing model boats, after all, but now he had burned them all and had none left. He'd have to find some new source of fun. He'd become bored with boats and butterflies.

The following year it would be birds and bullets, and the deaths in Verbrugge Woods would be noisier, the Goodchilds leaping into the air and dropping cups as the gunshots took them completely by surprise as they – or so they liked to imply – labored virtuously in their nearby house, biblical references never very far from their lips. The Goodchilds – this was to be quite understood – were not given to uttering frightful oaths as favorite cups and saucers shattered.

"The flowers appear on the earth; the time of the singing of birds is come, and the voice of the turtle is heard in our land," they'd have you believe they'd be uttering – not altogether appropriately – as Great Uncle Eugene blazed away just beyond the walls of The Old Pigpen, wreathed in smoke, his little beard vibrating. (Not a "Damn!," not a "Blast!" would escape their lips as crockery flew in all directions, bearded portraits trembled on the walls, and piano wires vibrated with an unmusical dissonance.)

"There's a special providence in the fall of a sparrow," Mrs. Goodchild would be intoning, unexpectedly quoting *Hamlet*, but firmly of the opinion that it was something from one of the Gospels, St. Luke or St. Matthew, one of those two. As the wife of a minister she knew such things, and made quite sure that everyone else knew that she knew them. "I speak as the wife of a clergyman," Mrs. Goodchild would inform all listeners when she spoke, and she spoke often and at length. It was a sentence usually repeated with a more-in-sorrow-than-in-anger intonation, and it was a sentence that really meant, "I know better than you do. Shut your mouth, you blathering idiot, and never open it again in my presence." It was the sentence at which you fell silent, overcome by gosh-isn't-she-wonderful admiration, a vague sense of a numinous beyondness hovering about you as you stared up into the darkness of her cavernous nostrils. The voice of the "Damn and blast!" would not be heard in the land (though there'd be plenty of blasting) when *she* was around, speaking of providence and sparrows, of whatever it was she chose to speak about. Whether they were from Shakespeare or from the Bible, the words weren't much consolation to the sparrows as Great Uncle Eugene let rip and many sparrows fell. ("I," said the Sparrow, "with my bow and arrow," but bows and arrows had no chance whatsoever against a shotgun, and the killing of Cock Robin was comprehensively avenged.)

Butterfly (after a while, Sorrow thought of her by this name, and not by the name of mother; she'd moved away from him, become small and remote in some point-of-infinity distance) had slit her throat, and her blood had run down the white kimono she had worn especially for the occasion – she'd assumed it like a bridal gown – and pooled in the hollows of her fragile neck, her tiny cupped hands. They'd had to replace two of the *tatami* mats in the room as they were so soaked in blood. The blood had been the one bright color in the whole bare room, all strewn with the pale petals of scattered dead and dying flowers. The night before, the night of watching and waiting, the night of joy, they – Butterfly, Suzuki, and he – had filled the room with flowers to make it beautiful for the return of the long-lost husband and father. The garden had been stripped bare, become desolate as a winter garden, but it had been springtime inside. "He loves me!" Butterfly had rejoiced, and dressed herself in her wedding garment, so that Pinkerton would see her as she had been on her wedding day. "Make me pretty!" she'd begged Suzuki. "Make me pretty!" Now her voice was stilled. It was as if, by choosing to die in the way that she did, she was attempting to cut out the voice that had so enchanted Pinkerton, her singing and her laughter, leaving a silence behind her that would never be broken again.

She couldn't have loved you if she killed herself and left you.

Ben and Kate Pinkerton never actually said this, but you couldn't help feeling that this was what they wanted Sorrow to believe.

We're your father and mother now.

That's what they actually *did* say.

They took him away with them, back to America.

They found him a new name.

A more suitable name.

Butterfly was soon forgotten.

They believed this to be true, though it was not.

Disturbing dreams troubled Sorrow. This was despite his

changed name, assumed like a disguise in which he could hide from her. She'd loved him too much, and love was a dangerous thing. Whether you were the one loving, or the one loved, it somehow weakened you, made you unguarded and vulnerable. You would have thought that love would make you strong.

Time passed.

Memories faded.

Ben — Benjamin Franklin Pinkerton — thought of Butterfly often, and — like his son — he dreamed, dreams that left him pale and shaking, dreams that were more real than the reality to which he awoke. Butterfly had died because he did not believe that anyone could love him as much as she did. He was not worthy of love. That was what he believed about himself. Love was like an unlooked-for blessing, and it was something for other people, something held in teasing reserve, a potential reward that only good boys got, or the confident ones who sought it out, like suitors undertaking a quest. That's what Charlie Whitefoord had done. You could just see Charlie scanning the horizon, looking — well, not confident, really — but hopeful and *patient*. Then he'd met Angelica Swenning. "I've met a girl." That's what he'd said afterwards, his eyes shining, a glow about him. The loved ones, the loving ones, were older and wiser and luckier than he was, and he would never be one of them.

Time passed, and time passed.

Memories faded further.

After a while, Sorrow had the feeling that there was something he ought to remember, something on the very verge of remembering, something pale and small and far away. It haunted him, nagged away at him. It was like trying to remember the title of a piece of music that was only just audible, something you strained to hear, even as you strained to remember its name.

He'd thought that he'd be able to remember it if he looked through a telescope, as if telescopes looked through time as well as distance. He'd looked through a telescope long ago, he knew that, looked down from a house on a hill, and out across an empty stretch

6

of water. Night had fallen, the sea had darkened, and there had been the smell of flowers in the room behind him. He'd been watching for something. He'd been waiting for something. If he looked through a telescope he would see it again, bring it closer, and all senses – not just the sense of sight – would be heightened. He'd smell that smell again, stronger than ever, feel those hands resting upon him from the unseen person standing behind him.

Then he'd come across the telescope at Aunt Charlotte's – she wasn't really his aunt, but this was what he called her – positioned on her piazza up on Hudson Heights, waiting to be found by him. He'd run straight to it, and Papa had had to lift him up, because it was too high on its stand for him to reach. Everything had been misty at first, the low clouds upon the water and the lower parts of the bluff entering the instrument, but Papa had turned something a little way at a time to focus it for him, his hand rotating slightly like that of someone winding a clock, the rough material of his sleeve brushing the side of Sorrow's face. (Sorrow no longer existed, but it was still Sorrow's face.) He'd felt the small vibration against the outer parts of his eye, in the bones of his eye socket, and it had been like looking through a kaleidoscope to see the brightly colored symmetrical patterns unfolding in front of him, the shifting shapes of the glass. The tips of his toes swung slightly, his feet weighed down by his boots, tapping against the stand, swaying from side to side with a tick-tock pendulum motion. It was like when he was hoisted up at the rail of the boat, his arms braced against it, his feet dangling.

It was the boat moving out of Nagasaki harbor.

It was the boat crossing the Pacific Ocean.

It was the boat moving up the Hudson.

"What can you see?" Papa had asked, as he had asked on the boat.

"What can you see?"

"What can you see?"

What he could see was the same as he had seen from the boat, the same as he had once seen – long ago – from another height.

There was nothing to see but an empty expanse of water stretching away into the distance.

"Emptiness," he replied.

It seemed it was what he always saw.

The telescope had not brought what he searched for any nearer. Emptiness.

Something had stirred inside him, come a little closer, when he had first read *Treasure Island* some years later. Like his father had been, he was drawn to books with maps, and it was his father's childhood copy of the novel that he had read. There were two dedications on the page after the title page. First there was Robert Louis Stevenson's dedication.

To S. L. O., an American gentleman . . .

(He had recently read *The Adventures of Tom Sawyer* for the first time, and had *The Adventures of Huckleberry Finn* – these were both books in which maps would have been helpful – all ready for when he had finished *Treasure Island*. "I remember *Tom Sawyer*," Papa had said. "We read it at school." He had held the book, but not opened it, lost awhile in musing, going away from him a little. You could feel it when this happened. For memory really to work, it had to be the same edition of the book, the same shape and color.

(It wasn't just the words that made memory work.

(Sometimes you didn't need any words at all.)

Below the author's dedication was the second dedication, written in his Aunt Alice's familiar handwriting.

For Ben, from his affectionate sister, Alice. Christmas 1887.

It was strange to see his papa given a name, Ben, another name rather than Papa, a Ben who was a little boy, all those years ago.

Over the page was the map of Treasure Island, and the first thing he read on the map – *Ye Spye-glass Hill* – was what caused the stirring inside him. He was vaguely aware of the shape of the island, the compass-points, the little sketch of a sailing ship, but it was these words on which he concentrated. He paused, very still, in case the feeling that he had was something that could be scared away, something that he wished to capture, like a bird in the garden sensing movement.

Spy-glass Hill.

The spy-glass.

He remembered his father holding him up when he was younger, too small to reach to see through Aunt Charlotte's telescope, the spy-glass that had been waiting for him.

Again, he could feel his father's left arm hooked under his arms to hold him up, as he used his right hand to adjust the focus.

Again, he could feel the cloth rubbing against his cheek, the sound and movement of his father's breathing, the shape of the eyepiece, his swinging legs. They were high up, above water, a morning of mists.

There were other arms, other hands. There was someone else breathing, and a strand of long hair – not his own – had fallen down across his face.

Again, he had that feeling . . .

Perfume . . .

The overpowering scent of flowers . . .

Breathing . . .

The sound of breathing . . .

The *feel* of breathing, a body pressed to his, breathing at the same time as he was breathing. Breathing *for* him. That was what it felt like.

What can you see?

What can you see?

What can you see?

The pattern in the kaleidoscope shifted and spun, shifted and spun, on the very verge of forming itself into a recognizable shape.

It was very close . . .

He was almost there . . .

He reached out his hand, slowly, so as not to scare it away, and his hand began to close around, to grasp onto . . .

. . . emptiness.

It was always emptiness.

It was not something that could be brought closer by a spy-glass.

Emptiness.

He began to think that what he needed to remember was hidden somewhere inside himself in that other emptiness, hidden away like the dreams, waiting to emerge when the right time came.

ONE

I

The only lessons that Ben had enjoyed at Otsego Lake Academy had been Chemistry lessons. This was not because he enjoyed Chemistry.

$$Zn + 2HCl = ZnCl_2 + H_2\uparrow$$

Dr. Brown, his nerves shattered by years of teaching Chemistry, wrote the equation on the blackboard in his shaky up-and-down printing. The ups – there were more ups than downs, and some of the ups hit the top of the blackboard – were where a noise had made him jump. A dropped pencil would make him jump. He tried to write, and to keep an eye on Year Three (*aleph*), at the same time, turning his head round accusingly each time he lifted the chalk from the board's surface, swiveling his eyes to encompass the whole of the twilit world of his laboratory.

Z – swivel – n – swivel – $+$ – swivel, swivel; one for the vertical stroke, one for the horizontal stroke . . .

Occasionally, he emitted a nervous, half-suppressed whooping sound.

(Who was that boy who kept dropping pencils?)

Its dark wood and high narrow windows gave the laboratory a somewhat alchemic atmosphere, in which generations of schoolboys had toiled like dwarfish necromancers, not to transmute base metal into gold or to discover the secret of eternal life, but (they were perfectly happy with these) to concoct the foulest possible smells, and the loudest possible explosions. Dr. Brown's beard, hands, and clothes were singed and stained by years of unremitting toil in his smoky chemical underworld. All his shirts and suits were patterned with little burned-edged holes, like those of a careless smoker, or a clumsy poker work enthusiast entirely lacking in decorative sense.

"Boys! Er . . . Men!" he would exclaim intermittently, between window-jarring booms.

It seemed strange to hear the sound of the English language in that subterranean Faustian darkness, where the many buttons of the schoolboys' uniforms gleamed like observing eyes. You somehow expected Latin. This seemed far more fitting.

"Men!"

All boys were addressed as "men" at Otsego Lake Academy. It brought The Beards ever closer, those ritualistic accoutrements donned as a symbol of entry into the secret world of manhood. This was the place to see the smallest and squeakiest men you'd ever see, Dr. Vaniah Odom – of course – always excepted. You had to bend down to see some of them. They were as small as the illustrations in a Lindstrom & Larsson catalogue, though not so stiffly posed. The artist in the catalogue was clearly incapable of drawing children correctly, and all the boys were drawn like miniature adults, perfectly proportioned poised pygmies, standing with great dignity next to full-sized men, who – somewhat understandably – completely ignored them, perhaps out of embarrassment, as the miniature men stood there, waist high, clad in miniature suits or miniature underwear (exact diminutive copies of the garments sported by their elders), like Tom Thumbs in training.

The miniature men seethed.

The miniature men squabbled.

The miniature men were *everywhere*.

It looked like a scene from a lavishly populated production of a Wagner opera, a demented smoke-filled Bayreuth Festival fitfully illuminated by flaring gas taps, as in a dimly recessed manufactory. The miniature men sought for methods of mayhem like high-pitched Nibelungen bashing away at their anvils with glee-filled malicious intent, and were completely beyond the control of the nerve-racked nicotine-stained Alberich who stood before them. He had explained what it was they were to do, and now they had been unleashed. They had full access to the means of destruction. In these smoke-filled white-tiled Wagnerian caverns, deep below the surface of the earth, *Götterdämmerung* could not be long delayed, and deep-voiced bearded basses would soon pronounce the destruction of the old world, the passing away of all that had been. Chemistry lessons worked wondrous changes on schoolboys, as Dr. Jekyll had gloomily confirmed a few years earlier.

As thunder and lightning rent the heavens, as the Rhine burst its banks, as Brünnhilde blazed like a Viking funeral or one of the late Albert Comstock's more ambitious barbecues, as Valhalla collapsed in flaming chaos, Dr. Brown ineffectually sought to subdue his scuttling dwarfs.

From time to time, stools fell over, and bodies hurtled into the air between explosions.

("Whoop!")

February 23rd, 1892. The Preparation of Hydrogen Gas.

Ben wrote this neatly in his exercise book in his best hand-writing – however much he tried, it was always a little boy's handwriting, rounded and carefully spaced – and underlined the title using his ruler. He thought for a while, and then copied the equation from the blackboard underneath.

No need to think for the word that came next.

Object.

Well, that was easy enough.

To prepare hydrogen gas.

He underlined *Object.* This gave him a real sense of progress, a feeling of being in control as knowledge inexorably advanced. That line was really straight.

Object.

(A memory of a hand reaching out to a blackboard and writing the word *Object.* He saw the hand with great precision, shadowed and three-dimensional.

(It had already written *Subject* and would soon write the word *Predicate*.

(The words held a Belshazzar's Feast-weight of significance, if only he could work out what it was.

(The hand chalked the three words over and over in the same handwriting, a hand compelled to write the same lines until it had covered every inch of space in front of it. It was not, however, the teacher who was being punished, assigned this repetitive task.

(*Subject, Object, Predicate*.

(There was no other sound but the scratching of the chalk, followed by a *tap, tap, tap* as the side of the chalk was rapped emphatically beneath each word.

(After a while, other words were written beneath the first.

(*Pater filium amat*.

(*Tap. Tap. Tap*.

(Latin had made its appearance in the Chemistry laboratory after all.

(*Pater filium amat*.

(*Tap. Tap. Tap*.

(The father loves his son, and hydrogen gas was being prepared.

(*Subject, Object, Predicate*.

(*Tap. Tap. Tap*.)

In front of him Oliver was arranging the equipment, with the air of an artist preparing a still life for a major commission. He insisted on "Oliver" instead of "Comstock," as if – and who could blame him? – to distance himself from his mother and his late father. He held the white pottery beehive shelf in front of him, looking at it speculatively, a customer who had just ordered one of the more ambitious concoctions at the ice-cream parlor, and was debating how best to consume it, planning his first crunch into that brittle shell. Linnaeus Finch and Charlie Whitefoord, the other members of their group, hovered beside him, offering their suggestions. From time to time Oliver stood back, leaning musingly to judge the effect with his head on one side, shifting things minutely to and fro, seeking to satisfy some inner sense of beauty.

Opposite them, across the adjoining dark wood bench, all its gas jets hissing out purply blue flames, the atmosphere swimming with heat-haze and the slowly unfurling smoke of ignited spills, William French had been imprisoned in the glass-fronted fume cupboard, squashed in like a specimen ready for dissection. He squatted with his arms wrapped around his knees, his chin on top, his head lolling disconsolately, employing the time usefully by reading a Captain Mayne Reid novel. This was the third time this had happened in two weeks, ever since he had overenthusiastically applied rather strong-smelling hair oil.

Huh!

You might have guessed he'd be named *French!*

It was bad enough having to be in the same room as a Charlotte Anne like Comstock!

Violently objecting to this vile hair-oiled challenge to the proprieties of manhood, the manlier pupils in the class had taken to cramming French behind thick perfume-proof glass to make themselves feel safer, and Dr. Brown hadn't noticed yet. Brinkman – of course (need anyone be in any doubt about this?) – was one of the valiant manly ones, joined in deep-voiced (or as near as they could manage) trainee biceps-bulging by Adams, Bradstone, and Swartwout. Bulge, bulge, bulge went the trainee manly muscles, like heroic nervous tics, and scowl, scowl, scowl went the trainee manly facial expressions. No smile whatsoever, and you were halfway to being a man. (No hee hees and no heehaws from he-men unless utilized for the acceptable purposes of mockery.) One or two of the more ambitious newer boys in the class had taken to hanging around in their virile vicinity, flexing their arms, and looking sulky, all teeth secreted from sight.

Men didn't wear hair oil that smelled.

This was the point that they were making.

Men just . . .

Men (real *men, men* with italics) just – er – *smelled.*

A beard and a smell were the proud proofs of manhood.

Excessive hair oil and a lack of italics struck at the very foundations of all that was most commendable in the male.

The offending hair hung down across William French's eyes as he read, seemingly engrossed in the book, the reflected flames gushing across in front of him. The hero would be fencing with astonishing skill, his enemies falling powerless before him, as a spirited beauty watched breathlessly.

Just you wait!

This was what William French would be thinking to himself, gripping his ruler with ferocious intent.

Just you wait!

He looked like one of the stuffed animals in glass cases in the other laboratory.

Equipment.

Ben underlined this next word – this was going really well – and began to list what had been ranged across the bench, the objects become printed words. Oliver adjusted everything carefully and neatly, so that it was precisely parallel with the front. He was by far the cleverest boy in the class – though he cultivated a manner that made this seem unlikely – and Ben knew that everything would be correct, and correctly arranged. Cleverness was not a quality that met with approval at Otsego Lake Academy. Anything but. It was the magical land where cleverness and imagination were snip-snapped as snip-snappily as if the task had been vigorously undertaken by Oliver's grim-faced mother at her fiercest, unleashed with freshly sharpened scissors upon an overgrown garden crammed with dubiously underdressed statues.

Snip-snap! Snip-snap! Snip-snap!

Tinkle! Tinkle! Tinkle!

He wrote down the first piece of equipment, feeling wonderfully alert and in control.

Flat-bottomed flask.

(Mrs. Albert Comstock wouldn't be too keen on "flat-bot-tomed." She would sense – ahem – *innuendo* and take offence. Mrs. Albert Comstock was the sort of woman who could sense – ahem –

innuendo in the poetry of Isaac Watts and Eugene Field. She was clearly a woman in possession of a rich inner life denied to the majority of the population, and it seethed like a jar crammed with maggots.)

Thistle funnel.

Delivery tube.

Bung. (Should you list the bung separately, or assume that the thistle funnel and delivery tube would automatically need a bung to hold them in position at the neck of the flask? "Never assume." That was what Dr. Brown had once said, after a particularly spectacular explosion one afternoon. He listed the bung.)

Pneumatic trough.

Beehive shelf.

Test tube.

He used a new line for each piece of equipment, to make it look as if he'd written more.

Thistle funnel. Beehive shelf. There was an unexpectedly rural ambience to the production of hydrogen gas. The shiny white beehive shelf – placed in the pneumatic trough – was a piece of pottery with an arch in one side of it, penetrated by the end of the delivery tube as it ran across from the flask. It looked rather like something in which spring bulbs might have been planted, though it was turned the wrong way round for this.

Materials.

This was the next underlined word.

Zinc granules. These – a disappointing silvery gray (experiments with brighter colors tended to be more interesting) – had already been placed at the base of the flask. There was the *Zn.* Oliver had agitated the flask until the little pyramid of granules had settled into a perfectly smooth layer across its base. He had developed demanding visual standards ever since he had decided to become æsthetic.

"I am an æsthete," he had announced some time ago – a risky pronouncement at Otsego Lake Academy – in the way that some boys would have announced a career choice, discovering a compelling vocation for the priesthood (as risky a choice as æstheticism to the baying hordes that thundered up and down the corridors of their school), or (*far* more acceptable) the navy. It had been Ben, in fact, who had ended up choosing the latter, though it had not been something that he had announced. He did not possess Oliver's theatrical flair.

Water. The pneumatic trough had been filled with water, completely covering the beehive shelf, and the inverted water-filled test tube had been placed over the opening in the top of the shelf.

All that was missing was the *HCl,* and Oliver stood ready with the bottle of hydrochloric acid. He paused a moment, tapping the bottle up and down on his jacket buttons, playing a xylophone on which every bar produced the same note, humming under his breath. It was the moment on the top board just before the dive. After *Materials* there would be *Diagram* (he must remember not to draw lines across the tops of the thistle funnel or the delivery tube, as Dr. Brown always deducted marks if he did this), followed by *Method* and *Observations.* All these were words that had to be underlined. The lack of an underlining meant the loss of more marks. Dr. Brown sought to bring order to his disordered domain by insisting at all times that every pupil obeyed a set of minor but inflexible rules in his written work. A thunderous explosion resulted in a quavering "Whoop!" but a diagram depicting a pencil line closing off the top of a thistle funnel meant an aggrieved red circle, and a mark deducted.

Method would consist of Oliver pouring hydrochloric acid down the thistle funnel onto the zinc granules. Dr. Brown's preferred wording for this action was: *Hydrochloric acid was introduced to zinc granules.* *Observations* would then follow. The word had a nicely scientific sound to it, the sound of something being discovered for the first time, explorers scanning distant blue-tinged unnamed mountains, astronomers descrying a new planet swimming into view, excitedly adjusting the focus of their telescopes. The reality, of course, was somewhat different.

Oliver removed the stopper from the bottle of acid. He sniffed fastidiously, with the air of a connoisseur.

"Slightly corky, I suspect," he commented. "Not one of the better years."

He had a crisp, elegant way of speaking. Years later, when he first heard someone use the word "posh," Ben immediately thought of Oliver Comstock, and saw him – heard him – as he once was, long, long ago. Oliver, though perfectly oblivious of the fact, undoubtedly had a posh voice. This was the perfect word with which to describe it. It was something he had somehow constructed for himself – he spoke nothing like his awful parents, although Mrs. Albert Comstock essayed an eye-wateringly unconvincing attempt at poshness – and it was connected with his love of quotation and florid words, and his startlingly undisguised dislike of his Mama and (alive or dead) Papa and his Big (Big and Getting Bigger) Sis. In the days when he had been strapped into his Little Lord Fauntleroy outfit – gloweringly rebellious – the aristocratic voice of the heir to Dorincourt Castle (and Wyndham Towers *and* Chorlworth: Oliver was not a boy who went in for half measures) had emerged to stun all who listened. You were left in little doubt that any sentence he chose to speak – grammatically correct, and often making use of sub-clauses – would be perfectly punctuated. The fingers of ambitious members of the lower orders – hopeful of tips and condescending acknowledgement – leaped straight into fawning forelock-tugging position, as soon as Oliver opened his mouth. They assumed abased postures and servile expressions, and their voices – lowered to a respectful hush – lingered caressingly over the words "your lordship" and "young master." Oliver took it as his rightful due. He wasn't very tall, but he seemed to take up a lot of space whenever he was in a room.

Ben stopped writing, and watched with Linnaeus and Charlie. They were Finch and Whitefoord in the usage of Otsego Lake Academy, but Ben thought of them by their Christian names. It was a link with the past, the time when they had been schoolboys together at their previous school, Crowninshield's.

"Are you observing?" Oliver asked, and – serious-faced, scientists poised to discover – they assumed attitudes indicative of observation, the slightly heightened poses Oliver preferred, looking not unlike a row of Reynolds Templeton Seabrights, searching – in old actorly fashion – for something vaguely discernible in the far distance. They held their hands – right hands for Ben and Charlie, left hand for Linnaeus, rather spoiling the unity – above their eyes, and turned their heads slowly to the right (always beginning with a turn to the right), their observation moving from the flat-bottomed flask, along and down the delivery tube (heads dipping in unison) to the pneumatic trough. They then moved their heads slowly back again from right to left (heads lifting in unison), and then slowly once more from left to right.

"We are observing," they confirmed.

"Hydrochloric acid, meet zinc granules. Zinc granules, meet hydrochloric acid," Oliver said, in his most polite tones. He always did this. The hydrochloric acid had now been introduced to the zinc granules, and they could continue. He checked once more that the end of the thistle funnel was close enough to the bottom of the flask for it to be under the surface when the acid was added.

The rabbit was about to be produced from out of the hat, the wing-whirring fan-tailed pigeons from the pockets.

"I shall now *liberate* the hydrogen," Oliver announced. The phrasing used by Dr. Brown – "the liberation of hydrogen from hydrochloric acid by the action of zinc granules" – had rather appealed to him. He had come to bring freedom to entrapped, unjustly imprisoned hydrogen, suffering for its firmly held beliefs. A moral dimension added to the interest of the lesson, he always felt.

"*Observations*," Oliver added – you could hear the italics – and (after a moment in which he seemed to be considering dabbing the glass stopper against his wrists, a connoisseur genteelly applying cologne) poured the acid down the thistle funnel onto the zinc crystals. They watched the resulting effervescence in the flask, fizzing like white-foamed boiling water, and then – a little later – the bubbles beginning to rise from the end of the delivery tube, as the hydrogen gas produced began to enter the test tube, displacing the water.

"Come on, hydrogen! Come on, hydrogen!" they urged the bubbles encouragingly, loyal supporters massed beside the racetrack. This was a dash to freedom, a brave sprint for liberation, and all right-minded men must applaud.

"Bubble, bubble," Oliver said – he'd read *Macbeth* – uniting Literature and Science in an effortlessly Renaissance moment.

At other benches, other groups – groups with less demanding æsthetic standards, and therefore ahead of them – were already removing test tubes filled with hydrogen gas, and (it was what they had been waiting for) hastening to apply naked lights to cause explosions. All across the laboratory, boys were carrying lighted spills in one hand, with their other hand cupped protectively around the little flame. They had the look of choirboys, deprived of their frills (the very thought of frills at Otsego Lake Academy!; things would get rough if you indulged in a ruff), massed ranks of Frank Stoddards taking part in some small religious procession in one of the Mediterranean countries. "Ave Maria," they should be intoning, with downcast eyes, and pious faces lit from beneath, or "Oh, for the Wings of a Dove." If any doves had appeared, summoned by the shrill-voiced supplicants – drawn from the sanctuary of their half-timbered dovecote in Mrs. Alexander Diddecott's garden – they'd have been blasted from the skies in clouds of entrails-spattered feathers. The bigger the bangs, the more impenetrable the clouds of smoke, the louder the screams, the whoopier the whoops from Dr. Brown, the more successful the experiments had been. That, more or less, was the philosophy of these trainee mad scientists. Choirboys had no place here. This was the place for Dr. Brown and Dr. Frankenstein, haunted men grappling with the dangers of science.

Dr. Brown knew all about the dangers of science.

Dr. Brown also sometimes prayed for the wings of a dove, to fly away and be at rest.

> *Hear my prayer, O God, incline Thine ear!*
> *Thyself from my petition do not hide!*
> *Take heed to me!*

The exclamation points reeked of desperation, as he prayed in his loudest voice to ensure that he was heard. Trapped in his glassy prison, William French lowered his novel, and peered out into the laboratory, shading his eyes.

Whoop!

Whoop!

Whoop!

Suddenly, from every direction, there came a series of high-pitched farty whoops, accompanied by shrieks of laughter, and you'd have thought that Dr. Brown was everywhere, and everywhere leaping nervously into the air. For a moment, he appeared to have discovered the secret of omnipresence, that most useful attribute for a schoolmaster. There would be *Method* and *Observations* worthy of the neatest of underlinings, and of a carefully labeled *Diagram* drawn with the most sharp-pointed of pencils.

Whoop!

Whoop!

Whoop!

The whoops were not, however, from Dr. Brown, but were the sounds produced by ignited hydrogen gas. This was today's explosion. Not a *Bang!* Not a *Boom!* Not — these were special treats, doled out on days when the men were exceptionally restless, days of high winds and thunderstorms — a *Ker-boom!* or a *Whumpf!* Just a *Whoop!*, a sound they heard every lesson (if slightly more restrained, partially suppressed) from Dr. Brown himself, without the need of any specialized equipment.

It was rather disappointing.

Ben had expected something a little more spectacular. The rest of the class was happy enough. They found farts hilarious, and the high-pitched squeaky whooping sounds clearly appealed to some deep inner need. They joined in, pitching their voices to ear-splitting falsettos. They had not had access to explosives when they had been schoolboys at Crowninshield's school, and such pleasures had previously been denied to them.

"Whoop! Whoop! Whoop!"

In echo, Dr. Brown leaped into the air, with his own – more discreet – whoops.

"Men!" he tried, rather hopelessly.

Whoop!

"Whoop!"

("Whoop!")

"Men!"

> *Without Thee all is dark, I have no guide,*
> *I have no guide, no guide, without Thee all is dark . . .*

The men carried on whooping, with voices that were not the voices of men. It was a long way from "Ave Maria" and "Oh, for the Wings of a Dove." It was *distinctly* disappointing. No frills, and no thrills, from this defrocked choir. They hastened for more zinc granules and more hydrochloric acid, avid for more of the farty whoops. "Whoop!" they kept on caroling in the interim, reminding themselves of the exact sound they wished to reproduce, like musicians asking for a certain note to find their key.

> *The enemy shouteth,*
> *Hear my prayer, O God, incline Thine ear!*
> *The godless come fast!*
> *Iniquity, hatred, upon me they cast!*

Oliver seemed to share Ben's sense of anticlimax.

As an epicure of explosions, he had heard better than this, and he was pursing his lips critically. A whoop wasn't very exciting. *WHOOP!* would be more like it. *WHOOP!!* would be an improvement, almost as good as a *WHUMPF!!* Most of Oliver's explosions required capital letters, and several exclamation points to cope with them. Even though their test tube was not yet full of gas, the water not fully displaced, he flicked it away to lie at the bottom of the water in the pneumatic trough, not even bothering to ignite what had been produced. He seized a gas jar and submerged it to fill it with water, positioning it on top of the beehive shelf in the test tube's place. Something on a bigger scale than a mere test tube was clearly called for, to edge them ever whumpfwards. There was a gleam of ambition in Oliver's eyes, and all who knew him as well as they did would be torn between excitement and panic, though excitement would be the predominant emotion.

"I'll hurry things along a little," he muttered – Oliver always hurried things along a little – and reached across for a bottle of copper sulfate solution, labeled (like everything else in the laboratory) in Dr. Brown's agitated script. The *f* of *sulfate* went right off the top of the label and onto the bottle, suggesting that he had been misguidedly attempting to complete his identifications in the course of a particularly explosive lesson. Linnaeus and Charlie moved a little further away, dragging their wobbling wooden stools with them across the undulating surface of the singed and stained parquet floor, bracing themselves slightly. They were used to things being hurried along a little, and knew what to expect. Discreetly, they took a tight grip of the edge of the bench with one hand, and held onto a leg of their stools with the other. Men fearlessly risked their lives in the cause of science. That was what their firm stance was saying. They looked like experienced "At Home" visitors preparing for the worst as Mabel Peartree took a deep, deep breath just before she unleashed her voice in song. William French, noticing what was happening, wriggled himself a little closer to the white tiles behind him, and held *The Scalp Hunters, or, Romantic Adventures in Northern Mexico* up before his face. He didn't want to miss too much, and peeped over the top. The rest of the class was too absorbed in preparing whoops – not many _Observations_ going on here – to notice the *WHOOP!* taking shape amongst them. It might even be a *WHOOP!!*, necessitating more than one exclamation point. A bigger container and a more violent reaction were needed to burst into capitals and multiple exclamation points. On Oliver's more ambitious days, structural damage could not be ruled out.

Dr. Brown, all unaware of this, was drawing a large-scale labeled diagram of the apparatus on the blackboard. It helped to pass the time – only fifteen minutes to go, one more lesson almost over and still alive – and helped him to ignore the noise behind him. His diagrams were always carefully and beautifully drawn, and he sometimes found it difficult to erase them after a lesson. They were a consolation for the chaos behind him, and it hurt to realize how transient even achieved perfection could be. He had, by now, stopped turning round for accusing looks. The class had rather moved beyond the power of accusing looks. Not even a threateningly angled retort stand would cow them now, not even a machine gun, though he'd have preferred the machine gun.

> *The wicked oppress me,*
> *Ah, where shall I fly?*
> *Perplex'd and bewilder'd,*
> *O God, hear my cry,*
> *O God, hear my cry!*
> *The enemy shouteth,*
> *The godless come fast!*

He'd reached the stage where his whoops were starting to become as loud as theirs. This was always a bad sign. He'd need to buy another large can of cocoa powder from Comstock's Comestibles to aid his sleep. It was kind of Oliver Comstock to offer to supply him at wholesale prices. (He was right out of wodka.) Carefully, with a perfectionist's meticulous attention to his workmanship, Dr. Brown drew spiky little arrows with feathered tops all over the apparatus, making it appear that it was under attack from massed Red Indian hordes, killing the White Man's science. The war whoops from all around the room provided an appropriately atmospheric accompaniment. Drawing the arrows was his favorite bit. He drew all the arrows, and then he added the labeling. The labeling was his least favorite bit.

Whoop!

"Whoop!"

("Whoop!")

That last whoop had bent one of the arrows. He rubbed it out, and started it again. He was proud of his sharp, decisive arrows. He'd allow no nonsense from his arrows.

He looked again at the equation, the first thing that he had written on the blackboard after he'd written the date, the little grouping of symbols that had unleashed the anarchy around him as assuredly as a declaration of war.

$$Zn + 2HCl = ZnCl_2 + H_2\uparrow$$

He looked more closely at the equals sign, and touched at it with an air of tenderness.

("=," he was thinking to himself. "=."

(When all else failed, when chaos erupted around him, he thought of the equals sign. He concentrated on this sign, his little pathway into peace. For some reason, it seemed to lead him away from everything around him and into a better place. It was like a bridge, neat and safe-sided, built across chaos and torment. He'd hold firmly onto the handrail with both hands, drawing himself across to a better place, like someone hanging onto the rail of a ship in a storm, and he wouldn't look down. He *definitely* didn't wish to know what lay beneath him if he fell.

("Equals," he was thinking.

("Equals . . ."

("Equals . . ."

(=

(=

(=

(Sometimes, as he cowered in his laboratory, nervously awaiting the arrival of one of the rowdier classes – they were *all* rowdy classes – he drew equals signs all over the blackboard until his hand was completely covered in chalk.

(*Whoop!*

(=

("Whoop!"

(=

26

("Whoop!")

(=

(If "=" failed him, he would linger over his chemical mantras, repeating the equations to himself like a prayer imploring for peace.

(Cesium.

(Rubidium.

(Potassium.

(Sodium.

(Lithium.

(Cesium first . . .

($2Cs + 2H_2O = 2CsOH + H_2 \uparrow$.

(Then rubidium . . .

($2Rb + 2H_2O = 2RbOH + H_2 \uparrow$.

(Then potassium . . .

(If even this failed him – it increasingly failed him, these days – he would think of his favorite equation of them all.

($NaOH + HCl = NaCl + H_2O$.

(*This* was his favorite equation.

(He filled his mind with thoughts of sodium hydroxide and hydrochloric acid, their amicable union, free of all bangs and unpleasantness. If only his life could be like sodium hydroxide uniting with hydrochloric acid.

($NaOH + HCl = NaCl + H_2O$.

($NaOH + HCl = NaCl + H_2O$.

(Sometimes this helped.)

Oliver held the bottle of copper sulfate solution irresolutely in his hands. For a while there was an obvious struggle between his æsthetic side and his scientific side. His æsthetic side was clearly urging him to pour the deep blue copper sulfate solution (the same color as his eyes: Symbolism could be so satisfying) on to the white of the beehive shelf. He hovered between the Devil and the deep blue catalytic sea. Blue and white china ever formed the higher slopes for those laboring upward to achieve æstheticism, but on the beehive shelf – though it might provide a feast for the eyes – it would have no scientific effect. It was the word "catalyst" that swayed Oliver from the æsthetic to the scientific. If – as he must, in order to achieve the result he wanted – he poured the copper sulfate solution into the flask, and onto the zinc granules, it would act as a catalyst and speed up the reaction dramatically. Oliver could not resist the thought of acting as a catalyst, an agent provoking change without itself being permanently changed. That was Dr. Brown's definition, with the addition of the word "chemical" in one or two places. It described so well what Oliver always tried to be in social situations, and he was further seduced into action by the word "provoking." He would be – ooh good, it was in French, that would annoy his mother – an *agent provocateur*. He liked being "provoking." According to his mama he was always being provoking. It was either provoking or satirical, one or the other – he preferred "provoking" – and neither of them was good. Good. On this occasion, æstheticism lost.

Oliver took a deep breath, and poured out the color of his eyes. Into the flask went the solution, even though it would have looked far more attractive in the pneumatic trough. In Oliver's hands it was more of a problem, than a solution.

They watched – they *observed* – the dramatic effects of the catalyst, as the contents of the flask surged and boiled. The flask didn't actually rock from side to side, though they couldn't help thinking that it probably should. The entire bench should rock, the whole room, in the first tremblings of an earthquake. The word "cataclysmic" should surely be derived from "catalyst," as the alchemistic powers were unleashed. Gas whizzed along the delivery tube and roared down into the pneumatic trough, as bubbles the size of underwater screams gushed up into the gas jar. They could actually hear the violent agitation of the water, the sound of doomed explorers rafting down through white-foamed wildness. They scarcely noticed what was happening to the zinc: this was far more exciting. Had Oliver overdone the copper sulfate solution, his keenness to achieve a deep shade of blue leading to a tragically early – if æsthetic – death for them all? The prospect rather appealed. Oliver had his spill all lit and ready, like an anarchist poised to ignite the fuse of his explosive, ready to die for a cause in which he believed. So would Guy Fawkes have stood beneath Parliament amidst his barrels of gunpowder.

The moment the gas jar was completely filled with gas, Oliver fearlessly upturned it, and plunged in the burning spill, with the expression of a hero plunging his sword-point into the heart of a hated enemy.

It was definitely a *WHOOP!!*

The high-pitched shriek sounded as if a very large, and very cold, hand had launched itself unexpectedly upon Oliver's gigantic mother and comprehensively goosed her. Never had a more unwilling goose been more forcibly stuffed. Here was a goose crammed full of *pâté de foie gras*, a goose fit to bust, though "bust" was a word you generally attempted to avoid whenever your thoughts strayed unwillingly in the direction of the massively bosomed Mrs. Albert Comstock. It was *very* loud, and – in strict defiance of the laws of Physics (though obeying one of the essential rules of an interesting Chemistry lesson) – it seemed to get louder and louder as it bounced around the room, echoing between the white tiles, galvanizing the shrieking hordes of Dr. Jekylls, all – schoolboy-sized and dressed in uniform – caught in mid-transformation to massed Mr. Hydes.

It was the very sound guaranteed to give Oliver the most possible pleasure.

Not much pleasure for Dr. Brown.

He, in his turn, whooped an unguardedly shrill whoop – his best effort for ages – (most of the class whooped, echoing it as they had echoed the whoops of the ignited hydrogen gas) and one of his arrows (for *Inverted test tube of water*) shot right across the diagram from left to right, into *Flat-bottomed flask*. It should have remained there, quivering, but – as Dr. Brown lost his balance at the end of his little wooden platform – the arrow plummeted earthward, followed by Dr. Brown. The class – unusually attentive, for a change – watched, *observed*, as their teacher tottered. He seemed to sway for a surprisingly long time. There might even have been time for a miniature man to have sprung forward and caught him before he fell, in a touching display of protectiveness, but no miniature man sprang. It was much more fun to see him crash to the floor. There was little doubt they'd all be producing neat diagrams, with every angle correctly entered (Arithmetic blending seamlessly with Chemistry) of Dr. Brown's whooping pearl-diver plunge.

Object they'd be writing, with a zest they hadn't felt for quite some time.

Equipment.
Materials.
Diagram.
Method.
(_Dr. Brown was introduced to the floor._)
Observations.

Oh yes, they were observing all right.

With a final, despairing, long-drawn-out whoop, Dr. Brown — no time even for "Dr. Brown, meet floor. Floor, meet Dr. Brown" — fell, grabbing at the engraving of Abraham Lincoln that hung alongside the blackboard as he launched himself sideways off the platform.

(=
(=
(=
(= had failed Dr. Brown completely.)

> _My heart is sorely pain'd within my breast,_
> _My soul with deathly terror is oppress'd,_
> _Trembling and fearfulness upon me fall,_
> _With horror overwhelm'd, Lord hear me call,_
> _Lord hear me call!_

Things had been going so well.

There had been (for the first time all week) no _Three Musketeers_ swashbuckling sword-fights around the laboratory with retort stands as weapons. No one had been set on fire during a Bunsen burner duel, leaving that unpleasantly lingering smell of scorched hair and singed school uniform. Not one pane of glass had been broken, and all windows were intact.

But things were well no longer.

Dr. Brown, with his arms locked around Abraham Lincoln, crashed to the floor beneath President Harrison.

There was an impressed silence.

"I think that went rather well," Oliver said, displaying modest pleasure at the improved quality of their teacher's whoop.

You couldn't help but feel an awestruck reverence for his exalted intellectual qualities and his majestic personal appearance. Linnaeus's sister had described Oliver in these words once. It was probably — like many of Charlotte's quotations — from one of the Gilbert and Sullivan comic operas.

"Should we continue to write up our notes?"

Year Three (*aleph*) seemed to think that this was a good idea. It meant that there'd be less to do at home. There was a studious silence in the laboratory — a rare occurrence — as twenty-two right hands, and one left hand (William French, in no position to write, would have to copy up everything at home: serve him right for smelling like a girlie), simultaneously wrote *Diagram*. Twenty-three hands had already written *Object*, *Equipment*, and *Materials*.

"Remember to underline the title," Akenside said helpfully, "and not to draw lines across the top of the thistle funnel or the delivery tube. You know how he goes on about it."

They had completely forgotten about Dr. Brown.

Year Three (*aleph*) was one of three classes in Year Three.

There was *A*, there was *alpha*, and there was *aleph*. Parents didn't like the thought of their sons being placed in classes labeled *B* or *C* — such classes smacked of unsatisfactory lower grades — and parents — they made this quite clear — were not forking out generous sums of money for their sons to be privately educated and then see them placed in a class bearing a letter from lower in the alphabet than *A*. All classes, consequently, were *A* classes at Otsego Lake Academy, though one was described as *alpha*, and another as *aleph.* In doing this, the first headmaster had demonstrated his linguistic prowess, and persuaded ambitious parents that here was a school worthy of – at this point he tended to assume a twinkly avuncularity of manner – their gifted child. Parents tended to prefer the *A* class. You knew where you were with *A*. *Alpha* and *aleph* had the suspiciously foreign ring about them of something not quite as it should be, something a little too Lower East Side. Though they sounded like the first letters of alphabets, which, of course, both were, they were – you had to say – from *inferior* alphabets, alphabets that used those funny squiggly symbols instead of proper letters, not like proper alphabets at all. A few realized that *alpha* was from the Greek, though hardly any that *aleph* was Hebrew. Mrs. Albert Comstock would have had a fit if she'd found *that* out. *Hebrew!*

A disturbing sound broke upon their studious pen-scratching silence.

"Men!"

That was the sound they heard.

Everyone looked about.

"Men!"

There was a voice coming from behind the teacher's bench at the front of the class.

"There is another way of liberating hydrogen that I have not yet demonstrated."

It was Dr. Brown's voice.

He was lying flat on his back on the floor, in a compromising position with Abraham Lincoln, but – what a professional! – he kept on talking. He couldn't see them, and they couldn't see him, yet Dr. Brown kept on talking. He was hoping to create an impression of order and control. If you didn't show the fear in your voice, all would be well. The students most anxious to impress assumed expressions of keen alertness.

"You will all need to go to the *very* back of the laboratory."

It was always a good sign when Dr. Brown said this.

It meant danger.

It meant major explosions.

It meant extensive charred areas in Dr. Brown's beard and clothing.

A popular request from his students (he liked to think it demonstrated the way in which he brought the subject thrillingly alive for them) was, "Will you do something where we have to go to the *very* back" – the addition of the word "*very*" (in italics) made all the difference – ". . . of the laboratory?" You felt that the widest possible distance between Dr. Brown and his students was a special treat, eagerly anticipated by both sides. He sometimes held it out as a bribe to ensure good – well, slightly improved – behavior, and here he was offering it for free. With the usual rising roar, the whole mass of schoolboys hurled itself at the back wall, scrambling up on to the bench beneath it, an out-of-control army attempting to break the siege of an enemy city. It was the Storming of the Bastille with added smells and sizzles. Bodies were dashed to the floor – Dr. Brown had demonstrated the *Method* – as rivals jostled for the best position from which to witness the catastrophe that was sure to follow. Scattered across the dark wood surfaces of all the abandoned laboratory benches – startlingly white in contrast – were the open pages of Year Three (*aleph*)'s exercise books and their incomplete, spindly, as-yet-unlabeled diagrams, beset about with pens and pencils at peculiar angles. It was like the collapse of a civilization.

In the adjoining Biology laboratory, the stuffed rabbits, wolves, cougars, and (there was a sad story behind this) hens trembled in their glass cases. Mr. Caswell's class watched as he picked up a beaker (checking it contained no corrosive contents: he'd had an unpleasant experience the previous year), and pressed it against the wall, his ear against the base, listening to what was going on next door.

"Quiet, class!" he commanded, and they were quiet. They wanted to hear as much as possible, and they didn't have beakers.

It was his duty – Mr. Caswell felt this quite firmly – to report inappropriate behavior on the part of other teachers to the headmaster.

At the end of each week he submitted a neatly written file of observations – **Observations** of many kinds found their place in the Science department of Otsego Lake Academy – to Mr. Scrivener, with his very best Obadiah Slope simper. He was an odious little toady, anxious for promotion, so toad-like that he'd have passed as yet another gruesome-faced member of the massed Goodchild and Griswold families. He'd dissected so many toads in the course of his biological career that he had somehow – osmosis was a process he'd described, complete with baffling diagrams, many and many a time – assumed some of the least attractive traits of the creatures he so zestfully flayed. He rather enjoyed pinning down the flapped-back skin, exposing the oozy innards, fully alert to any signs of nausea in his pupils so that he could denounce their unmanliness. He'd blood them like tyro foxhunters being initiated after their first kill, a dripping red cross upon their foreheads like the mark on the door of a house where plague dwelt. *Beware!* the cross warned, *Danger of Infection! Do Not Approach!* He'd blooded Comstock in this manner (æsthetic shudders had no place in a Science laboratory), and there could have been – *Snigger!* – no better choice than he to hedge about with warnings.

Keep Well Clear!

Avoid!

(Would that Mr. Caswell had thought to whisper these discreet words of chappish advice to Mr. Rappaport about Oliver Comstock!

(Would that Mr. Rappaport had thought that any words from Mr. Caswell were worthy of note!

(Impossible.

(The Humanities – amusing to think of any subject taught by Mr. Rappaport as being linked with humanity – were the Capulets of Otsego Lake Academy, and the Sciences were the Montagues, and in Mr. Scrivener's ill-governed Verona the undisciplined disciplines, the rebellious subjects, wouldn't dream of leaning across the sharp-edged borders of the timetable to lower themselves to speak to each other, and Mr. Rappaport would not have listened to

Beware!, even if Mr. Caswell had chosen to speak it. Mr. Rappaport would not even have heard *Do Not Approach!* or *Keep Well Clear!* Mr. Rappaport failed to *Avoid!*, and Mr. Rappaport, consequently, was infected, and paid the price, more bloodied than blooded.

(Two years later, it would happen.)

Mr. Scrivener accepted Mr. Caswell's observations with an expression of intense gratitude, and tottered home to his waiting wife. It was their Friday evening treat. "Here are the latest dispatches from Creepwell!" he'd announce as he entered, and his wife would pour the tea and distribute the neatly-sliced lemon cake, as he read them out in a sycophantic voice. "I observed that Dr. Brown did not think it necessary to wear a clean shirt in the entire course of the week that has just drawn to a close . . ." This was a typical beginning, demonstrating the usual level of significance in Caswell's observations, and Mr. Scrivener managed a fair approximation of the teacher's obsequiously cringing tone, Uriah Heep with a microscope. It was the one thing that kept them together, the only time he made her laugh.

Mr. Caswell leaned in closer, pressing the beaker more firmly against the wall, concentrating, gesturing with his other arm at the class to remain absolutely silent. They gestured back, in ways they would not have chosen had he been facing them.

"Men!" the voice said again in the other laboratory.

From the very back of the laboratory, the men watched, the men listened.

"Men!"

Dr. Brown – as if nothing had happened (he'd have attempted an insouciant whistle if he hadn't banned whistling in the laboratory) – emerged, with immense *sangfroid*, from behind his bench. First one hand, then the other; the whole bearded head, then the body. He propped Abraham Lincoln at a dignified angle beneath President Harrison, and turned to face his students across the whole length of the laboratory.

"Another way of liberating hydrogen."

He inserted the plug, and turned on the faucet of the biggest sink in the laboratory, a sink big enough for a refreshing early morning swim. As it filled, he went into his storeroom, and emerged with a chunk of sodium securely contained within its bottle. A jinnee was about to be unleashed. That was the impression conveyed by the cautious way in which Dr. Brown gripped the glass. There it lay, yellowy-brown beneath its covering of oil, as swollen and putrescent as a portion of long-drowned corpse. When the sink was filled, he turned off the faucet, and stood in front of it, hefting the bottle in his hands, with the look of someone contemplating throwing a grenade at too close a target. Oliver rather hoped that – when he removed the sodium – he might cut into the soft putty-like substance, to reveal its silvery metallic sheen, giving it a more weapon-like look, a more aggressive war-colored, gunmetal luster. But Dr. Brown was beyond the reach of Symbolism.

He was about to succumb to a reckless impulse.

The enthusiastic roar from the men urged Dr. Brown ever onward to foolhardy excess. He had the air of an impoverished magician driven to ever more risky feats of prestidigitation. On the other side of the wall, Mr. Caswell winced as his beaker vibrated on a shrill note near to shattering.

Dr. Brown poured a complete bottle of litmus solution into the sink, with the air of a man downing the contents of a poison bottle, and the water turned a reddy-mauve color. You'd have thought that a guilty man had washed his bloodstained hands in it, a little water clearing him of this deed. *Macbeth* was proving most useful today. It must be Act Four, Scene One, the witches blending their concoctions in the cauldron, which gave it this close kinship with Chemistry. There was sure to be some baboon's blood in the bottle next to the hydrochloric acid.

Toil and trouble were undoubtedly about to be double, doubled.

Dr. Brown had that look in his eye.

Fire would burn, and the cauldron would bubble.

Perhaps Dr. Brown had a sense of Symbolism after all.

This looked promising.

The litmus-tested class – *tick, tick, tick*, here was a test they'd passed – watched expectantly. They were never as attentive as just before a major disaster, savoring what might be their last seconds of life. William French, trapped like another Snowdrop within his glass coffin, was showing signs of panic, attempting – with limited success – to shield the whole of his body behind Captain Mayne Reid. Doomed to die because of hair oil! What a dramatic demonstration of the evils of Pride, the punishment of sin!

Akenside, always keen to impress, had his hand in the air.

"What is the equation for this, Dr. Brown?" he asked, with a note of enthusiasm.

Dr. Brown, not choosing to reply, plunged his hand into the bottle like an unhygienic diner helping himself to a gigantic pickled gherkin. Most of his arm disappeared from sight, shoved well in. In his eagerness to impress he'd forgotten the vital little rule about sodium that he vainly attempted to hammer into the heads of the miniature men.

Do *not* handle sodium!

Do *not* handle sodium unless you can be certain that your hand is completely dry!

(The withering, sandstorm arid touch of dry fingers.)

Touch it only with an arid hand!

If you sweat, it *sizzles*!

Dr. Brown spent every lesson in a sweaty lather of panic, and he clutched the sodium in his hands, beginning to wipe off the oil caressingly.

He sweated, and . . .

(How reassuring this proof of scientific certainties.)

. . . the sodium *sizzled*.

With an agonized cry, Dr. Brown threw the generously proportioned chunk high into the air – as if to ensure a splash that would reach the *very* back of the laboratory – and it dropped spectacularly into the water with a splash that sent tidal waves sweeping across to the front row of benches.

Sometimes experiments produced a *Pop!*

Sometimes there was *Whoop!*

There was *Bang!* and there was *Boom!*

Sometimes — stormy weather days of restlessness — there was *Whumpf!* and there was *Ker-boom!* (with and without capital letters and exclamation points).

And then there was the noise produced by dropping a brick-sized chunk of sodium into a large sink full of water in a laboratory crammed with high-pitched, overexcited schoolboys.

This cauldron didn't just bubble.

It seethed.

It roared.

It smashed.

It *stunned.*

There was an ear-shattering *SIZZLE!!!* loud enough for a score of lightning-bolts from the most bad-tempered and malicious of gods, followed by the most tremendous *CRACK!!!* of an explosion, and the chunk of sodium — glowing menacingly like an approaching meteorite, like thunderclapping quicksilver, mercury at its most mercurial — began to zoom uncontrollably around over the surface of the water with a power that threatened to launch it right across the room to obliterate swathes of the screaming, cowering school-boys, as they fell off the bench in writhing heaps, thoroughly enjoying the sensation of mass hysteria. They weren't offered the opportunity for this quite often enough. They felt vaguely cheated that the sink hadn't shattered — it had been a near thing — and sent chunks of jagged debris hurtling through the air to mow them down, piercing heads and limbs in a blood-misted massacre. Survivors could have proudly flaunted interesting scars for years to come, whipping up their shirts at the slightest sign of encouragement. Clouds of acrid caustic soda fumes hellishly enveloped them all in corrosive clouds — they could feel their scoured lungs withering — and they coughed and choked and fought and struggled and screamed in this most unforgiving of biblical cleansings. Deoxygenated, litmus-changed to blueness, blue-bloodedly dying like ousted aristocrats in a violent uprising, they sank shrieking to the floor. It was the most fun they'd had for ages.

"We're all going to die! NaOH!" screamed two of the cleverer boys (there were a few of these, enough to keep Oliver balletically balancing on his intellectual toes). "We can't breathe! NaOH!" utilizing an appropriate formula as a scientifically accurate scream of terror.

Akenside — what an example that boy was! — wrote carefully in his exercise book, oblivious to the mayhem around him. *The water in the sink turned blue* — such was one of his *Observations* — *thus demonstrating . . .* — Akenside was fond of *thus* — *. . . the presence of an alkali. It might be supposed that . . .* He was also a great supposer. He lost marks for this.

The explosion seemed to have recalled to mind some suppressed memory of the Civil War for Dr. Brown. His whoops seemed to increase, and became louder, with a permanently higher pitch. What had once been a *Whoop!* now became a *WHOOP!*, and a *WHOOP!* it remained. The entertainment level of Chemistry lessons improved significantly. "WHOOP!" the class echoed. "WHOOP!" *WHOOP!*s bounced from white-tiled wall to white-tiled wall, and the chalked ups and downs of Dr. Brown's already unsteady chalky handwriting began to look more and more like the seismograph records of a catastrophic city-obliterating earthquake.

But Dr. Brown was not defeated, *WHOOP!*-haunted as he was. He possessed as yet unutilized reserves of destructive power, a power that would go far beyond the capabilities of sodium. Classes would need to go to the *very* back of the laboratory for some time to come. It would — indeed — not be too long before his classes would be offered the opportunity to go so far to the back of his laboratory that they would be bursting through the wall, and into Mr. Caswell's laboratory (trampling with unnecessary emphasis upon his crumpled brick-strewn body, the beaker still clutched in his death-clawed hand), as if they had become the newly activated rabbits, wolves, cougars, and hens, fleeing a hastily evacuated ark. "You will all need to go to the *very* back of the laboratory," he would say, filling the sink with water, as enthusiastic for a splashy baptism as a born-again high-diving champion. Potassium would follow sodium, rubidium would follow potassium, and – his farewell to the world, his school-shattering conclusion to his chemical career – cesium (the biggest chunk he could carry; he might seek help to heft it) would follow rubidium. He'd leave the door of his laboratory open for a hasty exit, and (his regular runs with Dr. Twemlow having honed him to a peak of physical perfection) smash his existing record, as he sped away (*faster, faster, faster!*) – just a blur – from the spectacularly exploding school. He'd be wearing his new running shoes, size eight, leather, spiked (a dog's claws *click, click, click* as he first entered) – they'd cost him $3.50 – and they'd speed him ahead of the impending *KER-BOOM!!!* as he hurtled across the park.

("Observe *that*, Caswell!")

(At last – at long, long last – he'd be granted the wings of a dove for which he'd prayed so devoutly, so loudly, and so many times.

(Far away, far away would he rove!

(In the wilderness he would build him a nest, and remain there for ever at rest.

(=

(=

(=

(At last he'd have crossed his little pathway into peace.)

Cesium – *cæsius*, bluish gray: it didn't say much for the complexions of the Cæsars – would lay waste to most of north Manhattan when it exploded into the water. The Ides of March might be an appropriate choice of day. Men, wives, and children would stare, cry out, and run, as if it were doomsday.

2

Of course, it hadn't really been like this, though Ben wished it had.

This was what it was like when his oldest sister wrote it down for him, to cheer him up when he was feeling low, describing it in the way he would have liked it to happen.

Alice would sniff the air sometimes when he arrived home from school.

"Chemistry today, I notice," she'd say, as if he still reverberated from the aftershock of explosions, though it was the fumes that informed, these and the reminiscent smile. "Was Oliver on good form?"

Oliver was usually on good form.

He'd tell her about Oliver. She always liked to hear what he'd been doing, like an elderly indulgent aunt, though she was only ten years older than they were. Oliver would sit and talk about books with Alice, and Ben wouldn't be able to follow most of what they were saying.

He'd tell her about the lesson.

Papa hadn't liked him to be near Oliver, had told him not to talk to him. This was years before they'd started at Otsego Lake Academy. Ben and Oliver's fathers had both died before – only just before in Ben's case – they'd entered Mr. Scrivener's demented domain. Papa disapproved, also, of Ben's talking to his sisters at any great length, or – most of all – to his mother. "Mama" was a word that soon had him snorting, if Ben spoke it. Conversations with Mama were guilty, hurried, words spoken after other rooms – and the street outside – had been checked. Papa had made it quite clear to Ben that Ben wasn't a manly enough son, and Comstock was the very last sort of companion with whom he should consort. He imbued the word "consort" with a sense of unspeakable filth. Here was a source of potential disease besides which sneezes and dubiously unidentifiable spots faded into insignificance. Here – unmistakably vivid – should be the red cross, the *Beware! Danger of Infection! Do Not Approach!* Oliver's own mother could scarcely have equaled Papa's appalled intonation of unsayable ahemness, though – confusingly – he urged Ben to cultivate every appearance of friendliness toward Oliver when they were at one of Mrs. Albert Comstock's "At Homes," a lesson in useful duplicity that came straight from the heart of Papa's deepest-held beliefs. Papa wished to be thought well of by Mrs. Albert Comstock, even if this –

Shudder! – meant having to look at that – *Shudder!* – prancing little pretty boy with an air of paternal benevolence.

(If Papa had looked so askance at Ben's alleged daintiness of manner, how on earth had the uncouth Albert Comstock regarded Oliver, that sturdy exotic orchid in the Comstock nettle-patch? Whatever the reaction, it hadn't seemed to bother Oliver. "Bertie Buttocks has been on the warpath again," he'd sometimes comment mysteriously to Ben, in reference to his father, giving the impression that some minor inconvenience had been neat-handedly overcome, bare hands fearlessly dashing arrows aside.)

Ben and Oliver had worked out a strategy to deal with the situation. He hadn't needed to tell Oliver what Papa had thought of him. The pat-pat-pats on what Oliver referred to as his "curly locks" hadn't *quite* made contact; the smiles at Oliver's *bon mots* had been strained and sweatily conscientious (Papa hadn't *understood* most of them); and his applause and enthusiasm at some performance (when his sister Myrtle let Oliver get a look in) had been less and less convincing the noisier they got. He had described Oliver as a "mama's boy" in an incautiously loud voice to the Reverend Goodchild – you needed a loud voice to get a word in when the Reverend Goodchild held forth, dingy grin on full display with cheesy chumminess – and Oliver had overheard him. Oliver heard *many* things boomed out by the Reverend Goodchild in his Tremble-Ye-Sinners-And-It's-*You*-I'm-Talking-About tone of voice. Oliver – in his turn – had shuddered, appalled at the thought of being seen as in thrall to his formidable and much-loathed mama. "It's the *worst* thing anyone has ever said about me," he'd complained. "And they've said plenty." Surely everyone knew what he thought about his mama!

Ben hadn't told him the far worse thing that his father – a connoisseur of carelessly (or carefully) hurtful comment (*carefully* would have been more *à propos*) – had recently said about Ben himself.

I have a son who is prettier than any of my daughters.

That was what he had said, jeering, at Ben, at Alice, at Edith, at Allegra, at *all* of them.

There were some comments that you did not wish anyone to know about, even though Oliver could be trusted not to repeat them. There were some comments that you turned over and over in your mind as you lay in bed at night and tried to sleep. Ben had been nine at the time. Over and over he heard the witheringly amused note in Papa's voice as he spoke — *prettier, prettier* — and the stress on that one word, *prettier*. It was the voice of a sadistic spoiled child (a Sidney Brinkman with a beard) baiting a pet parrot through the narrow bars of its cage in an attempt to ward off boredom. "Pretty Polly!" the sneering voice repeated tauntingly, as the sharp stick or steel nib stabbed at the cowering bird. "Pretty Polly!" It had been far worse because it had made him blush. He blushed easily. It was shortly before he began at the academy, and was one of the last things he could remember his father saying. He had been a delicate and nervous small boy, sensitive in his awareness of others, and — for years — had suffered mildly from what might have developed into consumptive symptoms. He had a tendency to faint, and had sometimes done so in the presence of his father. His Papa's reaction had been disgust. You'd have thought that he'd done it on purpose, an airy-fairy frippery on a level with playing the piano, reciting, or — particular scorn was reserved for this — *singing*. "Don't forget the smelling salts!" had been added to his father's extensive repertoire of mockery. For a time he had expected his father's large hairy-backed hand to grasp him around the mouth and pinch his nose (it would cover almost the whole of his face), to stop him from breathing, to make him faint again, just so that he could laugh at him. You could do it quite easily one-handed. Ben had experimented, bringing himself to the verge of fainting, alone in his room, feeling everything around him starting to fade, a high ringing sound in his head. He'd started to take deep breaths when his father approached close to him, in case a cigar-smelling hand descended to stop him from seeing, to stop him from breathing, a hand to cover his eyes, his mouth, his nose. One hand across the face, and one hand around the throat. He'd be held from behind, the beard pushing into the back of his neck. If he took really deep breaths it would be quite some time before he fainted, and his Papa would not laugh at him immediately. There would be a time — before the blackness descended — when his father would have his hands around him, and would not be laughing at him.

He'd seen a painting of Abraham and Isaac in an exhibition of Christian art, Abraham's hand pressing down hard upon the face of his son as he prepared to sacrifice him, covering it so completely that no trace of his features could be seen, and it had made him think of these feelings. He'd found himself preparing himself, beginning to take the deep breaths, a diver about to plunge deep into dark waters. He'd wanted to examine the painting closely, to see it happening from outside himself, but Isaac had been naked, and he'd been embarrassed to be seen looking, bending forward. He knew what his father would have said if he'd seen him doing *that*. He said really dirty things sometimes.

Always, as a small boy (as an even *smaller* boy) (he was conscious of his lack of height, and had to bend back to look up at Papa, Papa the preacher high in his pulpit speaking the words that had to be obeyed) — he was slight, with straight blond hair that brushed his shoulders — he would unconsciously adopt graceful little postures with his hands, or with the way he held his body. He folded his hands precisely one upon the other as he sat upright on a high-backed chair; he clasped his hands around one knee as he sat on a footstool; he folded his arms carefully in front of him on the dining table after a meal, each hand cupped around the elbow of the opposite arm, his face grave and intent like someone posing for a portrait or a photograph, neat in his movements. His mother had studio photographs by Henry Walden Gauntlett of such poses: they seemed like poses, though they were the natural way his body paused.

Such postures, such photographs, angered his father, although he never said why. Ben had found photographs of himself — those judged not to be acceptable, those not hidden by Mama — neatly and firmly torn across (not crumpled up in a fury: that would not be like his father) and left to be taken out with the other trash by the maid, their surfaces wrinkled by the dampness of the potato peel-ings or outer leaves of cabbages, stained by coffee grounds or the seepage from eggshells. His father had the habit of, without saying a word – it was a house in which things were rarely spoken aloud – reaching across and adjusting Ben's body, pulling an elbow to one side, pushing his hands apart, treating his son like a picture on a wall, or an ornament on a dresser, which offended some private sense of symmetry, an object to be rearranged. When his father came into the room, he would find himself – it became an auto-matic, instinctive action – holding his arms away from his sides, like someone preparing to be searched, waiting to be pushed and pulled into a permissible position.

These were the occasions on which his father touched him.

Touch it only with an arid hand!

A voice in a laboratory at the beginning of an experiment.

A voice struggling to be heard amidst shouting.

Touch.

It made him think of small, unfledged birds being caressed in their nests, and doomed to die – abandoned by their parents – because they had been touched by human hands. It wasn't the right image to use – "caressed" was not the word to describe the way in which his father touched him, and even "human" scarcely qualified (it was he who was made to feel scarcely human, as much as his father) – but it was the image that came inescapably into his head. He couldn't remember who it was who had told him never to touch birds in their nests. It could have been Mama. It could have been Mrs. Crowninshield during a nature ramble. Someone had even told him that the young birds weren't just abandoned; they were actually pecked to death by their parents because they had become alien, tainted by touch.

It was like the time when the Comstocks' parrot had made a bid for freedom – you felt inclined to cheer it on, foul-tempered thought the bird was, a bird of prey as much as a parrot, with a distinct taste for human flesh – and Oliver had walked around Longfellow Park all day carrying the large cage, its door left temptingly open, his arm aching. "Hilderbrandt!" he'd called seductively. "Oh, Hilderbrandt!" Flocks of other birds, drab-colored, bird-colored birds, had mobbed Hilderbrandt on the rooftops, stabbing at the bright-feathered interloper into their high, clouded domain, and – as night fell – Hilderbrandt had crept back into his cage, disheveled and shivering, loose feathers falling to the floor, his brief taste of freedom at an end, rejected by his unkind kind, who had refused to recognize him as one of their species. The sharp sticks, the steel nibs, the beaks: they all penetrated between the close-set bars. "Pretty Polly! Pretty Polly!" the voices jeered. He'd seen an engraving – seventeenth-century? eighteenth-century? – in one of Alice's books, a physician treating plague victims, his face entirely obscured by a bird-like long-beaked protective mask, and he saw the sharp beak rising and falling, rising and falling, bringing death to the infected, destroying them to protect the pure.

He didn't know why these thoughts came into his head.

How strange that people rarely knew the thoughts that were inside you, the words that you carried within. He was never entirely sure that these thoughts were not betrayed by the expression on his face, and he learned to control what his face revealed. He learned to control the emotions that had once been reflected in his face.

Best not to show them.

Best not to *experience* them.

His father had started this process, and Otsego Lake Academy – prompted by his expressed requirements – had continued it. "Go to the inner room," he'd whisper when he sensed the beginnings of an emotion, and it would go to the place of banishment. He visualized – he *smelled* – the inner room as being Papa's dressing room, the suffocatingly windowless interior lined with silent hanging rows of clothes that had not been cleaned often enough, dark, all of them, the sensation of a huddled mass of shrouded, disapproving mourners. Each time he went in there – he found himself returning, as if drawn – he would begin to hold his breath. It wasn't just to avoid the musty, slightly rancid smell, it was also because here (though it was a place imbued with more of a sense of absence than of presence) he felt — closer than ever — the hand across his face, the hand around his throat, the scratching of the beard on the back of his neck.

Animal-smelling fur-collars.

Sharp-edged horn buttons.

It felt more like a place of sacrifice than a place of sanctuary.

The naked boy with his face erased.

There he'd sit, feeling that he'd crawled in on his hands and knees, his arms wrapped around himself, his head lowered, his eyes closed, trying not to breathe.

Long periods of time went past like this.

Go to the inner room.

There, deep inside him, a place on which the door remained perpetually closed, slammed-to and bolted, the emotions became trapped like prisoners in an oubliette, labeled like the skull of a dustily untouched phrenological head, slowly suffocating in the crammed-in darkness as they were pushed in closer and closer upon each other. There — safely inaccessible — were emotions that were not to be experienced, words that were not to be spoken, words such as "beautiful," "sad," "wonderful," or "lovely."

Those sorts of words.

Oliver Comstock sorts of words.

He was quite lucky, he supposed, that his handwriting was so childish, and his spelling and punctuation so poor. There was something a little suspect about a boy who wrote beautifully and accurately.

Oliver Comstock sorts of accomplishments.

As Ben's body was corrected, so were the words he spoke, the thoughts he thought, and many words were words that he was not allowed to speak or think. He was never touched with tenderness or affection; neither was he beaten: his father preferred the use of words, enjoyed them more. It was more satisfying, it was more skillful, the ability to cause pain without striking the one you sought to hurt.

There was something magical about it.

Papa spoke the right words, and tears spilled from Ben's eyes, sobs shook his body.

Papa experienced the delirium of godlike power.

With the beard of Michael Angelo's God, he hovered in the air, his finger stretched out accusingly in front of him. This was not a finger to bring life with a touch, to animate the limp fragility of a human form. It was a finger to prod, to jab, to object, to adjust, to ensure the acceptable.

There was no comment, no rebuke or explanation for his father's actions, but they happened every time his father saw him, even when he had attempted to assume an attitude that would be found satisfactory. A firm hand would descend silently, there would be a little push – not quite a chastising shake, not quite a slap – and he would be made to alter the way he sat, or stood, or moved, like the way in which – at Otsego Lake Academy – Linnaeus, though left-handed, would be compelled to hold a pen in his right hand by Mr. Rappaport. Like Ben's father, Mr. Rappaport gave no explanation for what he did (the obvious enjoyment it gave him was clearly reason enough as far as he was concerned); like Linnaeus, Ben thought that what happened was what should be, that something wrong within himself was being cured, to make him grow the right way. The power of adults over children was absolute. He gradually learned what it was he had to do. The photographs which showed how he once was – the ones kept by his mother – remained, like the photographs taken by doctors to record scars or deformities before corrective surgery; but he himself changed, between the ages of five (it probably began earlier than that) and fifteen, and adapted, like those creatures – insects, moths, birds and animals in the forest – that change their coloring to blend in with their surroundings in order to survive. Like his long blond hair, part of him was cut away in order for him to become invisible, to be safe, even if his own *coloring* – his shameful inability to control his frequent painful blushing – did not change. He belonged in a place of redness, a place the color of blood and embarrassment. That was the place in which he could become invisible, and hide himself away in unremarked-upon obscurity.

48

Gradually, every movement of his body, every word he spoke, was considered before he made or uttered it, so that no gesture, no stance, no expression would be found unacceptable to his father, or – after he started at Otsego Lake Academy – to Mr. Rappaport, and he tried to cultivate a studied gracelessness, a conscious awkwardness. It hadn't happened consistently; it hadn't happened all at once; but it had happened. It had taken a long time. You would not have thought that something that was so weak, something that you thought could have been easily overcome, could have been so strong. He was not damaged in his speech, like Linnaeus (his occasional stuttering had always been a part of him), though he knew few words of tenderness; he was marked in the language of his body, where no spontaneity remained, and he was unable to express emotions unthinkingly. He moved as if upon a stage, each action imposed by a director, each word learned from a script, taught so as to appear natural. "Prompt" he felt like calling sometimes when words and movements failed him, peering across into the darkness beyond the small area of illumination in which he walked. "Prompt!"

A Particularly Handsome Article That Walks in a Manner That Looks as Natural as Life. It Looks as Much Like A Real Boy as it is Possible to Make It Appear.

These were the words on the brightly colored cardboard box in Papa's study, elaborately emphatic, beset about with ascenders and descenders, curling like the tendrils of plants seeking the sun; these were the words that summed up his whole philosophy of what a father should strive to create – it was his bearded parental duty – if he had a son.

Prompt!

It had to look natural.

Prompt!

It had to look like a real boy.

Prompt!

As far as it was possible.

As promptly as possible.

The words in the script were learned by heart – like a Latin vocabulary – and repeated many times. He must have forgotten the script that time he fell over in the street, forgetting how to move his legs as his father watched him walking, unable to remember what he had to do so that he walked in a manner that looked natural, unable to think of the right way he should scramble to his feet, unable to think of the right words to speak. "Frightened" was another word that he was not allowed to use.

Prompt!

Prompt!

Prompt!

But these were not the words that had been hissed at him from the darkness, telling him what to say and do.

Other words, quite other words, had been spoken.

When Ben and Oliver met in public (aware that their comportment was being carefully observed) they spoke to each other with distant politeness, boys only just meeting for the first time, not too impressed with what they were seeing. That was the impression that they sought to convey. You could see Papa grappling with the agonizing thought that perhaps it might look best if Franklin (Papa chose to refer to Ben by his middle name) gave the impression to Mrs. Albert Comstock that he was – *Shudder!* – Oliver's special playmate.

"Golly! It's Olly!" Ben would whisper secretly as they coolly shook hands in an exaggeratedly manly fashion (they'd practiced), like burly youths about to start arm-wrestling, Oliver only just preventing himself from bowing politely, and "I think it's Pink!" would be Oliver's whispered reply. You could hear the slight intake of breath from Papa at the wanton physicality of a handshake, the touching of the flesh. He'd have been furious to find that Ben was once again – had always been – in the same class at school as "that little Johnny-jump-up." There'd been no escaping this unsavory proximity at Crowninshield's – a one-class school – but he'd have hoped for better from Otsego Lake Academy.

Alice could tell when Ben had been enjoying something. She could also — with even greater accuracy — tell when he was feeling unhappy, and he was often unhappy, particularly at Otsego Lake Academy. She would come and find him in the front parlor, the room in which he labored at his schoolwork, and sought him out more — perhaps it was something to do with the age he then was, the age she then was — after he had started at the school. They neither of them pretended that his unhappiness had anything to do with the recent death of their father. They both knew what each felt about that, though it was something that they did not put into words.

Sometimes — if things were especially bad — he would go to her in the schoolroom, which was what they still called the room at the top of the house that was the domain of his three sisters. It was Alice he went to, not his mother, and even though he went to her he did not talk about his worries. This was his concession to manliness, a lesson remembered from his father. His father had never shown much interest in how he had progressed in his lessons at his first school, Crowninshield's (though he had worked hard, and tried his best), but this was one lesson Ben had been well taught, and taught by his father. *Franklin tries his best*. There it was, written down as a fact by Mrs. Crowninshield, who sometimes helped her husband with his reports, but Mrs. Crowninshield was a woman, and Papa did not take much heed of women. ("Women!" and "Girls!" were words invariably accompanied by contemptuous snorts as a part of the pronunciation, foreign words imperfectly assimilated into English.)

"Yes, Lincoln," Mama would say, bowing her head.

"Yes, Papa," Alice, Allegra, and Edith — big, grown girls — would say, bowing their heads, worshipers abasing themselves before their idol.

"Women!"

"Girls!"

He'd look at Ben for a conspiratorial response, and Ben had

never been quite sure what to do. He loved his Mama. He loved his sisters. Perhaps he – also – was a mama's boy, a prancing little pretty boy. He was, after all, *pretty*, prettier than any of his sisters. Ben might be doing the unthinkable, and feeling emotions, despite telling them to go to the inner room, but at least he wasn't talking about worries, and – even worse, far worse – talking about them with a *woman*, and at least he didn't cry. He didn't cry *much*, and did it only when he was alone, apart from those few – those shameful few – occasions in Mr. Rappaport's Latin lessons in Room 37.

Alice's illness – intermittent at first – had displayed its first symptoms at about the time he had entered the academy, when he was ten and she was twenty. Mrs. Albert Comstock and Mrs. Goodchild, elbows all of a nudge, had flocked, had peered, had jostled eagerly for access.

It was Alice who'd found Papa's body after he'd killed himself, Alice who'd been alone in the house with the body for those days during the 1888 blizzard, just before Ben started at the academy. Perhaps – an uncharitable thought, but just think who the thought was about – the two women were eager to hear fuller details of Papa's death than they'd been able to glean from their contacts. In a spirit of Christian compassion – this took some imagining – they'd press Alice (it was to help her to come to terms with the anguish: they'd sound really *convinced* about this) to give them the details, the details, *every* detail about what had happened. Charlotte Finch and Miss Ericsson were regular visitors to see Alice Pinkerton, but what was the point of their going to see her when they flatly refused to tell other people all about her when they'd been? Where was the pleasure in that? Charlotte Finch had been positively *rude*. (Let's face it, she was virtually as batty as her ha-ha-ha-ha friend was. That particular belfry was dark and crowded, noisy with high-pitched squeaking.)

Well before Alice had found herself under the care of an alienist (Dr. Severance of Staten Island, just managing to trip up and stun Dr. Wolcott Ascharm Webster, and walk into the house over his prostrate form), two rival alienists — two *very* alien alienists — had got themselves well established, the ends of their large feet firmly poking into the dark spaces beneath the bed. Fearlessly, they'd sat quite close to Alice Pinkerton in their avid quest for *details*, and, recklessly, they'd prodded about in the obscurity as far as their feet could reach, hopeful of chamber-pot clinkings, hidden, secret things being unearthed. They'd come in a twosome, to feel safer.

Mrs. Albert Comstock and Mrs. Goodchild were not women to waste time.

Right.

Off we go.

You first, Mrs. Comstock.

No, after *you*, Mrs. Goodchild.

Off they went.

"Was it a razor he used to cut his throat, or was it a knife?"

"Or something else? A piece of broken glass, a bottle?"

"After all . . ."

". . . he'd always have plenty of bottles around . . ."

". . . wouldn't he?"

"Was it really, really awful?" Mrs. Albert Comstock or Mrs. Goodchild asked hopefully (hopeful that it *would* be really, really awful, and wishing that she'd thought to bring a phonograph with her to make a recording of Alice's reply, solving the difficulty of deciding upon the entertainment that she was to offer at her next "At Home"; you'd had enough of piano-playing after a while, particularly if it were Myrtle Comstock doing the playing).

Alice would lean up on her pillows and stare at them politely, thinking thoughts that were not polite, and saying nothing.

"Was there lots and lots of blood?" Mrs. Albert Comstock or Mrs. Goodchild was even more hopeful when she asked this one. ("Two pints?" she'd be prompting helpfully. "Three pints? Four pints? *Gallons?*" She'd be really hoping for gallons. Gallons sounded gruesome and gallons were good.)

Silence.

"Did it splash *very* far?"

Silence.

"Was his head *really* you know, was it *completely* . . .?"

Silence.

"How many times did it bounce? Once? Twice? You could nod your head when I get the right answer, if you like."

Silence. No nods.

"How far did it bounce? Two feet? Three feet? Just nod your head. You needn't do it very vigorously, Alice dear."

"What sort of sound did it make as it bounced?"

"Was it a sort of *boing*?"

"A *boing, boing*?"

"A *boing, boing, boing*?"

"Depending . . ."

". . . of course . . ."

". . . on the number of times it bounced."

"Or was it more . . ."

". . . a sort of . . ."

". . . *squelchy* sound?"

"Tell us!"

"Tell us!"

"Give us the details!"

"Give us *all* the details!"

Silence. Still no nods. That Alice Pinkerton could be damned annoying at times.

(They'd be furious.

(*Damned* they'd think, not *d——d*, the version favored by the better novels. When you were really annoyed your standards tended to slip a bit. You didn't have the time to insert dashes in all curse words stronger than *Dash!* You just came out and thought it.)

"Did you go mad straightaway, or did it take time?"

Silence.

"Five minutes? Ten minutes?"

Silence.

"Did you gibber and become dangerous . . ." – shifting her position slightly at this point, clutching her purse defensively, showing every indication that you couldn't be too careful – "... or did you just sort of lie on the floor and moan a bit?"

Silence.

"What was the moan like *exactly?* Could you give a demonstration? A *loud* demonstration? Just for us?"

"Was it a sort of *Waaaagh!?*"

"... or more of an *Oh! Oh! Oh!?*"

Silence.

"We've come out to see you *specially*. You could say *something*."

(Voice slipping slightly, tone of a concerned Christian fraying at the edges. The height of Mrs. Goodchild's ambitions never varied. All she asked for was to discover something absolutely appalling so that she could take it back to share with her sister.)

Judging by the expression on the faces of Mrs. Albert Comstock and Mrs. Goodchild as they emerged from the schoolroom, Alice *had* said *something*. Judging by the expression on the faces of Mrs. Albert Comstock and Mrs. Goodchild, that *something* had not been the something that they had been hoping to hear. The expression was a well-it-looks-like-it's-back-to-Myrtle-on-the-piano expression, and it was a distinctly annoyed and disappointed expression. Mrs. Albert Comstock had brought a hideous purple plant from her conservatory with her the first time they'd called (it looked the sort of plant to leap upon and devour passing cattle), and – a sulky expression on her face – she'd taken it back home again with her, firmly clamped to her bosom (it was a particularly hardy variety of plant), pointedly withholding it for unsatisfactory behavior. Alice, undoubtedly, had failed to *earn* her beneficence. Perhaps Mrs. Albert Comstock was going to feed Chinky-Winky to the plant. It was about time that a purpose was found for her revolting Pekinese.

They'd salvage something from their visit.

It hadn't been worthy of a purple plant, but they'd salvage something.

"She was just sort of *lying* there ..."

"Dr. Twemlow's made her stay in bed, of course ..."

"Though I'm not sure that it's a *doctor* she needs at the moment . . ."

"Dr. Wolcott Ascharm Webster . . ."

"It seems to me that he, *he* of all people . . ."

"The – ahem – Webster Nervine Asylum . . ."

"The *very* place . . ."

"She looked . . ."

"Didn't she!"

"She looked really *strange*. There was a sort of . . ."

". . . a sort of – whatdoyoumacallit – *strange* atmosphere . . ."

"I would have not have liked to have been there on my own . . ."

"*Just* what I thought!"

"She was lying there . . ."

"You know what she's like . . ."

"Lying there . . ."

"Just sort of *lying* there . . ."

When he was sure that there was no one else there – there was rarely anyone else there – Ben would knock at the door, and go into her room.

Alice didn't go in for pale and picturesque invalidism, lying back against her pillows in a prettily crocheted jacket, eyes closed with saintly forbearance, sighing gently. Pretty crocheting played no part in Alice's plans. She was decidedly unacquainted with saintly forbearance and gentle sighs. She looked *furious* at being ill, most of the time. Elizabeth Barrett Browning's supposed demeanor did not come to mind, though some of her words might.

"The works of women are symbolical.

We sew, sew, prick our fingers, dull our sight . . ."

– he'd actually heard her quoting these words to Charlotte once, a distinct note of acrimony in her voice –

". . . Producing what? A pair of slippers, sir,

To put on when you're weary – or a stool . . ."

56

"'A sort of birdcage life,'" Charlotte had replied, and these words — it was clear — were also the words of Elizabeth Barrett Browning. Perhaps he'd been wrong about Mrs. Browning. Perhaps she was another one who had seethed and muttered in the way that Alice tended to do. Perhaps she'd swung sew-sewn, finger-pricking slippers, and footstools, and trays, and tea sets — and Flush (ears flapping vigorously) — around her head, and hurled them across the room to bounce off Robert Browning's head, disarranging his carefully combed beard. "That tea's cold, and you've cut the toast *far* too thinly! I want something I can get my teeth into!" This thought gave a whole new insight into his motivations for writing "My Last Duchess" or "Porphyria's Lover." Ben had heard about these from Oliver, who went in for dramatic declamations, and performed them with bloodcurdling verve.

Alice would be lying in bed, pulled close to the window looking out onto Chestnut Street, near to the gold stars from All Saints' on the window-ledge, and the pieces of colored glass and terracotta sculpture from the demolished Shakespeare Castle, a building he had never seen. Her books would be open on the bed around her, her scattered pages of writing in their blackest of black ink. She'd start gathering up the pages if anyone entered the room, hiding them away. She, also, had learned lessons from Papa. She, also, had her inner room.

"Moonshine!"

That was what Papa thought of Alice's writing.

"'The pleasant land of counterpane,'" Ben said to her. He'd checked the words in the copy of *A Child's Garden of Verses* that she'd bought for him. This was not a book — *Poetry!* — to have ever shown to Papa; this was not a book — *POETRY!* — ever to take to school with him. Otsego Lake Academy was a two-twos-are-four sort of school, a the-capital-of-Oregon-is-Salem sort of school, a the-third-president-of-the-United-States-was-Thomas-Jefferson sort of school, an *amo-amas-amat* sort of school, and it had no place for poetry. You could hear the antiphonal voices echoing from behind closed doors as you marched (you always marched) down the narrow windowless corridors, the tramping of your boots sounding from bare wall to bare wall. The dominant sound was the tramping, and the shouted orders, "No talking! No talking!" (there was a Trappist monk insistence about this that would have worried Oliver's mama) and — urgent as a political imperative — "Keep right! Keep right!" (this would have appealed rather more to Oliver's mama), but the chanting voices were always there in the background.

It was ever a place of certainties.

The voices sang like the voices of chanting monks in a secular monastery, this most undecorated of plainsong celebrating the triumph of factuality.

"'The pleasant land of counterpane.'"

"'Pleasant'?"

"Is it pleasant?"

"'All my toys beside me lay,'" she replied, "'To keep me happy all the day.'"

Pen.

Paper.

The open journal.

More than toys to Alice.

The more recent section of writing still gleamed faintly, still wet, the pen only just placed down.

"Have they kept you happy?" he asked.

"Sort of happy." Then, "Happy?" she asked.

"Not really."

He still felt slightly jumpy talking to Alice in this sort of way.

Women!

Girls!

"Pass the mustard," was acceptable (less acceptable if you added "please"), as was, "I think girls are *silly*," but *talking* was distinctly more hazardous.

He kept expecting Papa to appear through the door suddenly, in that way he had, waiting for the right moment to pounce. Death did not put an end to pouncing. Ben had found that out.

Resurgam.

That was the threat spelled out in the darkest place in the grave-yard.

"Discussing the right sort of flounces to add to your nice new dress with the girlies, Franklin?" (If it wasn't pounces, it was flounces.)

That was the sort of comment Papa would make, as he returned from the Occidental & Eastern Shipping Company in the evening, to find his son in that house of women.

"Discussing how much rouge to add to your cheeks with the girlies, Franklin?"

"Discussing the latest pretty little waltzes with the girlies so that you can learn to play them on the piano, Franklin?"

"Discussing an exciting new love story with the girlies, Franklin?"

That sort of thing.

The word "girlies" was always spoken with infinite scorn. Papa made a little exaggeratedly effeminate twirl round on one foot, coyly resting the side of his head on a limply extended finger. His There-Goes-Oliver-Comstock gesture had turned into his Here-Comes-Franklin-Pinkerton gesture, fragile fairy Franklin, giggling with the girlies.

Papa seemed to expect Ben to sit apart in manly silence until he appeared, all poised for bearded camaraderie.

At first he had tried to protest a little, in the sort of way that Allegra did.

"Papa!"

"Papa!" his father would mimic shrilly, with surprising energy, waiting all day for just such a moment.

"Papa!"

"Papa!" (Shriller than ever, and all his sisters hearing. This would be enough to start the blushes.)

"What an *attractive* blush, Franklin!"

"Papa!"

(Blush deepening.)

"Quite the cutie!"

"Papa!"

(So much redness flooding his face that he expected blood to begin pouring from his nose and eyes.)

"All pink and pretty and pouting!"

"Papa!"

"All rouged-up and raring to go!"

"Papa!"

After a while he stopped protesting, as they all did.

Silence was safer.

Sometimes — when he was smaller, not now — Alice talked about what she'd written.

She'd always wanted to be a writer, and had written stories for him when he was a small boy, though they were not children's stories, reading them to him at bedtime. She'd written other little things over the years especially for him, little presents like the books she bought him, and gave them to him in the way that other people gave a little treat to cheer someone up, chocolate or cookies, or in the way that Harry Hollander sometimes wrote songs. One particular favorite — "An Ambition Achieved" — had started: *Jessica Philadelphia Tennyson — a girl of poise and determination, one worthy of emulation — wanted, more than anything else, to be an orphan. By the age of seven she had achieved her ambition. She'd hurried things along a little, but it still counted* . . . This was one he'd asked her to repeat to him several times. Papa would not have approved. It was bad enough — *Moonshine! Moonshine!* — that Alice was writing stories, but to be *reading* stories — *about a girl!* (you could hear the outraged wheezy roar, smell the expelled cigar fumes) — to his namby-pamby slip of a son!

Ben had particularly liked the *hurried things along a little*. Even at that early age, long before Chemistry lessons at Otsego Lake Academy, Oliver had been all in favor of hurrying things along a little, and to hear those words in a story (particularly when describing a captivating 7-year-old mass murderess) was oddly liberating. He'd told Oliver about it, and Oliver had written to ask Alice for a copyright fee of one dollar — he felt as strongly about copyright as

Charles Dickens, he'd informed her, *hurried things along a little* was definitely *his* copyright phrase – and Alice, who'd been seventeen at the time, had paid him.

Some years later, just after his father had died, shortly before Ben's, he had written to Alice. *Halfway to being an orphan* – he informed her (Oliver liked to shock) – *I've never been the same since I read "An Ambition Achieved." I blame you. Jessica Philadelphia Tennyson has long been my inspiration, and is unquestionably a girl worthy of emulation, the source of my widely admired poise and determination. Just Mama to dispose of now. Any suggestions?* He'd obviously heard about Alice and Charlotte, when they were little girls, drawing up their sadly thwarted plans to commit Sybilicide, slaughtering Sibyl Comstock to earn the thanks of a sobbing and grateful nation. They'd tried and tried again, girls who'd clearly taken against needlework and flower-arranging, girls eager to *STAB ENORMOUS SIBYL,* and see Mrs. Albert Comstock as packed with knives as a cutlery drawer.

Oliver had enclosed a dollar with his note, returning the same one that she'd sent to him three years earlier. Anyone who'd tried to murder his mother qualified as a best friend, as far as he was concerned.

Later – when they were fourteen, and in Year Three (*aleph*) at Otsego Lake Academy – Ben had shown Oliver the version of a Chemistry lesson that Alice had written, when things had been hurried along a little yet again.

Oliver read it, and assumed an expression of horrified incredulity.

"Note the expression of horrified incredulity," he said. "This is *frighteningly* accurate. Your sister clearly keeps a servant fee'd in Scrivener's Workhouse." "Scrivener's Workhouse" was Oliver's term for Otsego Lake Academy. He was all too conscious of the literary antecedents of his Christian name, and probably kept a list of all the novels he'd read that contained the name, in the way that Charlotte Finch – Alice's friend, Linnaeus's sister – collected Alices and Pinkertons from her reading.

"'Servant feed'?" Ben asked, not sure if he'd heard correctly, thinking of poorer cuts of meat, some reference to the low quality of the lunchtime meal at the academy. This was an establishment in which no boy would think to ask for some more.

"It's a reference to *Macbeth*."

He was currently involved in a particularly ferocious battle with his mother, and was in skittish mood.

"*Macbeth*?" Ben asked.

"*Macbeth*," Oliver confirmed, as if that explained everything. "Alice will understand what I mean. She's quite keen on *Macbeth*. Bubble, bubble. Don't forget to tell her. *Halfway*, tell her. *I am in blood*, tell her. *Strange things I have in head. Worthy of emulation. I've been bloody, bold, and resolute.* Tell her all these."

It was not always easy to follow what Oliver was saying.

"*Bloody!*" Ben repeated, in the tone of one shocked at a daring choice of word.

"*Very* bloody. *Bloody* bloody."

Oliver was in a let's-frighten-the-fragile mood. It often happened after a *contretemps* with his mother.

"What are you going to tell Alice?" he asked, testing him out.

"*Halfway. I am in blood. Strange things I have in head. Worthy of emulation. Bloody, bold, and . . .*"

". . . *resolute*."

". . . *resolute*."

"Tell her."

Oliver looked again at the description of the Chemistry lesson.

"This is jolly good," he said, smiling. ("Jolly good" was very much an Oliver sort of phrase.)

"*He was by far the cleverest boy in the class*," Ben quoted.

"*Frighteningly* accurate. As I've already remarked."

"She also thinks that you have a really nice smile. She said so."

The following day Oliver gave Ben a story he had written, to take to Alice. It was called "A Really Nice Smile."

"Tell her I haven't been snip-snapped," was the message Oliver had given him with the beautifully italic-scripted pages, curled round in a cylinder-shape and fastened with a ribbon, like a message from a king in a Shakespeare play. "Not yet, anyway, though Mr. Rappaport lives in hope."

"He's sharpening his scissors at this very moment."

"Sparks illuminate the night sky, and gaping crowds gasp and point."

Oliver thought for a moment, and then spoke decisively.

"Mr. Rappaport is a *shit*," he said.

It was the worst word Ben had ever heard anyone speak, and he gasped a little, rather impressed. As if the word in itself wasn't enough, he'd also utilized italics. It was probably the use of "bloody" that had done it, nudging him over the edge into astonishing the bourgeois, long before he'd come across Baudelaire during his æsthetic phase.

(The worst word he'd ever heard anyone speak . . .

(Apart . . .

(Apart from . . .

(Apart from Papa.

(Papa hadn't said the words in front of his sisters.

(Usually.

(Though he had in front of Mama.

(*At* Mama.

(And all the time when he was with Ben.

(He'd say the words, and look at Ben for Ben's reaction.

(Ben was the brightly-colored bird in the cage – *too* brightly colored, that was the problem – and Papa was teaching him the right words to speak, the *manly* words, even though Ben's voice was not yet deep enough for authenticity, even though his beard would be a long time coming. Alice had once said to him that the language of The Bearded Ones – this was how she referred to men, with an unconvincing note of awe in her voice – was Latin, but Ben thought that another language was involved, another private code for use in girlie-free rooms with closed doors and a smoky atmosphere. It was a language he would have to learn in order to be comprehensible to The Bearded Ones, to enter that fuzzy-faced freemasonry. Papa would prod him, and repeat the word, prod him, and repeat the word, the sweetmeat held as his reward against the bars of the cage. Most of the words were quite short words, ugly-sounding words, and they had to be learned as carefully as any Latin declension.)

Oliver looked at Ben again, the cute pretty face that called forth coos.

"I said *shit*," he repeated, with some relish. "Not *twit*."

He'd said it *twice*.

They'd had Mr. Rappaport as their Latin teacher for almost four years by this time, and — considering the wide choice of appropriate nouns available — it displayed remarkable restraint on Oliver's part to choose to describe that tall trim turd, that sleekly poisonous sneerer, as no more than a *shit*.

Three times.

Ben hoped that he wasn't blushing.

Even having certain *thoughts* was enough to make him blush sometimes.

He'd blush, and Papa would pounce.

Even though he was dead, Papa would pounce.

"Having girlie thoughts, Franklin?"

"Overcome by girlie modesty, Franklin?"

"Don't forget the smelling salts! You look all fit to faint."

He'd rattle the bars of the cage, blow cigar fumes, and hold out the glowing end as if to ground it out on his face, anything to make the exotic pet bird say what it had been taught to say, and entertain them all. It was the reason it had been bought in the first place. The brightly colored bird glowed brighter as it blushed.

A sort of birdcage life.

("Pretty Polly! Say it!"

(*Rattle, rattle!*

("*Pretty* Polly! *Say* it!"

(*Rattle, rattle!*

("*Pretty* Polly!"

(*Rattle, rattle!*

(*"Pretty! Pretty! Pretty!"*)

(The foul-smelling breath enveloped him.)

Perhaps the brightly colored bird was a canary, and not a parrot, its cage brandished in the vicinity of poison gas, testing the quality of the air for safety. If the bird plummeted from its perch, you dropped the cage and ran. Why this choice of a canary? Why this impulse to stifle song?

He'd be lying on the floor of his cage, silenced forever. He'd never say "Pretty!" now.

Years earlier.

"Hilderbrandt!" Oliver shouted, shaking the cage like a maraca, hearing no sound but a feathered rustling. "Hilderbrandt!" Everyone hated Hilderbrandt, but Oliver was quite fond of the parrot ever since he'd gouged a great lump out of his mama's elbow. The fondness was mingled with considerable respect. A bird that had swallowed a hunk of Mama, survived, and come back for second helpings! It was clearly indestructible! Great shrieks had rent the air at 5 Hampshire Square, and they'd virtually had to prize Hilderbrandt off Mama with a crowbar. Once that bird tasted human blood it became insatiable. It had been just like Prometheus and the eagle, according to Oliver, though – Oliver was a perfectionist, quite strict about classical accuracy – he'd train Hilderbrandt to go for the liver next time. "Lodged into her liver!" he'd be repeating to the keen-to-kill parrot, eager to expand its short-tempered vocabulary, subtly (by gradual stages) leading the bird onto more lethal lungings. The description of the death of Eurymachus had created a sensation amongst the Crowninshield's boys when they'd recently read *The Odyssey*. (After Odysseus' arrow had twanged into Eurymachus' chest, beside his nipple, it had – they'd consulted dubious medical books, with rather off-putting illustrations, to grasp the concept – lodged into his liver. Rather a long arrow, they'd decided. You didn't get that sort of thing in Captain Mayne Reid or James Fenimore Cooper, both determinedly nipple-free zones as far as they could make out, though they hadn't yet seen the paintings of Cora and Alice Munro in the cupola at Otsego Lake Academy. "I've got nipples! I've got nipples!" That's what the Munro sisters seemed keen to demonstrate, breasts held out for inspection. They'd make a popular attraction at Brinkman's Papa's club, "Look! Look!," all fingers pointing – Dr. Brown emphasizing a particularly vital equation – bold as ships' figureheads. It quite put you off what Mr. Scrivener was saying of a morning. You'd stand there, trying not to blush, horribly embarrassed to think that you were a chap, and that – there was no denying it – you, also, were in possession of nipples (two of them). It was a distinctly disturbing discovery.

"Lodged into her liver!"

Hilderbrandt wouldn't need too much encouragement to get his beak bloodsoaked in a wet frenzy of liver-ripping.

Oliver was as keen to kill his mama as Alice and Charlotte had been when they were little girls. It was all the fault of Little Lord Fauntleroy.

Oliver, at the age of eight, years earlier, had been the Fauntleroyliest of all the Little Lord Fauntleroys of Longfellow Park. From the moment it was published, *Little Lord Fauntleroy* had rested on the Comstock Bosom, lain upon the Comstock table, had the Comstock bookmark inserted within it, and been endlessly discussed. First the copies of *St. Nicholas* magazine had mounted up during the serialization, from the end of 1885, and through 1886, and then the complete published novel. It had lain at the correct angle in the music room at about the same time as *War and Peace* and *King Solomon's Mines*. Mrs. Albert Comstock had become deeply enamored of Little Lord Fauntleroy, a complete thralldom far more powerful than anything she experienced for Prince Andrey Bolkonsky (despite the superior title) or Allan Quatermain. Here was the pattern for what Oliver ought to be, and for what Oliver would become. She labored to achieve this end, a besotted behemoth.

He was so like Little Lord Fauntleroy already that Frances Hodgson Burnett must surely have patterned her character upon him, and it was surely a portent (Mrs. Albert Comstock, encouraged by Mrs. Alexander Diddecott, was a great one for portents) that Oliver's middle name should be Francis, linking him in christened kinship with *Frances* Hodgson Burnett. Oliver's curled blond hair was tended obsessively by his mother — she seemed to regard it as a sort of outgrowth quite independent of the boy (it was "the hair," not "Oliver's hair") — in the way that the Japanese were said to lavish years of their lives in tending a single bonsai tree.

Oliver was the first, the true, the only Little Lord Fauntleroy of Longfellow Park, knitted, embroidered, and primped by Mama. He found himself — a year or so later — repeatedly hauled off to a theatre packed with other small boys. All of them equally glum, all of them with long blond curly hair, all of them dressed in lace-collared velvet knickerbocker suits, they watched, with horrified incredulity, as an *actress*, dressed exactly as they were dressed, flitted about the stage like a miniaturized Oscar Wilde fully formed in childhood.

She spun around, and exclaimed, "Dearest is my *close* friend, and we always tell each other everything."

Jaws sagged.

She, winsome as anything, struck a pose on the staircase, and coyly announced, "I am a very little boy to live in such a large castle, and have so many big rooms."

Jaws sagged further.

She looked limpidly at Miss Vivian Herbert and piped, "Of course I couldn't think anyone *quite* as pretty as Dearest. I think she is the prettiest person in the world."

Jaws crashed onto knees with eye-watering whacks.

("Dearest" was her *mama*, for God's sake!)

It was astonishing that there were not long lines of desperate, haunted youths outside Dr. Wolcott Ascharm Webster's, all of them with long blond curly hair, all of them dressed in — rather tight-fitting — lace-collared velvet knickerbocker suits, and all of them begging for help: electrotherapy, baths (hot), baths (cold), massage, hypnotism, the Weir Mitchell Treatment, cloud reading, picture reading, dream reading, *anything*.

"This is the Fauntleroy Ward," the well-muscled nurses would explain, to the horrified visitor to the Webster Nervine Asylum, as the heavily bolted doors creaked back, and the grotesque knicker-bockered creatures thus exposed to sight skipped about from barred window to barred window, the more hopeless cases bound in lace and velvet straitjackets. They made little steps forward toward their visitor, flushing rosy red with pleasure up to the roots of their bright hair, and (those unencumbered by straitjackets) flung their arms around his neck.

"Dearest! Dearest!" they cried. "Live with us! Live with us always!"

Oliver, of course, had known precisely what to do.

"Dearest!" he greeted his mother enthusiastically in the house whenever she had visitors.

"Dearest!" he called across the street to her.

"Dearest!" he exclaimed in the tone of someone overcome with surprise and delight whenever he saw her. He made special detours just to shout "Dearest!"

(He hadn't said, "Dearest is my *close* friend, and we always tell each other everything."

(He hadn't said, "Of course I couldn't think anyone *quite* as pretty as Dearest. I think she is the prettiest person in the world."

(*Mrs. Albert Comstock!*

(That *would* have been worrying.

(That *would* have led to running up and down in corridors, and raised voices as overworked doctors were hastily summoned.

(*Mrs. Albert Comstock!*

(*The prettiest person in the world!*

(*Crikey!*

(The Fauntleroy Ward would have prepared its deepest, darkest padded room. Nurses flexing their biceps would have gathered in serried ranks, bracing themselves for the most dangerous patient they had ever encountered.

("Don't panic," they'd be muttering to each other encouragingly, trembling. "Don't panic. We *can* handle this one. We *can* handle this one . . ."

(The voices from the Fauntleroy Ward, audible through the thick well-guarded walls, the lace and velvet loonies.

(*Dearest!*

(*Dearest!*

(*Live with us!*

(*Live with us always!*)

"Lodged into her liver!"

Hilderbrandt would need no encouragement whatsoever.

If Oliver could teach Hilderbrandt rude words – there'd been much blushing at the most recent "At Home," and Mabel Peartree had had to leave the room – then he could teach Hilderbrandt to rip out his Mama's liver. Hearing the word "Shit!" shrieked by a parrot in a room jammed with the genteel had a far more spectacular effect than just hearing Oliver say it to you with no one else in the room. Small boys had fallen off sofas in shrieking heaps, and the Reverend Goodchild had emptied an entire teapot of tea into his lap, spending the rest of the afternoon looking as if he'd wet himself. He probably *had* wet himself. (You could always hope.)

The effect of a foul-mouthed parrot was up there with cesium.

$2Cs + 2H_2O = 2CsOH + H_2\!\uparrow$.

(Oliver always knew the correct equation for any experiment you cared to mention, the secular equivalent of Bradley and biblical references.)

It was up there with *nitroglycerine*.

$4C_3H_5(NO_2)_2 = 12CO_2 + 10H_2O + 6N_2 + O_2$.

(Just *looking* at this equation had you bracing yourself, and taking precautionary measures.)

Oliver's "Shit!"-filled pleasure would have been complete if the spilled tea had only been somewhat hotter. The water, sadly, hadn't been at boiling point. You couldn't have everything, though everything would have been nice. Two hundred and twelve degrees Fahrenheit would have been just about perfect. An incensed and scalded clergyman – soggy, steaming, *furious* – would soon have outdone the best efforts in filthy language from Hilderbrandt. Oliver would start Hilderbrandt's liver-gobbling training with

Chinky-Winky, and work his way up. First Chinky-Winky's liver, then his sister Myrtle's (pleasure increasing all the while), then (the summit of his ambitions) Mama's. Oliver was a boy with a purpose. For the first time in his life, Ben began to look forward to the idea of an "At Home" at Mrs. Albert Comstock's.

Perhaps he *should* have told Oliver about "I have a son who is prettier than any of my daughters."

He knew how Oliver would have responded.

"I find that *most* offensive!" he would have exploded, in tones of deepest outrage. "Everyone knows that *I* am far prettier than you are! How *dare* he say that! I feel positively insulted, my superior charms spurned!"

He'd have swayed from side to side, like a parrot on a perch.

"Pretty Olly!" he'd have said, in a squawking Captain Flint, pieces-of-eight voice. "Pretty Olly!"

He would have made Ben laugh.

("What on earth can you be thinking about to cause that *attractive* blush, Franklin?"

("Please feel free to share your thoughts with us, Franklin. We're men of the world here, aren't we? Some of us. Come on, tell us what you're thinking.")

It was as if his father was inside his head, rummaging about, seeing his thoughts, not liking what he saw. First you rearranged the body, then you rearranged the thoughts. One followed on from the other, each an essential part of the multi-faceted tyranny of the purposefully unæsthetic.

Ben would shake his head.

He'd blush more than ever.

(Short, blond, little-boy gap in front teeth, occasional faints, prone to blushing.

(Perhaps his father had a point.

(Pretty Pinkie.

(Pretty Pinkie.

("In the *Pink*!"

("In the *Pink*!"

("In the *Pink*!")

Shit.

Four times.

4

A Really Nice Smile

The week after the Chemistry lesson – his ears still ringing, the smile still on his face – Oliver opened his black notebook on the desk in his room, and turned to a fresh page. He wrote in his very best handwriting. He had to make himself write slowly to do this; his hand usually sprinted across the pages with a looping scrawl.

Akenside had his hand in the air.

"What is the equation for this, Dr. Comstock?"

"Thank you for asking, Akenside," Dr. Comstock replied, with kindly condescension. The young genius had received his doctorate at a precociously early age.

He wrote it down like a declaration of intent, with firm defiant strokes.

$2Na + 2H_2O = 2NaOH + H_2\text{\textsh}$

After a moment, he added his first heading.

Object.

He underlined this, using his ruler in the way that Ben did.

To demolish Mama.

He thought about this for a while, and his smile broadened. This object was a subject on which he liked to dwell. He thought for a while longer.

Equipment.

No difficulties here.

No special equipment is necessary.

He almost underlined this, also – for the sheer pleasure of it – but it was not a heading, and he didn't want to lose a mark.

Materials.

This was underlined, and under this he wrote just two words, one in capital letters.

Water.

SODIUM.

The capital letters made him feel resolute.

Next there would be *Diagram.* He'd enjoy drawing the diagram. If the window above the bathroom door was left open as Mama took her morning bath, and he stood on a chair – should that be listed as a piece of equipment? – he would be able to project the chunk of sodium straight into the bath if he gave it a good hard shove. He was a boy who was a stranger to inelegant sweating, and his cool dry hands could handle sodium in perfect safety. A graceful balletic arc would be required of the descending sodium. The window – no more than one foot high and two feet wide – was disappointingly small-scale in size when he'd set his heart on a major explosion. He wished for as large a block of sodium as possible. He'd been a little anxious about the possible hazard of the block bouncing off Mama's head, and shooting straight out through the other, larger window into the garden, and probably killing the gardener as he lopped at the vegetation beneath. (He'd definitely lose a mark for that, *and* he liked the gardener, a man refreshingly free of all signs of respect for Mama.) A little subtle questioning had established that Mama was in the habit of sitting with her back to the outside window, and so her head would *not* be in the way of the descending block. What a relief that was!

He'd pour litmus solution into Mama's bathwater. The resulting maroon color – one of her favorites – would lure her into an enthusiastic plunge. "What a subtle fragrance," she'd mutter to herself – she couldn't stop talking even when she was alone in the room – as tidal waves obliterated coastal settlements around her. (The thought that a maroon was also an exploding distress signal was a definite linguistic bonus.) As she lay there, semi-submerged – there was, after all, a limit to the size of bath you could fit into a bathroom, and *semi*-submerged was about the best you could hope for –

the sodium could be introduced to the bathwater. He would shunt the Na into the H_2O, and the $2NaOH$ and H_2 would be liberated, along with a large part of Longfellow Park. What were the possibilities of a naked flame being introduced to the hydrogen, to hurry things along a little?

"Sodium, meet Mama's bathwater. Mama's bathwater, meet sodium."

He'd avert his eyes from the field-of-vision fleshiness on display within, alerted by the warnings within Greek myths. He didn't want to embrace the fate of Actæon after he'd seen Diana bathing, and be devoured by a maddened pack of Chinky-Winkies, all past and present pet Pekinese leaping into being at the same moment in time.

Then . . .

Then . . .

It would happen suddenly, completely out of the . . .

Blue.

KER-BOOM!!!

The bathwater would turn . . .

Blue.

SIZZLE!!!

Asphyxiating in the fumes, unable to breathe, Mama would go . . .

Blue

In the face, and

The air would turn . . .

Blue

– WHUMPF!!! –

As Mama's language became . . .

Blue

– AAAAGHHHH!!! –

As she disappeared through the roof, and soared into the . . .

Blue

Sky, her skin turning . . .

Blue

73

In the cold, the nearest she would ever approach to being a . . .
Blue
Stocking.

All that would be visible of Mama in the diagram would be her feet (he'd need a lot of pencil for these), at the very top of the page as she shot up high into the air. She'd look rather like St. Barbara's father in the stained-glass window in All Saints', as the bolt of lightning bounced off his bald head, galvanizing him into a gigantic leap. Even Dr. Brown's chalked ups – in his up-and-down printing – were never as up as this, even after the loudest of noises. How on earth could the necessary force be generated to shoot the enormous mass of his mother so high into the air that she would go through the roof? Would it be possible – oh, please, please! – to create enough force for his mother to be shot completely into orbit? She would circle the earth, another moon to join the first – as dead, as pale, as spherical – and the two of them would be like another pair of heavenly twins, another Castor and Pollux shining in Gemini, rotating silently (*silently!*) in space. He'd be like Keats, on first looking into Chapman's Homer. He'd feel like some watcher of the skies when a new planet swims into his ken, as Sibyl took up her position alongside Mars and Venus (with whom she had so much in common). There might well be climatic changes, if this huge new planet interposed itself between the sun and the stricken earth, and primitive tribes, panicking, would bow down in worship as darkness descended.

Enough force to break free from the earth's atmosphere . . .

For a long, tantalizing moment, Oliver hovered on the verge of making a momentous discovery, and changing the future course of science. An equation mistily began to take shape, like too faint chalk on a too far-away blackboard – distant pinging sounds in the more remote regions of his brain, a slight feeling of breathlessness – but then he lost interest, as he was far keener to begin drawing the diagram. He was wondering what would be the best and most appropriate noises he ought to employ when it came to adding his labeling. This was *far* more important.

He would use an expressively jagged style of printing right in the middle of the page, surrounded by a cloud of smoke – he was quite definite about this – but he was assailed on all sides by seductively competing examples of onomatopoeia. He'd rather set his heart on *KER-BOOM!!!* It seemed a pity, however, to miss the opportunity for a *SIZZLE!!!*, and he really would have liked a *WHUMPF!!!* and an *AAAAGHHHH!!!*

All the possibilities employed capital letters and three exclamation points.

All were attractive.

He thought for a while further.

His smile broadened again.

He'd use all four.

KER-BOOM!!!

SIZZLE!!!

WHUMPF!!!

AAAAGHHHH!!!

That would sum it all up nicely. He said the words in his head, over and over, occasionally saying them out loud in a subdued sort of way, like a small boy – not wishing to be overheard – secretly practicing the sound of gunfire with his toy gun.

And he wouldn't be using a measly bathroom-window-sized, far-too-small-sized chunk of sodium.

He wouldn't be *using* sodium.

He wouldn't be using potassium.

He wouldn't be using rubidium.

No, no, no.

Sod sodium!

Pooh to potassium!

Rubbish to rubidium!

He set his sights far higher than weedy whoopings and boring bangs.

He'd be causing a sensation with cesium.

He would not allow himself to be restricted by the size of the bathroom window.

Forget the open window.

Forget the carefully positioned chair.

The greatest experiments were the simplest. The simpler the materials, the fewer the pieces of equipment, the better.

If he shoulder-charged the door – that manly sense of mediæval warfare maneuvers as he black-and-blued his amazingly muscular body – he could carry a chunk of cesium that was the size of a sideboard.

Introductions would be brief and breathless, politeness reduced to a terse formula.

"Cesium, bathwater; bathwater, cesium."

There'd be a squawk, a splash, and then . . .

And then . . .

(A long, lingering moment of imagining.)

And then . . .

KER-BOOM!!!

SIZZLE!!!

WHUMPF!!!

AAAAGHHHH!!!

Mama would shoot skyward with the velocity of a rocket, never to be seen again.

The strange things in head would become the strange things to hand.

And then . . .

And then . . .

An ambition achieved.

Little Orphan Olly.

He'd be all the way there.

After the anguished-filled (and highly-enjoyable) *AAAAGH-HHH!!!*, there would be blissful, long-lasting silence.

He'd have been in blood.

He'd have been bloody, bold, and resolute.

Bloody bloody.

He'd have demonstrated his poise and determination, his worthiness of emulation. If Jessica Philadelphia Tennyson could do it, then so could Oliver Francis Comstock.

"You're a genius, Dr. Comstock!"

The great scientist bowed modestly.

"Thank you, Akenside."

He smiled encouragingly at his awed acolyte.

His smile was so broad that his eyes crinkled up completely, became invisible.

He was yet but young in deed.

But . . .

Blue. Blue. Blue. Blue.

Blue. Blue. Blue. Blue.

The color of his eyes was everywhere.

Slowly, carefully, he began to sharpen his pencils.

He'd be needing lots of pencils.

It was time to begin the diagram.

He had a really nice smile.

O. F. Comstock

5

Blue. Blue. Blue. Blue.

Blue. Blue. Blue. Blue.

The color of his eyes was everywhere.

Papa had made his feelings clear – *perfectly* clear – when Ben had once made a reference to the color of Oliver's eyes. It had been nothing rhapsodic (he knew to be careful in his choice of words) but Papa had pounced, roaring, almost gagging with disgust. Papa had long grown suspiciously weary of "Oliver said . . .," "Oliver said . . .," "Oliver said . . ." – these were Ben's attempts at opening a conversation with him – and Papa did not mince his words. Papa rigorously resisted mincing in all its forms. Boys did *not* notice the color of other boys' eyes, Franklin. That was more or less the gist of it, and Papa rammed the message home like a dagger going for the heart, beard bristling with outraged revulsion.

77

"'Oliver said!'" Papa repeated in a swoony sort of voice, his hands clasped to his chest in an enraptured sort of way, fingers loosely curled and quivering, his eyelids fluttering like fans in a hot room. "'Oliver said!' 'Oliver said!' You're just like a lovesick *girl*!"

Ben

(of course)

had blushed, not the most recommendable of reactions in the circumstances, and Papa pounced.

For a while

(and not for the first time)

the voices down the corridor

(and not for the last time)

followed him from school and came into the house, into the most private places where he lived, and there was no place where he might escape them.

(*Ooh!*

(*Ooh!*

(*Ooh!*)

That was what these voices were saying.

Papa had been unsparing.

He would make a man of him.

If it killed him.

Chaps approached other chaps in a curiously evasive circuitous manner, it seemed, carefully avoiding any suggestion of — *shudder* — seeing into their eyes. Perhaps that was part of the reasoning behind the design of gigantic manly beards. They were there to keep other chaps at a safe distance, like the protective metal cages that were placed around vulnerable or injured parts of the human body when battered victims lay groaning on their hospital beds. The eyes were safely shrouded beneath jungle-like eyebrows, protectively guarded by enormous side-whiskers. ("You're quite safe with me!" from the right side. "Nothing to be alarmed about!" from the left side.) These bearded Sleeping Beauties carried their very own defensive hundred-year hedges about with them to ward off marauding princes, to shatter their upraised swords.

"Good morning."

(Awkwardly unfocused gaze over right shoulder.)

"Chilly again."

(Left shoulder.)

This was what you said to other chaps in a brisk, no-nonsense sort of a way, keeping your eyes unfocused. You had to be careful not to knock into the furniture. Conversation was best when restricted to the vocabulary of Alexander Diddecott: short-sentenced uncontroversial references to the state of the weather; no references whatsoever to the existence of eyes. Sometimes – by way of an experiment – he and Oliver made forays into manly conversational areas, but they couldn't keep them going for long. There'd be a few awkwardly desultory comments about baseball or horses, that sort of thing, and then there'd be a pause. "Well, that's the manly talk out of the way," Oliver would say, with a note of relief in his voice. "Wasn't it *boring*? Perhaps it's better when you have cigars."

(*Swisssh!*

(*Swisssh!*

(*Swisssh!*

(The predatory princes – ignoring the *ahems*, the *tut-tut-tuts*, the "I say!" exclamations of displeasure – grew bolder, slashing at the vegetation with their weapons.

("I'm coming!" they trilled, unabashedly raising their voices. "I'll soon be with you!"

(*Swisssh!*

(*Swisssh!*

(*Swisssh!*

(Lips poised.

(Lips positioned.

(Lips limbering up in preparation, like those of a woman about to apply lipstick.

(Tip of the tongue emerged.

(Tip of the tongue discreetly moistened lips.

(Top lip.

(Right to left lick.
(Bottom lip.
(Left to right lick.
(Lips gleamed moistly.
(Lips put to use.
(Awakened eyelids lifting tremulously, the sense of sight dazzled.
(Eyes gazing into eyes.
("Your eyes are a lovely color!"
(*Shudder.*)
Blue. Blue. Blue. Blue.

Sometimes – summer and winter – he lay on his back on top of Grandpapa Brouwer's old ship's figurehead of Iphigenia, at the end of his "quarterdeck" in his grandparents' garden at Great Neck. Iphigenia's father had led her to her death. That was what Alice had told him. There was a poem about it. He'd lie there, listening to the snap-snap wet-sheet-on-clothesline sound of the flag on its pole, the wind rustling through the trees, and – most insistent, always there beneath all the other sounds – the sea roaring at the end of the garden. It was the winter when he was fourteen, when he'd been ill. He'd been ill, but he'd repeatedly been drawn outside, to lie and look up into the blueness of the sky, listening to the lonely sounds of the wind and the sea.

We were the first that ever burst
Into that silent sea . . .

These were the words that went through his head, the words that he'd memorized when he'd seen them in one of Alice's poetry books. Alice had made a mark in the margin beside these words – all her books were full of scribblings and comments – noting lines with a special significance. They were some of the words that he repeated to himself to make himself feel calmer. This worked, if he chose the words carefully. Sometimes it was music, and sometimes it was words, but since the time when he'd stopped playing the piano because of the things that Papa had said about him doing this,

80

it was almost always words.

The silence of the sea . . .

That was another line from the same poem.

Down to a sunless sea . . .

And that.

He liked the thought of emptiness and silence, the being-alone feeling that this produced, the sound of the sea – sunless, though not silent – making him believe that he had entered into the poem, or the poem had entered into him.

He was all wrapped up in his warm clothes, wearing his fur hat and his earmuffs, his gloves, and his muffler but – because he was lying so still, because he lay there for so long (Mama sometimes called him into the house) – he was shivering with the cold. He lay on the wooden figurehead for long stretches of time, cold, but feeling safe. He looked up at the sky, losing himself in the blueness there, finding the areas free of clouds, trying to think things out and make them clear in his mind, trying not to think of certain things.

The silence of the sea . . .
The silence of the sea . . .
The silence of the sea . . .

He looked up at the sky as he repeated the words about the sea to himself, the heavy weight of undescended waters hanging in the air above him. He breathed the words, and his white breath moved across the blueness. It was the idea of silence that became important to him, that feeling of there being no words, nothing written (seeing words written down broke the silence inside his mind), nothing spoken. He liked the silence. That, and the cold.

The flag.

The wind.

The sea.

Blue.

Blue.

Blue.

Blue.

The only footsteps in the snow would be the ones that he'd made, leading to the place where he was.

He concentrated totally upon the emptiness, the blueness, seeing nothing else. It became everything that he could see, filling his whole field of vision, entering and suffusing everything inside him. It was like holding something so close to his eyes that he was unable to focus them, unable to see anything else.

He'd do the same thing with Grandpapa's atlas, the same old-fashioned atlas that he'd seen at the Reverend Calbraith's house, the one in which the countries had different shapes, and their names were spelled different ways, where the world was not the same world as the world in which he lived. (He often had the feeling, even without the atlas.)

Polynesia or Islands in the Pacific Ocean.

That would be the page that he would choose, the double-page spread that was almost all ocean.

He'd lean toward it as if contemplating drowning himself in all that ocean, a suicidally inclined Narcissus drawn to water, wishing to lose himself in blueness. The larger areas of land (one of the islands of Japan, part of Australia, a sliver of California) were insignificant and unlettered, pushed out – pale and peripheral – into the edges of the map, and soon lost from sight as he leaned in closer. Inside or outside the house, it was nothing but sky or water, and if it wasn't *blue, blue, blue, blue* it was *white, white, white, white* as he lost himself in the unprinted emptiness of the margins.

Sometimes, he'd try to focus his eyes as he lifted his head away, to discover the first word that he would read, like Mrs. Alexander Diddecott opening a Bible at random to find words fraught with significance. He was filled with foreboding when – several times in succession — he opened his eyes to see what he thought was the ominously warning word *Sh!* printed in several places.

Sh! Sh! Sh!

We were the first that ever burst / Into that silent sea . . . he thought.

The silence of the sea . . .

Sh! Sh! Sh!

These officious shushings seemed to emphasize the thoughts of an imposed, an insisted-upon silence across the waters, but when he examined the words more closely he realized that the word that he was seeing in the emptier places of the map was *Shl*, a warning abbreviation for *Shoal*, like the truncated *Isld*, *Isld*, *Isld*s of all the nameless places that littered the ocean. This was a little disappointing.

Several times — it was right in the center — the first word he saw was *Equator*.

Once it was *Port San Francisco* — the only city named in all of California — and the coastline of the state awoke thoughts of *Two Years Before the Mast*, recently read, more sea, more endless blue. Most times it was the name of one of the tiny countless islands, as alone and faraway as stars in a winter sky.

Jesus Island.

Handsome People Island.

Coral Island.

Atlantic Island.

Elizabeth Island.

Deliverance Island.

Solitary Island.

(He liked the sound of this last one. This was the one he liked best of all.)

A bed had been made up for him in Grandpapa's study, and all around him were the books and the maps and prints. It was the time when he'd come across the copies of *Madame Chrysanthème* in Grandpapa's bookcase, the copy in English, the copy in French (the heart-in-mouth moment of balance as it slid from its hiding place on the high shelf).

Precisely at dawn of day we sighted Japan.

Precisely at the foretold moment Japan arose before us, afar off, like a clear and distinct dot in the vast sea, which for so many days had been but a blank space . . .

He remembered these words, and the words that followed, the first moment of entering that hidden place, that silent sea.

TWO

I

Three o'clock.

What Ben hoped wouldn't happen, that was what happened.

It was Oliver, and not a servant, who opened the door to them for the "At Home."

Ben concentrated on thinking of nothing but the present moment, nothing but the clenched fist of the bell-pull (a curiously aggressive choice of design, unsettling for the nervous first-time visitor), the steps swept clear of snow (he'd lowered his eyes), the gleaming black paint of the boot-scraper, the wet footprints. He studied the footprints. Some fortunate earlier caller at the house had not actually entered, but had turned away again – he could make out the outlines of the heels, swiveling round – and headed back down the way he had come. *He.* They were large feet, a man's feet, unless Myrtle – Oliver's lumbering sister – had been unleashed.

A Pinkerton was trained to notice such things.

We Never Sleep.

That was the slogan of the Pinkerton National Detective Agency.

It had haunted him in childhood, that threatened eternity of sleeplessness that was the heritage of all Pinkertons, waiting for the first light of morning, the furniture slowly assuming form around him in his room, the tentative first sounds of birds. The words had been going round and round in his head, and he unable to lose himself in sleep and forgetfulness, his ever-open eye dazzled by the coming of the light, the glare of the sun. Sometimes it was his own eye that never slept; sometimes it was the eye that watched him – like Papa's eye – noting everything that he said and did and thought, never at rest, never closed in dreaming.

Nothing but the present moment.

He hoped that he wasn't starting to flush.

He knew that Alice could sense his awkwardness.

You'd have thought – by the way in which he was behaving – that it had been years since he'd spoken to Oliver, that they'd never met since the time when they'd been schoolboys together, first at Crowninshield's, and then at Otsego Lake Academy.

The three of them – himself, Alice, Miss Ericsson – had been standing there as the door opened, visibly bracing themselves for the unenticing prospect of hour upon hour of Mrs. Albert Comstock in top vivacious form, Chinky-Winky, Myrtle Comstock and Childe Roland, Reverend and Mrs. Goodchild, Mabel Peartree, Mrs. Alexander Diddecott, the crack-of-doom line of them . . . Already (though you were always the first to arrive if you accompanied Miss Ericsson) he imagined that he could hear the ha-ha-ha-*ha*, the sound that demonstrated that hilarity was being experienced. The others were probably thinking the same as he was. If they'd thought about it at any length, they'd have turned tail and sprinted back the way that they'd come, clambering back into the carriage in the panic to escape. After a whole afternoon of the worst that Hampshire Square had to offer, he would then be dragged off to the theatre for an entire evening of cultural chit-chat with his hostess – you couldn't avoid either chit or chat when she got going, her commentary sometimes drowning out whatever was being spoken or sung upon the stage – and a selection of hangers-on from the inner circle of sycophants, though Kate would be there.

Kate . . .

"Allow me to open the door," Oliver said. "I can be humble; the noble spirit is not inflated by prosperity."

The present moment.

He did not look humble. Mrs. Albert Comstock may have beaten the servants into submission, but her son remained completely beyond her control. His long hair was neatly combed, but there was a shock-headedness in his nature that his mama was quite unable to suppress. He was twenty-five now, the same age as Ben, but he still possessed the manner of a clever bright-eyed boy eager to impress (and, preferably, appall) the adults around him, perkily schoolboyish in appearance. He always talked to Alice conspiratorially, as though they were sharing a secret, and he leaned smilingly inward, a *confidant* on the point of whispering.

Alice sometimes teased him about how little he changed.

Several of the women teased Oliver, because he (the Dorian Gray of Longfellow Park, one of – this was their joke – New York's leading seekers-out of æsthetic sensation) always looked the same.

Dorian Gray.

He wondered if any of them knew about Oliver's sixteenth birthday party, the things that had happened then.

The women claimed to be jealous of him.

Strange, that changelessness should be seen as something desirable, something to envy in others. It was one of the things that worried Ben most about himself, that ineluctable taint of childishness in his body and behavior, that shameful, piping incongruity blundering haplessly into the world that belonged to men, that knowledge that he wasn't man-like, was still slight in build, still small in stature. Change was what Ben prayed to happen to him.

What the women said was not – in fact – true any longer of Oliver. He was still a very good-looking young man, but there was a darkness under his eyes (*in* his eyes) that hadn't been there a year or so earlier. There was a certain flush to his cheeks, an overbright glitter in the eyes. He'd developed a fondness for alcohol early – Ben knew all about this – but more than alcohol seemed to be involved. Ben knew about this also.

He . . .

Things had happened. You could tell that things had happened, and the things that had happened had involved rather more than an enthusiastic pursuit of the too-too intense or the utterly quite.

Alice chose to tease Oliver in the usual manner now, as if things were the same as they had always been. She'd got on well with Oliver, even when he was a small boy.

"How's the p-p-picture in the schoolroom, Oliver?" she asked.

Ben winced at the stuttering. Many things embarrassed him about his sister, and this was one of them.

"The picture is hideous," Oliver replied cheerfully. "Absolutely hideous. I took one look at it, and hastily replaced the tapestry. It is far far worse than it has ever been hitherto." He thought for a moment, and then added, "I don't often get the chance to say 'hitherto.'" He then – conscious of neglect – greeted them all formally. "Good afternoon, Miss Ericsson, Miss Pinkerton, Lieutenant Pinkerton." He made a little bow to each of them in turn, polite but half-joking – a page boy not quite trained, not fully broken in, the whip withheld in the wielder's hand – and beckoned them through into the entrance hall.

The present moment.

The present moment.

"How is your mother today?" he asked of Ben and Alice, the question that everyone asked politely when they saw them.

"A little better today, thank you," Alice replied, after a short pause.

It was the answer she always gave, though it wasn't always a true answer.

"Lieutenant Pinkerton," Oliver said again, teasingly ceremonious, stressing the "Lieutenant" part of Ben's name in the tone of someone who could hardly believe it. He stepped back a little, seemingly to better appreciate the look of Ben in his uniform, his head on one side and then the other, lost in æsthetic musing. He looked like someone in an art gallery. For a moment Ben had the feeling that he was going to walk all the way around him, in order to inspect him from all angles.

He hoped that he wasn't . . .

Wasn't starting to . . .

He flushed.

He'd always blushed easily. It was one of the things that made him suffer.

His smallness.

His blushing.

Other things.

There were other things, plenty of other things.

The blushful Hippocrene.

That's what Oliver had called Ben for a while, after coming across the phrase in Keats, using the words like a term of endearment.

"Is the blushful Hippocrene in residence?" he'd ask, and Ben would smile, a bashful, secret smile, liking the name because it was Oliver speaking it.

This seemed a long time ago, a longer time than he'd been living.

Unexpected as such moments always are, he had a brief sensation of life being longer than you thought it was, of a whole history, a compacted mass of memories, of which he was the possessor. Childhood summer days – late afternoons – had been full of such moments, time palpably upon him.

Oliver held out his hand to Ben, in an oddly formal sort of way. You'd have thought that they were strangers meeting for the first time.

He and Ben shook hands.

More awkwardness.

It was not so much that they were shaking hands, but more a matter of Oliver shaking *Ben's* hand, the movement all on one side, up and down three times.

Ben – that feeling of Papa still being alive – heard Papa, the Reverend Goodchild, and Dr. Wolcott Ascharm Webster sniggering together, making manly jokes, and it made him constrained in his response. His was the inner hand in the handshake, and he gripped his hand tighter, to form a fist, to withdraw himself from Oliver's touch and assume an acceptable posture.

(The clenched metal fist of the bell-pull.

(*Made of Iron.*

("Look, Papa. I'm not *really* friends with him."

(*He's very "musical."*

(That's what Papa would be saying in reply, making use of a tone of amusement, though amusement would not be what he was feeling.

(He heard the voice.

(It was speaking from inside him.

(It seemed to be speaking with his own voice, as much as with his father's.

(He could feel the beard against the back of his neck, as Papa leaned in close to whisper.

(*My Brave Boy.*

(*Almost Six Inches in Height.*

(*Guaranteed to Delight Any Boy.*

(This was what the voice was speaking, and the last phrase was given particular stress.)

"Golly! It's Olly!" he found himself whispering automatically at the end of the third handshake, just before they unclasped their hands, hardly knowing that he was saying it.

"I think it's Pink!" Oliver replied, instantly. Ben had once liked that "Pink," that jokey abbreviation of his surname by which Oliver had almost always addressed him.

("In the *Pink*!"

("In the *Pink*!"

("In the *Pink*!"

(The voices down the corridor of the academy.)

"Golly! It's Olly!"

"I think it's Pink!"

It's what they had said to each other when they were schoolboys. It's what they had said to each other when they met at Linnaeus' funeral, another day of snow, in the very first days of 1900, three years earlier. It was a sort of secret thing between them, to show that nothing had ever changed, and things were still the same, though they both knew that this was not true. Something would have ended forever on the day that Ben didn't say, "Golly! It's Olly!" and he still couldn't quite bring himself to stop.

Linnaeus' funeral.

He remembered the New Year's Eve sign – constructed out of fireworks that were now hollow and burned-out – still standing in the park as the carriages drove past in line on their journey to the distant cemetery: *Welcome To The 20th Century!*

It was just about his first memory of the new century, the dark snowbound cemetery well away from All Saints' (more like a park than a place of burial), the funeral for the young man of twenty-one, a year younger than he had been, than both he and Oliver had been. *Safely* away from All Saints': that was probably the way in which the Reverend Goodchild would have thought of it, made moral and self-righteous by an ambiguous death. The Reverend Calbraith would not have been so smugly censorious if he'd still been there. A death gave the Reverend Goodchild an opportunity to display his power, and he – like a man who controlled both life and death – ensured that all around him were made fully aware of this power, and what it was he could do with it. News of a death must quite perk up his sense of importance. Sometimes – but not always – he managed to assume a suitably solemn expression (looking sad would have been overambitious), and always, *always*, he felt it incumbent upon him (this was his choice of words) to analyze the character of The One Who Had Gone Before (these, also, were his words) as he appeared to decide then and there if The One was worthy of being interred in All Saints' churchyard. As if he hadn't already decided. Charlotte had been all the family that Linnaeus had left at the time of his death and she had gone to plead with the Reverend Goodchild several times. She'd wanted her brother to be buried alongside their parents.

Sadly, no.

That had been the Reverend Goodchild's choice of words this time. Sadly, no, he didn't feel that it would be appropriate for Linnaeus to be buried there, *in view of the circumstances.* (Meaningful stress on these words.)

Sadly, no, the first time.

Sadly, no, the second time.

Sadly, *no*, the third time, even when Charlotte wept.

Sadly.

He must have heard of the concept of grief from somewhere. Perhaps he'd read about it. Even when you didn't fully understand something, vague glimmerings could give you a rough general idea, useful when it came to expressing an opinion that was seemingly the result of deep and restless agonizings (Halitotic Herbert — Alice's name for him — was quite keen on agonizings), and fostering an imposing — and usefully impressive — sense of wisdom.

In the cemetery they'd talked with Charlotte for a while, and with other people there, some they hadn't seen for a few years — Charlie Whitefoord had been there with his wife (*wife!*), and Frankie Alloway had been there, quite lost without his mama — and then Ben had walked through the snow to where the carriages were waiting, drawn up in a line before the gates. Oliver walked beside him. He had been crying. Oliver seemed to play a part much of the time, but had not been doing so then. He was never self-conscious about emotion. Ben had never realized before how much he envied him this.

They were going back to Delft Place — Charlotte now all on her own in the large house on Hudson Heights — to stand in front of Linnaeus' paintings, to remember him this way. That was what Charlotte had suggested. Charlotte had wanted to bury Linnaeus' lucky silver dollar with him, but she'd been unable to find it. He had — without her knowing it — destroyed, or somehow disposed of, all his possessions except for his paintings in the weeks before his death. Cupboards, closets, drawers: all were empty, even his pockets had been empty, and all the walls of his room were bare, like those of someone who had already died, a long time before his death. His only remaining clothes were the ones he'd been wearing, as if he'd chosen his best clothes for death, combing his hair, adjusting his necktie meticulously. Ben saw his fingers trembling as he prepared himself, making himself do it by a supreme effort of will, in the way he'd done when he'd been working himself up to reciting in front of the class at school.

"Oft in the st-st-stilly night . . ."

— Linnaeus was saying, his hands clasped firmly on the book he was holding in an attempt to stop the trembling, staring unseeingly at the drawings of Ancient Roman architecture thumbtacked to the back wall when he looked up from reading, trying not to catch anyone's eye —

". . . Ere slumber's chain has bound me,
Fond m-m-memory brings the light . . ."

— His lips tightened as the stuttering flared up, and you could hear his breathing change, like that of someone readying himself to leap or race or jump —

". . . Of other days around me . . ."

These words came into his head. He could hear Linnaeus saying them.

Charlotte didn't even possess an example of her brother's handwriting. All his books had gone, all the bundles of long letters that he'd spent Sunday after Sunday writing from his boarding schools in Massachusetts, and New Hampshire, and Maine. (Each time he'd been sent away from home, he'd been sent further.)

Charlotte, Alice, and Kate Calbraith were walking arm-in-arm behind him and Oliver, talking quietly. He'd stood beside Kate at the graveside, seeing her profile against the white snow-filled sky in the same way that he had seen it against the stained-glass window in her father's church. A sense of seeing her in a different way, of wanting to talk to her, to say something, but not knowing how to start. She'd stood beside him and he'd felt that she was supporting him, and not he her, and he'd thought of the way in which she'd looked at her father during his sermons, letting him know that she was listening, that she thought him wise, despite the machinations of the Goodchilds.

At the grave — a grave with no gravestone, nothing but the trench in the earth to reveal what it was — Oliver had whispered something, leaning forward, looking down at the coffin with the one gleam of brightness from its brass plate with Linnaeus' name upon it. Charlotte hadn't thrown flowers in, hadn't scattered earth, though there was a sensation that this was the sort of thing that you ought to do in a display of accepting what had happened.

"Hearing many tongues . . ."

Ben, straining to hear, had heard the first words, thinking that Oliver was whispering to him. When he realized that it was Linnaeus to whom he was speaking, Ben stopped listening, feeling that he was eavesdropping on something private, though he recognized the words, and knew the words that followed.

Catullus.

That's who it was.

Catullus saying his farewell at his brother's grave.

Oliver's translation.

Poem 101.

No.

Poem CI.

Roman numerals.

> *Hearing many tongues, sailing many seas,*
> *arrived at last, a world too late, I stand*
> *laden with love and duty at your grave.*
> *Fate sheared us stupidly apart, leaving one*
> *brother choked with dust, the other in desolation.*
> *Here they are, the ancient gestures . . .*

Thoughts of another Catullus poem.

Poem 5.

No.

Poem V . . .

He shouldn't be thinking of such things.

Not here.

Not now.

Linnaeus.

("I'm a bit worried about the Latin," Linnaeus was saying. "Latin and Sport." They were 10 little boys, standing in front of the pillars at the entrance to Otsego Lake Academy, surrounded by snow. Latin and Sport had always worried Linnaeus, and – on that first day there – cricket had been a particular source of uneasiness.

("*Amo!*" they declaimed, Oliver setting them chanting, Oliver reminding Linnaeus that he did know Latin and that there was nothing to worry about.

("*Amas!*"

("*Amat!*"

("*Amamus!*"

("*Amatis!*"

("*Amant!*")

Hampshire Square.

The music room.

Books all around Ben and Oliver on the table, neatly aligned.

> *Multas per gentes et multa per aequora vectus*
> *advenio has miseras, frater, ad inferias,*
> *ut te postremo donarem munere mortis*
> *et mutam nequiquam alloquerer cinerem . . .*

(*Would you like me to help?*

(That was how the Latin coaching had started.

(*I'm a devil with irregular verbs.*

(*Yes?*

(*Yes?*)

"'He has gone over to the majority,'" Oliver said. This time he *was* speaking to Ben. Ben, trying not to listen to Oliver's whispers, had been attempting to hear what the women were saying – he had the feeling that when you listened to someone speaking to others, and not to you, it gave you a clearer sense of what that person was really like – and he hadn't heard what Oliver said the first time. He had to ask him to repeat it. It was usually Ben who had to repeat things because he spoke so quietly.

"'He has gone over to the majority.'"

It was clear that Oliver was speaking about Linnaeus. It was clear, also, that – as so often, like Alice – he was quoting the words of someone else, giving the words a peculiar stress, a weighted significance, giving them an application to what was happening at that moment.

"Petronius Arbiter," he explained, identifying the words, "Nero's personal arbiter of elegance, a sort of Ancient Roman Mama, in some ways. He said it when Seneca died. I won't say it in Latin. Linn was always worried about Latin. You'll remember that."

He chose not to add that Seneca had committed suicide.

A Roman death.

They walked in silence for a while. Ben didn't know what to say. Oliver.

He was walking side by side with Oliver.

(He remembered walking – young-men-about-town fashion – arm-in-arm with Oliver when they were schoolboys. He remembered himself, Oliver, and Linnaeus, as little boys at Crowninshield's, walking along with their arms around each other's necks like Tweedledum and Tweedledee, trying to coordinate their steps. Tweedlethree. That's what Oliver had called them, when they were not being The Three Musketeers.

(Linnaeus . . .

(Oliver . . .

(He kept his mind on his surroundings with great precision – aware of the snow, the dark gravestones, *Beloved Father, R.I.P.* – like someone concentrating on a few words in a book to shut out everything else, the possibility of thought.

(*Lounging in the belvedere lately, at night, we saw torches gleaming in a distant lane. Presently, the sounds of the funeral chant reached us; these gradually deepened, until . . .*

(Those words.

(His feet crunched through the snow, making the first tracks.

(One . . .

(Two . . .

(Three . . .)

"I keep thinking of the illustrations in *Tom Brown's Schooldays*," Oliver continued, unexpectedly.

Ben thought of cricket, football, words spoken at the entrance to Otsego Lake Academy on another day of snow.

"Three in particular."

Oliver paused.

"I still have the copy that Alice bought me, when she'd seen how much I liked the illustrations in your book. There's the one of East pouring out his heart to Tom, and then — most of all — two of Tom and Arthur, the one where Tom's comforting him, and the one where Tom's visiting him after his fever."

Ben couldn't remember the illustrations, but didn't like to say so.

"Why those in particular?" he asked.

"I don't really know. In all of them it's as if they're alone in the world, with no one else to speak to, no one else to listen to them. There are just the two of them in the room. In one of them they're sitting side by side at a table in front of a bookcase, and the chair beside the table is drawn so beautifully. In the other there's an open window. They make you think that . . ." He thought for a while. He liked to use the most accurate word to describe his feelings. "They make you think . . ." Oliver had no qualms about long silences in conversations, though they weren't very usual once he was in full flow. He abandoned the search for the words he'd been seeking. "They just make me think of Linn. I don't think that I really spoke to him, or listened to him."

"Me too."

"I never really knew him. I felt that I wanted to. But I never really knew him."

Me too.

Ben didn't speak the words this time.

Two boys at a table.

The mention of Nero.

He and Oliver were working on the translation of a passage of Latin together, the description of a death.

The Death of Britannicus.

The first time he'd gone to Oliver's so that they could work on their Latin together. Instead of walking round the lake they'd gone across the ice, gone by a way that wasn't usually there.

He couldn't stop shaking at first, he was so cold after their journey, even after their bit of silliness, the dancing around the room, the chanting of the Italian words that they'd found hidden in Oliver's new mandolin.

He tried to circle the words that were giving him the most difficulty, but he could scarcely hold the pencil.

. . . *libata gustu* . . .

. . . *fervore aspernabatur* . . .

. . . *Trepidatur* . . .

. . . *At quibus altior intellectus resistant* . . .

("Why are your hands always so cold?"

(That was what Oliver has asked him.

(That had come later.)

Like George Arthur in *Tom Brown's Schooldays*, translating from Latin for the pleasure of the story, Oliver wanted to know what happened, taking delight in discovery. He played the piano in the same sort of spirit. With a dictionary on the table beside them, they'd worked their way down the page, Oliver doing most of the work. They'd felt quite at ease together then.

When they were translating, Ben tended to grasp at words here and there, words he recognized, but Oliver seemed to possess a sense of meaning, as if he knew the place where the words should be. Ben remembered the growing excitement as they began to understand what it was that the text was conveying, the gradual emergence of meaning, word by word, line by line.

Tacitus.

That was who the writer had been.

("Shall we tackle Tacitus?")

The death had been a murder, and the victim had been a boy. There'd been the word for "blush" — he remembered that — "*ruborem*." That was certainly a word he would remember.

(A hot drink had been tasted, and declared safe, but it had been deliberately made so hot that cold water had to be added before the boy could drink it, and the poison had been administered with the water.

("He lost his voice, and he lost his breath . . ." Oliver was saying, and then tried again — "his voice and likewise his breath were taken away" — and then again. "He simultaneously lost his voice and his breath . . ."

("Their eyes fixed upon Nero . . ." Oliver was saying.

("The prince's sister . . ." Oliver was saying.

("She had learned to hide her sorrows, her affections, every one of her emotions . . ." Oliver was saying.

("Your main difficulties are with verbs," Oliver told him.

(Irresolute, not quite sure of what to do, not sure what to say: that was Ben. What better parts of speech to pose difficulties for him than verbs?

(Gradually, they translated the description of how Nero — at the age of seventeen — had murdered Britannicus, his 14-year-old stepbrother.

(There was a moment — when they'd finally completed their task — in which Oliver made the meaning of the words emerge complete, all in one piece, and Ben felt like applauding. It was like a puzzle-picture. Once you'd seen what was hidden there, then you always saw it.

(Translating Latin.

(Side by side at a table.

(Catullus.

(Poem V.

(*Give me now a thousand kisses.*

(Those words.

(Again he made himself concentrate on what he could see around him, not what was in his mind.

(*Beloved Father.*

(*R.I.P.*

(The dark tracks in the snow.

(One . . .

(Two . . .

(Three . . .)

"They make me think of other things," Oliver was saying. "The illustrations . . ."

They'd reached the carriages by now. Oliver, who'd seemed on the point of continuing his train of thought, explaining what he meant a little more, fell silent, as he'd fallen silent earlier, and they waited for the three women to walk toward them.

"What I wanted to happen," Oliver began to say to him, lowering his voice, the words seemingly a continuation of what he'd started to say, "what I *really* wanted to happen . . ."

Linnaeus' funeral.

Three years ago.

Snow on the ground then, snow on the ground now, as if it had snowed without ceasing through all the months and years in between.

Now they were indoors.

He had the feeling for a moment that he was alone with Oliver, and that Alice and Miss Ericsson were not beside them.

He was sixteen again.

He'd come for his Latin lesson.

(*A Particularly Handsome Article That Walks in a Manner That Looks as Natural as Life.*

(*It Looks as Much Like a Real Boy as it is Possible to Make It Appear.*

(This was the voice that he was hearing now.

(Papa's voice.

(A sense of something else that needed to be translated.

(Ben tried to believe that these words were being used to describe Oliver.)

2

He could hear Oliver's voice floating up from the hall. You could tell that he was talking to someone on the telephone, and not someone who was actually present. "Hello Central, give me heaven," he sang, once or twice, in an interrogative sort of way. Ben felt himself listening in, straining to catch the words.

"Hello Central, give me heaven . . ."

The portières had not been pulled fully to, and he could see through onto the wide landing, and a section of the elaborate balustrade.

"Hello Central, give me heaven . . ." he sang again. "Hello?" It sounded as though he had been doing this for quite some time.

He laughed, and Ben thought of him – he had seen him do it – straightening up, like someone preparing to greet the person to whom he was speaking.

"Do you mean to say that you've never had anyone sing that song to you before?" he said. "How very surprising."

Oliver did not bellow into the telephone, as so many people seemed to do, attempting to communicate across distances by the sheer power of their lungs. He spoke rather intimately, whispering into the ear of someone close to him. When he listened, he held the earpiece closely against himself, the pose of someone listening to indiscreet confidences. Ben saw him hissing into the mouthpiece with an air of furtive intensity, as if it were a narrow pipeline into another place, a hollowed hole in the wall between adjacent cells, where secret messages were exchanged between prisoners, the way in which Edmond Dantés had communicated with the Abbé Faria in *The Count of Monte Cristo*.

He wondered whom it was that Oliver was preparing to telephone.

Would it be Arthur Vellacott?

(*The other room.*

(*The other room.*)

Dr. Severance of Staten Island and Dr. Wolcott Ascharm Webster would – if they had possessed them – have sold their souls for such confessional whisperings from Oliver, something prolonged and juicy, so that they could listen bug-eyed as they risked writer's cramp. You'd have thought that the two alienists – with the huge potential for profit from Oliver's mama – might have come to some sort of amicable agreement to share the spoils, the two of them sitting side by side (each chaperoning the other: you had to be braced for pouncing with a Charlotte Anne in the vicinity) as they scribble, scribble, scribbled, with only the occasional stunned "Crikey!" to break the silence.

(*Oliver Comstock!*

(*The boy who needed TWO alienists!*)

You had to admire a boy who'd fought them off in the way he had. (No one tamed Oliver.) Years of battling with his formidable mama had made him equal to anything, and there had been *plenty* for him to endure.

If it hadn't been Mr. Rappaport, the nudging elbows, or the mocking public serenades frightening the sparrows and pigeons off the statues, it had been Dr. Severance of Staten Island or Dr. Wolcott Ascharm Webster launching into the attack. These latter two grappled for dominance with Mrs. Albert Comstock just as they had with Mama, seeing Oliver as a potential patient, another Alice, another potentially lucrative source of income (and Mrs. Albert Comstock had far more money than Mama had).

Dr. Severance of Staten Island (although ultimately ousted) had got to Alice first, but Dr. Wolcott Ascharm Webster had had high hopes of Oliver. There wasn't such blatant touting for trade again until G. G. Schiffendecken arrived in Longfellow Park, and rapidly established his breathtakingly expensive false teeth as the *ne plus ultra* of extravagance, the Holy Grail of grinning. You found yourself surprised to find that G. G. Schiffendecken grins were not tastefully displayed in Twelvetrees & Twelvetrees, amongst the cuff links and earrings in the excitingly barred display-cases near the main cash register, where all the prices were written in the tiniest of handwriting to make them appear smaller. When he wasn't laughing about Oliver with the Reverend Goodchild, Dr. Wolcott Ascharm Webster was laboring to extol the excellence of his wares to Oliver's mama. Mr. Caswell, the Biology master at Otsego Lake Academy and chief source for sneaking – he was probably on commission (he'd be perfectly happy to be a 5% man) – had given him useful tips about the Rappaport scandal, and he'd sensed possibilities.

He'd made his notes like his chum, the Reverend Goodchild, preparing for a sermon.

Oliver's unfortunate and damaging experience.

(He was not a man who went in for evasive ahems in the crimson-faced tradition of Dr. Twemlow.)

Lingering vileness.

My specialized skills in dealing with this delicate area.

A boy who – not that many years ago – was so sadly deprived of the essential manly influence of his Papa.

(You pictured Albert Comstock, well soaked in brandy, belching, farting – if it wasn't Chinky-Winky it was him – grunting fatly, thwunking his cleaver down onto the slaughtered animal on his chopping board in the shop on Hudson Row, his bloodsoaked fingers tugging at the frizzy tufts of armpit-like hair that projected from his nostrils and ears as he hawked thickly: this was the sort of presence that all young chaps craved, and strove to emulate. No wonder Oliver was drawn, fascinated, to gaze at the statue of his father in The Forum. No wonder Oliver had shoved a bicycle up its bottom, with a vigorous twist of his wrists.)

A vulnerable young man who needs to be helped through the months ahead – the years *ahead* (Dr. Wolcott Ascharm Webster believed in careful long-term financial planning) *– with firm but friendly advice.*

As you know, I am myself the father of two young sons – he hauled in Theodore and Max (still very small boys at this time) when it suited his purposes, holding them up by the ankles (or so it seemed) for inspection — *and so am fully conversant with the importance of a father's presence in the upbringing of a male child* — and vaguely biblical resonances did not go amiss — *to ensure that he develops in the way that one would wish.*

He needs a skilled mentor to guide him, a man to whom — a "whom" always impressed Mrs. Albert Comstock — *he can speak with complete trust and openness, so that hidden things will not fester and cause life-long lasting damage, with fearful possibilities.*

His choice of words made him sound more and more like Anthony Comstock, the founder — and most enthusiastic member — of the New York Society for the Suppression of Vice. This was not altogether accidental. He knew the high opinion that Mrs. Albert Comstock had of her namesake, the man upon whom she modeled her seek-out-and-destroy policy on anything remotely mucky. He was the man for whom ("whoms" multiplied mightily as vague impressive gestures made far-beyond-this-place movements) dirty books burned like the library at Alexandria (you could guarantee that there'd have been *plenty* of dirty books in that one!) or were drowned in deep water, the man who sought out muckiness in the mail, and — you couldn't help feeling — sulked and stamped his feet and howled like a toddler unleashing a tantrum if he failed to find it. ("I *want* dirty books! I *want* dirty pictures! *Now! Now! Now!*" This was the implacable imperative from the single-minded finder of filth. If it wasn't filthy, he would always find a way of *making* it filthy.) Dr. Wolcott Ascharm Webster tried to hint at the muckiness *seething* within Mrs. Albert Comstock's son, to get her waddling urgently in search of her checkbook and diary, and a well-filled fountain pen. There he sat in the music room at 5 Hampshire Square, knee-to-knee with Mrs. Albert Comstock (Mahomet coming to the mountain), teacups tinkling, circling round and round the — ahem — *delicate* subject that he could not quite put into words in the face of Mrs. Albert Comstock's bafflement.

"'*Mentor*'?" she'd repeat, as if the word was unfamiliar to her. It probably was.

(*Tor*mentor, more like, when you were faced with attempting to have a conversation with that woman.)

"'*Hidden* things'?"

"'Lasting *damage*'?"

"'*Fearful* possibilities'?"

The way she went on, he wouldn't have been surprised if the words she'd selected to suggest were causes of bafflement had been "father," "son," or "male child." Dr. Wolcott Ascharm Webster was itching to haul Oliver off to the Webster Nervine Asylum, strapping him down, and administering enough electrical energy to power a small city, humming like a concert hall crammed with tuning-forks. As Dr. Twemlow was with the body, so was he with the mind, readily recognizing that the biggest bucks were to be made with female patients. Most of his patients (virtually *all* his patients) were women (an inevitable result of being an alienist), but as Oliver Comstock was already more than halfway to being a woman (this was the shrewd analysis) he'd be the perfect choice for whom to offer his services as his urgently needed – hurry, hurry, *hurry*! – physician.

He knew what the long waves were singing so mournfully evermore.

He knew what they were singing so mournfully as they wept on the sandy shore.

"Olivia, oh Olivia!"

That's what they were singing.

What else could it seem to be?

(Mr. Caswell had told them all about "Olivia," and about "Little Lord Fauntleroy," "Oscar Wilde," and "Dorian Gray," the mocking names he had heard echoing down the corridors after Oliver, the names that had been accompanied by wet kissing sounds, and "Oo! Oo! *Oo!*"

(Hell, he'd have done it for 1%!

(He'd have done it for *nothing*!

(He just liked the feeling of being useful.)

Dr. Wolcott Ascharm Webster and the Reverend Goodchild

had, with amused snorts, watched Rappaport – brassy as you like – breezing past on Indian Woods Road a week or so after the *débâcle*.

Booted out of Otsego Lake Academy!

Everyone knew about it by then.

Mr. Rappaport and Oliver Comstock!

The Latin teacher and the schoolboy!

The Latin teacher with his unconventional approach to – ahem – irregular verbs!

(These were exclamations that did not require a verb.

(Verbs were – *wince!* – the very things you didn't like to think about, grammatically traditional though they might be when it came to constructing sentences.)

Some said that Mr. Rappaport had – brace yourself for a verb – pounced upon Oliver Comstock.

Some said that Oliver Comstock had – here it comes again – pounced upon Mr. Rappaport.

Whoever had done the pouncing, it had been a verb athletically and enthusiastically deployed.

Perhaps they'd met in midair, licentious balletic leapers hurtling toward each other.

Ballet sounded an appropriate sort of subject to come to mind for this *pas de deux* of perversion, something frothy and feminine, frou-froued with frills and swisssh-swisssh-swisssh, certainly not the sort of thing that went on – week after week – in the room above the ice-cream parlor, grim-faced and graceless small girls hurling themselves in all directions and disturbing clouds of dust.

First position.

Second position.

Third position.

All sorts of positions.

(*Snigger.*)

The Reverend Goodchild watched Rappaport in the same sort of delightedly appalled way as his wife chose to stare at girls from The House of the Magdalenes.

"'Olivia, lost Olivia, will never return to thee!'"

He'd suddenly quoted the line in a mincing (but manly) sort of way, with a toothy chortle, showing an unexpected knowledge of popular poetry, and Dr. Wolcott Ascharm Webster had joined in with enthusiasm.

"'Olivia, lost Olivia!' – what else can the sad song be?"

They hadn't bawled it out across the street, in the way that the members of All Saints' choir would do to Oliver when they later serenaded him in public. It had been more fun to chant it in the manner of someone casting a malevolent spell, the hissed words private between them, and unheard by their victim.

"'Weep and mourn, she will not return, – she cannot return, to thee!' . . ."

When G. G. Schiffendecken, the dentist, arrived in Longfellow Park – Mrs. Albert Comstock had already purchased one of his grins, and unleashed it at every opportunity like a new star in the east – he walked his dog, morning and evening, calling his name after him as he made enthusiastic escape bids.

"Olivia!" he called, rather hopelessly, "Olivia!"

The fact that Olivia was a male dog with a female name (no one had quite worked this one out) seemed entirely appropriate in the circumstances, and added to the pleasure. "Olivia" for the dog, and "Olivia" for Olivia – *snigger* – Comstock.

"Olivia! Olivia!"

The first time that they had heard this, Dr. Wolcott Ascharm Webster had looked at the Reverend Goodchild, and the Reverend Goodchild had looked at Dr. Wolcott Ascharm Webster.

"Another one of them!" the Reverend Goodchild had said with some acrimony – his wife was demanding a set of false teeth just like Mrs. Albert Comstock's, and they cost a fortune! – "The buggers are everywhere about us!" and they both guffawed, in the full-bloodedly manly way to which Brinkman had prematurely aspired some years earlier.

"Olivia! Olivia!"

Whenever they'd seen Oliver in the future (generally on his way to or from Otsego Lake Academy) they'd looked at each other meaningfully, and hissed, "She will not return!" – they'd felt particularly naughty employing that "she" – or "Olivia, oh Olivia!"

(Ben knew that look.

(He knew that tone of voice.

(It was the way that Papa had looked at *him*, the way he had spoken to *him*.

(The way that he made him walk around the table so that everyone could see the way that he walked, the way that did not look as natural as life.)

The thing to do if they happened to find themselves in the vicinity of Oliver Comstock in public was to avoid eye-contact, and to move ostentatiously away from any physical closeness. It probably helped if they held their hands high in the air so that everyone could see where they were, and cleared their throats loudly, enough to cram a cuspidor with three squelchy squirts. It made them heave just to *think* about it, and they often thought about it, hovering athletically on the very point of heaving like a brace of well-trained tumblers. (It was rather different in private, where there was a potential source of revenue; in private you sidled up with a winning smile and a friendly, encouraging manner. That was Dr. Wolcott Ascharm Webster's method.) If they were feeling especially daring, and if the wine had been flowing freely, they'd sometimes whisper to each other behind Oliver's back at 5 Hampshire Square.

"Olivia, lost Olivia!"

(Oliver, of course, heard them.)

Olivia.

Dr. Wolcott Ascharm Webster flirted with the possibilities of explicitness, to ram home his message to the uncomprehending vastness that was Oliver's mother.

"*Everyone* knows he's a Charlotte Anne!" he should be bawling. It would give him enormous pleasure to say the words out loud, but – inevitably – they'd be met with a total lack of understanding.

"'*Charlotte Anne*'?" she'd be repeating in the same bland, vaguely puzzled voice, with an air of trying to recall the name of a distant acquaintance not seen for years, her fan starting to work like a long-silenced engine. All his meaningful phrases would be repeated, the extra emphasis he'd given them lodging them in her – for want of a better word – brain.

"'*Olivia*'?"

(Another what-on-earth-does-that-mean? tone of voice.)

"'We all know what he *gets up to*'?"

(Still the labored air of bafflement.)

"'Personally *castrate* the filthy little beast'?"

(Even that would be beyond her comprehension.)

"'*Dirty little bugger*'?"

(And that.)

How *simple* did the spelling-out have to be, for God's sake? "B-U-G-G-E-R."

That's what it would be coming to, and you could bet your bottom dollar that he'd be no nearer making himself understood.

"'*B*'?"

That would be the next question.

"'*U*'?"

"'*G*'?"

(A woman unacquainted with the alphabet.)

"Oliver is most provoking," she'd say from time to time, her expression signaling that this was her final word on the matter.

"Oliver can be quite a trial."

"Oliver is most satirical."

The opportunity to insert a "bugger" never seemed to present itself conveniently.

He'd once found Oliver by himself, learning the words of part of *Elijah* as he picked out the music on the piano. (Music. *Shudder.* You might have known it!) The Reverend Calbraith was a great lover of Mendelssohn – not so, the Reverend Goodchild: "Mendelssohn! You don't expect too much from someone with *that sort* of name," he snickered, with all the self-conscious naughtiness of a small boy coming out with a curse word – and All Saints' choir was preparing for a concert. Dr. Wolcott Ascharm Webster seized the opportunity to pounce. He didn't pounce in quite the uninhibited manner that Mr. Rappaport had so disastrously chosen, but he pounced.

"Ah, Oliver!" he remarked, as if Oliver's Christian name had just presented itself to him.

"'See, now he sleepeth beneath a juniper tree . . .'" Oliver responded, not terribly encouragingly, though he looked up – politely enough – from the sheet music. He didn't bother to swivel himself round on the piano stool.

"Oliver, I have been talking to your mother. To your *mama.*" He wielded the word like a weapon.

"Did you manage to say much?"

"Yes. We have spoken a great deal. About *you*, Oliver."

He assumed an unconvincing expression of paternal benevolence. He was working his way up to "firm but friendly," though he'd always had difficulties with the "friendly" part.

Oliver immediately looked suspicious.

"Oh yes?" (*Sotto voce*, he added, "'. . . in the wilderness; and there the angels of the Lord encamp round about . . .'")

The thought of the angels of the Lord encamped round about did not seem to encourage Dr. Wolcott Ascharm Webster.

"We share *concerns*."

"Oh yes?"

"*Grave* concerns. About *you*."

"Yes. I'd gathered that much."

It was almost as bad as trying to talk to the wretched boy's mother.

"After your unfortunate and damaging experience." (Like the Reverend Goodchild, once he'd come across a useful phrase he stuck to it.)

"What experience might that be?"

He was spending most of the conversation in talking to Oliver's back. The boy was bent over, absorbed in the music score, his attention desultory.

"You know to what I'm referring, Oliver."

(Dr. Wolcott Ascharm Webster measured the distance between himself and Oliver, and found himself — with emphatic clarity — picturing Mr. Rappaport's pounce. His visualization was based upon something he'd seen in a circus once, a tumbler hurling himself to the ground in a forward roll, and then leaping high into the air to land on someone's knees. Mr. Rappaport was wearing brightly colored silk, and his cheeks were smeared with bright circles of rouge like a pottery doll's. Oliver — similarly clad, but with even more rouge (rouge would *definitely* come into it) — sat braced against his chair-back, with his legs helpfully apart to provide firm places for landing, his hands held encouragingly forward for support. There was something a little — er — there was something a little — ahem — *troubling* about that inviting, open-legged stance.

("Hoopla!" he was calling, cock-a-hoop, shamelessly soliciting applause. Amongst other things. His groin was thrust forward, as if for a dog's sloppy licking, hootchying and kootchying in short staccato thrusts.

(Dr. Wolcott Ascharm Webster suppressed a shudder.

(He pictured the scene again, in rather more lingering detail.

(He shuddered, all suppression cast asunder.

(It was a scene he pictured quite frequently, with varying degrees of explicitness, and he was conscientious about always remembering to shudder. Once he got started, he'd quiver like Mrs. Albert Comstock's automobile — coyly christened Dimmesdale — after a few vigorous turns of the starting-handle, or whatever it was that implement was called.)

"You know to what I'm referring, Oliver."

"I do?"

"Yes. Perhaps you are attempting to deny that it ever happened." (He'd just read an article about this kind of thing in *Brain*.)

III

"*What* happened?"

Three questions in a row, and what he really wanted was answers.

"It's perfectly understandable that you should do that."

"It *is?*"

Four questions.

With his right hand, Oliver was silently practicing the same few bars of music, clenching and unclenching his fingers. It looked slightly aggressive. (There'd also been a most illuminating article about aggression. "Aggression", and what it *really* meant. His wife, Hilde Claudia, seemed to go in for novels, but you couldn't beat a good article in *Brain* for stimulation. That was what he always said, though certain novels seemed to encourage an unwelcome restlessness in women, an untoward pertness of manner. Two hundred pages of *Jane Eyre*, and they weren't fit for anything. He had had to speak to Hilde Claudia quite firmly on several occasions. Dr. Twemlow had muttered once or twice about a consequential acerbity in his mother – Dr. Twemlow was *always* muttering about his mother – and Mrs. Scrivener had never been quite the same docile creature since she discovered poetry. Imaginative literature was an unsettling influence, a curse to composure. Bugger the lot of it. That was his opinion on the subject.)

There was the sound, outside, of floorboards under enormous strain, and a chain-like rattling, a sound like that of a gigantic dray horse hauling a fully laden barge across the landing at the top of the first flight of stairs. Dr. Wolcott Ascharm Webster did not have much time.

Mama was on her way.

"I know it must be embarrassing – indeed, probably impossible – for a young chap like yourself to discuss this sort of thing . . ."

He paused, and was rather thrown when Oliver (too absorbed in clenching and unclenching his fingers, peering closely at one of them with the air of just noticing something for the first time) failed to say, "This sort of thing?" "Young chap" hadn't come across with quite the air of manly camaraderie that he had aimed for.

Dr. Wolcott Ascharm Webster repeated his last phrase meaningfully.

". . . *this sort of thing* with your mother, with a *woman*. Now, I am a man . . ."

"Hence the beard."

Not a question this time.

Encouraging progress.

The dray horse came closer. It was a *very* large barge, and so crammed with cargo that it would have considerable trouble in negotiating a tunnel. It might very well become jammed in the entrance.

Floorboards on the point of splintering.

Not much time left.

". . . and I think you should open yourself up when you are offered the opportunity to discuss your innermost worries, the things that have preyed upon your mind in the small hours of the morning . . ."

Dr. Wolcott Ascharm Webster was particularly proud of this last sentence. It tended to unleash the floodgates when proffered to rich neurotic women as a good excuse for gossiping. Rich irrational women clearly chose the small hours of the morning as the perfect time for self-flagellating agonizing, the only available moments in their busy-busy-busy but oddly unfulfilled lives. Most of what they said was very boring – the precise shade chosen for fashionable dresses, the cost of jewelry, the superior charms of a despised rival: this sort of thing – but it kept them talking for ages, and filled in his fifty-five fee-filled minutes nicely, as he scribbled away in his consulting room on Park Place. If he looked as if he was listening with an air of rapt attentiveness, they were perfectly happy. Some of them virtually begged to be accepted into the Webster Nervine Asylum, seeing it as a treat for good behavior, a place for talking and talking and talking with barely a pause, a nice little holiday up the Hudson, and a way of making themselves interesting. They nurtured their neuroses like pampered pets.

"Innermost worries?"

Five questions.

The portières were trembling on their rings, the hoops vibrating on the pole.

Dr. Wolcott Ascharm Webster – thinking of the potential for fees – seized the moment.

"Oliver! Turn around, and let me see your face! I should like to be the man to *cure* you!"

"Cure me?"

Oliver did turn around for this.

Six blasted questions.

"Yes!" He spoke in the impressive accents of one offering the opportunity of a miracle cure, like Mrs. Goodchild producing a bottle of Griswold's Discovery and a very large spoon.

"Yes, Oliver. I *can* cure you."

He was speaking more and more rapidly. Time was on the point of running out.

"Cure me of what?"

Oliver, also, spoke more quickly.

Their dialogue developed the touché, touché rapidity of a duel.

Seven.

"You *know*, Oliver."

"I haven't a *clue* what you're talking about. There is nothing whatsoever wrong with me. I am in the pink. What *are* you talking about?"

("In the pink." Now *there* was a revealing choice of phrase. *Too much* pink was precisely Olivia Damn-and-Blast Comstock's problem. Too much pink, and not enough blue.)

"You know *exactly* what I'm talking about. Yes, Oliver! Yes! You *know*! I should like to start seeing you regularly. You wouldn't really be a patient. My little boys . . ."

He paused, waiting for a bright fire-flickering image to take shape in Oliver's mind, a warm room in which he chucklingly gamboled with two delightful small boys (they bore little resemblance to Theodore and Max Webster), forming decorous correctly spelled short words with neatly aligned lettered building-blocks. On a side table there were wedges of fruitcake (Dr. Wolcott Ascharm Webster was not averse to a little subtle Symbolism) and dark bottles of ginger beer. Pillow-fighting might come into it, romping, and jolly singing around the piano. It was a pity it wasn't near Christmas.

"It would be an opportunity to *find yourself* . . ."

"Like the lost Olivia?"

Eight.

(*Olivia?*

(The significance of Oliver Comstock quoting this word was not lost on Dr. Wolcott Ascharm Webster. He was a man trained to seek significance in the most casual of utterances, and this utterance was anything but casual.)

"Er . . ."

He knew the significance of "Olivia."

Goodchild always talked as if he was addressing the very back of the church, booming out another of his sermons.

Olivia.

Oliver gave him a very direct look. "I know what you think about me. I've heard what you say about me." That was what the look said. "Why are you *pretending*?" It said this, also. No words were spoken, but he heard them loud and clear, nicely enunciated.

Not very lost, this one.

Oliver Comstock had heard *everything* that he and Goodchild had said about him. There wasn't any sign of a threat on Oliver's face, but – even more worryingly – there was every sign of amusement.

"Er . . ."

"Er . . ."

Dr. Wolcott Ascharm Webster was having to think so quickly that he almost whimpered.

Rattle, rattle, rattle.

The portiéres were drawn open by a maid, and Mrs. Albert Comstock's face came into view.

It was always a shock, even when you braced yourself.

Er . . .

Er . . .

Dr. Wolcott Ascharm Webster saw the look on Oliver's face.

He hastily checked through what he'd been saying, all systems on full alert for potential *double entendres*. Sometimes, his alienist's training inhibited all natural conversation.

He saw the humorous set of Oliver's lips, sensed the deep breath about to be taken, the sentences about to start pouring out, accompanied by an expression of innocent fearfulness, a mere child bewildered by the muckiness of a grubby groper.

What had he just said?

What had he just said?

He remembered what he'd just said.

Bugger!

He remembered all too well.

Bugger! Bugger! Bugger!

"Mama," Oliver would be saying shortly, with an air of bemused puzzlement. "Dr. Webster wanted me to turn round and let him see my face . . ."

"Mama, Dr. Webster wants to start seeing me regularly . . ."

"Mama, Dr. Webster says I wouldn't be a patient . . ."

"Mama, Dr. Webster wants me to open myself in the small hours of the morning . . ."

Bugger! Bugger! Bugger!

There had been — that would be the implication — little to choose between Dr. Webster's behavior, and that of Mr. Rappaport, just before his ill-advised chalky-handed pounce. Oliver would be cultivating a heart-clenching tremulousness, shielding his nether regions with awkward doe-eyed diligence. "Ouch!" he'd be saying, an injured child after an unfortunate accident with a baseball bat. "Ouch!" He'd be wincing tearfully, bruised but brave, pointing accusingly with a firm — if trembling — digit.

"Mama!"

"*Mama!*"

"It's happened *again*!"

"Another one of them!"

"*That* one!"

Er . . .

Er . . .

Dr. Wolcott Ascharm Webster hastily abandoned his prepared script.

He rose to his feet with a delighted smile, bowing like a humble inferior unexpectedly honored, recognized by a godlike being far above him in social status. This was — most conveniently — *exactly* how Mrs. Albert Comstock interpreted their respective positions. She was all in favor of bowing and scraping from everyone around her when she was present, the center of all attention. She wasn't quite sure what the "scraping" consisted of, but she just knew that it was appropriate. Her permanent expression of sour suspicion — honed by years of attempting to deal with Oliver — always gave the impression of being on the point of sensing insufficiently servile scraping.

"Mrs. Comstock!"

He liked an opportunity to demonstrate his keen observational powers.

Mrs. Albert Comstock's head moved briefly as proof of recognition.

She looked beyond him to Oliver, showing no sign of knowing who he was.

"It's me, Mama. Your little lost child," Oliver said helpfully.

Mama failed to display any enthusiasm, and ignored Oliver completely.

"Oliver has just been demonstrating his musical prowess to me." Dr. Wolcott managed quite a good indulgent chuckle as he said this.

Oliver, recognizing what was *really* being said here, turned back to the music rack and leaned toward his sheet music.

"'See, now he sleepeth beneath a juniper tree in the wilderness; and there the angels of the Lord encamp round about . . .'"

"Delightful!"

Dr. Wolcott Ascharm Webster got this in quickly, though Mrs. Albert Comstock looked less convinced.

"'A *juniper* tree'?" she asked, clearly baffled.

Was there *anything* this woman understood?

She turned to one side, as she made her way over to the chair she favored, and sat down heavily. Dr. Wolcott Ascharm Webster's heart winced in sympathy even for a piece of furniture. It was the kind of man he was, his heart overflowing with a natural sympathy for all that lay beneath heaven.

"Oliver," she said, "Dr. Webster and I have things to discuss. Your presence is not required."

(What on earth was he going to talk about with Oliver's mother?)

"I tremble to comply." This was Oliver's response. He tended to say this absently whenever his mama boomed an order, showing precious few signs of either trembling or compliance, but this time – although he failed to tremble – he complied.

He gathered up his music.

"I can sense when I'm not needed," he said.

"Delightful!" Dr. Wolcott Ascharm Webster said again.

(Was he overdoing the "Delightful"s?)

"I enjoyed our little chat," Oliver said to Dr. Wolcott Ascharm Webster as he went out, the portières swissshing out behind him like a departing nobleman's cloak – "Most illuminating."

"*Swisssh-swisssh-swisssh*," Dr. Wolcott Ascharm Webster found himself thinking automatically, but he wasn't in the mood to manage a snigger.

Mrs. Albert Comstock did not look too pleased about this. If there was any chatting to be done in that house, she was the one to do it. That was to be clearly understood.

Why on earth was he worrying about what he should talk about? *He* wouldn't get a word in once she got going.

She didn't waste a moment.

"A little bird tells me that Alice Pinkerton was in the vicinity of your consulting room just the other day . . ."

She eyed him coyly, waiting to hear what he had to say. There would — you couldn't help feeling — be bonus points for photographic evidence, or phonograph recordings.

Little birds were always telling Mrs. Albert Comstock things, and the little birds were always getting things wrong. Alice Pinkerton was still in the grip of Dr. Severance of Staten Island at this time, though Dr. Wolcott Ascharm Webster lived in hope of prizing her free for his own utilization before very much longer.

He did not say anything, however. He just grinned, knowingly and evasively, in his well-rehearsed I'm-too-much-of-a-professional-to-divulge-any-secrets sort of way. This always went down well with Mrs. Albert Comstock, as long as he followed it up — before trying her patience too much — with oh-all-right-then-if-you-insist-I'll-divulge-a-few-secrets-after-all. The coy initial hesitations whetted the appetite for what was to follow, the delicious smells from the direction of the kitchen setting the mouth salivating.

The little birds flocked around her in the way that they swarmed upon her late husband's statue in the park, though — disappointingly — they did not leave the evidence of their passage with the same massed piles of excrement. Albert Comstock had the look of a partially melted snowman half the time, great mounds of bird-droppings dripping from his head and shoulders like the worst case of dandruff you'd ever seen in your life.

The little birds (some of them were quite big birds) were telltale parrots, repeating all that they had overheard, ruffling up their brightly colored feathers with shrill, discordant cries. They wore earrings and feathers, and carried feathered fans that flurried as they squawked. The words they said over and over were usually the names of residents of Longfellow Park, and they were usually spoken with a nudge-nudge knowingness, a dot-dot-dot invitation to fill the unspoken emptinesses after the names had been spoken.

"Alice Pinkerton . . ."

(That was a popular choice.)

"Mrs. Twemlow . . ."

"Mrs. Italiaander . . ."

"Mrs. Dibbo . . ."

"Arthur Vellacott . . ."

"Mabel Peartree . . ."

"Linnaeus Finch . . ."

"Oliver Comstock . . ."

(That was another popular choice.

(But not in the hearing of Mrs. Albert Comstock.)

If she could have lowered herself to speak to a Roman Catholic priest she'd have been round to Father Gallaudet at Corpus Christi (some of the Roman Catholic churches didn't even have *English* names!) like a shot at regular intervals. She'd have had to travel across to Elswijk Hill — Longfellow Park was a high-toned area and had no Roman Catholic church — but she was quite prepared to travel a considerable distance if the entertainment on offer sounded suitably diverting. She'd be fearless in her quest — the novels of Marie Corelli had fully alerted her to the hazards attendant upon loitering within the vicinity of a Roman Catholic church (she'd vague visions of nuns with chloroform, threateningly tightened rosaries) — and fix Father Gallaudet with her steely Protestant stare.

"A little bird tells me that the tall blonde girl from The House of the Magdalenes was in your confessional for *ages* last week . . ."

That was how she'd begin, eyes coyly lowered, the inviting dot-dot-dot leading the way invitingly to further confessions, as Father Gallaudet squirmed with guilty evasiveness. She'd sit there, her notebook open at a nice new page, the cap of her Tiffany fountain pen dauntlessly unscrewed, all ready for startling revelations.

("Tell me!" That was what she was ordering. "Tell me! Give me *all* the details! Don't miss *anything* out!"

(Sibyl Comstock, doughty investigative journalist.)

"That nun with the limp . . ."

"Tell me! Tell me!"

"Carlo Fiorelli . . ."

"Tell me! Tell me!"

You'd have thought that she'd studied Dr. Wolcott Ascharm Webster's own methods, lingering outside the consulting room at 11 Park Place, listening avidly, and taking notes, attempting to give the impression that she'd been accidentally detained on her way to see Hilde Claudia.

Father Gallaudet would grip his crucifix until his knuckles turned white, and his rosary beads would be pulled to the point of snapping. Perhaps if Sister Bernard of Clairvaux from The House of the Magdalenes arrived early for their meeting she'd be able to save him from this crazed fanatic. If she crept in soundlessly, she'd be able to brain her with one of the plaster statues of the minor saints. She was one of the heftier nuns, and wouldn't have looked out of place as a quarterback, even if she'd still been wearing her habit. He could only pray that she wouldn't be singing "The Picture That Is Turned Toward the Wall" with its – slightly worrying – implications of a – ahem – colorful past. She'd been singing it for weeks now, the words appearing to contain a special resonance for her. Perhaps it was something to do with her close proximity to all the Magdalenes. Her misguided devotion to popular music might be the death of them both. He tugged tighter at the rosary, and beads pinged harmlessly against the well-armored bullet-proof bosom.

Hmm.

Absent-mindedly, Mrs. Albert Comstock caught at the small dark projectiles, a handful at a time. Thus would she have dealt with real bullets.

Crunch! Crunch!

She munched with Epicurean fastidiousness.

Yum-yum!

From the porch came the shuddering slam of a door hurled back against the wall, and the deep voice of Sister Bernard of Clairvaux blasting out like a foghorn from a mist-shrouded hostile coast. Saints teetered in their teeny niches.

". . . There's a name that's never spoken and a mother's
     heart half broken,
There is just another missing from the old home, that is all;
There is still a memory living, there's a father unforgiving,
And a picture that is turned toward the wall.

"They have laid away each token of the one who ne'er
     returns,
Every trinket, every ribbon that she wore . . ."

It wouldn't have sounded half so bad if Sister Bernard of Clairvaux
hadn't sounded quite so — well — *enthusiastic* about the situation.

". . . Though it seems so long ago now, yet the lamp of
     hope still burns,
And her mother prays to see her child once more . . ."

Some prayers were not answered.

You had to face up to that fact.

Sister Bernard of Clairvaux — she was actually Sister Bernard of
San Juan Capistrano, California, and you couldn't help worrying
about all that sunshine — was singing even more loudly than usual,
sensing an increased audience.

There was no chance *whatsoever* of a discreet and subdued brain-
ing. St. Bartholomew would have been ideal for the purpose. He
stood, waiting for repair, just inside the door, the first thing you saw
as you entered. You invoked him against twitching and nervous
afflictions.

". . . Though no tidings ever reach them what her life or lot
     may be,
Though they sometimes think she's gone beyond
     recall . . ."

Sister Bernard of Clairvaux sang as if this was the best news she'd heard all year. "I'm jolly," she sometimes said defensively, not at all jolly, "I can't help being jolly." She'd smash your face in if you expressed any doubts about this. She made this perfectly clear.

The significance of the words was not lost on Mrs. Albert Comstock.

Gone beyond recall.

This, from a nun!

A nun from The House of the Magdalenes!

Scribble, scribble, scribble.

This was well worth the trip out to Elswijk Hill! Marie Corelli had been so right! As soon as she got back to Longfellow Park she'd be letting all and sundry know what the little bird had told her. The skies were black with swarming. All she needed now were a few confirmatory details, and she'd soon squeeze some juicy ones out of Father Gallaudet.

"Tell me! Tell me!"

More of a threat now, the massive bulk impending dauntingly, the lowered eyes now raised and focused intimidatingly.

Hers was a picture he'd turn willingly toward the wall, though it would probably take both hands – and the risk of rupture – to turn it. Picture after picture, mirror after mirror, he'd turn them all toward the wall until the room was darker but safer, with no risk of frightening glimpses, heart-stopping reflections, a features-free infinity of blank wall. Would that the name would never be spoken, and that Mrs. Albert Comstock would become the one that ne'er returned!

"Er . . ."

Father Gallaudet leaned to one side to see if he could catch a glimpse of St. Bartholomew. He had to lean a considerable distance to one side to see past Mrs. Albert Comstock, and almost lost his balance.

"Tell me! Tell me!"

"Er . . ."

If he grasped St. Bartholomew firmly around the neck with both hands, he'd be able to bring him down with considerable force . . .

". . . there's a father unforgiving . . ."

"Er . . ."

"Er . . ."

Sister Bernard of Clairvaux was zestfully launched into the chorus again.

"Tell me! Tell me!"

Arrows darkened the air, and the little birds fell. They'd be telling with their dying words, but they'd be telling.

"I," said the Sparrow, "with my bow and arrow."

"I," said the Owl, "with my pick and shovel."

"I," said the Rook, "with my little book."

"I," said the Lark, "if it's not in the dark."

Mrs. Albert Comstock was never in the dark for very long.

She sat there, pen perkily poised, all agog for scribbling.

3

Just as Mrs. Albert Comstock circled round and round the sources of gossip (*encircled* them if she positioned herself just right) so did Dr. Wolcott Ascharm Webster circle round and round her son. Time and time again he'd launch himself into a manly chat —

for which he was not being paid — and time and time again the little bugger evaded him.

(*Mama, Dr. Webster wants to start seeing me regularly* . . .

(*Mama, Dr. Webster says I wouldn't be a patient* . . .

(That had been a near thing.

(But he kept on trying, floundering about like one blindfolded.

(Think of the money.

(Think of the money.

(Think of the *pleasure*.)

He'd never been much good at blindman's buff as a child. He'd preferred to refer to it as "blindman's *bluff*," already marking himself out as a future alienist, the skilled interpreter of the unspoken, the half-said, the half-meant meaning, and he was fully aware of the significance of bluffing. Whatever he called it, he wasn't much good. Disorientated by his blinding, he'd flounder about, his arms reaching forward hopelessly, and closing in on nothingness. There'd be the sound of faint laughter from unseen mockers elsewhere in the room, in other rooms. This was just what it felt like with Oliver Comstock.

He could never tie him down — he'd have done it tightly, the rope well knotted and digging into the flesh — to agree to ask his Mama to allow him to become one of his patients. He'd soon abandoned visions of a tearful Oliver begging his mama to seek help for him with the only man who could offer him the possibility of anything like a natural future life. No chance of that. He'd settle for a half-mumbled suggestion that they might as well give that Webster fellow a go. Even when Alice Pinkerton became his patient, wrested from beneath the eyes of Dr. Severance of Staten Island — ha, ha, ha! — he still had hopes of Oliver Comstock.

("A daunting challenge!" the Reverend Goodchild had joked to him, indicating Oliver walking into the park entrance as they stood at the window of the consulting room. That was what he saw.

("A considerable fee!"

(That was what Dr. Wolcott Ascharm Webster saw, as the two of them stood side by side. He did not, however, speak these words out loud. He chuckled, and nodded in agreement.

("Quite!")

Oliver was sixteen, seventeen, eighteen, and Dr. Wolcott Ascharm Webster kept on trying. He kept on trying even after Oliver had left school, and the friendly firmness had been worn to a frazzle.

He was invariably rebuffed.

Week after week he'd called in at 5 Hampshire Square, and week after week Oliver would adroitly slip away, if he was there in the first place. More and more he was absent. Arthur Vellacott had a lot to do with this. Arthur Vellacott had a lot to do with — ahem — *all sorts of things*. Week after week Mrs. Albert Comstock was quick to inform him what the little bird had told her, and week after week he grinned his grin, furious though he was.

There'd been some awful moments, even worse than Dr. Webster-wants-to-start-seeing-me-regularly . . .

Once, he thought he was starting to make progress, promising inroads into Oliver's ostentatious incomprehension.

"Mama has been talking to me about your little chat yesterday," he began, quite promisingly, regarding Dr. Wolcott Ascharm Webster with the eyes of one seeing him for the first time. A veil had been lifted from his eyes, what had once been shrouded in the mists of unknowing suddenly made dazzlingly clear.

"Yes, Oliver?" he responded, in his best tell-me-everything tone of voice, his brow thoughtfully furrowed, his fingers twitching for a notebook and pen. When he used that tone of voice, he tended to be scribble, scribble, scribbling.

"She was quite excited about what you had to say to her . . ."

(At last!

(Patience had been rewarded.

(Dr. Wolcott Ascharm Webster began to make plans.

(His appointments book was rather thin on Friday afternoons. He could book in fifty-five minutes for Oliver Comstock with no difficulty whatsoever. He could easily persuade Mrs. Albert Comstock that Oliver would undoubtedly benefit from at least *two* appointments a week – a sense of urgency always helped to increase the willingness to pay – and he could shunt that woman from Morningside Heights along an hour or so to free a good time on Tuesday morning . . .)

". . . but – this is rather a – ahem . . ."

(Oliver making use of an "ahem" should have alerted his listener.)

". . . troubling matter – she is a little *confused* . . ."

Dr. Wolcott Ascharm Webster emerged from his self-imposed brackets like a tortoise peering out from its shell, and blinked.

(*Troubling?*

(*Confused?*

(He'd expressed himself – he'd grown rather desperate by now – in fairly unambiguous terms about Oliver, Oliver's *needs*.)

"Mama was – as I have said – *excited* by your offer . . ."

(*Offer?*)

". . . as – after all – it is eight years now since Papa was sadly taken from her . . ."

(Alarm bells started ringing.

(*Loud* alarm bells.

(*Frantic* alarm bells. Dr. Wolcott Ascharm Webster jumped, as if he'd heard them right in his ears.)

"You expressed yourself with a delicacy that touched Mama deeply. She has been so lonely . . ."

Oliver stared limpidly into Dr. Wolcott Ascharm Webster's eyes, with all the sincerity of a fortune-teller informing a potential customer that he had a lucky face, and quick-give-me-the-money. A worrying edge of filial soulfulness had been skillfully introduced into his voice.

". . . just as I, of course, have been deprived of Papa's love for all that time, and a father's presence is so important in the upbringing of a male child . . ."

(The very words he'd used himself!)

". . . but surely – ahem – you are already married?"

(*Married!*)

"Mrs. Webster, Theodore, and Max. An enviable picture of domestic concord, the envy of less happy households. Mama has become confused, all-of-a-flutter with imaginings . . ."

(You tried to prevent yourself from visualizing Mrs. Albert Comstock all-of-a-flutter, feathers flying in all directions like an uncooperative buzzard being prepared for stuffing.)

". . . but if you recall some of the expressions you employed yesterday afternoon, as you were ensconced alone in the music room with my mama . . ."

(Dr. Wolcott Ascharm Webster knew *exactly* the expressions he had employed. As did Oliver, who'd been listening from outside, sitting on the conveniently positioned sofa alongside the wall and apparently absorbed in reading one of his dubious French-looking novels. He had drawn the portières to behind him when he'd left the room, but failed to draw the doors completely together.

(*What had he said?*

(*What had he said?*

(He remembered what he'd said.

(*A woman on her own.*

(He'd said that.

(No.

(It had been *worse* than that.

(*It can be lonely for a woman on her own.*

(*That* was what he'd said.

(*What she needs is the guidance of a man.*

(And he'd said that.

(*Bugger!*

(*Bugger! Bugger! Bugger!*

(You were never very far away from a bugger, one way or another, when Oliver Comstock was around.

(Mrs. Albert Comstock — beset about by the shrill cries of the little birds — had, in fact, registered none of what he'd said, but Dr. Wolcott Ascharm Webster readily believed that every word he'd uttered had entered into that endlessly capacious bosom, and given rise to agonized hours of painful ponderings, flutter-hearted speculations.

(*So that no one may take advantage of her natural feelings, her vulnerability.*

(And he'd said *that*.

(*Your son is of the very age when he might prove most troublesome to a woman on her own.*

(That was *twice* he'd said "on her own."

(He looked at the expression on Oliver's face.

(The *rather pleased* expression on Oliver's face.

(The awful, awful thought of possible ambiguities came into his head, possible misinterpretation of his large-minded ministrations . . .

(Damnation.)

"I have longed for a new papa to guide me, " Oliver was saying, employing a tone of guilelessness, "ever since I was so cruelly deprived of the essential manly influence of my papa. I was – and remain – a vulnerable young man who needs to be helped through the months ahead, the years ahead, with firm but friendly advice."

Dr. Wolcott Ascharm Webster's head began to nod rather angrily.

He *knew* these words.

He'd used them often enough.

He could now see where this was going.

As Oliver intended.

The little *bugger*.

All that time *wasted*.

The time *for which he was not being paid*.

The panic began to subside slightly, but . . .

(*Damnation.*)

"I need a skilled mentor to guide me . . ."

The expression on Oliver's face was exactly the same as the time when he'd asked, as if ingenuously, "Like the lost Olivia?"

Weep and mourn, she will not return, – she cannot return, to thee!

"Yes!" Dr. Wolcott Ascharm Webster was starting to say sarcastically, his head nodding more and more emphatically, his beard bristling. "Yes!" As with the words spoken by Dr. Wolcott Ascharm Webster's patients in 11 Park Place, each phrase employed by Oliver reverberated with hidden meaning. Unlike the patients – amongst whom, the alienist now knew, Oliver would never be numbered – Oliver was entirely aware of the hidden, the not terribly well hidden (hopeless at blindman's buff, hopeless at hide-and-seek, that was the seeker-out of symbols) implications of the words he chose to speak. He must have chosen them as carefully as Dr. Wolcott Ascharm Webster chose the words when he was preparing his secular sermon of entrapment.

Unfortunate and damaging.

Lingering vileness.

Hidden things will not fester.

Oliver wasn't hiding much; neither was he lingering. He was making his feelings perfectly clear. It was unfortunate. It was damaging.

"Yes!" Dr. Wolcott Ascharm Webster kept on saying angrily. "Yes!" Each "Yes!" was an admission that he heard what Oliver was *really* saying to him.

He knew when he was beaten.

". . . a man to whom I can speak with complete trust and openness . . ."

Swisssh!

Touché!

"Yes!"

". . . so that hidden things will not fester . . ."

Swisssh!

Touché!

"Yes!"

". . . and cause life-long lasting damage, with fearful possibilities . . ."

(A shudder at this last phrase from Dr. Wolcott Ascharm Webster.

(*Fearful!*

(*Fearful* possibilities!)

Swisssh!

Touché!

"Yes!"

(The yesses were becoming quieter and quieter, the angry bow of the head lower and lower.)

". . . a man who will not address me as Olivia . . ."

Swisssh!

Touché!

"Yes!"

". . . or Oscar Wilde . . ."

Swisssh!
Touché!
"Yes!"
". . . or Dorian Gray . . ."
Swisssh!
Touché!
"Yes!"
". . . I need a man who will not refer to me as a dirty little bugger . . ."

(A modest enough requirement.)

Swisssh!
Touché!

(Too many *swissshes*, too many *touchés*, particularly in relation — he winced at "relation" and reordered his thoughts hastily — to someone he'd never dream of touching, not even with a well-disinfected ten-foot pole. A *twenty*-foot pole.)

"Yes!"

Dr. Wolcott Ascharm Webster found himself remembering — too late, far too late—that Oliver was a skilled fencer. Inspired by the time he'd been a ten-year-old Brutus when Dr. Crowninshield had unleashed *Julius Cæsar* on his school (stabbing with a twelve-inch ruler had awoken dormant skills), Oliver had been taking fencing lessons for years, and was ruthlessly proficient.

A little boy with long blond hair, dressed all in white in his fencing clothing, stood in the music room in front of the piano, and prepared to demonstrate his newly acquired skills. Every piece of equipment was immaculately in place except the mask. Oliver liked to have his face fully visible, and the face had a characteristic expression of rebelliousness. Mama had insisted that he illustrated what she'd been spending money on, and he hadn't been enthusiastic. The gathered æsthetes of Longfellow Park, crowding the sofas and chairs, watched the movements of the *épée* with keen appreciation, heads angled a little to one side, in the attitude of those listening to one of the more minor musical instruments (a dulcimer or a celesta, that sort of thing), straining to catch the notes quite beyond the pitch for human hearing, the unheard music beyond the silence. Not *quite* a silence. Oliver was rather laying on the heavy breathing and the agonized grunts to impress them with his athleticism, and Myrtle kept dropping her heaviest fan (hurled down like a challenging gauntlet) in an attempt to turn the attention more upon herself. She was wearing most of her mama's crocodile teeth jewelry, and, though the face was characteristically scowling (dark, dark cumulonimbus clouds with a faint tinge of green filled the upper levels of her face, and faint internal thundery sounds threatened a storm), she looked like a gigantic grin in a drab dress. If you ignored the grunts and the crashes of the fan you were well on the way to an æsthetic experience. Fencing was the sport nearest to Shakespeare. That was the epigram being polished beneath the beards.

The Reverend Goodchild had positioned himself right in the middle of the front row, his chair projecting forward from all the others. He liked to be noticed, and Oliver had indeed noticed him. A gleam had come into Oliver's eye, a just-what-I-was-hoping-for expression, an *exactly*-why-I-agreed-to-do-this expression, an I'm-going-to-enjoy-this-more-than-I-expected expression.

Oliver struck a graceful pose in the way that he did when he was reciting something, though deeds and not words were what were on display today. He extended his right hand, holding his *épée* in front of him, and slowly held his left arm at an angle into the air, to one side of him, cupping his fingers elegantly over. He bent his knees slightly. There was something slightly (disturbingly, if you were a chap) balletic about the posture. The Reverend Goodchild, smirking in a knowing sort of way, looked about the room and tried to catch the eyes of Dr. Wolcott Ascharm Webster and Mr. Pinkerton. A shared moment of chappishness.

Olivia!

Snigger.

Olivia!

Snigger.

Swisssh-swisssh-swisssh!

Snigger.

It was long before "Olivia," but this was the sort of thing that he was attempting to convey. He was a chap, and chaps sniggered.

"*Pronation*," Oliver explained.

Applause for *pronation*, rather louder from the ladies present than from the gentlemen. They were men with beards to live up to, most of them, and they did not wish to be seen applauding anything unsuitable.

"Lunge!" Oliver said suddenly, loud enough to make everyone jump – another crash from Myrtle's fan – and – *Swisssh!* – the *épée* darted forward with dizzying speed to remain, quivering in the air, about half an inch from the Reverend Goodchild's left eye.

Whimper from the Reverend Goodchild, and applause – noticeably louder applause – from everyone else, the gentlemen displaying far more enthusiasm for a lunge than they had for *pronation*.

Oliver always throve on applause, and though there had been no cries for encores, he encored.

Lunge.

Swisssh!

(Quarter of an inch away.)

Whimper.

Applause.

Lunge.

Swisssh!

(An eighth of an inch.)

Whimper.

Applause.

With each lunge, with each *swisssh*, with each whimper, the applause (like the whimpering) grew in volume, until some of the younger, rowdier elements – you shuddered to convey appalled disapproval – actually began to shout "Encore!", those of them who weren't too busy whistling, fingers thrust enthusiastically into mouths in a manner that was not quite the thing. It was a perilously thin dividing line, the one between civilization and barbarity. Even some of the most eminent of The Bearded Ones, hearing those

Goodchild whimpers, sniffing the armpitty whiff of terrified cleric, began to consider that they'd perhaps been too hasty in their stern condemnation of all things swissshy. So much depended on the context of the swisssh. They were starting to recognize that now.

Oliver moved in closer to the Reverend Goodchild.

"Oliver!" his mama was beginning to say, recognizing the warning signs, her attempts to sound chucklesome rather getting in the way of the urgent warning in the word. "Oliver!"

Oliver wasn't listening.

There might be something Shakespearean about fencing, but there was nothing Shakespearean about Oliver's face. A Shakespearean face – vague memories of Reynolds Templeton Seabright as an immensely aged actor staggering about the stage (his twilight in the limelight) for the older members of the audience – involved disheveled hair, rolling eyes, an open and aghast mouth, bared teeth and tonsils, but Oliver maintained an expression of mild equanimity as he set about the Reverend Goodchild with his *épée*. Another day of scything down the weeds for the æsthetically inclined gardener, as he swissshed about him with *touché!-touché!* forcefulness, *corps-à-corps*ing, *passato sotto*ing, straight thrusting, accompanied by whimpers, hissed "Oliver!"s, and applause.

For an enthralling five minutes the Reverend Goodchild found himself become a bearded bull's-eye. The more knowledgeable of the audience, chaps who were sports and built up a sweat on a regular basis, strained to see if Oliver had removed the button from the tip of the blade – if only they'd thought to bring their opera glasses! – hopeful of blood and screaming. *VICAR SLAIN IN MUSIC ROOM HORROR.* Readers of the *New York Herald* were seeing the headlines across three columns on one of those interesting inner pages, where the more dubious items of news were tucked away for finding. It made you feel even more pleased when you found them; little rewards for patient seeking, triumphant cries as you grubbed out the grubby nuggets. The Reverend Goodchild sat frozen into immobility, showing his ghastly grin, in the rigidly clenched posture of someone unwillingly thrust – and "thrust" was the very last word he wanted to hear at that moment — into the position of demonstrating his sense of fun. You half-expected to see him strapped upright against a spinning circular board, something of a roulette wheel on its side about it, revolving faster and faster as Oliver — smiling like a glamorously spangled magician's assistant — turned it vigorously until the clergyman's beard flapped in the wind, and all his features blurred. (The more you saw of the Reverend Goodchild, the more appealing this thought became.) Oliver, smiling and bowing, smiling and bowing, spun him ever more speedily, just before the knives started to swisssh across the room. No number was lucky (for the panic-stricken vicar) with this wheel, and the only winning color would be red.

"Thrust!"

Swisssh!

Whimper.

"Oliver!"

Applause.

"Dérobement!"

"Coulé!"

"Feint!"

(*Faint,* more like, judging by the Reverend Goodchild's pallor, his rigidly exposed teeth, his fingers clutching the arms of his chair with a strangler's grip.)

Applause.

Applause.

Applause.

They began to visualize the Reverend Goodchild's beard as being ruthlessly topiaried by the swissshing blade, razored into the fantastical shapes of the bushes that had once adorned the grounds of the Shakespeare Castle, demolished ten years earlier. Beneath the bulging, terrified eyes, and all around the aghast grin, the foliage magically assumed the shapes of heraldic figures, chivalric shapes, the knights and bishops (ecclesiastical promotion!) of a chessboard.

"Checkmate!" Oliver would be shouting triumphantly.

"Checkmate!"

"Checkmate!"

His opponent, speechless, his piece clutched in his hand with a *rigor mortis* rigorousness (all his pieces were pawns), stared fixedly ahead, too terrified to move a fraction of an inch in any direction.

(Swissshed to death.

(What a fate for a man with such a big beard and such a deep voice and such manly credentials.)

". . . I need a man who will not refer to me as a dirty little bugger . . ."

Swisssh!

Touché!

"Yes!"

The vorpal blade went snicker-snack!

Oliver – it had become perfectly clear – listened carefully to everything that was being said around him at his mama's "At Homes."

Unlike his mama.

(Phew!

(That had been Dr. Wolcott Ascharm Webster's first thought when he managed to rearrange his feelings into some sort of logical order. Just as Oliver had learned the words he had used by heart, so some of the words used by Oliver had been committed to the alienist's memory.

(*Ensconced alone in the music room . . .*

(*Mama has become confused, all-of-a-flutter with imaginings . . .*

(Phew!

(That had been a real scare.)

4

If that had scared him, then Anthony Comstock nearly finished him off.

You might have known that Anthony Comstock would have something to do with it.

Mrs. Albert Comstock had hauled him along to a lecture given by Anthony Comstock, beaming approvingly all the while – the man must have had nerves of steel – at her namesake from the front row. Mrs. Albert Comstock had been on one side of Dr. Wolcott Ascharm Webster, and Mrs. Goodchild – to ensure that he could not escape, overcome by his guilty secrets (Oliver gave the distinct impression that he saw him as a man with guilty secrets) – had been on the other, ahemming him in. Oliver – looking worryingly keen, with his pocket book and fountain pen all ready for action – had been on the other side of his mother. Dr. Wolcott Ascharm Webster may have abandoned all hopes of launching any further attacks, but Oliver had the expression of someone just about to start.

"Of course I'd like to come, Mama," he'd said, making it sound like the best suggestion she'd made for ages. Mrs. Albert Comstock had become more and more concerned about the lurid reading material favored by her son, and thought that a quick burst of Anthony Comstock would make the scales fall from his eyes and alert him to the peril that threatened his soul. She really was a very stupid woman.

Oliver Comstock had come to fleer and scorn at Anthony Comstock's solemnity. That much was clear to Dr. Wolcott Ascharm Webster. Most of the people in the Athenian Hall (pillars, echoing acoustics – the more unfortunate members of the audience heard Anthony Comstock say everything twice – hard wooden chairs) had been women. Anthony Comstock – he went in for an expression of stern resolve, beard bristling challengingly – had been returning to the scene of one of his earlier triumphs, *Traps for the Young* (well done, Funk & Wagnalls!), his searing exposé of the dirty books that had placed an entire nation in danger of imminent attack from rampaging bestialized schoolboys.

This was the very thing for Oliver to hear, the sooner the better. This was Mrs. Albert Comstock's firm belief. She could never get enough of it.

(Beam, beam.

(Make sure you speak nice and loudly, Anthony Comstock!
(Don't hold back!)

Anthony Comstock stood before them, his side-whiskers coyly brushed inward, like hairy drapes attempting to conceal the wanton bareness of his chin. There'd be no flaunting of uncovered flesh whilst *he* was in the room. As a speaker, he was of the school of Dr. Vaniah Odom. Spit, and tremblingly half-suppressed anger, were the outward manifestations of sincerity, amply compensating – in the eyes of the faithful – for a lack of clarity, or (indeed) coherence.

(Anthony Comstock spoke nice and loudly.
(Anthony Comstock didn't hold back.)

After a quarter of an hour, Anthony Comstock was well away, clutching his book threateningly before him like a more virtuous version of the Bible, driving sin into cowering, slobbering submission. If all else failed, he'd at least give it a good whack over the head. The atmosphere grew so like a revivalist meeting that you half expected sobbing sinners to leap to their feet, and sprint to the front of the room to confess themselves, beating their – ahem – breasts, and tearing at their hair.

"Brothers and sisters, I have sinned!"

Hallelujah!

"I have sinned *grievously*!"

Hallelujah!

It was rather disappointing when it didn't happen.

In front of them, the dirty books were relentlessly being berated.

(Sniggering over their dirty books, Brinkman, Adams, Bradstone, and Swartwout – Oliver's memories of his schooldays were utterly precise – out-did the sparkling waves in glee. Beside the lake, beneath the trees, the pages were fluttering and dancing in the breeze. Tossing their heads in sprightly dance, they gazed and gazed.

("Page one hundred and sixty-three!" Brinkman recommended, with the air of a connoisseur, activating his expression of neophytic salaciousness. Quite a good effort, with a suspicion of drool.

("Page one hundred and eleven!" Adams.

("Page eighty-nine!"

("Page seven!")

". . . This moral vulture steals upon our youth in the home, school, and college, silently striking its terrible talons . . ."

– a good use of alliteration here –

". . . into their vitals, and forcibly bearing them away on hideous wings to shame and death. Like a cancer, it fastens itself upon the imagination, and sends down into the future life thousands of roots, poisoning the nature, enervating the system, destroying self-respect, fettering the will-power, defiling the mind . . ."

Anthony Comstock was really living this. You couldn't help feeling that he was rather enjoying himself.

(Poisoned nature.

(Enervated system.

(Destroyed self-respect.

(Fettered will-power.

(Defiled mind.

(Anthony Comstock was clearly a close acquaintance of Brinkman.

(The description was unmistakable. He'd be bringing him out, any moment now, as an appalling example of the fearful symptoms that he was so graphically describing, the results of unspeakable muckiness marked out upon his face with graphic indelicacy for all to see. It would be just like the way in which doctors – rather proudly – produced stomach-churning gonorrhea or syphilis patients – minus most of their noses, not much brain left, vacant-eyed, dribbling – into the lecture theatre to set their students fainting in waves.

("See what I mean?"

(*Prod.*

(Grunt from Brinkman.

("See what I mean?"

(*Prod.*

(Grunt.

(The terrible talons had silently struck.)

Oliver, looking fascinated, began to lean forward. He must have leaned forward a long way, because Dr. Wolcott Ascharm Webster was able to see him appearing on the far side of his mother.

Dr. Wolcott Ascharm Webster's heart began to sink.

Oh no.

". . . corrupting the thoughts, leading to secret practices of . . ."

Anthony Comstock launched himself headlong into italics, fearless of their spiky edges.

". . . *most foul* . . ."

Interest definitely increased on "*foul*."

Men who had been nodding gently were galvanized into eager attentiveness.

". . . *and revolting* . . ."

"*Revolting*" had them leaning forward.

"*Revolting*" had them verging on the enthusiastic. Was he going to give details? *Detailed* details?

". . . *character, until the victim tires of life, and existence is scarcely endurable* . . ."

Oh *no*.

Oliver's hand was in the air, waving frantically.

The italics faded a little.

Anthony Comstock did not like being interrupted. When he spoke, others listened. When he spoke, all others were struck dumb, rapt in their listening. Others did not *wave their arms about* (Anthony Comstock even *thought* in italics) as if desperately *begging to be excused* from a schoolroom.

(*Please, sir!*

(*Please, sir!*

(*Please, sir!*)

". . . It sears the conscience, hardens the heart, and damns the soul. It leads to . . ."

The italics excitedly crept back, into speech as well as thought.

". . . *lust* . . ."

"*Lust*" went down well.

". . . *and lust* . . ."

140

It went even better the second time. He knew how to get their attention, all right!

"... *breeds unhallowed living* ..."

Oliver was half standing, his whole arm waving from side to side, a young man signaling across a great gulf, rather like dear Theodore and Max practicing their semaphore in that wholesome way of theirs. Some Young remained resolutely Untrapped, their minds as pure and ethereal as their unbroken (how symbolic a word that one was!) voices.

(Oliver Comstock was broken beyond repair, that much was certain. Arthur Vellacott had definitely damaged – *snigger!* – the more delicate working parts of this particular model. *Snigger.*)

"... and sinks man, made in the image of God, below *the level of the beasts* ..."

"Could ... ?"

Oliver was fully on his feet now, starting to call out like one in the grip of an irresistible compulsion. Perhaps a sinner really was going to confess himself after all. *Hallelujah!* This should be good. "Brothers and sisters, I have sinned! I have sinned *grievously!*" It would take hours for Oliver Comstock to unburden himself in detail. It might very well – at long last, after all his patient years of waiting – be *scribble, scribble, scribble* time. He had his notebook with him. He had his fountain pen. He'd filled it just before he'd set out. The detail would be full, frank, and unblushing, though – come to think of it – he wouldn't mind a little blushing. He'd rather enjoy a little blushing, and the blushing wouldn't be coming from him. Perhaps they really ought to insist that all the ladies present should leave the hall ...

"Could you ... ?"

If the ladies left the hall, then there would no need for shame-faced Silly-Billy shilly-shallying ...

Though perhaps it might suit his purpose best if Mrs. Albert Comstock remained in the hall and heard every word of Oliver's lurid babblings. Shocked, reeling, dazed: she'd be in the perfect condition for hearing how he was the one man who held out hope for Oliver Comstock's being repaired and returned in full working order. "It's your *duty*, as a mother . . ." That sort of thing. He could keep going for hours with that sort of thing. He'd totally failed with the son; perhaps he was to be given another opportunity with the mother, and it was the mother who had access to the money, and his fees were just about to increase dramatically.

Oliver's right arm was whirling round and round in a circle. People in the row behind were ducking. No sign of – ahem – breast-beating or hair-tearing, and – heaven knows – Oliver Comstock had plenty of hair to tear, too much hair (you had to admit) for a young man.

(*Long hair was shame unto a man*.

(St. Paul had the right idea.

(*Shame*, Oliver Comstock!

(*Shame!*

(He'd rather enjoy sounding shocked and shouting "Shame!"

(Dr. Vaniah Odom had once preached a splendid sermon on this text, long before Oliver was born, unfortunately. It had gone on for one hour and eleven minutes. He had – in the course of it – used the expression "I see hell!" forty-seven times.)

"Could you tell us . . .?"

If the ladies left the hall, he could tell them *everything*. The italics were quite infectious.

Anthony Comstock – once started – was hard to stop, a veritable Juggernaut of gentility.

". . . From the first impure thought till the close of the loathsome life of the victim of lust, there is a succession of . . ."

(*Impure!*

(Oh!

(*Loathsome!*

(Oh!

(*Lust!*

(Oh!)

The italics leapt back in full force. He always became more

animated when he spoke in italics, attacked by their jagged edges, invigorated by their pleasantly painful pokings.

"*. . . sickening, offensive, and disgusting scenes before the mind . . .*"

(*Sickening!*

(*Offensive!*

(*Disgusting!*

(Oh! Oh! Oh!)

He paused, allowing – this was a bit risky – the imaginations of his audience to picture what he was describing. It went very quiet in the hall, everyone concentrating.

Sickening.

Offensive.

Disgusting.

Some of his male listeners shifted their positions, made themselves a little more comfortable. This was rather better than they had expected. Reminiscent smiles appeared on the more unguarded faces. Those with observant wives would have some explaining to do when they got back home.

". . . until life, to such a one . . ."

There was a slight, but distinct, hiss of annoyance as concentration was broken when Anthony Comstock steamrollered ever onward. Oliver was still trying to ask his question.

"Could you . . .?"

". . . must be made up of *disease, wounds, and putrefying sores*. Suicide dances before his vision . . ."

My word!

". . . in his moments of despondency as the only means by which to hide his shame . . ."

Crikey!

". . . and the sole cure for his wretched condition. The turgid waters speak louder with the death stillness which they promise than does hope, with its beckonings to a better life . . ."

"Could you tell us . . .?"

This had clearly been one of Anthony Comstock's favorite passages. Perhaps the appearance of the word "suicide" reminded him of the many varieties of pleasure he had experienced because of his unimpeachable moral stance, all those dirty devils he'd driven to take their lives. Now that he had managed to read the passage – he did so enjoy reading this passage – he appeared to be a little more receptive to an interruption, though he was clearly not enthusiastic. It disturbed his flow. Once he got going he was *possessed* by the intensity of his feelings. Powers greater than himself took complete control. This is what he told his audiences, the words he spoke the result of a Pentecostal gift of tongues, and not of careful study.

He placed his book down on the lectern with an impatient little whack. His tone of voice was not inviting, prickly and italicized.

"*Yes?*"

Anthony Comstock, not pleased, not pleased at all, glowered down from the platform. The syllable was spat out, the question mark wielded like a scythe. Behind him, the life-size photograph of President McKinley – all nicely red, white, and blued with ruffled patriotic bunting – glowered supportively.

"*Yes*, young man?"

"Could you tell us the name of the filthiest book you've ever come across?"

"I . . ."

"The really *filthiest*."

Oliver's pocket book was open, his fountain pen – cap neatly clicked onto the base of the barrel – all ready for writing. He looked like an ace reporter on the verge of an exclusive. All over the hall, the men seemed to bow down in worship to Anthony Comstock as they leaned forward so that their jackets would gape open, giving them discreet access to the tops of the pens that were clipped in lines inside the inner pockets. All that they had to do was slip their fingers a little way across, and flick out the nearest pen.

"The really, *really filthiest*."

Pen caps were unscrewed as furtively as the tops of illicit bottles of spirits. The tips of straining fingers moved in a counterclockwise direction, as slow and nerve-racked as if tick-ticking short-term time bombs were being urgently disassembled.

Frantic searches began for scraps of paper. Those who'd kept the handouts with which they'd been issued at the beginning of the lecture – *Anthony Comstock: "Eternal Vigilance is the Price of Moral Purity!"* – turned them over to give them a nice big space for writing. It made a sound like the one you heard in church – here was an appropriately high-minded comparison – when a congregation, taking a breath in mid-verse whilst hymn-singing, suddenly realized that the rest of the words were on the next page, and flicked over to it with a deftly wielded digit as they inhaled.

"Well . . ."

Anthony Comstock was starting to look a little mollified. This was the sort of question he liked to get. He was almost on the point of saying, "That is an intelligent question, young man," but he hadn't been too keen on the arm-whirling, so forbore.

"I have seen a great deal – *a great deal* – that has indeed been *deeply* shocking. I can imagine the effect of such a book or *such a picture . . .*"

He almost lost control there for a moment, giving the distinct impression that he had a particular picture in mind. You'd have thought that it might have occurred to him to have copies to pass around so that everyone present could share his horror. They'd have studied it in comprehensive, lingering detail, trying to remember to say, "Well, I never!" and "How disgusting!" at regular intervals. It wouldn't have been that much trouble for him. It would have been a nice little souvenir to take home afterwards.

Foul, they remembered.

Revolting.

Sickening.

Offensive.

Disgusting.

Some of the men looked positively cheated.

". . . on vulnerable and impressionable boys . . ."

Mrs. Albert Comstock stared speculatively up at Oliver at this point. She could *certainly* imagine the effect.

". . . The hideous appearance at first shocks the pure mind, and the poor victim would fain put it out of existence . . ."

Anthony Comstock was one of those speakers who was incapable of speaking unless he had already written down what it was he was saying, a *reader* rather than a speaker. Like a lazy amateur pianist, he played the same pieces over and over, rather falteringly, and not very well. What he lacked in finesse, he compensated for in volume, his foot jammed down on the pedal as if it were the accelerator pedal in one of Samuel Cummerford's automobiles, and he was accelerating away at top speed — fleeing the scene of a crime — leaning back at a dramatic angle, tires shrieking, comforter whizzing back.

Make way! Make way!

Hesitate, and I'll knock you down!

He did not answer direct questions; he quoted vaguely applicable passages that came to mind. It was slightly surprising that he did not riffle through his copy of *Traps for the Young* to find the section that he was visibly recalling. He almost had his finger (print-side forward) up in front of him — it would have borne a disturbing resemblance to a blessing — as he ran it beneath the line he was reading in the air. He was one of those readers who had to hold his finger under a word as he read it with dutiful, forehead-wrinkling endeavor. A slightly protruding tongue could not be ruled out. Pornographers with larger vocabularies, and multi-syllabic capabilities — here was a useful tip — would baffle this sniff-sniffing seeker-out of sinfulness.

". . . But the tempter says . . ."

Anthony Comstock, demonstrating his histrionic abilities — and sounding exactly the same as he had done before — attempted the insinuating tones of the vile seducer.

". . . 'It can't hurt you; you are strong. Look it over and see what it is. Don't be afraid . . .'"

Anthony Comstock stood there like a particularly unfortunate Doctor Faustus, with a double dose of Bad Angels, one on either side of him, and no Good Angel to warn him away from temptation, to beg him lay that damned book aside and gaze not on it lest it tempt his soul.

"... Thus beguiled, a second look, and then a mighty force from within is let loose ..."

— time for italics again, deep breath, look really serious —

"... *Passions that had slumbered or lain dormant are awakened, and the boy is forced over a precipice, and death and destruction ...*"

Crumbs!

"... *are sure, except the grace of* God *saves him. An* indelible *stain* ..."

Gosh!

(*Stain!*

(*Indelible stain!*

(Audible whinnies at this point from some of the less restrained male members of the audience, starting to feel quite glad that they'd been persuaded to come along.

(This was unexpectedly explicit. If they were lucky, more might be on the way.)

"... has been placed upon the boy's imagination, and this vision shall be kept like a panorama, moving to and fro before his mind *until it has blotted out moral purity*, and the lamentable condition before described is experienced. Parents and teachers must *keep watch for these traps*. Evil things may be found *lurking in pocket, desk, and private box* of the child ..."

— it sounded as if he'd had a good rummage around, knowing where best to look; he'd patted pockets (*What have we here?*), he'd thrown open desks and drawers (*What's this? What's this?*), those Pandora's boxes of *filth*! —

"... they *cannot bear* the light of day."

He paused.

That had got them.

Some of the women had gone quite pale. Most of the men — clearly overcome by reminiscent guilt — had their heads bowed. Shoulders shook. Anthony Comstock always enjoyed it when shoulders shook.

He looked down on Oliver – who was still standing – with a labored smile of sweet condescension. A firebrand plucked out of the burning (Amos, Chapter IV, Verse xi), but definitely a bit singed at the edges.

"Does that answer your question, young man?"

The correct answer was clearly, "Yes! Yes! A thousand times yes, Anthony Comstock! Blessings upon thee, O wise counselor!"

Oliver did not give the correct answer.

"Not really," he said. "I was hoping you might give me a title." He held his pocket book at the ready, poised his pen. "The really, *really filthiest* book you've ever come across. I mean, you must have read more filthy books than anyone else in this hall . . ."

Oliver paused, and looked at Dr. Ascharm Wolcott Webster with peculiar emphasis. He leaned right over to do it.

". . . with possibly one exception . . ."

Oliver paused again, his look intensifying, his angle of lean increasing. All that was missing was the large illuminated pointing hand, and the ornate decorative lettering beneath it reading: *This way! This way!* All around the Athenian Hall heads turned to see the face of the man thus indicated. Some people rose to their feet so that they could have a good view of him. Fingers pointed. Whispering. Not very subdued whispering.

The man behind Dr. Wolcott Ascharm Webster began to write furiously, his pen nib scratching itchily.

A firebrand that was *still* burning, one that could spread the blaze and engulf the unwary.

There was a discreet tap on Dr. Wolcott Ascharm Webster's shoulder, and a hand appeared in the gap between his left arm and his body. There was no gap on the right-hand side, of course, as Mrs. Albert Comstock was sitting there, crammed into every available square inch of space. The man behind him was passing on what it was he had written. The hand thrust its way forward – all the arm up to the elbow following – with a visiting card firmly held between the tips of the index and middle fingers, all poised to be dashed downward like a perfectly timed trump card in a game played for high stakes. There was a self-conscious grace in the way the card was held, in the manner of a magician producing a playing card at the climax of a trick.

"And the card you chose is . . ."

Automatically, he found himself taking the card, whispering polite thanks.

"And the card you chose is . . ."

Mrs. Goodchild – rearing away to her left – reacted as if something disgusting were being cheekily flourished in her face by a beaming, rather proud, exhibitionist (a – ahem – "meat-flasher" was, she believed, the appropriate terminology) in the warmer weather. She had a good look at the man's face. Thank heaven she was wearing a veil. Her knuckles tightened around her umbrella.

The card he chose had writing on it in green ink, and many underlinings. Underlinings and green ink was not a combination that invited confidence.

On the front of the card, the man's address had been meaningfully underlined in green ink. On the back of the card there were more underlinings, more green ink.

I see that you are a collector also. Shall we meet, to discuss our collections?

". . . and so you . . ." Oliver was continuing, standing completely upright again, but leaving – or so it felt like – *This way! This way!* still blinking and popping in the air, the extended pointing finger digging Dr. Wolcott Ascharm Webster knowingly in the small of his back. Unless that were the man behind him, matily establishing a closeness, drawn toward him by a shared interest.

Thinking quickly, Mrs. Goodchild dropped her gloves on the floor, and leaned across for a good look at the card as she bent to recover them. Scrabbling blindly – she was too interested in the visiting card to look at the floor – she ran her fingers across Dr. Wolcott Ascharm Webster's well-polished (Hilde Claudia-polished) shoes, her ring catching tuggingly in his laces. He was being assailed from all sides!

Evil things may be found lurking.

They were hardly *lurking*. Mrs. Goodchild lunged against him, and tugged the lace of his left shoe open as she pulled away. There was an insistent prodding in his back from someone anxious for a prompt response. They were out in full force, unabashed and brassy.

I'm sure that we shall have much of interest to discuss! You saucy boy!

The exclamation point was worrying. Punctuation could so easily spread unease in the mind when thoughtlessly lavished upon an otherwise unprepossessing sentence.

Mrs. Goodchild leaned right up against the card – her nose virtually touched it – grabbed her gloves, and hauled herself upright, gratifyingly appalled.

She'd seen the green ink.

She'd seen the underlinings.

She'd seen the exclamation point.

She'd seen *You saucy boy!*

Mrs. Albert Comstock – without saying a word – asked Mrs. Goodchild a question with a look, a tilt of the head, the eyebrows.

Mrs. Goodchild – without saying a word – answered.

They'd have a great deal to talk about afterwards. They'd need to sit down. They'd need to sip sherry. They'd need to utilize their fans at full force. They could hardly wait.

". . . more than anyone else – *virtually* – . . ."

Ouch.

The digging from the pointing finger intensified. Its nail needed the urgent attentions of a fully trained manicurist.

". . . should be the *best qualified of all of us* . . ."

Anthony Comstock detected a compliment in the italics.

". . . to name the *filthiest book ever written.*"

There was a pause.

Anthony Comstock wasn't too sure about the last set of italics.

"I ask you to share the benefit of your expertise with us. I ask you to *give us its title.*"

Oliver's pen hovered in the air above his pocket book.

All the men leaned forward. Pens were poised.

"Its title? . . ."

"And the author!" a man's voice added, anxiously, from several rows back.

There was a flurry across the hall as pens drew closer, hovering, over scraps of paper. It was like the beginning of a short timed examination.

This was more like it.

This was what they had all come to hear.

Well done, that young fellow with the long blond hair.

"Ah!"

Anthony Comstock was equal to the occasion.

"Our youth are falling on every side!" he informed them, his voice infused with urgency. You expected to hear dull thuds from all sides as our youth fell. "Lives that otherwise might shine as the stars in the firmament are shrouded with a veil of darkness, with horrors to the victim's mind which no pen can describe!"

Pens faltered in disappointed hands. They'd have appreciated being given the opportunity to make an attempt to describe the horrors to the victim's mind. They were really interested in the horrors.

"The title . . ."

Pens quivered back into life, as Oliver spoke again. The hymn-book hiss of turned pages intensified.

". . . of the *really, really filthiest book* . . ."

"Could I borrow it?" a voice – rather desperate – called from the side of the hall. The speaker (by accident or by design) was hidden behind one of the pillars, but was clearly anxious to get in the question before Oliver did. "I'd look after it very carefully. I wouldn't snap the spine."

Anthony Comstock ignored the question. If there were to be any spine-snapping going on, he was the man who would do it, thank you very much. He flexed his fingers experimentally, keen to get started on the snapping. This young man with the unfeasibly long hair was really starting to try his patience. This was a youth that should be falling with immediate effect, shrouded with a veil of darkness, with indescribable horrors to his mind. That would go down *very* well.

"You cannot handle fire and not be burned," he said — he quoted — officiously, "neither can the black fiend Lust touch the moral nature without leaving *traces of defilement*."

That was his clinching line. That would shut them up.

It never failed.

(*Snap!* he was thinking, *Snap! Snap! Snap!* Spines snapped like fresh celery sticks being prepared for a *really* large salad. Veils of darkness. Indescribable — *Babble! Babble!* gibberings — horrors. He bared his teeth — this was a smile — as if all ready to start crunching that celery, wolfing down that Waldorf. He'd got the celery, he'd got the apples — that potent symbol of lost innocence — and he'd got the nuts. He'd *most certainly* got the nuts.)

"Is that some kind of confession, Mr. Comstock?"

The smile vanished.

Anthony Comstock's mouth gaped.

"You have handled fire. Are *you* burned?"

The firebrand crackled with a fierce blaze.

"Has the black fiend Lust touched *your* moral nature?"

No supporters of Anthony Comstock intervened. No one attempted to silence Oliver, or hurry him out of the hall. They were all too interested in hearing the answer. Several people near the back, who had been discreetly attempting to slip out of the hall, had returned. They hovered with expressions of keen appreciation. Anthony Comstock's beard was all of a quiver.

"Have you been *defiled*?"

Furtive nostrils sniffed the air, alert for telltale whiffs. Something sewagy and penetrating, with the eye-watering edge of last week's soiled linen. That was the sort of thing they had in mind, the unmistakable *ding-dong-dung* (especially the *dung*) of defilement.

Oliver leaned right over again.

This way! This way! hissed and crackled as the voltage increased to a dangerous intensity. Sparks showered down, and there was the unmistakable smell of just-singed beard in the air.

A firebrand . . .

A firebrand . . .

A firebrand to ignite a cleansing blaze.

The pointing finger prodded and prodded with unignorable persistence, until Dr. Wolcott Ascharm Webster's back vibrated with the handles of well-insulated stabbed-in daggers.

You saucy boy!

Stab!

You saucy boy!

Stab!

"Have you been *defiled*, like *Dr. Wolcott Ascharm Webster of 11 Park Place, Longfellow Park?*"

That was how Oliver would have liked it to happen.

5

Ben turned a little to one side on the sofa, drawing himself closer to the sound of Oliver's voice, though he'd unconsciously crossed his arms, leaning in against himself. His right hand – he didn't know that he was doing it – began to creep up the outside of his left arm, and began to rub away at the top of it over his biceps, a gesture to erase a stain, soothe a hurt, or bring warmth. This movement had become habitual with him, and yet it remained curiously unlike him. His movements were usually so thought out beforehand, so controlled. He bowed his head, to concentrate better on what Oliver was saying. His face had its cool, distant look, a face from which emotion had been carefully eradicated. "How interesting," that face would say, when it wasn't interested. That face would turn away with no expression to reveal the thoughts within the mind. It had taken many years to achieve this degree of control.

He listened for a while. They were all listening. His mouth was slightly open, like that of a concentrating child.

"'F' as in 'photograph,'" Oliver said. "'R' as in 'wreckage' . . ."

He was, Ben realized, spelling his middle name, Francis.

"'N' as in 'pneumonia.' 'C' as in 'seesaw' . . ."

He paused, and started to laugh again.

"No," he said. "Definitely not. That would be silly."

What had he said for "A"?

They continued to listen.

Another laugh from Oliver.

("Golly! It's Olly!"

(It had been as if he and Oliver were friends again, boys still at school.

("I think it's Pink!")

THREE

I

Ben didn't tell Alice about many things.

He didn't tell her about school.

He didn't tell her about Mr. Rappaport.

He didn't tell her about the things that he could not understand, the things that were worrying him.

It was a part of his attempts to be a manly chap, to please his Papa, even though his Papa was dead.

Ben had entered Otsego Lake Academy at the age of ten, the week after his father had died during the 1888 blizzard, with a black band around the upper part of his left arm, marking him out as a child who had had a death in the family. The black bands – there were three boys wearing them – as well as being an outward demonstration of mourning, like lowered blinds and black-edged writing-paper, might – generous-hearted souls could have chosen to believe – also have been designed to alert masters and other boys to treat their wearers with particular gentleness. The effect they actually produced was to identify easy targets for teasing, enticing little treats for the likes of Mr. Rappaport. Black bands were bull's-eyes for Brinkman, targets at which he aimed with all the sharp words of weaponry.

They approached the academy through a snowbound, high-walled maze, shivering in the cold, seeing nothing but the dirty sides of the rough-cut snow tunnels on either side of them like the approach to an Ice Queen's palace. It was Monday, March the nineteenth, his sister Alice's twentieth birthday. There was only one route by which they could approach the school beside the ice-covered lake, the same narrow ash-scattered track that had been trodden by all the others who had gone before them that morning. The darkly enclosed pathway, cut through the deep snow that was still there after the blizzard, shut out all the views around them. It seemed an appropriate symbol of the years that were to follow in that building, as they trudged along with their heads bowed, their feet crunching and slithering, their boots whitened. They'd all been taken to Oldermann & Oldermann (*Particularly To Be Recommended For Boys' School Attire!*) and he was walking along in his stiff new uniform with Oliver Comstock and Linnaeus Finch, all their buttons gleaming in the white, cold light, their jackets dark against the snow. From time to time, they looked at the dark-clad figures ahead of them when there was a straight stretch, looking for people they recognized, the other Crowninshield's boys, someone familiar so that they felt less lost.

Occasionally a boy would slip and fall on the slippery surface, sometimes grabbing at a friend to drag him down with him. The laughter sounded unnaturally shrill.

> "Alas, regardless of their doom,
> The little victims play!"

Oliver, who was in poetic mood, was suiting his declaiming to the occasion.

"Ooh, good!" he added when Sidney Brinkman – in attempting to trip up Charlie Whitefoord – fell heavily onto his front. "I hope he's permanently disfigured. That'd be quite an improvement. A broken nose, at least." They'd been running – fearful of being late on their first day – and were out of breath, capable of only short sentences.

"*Festina lente!*" Oliver had been urging them – reminding them that, as Dr. Crowninshield had demonstrated, they (it was an encouraging thought and made them feel less nervous, a *little* less nervous) all knew Latin — and they'd hastened slowly. He was sporting his bank-robber look, his muffler wound round and round the lower part of his face — only his eyes were showing — but the muffler failed somehow to muffle his voice. It took advanced skills to muffle Oliver's voice, once he was in talkative mood.

Brinkman tried to get to his feet, and fell again, a spectacular collapse, with both feet high in the air, a square-shaped athlete experimenting with a new technique for jumping over a bar. This was quite good timing on Brinkman's part. They needed something to cheer them up.

"Even gooder!"

Brinkman had been their resident bully at Crowninshield's. Schools seemed to require them, along with canes and globes of the world. In a spirit of helpfulness, the new boys had brought their bully along with them, as a sacrificial offering to appease the gods of their new school. That was Oliver's plan. The Brinkmans would be furious that the deep snow had prevented them from showing off their new carriage to assembled crowds of awed and envious lesser mortals.

The academy had only just reopened after the temporary closure forced upon it by the blizzards that had brought New York to a standstill.

This was to be their new school.

Their old school — Dr. Crowninshield's — had closed unexpectedly, and the parents of its pupils left searching for a new private school. Mr. Scrivener (or minions working upon his orders) had pounced (Mr. Scrivener himself was long past the age for pouncing; if he pounced he'd need help to haul himself back upright again) — Otsego Lake Academy masters tended to go in for pouncing, they were to discover — and grabbed all the former Crowninshield's pupils to add to the numbers of his establishment, even if they were not quite of the usual age. It was numbers that mattered. Numbers meant finance, and there was no reduction in the fees for younger boys.

The "Dr." part of Crowninshield's name had been a fiction — that had been discovered shortly before the school had folded — as, indeed, had been the "Crowninshield" part. So, also, had been the long string of letters after his name that looked like a very complicated date in Roman numerals, some eighteenth-century battle in which the cavalry had come galloping into the attack with the sun dazzling on the uplifted blades of sabers. It was full of Ls and Ds, and Ben had sometimes seen it as a Roman arithmetical puzzle, crammed with challenging fifties and five hundreds. No half-measures with Dr. Crowninshield. The owner of the school — whatever his real name was — had designed his title, and his splendidly heraldic name (there was a coat of arms on the school notepaper, and above the entrance) to inspire respect, and they had succeeded in their purpose. Both Ben's and Oliver's fathers had always been impressed by titles — Oliver's papa had invariably simpered over his sausages when a *grand dame* with cowed maid-servants swept into his shop and spoke to him as if he were the third gardener on her vast estate — and they hadn't been able to resist shoving their sons into a school with a coat of arms. Both papas had rapped on the impressively stiff headed notepaper with their knuckles so that both mamas — Oliver's mama had become the grandest of *grand dames* herself, after years of practicing — had noted the crown, the shield, the lion and the unicorn. Ben's three sisters, Myrtle Comstock, and Charlotte Finch had all been pupils at Miss Pearsall's School for Girls, and now here was the *very* place to prepare their brothers for Otsego Lake Academy. Ben and Oliver had always been destined for Otsego Lake Academy. Throughout their childhood, there it had been beside the lake, with its rows of windows and its central dome — "a stately pleasure-dome" Oliver had once mused as they saw it rising up above early morning mist, not sounding as if he meant it — like a destination from which there would be no escape.

Dr. Crowninshield's school had been a small pillared stucco building set behind railings on Indian Woods Road, not very far away from the chiropodist's, and Mr. Brczin's, the optician's. The gaudy coat of arms above the entrance – the gold paint had been applied with a lavish hand and gleamed in the sunlight – gave it the look of an embassy for some minor European power. You felt slightly cheated that there wasn't a flag snapping – Independence Day celebratory fashion – from a white-painted pole that inclined at an angle above the portico, a flag with colors selected from the brighter hues of the paintbox, and with a simple pattern involving broad stripes. Most of the parents – unless it was just that they were dazzled by all that gilding – were clearly in need of Mr. Brczin's services, and failed to notice the cracks in the stucco, the decayed sections that had fallen away from the walls, the bare brick beneath, the provocatively revealing Symbolism that displayed – for those with eyes to see it – the true state of financial affairs with Dr. Crowninshield in the vital couple of years before he was exposed as "Dr. Crowninshield," a nonentity nullified by carefully applied punctuation.

They'd been happy there. They'd been *very* happy there. Dr. Crowninshield might have been an imposter, but he had possessed a sprightly, good-humored manner (probably a prerequisite for successful fraud), and they'd enjoyed reenacting battles out of ancient history all the way down the steps from the second-floor classroom, and out through the front door. Many a tyrant had met his doom alongside the railings outside the chiropodist's. "Die, you bunioned blackguard! Die!" Oliver had been fond of declaiming, as his twelve-inch ruler plunged its full length under a defeated despot's arm, a cardboard crown rolling down the sidewalk as a sure sign of the impermanence of all sublunary power. "Dr. Crowninshield" soon found out about that.

Now they were on their way to their new school, rather earlier than had been originally intended.

They had heard about Otsego Lake Academy – long, long ago they'd heard *all* about Otsego Lake Academy – and they were not enthusiastic, though Oliver – just to be provoking – cultivated an air of keen anticipation.

Papa had made all the arrangements for Ben to enter Otsego

Lake Academy. Papa wasn't actually alive now to see him entering the school, but he had made all the arrangements, as if the unhappiness that followed had been something willed to him, his inheritance from his father, longer-lasting than any money might have been (there hadn't *been* any money), more deeply rooted, more *meant*. Papa had had long conversations with Mr. Scrivener and with some of the teachers – certainly with young and enthusiastic Mr. Rappaport, a new teacher keen to make his mark – and given them helpful hints on how to make a manly little chap out of him, strict instructions on how to snip out the incipient girliness that ever-threatened the austere battlements of the bearded.

"Say *this*," he'd said, and they'd say it.

They'd be saying it over and over.

"Do *this*," he'd said, and they'd do it.

They'd be doing it repeatedly, doing little else but those same repeated movements of hurting.

His father had talked to the headmaster (telling him what it was he had to say and do), and the headmaster would have talked to all the masters, and all the masters would begin to correct his movements, his voice, if he forgot to move the right way, speak the right words. He just *knew* that Mr. Rappaport would be particularly ingenious and thorough in doing this. Not only would he be carrying out the sacred duty of obeying the wishes of a dead man, but he'd also be thoroughly enjoying himself. He'd seen that look in Mr. Rappaport's eyes, that gleam of complicity. At school, as at home, he would have to sit, to stand, to move, to speak, in the way that was deemed to be correct, and they would make comments about him – the boys, as well as the masters, for Mr. Rappaport would be nothing if not meticulous in carrying out instructions – if he forgot the right way. "Pinkie!" the other boys would jeer in high falsetto voices, and it wouldn't just be "Pinkie!" that they'd select for their means of mocking. They'd think Pink, and all the other words and phrases, the ones tried and tested by Papa. They'd have been told the best ones to use, the ones guaranteed to produce gratifying results: blushes, tears.

He didn't want to go.

He was dreading what would happen when he got there.

He could have claimed to be upset by Papa's death.

He could have said that it was *far* too early to go to school, just a week to the day since it had happened, but Mama had said she thought it would be best if he went.

"I'm upset," he could have said.

He could have attempted to force out a few tears, despite the risk that the sight of his son *crying* might have resurrected his father, and brought him roaring back to life, eager to mock and punish.

Resurgam!

"I'm *really* upset," he could have said, though he wasn't upset.

He couldn't say what he was.

He . . .

He felt *nothing*.

He . . .

He did feel something.

He felt *safer*.

He didn't want to go, but he went.

It would be awful, but it would be far worse to arrive by himself, days or weeks after the rest of the Crowninshield's pupils had settled in, if "settled in" was ever the expression to use of the experience of being in that school. Instead of being just one of a whole crowd of new boys, he'd be *the* new boy, all by himself. The others would have become *used to it* – you could become accustomed to anything – and he'd be just starting to make that change. The others would have learned to *know what to expect* – that had been Mr. Scrivener's expression – and he'd be just starting to find out what to expect. (It wouldn't be good.) He couldn't have borne the thought of that.

So he didn't claim that he was upset.

(He wasn't.)

He didn't force out some tears.

(He wouldn't have been able to manage them.)

For a week now he'd stopped being called Franklin.

(He'd never known why Papa had opted for "Franklin" instead of "Ben." He'd never recognized himself in "Franklin." That name was not who he was, though he'd not yet found a name that seemed to suit him. It wasn't "Ben." That's what he felt some-times, only sometimes, seeing himself as something nameless.)

For a week now he had been Ben to *everyone* who knew him, apart from those who addressed him as "Pinkerton." There were too many opportunities for taunting in the name "Pinkerton."

It was like being given the opportunity of being born again, being someone new, although Papa had taken the necessary steps to ensure that — after his death — there would be no possibility of a rebirth for his son. Otsego Lake Academy had been fully briefed (and the briefings had not been brief ones) as to *what to expect* when Pinkerton, Benjamin Franklin arrived there to be ticked off on lists. (Ticking off would *certainly* come into it.) *What to expect* would have been closely followed by *what to accept* and *what not to accept* from Pinkerton, Benjamin Franklin. Mr. Rappaport would be poised for action, knees slightly bent, arms reaching forward, pant-ing eagerly. He'd have been assiduously practicing.

There was the name, printed with all the others, in the columns with their straight left-hand margins.

Pinkerton, Benjamin Franklin.

Tick.

It didn't seem to have much to do with him.

Ben was on his way to his new school with Oliver Comstock and Linnaeus Finch, with them and all the other new boys, the Crowninshield's boys now walking in quite the wrong direction, away from the school that they had previously known.

Oliver began to spin his satchel of schoolbooks in the air around him on the end of its strap, a sudden impulse seizing him — this could not be discounted — to hurl the books as far away from him as possible. Ben and Linnaeus had to dodge to one side to avoid Oliver's swings, as they gathered momentum. It was quite impress-ive that he was managing to do this with one hand. There were so many books, and their satchels were so heavy, that they had all sunk perceptibly deeper into the snow when they had started out on their journey with them. Oliver – in numerous ways – was rather stronger than he appeared.

More poetry.

> ". . . A youth, who bore, 'mid snow and ice,
> A banner with the strange device . . ."

– he chanted, and –

> ". . . Excelsior!"

Ben and Linnaeus added the last word, sensing their cue.

They continued with this for a few yards, Oliver leaping from verse to verse of "Excelsior" as the mood took him. His mama had made him recite the poem to entertain the guests at her most recent – you struggled for an adjective – celebrated cultural gathering. "Made him" wasn't really the correct phrase to employ. Oliver's mama couldn't *make* him do anything he didn't want to do. She'd asked him to recite "Excelsior," making it sound like an order, and – as it was something that he had actually wanted to do – he had agreed to do it. It had quite taken her by surprise. "Why *not?*" she'd snarled automatically, when he'd actually said yes. She'd had to think for some considerable time before she could produce a suitable next sentence.

Reciting "Excelsior" had been a part of Oliver's preparation to become a fully trained new recruit for Otsego Lake Academy, and whenever Oliver chose to do something, he chose to do it *properly*. He had wanted to do it as soon as Alice had told him that she'd heard an Otsego Lake Academy pupil – William Blennerhasset (William and George Blennerhasset had cousins who were pupils at the school now) – recite the poem years ago, before he and Ben were born, when she had unveiled *The Children's Hour*, the statue that depicted her and Ben's two other sisters, in the park. *And* "Excelsior!" – they knew – was a word in Latin, a proclamation of their academic suitability for their new school. "Ever upward!" That was what they were chanting, given extra courage by that optimistic declaration of unshakeable resolve, that defiant exclamation point. They were not going to be cowed by the thought of what lay ahead of them. They were fearless, invincible! *Excelsior!* (Two more morale-boosting exclamation points.) Ever upward, they'd scale the intellectual heights of Mr. Scrivener's rigorous establishment, as whips cracked at their heels, just missing them.

Several weeks before they'd started at the academy, Oliver (his mama, inevitably, had been the first parent to purchase one) had called round – grimacing – to demonstrate his new school uniform, marching up and down like someone on sentry duty, wriggling from side to side to make all the buttons bobble and tinkle and catch the light – "Listen to that!" he'd said. "I feel like a sleigh!" ("I feel like *slaying*," he'd added, seconds later, spotting the pun) – and she had told him then. She'd been a little girl, and – on a bitterly cold day like today – she had been surrounded by the massed buttons of the assembled academy, glinting frostily.

A week after its first appearance he'd stood there in the music room at 5 Hampshire Square with an appropriately sad mood-creating expression, wearing his school uniform again, creatively jingling his bell-like buttons to help create a suitably icy atmosphere. An idea suddenly came to him. "The bells!" he gasped, assuming an expression of torment, enthusiastically essaying his Sir Henry Irving gestures, Mathias hearing the approach of the man he was doomed to murder. "The bells!" (Even Reynolds Templeton Seabright, slightly sulky, would have applauded his wild-eyed, disheveled-hair hamminess.) He rolled his eyes and staggered about a bit, and then – "The shades of night were falling fast . . ." – launched himself straight into "Excelsior." You always got good value from Oliver.

Dr. Crowninshield would have enjoyed the recitation, buoyed up as he was by his enthusiasm for Oliver's versions of Mrs. Alexander Diddecott's poems. The literary ladies hadn't, however, been enthusiastic about the banner that Oliver had dramatically unfurled as the stupendous climax of his performance. (Oliver went in for stupendous climaxes whenever he performed something.) "He's used a *great deal* of paint." That had been Mabel Peartree's summing-up, the thoughtful verdict of a true connoisseur of the arts. Mrs. Goodchild had just shuddered, and (in simultaneous motion with Oliver's mama) raised her fan to shield her eyes, but Dr. Crowninshield – in no need of shielding – would have enjoyed this, also. It was generally agreed that the device Oliver had designed upon the banner was perhaps a little too – ahem – *strange*, a little too – ahem – *graphic*.

As they all lived in Longfellow Park, they *had* to listen to a bit of Longfellow's poetry from time to time. That was Mrs. Albert Comstock's belief. Each neighborhood of New York brought its own attendant hazards to its inhabitants.

> ". . . A traveler, by the faithful hound,
> Half-buried in the snow was found,
> Still grasping in his hand of ice
> That banner with the strange device,
> Excelsior! . . ."

Oliver paused at this point. Time for a textual clarification.

"The 'faithful hound' is *not* a reference to Chinky-Winky," he informed them. (He loathed his Mama's Pekinese: the feeling was mutual.) "Chinky-Winky would pee on me, for several minutes, gallons and gallons of steaming pee . . ." – Oliver was a connoisseur of unsuitable detail – ". . . and then complete the burial. That's all I could expect from him. They shall find me in the twilight cold and gray, lifeless, but beautiful. You may wipe away a tear at this point, if you wish." He added, in his Shakespearean voice, to reassure them that what they were hearing was cultural, "I do smell all dog-piss at which my nose is in great indignation."

The original intention had been that the new influx of pupils should start at the school at the beginning of the Summer Term, but then Mr. Scrivener had decided that it might be a nice idea to "welcome" – he used the word with no sense of irony – all the new boys for the last two weeks of the Spring Term, so that they'd "already be at home" – Mr. Scrivener had no sense of irony *whatsoever* – when the Summer Term eventually arrived.

In describing his nice idea, Mr. Scrivener had also declared that the nice idea was also a good idea, as the new pupils would thus be well prepared for what was to follow, and would "know what to expect." He employed a deeply manly chuckle that vibrated his beard as he said this, making it sound like a not very veiled threat, which is what it probably was. "They'll know what to expect." This was exactly what they feared. It seemed like a good way to ruin the approaching vacation, knowing what to expect. That was Oliver's opinion. ("A jolly good way to ruin the vac for us chaps." Those were Oliver's exact words. He had researched the correct vocabulary to employ when you were a pupil at the likes of Otsego Lake Academy. Oliver always liked to do things the right way, or – failing that – the *annoying* way. To be quite accurate, he *preferred* the annoying way.)

The blizzard had rather put paid to the original plan, but here they now were – with just *one week* left of the Spring Term – starting their new school. It seemed a silly thing to be doing, but Mr. Scrivener had said they should do it, and so it was what they were doing. "Spring Term" seemed the most misnamed of all terms, starting as it did with snow on the ground (*finishing* with snow on the ground in this particular year), and no signs of greenery (entirely appropriate though this desolation and coldness was for what lay within the walls of the academy). With all its pretensions to academic grandeur, you'd have thought that Otsego Lake Academy would have had terms named "Michaelmas" and suchlike. This was the sort of thing to persuade parents that they were getting value for money. Perhaps the founder of the school had thought that using such expressions as "Year One" and "Year Two" for the different grades within the school (Otsego Lake Academy did not go in for "ninth grade" or "tenth grade," eschewing grades completely, as it was too refined to dabble in such *hoi polloi* vulgarity) – not to mention the multi-lingual refinements of *A* and *alpha* and *aleph* to distinguish the classes within each grade – was enough of a flirtation with the higher echelons of academe for the more conservative-minded (or dimmer) of the parents. When they entered the school – walked up those steps, walked between those pillars, walked through those doors – and became Year One (though they were not, however, destined to bear even that lowly name) they were being told that everything that had happened to them before they arrived at that place was of no consequence. Only now was the meaningful, chronicled part of their lives about to begin.

"That sunny dome!" Oliver was declaring, rather mysteriously, as they drew closer, straining to catch his first glimpse of the school above the banks of dug-out snow.

(There wasn't much sun.)

"Those caves of ice!"

(Now *this* made sense.)

"Beware! Beware!"

(As did this.)

They were fully on the alert for warnings, and "Beware! Beware!" was what they felt. All the Crowninshield's boys had been told to report half-an-hour later than the rest of the school, so that a special "welcome" (you flinched at the possibilities) might be prepared for them by the rest of the school, and Oliver – who had borrowed Ben's copy of *Tom Brown's Schooldays* to read as part of his preparative research – claimed to be looking forward to the wealth of new experiences that would be on offer. He casually mentioned – as everyday occurrences – that being thrown up against the ceiling in blankets and being roasted in front of roaring fires (fires tended to roar in this context) were probably essential parts of beginning a day at Otsego Lake Academy, like singing "The Star-Spangled Banner" in ringing patriotic tones, good healthy exercise, and integrated torture. It was a school that catered for the most muscular of Christians, with bulgy muscles and not much brain. Christianity – Oliver described the Otsego Lake

Academy version of this as "Inanity" (like a fiercely independent small state it nurtured its own language and its own religion) – did not play much of a part in what went on there, but bulgy muscles and not much brain were definite assets. With Otsego Lake Academy in one part of Longfellow Park, and the Reverend Goodchild growing in power at All Saints' in another, it was a miracle – this was a very precise choice of word, you felt – that Christianity survived in their neighborhood at all. At least they were spared a Roman Catholic church. (That was Mrs. Albert Comstock's firm opinion.)

Roasted.

However welcome a little heat might be in weather like today's, that did not sound too encouraging. They pictured being skewered on spits and rotating slowly. Dizziness and severe burns was not a combination that invited enthusiasm.

"Beware! Beware!" Oliver said again, with some relish.

Blankets.

Another tantalizing glimpse of out-of-reach warmth, wantonly misapplied.

Oliver would quite enjoy being tossed high into the air on a blanket, just to be aggravating. Alice had bought *Tom Brown's Schooldays* for Ben, but Oliver had seized upon it as a guide to behavior, with all the etiquette of education clearly explained within its covers.

"Higher!" he'd be shouting – he'd be the one giving the orders, you could guarantee that – "Higher!" He'd have them all exhausted, begging to be excused as he soared twenty feet, thirty feet, as he approached ever nearer to banging his head against the painted breast of Cora Munro in the cupola above the main hall, the achievement to which he aspired.

He'd bring chestnuts with him – his pockets were probably *crammed* with chestnuts – to make full use of the roasting.

"Now the other side, chaps!" he'd demand, when he felt that one side of him was well cooked. "Has anyone brought any decent wine?"

The massed men of Otsego Lake Academy were probably giving the spits a few experimental twists at that very moment. They'd be looking forward to welcoming Oliver Comstock, making him feel at home, letting him know what to expect. They'd be all in favor of spitting, in one form or another. Oliver wouldn't be the slightest bit alarmed.

"It's jolly decent of you chaps to offer," he'd say – they'd be staring, open-mouthed (*What language was that?*) – "but I don't want to disappoint Brinkman. He's been so looking forward to being roasted. He's been practicing at home. I'd hate him to be disappointed. Come on Brinkman, old chap . . ." – he'd start to empty out all the chestnuts as a further inducement to sway the Otsegoans (was that what you called them?) onto his side – " . . . come and be skewered. I'll render assistance." (He'd be rended from limb to limb if Brinkman got hold of him.)

("Otsegoans" sounded like some primitive tribe.

(This was entirely appropriate.)

"Beware! Beware!"

"'That really helps," Linnacus said, rather plaintively. He was always a nervous boy. Some of the Otsegoans – latecomers dawdling along through the snow – had already seen the new boys starting to approach, and they were all covered in the remains of snowballs. The welcome had already started. The front of Linnaeus's jacket was almost completely wet and whitened. One snowball had hit him in his right eye, and tears were still welling up in that eye, the first of the many tears that he would shed at that school. You'd think that they would freeze on this morning.

"His glittering eye!" Oliver said, indicating Linnaeus's bright eye, brimming with water. You couldn't understand what he said sometimes.

Linnaeus Finch lived on Hudson Heights, but he had come to Crowninshield's from New Hampshire, from *another* school that had closed down. His father – Colonel Finch – had sent him away to boarding school when he was very young. You imagined him being packed and posted – a tiny child rigidly enclosed in tightly folded brown paper in a well-strung and knotted swaddling-clothes sort of way – and placed in the hands of the U.S. mail service. It wouldn't have cost much to post him. He'd be looking from side to side hopefully as his peripatetic cot was hurled from hand to hand, seeking for a kind face, smiling tentatively, well behaved and biddable. Linnaeus's *two* previous schools had closed down, and they were trying to build their hopes upon that basis. On his first day at Crowninshield's he'd come up to them and told them his name, and you'd have thought that they'd never met him before, or that no one would ever remember who he was. He was something of a stranger, even though he lived so close, even though he was the brother of Alice's best friend, Charlotte, more of a holiday acquaintance than someone they could be said to have known at all well. They knew who he was, but he'd told them his name, assuming that they wouldn't remember him.

"Finch," he'd said, "Linnaeus Vorhees Finch," and waited with patient resignation for them to start singing, "Vorhees a Jolly Good Fellow."

When they didn't – revealing that they, in fact, were the Jolly Good Fellows – he'd visibly relaxed. He didn't say much about his school in New Hampshire, but you could hazard a guess at what it must have been like for him there. There was something rural and gentle about him, though his face was a pale, city, indoor face, his skin the color of milk, and they liked his slow way of speaking. All his nervousness seemed to be concentrated into his long, thin fingers, fingers that were rarely at rest, tugging at his collar, fiddling with buttons, forever tracing the outline of his lips, shaking even when they were supposedly still. It was as if he knew already what would be brought upon him by being left-handed and prone to tears at Otsego Lake Academy, the hands already trembling with the knowledge of what was going to happen to him. His nails – hidden, now, by his gloves – were bitten down, and even the edges of the skin, as much as of the nails, were nibbled. They were nearly in as bad a state as Ben's, and Ben's were *really* bad. ("Dear, oh dear," Oliver would say, all his æsthetic feelings shaken, whenever he studied Ben's fingernails. "Dear, oh *dear*.") He was a quiet, inoffensive boy – amicable and unostentatiously studious – and Ben and Oliver were taken with the strange power of doom he seemed to bring with him to educational institutions. He was, you felt, the sort of boy who'd labor long and hard – with infinite patience – over something that caught his interest. They were rather counting on him to exercise his occult powers yet again.

"Go on, Linn," Oliver was urging. "Make it three in a row! Close down Otesgo Lake as well! Employ the Mystic Malison of Linnaeus, the Fearsome Force of Finch! Thou shalt be richly rewarded!"

Linnaeus was a little uneasy about teasing – to him it still meant mockery – but he was starting to smile more.

They were very close to Otsego Lake Academy now. They could see the pillars of its frontage, and the flight of steps leading upward. The final stretch of the pre-cut tunnel ran through the snow straight ahead of them, and there was no other direction in which they might walk.

No escape.

There might still be time to make a dash for it, to sprint desperately across the ice . . .

Then . . .

"Excelsior!" Oliver chanted again, ever encouraging. He was reminding them. Their direction was going to be ever upward with an exclamation point. They could speak Latin. Otsego Lake Academy held no fears for them of shadowy Beards speaking a language they could not understand.

"*Amo!*"

Oliver again, this time starting an incantation of the one Latin verb they knew how to conjugate, a proud declaration of defiance. They were like Christian martyrs going to their deaths singing hymns. With his strongly developed sense of irony, he would be well aware of the incongruity of their approaching the abode of The Beards chanting words that expressed all the varying ways they knew of declaring love.

"*Amas!*"

"*Amat!*"

"*Amamus!*"

"*Amatis!*"

"*Amant!*"

And that was it, as far as they and Latin verbs were concerned. The first verb you always learned in Latin was the verb "to love." That had been Dr. Crowninshield's impression. It did not altogether square with what they knew about Otsego Lake Academy, or – in Ben's case – what he knew about Mr. Rappaport, the man who was waiting to lead them deeper into the mysteries of the dead language, further into the more complex tenses of loving.

"*Et cetera!*" This was Oliver's next chant. They may have run out of verbs, but they knew *lots* of other Latin words. Dr. Crowninshield had made them realize this, had demonstrated to them that they – without ever knowing it – had virtually been bilingual, fully capable of interesting conversations with a passing centurion.

"*Dramatis personae!*"

"*E pluribus unum!*"

(The Three Musketeers ring of this last phrase – with its echoes of "All for one, one for all!" – was particularly comforting. If they'd have had swords, or if their rulers had not been securely fastened within their satchels, they'd have flourished their weaponry with theatrical *élan* to boost their sense of invincibility. Olly, Pink, and Linn were perfectly capable of holding their own with Athos, Porthos, and Aramis. That's what Oliver was reminding them. In lieu of Richelieu they had a Latin teacher as a villain, and well might that man tremble!)

They could speak *Latin*!

"*Exeunt omnes!*"

"*Tempus fugit!*"

"*Requiescat in pace!*"

Oliver thought for a moment after he'd chanted this last bit of Latin. "Not the best choice of expression in the circumstances," he admitted, nodding at what lay before them, toward which they were drawing closer every moment. Not much chance of resting in peace there. "*Mea culpa!*"

They chanted the words like a defiant challenge, all the Latin words they knew, three miniature Faustuses calling up – or dispersing – their swarming demons. They were not afraid of Otsego Lake Academy! (Yet another encouraging exclamation point.)

2

They had discovered their unsuspected skills in Latin just before they'd started to act *Julius Cæsar* in the schoolroom at Crowninshield's. They'd done their research. With Dr. Crowninshield they'd marched about Longfellow Park to look at all the new buildings erected in the classical style, the tall white columns and flights of steps of the banks and offices, to put them in the right sort of mood for killing Julius Cæsar. They were all dressed in their togas, supplied by Mrs. Crowninshield, sheets with neatly ironed square-edged creases clearly visible upon them, as if they were clad in all-ready-for-church clean handkerchiefs. Oliver, always a boy conscious of his clothes, had arranged his sheet so that it swept magnificently from his shoulders, and walked like a king at his coronation, rather enjoying the swathe of material billowing out behind him. *Swisssh-swisssh-swisssh.* No one had given them a second glance. A neighborhood that contained the Comstocks, the Goodchilds, the Websters, and Mabel Peartree, was inured to strange and frightening sights. They'd stood in The Forum in the park, surrounded by Carlo Fiorelli's statues – also toga-clad – of Reynolds Templeton Seabright, John Randel, Jr., and all the other laurel-wreathed worthies, striking heroic poses with their lethally angled rulers. They were going to return and play out some of the scenes from their play there, once they'd read it through and rehearsed it a little. Brinkman, sensing an opportunity, had gone straight to the recently erected statue of Oliver's papa, hideous in its too-short tunic, and bulgy-bulgy buttocks. You'd have thought that Dr. Crowninshield would have shielded his sensitive young charges from such potentially trauma-inducing sights. Even Dr. Vaniah Odom's – "I see hell! I see hell!" – sermons had not possessed the nightmarish sleep-no-more potential of *The Curse of Constipation*. The statue's half-squatting pose, and the expression of strained anguish on its face, made the sobriquet irresistible.

"He's got a backside like a rhinoceros!" That had been Brinkman's insightful artistic assessment. There was still a distinct whiff of the yogurt that had been applied to the statue to hurry along the tasteful patina of aging.

"It's even worse in real life." This was Oliver's reaction, not the sort of reaction for which Brinkman had been hoping. "Twice as big, and even smellier." Oliver was not a dutiful son, and all Brinkman's blunt barbs pinged off the target without impinging upon it. Horrified gasps from some of the more dutifully filial offspring around Oliver. Just what he liked to hear.

They'd ventured as far as Hudson Heights – Dr. Crowninshield's research was impressively far-ranging – to peer at the coldly gleaming Roman splendor of Pettifar's Orphanage, The House of the Magdalenes, and the North River Lunatic Asylum. ("Be careful, Alloway!" Brinkman had warned. "Don't get too close to the loonies! They might not let you out again!" He had a much more gratifying reaction than he had achieved with Oliver. Frankie Alloway, who had a cousin who was in the Webster Nervine Asylum up in Poughkeepsie, had started crying. Much encouraged by this success, Brinkman had continued chanting, "Be careful, Alloway! Be *really* careful!" for most of the rest of the day.) Heaven knows what any of the sad inmates of those establishments would have made of them if they'd looked out and seen the white-clad figures, gathered together like a group of squabbling ghosts. The Crowninshield's boys didn't tend to walk hand-in-hand in twos, all in a neat line, when they ventured out on their expeditions. They tended to *swarm*. You imagined them yelling, "This Cæsar was a tyrant!" or, "O noble Cæsar!" You could never rely on rabbles for consistency. The same voices, their speakers not clad in togas this time, would be demanding – with equally riotous insistence – "Barabbas! Barabbas!" Whenever he heard the passages in the gospels in which the multitude demanded the release of Barabbas, and the crucifixion of Christ, Ben always wondered why Jesus bothered spending his life in trying to save such people. He worried that he had such thoughts.

On Friday afternoon, they'd returned to the schoolroom, hair wind-disheveled and the lower hems of their togas mud-splashed, after a brief expedition to see the new library on Cross Hudson Row. Ancient Romans would have strolled up the steps in confident expectation of discovering a public baths, causing a sensation as, chatting informally, they brazenly wandered – completely naked (they'd cast their togas and tunics from them with the emphatic air of lifesavers about to plunge into a stormy sea) – into the non-fiction department without examining their surroundings in sufficient detail first. They'd step down from their plinths in The Forum, and John Randel, Jr., with his pointing finger, would indicate the direction in which they were to walk. They'd amble along behind him, blithely unconscious of the consternation in their wake as they sauntered through the Dewey Decimal System, pausing awhile – in nude and contemplative mood (a massed gathering of *Thinkers*) – at 937.06, 355.00937, or 394.30937, as they attempted to determine what on earth was written in this incomprehensible language, with no sign of a reassuringly familiar *amo*, *amas*, or *amat*.

There was equal incomprehension from the trainee Ancient Romans (fully clothed, but just as baffled) when they opened their copies of *Julius Cæsar*, and looked – with growing puzzlement – at the curious language in the opening speeches of Flavius (his name chummily abbreviated to *Flav*) and Marullus (*Mar*). Flav and Mar spoke in *poetry*, and said things like "Hence!" and "Know you not?" and "What dost thou?" and "Why dost thou?" and "What mean'st thou?" They seemed to ask an awful lot of questions. There was a rare silence as twenty-four nine- and ten-year-olds digested this information, and tried to work out what on earth it mean'st. This was not the manner in which people tended to speak in Longfellow Park, even at one of Mrs. Albert Comstock's "At Homes." Had the Ancient Romans all been Quakers? Those "thous" made them wonder.

They'd been starting to decide who would play what part.

Eyes had eventually strayed to the right-hand page, the first page of text opposite the list of characters.

It was Frankie Alloway's hand that had gone up first. Frankie was always amongst the first in the fearless quest for knowledge, mainly because he knew hardly anything.

"Is this the way that the Ancient Romans used to speak?" he asked, sounding a little daunted, the drapes of his toga drooping. "In this funny English?"

"The Ancient Romans wouldn't have spoken English *at all*," Dr. Crowninshield informed them.

Gasps from the more unsophisticated of their classmates. You could see them visualizing crowds of steerage class toga-clad figures thronging out of steamboats somewhere along the East River, holding up pieces of paper scrawled with the words *Mulberry Street* or *Mott Street*. They couldn't speak English *at all*, and most of them would be carrying daggers. Daggers and alcohol. (Some of them had heard Mrs. Albert Comstock holding forth at her most recent "At Home." Ancient Roman immigrants would not have felt at all at home at one of *her* "At Homes.")

"They'd have spoken *Latin*."

Further consternation.

(What was Latin?)

Frankie Alloway's hand went up again. This boy's thirst to improve himself was inspiring.

"And would they have understood each other?" he inquired, a little anxiously.

"Virtually every word," Dr. Crowninshield reassured him. "Though they had to concentrate."

"Did Shakespeare have to *translate* the Latin into this funny English?"

(Swartwout. His sister was rumored to be learning *French*. You couldn't help hoping that Mrs. Albert Comstock was not aware of this. She had her suspicions about Edeetha Swartwout.)

"Why didn't he translate it into *proper* English?"

(Petteys.)

A monumental task lay ahead of Dr. Crowninshield, a large, marble, ivy-clad, age-decayed Roman monumental task.

"Shakespeare didn't use Latin," he admitted. "He didn't *know* Latin. He couldn't *speak* Latin."

"Can *you* speak Latin?"

(Brinkman, always keen to find a weakness, and reduce Dr. Crowninshield to the low level of Shakespeare.)

Dr. Crowninshield was equal to the challenge.

"Not a word!" he cheerfully admitted. (So, not one of the Ls in the letters after his name was an abbreviation for "Latin." They'd often tried to find meaning in that clotted assemblage of – mostly – consonants. "Is it an anagram?" Oliver had asked once, seeking clues, all fired up after some word-game with Alice.)

"Not a word!" Dr. Crowninshield repeated.

"'Small Latin, and less Greek,'" Oliver said in his quotation voice. No one knew what he meant, but you could tell that it was something cheeky.

"Hmm," Dr. Crowninshield commented, recognizing this. He thought for a moment, and then added, lowering his voice, "Don't tell your parents that, boys. Don't betray my shameful ignorance!"

"Oh no, Dr. C.!"

Horrified. As if they would! (They employed "Dr. C." or "sir" when they wished to suggest particular politeness, for statements of special importance.)

Loyal solidarity. No one did betray Dr. Crowninshield, except – and what a surprise that was! – for Brinkman, who was bitterly disappointed by his parents' response to this rapidly imparted tidbit of scandal. They expressed *delight* that Dr. Crowninshield shunned Latin, and his reputation soared even higher in their estimation. They marched meaty-shoulder-to-meaty-shoulder with Mrs.

Albert Comstock when it came to Latin. Latin smacked too much of the incense-smelling breath of the Anti-Christ of Rome for their liking. Here was an Ancient Roman they'd have paid ready money to see assassinated. Why bother with Julius Cæsar when Leo XIII was around? (At least he hadn't had the nerve to call himself Innocent or Pius. *Innocent!* Ha! *Pious!* Twice ha! They couldn't even *spell* "pious"!)

Dr. Crowninshield thought for a moment after he'd just told them that he couldn't speak a word of Latin. You could tell that a Good Idea For A Lesson was forming in his mind. *Julius Cæsar* — with its troublesome funny English, its "What dost?" and "Why dost?" perplexities — was going to have to wait for next week before they began to uncover its mysteries. It was Friday afternoon, the last lesson of the week — they'd finished *The Adventures of Tom Sawyer* the previous week — and they were about to be sent home with something special to think about over the weekend.

"I have a confession to make," he admitted.

Ooh, good!

"I've just told you all a lie!"

Exaggerated gasps of horror.

"A teacher, *lying* to us?"

(This from Oliver, a sob in his voice.)

"I freely admit it, boys!"

"How soon are the fragile illusions of childhood shattered!"

"Very poetic, Olly. Good! Yes, I admit it." He spoke as if he'd just broken down after hours of torture. "I lied. I *can* speak Latin!" He looked at the toga-clad Ancient Romans at their desks in front of him. "And *all of you* can speak Latin!"

"*Can* we?" they chorused.

(Surprised pleasure at their own unsuspected intelligence. They could speak *Latin*! Whatever that was.)

"Yes, *all* of you!"

"Even me?"

"Yes, even you, Frankie."

Anxious expression on Frankie's face, and the unmistakable

signs of another question pushing itself forward – "Will it *hurt*?" Something like that – but before he could speak again, others had got in first, eager for enlightenment.

"Tell us some, sir. Speak some Latin."

They braced themselves, a preparation for the later explosions in Dr. Brown's Chemistry lessons. They'd had years of practice with this sort of thing, thanks to Mabel Peartree's singing. You couldn't be too careful. This Latin might be risky.

"Well . . ."

Even more held-breath, desk-grasping bracings.

"Think of *time*," he said. "That's a good start. Think of the *date*." Being *Ancient* Romans – on the very verge of decrepitude after so many years of living – they'd presumably know all about *time* and *dates*. "What time is it, Frankie?" All Saints' clock had struck two only a minute or so earlier, but Dr. Crowninshield was clearly in need of scientific precision.

Frankie Alloway took out his pocket-watch with a proud flourish. It had recently been a gift from his parents for his tenth birthday, and he was gratified at being offered an opportunity to display it to the whole class yet again.

"The time is two o'clock and . . ." – he paused, presumably until the second hand had moved exactly over the twelve, like someone starting a race – ". . . three minutes. Exactly three minutes past two." He sounded as triumphant as if he'd just learned how to tell the time. Always a possibility.

"In the morning or in the afternoon?"

"In the *afternoon*!"

(That was a teasing sort of question.)

"And how can you tell?"

"Because it's light and not dark."

(Once Frankie became enthusiastic, it would take a good deal of slapping-down to quieten him again, and Dr. Crowninshield was not one given to slapping. A winter's afternoon. It was light, sort of, though you could sense that darkness would not be long delayed. It already *seemed* to be on the verge of growing darkness.)

"Because it'll soon be time to go home!"

"Because we're not in bed!"

There was no shortage of suggestions as to why they were fully aware that it was three minutes past two in the *afternoon*.

"True. All perfectly true. But what if I wrote it down?"

He wrote 2.03 on the blackboard, aware that writing something down somehow seemed to help them remember it better.

"Is that light or dark?" he asked. (White chalk on a blackboard. A possible trick question here. Light or dark?) "How would you let someone know that you meant 2.03 in the afternoon?"

"*P.m.*"

(Oliver.)

"Exactly. Thank you, Olly. You wouldn't write *in the afternoon*, or *because it's light*, you'd write *p.m.* – much quicker and much simpler – and *p.m.* is *Latin*."

He wrote *p.m.* after 2.03.

They leaned a little further forward in their desks, slightly suspicious. They were looking at Latin. It remained firmly written on the blackboard, and seemed quite safe.

"It's an abbreviation. What do the letters *mean*?"

(They'd never thought of this.)

"*Post meridiem!*" Dr. Crowninshield announced triumphantly, getting it in quick to beat Oliver, who was starting to inhale. You never felt that Oliver was trying to show off, despite Brinkman's groans and gruntings. He always seemed keen to share what he knew with everyone, thinking that they'd be as interested as he was in learning new things.

Dr. Crowninshield began to write the words on the blackboard. He wrote as far as *post meridi* quite confidently beneath *p.m.*, paused infinitesimally, added *am* – looked discreetly across at Oliver (sometimes a single lifted eyebrow was enough of a signal) – and altered the *a* to an *e* as if an *e* had been what he had meant to write all along. Hardly anyone noticed. His spelling could be as fallible as his arithmetic.

"Now what do you think '*meridiem*' means? It's the same as . . ."

"... meridian?"

(Akenside.)

"Good, Tom. And 'meridian' means?"

"Noon."

Tom Akenside had become very fond of sailing. You could see him out on the Hudson most weekends. They'd watched him — Ben, Oliver, and Linnaeus — through the telescope on the Finches' piazza. It seemed to have given him a whole new vocabulary that few others could comprehend, *and* an impressive range of newly learned knots. Not the nautical mile sort of knots, the 1.15 miles per hour sort of knots — though he knew these also — but the reef, the sheet bend, the bowline sort of knots, and his fingers twitched to tie them. You didn't stand too close to Akenside if you were wearing a necktie, or you'd end up purple in the face, and gasping for breath. His handkerchief was so packed with experimental knotting that he could hardly use it half the time, so bulging and bursting was it, like a strong man rippling his torso to demonstrate his impressively defined groups of muscles, and his dripping nose remained unwiped. Sailing also seemed to have given him — it could be really cold out on the Hudson — an impressive variety of coughs and sniffles. This was another reason for not getting too close to Akenside. Perhaps "meridian" was a part of this newly acquired knowledge, the lone sailor plotting his course through unknown waters with the skilled use of a sextant, the positions of the celestial bodies, the horizon, and the hour of noon. Sailing seemed to involve advanced arithmetic, not much of a commendation, this, especially in winter. Snow, ice, frostbite, and arithmetic. All good training, they were soon to discover, for Mr. Stolley's Arithmetic lessons at Otsego Lake Academy, when Akenside — to the wonderment of all — would become the class prodigy, even when furthest away from the radiator in Mr. Stolley's bitterly cold room at a corner of the building round which winds whistled.

The knots also came in handy for Mr. Rappaport's lessons when, looking murderous (he was not alone in harboring — an appropriate choice of verb for a sailor like Akenside — such feelings for Mr.

Rappaport, you felt like cheering him on), he'd gaze at his Latin teacher with a look of utter loathing, and twist his handkerchief as vigorously as someone wringing out a dishcloth, as he enthusiastically practiced all the knots most suitable to use for strangulation. A figure-of-eight might do it, a sheepshank. *Any* knot would do it when he was in the mood, as long as he had sufficient rope. Give him enough rope, and he'd string up his teacher in no time. There'd be no hitches once *he* got going with a clove hitch or a half hitch. You'd forgive him any number of ruined neckties if ruining them had helped him perfect his technique for murdering Mr. Rappaport. You'd happily spend entire afternoons in Twelvetrees & Twelvetrees with Akenside, enthusiastically encouraging him as he worked his way through their entire stock of neckties, knotting with increasing ferocity. Ben always paused at this point, to savor the mental picture of Mr. Rappaport being strangled. Sometimes he had a viciously knotted necktie cutting so far into his neck that he was virtually decapitated, clearly all dressed up for a *very* formal occasion (you could rely on Akenside to do a job properly). Sometimes – it was more pleasurable to inflict a variety of agonies – the knots and the necktie were employed to suspend Mr. Rappaport upside-down by his left ankle, creakily swaying to and fro like the figure of The Hanged Man (*Le Pendu*) on Mrs. Alexander Diddecott's tarot card, looking like a mutineer who'd just been keelhauled – these nautical expressions could be *really* useful – seawater dripping out of his mouth and down from his flowing hair.

"Even better! So, if *meridiem* means 'noon,' what do you think *post* means?"

"After!"

(Charlie Whitefoord.)

"Yes!"

"Like *post mortem*?"

"*Exactly* like *post mortem*, Charlie, because *post mortem* means . . .?"

"After death?"

"Of course it does!"

"And *P.S.* in a letter." (Charlie was now dispensing with a question mark in his voice. He *knew*.)

P.S. went on the blackboard.

"Better and better! You're a fluent Latin speaker, Charlie!"

"*Post script.*"

"*Post scriptum.*"

(Oliver.)

"*Most* impressive!"

Post scriptum went down.

The blackboard soon filled up once Dr. Crowninshield got them going. He went through a box of chalk in no time.

"After writing." (Another question mark dispensed with. Linnaeus! Linnaeus didn't often venture to give an opinion or answer in class, and when he did he almost always armored himself with an upward inflexion to his voice. What *had* they been like to him in New Hampshire?)

"Splendid, Linn! Latin! Latin! *Latin!*"

They were rapidly discovering that they'd been speaking fluent Latin for *years*, and had never realized. The togas gave them strange power, the ironed-in square-cornered geometrical shapes vibrating with mystic energy. Like white-clad Druids, they were the rather young elders of a Celtic priesthood, versed in strange matters.

"And *a.m.*!"

Frankie Alloway must have been eating meat, meat in large helpings, with blood-red gravy dribbling down his chin. He was off and away, in baying pursuit of a gold star, the longed-for prize that awaited the schoolboy who had tried the hardest in school that week. Frankie Alloway wouldn't sleep a week for excitement if he was awarded a gold star. Ben – as a very small boy – had thought his sister Alice the cleverest girl in the world when he had seen the large gold stars balanced on their points on the window-ledge in her room, the stars that had fallen from the ceiling in All Saints'.

"And *a.m.*, Frankie. And if *p.m.* means *post meridiem*, then *a.m.* means . . .?"

"Something else *meridiem*!"

(Frankie Alloway at the very limit of his powers, but confidently dispensing with a question mark. He was following yonder gold star. Field and fountain, moor and mountain: nothing would impede his ceaseless quest.)

"*Ante meridiem.* It must mean 'before noon.'" (Linnaeus *again.*)

"I was thinking of *ante bellum*, 'before the war.'"

"*Exactly* right, Linn. More Latin! Whatever you had for lunch today, have it again!" (They went home for lunch at Crowninshield's. Meals were not supplied.)

Dr. Crowninshield turned back to the rapidly filling blackboard, and indicated that day's date written in the top right-hand corner. The day's date was already written on the blackboard when they arrived each day, to jog the memory of the more forgetful, so that they would know what day it was. It didn't always work. On this day — to put them in the mood for *Julius Cæsar* — the year had been written in Roman numerals, with signs of much correcting and rubbing-out before the final version. The final *versions*.

Febury 11th, MCCMLXXXVII.

This was one version.

Hedging his bets, he'd written in a second version of the date below the first.

Febury 11th, MDCCCLXXXVII.

He clearly hadn't been able to decide between the two. The rendition of the year varied, but the misspelled month remained the same.

Febury was Dr. Crowninshield's spelling of February. He kept on getting it wrong. It made it hard to be confident about the unlikely looking dates. Was either version of this Roman date correct?

Pronouncing them didn't bear thinking about, and none of them had tried. It was worse than Polish! Imagine what Arithmetic lessons must have been like for Roman schoolboys, with all that writing, all those hard words! That was what they'd all been thinking, anxious on behalf of rows of rather squashed-looking little

Tituses, Decimuses, Marcuses, and Caiuses rubbing away – rather dejectedly – at the mistakes on their slates with the corners of their togas. It would take *ages* to rub out a Roman sum. Would Roman schoolboys have had slates, like Tom Sawyer and Becky Thatcher? Slates with dates. Once they'd written the date, there'd be no space to write anything else.

"I said that we should think about *time*, and I said that we should think about the *date*," Dr. Crowninshield reminded them. "We've talked about time. Now let's look at the date, boys."

The Romans seemed obsessed with time and dates, as if they were confident that everything that they did was something that would be remembered.

"The two letters *a.m.* and the two letters *p.m.* tell us the time before and after noon. Now what two letters might you find in a history book before today's date, to tell us something about the year?"

"*A.D.!*"

(Bradstone, instantly.)

"*Anno Domini!*"

(Ben, harvesting the fruits of Sunday school.)

"In the Year of Our Lord. It is now one thousand, eight hundred, and eighty-seven years since the birth of Our Lord."

(Bradley.

(*Anno . . .*

(*Year . . .*

(*Annual . . .*

(*Annuity . . .*

(*Anniversary . . .*

(It was one of those occasions when you could feel your brain beginning to pulsate.

(Bradley was a rather pious boy, often teased by Brinkman for this reason. Year of Our Lord. The capital letters were reverentially enunciated, or – the word he would probably prefer – annunciated. The latter spelling would surely find greater favor with Bradley. He was Miss Augusteena's very own saint-in-training

185

and would do anything for a colored picture of a Bible scene. He loved demonstrating his Christian forgiveness, and – you couldn't help thinking – probably made himself deliberately infuriating to Brinkman in order to create ample opportunities for displaying meekness. He was as keen to inherit the earth as Alexander the Great or Genghis Khan – blessed was Bradley – and always turned the other cheek, with a seductive, come-and-get-it! simper, whenever Brinkman thumped him one. Brinkman – invariably – came-and-got-it!, thumping him even harder. There was little doubt that Bradley's ambition was for a death-scene of peerless piety, in which sobbing crowds gathered around his halo-illuminated bed, as he nobly forgave Brinkman for his murderous blow. "I forgive thee, Brinkman!" he'd utter with his dying breath, smiling serenely as Brinkman – his face contorted with fury – thumped him yet again with a satisfying squelch. He would – as angelic hosts chorused – join the ranks of the Children Who Had Found The Lord And Been Saved And Promptly Died In Consequence. Bradley had a whole shelf of Sunday-school prizes at home, and could give you the chapter and verse of any quotation from the Bible that you cared to throw at him. His parents were rather concerned, and were attempting to cultivate an interest in chicken-breeding in their son.)

"Yes! Yes! Yes! Thrice yes!" Dr. Crowninshield enthused, driven into biblical cadences by the nearness of Bible-Bashing Bradley. (This was one of Brinkman's more repeatable epithets.) "And what do the history books print after a date if it refers to a date *before . . .*" – here was a helpful hint – ". . . the birth of Our Lord?"

"*B.C.!*"

"*Before Christ!*"

(Distinct disappointment that 'B.C.' was not a reference to something in Latin, *another* Latin expression that they'd known without realizing.)

Dr. Crowninshield looked out at the Ancient Romans in their desks in front of him. He'd only just managed to stop them speaking in old men's tremulous voices when they answered him.

Crowninshield's had formed the distinct impression that Ancient Romans had invariably been old, old men (not a woman or child amongst them), well laden by the weight of years, centenarian centurions. Eager for authenticity, they'd automatically bowed over as they assumed their togas, converting themselves into doddery parodies of the immensely aged. These Ancient Romans would have been incapable of lifting their daggers, even two-handed, and they'd have fallen out of their chariots at the first jolt, with high-pitched caged-bird cries. They'd looked about XCIX years old, shrunken back into shrill-voiced small boyhood, a Roman rabble of Mr. Scriveners, the ancient monument of a headmaster at Otsego Lake Academy.

"I think," Dr. Crowninshield had said, tactfully, "that there has been something of a misapprehension here."

Another idea now had him in its power.

He leaned behind him, and lifted up a hefty volume from his desk. He barely managed it single-handed, and it nearly leaped out of his hand to crush Bradley. Not so much Bible-Bashing, as Bible-Bashed, or as near enough to a Bible as made no difference as far as some people were concerned.

"And it's not just time and dates!" Dr. Crowninshield told them. "Get ready to open your encyclopædias! They're *full* of Latin. Whenever you look something up, you find Latin. You all *know* Latin! Five minutes! Let's see how much Latin we can find in five minutes, boys."

Their encyclopædias – *Griswold's Discovery Medicated Soap Encyclopædia For 1875. Over 1,000 Pages! Discover With Griswold's Discovery!* – were the source of all knowledge at Crowninshield's. Even the front cover was educational. *The soap for man and beast!* it trumpeted, rather excited, eager to share what it knew. *Cures Cuts! Cures Burns! Cures Bruises! Cures Eczema! Cures Unseemly Imperfections Of The Skin! Cures Chronic Skin Diseases! Cures Chilblain! Cures Itch! Cures Freckles! Cures Liver Spots! Cures Eruptions!* Even Mount Vesuvius, you felt, was an eruption that would have held no fears for Griswold's Discovery Medicated

Soap, and ash and lava would have bounced harmlessly off well-washed Pompeians. Brinkman, a boy who (an inspiring example to others) rarely wasted a moment, could regularly be seen rubbing Frank Stoddard's spotty face with the cover of someone's encyclopædia (never his own). "Cures Unseemly Imperfections Of The Skin!" he'd crow. "Cures Chronic Skin Diseases!" Brinkman was clearly a boy with a highly developed imagination, capable of deriving hours of pleasure from the simplest of materials. Opposite the title page of the encyclopædia was an engraving of Ulysses S. Grant, a man who'd ceased to be president the year before most of them had been born, beneath the puzzling patriotic declaration *Our President.*

"Five minutes . . ."

Dr. Crowninshield paused dramatically.

They all waited, their hands on the edges of the front covers of their encyclopædias, runners with their toes just touching the chalky white line at the beginning of a race. It was a moment in which Frankie's pocket-watch might usefully have been employed again. The schoolroom clock possessed no second hand.

Tick-tock.

Click.

They waited . . .

On your marks . . .

. . . watching as the black, arrow-shaped minute hand vibrated and seemed to gather its power (it always seemed to jerk forward a whole minute at a time, making them jump in circumstances such as now) . . .

". . . from . . ."

Get set . . .

. . . before clicking decisively down to eight minutes past two . . .

Click!

". . . now!"

Go!

Dr. Crowninshield was perfectly correct.

Griswold's Discovery Medicated Soap Encyclopædia For 1875 was *full* of Latin. Ancient Romans seemed to write exclusively in abbreviations and italics, emphasizing everything all the time. It must have been exhausting conducting a conversation. Another – and much longer – list began to spread across the blackboard as they searched for more Latin, and each time Latin was identified they'd work out its translation. Dr. Crowninshield covertly consulted an inside page of another book to check these translations. Even *Griswold's Discovery Medicated Soap Encyclopædia For 1875* must have had a Teacher's Book, those mysterious sources of all answers.

The inescapable fact was soon fixed firmly in their minds.

They'd been reading and speaking and writing Latin for *years*, and they'd never realized.

e.g. = *exempli gratia* = *for instance*
i.e. = *id est* = *that is*
cf. = *confer* = *compare*
etc. = *et cetera* = *and so on*
c. = *circa* = *about*
viz. = *videlicet* = *namely*
et al. – *et alia* = *and others*
ibid. = *ibidem* = *in the same place*
N.B. = *nota bene* = *note well*
q.v. = *quod vide* . . .

The equal signs and the letters gave the list the look of something like advanced Arithmetic, faltering first footsteps on the lower slopes of algebra. They should be lightheaded and prone to breathlessness in such rarified air, but they felt absolutely fine, fully capable of climbing far higher.

Excelsior!

Ben, who'd confused *Excelsior!* with Excalibur, always tended to hear the sound of a mighty sword ringing thrillingly as it was whisked out of its scabbard and flourished challengingly aloft. Newly conquered peaks would be fluttering with so many flags that it would look like washday.

Excelsior!

Excelsior!

Click.

Twelve minutes past two.

They started to flag, wrists aching from wading through *Griswold's*; learning could be hard work, even if muscle-building.

Thirteen minutes past two.

Click.

"Time over, boys!" Dr. Crowninshield announced.

He scrawled *Q.E.D.* at the bottom of the well-filled blackboard (more white than black with all its chalked writing) with the proud flourish of a painter writing his signature beneath his masterpiece.

" *Quod erat demonstrandum!*"

"'Which was to be demonstrated.'"

(Akenside.)

"Splendid, Tom! And what was to be demonstrated?"

"That we all know Latin!"

Dr. Crowninshield circled *Q.E.D.*

" *Q.E.D.! Q.E.D.!*" he read. " *Latin!*"

(" *Q.E.D.! Q.E.D.!*" some of the boys repeated, in recited-arithmetical-tables voices, like armor-clanking legionnaires marching beneath the proudly displayed *S.P.Q.R.* on their battle standard. They *all* knew Latin.)

"We could have gone on for *ages* longer . . ."

(Groan from Brinkman.)

"Thank you, Sid, for your scholarly erudition."

"We could have gone on *ad infinitum*, sir."

(Linnaeus!)

Dr. Crowninshield was greatly impressed by this.

He scrawled *ad infinitum* on part of the small remaining space on the blackboard, adding = *to infinity*.

" *Latin!* Very encouraging, Linn."

"Or even *ad nauseam*, sir."

Ad nauseam = *to the point of causing nausea* went on the blackboard.

"Not *quite* so encouraging a choice of expression, Olly."

"But *Latin*."

"Indisputably Latin."

"*Nil desperandum*, Dr. C."

"I often do."

Conversations in Latin! Conversations in Latin that they were – more or less – understanding! The togas had the power of magic robes, conveying not invisibility, but the mystical ability to follow unknown tongues.

"Latin is all around us, boys!"

They were starting to form the distinct impression that there was more Latin than there was *English* in the room.

He walked to the back of the schoolroom, and looked ahead of him.

"I can see some Latin words *now*," he said. "They're in front of you every day of your school life."

The class scanned all the words they could see on the wall around the blackboard.

Is it *February*?" Frankie Alloway asked, keen for further commendation, as if he saw an eternity of Februarys before him, in which that would always be the word in front of him. He was not looking at *Febury 11th, MCCMLXXXVII* and *Febury 11th, MDCC-CLXXXVII* in the top right-hand corner of the blackboard, but at the *FEBRUARY* on the open page of the calendar – *National Costumes of Europe* – pinned to the wall beside the photograph of Abraham Lincoln. Abraham Lincoln regarded Ben steadily throughout his childhood. A man after whom his father was named was sure to keep an observant eye upon him.

("*Both* eyes."

(*Laughter*.

(He heard Mr. Rappaport's words to Papa in Papa's study. He heard the conspiratorial laughter as both men stood and looked speculatively at him, not impressed by what it was they saw.

(He was tugging at the bottom of his jacket, trying to stand up straight.)

191

On the calendar picture for February, a sultry Spanish *señorita* balanced a *mantilla* as big as the Alhambra on her head, her hands so crammed with a fan, castanets, and a tambourine that it looked as if she was about to start juggling.

"No, not February, Frankie. July would have been closer, though. Very appropriate for *Julius Cæsar*. What a pity it's not the summer."

"But we're much closer to the Ides of March now, aren't we?"

"How true. What a comfort you are, Olly."

"Is it *bard*?"

(Franny Darville, making a rare contribution, picking out a word he'd never heard of before on the off chance that it might be Latin.)

William Shakspeare, the Bard of Avon had been the main heading on the blackboard, in Dr. Crowninshield's rounded schoolboy hand (perhaps Ben's unalterably childlike handwriting was his young teacher's legacy to him), until Latin had taken over. He had missed Oliver's signaling eyebrow when he wrote *Shakspeare*.

"No, it's not something written on the blackboard."

"*Constitution?*"

"Warmer."

"*President Cleveland?*"

(Brinkman, being sardonic.)

"Warmer."

(A surprising answer. Even Brinkman looked surprised.)

"*Sahara?*"

(William French, looking at the map of the world – partially hidden behind the recently pinned-up map of Italy – pinned on the other side of the blackboard from President Cleveland.)

"Colder."

(The Sahara colder. This sounded like unlikely geography.)

"The Reverend Goodchild."

(Henderson, who'd just noticed the Reverend Goodchild walking past outside.)

"Certainly not, Harry. Never link the Reverend Goodchild with

Latin. And stop looking out of the window. Colder than ever. Positively icy. So cold that your mouth freezes as you speak."

Ben's row, the ones sitting closest to the windows facing out over the street, all – despite Dr Crowninshield's prohibition – looked across to their right, as the Reverend Goodchild (*colder than ever, positively icy, so cold that your mouth freezes*: the words were an appropriate accompaniment) strode majestically down the sidewalk of Indian Woods Road. He paused in his progress to All Saints', and stood beneath the windows of the school, his beard flapping frolicsomely in the wind, unaware that he was being observed from above. He didn't even notice the windows.

His mind was on higher things.

Much higher things.

Things *well* above the windows.

That was the impression he sought to convey.

"Now, where you're going wrong, God . . ."

This was probably the sort of thing he had in his mind, tactfully, but firmly, pointing God in the right direction.

He backed up against the railings, looked up and down the street, to left and right to check that there were no witnesses, and then – it was a regular ritual – he lifted up his coat-tails and began to give his bottom a vigorous scratch, stretching like a satiated cat. They'd have probably heard a low ecstatic moan if the windows had been open. It was a part of his preparations, some purification ceremony, before he walked up the street and into the church. Sometimes, if Dr. Crowninshield was absorbed in what he was writing on the blackboard, his back turned to them, the whole class would stand up on tiptoe and lean over to its right to get a good view. *Twenty minutes past two. Rev. Goodchild scratches bottom.* That was the entry in their mental diaries, though the impression gained was more of a comprehensive excavation than a superficial scraping. He wasn't scratching the surface; he was delving deep. There was the distinct possibility that some of the more advanced gardening implements might be involved.

His sister-in-law had married a Griswold. Surely he had access to vast supplies of Griswold's Discovery Medicated Soap at wholesale prices? A choir of boy sopranos should sing the tidings of great joy from the upper windows, a top right-hand corner scene from one of the larger Renaissance paintings. Angelic voices from the sky. "Cures Chronic Skin Diseases! Cures Chilblain! Cures *Itch*!" They should begin rehearsals, hone their skills all ready for the next time he hoisted up his coat-tails, and dug in. Lutes, they'd be holding, and halos would be their new school uniform.

Dr. Crowninshield had recently read them a story about the action-packed life of a fearless boy pearl-fisher, and it had made a great impression upon them, particularly a scene in which he had battled to save himself – armed only with his oyster-gathering dagger – from a giant clam that had snapped tightly shut across his ankle like a mantrap. The things that happened to Manabharana, the Ceylonese boy, made their own lives appear utterly colorless and uneventful. Before breakfast he thought nothing of plunging down into the depths a few times to emerge with pearls of great price, enough to bedeck most of the princesses of Europe with multi-stranded necklaces (ripping open the oyster shells with his teeth) and then – to pass the time – grappling courageously with a herd of maddened elephants. He was not a boy to be daunted by a giant clam. The long, long seconds had ticked away as he held his breath, and struggled to stay conscious, levering away in an intrepid sort of way with the point of his dagger. They'd held their breaths in instinctive sympathy.

They now found themselves imagining in queasily emphatic detail, despite their instinctive feelings of revulsion – if you swallowed poison your body's self-protection system made you vomit – that the Reverend Goodchild's whole hand had disappeared inside him up to the wrist. It was just as well that he was wearing gloves. They had the distinct sense of that giant clam – deprived of the small dagger-wielding pearl-fisher (it had been such a relief when Manabharana had escaped, shooting up to the surface for a great gulp of air) – locking its shell firmly (*Snap!*) across the wrist of this latest foolhardy intruder from the world above the water. Ankle or wrist, it made no difference to the joint-jammed clam. This victim would not escape like the other one had! "Die, you air-breathing invader!" the menacing mollusk muttered, keeping its shell slammed shut like a sulky toothless mouth. As they had done before, they held their breaths without realizing that they were doing so, and it became very quiet and still in the schoolroom. Frankie had held his breath for so long when Dr. Crowninshield read the story to them – he really *lived* what he heard – that he had turned dizzy and keeled over. Ben saw himself swimming down through the clear, icy February water, a dagger just like Manabharana's dagger clenched between his bared teeth, down toward the bivalved beast that held their vicar in its deadly, clammy embrace, his hair streaming out behind him. The word "clammy" was not very far from your mind, somehow, when your foolhardy thoughts strayed in the direction of the Reverend Goodchild.

Oliver had very firm views about the Reverend Goodchild. He'd probably use the knife to aid the mollusk, making quite certain that the Reverend Goodchild would never rise again from beneath the surface of the water, the water that was colder than ever, positively icy, so cold that your mouth freezes. He'd be shoving the Reverend Goodchild into the giant clam with both hands, like his papa feeding steak into a mincing-machine at Comstock's Comestibles. It would look as if he were feeding a tidbit to a pet goldfish in its bowl. "Who's a good boy, then?" he'd be cooing. "Who deserves a *very* special treat?" You began to feel sorry for the giant clam, crammed with clergyman. All that beard to digest. Those *teeth.*

"*Liberty?*"

(Henderson again, making amends for "The Reverend Goodchild." Concentration returned to what they could see on the wall in front of them. Their spiritual leader was left unobserved to his posterioric probings, rooting around and grunting and gasping and – in all probability – squelching.)

"Hot!"

Minds, even though they might be lower minds than that of the Reverend Goodchild (most minds were), began to calculate.

Constitution and *President Cleveland* were warm.

Liberty was hot.

Constitution, President Cleveland, and *Liberty* were words that were grouped closely together to the right of the blackboard, in Democracy Corner, the collection of words and illustrations displayed beneath the Stars and Stripes. Dr. Crowninshield's "warmer" and "colder" were words guiding them to this area of the wall. This was where Latin lurked.

It was Oliver who spotted it.

"*E pluribus unum,*" he announced, confident that he was correct.

"And *annuit coeptis!*"

(Ben.)

"*Novus ordo seclorum!*"

(Stoddard.)

(A veritable Tower of Babel on Indian Woods Road, a suitably reduced Roman version of the structure.

(The phrases were printed in large wobbly letters – Dr. Crowninshield had written them out – and looked like a display for parents to coo over on a visit to school to see their children's work.)

"*Red hot!* Yes. Well done, Olly, Ben, Frank. *That* is Latin, and you see those words in front of you every day." He paused a moment before he attempted to pronounce them. "*E pluribus unum*: the motto of our country. *Annuit coeptis* and *novus ordo seclorum*: words on the Great Seal of our country." (They weren't quite sure what the Great Seal was, though they heard the capital letters. Somewhere in Frankie Alloway's mind – he'd seen a seal spinning a large colored ball on the tip of its nose at a circus – the Great Seal of the United States began to revolve a spherical Stars and Stripes, the red, the white, and the blue merging, and the letters blurring until they made even *less* sense.)

"*E pluribus unum,*" they muttered doubtfully to each other. "*Annuit coeptis. Novus ordo seclorum.*" It seemed highly unlikely. In Washington, D.C., the men who held the reins of government wandered about in togas and spoke in Latin. No wonder that the buildings of office looked like constructions from Ancient Rome. Ancient Romans would have felt right at home on the banks of the Potomac and the Anacostia; build a few more hills, and they'd have scarcely noticed the lack of the Tiber. Frankie Alloway was originally from Washington, D.C., and they looked at him with new respect. No wonder he'd been galvanized into life at the mention of Latin! Ancestral voices were calling him, and they were not speaking in English.

Dr. Crowninshield pointed, with patriotic fervor, at the words that had been (they were a little vague on this point) spoken by the Great Seal.

"These words should rarely be absent from your lips!"

Dr. Crowninshield had a tendency to become overenthusiastic.

"Here you see even *more* Latin that all of you know. More or less."

"And what does it *mean*?"

(Bradley, hoping for something spiritually uplifting.)

Oh! It *meant* something!

"*You* can work it out, Charles." (Whitefoord might be Charlie, but Bradley insisted on "Charles." "Charles" was somehow more Christian, even if the scribes had unaccountably neglected to mention a Charles in the Bible. The New Testament, rather than the Old Testament, was the place where a Charles might most fittingly have found a place, you felt. A Charles would have been unexotically out-of-place in a crowd of Old Testament Chilions, Chedorlaomers, and Chelubs.) "*E pluribus unum. You* can understand Latin. *Unum.* What do you think *unum* means?"

"One?"

"Excellent, Charles. And *pluribus*?"

"A plurality?"

"*Nearly!*"

Eventually, they worked out that *e pluribus unum* meant "one out of many," and wandered into a philosophical discussion of the significance of the motto. Most lessons with Dr. Crowninshield seemed to ramble about down unexpected byways. These were the

times when Ben felt that he sometimes learned the things that interested him the most. Brinkman – with the nearest they'd ever seen
him approach to an æsthetic shudder – made it quite clear that he
wasn't altogether enthused about the idea of being one made out of
many, cast into the melting-pot promiscuity of what was clearly a
distinctly dubious phrase. He hinted at an appalled glimpse of
Hester Street, heaving masses of recently arrived *foreign* immigrants. Men with funny shawls with fringes. Men with funny beards
and hairstyles. Men with funny names. Men who couldn't speak
English. Men pushing *handcarts!*

"You'd get on like a house on fire with Mama, Sidder-knee,"
Oliver said. This was not an expression of praise. He was clearly
picturing a blaze that roared happily.

Warm.

Warmer.

Hot.

Red hot!

A sound of sizzling as Brinkman and Mama blazed companionably side by side in a crackling conflagration, one that produced
little light, and no warmth.

"You could sit on her knees like Chinky-Winky." Oliver spoke
like one offering a glimpse of an enticing prospect. "There *is* a
distinct resemblance." Brinkman glowered rebelliously at being
compared to a flatulent Pekinese. "She'd feed you on honey-dew,
and you'd drink the milk of Paradise. You'd love it! Beg, Sidder-
knee! Beg! Beg! *Beg!*"

He leaned across the aisle, his hand held high above his head,
dangling his pocket-watch, swinging it enticingly from side to side.

"Ha! Ha! Ha! *Ha!*" Brinkman enunciated with heavily unamused
irony. "*Very* funny, Comstock."

"You even *laugh* like Mama!" Oliver added, delighted, in an I-
rest-my-case tone of voice.

(Brinkman had sounded *exactly* like Mrs. Albert Comstock
clunkily demonstrating her ha-ha-ha-ha-happy gift for infectious
fun.)

"*Q.E.D.*," Charlie Whitefoord added. It was so *satisfying* to be offered the opportunity to demonstrate recently acquired knowledge.

"Why don't we speak Latin in New York?"

(Frankie Alloway, still baffled by the Great Seal.)

"But we do!"

Consternation.

"We all do!"

Sensation.

"As I have indicated."

A sweeping gesture encompassed the chalk-filled blackboard.

"You've *often* heard me speak Latin to you."

"You said you couldn't speak a *word* of Latin!"

(Brinkman, triumphant.)

"Yes, I know. I lied. I've admitted that. It was inadvertent, but I *lied.*"

"*Sob!*"

"Bear up, Olly! Act the Roman! Be a man!"

"That'll be the day!"

(Brinkman.)

Act the Roman!

They were *all* going to act the Roman. They were all going to speak Latin. They already had the togas for it

"*Have* we?"

"What?"

"Have we heard you speak Latin to us?"

"Yes. I don't *always* lie."

"And did we understand you?"

"I used Latin yesterday. I suppose I spoke it more to myself, but you heard me."

He looked at the baffled, not-fully-convinced Ancient Romans — (*Latin?*) — and assumed the stance for shameful confession, head lowered sheepishly, feet shuffling. He spoke in a just-audible mumble.

"Yesterday I made a mistake in one of my sums, boys."

"*Very* hard to believe, sir! Very like a whale!"

"I know, Olly, but – though it strains the bounds of credulity to believe it – I actually *made a mistake* in one of my sums."

Gasps.

"Nine times seven is sixty-three."

They hadn't forgotten, and were reminding him.

"You *always* get that wrong."

"A Moby-Dick of a whale, straining and spouting, heading straight for the ship to sink it."

"I shall ignore such petty recriminations," Dr. Crowninshield announced magisterially. "I made a mistake. That I *freely* confess. Don't take cruel advantage of my good nature, boys. And what do you say when you make a silly mistake, something that's entirely your fault?"

"'Oh, bugger!'?"

(Frankie Alloway, in like a shot, not thinking, keen but confused.)

"No, certainly *not*. I should certainly never say that, Frankie. You will never, *ever* hear me swear . . ."– they never did – ". . . unless, perhaps . . ." – a meaningful look at Frankie – ". . . a pupil drives me to swearing by making the outrageous suggestion that I swear." He thought for a moment. "There's something going wrong with my logic here," he admitted, "but I think you know what I mean." They knew. "No, Frankie, what *I* would say, what I *did* say, was not the unsavory phrase with which you have just polluted the atmosphere of this high-minded establishment, but the appropriately educational words *mea culpa*."

Mere culper?

Baffled expressions.

"*Mea culpa*," Dr. Crowninshield repeated, scribbling it on the blackboard. "Latin! I spoke Latin!" He sounded as proud and pleased as the schoolboys did, to discover that he could do this. "It means 'I am to blame! My fault!' *That's* what I said. I certainly didn't swear. Teachers *never* swear, as I thought you would all have realized. Any teacher who forgot himself and swore would face The Fearful Fate."

"Mr. Caswell swears." This from Brinkman, seizing an opportunity to speak forbidden words. He was distinctly envious of Frankie's "bugger." Mr. Caswell was one of the teachers at Otsego Lake Academy, one of the beings who wore a beard in the way that the Otsego Lake Academy schoolboys wore their many-buttoned uniform, a proud mark of his apartness. He taught Biology, and they sometimes came across him on their nature rambles, competing with them to capture specimens for class discussion. He had once stolen a whole pickle-jar full of frogspawn from Bradley. (Sulky expression, determined *thrust* from Mr. Caswell, as Bradley seized the opportunity to look forgiving. You wouldn't have been surprised if Bradley had squeezed in a couple more handfuls of spawn and flutily intoned, "I forgive thee!" "Thee" was the more authentic expression in such circumstances.) "I was behind him on Hudson Row on Saturday, and I heard him swear quite clearly. He said . . ." (Seeing the expression on Dr. Crowninshield's face, Brinkman had started to speak more and more rapidly, anxious not to miss his chance of saying something mucky.)

More and more rapidly, but not rapidly enough.

"We don't need to know what he said, thank you very much, Sid. I might swoon completely away if I hear it, a man with my moral sensitivity. I'm *shocked* to the very core of my being to hear you say that, however. A teacher *swearing*! It's quite unprecedented. The National Society for the Protection of the Good Name of Pedagogues should be alerted. The Fearful Fate must be instantly prepared for Mr. Caswell."

When Dr. Crowninshield launched himself into one of his tall stories, they strove to drive him into ever-higher flights of fantasy.

"What'll happen to him?"

(Awed whisper.)

"He'll be summoned to the Inner Chamber of the Society in its palatial headquarters on the Fifth Avenue. It's a magnificent room, one that never fails to draw gasps of wonderment from all who penetrate its carefully guarded mysteries. It has the tallest unsupported ceiling in the whole of the Northern Hemisphere, composed entirely out of discarded canes and the upper levels are quite lost from sight in low cloud. Here, in a ceremony that will torment his memory for the rest of his life, he will be *unteachered*, and reduced to the level of a mere mortal man."

"What happens to him?"

"Is it painful?"

(Swartwout, quite hopeful.)

"Are we allowed to go and watch?"

"*No one* can watch The Fearful Fate!" (Horror at the very idea.) "It's a deeply private, deeply humiliating secret ceremony, and not all who undergo it survive."

Gasp!

"They . . ." – Dr. Crowninshield's voice faltered a little – ". . . remove the chalk from between his fingers, and . . ." – he struggled to be able to continue – ". . . *snap it!*"

Gasp!

Dr. Crowninshield gazed at the blunt-ended stub of chalk between his fingers, and – as they watched – it began to tremble more and more.

"They break his cane across their knees!"

Gasp!

"They rip off his gown, and cast it to the floorboards!"

Gasp!

"They . . ." – courageous struggle for self-control – ". . . They even tear out all the answers from his Teacher's Books, boys!"

Gasp!

"He's reduced to nothing more than the wreck of the man he once was, barely able to survive the few wretched years that are left for him to live. *That's* what becomes of you if you're a teacher, and you swear! Mr. Caswell is *living on borrowed time!*"

"If you give them the name of a teacher who swears . . ." – Swartwout again, whose father was a teacher – ". . . are you allowed to watch what happens *then?*"

"No, Chas, no outsider is *ever* admitted to the Inner Chamber. He would probably not survive the horrors of what he witnessed."

"How do *you* know what it's like inside, then?"

(Brinkman.)

A tortured expression came across Dr. Crowninshield's face, and he shuddered.

"I'd rather not talk about it!" he admitted. "Please, *please* don't insist that I answer that question, boys!"

They insisted.

"*Mea culpa! Mea culpa!*" he said, beating himself upon the breast, an anguished penitent on the point of scourging. "I should never have revealed what I have done! I have betrayed sacred secrets to the unworthy! *Mea culpa!*" He turned to Frankie. "Latin, not swearing. I hope you noticed."

"*Mea culpa!*"

"Yes, that's *certainly* true, Frankie. You are to blame! Your fault!"

He picked up the copy of *Julius Cæsar* from his desk, artfully avoiding their questioning. He looked down at the open pages, and seemed to notice something for the first time.

"Oh!" he said. "I've just realized that I lied to you *again* when I said something earlier."

Gasp! (Even gaspier than earlier gasps.)

"Is there *nothing* in this world to which we can entrust our innocent idealism?"

"Very moving, Olly."

They forgot about the Inner Chamber. This sounded even more interesting.

"I said that Shakespeare didn't use Latin, didn't *know*, or *speak* Latin. I definitely used italics. But . . ."

"*Et tu, Brute?*" Oliver pointed out. He'd been saving that one up.

"*Et tu, Olly?*" Dr. Crowninshield intoned gloomily. "Yes, there's that, too, looming up ahead of me, but I'm not thinking about that now. I look down at the page in front of me, and what do I see?"

Not recognizing a rhetorical question when they heard one — Dr. Crowninshield was occasionally given to rhetorical devices — most of the class peered suspiciously at the first line of *Julius Cæsar*.

What did he see?

(What *they* saw was *Flav. Hence! Home, you idle creatures, get you home!*

(They were none the wiser.)

"What do I see?" After a dramatic pause, Dr. Crowninshield repeated his question, and then answered his question. "I see *Latin.* That's what I can see. And I told you that Shakespeare didn't use Latin. He probably didn't write this bit himself, but it's down here in his play."

Griswold's Discovery Medicated Soap Encyclopædia For 1875 was pushed to one side, or placed on the floor (a two-handed task), as *Julius Cæsar* was once more placed where it had been at the beginning of the lesson, open on the desk in front of them. They bent their heads, on the alert for more Latin, quite pleased with the thought of the intellectual heights they'd scaled – stoutly roped together, their leader fearless with his ice-pick – without even realizing it. They knew Latin!

"E pluribus unum" – more or less – they'd be announcing to their parents that evening, as if casually. "That's an *exempli gratis. Post scriptum, et alia, et cetera.*"

Novus ordo seclorum. A new order of the ages would certainly be upon Longfellow Park. *Nota bene.*

They could speak Latin, and their parents (with the possible exception of Franny Darville's papa and Frankie Alloway's mama) *couldn't.*

Q.E.D. Ad infinitum, possibly, both *ante meridiem* and *post meridiem.* They'd drive their parents *mad*, or at least *ad nauseum.* It was an appealing thought.

Now, where were these new words with which they would torment?

They were eager for more weaponry.

"Well?" Dr. Crowninshield inquired. "Have you found it?"

They peered at the opening words of the play, the *very* first words on the right-hand page, the ones above that *Flav* bit.

They were in italics, and italics seemed to be a sure sign of Latin lurking somewhere. That was something they'd *Discovered* with *Griswold's Discovery.*

Cures Ignorance!

Cures Lack Of Latin!

And there were whole words in *CAPITAL LETTERS.*

ACT I

Scene I

Rome. A street.

Enter FLAVIUS, MARULLUS, and certain Commoners over the stage.

"Is it *FLAVIUS?*" Ben asked, raising his voice because the word was in capitals. It always meant you had to shout when you saw a word in capitals.

"*MARULLUS?*"

"I suppose they *are* Latin words, sort of, but look at the opposite page."

All heads shifted slightly to the left, a little ripple of coordinated movement.

They looked at the list of characters, printed one beneath the other, more characters than there were people in the class. Some of them would be playing *several* parts. Surely *every* word was in Latin, sort of Latin, here, apart from some of the explanatory comments of who was who.

"The very first words."

"*Dramatis Personæ.*"

You could see Oliver brightening up at the sight of that *æ*. He – keen on diphthongy things – really liked words with ligatures. Julius Cæsar! Julius Cæsar! A whole play in which the title character carried a ligature within his name like a proud symbol of office. Lucky, lucky Oliver. He'd be styling himself Olivær Comstöck before much longer. (The name looked more Scandinavian than Roman, a whiff of snow and the elk about it, a *smörgåsbord* walrussy sort of a smell. You expected raw fish on the breath.) You could tell – by the little experimental scribblings on the covers of his notebooks – that the idea appealed to him no end.

"Yes, Tom. *Dramatis Personæ*. That is more Latin. And what does it mean?"

"Dramatic people?" Not quite sure. Question marks had made a return. "They were, weren't they? Dramatic people? Always fighting and killing each other?" (*Just* the same in Rome today. That was Mrs. Albert Comstock's opinion.)

"Sort of. Latin puts words in a funny order, as you might have noticed earlier."

"Like German."

"Very good, William."

(William French had been listening to Mrs. Webster speaking. Sometimes, Dr. Wolcott Ascharm Webster's Austrian wife had been known to speak.)

"People dramatic?"

"Hmmm."

"Persons in the drama."

(No question mark from Hugh Petteys.)

"*Red hot!* Just about *perfect*, Hugh! 'Persons in the drama.' Something *very* like that. *And* there's another Latin word at the bottom of the page, the very last word on the list, a Latin word that you *know*."

All heads tilted down, all faces vanishing from view. Dr. Crowninshield found himself facing the tops of everyone's heads. Frankie Alloway's red hair blazed out with a "Choose me! Choose me!" intensity.

Senators, Citizens, Guards, Attendants, &c.

&c.?
"Is that a word?"

"Yes."

"And see?" (Bafflement, the question mark returned in Frankie Alloway's voice.)

"It's an abbreviation."

"*Et cetera!*"

"Which means?"

Quick glances at blackboard.

"And so on!"

"*And* the last word of the first scene is in Latin!"

Dr. Crowninshield assumed a dramatic pose, recreating the statue of Reynolds Templeton Seabright that they had gathered around just after lunch. Not only had Reynolds Templeton Seabright been a famous Shakespearean actor – and hence an essential part of their preparatory pilgrimage – but in the statue he looked exactly like one of the characters from *Julius Cæsar* (he'd once *played* the part of Julius Cæsar himself!), even though Carlo Fiorelli had actually depicted him in the rôle of Hamlet. Dr. Crowninshield not only recreated Reynolds Templeton Seabright's pose, he also assayed an ambitious attempt at Reynolds Templeton Seabright's famous vowels, vowels that still lingered in Longfellow Park whenever one of the theatrical Blennerhasset family opened his mouth.

> ". . . These growing feathers plucked from Cæsar's
> wing . . ."

– he began, giving his all to the last speech of the scene, his right arm, holding his open copy of *Julius Cæsar*, extended so far out in front of him that he was struggling to read the words of the speech –

> ". . . Will make him fly an ordinary pitch,
> Who else would soar above the view of men
> And keep us all in servile fearfulness."

More funny English.

"'Fearfulness'?"

(Franny Darville, not sounding convinced. "The last word of the first scene." That was what Dr. C. had said, but "fearfulness" didn't *look* like Latin, didn't *sound* like Latin. Already, they were cultivating a connoisseur's sense of what Latin should look like, and sound like. A little more of Dr. Crowninshield at full stretch, and they'd be fully capable of distinguishing which of the Seven Hills an Ancient Roman came from as soon as he opened his mouth, each hill a sort of classical Brooklyn or Bronx, nurturing its own unmistakable accent and dialect.

("... in ...")

("Palatine!")

("... servile ...")

("Esquiline!")

("... fearfulness ...")

("Capitoline!")

"Not the last *spoken* word, Franny. The last *printed* word."

"*Exeunt?*"

(Still a question mark.)

Exeunt was written on the board, squeezed in between *q.v.* = *quod vide* = *which see* and *op. cit.* = *opere citato* = *in the work cited*.

"Yes. They've all spoken. The scene is over. The first scene was set in a street, and ..." – he tapped at the words in the text – "... the second scene is set in a different place, 'a public place' it says, so what do the actors from the first scene have to do before the second scene can begin?"

He held his book over the *eunt* of *Exeunt*, so that only *Ex* was visible.

"They ...?"

"*Exit!*"

"Exactly, Harry."

He added = *They leave the stage.*

"Sometimes," he said, "it says *Exeunt omnes* ..." – this went on the blackboard – "... and this means?"

"They *all* leave the stage."

Bradley.

"Brilliant!"

"I was thinking of God being *omni*potent," Bradley went on, explaining the secret of his success. "*All* powerful." Bradley thought of little else. They braced themselves for Bradley to fall to his knees, hands clasped in fervent prayer, the gift of tongues. A sermon almost followed, but – with an effort – he controlled himself.

Dr. Crowninshield mimed a tribunal *exeunt* – Mar and Flav, heads held so high that they were almost leaning backward – and then reassumed his Reynolds Templeton Seabright posture.

"Calphurnia!" he enunciated, all vowels vibrating. It was the opening of the second scene, the first word spoken by Julius Cæsar in the play. Dr. Crowninshield was obviously raring to go, as keen for assassination as Bradley.

"Peace, ho!" Oliver added. "Cæsar speaks."

"Calphurnia!" Dr. Crowninshield repeated. He lowered his book. "And scene two has started. Thank you for your Casca, Olly."

"A pleasure, Dr. C. Don't you think we ought to institute some similar phrase before your every utterance? As a sign of our deep respect, our servile fearfulness?"

"I'm all in favor of servile fearfulness," Dr. Crowninshield admitted. "Peace, ho!" he repeated experimentally, savoring the sound of the words. "Dr. Crowninshield speaks."

"Precisely, sir."

"I really liked the sound of that. Your idea appeals to me strangely. Something has long been missing in my life – I especially yearn for the servile fearfulness – and this could be the very thing to restore my sense of self-importance. A splendid suggestion! Your best for quite some time. You're clearly quite an intelligent boy, Oliver, despite what everybody says." (This was one of his regular jokes.) "We shall certainly experiment with its usage."

He flicked back one or two pages in *Julius Cæsar*.

"And *Dramatis Personæ* reminds me . . ."

"Peace, ho! Dr. Crowninshield speaks."

"I like it even better the second time! *Dramatis Personæ* reminds me that we need to finally make our minds up about who will play who . . ."

". . . or whom will play who . . ."

". . . or who will play whom . . ."

(This was something else that had baffled them all, Dr. Crowninshield included. When were you supposed to use "who," and when were you supposed to use "whom," and – er – who were the people to – er – whom it was so important?)

". . . so that we'll know before we reassemble, bright-eyed and eager (I live in hope) on Monday morning. Time is getting on, and we haven't quite finished. If we cast all parts now . . ." – Dr. Crowninshield impressed them all by his expert use of theatrical terminology – ". . . you'll be able to take your books home and practice before Monday."

(Latin *and* Shakespeare. Unsuspecting parents were in for an exhausting weekend.)

Casting the parts was what they'd been doing when they'd arrived back from Hudson Heights, before their eyes had strayed to the right-hand page of the book open in front of them, before Frankie Alloway had asked, "Is this the way that the Ancient Romans used to speak?" They'd been studying the *Dramatis Personæ*, trying to decide the parts they wished to play. They'd already been told the story the previous day, after a morning of drawing Roman buildings. William French – a great devotee of blood-and-thunder novels – had objected that Dr. Crowninshield had spoiled the suspense by informing them that Julius Cæsar was going to die, but when Dr. Crowninshield had informed them that *he* was going to play the part of the murdered man, interest had quickened, and fingers had flicked through the book to find the scene in which he was hacked down. (A lurid account of his killing – *lots and lots of daggers, blood everywhere, some of the daggers went in* this *deep*, Dr. Crowninshield could be unscrupulous in arousing their interest – had already whetted their appetites.) "Act

Three, Scene One," the more intellectual boys had whispered help-fully to each other, while the others muttered, "Page 108." Unconsciously they made stabbing motions with their rulers as they tried to work out which were the parts to ask for if they were to be in with a chance of killing their teacher.

Bru (definitely *Bru*, they all remembered this bit).

Cas.

Cin.

Dec . . .

(Those abbreviations were a bit confusing.)

Their lust to assassinate their headmaster was probably as a result of their being baptized – most of them – in All Saints' Church, in a font that was positioned beneath a stained-glass window depicting a teacher, St. Cassian – another *Cas* – of Imola, being murdered by his pupils. The more ambitious earmarked cer-tain parts in the play as theirs by inalienable right, forming a rather disorderly line for the killing. (Their daggers would go in *this* deep.) These aspiring assassins experimented with differing stab-bing techniques. Sometimes they favored overarm actions, and sometimes they stabbed upward from below. Some of the more enthusiastic boys went in for vigorous side-to-side hacking – you'd have thought that they were gutting a large fish (Jonah tunneling out of the whale) – and they held their rulers with *both* hands, accompanying their elbow-blurring gouging with the loudly unin-hibited sounds of squelchy spattering. A tidal wave of loosed intestines surged across the classroom. Dr. Crowninshield looked round with an expression of mild concern. "Perturbed," he com-mented. "That's the word. I'm definitely starting to become perturbed." Linnaeus – and the other shyer boys – had been flick-ing through the book to find the characters with the shortest speeches, all those who didn't have very much to say for them-selves, feeling that the only parts they could play would be the parts of people who were like themselves. (First Plebeian or Second Plebeian – *1 Pleb* or *2 Pleb* – was as high as their hopes aspired.) Ben – distinct increase in pulse rate – had found himself cast as

Octavius. He wasn't one of those who killed Julius Cæsar, but –
Dr. Crowninshield had informed him, wooing him round to the
idea that the part was the very one for him to play – he was the one
who defeated the conspirators, the one who spoke the last words in
the play, "The glories of this happy day."

(Cautiously, with Brinkman very much in mind, Ben had tested
the name for taunting potential.

(Octavius.

(Oct.

(Tav.

(Vius.

(It didn't seem too bad.

(But what did he *say*?

(Were there hidden torments in the words he'd have to speak,
words that could become sticks, words that could become stones? If
there were no more weapons, it was words that would be hurled.

(He'd been discreetly working his way through the pages, on the
alert for *Oct*, and he hadn't found him yet, so it couldn't be a very
big part. Some comfort in that thought.

(What would he have to *say*?

(In front of everybody?

("The glories of this happy day" was encouraging.

(Nothing to worry about with "The glories of this happy day."

(Unless . . .

(He began to think of the ways in which these words might
become embarrassing.)

It was the bottom of the *Dramatis Personæ* page that provoked
terror in the Ancient Romans.

At the very end of the listed persons in the drama – in recognition of their inferior, segregated status – were the names of the two
women in the play (Calphurnia and Portia), and the *women* would
have to be played by *two of them*! There'd been cries of revulsion
when Dr. Crowninshield had broken the distressing news. So much
for the comforting fiction that Ancient Romans had been an exclusively male society. *Women* were allowed to walk across the pages

of *Julius Cæsar*, disrupting the appealing atmosphere of masculine murderousness.

"Couldn't Mrs. C. . . .?"

John Drinkwater rarely spoke, but such was his fear of Calphurnia and Portia that he broke his long silence to make this tentative suggestion. The only person who spoke less than John was Len Merrill — Silent Len — who never said a word from day's end to day's end, and sat amongst them like a vacuum given form. "Foster-child of silence!" This was how Oliver greeted him when his enthusiasm for Keats was at its height. "Silent, upon a peak in Darien!"

The rest of the class eagerly seized upon John Drinkwater's suggestion.

"Mrs. C.!"

"Mrs. C.!"

(Drinkwater repeated it loudly several times, like a sports enthusiast attempting to encourage a chant in support of his team. His mother came from the South, and — poor devil — his middle name was Mississippi. Who on earth would wish to drink *that* water? Oliver always referred to Drinkwater's twin older sisters as North and South Carolina.)

"Mrs. C.!"

"Mrs. C.!"

(There was a certain panicky desperation about this attempt at insistence. Even Len Merrill joined in.)

She'd miss reading out *The Adventures of Tom Sawyer* to them, surely, now that they'd finished the book?

Wouldn't she be *delighted* to be offered the part of Calphurnia?

At that very moment, she'd be upstairs, *longing* to be offered the opportunity.

It would be unkind to deprive her of this chance to shine.

Calphurnia was Julius Cæsar's wife, and Mrs. C. was *Dr. C.'s* wife!

Mrs. C. would be an *excellent* Calphurnia.

She'd be perfect for the part.

(They sounded like employees from a theatrical agent's, gathered in eager disputation in a bar near Herald Square.)

She could, also – while she was at it – play Portia.

(Portia was a bit confusing. Some of them had the *distinct* impression that Portia was in *The Merchant of Venice*. When Dr. Crowninshield had proven to them on Monday that *all* of them knew some Shakespeare, rather like he had proven to them today that *all* of them knew some Latin, *The Merchant of Venice* had been mentioned. There'd been a recent popular production of the play, and several of the boys had been taken to see it.

("'All that glitters is not gold,'" Bradley had quoted, as tentative as a tyro attempting a foreign language. Shakespeare was up there with Latin when it came to incomprehensible utterances.

("*Almost!*" Dr. Crowninshield had said, rather bafflingly.

("'The quality of mercy is not strained.'"

(Ben.

(His mama had taken him. It had been a secret from Papa. *Moonshine!* That was what Papa would say about Shakespeare, and he'd probably have the same opinion about Latin, unless – because it was taught at Otsego Lake Academy – Latin somehow possessed a veneer of respectability.

(*The quality of mercy is not strained*.

(*That* had been a speech by Portia.

(Unless she'd said *strain'd*.

(Shakespeare, like Ancient Romans, seemed to go in for abbreviations.

(What on earth was Portia doing in *Julius Cæsar*? Wouldn't her presence spoil everything, confuse Bru, Cas, Cin, Dec, and all the others? "Why is *she* here?" they'd be muttering, impatient to get stabbing, but quite put off their stroke. They didn't want any talk about the quality of *mercy*, thank you very much, the mood they were in! Cæs would not be long for this world! There'd be plenty of *straining* going on once they'd started!)

Confusing as Portia may have been, Mrs. C. was the ideal person to play her.

She'd be an *excellent* Portia.

She'd be perfect for the part.

(She was a *woman*, wasn't she?)

Dr. Crowninshield was having none of this.

Just as they'd feared.

Panic rose at Dr. Crowninshield's imperturbable implacability.

"*Comstock!*"

(Brinkman, with immense enthusiasm. He'd been seething for quite some time about the "Sidder-knee," the Chinky-Winky references — *Beg, Sidder-knee! Beg! Beg! Beg!* — the spinning pocket-watch.)

"Why did you give Comstock the part of Brutus? He'd be perfect as a *woman*! If Mrs. C. can't play Calphurnia, then Comstock should. He'd be *perfect* for the part."

"Or the parts of *both* women? Calphurnia and Portia only appear in one scene together in the whole play, and in that scene Portia doesn't say a word. There'd be no difficulty whatsoever in one person playing both parts."

(Dr. Crowninshield.

(Brinkman should have been warned by Dr. Crowninshield's ingenuous manner, his mild affability, but he was far too eager to make a fool of Oliver. He *leaped* upon the suggestion.)

"Even better! He'd be totally convincing. They'd be the best-acted parts in the whole play! Everyone would believe that he really was . . ."

— Brinkman gathered his full powers for the most awful of all insults —

". . . *a woman!*"

"An interesting suggestion," Dr. Crowninshield replied, "but — unfortunately — I think it's perfectly clear that Olly is going to make an excellent Brutus. No, no . . ."

— His musing look at Brinkman should have alerted the beefy booby —

"No, the person I have in mind isn't Olly. They're not the parts for Olly. The person we need to play Calphurnia and Portia — yes, you've quite convinced me that the same person should play both parts — needs to be a boy who's big and tough and coarse, a boy with the muscular confidence not to be the slightest bit embarrassed by playing the parts of . . ." — he adopted Brinkman's lethal tone of sneering dismissiveness — ". . . *women*. This will be the real test of his acting ability! A boy who can carry off such parts with dignity. A boy who's rough and fearless and manly all the way through . . ."

"They're *certainly* not the parts for me."

(Oliver, in a well-that-lets-me-out tone of voice, primly dismissive.)

"A boy who can be rather cruel to others, a boy who likes to watch others blush or cry . . ."

(Horrified suspicion growing on Brinkman's face.

(The beginnings of hopeful narrow-escape smiles on other faces.

(Dr. Crowninshield *had* seen Brinkman make Frankie Alloway cry on Hudson Heights.

(Dr. Crowninshield *had* seen Brinkman rubbing Stoddard's face with the encyclopædias.

(Dr. Crowninshield *had* seen Brinkman . . .

(Ben started to blush, and looked down at his *Julius Cæsar* as if rapt in a study of Marullus' first speech.

(*Where is thy leather apron and thy rule?*

(Ancient Roman tradesmen were clearly expected to carry the tools of their trade about them at all times, like the saints in the windows at All Saints', forever displaying the emblems of their martyrdom.

(With their rulers, like the schoolboys before them, they'd be essaying all the angles of assassination. Why should the patricians possess a monopoly of murder?

(*What dost thou with thy best apparel on?*)

"Yes, Sid. You'll be an *excellent* Calphurnia. You'll be *perfect* for the part of Portia."

"I'm not playing any *women*!"

(Brinkman, flustered and *furious*, rebellious mutterings.)

"Yes, you are, Sid."

(No discussion.)

"You can't *make* me. I'll tell my papa."

"I'll be *delighted* to see your papa if he'd be good enough to call in to see me. I have seen far too little of your papa, and I've a great deal I'd like to discuss with him. For a start, there's what I saw you doing in the lavatory on Tuesday. Then there's what I heard you say yesterday to Miss Ericsson." Long pause. Long meaningful pause. You could tell by the changed expression on Brinkman's face that he'd grasped what the meaning was.

The message had been received. The message had been understood.

"You'll be a *splendid* Calphurnia," Dr. Crowninshield continued briskly. Not once had there been the slightest suggestion in his tone of voice that playing the parts of Calphurnia and Portia was anything other than an honor, a true test of someone's mettle. Dr. Crowninshield's punishments sometimes crept up on you without you realizing. He didn't punish much, and tended to contrive things so that the punishment appeared to be the very thing that you were longing to do.

"'Here, my lord.' That's all you say in your first scene. Three words. You begin with just three words. You *can* do it, Sid, and you can do it well. Think about this over the weekend, and if there is anything you'd like to discuss with me, I shall be available at all convenient times."

Dr. Crowninshield straightened up, and looked out across the rest of the class.

"And if anyone finds anything amusing in Sid playing those parts, then I shall have something to say to him. Something not altogether to his advantage."

"'When Dr. Crowninshield says 'Do this,' it is performed.'"

(Charlie Whitefoord. He was already examining some of his Mark Antony speeches.)

"Precisely. That's nearly as good as 'Peace, ho! Dr. Crowninshield speaks.' *And* you said it as if you meant it. This is

217

going to be absolutely splendid. A highly promising Mark Antony, a gifted Brutus . . ."

"A godlike Cæsar . . ."

"*Especially* the godlike Cæsar. What a feast of theatre lies ahead of us! A glittering cast, from *Julius Cæsar* all the way down to *Attendants, &c.*"

"*Et cetera!*" the Ancient Romans repeated.

"And so on."

"*Latin!*"

"Two tasks this weekend, boys . . ." – Dr. Crowninshield tended to describe the work he set them as "tasks"; they rather liked the sound of "tasks" – ". . . One: have a look at your part in *Julius Cæsar*. Two: don't forget that you *all* know Latin . . ."

"*E pluribus unum!*"

"*Dramatis personæ!*"

"*Et cetera!*"

They were virtually bilingual! Pshaw! to Mrs. Albert Comstock and her exotic French phrases!

". . . and try to find some *more* Latin to bring in to show the rest of us on Monday. This week's school will soon be over . . ."

He paused.

"I pause to hear the cries of disappointment, the dismayed realization that school has nearly finished for the week," he explained, and added, in a sad but unsurprised voice, "but I pause in vain."

Frankie raised his hand.

"*Where* shall we find the Latin?"

He spoke rather nervously, as if they'd be taking their lives in their hands by venturing too close.

"Latin lies everywhere about you," Dr. Crowninshield replied, an angel bringing good news to the huddled masses.

"Will we find more Latin?"

"*Lots!*"

Ideas started to come to Dr. Crowninshield. You could see it happening.

"I'll give you some examples. One: Mrs. Alexander Diddecott's sundial. Two: the lettering on All Saints' clock . . ."

"*Tempus fugit!*"

(Bradley. In like a shot when anything churchy came into things.

(A sundial. A clock. There was that Latin-like lingering on time again, though the sundial seemed the more authentically Roman method of measuring. Sundials and sandglasses came into Ben's mind. How strange, to mark the passing of the hours of life by silence.)

"*Time flies!* You'll see it – those of you who go to All Saints' – when you're at church on Sunday, and, whilst you're there, have a good look in the graveyard. You'll see a lot of Latin on the gravestones." (There were going to be some anxious parents this weekend.) A pleasing idea suddenly occurred to Dr. Crowninshield. "*Tempus fugit*, like many of the symbols and Latin words you will see on the gravestones, can be described as a *memento mori*." He wrote *memento mori* – it had to undulate up and down to fit – in the sole remaining space on the blackboard, hovering indecisively between *e* and *o* as the second letter of *memento*, finally deciding on *o*, clearly convinced that this was far more likely to be correct than *e*, despite Oliver's eyebrow. He then explained what *momento mori* meant.

"Euch!" from the Ancient Romans.

The incorrect spelling looked more correct than the correct spelling, just as – as Alice had once said – *miniscule* was always far more convincing as a spelling than *minuscule*, even though it was wrong.

"'Remember that you must die,'" Dr. Crowninshield repeated.

"Euch!" again.

"The skull on the desk in the study. The dead leaves in the painting."

Dr. Crowninshield could be quite poetic.

When you were Ancient, this was not the sort of thing you wished to have repeated to you. When you were a ten-year-old you *knew* that you were going to live forever and never die.

"Very cheerful!"

"*That's* brightened up my weekend!"

(Though, come to think of it, a useful phrase to employ against irritating sisters. First they'd be baffled; then they'd be depressed. It was an attractive combination.)

"Three: gravestones. Four: the lettering above the Manhattan & Brooklyn Bank. Five: the plaque on the wall outside the new library. I wonder how many of you noticed it earlier. Six: the lettering under the coat of arms outside this very building! *Don't* shout it out, those of you who can remember it. You can all turn round for a look behind you – a loving, nostalgic look – as you leave for the day, reluctant to leave the wonderful school in which you are lucky enough to be pupils, heartbroken that there is no school on Saturday and Sunday. I'm sure that this is an emotion that often has you in its power, boys, bringing manly tears to your eyes. Seven. Eight. Nine. You'll soon find seven, eight, and nine. Does that answer your question, Frankie?"

It did.

Dr. Crowninshield repeated what he'd said earlier. "Latin lies everywhere about you. Let's see who can produce the longest list."

Click.

Ten minutes to three.

A fundamental question entered Frankie's mind, and his arm rose into the air. He'd be *exhausted* when he got home.

"Where do they *speak* Latin?"

He'd heard Swartwout boasting about how his family would be marching about France, all *portes* (*porte* was French, he'd informed them) magically *ouvreﬅing* (something like that) before them as Edeetha opened her mouth and spoke like a native. (*Not* a native of France, unfortunately, as yet. "*Je suis, tu* – er . . ." This was about as far as she'd got so far, though she could count up to twenty with very little hesitation, and knew at least seven of the months. In French, as with Latin, you seemed to begin with time.)

"Apart from *us*, here?"

"Yes."

"In schools, in universities. You'll be speaking Latin at Otsego Lake Academy."

(A worried glimpse of a brass-buttoned future in which English was banned.)

"In what *country?*"

"In *all* countries."

"They speak *French* in France."

(Swartwout, still keen to advertise his family's Napoleonic European ambitions.)

"Isn't it only in *Rome* that they speak Latin?"

(They had the sense of Rome being a large country – full of tall white columns and marble ruins – somewhere in Europe, next to Greece, despite Dr. Crowninshield's best efforts to clarify matters with the globe and atlas. If they turned the pages of the *National Costumes of Europe* calendar to one of the warmer months, they'd surely find the photographic evidence there as unignorable proof: toga-clad, Latin-spouting Romans, assembled like another Longfellow Park Forum. They used hands a lot to talk if they were Romans, as if everyone were deaf, their sense of hearing weakened by the constant rumble of chariot-wheels, the rattling armored sound of perpetually marching armies, the chanting roar of the crowds in the Colosseum, those endlessly repeated lists of declensions and conjugations. They were *positive* about this.)

But Dr. Crowninshield was firm.

"They speak *Italian* in Rome."

It was very confusing.

Brinkman was convinced that they spoke exclusively in Latin in Rome. It was an integral part of Popish scheming. Why else would they employ Latin in their church services and call themselves *Roman* Catholics? This latter fact confirmed the presence of a provocatively pagan quality to goings-on at Corpus Christi, the clouds of incense decadently reminiscent of burnt offerings, dagger-slain sacrifices upon an alien altar. He'd quizzed Stoddard ferociously about this, torn between edging closer, and edging further away. "Are you a *Catholic?*" "Yes." "Are you a *Roman*

Catholic." "Yes." He hadn't even had the good manners to sound *ashamed*. It was rather disturbing, the way that he'd disguised himself, not even bearing an Irish or Italian name by way of warning. With an O'Rourke or a Fiorelli — or a Cohen or a Silverstein, for that matter — you knew precisely how things stood, the correct attitude to assume. A sense of sulky grievance had been building up inside him that Stoddard had been afforded an unfair advantage when it came to this Latin business. He'd have filled several notebooks with Latin by the end of the weekend, most of them packed with highly inflammable (all the more convenient for the pyre on which to burn him) religious propaganda.

"Isn't . . .?"

Frankie had a sense of approaching the heart of the matter that was concerning him.

"Isn't there a country where they speak nothing but Latin?"

"Not in *any* country. Latin is a dead language."

A dead language.

This was a worrying phrase.

A sense of an entire nation silenced, a gleaming white ruinous full-moon landscape of desolately infinite space and speechlessness, the buildings of the white-columned, white-stepped North River Lunatic Asylum curiously multiplied and stretching away for as far as they could see. They saw it in front of them, heard the wind moaning. It was like the model of the Holy City that some of them had seen in an exhibition of Christian art in the Athenian Hall (odd location), a strangely unpeopled city that they looked down on from above, hovering in the air. There was no other sound to hear, and certainly no spoken words, not even the distant echo of an echo.

They'd been told to look for Latin *in the graveyard*.

"You'll see a lot of Latin *on the gravestones*."

That was what Dr. Crowninshield had assured them.

Momento — his spelling of *memento* was the one that stayed in their minds (how sacred the duty entrusted to teachers) — *mori*.

That was something else he'd said.

In Latin.

Remember that you must die.

It was no surprise that *post mortem* was a phrase in Latin, because Latin — this was the horrified discovery — was the language you spoke *post mortem*.

The language of the dead.

A *distinctly* worrying phrase.

They'd quite gone off Latin, a language that withered up and died, a language that probably had the power to kill you if you spoke too much of it, a language that you spoke when you were dead. They'd quite gone off Otsego Lake Academy, where the words you spoke were words in the fatal language.

"*Et tu, Brute?*"

That's what Julius Cæsar had said.

He'd spoken Latin, and promptly died.

No wonder that necromancers — dabbling in the Dark Arts — favored it as the language with which to conjure up the dead. It was the only language they understood once they'd traveled beyond the veil, enticed back briefly into the world of the living when they heard it spoken, the words an allurement, a tidbit pressed against the bars of their cage.

Mrs. Alexander Diddecott assured everyone in Longfellow Park that the dead could talk. When she finally succeeded in bringing back Mrs. Italiaander's dead infant son during one of her séances (Mrs. Italiaander had searched for years and years), little Archer Italiaander would reach out his arms toward her in the way that Allie Crowninshield did to Oliver.

"Archer!" Mrs. Italiaander would whisper, the only word she was capable of speaking, reaching out yearningly across the polished circular table to take him in her arms again. "Archer!"

And Archer Italiaander would open his mouth and say, "*Post scriptum*" or "*Exeunt omnes.*"

And his mama would start screaming, screaming and screaming *ad infinitum.*

Click.

Five minutes to three.

Mrs. Crowninshield walked into the room behind them.

They all — Brinkman gracelessly — stood, and chorused, "Good afternoon, Mrs. C."

"Good afternoon, boys."

They sat down again as she walked to stand beside her husband. She was carrying the gold star on a red satin cushion. This was the final ceremony of the week, just before they went home. It was time to award the gold star to the one of them who had tried the hardest in school that week.

"No difficulties whatsoever in deciding this week, boys. I think you all know who it's going to be, who it *ought* to be."

Bradley simpered.

He knew who it *ought* to be.

You could see him flexing his modest expression, all prepared to put it to good use.

Dr. Crowninshield turned to his wife.

"Time for this week's award."

"'When Dr. Crowninshield says 'Do this,' it is performed.'"

"Exactly as things *should* be."

Mrs. C. was the most loyal of wives.

You imagined them rehearsing on Thursday evenings in their little upstairs parlor, in front of their intrigued baby boy. Not much escaped the notice of Allie Crowninshield. His sharp little eyes — he always looked gratifyingly fascinated by whatever it was he saw — lingered on everything, reluctant to stop seeing. He'd be reaching out to take hold of the gold star for himself, to examine it more closely, and find out precisely how it had been manufactured. Whenever he was brought into the schoolroom he expressed a distinct preference for Oliver, reaching his arms out toward him, and clasping him firmly round his neck. (More ammunition for Brinkman.) Allie's eyes would follow Oliver about the room, and he'd smile when Oliver went up to him. Ben thought of baby geese, following the first living thing that they saw, claiming it as their mother. There'd be a line of small boys behind Oliver, crawling determinedly toward him, and nothing would impede their progress as they reached out to grab an ankle with both hands. They'd be clinging on, dragged across the floor, polishing the boards to a highly reflective slippery gloss, eyes closed in bliss, Oliver struggling to keep walking. Allie would take firm hold of Oliver's nose, and turn it gravely in one direction, then back again in the other direction, listening with great concentration, a safe-cracker attempting to open a combination lock. "He ought to play with Stoddard's face," Brinkman would snigger. "He could swing from spot to spot, and get some exercise." If you ever longed for a boon companion who mixed witty repartee with generosity of spirit, then Brinkman was the man for you.

Mrs. C. lifted up the gold star – she made them out of metal, fastened onto safety pins – and beckoned.

She held it so that it caught the light and glittered alluringly.

"Come on, Frankie. It's *you* this week, and *well* deserved!"

All that glitters (*almost!*)

– *glisters* (*that* was the word!) Dr. Crowninshield had explained to them –

was certainly gold for Frankie Alloway.

There was an audible gasp from him.

He stood up with a look of rapture on his face – *the glories of this happy day!* – as the whole class (the whole *school*), with the usual predictable exception, applauded. Bradley applauded extra loudly so that they'd all notice he wasn't being the slightest bit jealous, that he was absolutely delighted on Frankie's behalf, that he was an inspiring example of unselfish Christian generosity, even if his lips *had* gone a bit thin. (*Let your light so shine before men, that they may see your good works.* Matthew, Chapter V, Verse xvi.)

Horas serenas!

Horas serenas!

(Those were two of the words on Mrs. Alexander Diddecott's sundial.)

Frankie's bright hour blazed.

"Well done!"

Mrs. Crowninshield pinned the star on Frankie's chest, another Wild West sheriff — *gold*, not silver, for *his* star! — appointed to rid the town of evildoers. Those six-shooters would be blazing like firecrackers on the Fourth of July.

He walked back to his place, beaming, polishing the gold to an even brighter shine. He couldn't *wait* to show his mama.

Dr. Crowninshield picked up his copy of *Julius Cæsar*.

"Don't forget," he said. "*Julius Cæsar*. Latin."

He opened the book, and read the first line of the play.

"Hence! Home, you idle creatures, get you home!"

Something occurred to him, and he looked pleased.

"I told you that Shakespeare had the right words for everything."

(Dr. Crowninshield spoke the truth.

(The *astonishment* when they reached Act Three, Scene One.

(Cassius, after the killing of Julius Cæsar, stooped to bathe his hands in the blood up to his elbows — they'd liked this bit, even if it wasn't quite as gruesome as the death of Eurymachus — and said the bit that made them gasp:

("... How many ages hence
(Shall this our lofty scene be acted over
(In states unborn and accents yet unknown!"

(This was a reference to *them*!

(That's what Dr. Crowninshield had told them.

(Shakespeare *had known* about *them*.

(*Ages hence.*

(Julius Cæsar.

(100–44 BC.

(These BC dates, like minus numbers in Arithmetic, were a bit confusing, and seemed to go the wrong way round.

(Shakespeare.

(1564–1616.

(Crowninshield's.

(1887.

(*Acted over.*

(*States unborn.*

(United States of America.

(1776.

(*Accents yet unknown.*

(This was probably a reference to John Drinkwater's Mississippi way of speaking.

(Vowels prolonged into strange sounds.

(You never heard a Cassius like him.

(That was Oliver's theory.

(Shakespeare *had known.*

(They were *really* impressed.)

"I told you that Shakespeare had the right words for everything."

"Thou naughty knave! Thou saucy fellow!"

(Oliver had been reading ahead in the play.)

"I'll cobble *you!*"

(Dr. Crowninshield made to bounce his book off Oliver's head.)

Click.

With impressive synchronicity, the schoolroom clock clicked up to *XII* – *more* Latin! – at the exact moment that the first chime of three began to sound from All Saints'. Ben always liked it when things like this happened. It made it seem as if there was a pattern in the world, and that things were meant to happen in a certain way.

"*Tempus fugit!*"

(Frankie, rubbing his star like an Aladdin's lamp, thought his wishes had already come true.)

"Splendid! No wonder you won the gold star!"

He tapped at *Julius Cæsar.*

"And what is it that *you* do now?"

"We *exeunt.*"

"You do indeed, Charlie. In fact – come on, let's clear this place! – you . . ."

227

"*Exeunt omnes!*"

"And Mrs. C. and Allie and I will remain. *Manet*. That's *another* Latin word you'll find in *Julius Cæsar*. It means, 'He remains.' Sometimes people *exeunt*, and sometimes people *manet*."

"Unless they *exeunt omnes*."

"In which case the stage is empty. As this room will be shortly. Nothing will remain but drawings of Roman columns on the walls, and wet footprints, to show that you've been here." Dr. Crowninshield could be quite philosophical, in a *momento mori* sort of way. (They were virtually all convinced that *momento* was the only possible spelling of *memento*.)

("*Very* wet footprints near Akenside's desk!"

(Brinkman would go home with a warm, grateful glow inside him. Yet *another* opportunity offered to him to mock someone. He'd made sure that everyone knew that Tom Akenside wet the bed.)

Manet went down on Frankie's list. He had no hesitation about the correct way to spell it. Manet was his mama's favorite painter. He was French. French *and* Latin. A sense of confusion again. Mrs. Albert Comstock had told his mama, quite firmly, that she did not approve of Manet. First of all he was *French*, and then, though this was quite enough all by itself, he painted – ahem – Mrs. Albert Comstock invariably ahemmed at this point, *quite unsuitable* paintings.

Frankie studied the paintings conscientiously, seeking the muckiness, like Brinkman on one of his tit-seeking art-gallery expeditions, but had failed to find it. Slight sense of disappointment. "Eleven, twenty-three, *thirty-seven!*" Brinkman would announce with a smutty smirk on Monday mornings, seeking to impress them with his latest tally from tit-trawling, sounding like a weekend sportsman boasting of his bag at a shooting-party. His totals – rather worryingly – tended to be odd numbers, and you couldn't help speculating about all those lopsided women captured on canvas by the Old Masters. Old Masters. Ancient Romans. You were never far from tits when The Beards gathered gruntingly together in groups. Perhaps the odd numbered tit sporters were all Amazons. He'd heard somewhere – blushes contending with giggles – that this fearsome tribe of women warriors lopped off one of their (blush) breasts to stop it getting in the way when they were unleashing arrows from their bows in battle. (Shrill Amazonian shrieks echoed through the parrot-haunted dimness of the tropical forest as whipped-back bowstrings twanged on tits.) Long biological speculation had followed this discovery, as he tried to decide which (darker blush) breast would be the one that got in the way, and sent arrows off at tangents. Here was a curious new method of identifying left-handed Amazons. Amazons were the very sort of women to get artists reaching enthusiastically for their paintbrushes. Any excuse to paint women with no clothes on. *Thirty-seven!* It was just like Mrs. Albert Comstock arriving home after a hard day's darkie-counting in New York City, though – the complete reverse of Brinkman – the higher the total, the more total the hissing displeasure from Olly's mama. Brinkman had even (slight pinkness about Frankie's cheeks) starting making comments about Mrs. Crowninshield's *tits* – it was a word he tended to employ in italics, to stress how daring he was being – and they'd all been embarrassed, especially when he'd developed a smutty obsession with the idea of baby Allie being breast-fed. ("*Breast-fed.*" Italics again. That was the way that Brinkman pronounced it.) Frankie had been baffled. How on earth would a baby be able to eat *that* much? Charlie – who possessed a gentlemanly sense of decorum – had spoken firmly to Brinkman (quite right too, they all thought) about the respect due to Mrs. Crowninshield (he'd spoken *very* firmly) and her name had not been sullied again. Frankie looked across the classroom at Brinkman, and Brinkman glared sulkily back at him. (Alloway with a gold star! *And* he had red hair! A *shitty* state of affairs!) Olly had been perfectly correct. Brinkman really was developing into a frighteningly convincing duplicate of Mrs. Albert Comstock's sour-tempered lap dog, wagging his tail or snarling in all the right places to get the little treats dropped into his gaping cuckoo mouth.

(1. *Manet.*

(That was the beginning of Frankie's list of Latin.

(Frankie wrinkled his forehead in ferocious concentration. It was something Linnaeus Finch had said. Another Latin word that no one else had appeared to notice.

(*Ante bellum.*

(That was what it had been.

(Before the war.

(That was what Linnaeus had said that it meant.

(2. *Bellum.*

(Frankie's list was coming along nicely, though *bellum* didn't sound at all right for "war." It sounded too like "belle," too like something pretty and desirable, which it probably was to some people, Brinkman, for example, or Ben's Uncle Eugene. Unless the word was something to do with "bells," strident warnings of imminent hostilities ringing out from all church towers.

("... Hear the loud alarum bells —
    Brazen bells!
What a tale of terror, now their turbulency tells!
In the startled ear of night!
How they scream out their affright! ..."

(That was what Olly had been reciting last week, though it seemed to have been more about fire than war.

(Brave clergymen swung perilously on the bell ropes, all those clerical Quasimodos risking their lives to save their parishioners as war thundered down upon a sleeping city. You couldn't imagine the Reverend Goodchild doing that ...

(Frankie could actually feel his brain starting to ache sometimes when he was over-ambitious with his thinking, a dull throb like the beginnings of a headache.

(He held his hand against his gold star to comfort himself.

(The agony abated somewhat.

(Mama would be so *pleased*.)

Have a good weekend, boys!"

"You too, Dr. C., Mrs. C.!"

The idle creatures got them hence.

The idle creatures got them home.

The idle creatures exeunted.

It was a holiday.

Manet — could you use this for the plural? — *Dr. and Mrs. Crowninshield.*

They didn't forget to turn back at the bottom of the steps to check the Latin on the school coat of arms. They'd have plenty with which to impress their parents when they got home. School could be so — what was the correct choice of word? — *educational.*

FOUR

I

The closer they approached to Otsego Lake Academy, the more they slowed down. They'd been so anxious not to arrive late that they'd arrived distinctly early. The Crowninshield's boys ahead of them had already entered, but they lingered, savoring their last moments of freedom. Here was the place where they would be taught Latin, and how to become men, with a sensation that the two things would not be unconnected. Up the steps they walked – the single narrow path cut out of the snow – and between the Corinthian columns that supported the central portico. This was the frontage that Ben had chosen to draw when they had been researching – they'd used the word a lot, feeling scholarly and Yale-like – Roman architecture, and his picture had been fastened to the wall with thumbtacks, like all the others. Dr. Crowninshield was not a man with a particularly strongly developed visual sense, and he'd thumped in the pictures – thumb splayed – with his eyes looking elsewhere, keeping an eye on Brinkman, so that all the buildings had been at dramatic, stomach-heaving angles, Ancient Rome – or its likeness in the New World – devastated by a cataclysmic earthquake. Only Linnaeus's pictures – they all readily acknowledged that Linn was by far the best artist in the school – were displayed with any conscious care, Dr. Crowninshield unable to bear not

232

showing them to their very best advantage. He would look at them again and again, and he'd say, "These are really special!" Once, when Allie had been ill, Linn had given him a drawing he'd made of the baby boy – like a talisman to make him well – and Dr. Crowninshield hadn't been able to speak. Linn's Ancient Roman drawing – the front perspective of the North River Lunatic Asylum (a choice that was a gift to Brinkman; Linnaeus always seemed to leave himself undefended) – had the detail and precision of an architect's plan, with all the decorative acanthus leaves beautifully inked in. Oliver – "*The Fall of the Roman Empire*," had been his only comment – hadn't been able to stop himself from going round in Dr. Crowninshield's wake, and repinning all the clumsily slanting pictures in more pleasing positions, restoring the necessary equilibrium. If you were training to be an æsthete, you had to embrace an awesome range of responsibilities.

Linnaeus – in every one of his drawings – always hid a little portrait of himself, waving out at whoever was examining his artwork. What would be the correct term for such a person: a viewer, a spectator, a *reader* (even though there were no words)? Each portrait was always tiny, but quite recognizable: the slightly awkward stance, the rueful twist of the mouth, the mussed hair hanging low over his forehead and almost hiding his eyes. Linnaeus's hair was always untidy. Whenever he made a mistake, or said something that embarrassed him (he'd often do this), he'd bow his head down and press his face into the inner part of his left arm, to hide his features. He'd reach a hand across the top of his head, and clutch the back of his skull with it, wincing, bending down, a gesture that seemed made to ward off expected – and (he clearly felt) fully deserved – blows. After he'd first noticed the miniature figure of Linn with his gesticulating left hand ("Here I am!" he seemed to be saying. "Can you see me?") – ingeniously hidden, as in a puzzle picture – Ben always found himself looking for him. He wondered if anyone else had noticed. Sometimes Linn was at the back of an inner room, just visible through a window; sometimes he would be partially hidden behind a tree or in shrubbery; sometimes he would

233

be in the far distance, only just visible to the naked eye. He was always present, always waving. In the drawing of Allie he was the smallest of manikins clutching at the edge of an egg-dipped slice of bread in the little boy's hand, waving bravely out at Dr. Crowninshield as Allie — seemingly — prepared to bite his head off with considerable relish. Allie would eat anything, or demonstrate ambitious attempts to do so. They kept him well away from the Nature Table, or he'd have been cramming in the fruits of their rambles: frogs — vigorously resisting, shooting out their long back legs like synchronized chameleons uncurling tongues — and half-wilted catkins from a pussy willow.

As they picked their way up the steps, Ben felt that he was walking into his own drawing, the drawing of the place where he had once felt that he wanted to be, but he couldn't rub any of it out anymore. What once had been drawn could not be amended. Their boots crunched on the wet ashes that littered the darkened stone. It was strange to be reminded that — beneath all the snow — there was stone. They were already starting to believe that the snow was deep and endless, nothing but snow beneath them wherever they were, nothing solid beneath the shifting surface. It was here that they paused, and looked back the way they had come, the single track through the dirty-looking snow, cut as deeply as the pattern of a maze, the only route to or from their new school.

Latin, and becoming a man.

Acting the Roman.

That meant killing yourself.

That had come as a shock.

That was the impression they'd formed after Brutus had committed suicide with the assistance of Strato. Linnaeus (Stra) had stood beneath the blackboard holding his ruler at a helpful angle, and Oliver (Bru) had run the full length of the aisle to hurl himself upon it, and meet his end like a Roman. "This was the noblest Roman of them all." That was what Charlie Whitefoord (Ant) had announced, standing upon Dr. Crowninshield's desk. "This was a *man*!" ("Huh!" from Brinkman.) Ancient Romans — it became perfectly clear — considered it *noble* to die with self-chosen dignity, but the Crowninshield's apprentice Ancient Romans had not been too keen on the idea. They weren't keen *at all* on the idea of killing themselves. This was a *momento mori* (they ignored Oliver's intermittent attempts to impose *memento mori* upon them) that they had no wish to remember. New academic accomplishments sometimes seemed to expect a commitment so total that it was difficult to guarantee wholeheartedly, and Latin was no exception to this.

Latin . . .

A different morning . . .

2

Latin . . .

A different school . . .

They'd walked up Indian Woods Road on the Monday morning after their discovery of the dead language, comparing the lengths of their Latin lists, far more eager then — as they approached Crowninshield's — than they now were as they approached the academy. It was generally agreed that Franny Darville — whose papa was a doctor — had an unfair advantage, though Frankie Alloway (inspired to ambitions of an unprecedented two gold stars in a row) had sheet after sheet of Latin names for plants that had been supplied by his mama, a keen gardener. You wouldn't have had a very far-ranging discussion with an Ancient Roman taught his Latin by Mrs. Alloway, but you'd certainly end up with a colorful and well-weeded garden. The flowering of pastoral poetry might very well have blossomed from such humble beginnings.

They'd walked into the schoolroom full of ideas. Fearlessly, they'd wandered into the *terra incognita* (Latin!) of Latin, and now it was time for their *viva voce* (Latin!).

Dr. Crowninshield hadn't lied to them — *this* time, they stressed — and Latin had indeed lain everywhere about them. Not only would the sight of most of the new public buildings of

Longfellow Park have gladdened the hearts of all homesick Ancient Romans – homesick in time, homesick in space – but the very words of their once-alive language could be glimpsed in even the most casual of glances. "Ooh, look!" they'd be saying, like Mrs. Albert Comstock – a great one for ooh-looking, making sure that everyone·else had fixed their eyes unwaveringly upon whatever it was that had temporarily caught her attention – (but in Latin), "Ooh, look at that, Marcus! . . ." – or Quintus or Publius or Numerius (pity the Numerius with a pun-loving Arithmetic teacher) – ". . . *Latin!*" Longfellow Park prided itself on catering for the needs of visitors, as long as they weren't *too* foreign, had hygienic habits, and spent freely.

Linnaeus had brought in his lucky silver dollar that his grand-papa had given him for his sixth birthday in 1885 (he was a year younger than they were) when he'd first been sent away to school – Linnaeus hadn't needed to read *Tom Brown's Schooldays* – and they'd passed it around the class. It was quite warm by the time it had returned to Linnaeus. Dr. Crowninshield was always delighted when you brought him something that you thought might interest him. "Look, boys!" he instructed them, indicating the words – the *Latin* words – that curved around the top of Liberty's head like a halo. "*E PLURIBUS UNUM.* Those are words that should ring a bell. It might be a faint and faraway tinkle after a riotous weekend of freedom, but . . ."

They were ahead of him.

They often were.

He encouraged this, and seemed to thrive on it.

"One out of many!"

Brinkman sniffed at this hubristic assertion. What a slur on the pedigree of the United States! The rest of the class was perfectly happy, however. As they had just discovered, two days had gone by and they *still* knew Latin!

The Great Seal began spinning its ball again in Frankie's head, but it had lost much of its sinister power. His *five* sheets of Latin – Mama had written in her largest handwriting (and on one side of the paper) to make the list look longer – had been received with great acclaim. After *1. Manet,* and *2. Bellum,* there'd been *3. Euphorbia griffithii* and *4. Lilium candidum,* followed by all the others, enough to fill every conservatory in the district, and bring about a glass-shattering plague of hay fever.

Ben, also, had gathered in a harvest.

(Come, ye thankful people, come!
Raise the song of harvest-home!)

The one disappointment in an invigoratingly brain-expanding weekend (Latin, Shakespeare, much praise from Mama for his performance as Octavius, much – he'd been quite right about this – repeating of "Let me hear you again!") had been with the falsely alluring promise held within the sixth book of the New Testament. After church yesterday, he and Mama – it was something they always did when Papa was not around – had reread the text that had been taken for his sermon by the Reverend Goodchild during one of his early guest appearances as a preacher at All Saints'. Not all Trojan horses were made of wood; not all Trojan horses unleashed fire and swords. (*Go unto this people, and say, / Hearing ye shall hear, and shall not understand; / And seeing ye shall see, and not perceive: / For the heart of this people is waxed gross:* that had been the choice. The Acts of the Apostles – Chapter XXVIII, Verses xxvi–xxvii – had received the usual Goodchild pummeling.) He and Mama had decided – Mama was a daringly advanced freethinker – that, even with St. Paul in the vicinity, these words had not been chosen for the sole purpose of describing Longfellow Park and its inhabitants. Once the Reverend Goodchild had been laid low, Ben's attention had wandered idly across to the next page of the Bible, and – a little leap of his heart – had noticed the importantly capital-lettered name of the book that followed The Acts of the Apostles.

ROMANS.
ROMANS!

An impressive list of Latin already committed to paper (he'd spent *hours* in the graveyard), and here were – he checked hastily – *twelve* more pages (double-columned, small print) full of the alluring promise of even more Latin! He'd be writing out six pages, seven pages, eight pages, *nine* pages more of Latin: he'd be writer's cramped, writer's clamped to his pen with an excess of Sunday afternoon scribbling.

That's what he'd thought.

Huh!

What a disappointment Romans had turned out to be!

He spent hours after lunch in plowing through Romans (his furrows deep, though not straight, like the ones on his forehead, carrying the dictionary to and fro across the red and purple Brussels carpet to the Bible), to make the discouraging discovery that here were Romans with not one word of Latin between them, as far as he could make out. Say *"Post meridiem," "nota bene,"* or *"Quod erat demonstrandum"* (*et cetera*) to these Ancient Romans, and they'd stare uncomprehendingly, nudge each other meaningfully, make feeble excuses, and beat hasty retreats, breaking into a run as soon as they'd reached the door, *Dramatis Personæ* quite incapable of grasping the fact that they were performing parts in a drama.

There is none that doeth good, no, not one.

This was the sort of thing you got instead of Latin. Romans had a lot of worrying assertions like this in it, things that made The Acts of the Apostles appear positively jolly in comparison. *Their throat is an open sepulchre; / With their tongues they have used deceit; / The poison of asps is under their lips: / Whose mouth is full of cursing and bitterness: / Their feet are swift to shed blood: / Destruction and misery are in their ways.* If this wasn't enough in itself to finish you off (jolliness was in distinctly short supply, let alone Latin), there seemed to be a great stress on – he was conscious of sort of lowering his voice, even though he wasn't speaking out loud (it was the sort of word that seemed to demand such precautions) – *circumcision* in Romans.

For circumcision verily profiteth, if thou keep the law: but if thou be a breaker of the law, thy circumcision is made uncircumcision. Therefore if the uncircumcision . . .

That sort of thing.

He'd never *seen* the word written down so much in all his life. He wasn't entirely sure what it meant, but he didn't like the sound of it. It somehow sounded like a Brinkman or a Swartwout sort of word, a word seldom spoken without the accompaniment of sniggering. It was linked with garters and drawers and tits. *That* sort of word.

Another walk across the room to fetch the dictionary.

Mama was in the back parlor with Mrs. Swartwout.

It should be quite safe.

An attempt to look casual, a swagger to his shoulders, a (failed) reach to slide the book off the shelf without really looking at it. He'd debated about employing a light-hearted whistle, but decided that it might draw attention to what he was doing, and forbore.

Mama and Mrs. Swartwout, summoned by the whistling, would scurry into the room and catch him at it, seeing the telltale blush of the sinner.

Aghast mouths.

Pointing fingers.

Circumcision verily profiteth.

Circumcision is made uncircumcision.

Therefore if the uncircumcision . . .

Garters.

Drawers.

Tits.

On a Sunday.

(*Circumcision.*)

A pause before the plunge.

(*Circumcision.*)

The plunge.

cir-cum-ci-sion, *n. the act of circumcising [O.F. circumcisiun]* . . .

Cir-cum-ci-sion.

He felt like a tiny boy again, just learning how to read, when all the syl-la-bles were sep-a-rat-ed like that.

"Jack, Jack, look at the rab-bit!"

He heard his mama's voice saying those words over and over to him at bedtime on the times when she was able to come to his room, her fingers indicating the words as she read them out to him, his fingers stroking at the appealingly soft-looking ears of the illustration of the rab-bit at which Jack was being implored to look. When Mama read the words he could feel the warmth of the fur, the pulsing blood beneath – that's what words could do – but when he touched the picture, all that was there was paper.

Always this disappointment.

That was reading for you.

He seemed to have spent the secret times of his early childhood (some of them) in being urged to look at the rab-bit with Jack, and his mama had always sounded really excited when she read it out to him. Learning to read – like (later) reading itself – was something that had to be kept secret from his father. That was what it had felt like, a whispered concealment, a sense of something suspect in literacy.

Jack, Jack, hide the rab-bit.

(Sometimes, after she'd read this story to him again – just before she blew out the candle – she'd make rab-bit shadows on the wall with her hands, wiggling the rab-bit's ears, twitching the rab-bit's nose to make him laugh. "Ben, Ben, look at the rab-bit!"

(That was what she did when Papa was not in the house at bedtime.

(Alice would be in the front parlor, reading.

(Edith and Allegra would be scurrying up and down the stairs, quarreling with each other, seizing an opportunity to make some noise.

("Shh!" Mama would call out to them sometimes. "Shh!"

(Alice, Edith, Allegra.

(But Mama was with him.)

Ben would lie there in bed, watching the tall rab-bit's head-shaped shadows — alert, inquisitive — watching from the wall beside him. Sometimes, he'd be so convinced by the shadows that he'd turn to see the baby rab-bit that he thought his mama was holding in her hands, though he didn't tell her this. After Mama had kissed him and left the room — door slightly ajar, a light left on in the corridor, the smell of just-extinguished candle in the air — he'd reach up to touch the place where the rabbit had been, and all that was there, just as happened with the book, was the feel of paper under his fingertips.

"Oh dear! Oh dear! I shall be too late!"

That's what rab-bits said.

He felt for the ears, he felt for the whiskers.

Nothing but paper.

Too late.

"Jack, Jack, look at the rab-bit!" were the very first words that Ben ever remembered being able to read, though they had not been of great practical use in his life so far. It was a long academic haul from "Jack, Jack, look at the rab-bit!" to the rather more worrying, if exclamation-point-missing *cir-cum-ci-sion*. (No exclamation points, but the bold type seemed to flaunt in its indelicacy, bawling out a dirty word in church in its loudest voice.)

Cir-cum-ci-sion.

The act of circumcising.

Hmm.

Not what you'd call a terr-ib-ly in-form-a-tive def-i-ni-tion.

What was it that they were trying to hide?

Slight increase in heartbeat.

Perhaps *O.F.* was Latin. It was an abbreviation, so it was clearly virtually halfway to being Latin.

Eager search in the list of abbreviations at the beginning of the dictionary. *O.F.* was between *O.E.* and *O.H.G.* He was virtually trapped in his chair when he opened out the dictionary on top of the Bible, his circulation stopped by the hard-edged spines, the sheer *weight*, of the books. His toes would be turning blue.

Droop to shoulders.
Not Latin.
And, even worse than that.
Old French.
That was what was meant by *O.F.*
French.
Slight pinkness about the cheeks.
It was becoming worse all the time, but he couldn't stop himself.
He knew where he had to look next.

> **cir-cum-cise**, *v.t. to cut off the foreskin as a religious rite* . . .

Increased pinkness.

Even though he was alone in the parlor, he curled his hand secretively around the column he was reading, the gesture of one hiding the answers to a test from an angled-over cheating classmate. Faintly, he heard Miss Augusteena's voice in the Sunday-school. Faintly, he heard Brinkman sniggering – *"Look at this bit! Look at this bit!"* – grubby index finger jabbing at the juicy gobbets.

It got worse..

> **fore-skin**, *n. the fold of skin covering the end of the penis* . . .

Pinkness deepened to redness.

Redder and redder the cheeks.

Bluer and bluer the toes. They'd be dropping off, frost-bitten in the snow-bound sinfulness that stretched alluringly in front of him.

He couldn't *stop* himself.

And it was *Sunday*.

The search for Latin inevitably led to decadence. That was Mrs. Albert Comstock's opinion on the matter.

Cursing and bitterness.

Destruction and misery.

To be on the safe side, he placed the Bible on the table, so that he was not holding the Bible and the dictionary in his lap at the same time, pinned down helplessly as GOD unleashed his fury. The Reverend Goodchild left you in doubt about how tetchy and malicious GOD was most of the time, filling all the boredom of eternity with spiteful smitings to keep himself entertained in various colorful and inventive and painful (to those smitten) ways. Reverend Goodchild was all for GOD doing this, and never failed to comment approvingly when something nasty happened to someone in the Bible. He and GOD were great chums.

pe-nis, n. *the male organ of copulation [L]* . . .

Redder and redder.

Bluer and bluer.

Blue certainly seemed the right sort of color for the paper-trail he was now following, haring and hounding after the forbidden, head poised to hear the tally-ho cry of the hunters.

He knew what *[L]* meant.

[L] meant Latin.

He *had* found a Latin word, but he did not feel particularly triumphant about this fact. Was it a Latin word he could ever admit to knowing, an acknowledged part of his vocabulary, a word he might actually be known to *speak?*

You could quite understand why it was placed within square brackets in this context – there was something no-nonsense and firm about *square* brackets – though they did make the word rather taboo and touch-not. These last were two expressions that began to make him feel increasingly uncomfortable the more he thought about them.

Taboo . . .

Touch-not . . .

He'd feel far worse if he worked out why. He was quite certain about that. He shifted in his seat awkwardly, the warm buttery taste of his dessert pie-crust quite banished from his mouth, trying to think of something else. Only *one word* of Latin! And that one word was a word he could not possibly – he now decided – ever admit to knowing.

He knew what was going to happen on Monday.

"Ben and Franny have exactly the same number of Latin words!" Dr. Crowninshield would announce, after the words had been totaled. Ben had decided that Franny — with the eager assistance of his papa — might be capable of topping even Oliver's tally. "They have far more words than anyone else in the school! Far more words than I ever thought possible!"

Pause.

Breathless excitement.

"Whichever one of them gives me another Latin word first will be the winner! He'll be able to wear the gold star all this week!"

(And all next week.

(All *month*.

(Forever.

(Mama would . . .)

"The first Latin word! Just *one* word! Franny?"

Silence from Franny.

Agony from Ben.

"Ben?"

"Ennis."

A dormouse squeak.

"Ben?"

"Ennis."

Communication was hampered not only by the fact that Ben's whisper was almost inaudible, but also because he was under the impression that "penis" was pronounced "pennis."

"A little bit louder, Ben, please."

Agony.

"Pennis."

"A little bit louder."

"*PENNIS!*"

"Pennis . . .? Pennis . . .?" Dr. Crowninshield mused, half-suspecting that this was a tip-of-the-tongue Latin expression that he really ought to know, one most probably connected with something that you found in a garden, something to do with gazebos or belvederes. All the names of flowers in Frankie's list had entered his head, and all he could see around him was an Eden-like garden, in which – without his having realized – the subtle serpent had started to unloose its coils. "Hiss! Hiss!" from the serpent. You imagined a boa-constrictor, something that crushed.

("There's my pennis!"

(Mrs. Alexander Diddecott spun round in her garden, briskly indicating something in the distance with her earth-coated trowel, almost decapitating a low-flying dove as it made its final approach to the dovecote.)

Dr. Crowninshield's face assumed its make-a-quick-decision expression as he tried to work out what on earth was meant by *PENNIS!*, the expression that was shortly to develop into his entreating "Help from on high!" expression, his "*Auxilium ab alto!*" invocation when Latin began its irresistible advance throughout the school.

"Could you explain what that means, Ben? It's not one that I've come across before."

And . . .

Pause.

"The male . . ."

Pause.

"The male or-gan of cop-u-la-tion," Ben would have to reply, if he was to be in with a chance of a perpetually shining gold star. He'd have to say it a-little-bit-louder-Ben-please, a-little-bit-*louder*, in front of the whole class.

Ben shuddered.

It was bad enough when it was Olly's parrot squawking out the mucky words, with that unmistakable note of distinct enthusiasm.

Doc-tor Crown-in-shield would not re-spond with much en-thu-si-asm to such bra-zen bran-dish-ings.

It was bad enough with the mucky-minded Brinkman and Swartwout, but you, *you*, as well, Ben? That would be the sad, unspoken accusation. (*Et tu, Ben?*) This Lat-in was the statue of Olly's papa with the exposed buttocks and bosom, ghastly and gigantic for all to gape and gag at.

This was Lat-in with a too-tight toga.

This was Lat-in with a too-short tunic.

Dr. Crowninshield would not let in this Lat-in.

He'd slam the door in its face.

He'd banish the menace of pennis.

Only one word — one *unusable* word — of Latin! He'd spent *hours* looking! It had been an exhausting weekend. And that dictionary weighed a ton. Back and forth he'd toted it. *And* the Bible. He'd be bulging with manly muscles on Monday. Latin and muscles: that would be him.

He listened carefully.

Mama was still in conversation with Mrs. Swartwout, who was really very nice, despite being the mother of mucky-minded Chas Swartwout. Who was Ben to accuse others of being mucky-minded, poised as he was between *pen-is* (he hastily stifled the bold print with his thumb to suppress the shouting) and — he knew it had to follow — *cop-u-la-tion?* (Another hastily applied stifling thumb.) Mrs. Swartwout had brought him a miniature mint walking-stick, striped like a barber's pole, and he'd been using it as a sort of ruler to hold under the words as he'd read them. All the dirty pages in the dictionary would be smelling of mint, exposing his dirty dabblings to all seekers of sin. Specially trained bloodhounds would be brought into action, nostrils honed to a peak of physical fitness, missing nothing sniffable. They'd be exhaling with noisy sounds of doggy disgust, fluttering all the thin pages. He began to sniff at the *pe-nis* (a wince as if the word had shouted) page. Betrayed by minty muckiness! He couldn't distinguish whether the minty smell was from his fingers or from the page, and began to lick his fingers, hoping to remove all traces of dubious behavior. Mrs. Swartwout was *very* nice. This was one of the many puzzles in Ben's mind, the fact that nice parents could have awful children, and that awful parents could have nice children. Awful parents and awful children — the pattern adhered to so religiously by the Brinkmans — seemed so much more as things ought to be, so much more comfortingly pedigree and distinguished, so much more Darwinian and the Law of Nature.

Another sniff at his fingers.

Still the smell of mint.

Another sniff at the page.

Mint.

Mama and Mrs. Swartwout were not discussing The Acts of the Apostles. Mrs. Swartwout was experiencing difficulties with her dahlias. An intense conversation was taking place, in which Mama (repeating a tip from Frankie Alloway's mama) appeared to be recommending, with considerable fervor, the generous application of well-rotted manure in vast undulating piles. Chestnut Street was a hotbed of controversy that Sunday. Front parlor or back parlor, saucy topics abounded.

cop-u-la-tion, *n. sexual intercourse, coition*

Redder and redder.

Bluer and bluer.

Toes would be dropping off like well-ripened blueberries. He could munch upon them as he browsed through the more unsavory pages of the dictionary, leaving appropriately colored telltale fingerprints to mark his promiscuous progress up through the fruit-laden branches of the Tree of Knowledge. It was more like a forest than a single tree. He really, really couldn't stop himself. **Co-i-tion** beck-on-ed, and it was not calling with a quiet voice. He didn't like the sound (the clamorously assertive cooee! sound) of **co-i-tion**; there was something peremptory and bossy about it. Caution with **co-i-tion**! That was his motto. He began to turn back the pages to earlier in the dictionary, hefting the volume up from his knees. His arms would be *aching* on Monday. He didn't really feel strong enough to tackle **sex-u-al in-ter-course**. He didn't really feel that he could face that one.

. . . shall not his uncircumcision be counted for circumcision? And shall not uncircumcision which is by nature . . .

He'd felt safer with Shakespeare on Saturday, and thought back again to Mama's comforting words of praise.

"That was nice and loud, Ben!"

That was one of the things she'd kept repeating.

"That was nice and clear, Ben!"

That was another.

"That was *very* dramatic!"

All afternoon, she'd been full of praise.

A weekend of praise from Mama.

A weekend without Papa.

This happened sometimes, the days become red-letter days, highlighted in his mind like saints' days in almanacs, days of feasting.

Together, in the front parlor, they'd gone through every one of Octavius's speeches. He didn't really have all that many speeches — nothing at all, really, when compared with Brutus or Mark Antony — and (this was quite a relief) he had none of the long, long declamatory utterances that they seemed to favor, but it was a *really* important part.

That's what Mama had said.

Vital.

She'd said that as well.

Octavius didn't appear until Act Four, but his late entrance meant that he could make a *tremendous impact* when he eventually appeared, and Ben was all in favor of making a *tremendous* gold-star-worthy *impact*. Mark Antony had talked about Octavius at the end of Act Three, when a servant came in to announce that he had arrived in Rome. "He comes upon a wish." That's what Mark Antony had said. "Bring me to Octavius." He'd said this, also. This showed how important Octavius was. Mama had explained how the words ought to be pronounced, so that he'd be able to create a sensation and make a gold star within his grasp. He'd been awarded a gold star on only one occasion, a year ago, when he had developed an intense, fleeting, interest in writing poems about the sea. Papa had soon put a stop to that nonsense. ("Show me your gold star again, Ben." He'd heard that sentence a lot from Mama during the week that he was wearing it.)

He'd certainly needed help with the pronunciation. "Proscription." That was one of the words Octavius had to say in his first scene. "Conspirators." That was another one he said later. Really hard words. Were these words written down to be read from a book, or were these words that people had once actually chosen to speak out loud, making up the sentences as they went along, as if they were buying a bun at Washington Thoroughgood's?

"That was nice and loud, Ben!"

"That was nice and clear, Ben!"

"That was *very* dramatic, Ben!"

"'One out of many!'" Dr. Crowninshield was repeating after them. "And here are those very same words on Linn's dollar!"

Bradley was more drawn to the reverse side of the coin, you could tell.

In God we trust.

That was more the sort of message that spoke to Charles Bradley.

And – a great point in its favor – it was in English. He nodded his head in vigorous approval – hoping for witnesses – as he read the words between the eagle's outstretched wings. In God he trusted, and – he was quite confident about this – God trusted in *him*, relied on him in a manner that was a touching testament of faith. God would struggle to manage without him. That was what he thought. He and the Reverend Goodchild grappled for God's undivided attention.

Me first!

Me first!

They leapt up and down in the air and wiggled their fingers so that they'd be seen, avid for gold stars from God. He'd pluck them from the heavens, and personally pin them – still warm – upon their proudly inflated chests.

"I'm so glad you're here!" God would be saying, a great weight lifted from his troubled brow. "There's something that's been worrying me . . ."

"Calm down," Bradley would say, with patient understanding, "take a deep breath, speak slowly. Don't worry."

It would be such a *relief* to God! The Reverend Goodchild, driven mad by jealousy, would be cramming his own beard into his mouth with the air of a desperate man for whom life had lost its purpose.

Ben — as his personal Latin possession — had brought in the framed Pinkerton coat of arms that Linnaeus had drawn for Alice, *a rose gules, stalked and leaved, vert* (this description, in itself, verging on the Latin-like), with the Pinkerton motto (in *genuine* Latin) neatly printed beneath. He'd wrapped it in a pillow sham to protect it, folded elegantly like pretty paper around a birthday present, and Dr. Crowninshield had expressed as much delight as if it had been a gift just for him.

Post nubila sol.

Ben had traced his finger along the words with a certain sense of proud possessiveness.

His family motto!

In *genuine* Latin!

After clouds, sunshine.

That was what it meant.

It linked up nicely with Mrs. Alexander Diddecott's sundial, and the Latin motto there. He'd gone especially to look at it with Oliver, and they'd peered at the pigeon-droppings-coated stone of the rim, digging in with their fingernails, picking away at the encrusted layer as if working at a scab.

Horas non numero nisi serenas.

I remember none but bright hours.

Oliver had worked out what it meant, and they'd paused for a while at the ingenuity of these words on a sundial, feeling superhumanly brainy, though there'd been few bright hours *that* cold, wet weekend.

More clouds clearing.

More warmth.

More sun.

He felt on the very verge of chatty articulateness when it came to Latin (which was more than he'd ever felt about speaking English).

Give him a charioteer, a gladiator, or a centurion, and they'd be greeting each other like long-lost friends. Clouds, they'd be talking about; sunshine, they'd be talking about. Things like that. If the weather cooperated there'd be no shortage of conversation. If Alexander Diddecott could get through life by talking about nothing but the weather, then so could he.

He had his motto, and Linnaeus had his silver dollar.

Linnaeus really did believe that his silver dollar was lucky, and held it to reassure himself when he felt nervous. The coin was smooth and shiny — Liberty's features blurred by years of weathering. (You thought of clouds again when you thought of the weather that had surrounded Linnaeus throughout his life, dark clouds that threatened. You thought of downpours and coldness, Linnaeus's profile dimmed and unrecognizable after years of rainfall, smudged like Liberty's.) The details of her hair were quite rubbed away — worn by much worrying — and it possessed a satisfying weight and solidity. You imagined Linnaeus closing his eyes, and holding onto this weight, anchoring himself. Brinkman had made a pounce for it at the end of the day, but Dr. Crowninshield — even though he had had *his back turned to them* — had quietly said, "Remember what I told you on Friday, Sid. 'I'll be *delighted* to see your papa if he'd be good enough to call in to see me. I have seen far too little of your papa, and I've a great deal I'd like to discuss with him.' That was exactly what I said, and what I said still holds. I have an *excellent* memory for remembering what I've said, particularly when I *really* mean it."

It had all been spoken in an unemphatic, conversational sort of way. The italics had barely slanted.

Brinkman had slunk off without another word.

When Dr. Crowninshield said "Do this," it was performed.

John Drinkwater — they'd been keen to suggest further sources of Latin — announced that Miss Peartree had sung a song that had sounded *just* like Latin the last time he had been to an "At Home" at Olly's mama's. (People tended to refer to Oliver's house as "Olly's mama's," even when his papa had still been alive.)

"*Latin?*" Dr. Crowninshield had queried. He was not convinced.

"Latin. I'm *sure* it was Latin. It was from an opera. She said so." He thought for a while, and then clarified matters. "She said that last bit in English."

"It was probably in Italian, in that case, John, I should imagine. Opera tends to be in Italian rather than Latin. Can you remember the tune?"

John quailed slightly, suspicious that he might be requested to sing the song he'd heard. He began to wish he hadn't been quite so keen. ("Why don't *you* ever get a gold star?" his papa had been asking him, with nudging insinuations in his voice.)

No. He couldn't remember the song.

"But," he added helpfully, "she sang it *really* loudly."

She always did.

Those of a fragile constitution, or those possessed of any æsthetic sense, would be strongly advised to leave the room, to leave the *building*, before Mabel Peartree let rip. Old-timers braced themselves in positions that reduced the possibilities of permanent damage, and avoided sitting near large areas of glass.

"Perhaps," Frank Bradstone suggested, "you could ask Miss Peartree to come and sing her song for us here." Miss Peartree, as they all knew, was so keen to sing in public that she'd have performed outside Comstock's Comestibles, advertising the latest bargains in cheap sausages. She was, she liked to suggest, a true *artiste*, possessed totally by the power of her God-given talent. You went right off God sometimes, even without Bradley being around.

"*Gosh!*" Oliver exclaimed. "Miss Peartree singing *here*, in front of us, *close up!*" He looked at Dr. Crowninshield. "We'd have to lash you to the mast, Dr. C., so that she doesn't lure you toward her!"

This was a distinctly saucy comment. Mabel Peartree was no siren. She was a lady of a certain age, and of quite startling plainness. Flocks of birds, open-beaked with horror, would abruptly veer off sideways if they caught sight of her in front of them, and nervous horses reared and bolted. If the homesick Ancient Romans had been joined by crowds of homesick Egyptians – *Antony and Cleopatra* following *Julius Cæsar* – the Egyptians would have tearfully greeted the sight of Mabel Peartree's nose as an eye-misting misspelled *momento* of the land from which they were estranged. "The Great Pyramid!" they'd whisper sentimentally to each other in Egyptian (an even *more* exotic language than Latin, and one unlikely to yield very long lists in Longfellow Park) indicating the opera-singing Miss Peartree's monumental olfactory organ. (More *factory* than olfactory, one with gigantic sooty-bricked chimneys, casting vast shadows to blight half a landscape, and belching clouds of sooty black smoke.) "The Great Pyramid!" They might have been standing outside Twelvetrees & Twelvetrees on Hireling Road as Mabel Peartree breezed past in pursuit of a new hat, but in their hearts they were back in Giza, hearing the rustle of the Nile's breeze through the palm trees, the plash of disporting crocodiles. Well-wrapped mummies would twitch inside their multi-bandaged cocooning as the Great Pyramid sashayed past, its hands clutching a prominently displayed book of sheet music.

I'm Mabel Peartree! I sing songs!

That's what she was hopefully promoting to all potential members of an audience, parading up and down advertising her wares like the Oldermann & Oldermann sandwich-board man.

Particularly To Be Recommended For High-Pitched Shrieks!

That would be her alluring siren song.

"Give us a song, Mabel!" you'd find yourself unwisely requesting. And Mabel would give you a song. As Mrs. Goodchild had thoughtfully remarked after one of Mabel's songs – every object in the room still vibrating, and Hilderbrandt lying inert at the bottom of his cage (it was like the scene of carnage in the aftermath of one of Chinky-Winky's more lethal unleashings) – "Once you've heard Mabel sing a song, you somehow never want to hear that song sung again." The more you thought about these words, the less they sounded like a compliment.

They watched Dr. Crowninshield's face closely as he considered the idea of Miss Peartree singing *here*, in front of them, *close up*, hoping to detect signs of revulsion. He'd *definitely* faltered slightly – they'd *all* faltered, and not all faltering had been slight – at the thought of her singing in Italian, *really* loudly. They'd tried repeatedly to trap him into passing slanderous comments about some of the more stomach-heave-causing grown-up inhabitants of Longfellow Park – thus breaking the worrying solidarity of adult-hood – but he proved adept at evading all their artful wiles, and annoyingly incorruptible. Even when (like Harry Henderson) they cunningly brought the name of the Reverend Goodchild into a conversation, it failed to elicit encouraging signs of censure, though you could tell that Dr. C. was sorely tempted to tell them what he *really* thought of that bubonic-plague-breathed baboon, that bottom-scratching barbarian. (They'd memorized some of Oliver's more evocative descriptions, and derived great comfort from them, in the way that the faithful repeated certain prayers in times of trial.)

"You could always lash *us* instead, sir, if you preferred."

"Yes, you could do the lashing, sir," Charlie Whitefoord suggested. "You could be the one to lash us all to the mast." ("Sirs" and "Dr. C.s" – their weapons of politeness – were often also brought into play as ruthless tools of beguilement.)

"And when you'd lashed us, you could *lash* us."

("Lash" had a puzzling number of possible meanings.)

"You could lash us *really* hard, sir."

(Oliver again, offering an added inducement.)

"Well I can't say I'm not tempted," Dr. Crowninshield admitted.

"We'll pour wax into *your* ears, sir."

"We'll melt some candles down especially, sir."

"So *you* wouldn't have to listen, sir."

"If you wish, sir."

"*We'd* be the ones who'd listen, sir."

"Unless you'd regard that as pearls before swine, sir."

"*Honk, honk!* sir."

They'd read *The Odyssey* before *The Adventures of Tom Sawyer*, and were keen to demonstrate their familiarity with Homer. After they'd read Homer – beguiled by his wine-dark linguistic repetitions – they'd developed a taste for describing Oliver as "Oliver of the slim ankles," and Frankie as "Frankie of the white arms" after the descriptions of Hebe and Nausicaa. ("Brinkman of the tit-spotting" hadn't featured in *The Odyssey*, but this also had become a popular usage – Nausea, rather than Nausicaa – a small act of literary homage to Homer, one of a number, so readily might schoolboys be nurtured into a sensitive literary response by a gifted teacher.) They'd also been particularly struck by some of the gruesome details in Book XXII, when Odysseus had set about the suitors, relishing the deaths with the keen critical eyes of connoisseurs. Antinous' end – an arrow through his neck, his final convulsions knocking the table back and jerking the food onto the floor, blood spurting thickly out of his nostrils – had drawn much approving comment. ("Euch!" was high praise in this context.) Even better – "Euch! Euch!" – was the death of Eurymachus (Eury to his chums, they speculated), when Odysseus' arrow went into his chest beside his nipple, and lodged into his liver (this last phrase a convincing demonstration of the pleasures of alliteration: "Lodged into his liver! Lodged into his liver!" they'd chanted with incantatory relish). As if this wasn't enough, Eury then squirmed and thrashed across the table, beat his head against the floor in agony for a bit, and *writhed* his legs about. Euch, *euch* for Eury! It was nearly as good as the death of Jezebel.

For several worrying weeks, the chiropodist and the optician had looked out disapprovingly from their respective windows – drawn from their chaste grapplings with corns (the chiropodist disturbed in mid-pour from his bottle of The Great Russian Corn and Bunion Exterminator, $1.68 per dozen bottles) and myopia (Mr. Brczin barely able to hear his patients' tentative readings from the sight-test: "*A* – er – *H* – er, er . . ."; God, it got boring) by unignorable shrieks from beyond the railings – to see massed Odysseuses and Eurys hoisting up shirts in search of nipples (the mention of a nipple had somehow made this death particularly commendable) before enthusiastically unleashing the final fatal wounds upon the correct location. It was important to get these things right. Some of the more ambitious boys made pillows out of their rolled-up jackets so that they could beat their heads against the floor in comfort. Shrieks became even more piercing, and heels drummed in competitively prolonged death throes. Oliver – *Oliver* he became for a while ("Lodged into *Oliver*! Lodged into *Oliver*!") – was incomparably Top Eury when it came to Euch-inducing, and had briefly sported a target painted on his chest, with his nipple as the bull's-eye, in a commendable attempt to encourage Odyssean accuracy in his eagerly competing assassins. Judging by the prolonged death cries, you'd have thought that a dentist had established a practice alongside his professional compatriots, and it was a noise that would not have increased the confidence of ner-vous bunion nurturers. Rail, rail, beyond your railings, ye men of Indian Woods Road, but consider yourselves lucky that the death of Melanthius (dragged through the court, nose and ears lopped away, his privates ripped off, and fed raw – little, fastidious shudder on *raw* – to the dogs) was tactfully omitted from the edition of *The Odyssey* that had so inspired the Crowninshield's boys. The sight of massed Mels being dragged to their deaths – all those barking, sali-vating dogs slobbering and crunching! – would have put paid to the more genteel patients in no time. *Raw!* Carriages would have been reversing back all the way to Park Place.

It was Frankie who made the "pearls before swine" comment, thinking of Circe, and becoming confused.

Bradley winced. ("Matthew, Chapter VII, Verse vi," he mut-tered censoriously, thinking really loud pious thoughts so that God could hear them.)

"I have decided, after long and agonized thought," Dr. Crowninshield had informed them, when he'd first introduced *The Odyssey*, "that we'll study Homer in translation, rather than the original Greek."

The Odyssey had then been placed triumphantly in front of them. They'd been really impressed.

"'On first looking into Dr. Crowninshield's Homer,'" Oliver had commented when they had opened their ancient translations, blowing off the dust and making each other sneeze histrionically. It was like being trapped in a desert sandstorm. Very atmospheric. This was the first time that Ben remembered hearing a reference to Keats's poem. It was probably the first time he had heard a reference to *Keats*. He'd learned many of the words he knew from hearing Oliver say them, though usually his new words tended to come from reading. Most of the inhabitants of Longfellow Park – with the suicidally experimental exception of Mrs. Goodchild (conversations with Mrs. Goodchild verged on the incomprehensible once she ventured beyond three syllables) – seemed to confine themselves to short, simple words, most of which they could spell, and conversations held few challenges.

"Can *you* speak Greek?" Brinkman had asked, just as he'd later asked, "Can *you* speak Latin?"

This time the answer hadn't been "Not a word!" because Dr. Crowninshield *did* know a word in Greek. *Several* words. Small Latin, but more Greek. That was Dr. Crowninshield. "*Eureka!*" he'd demonstrated. *Just* the right choice of word in the circumstances. "*Acropolis! Amphora!*"

"*Halvah!*" Petteys – whose parents were fearless in their choice of restaurant – had added. "*Baklava!*" The blackboard became unusually exotic in its vocabulary. They'd rather liked the sound of *baklava*. Nuts and honey! Frankie Alloway, who thought that this last word was "balaclava," rather boggled at the Greeks' oddity of diet. It quite put him off any idea of wandering about in the footsteps of Odysseus. The thought of chewing wool always set his teeth on edge. Throughout their reading of *The Odyssey* he'd pictured Odysseus and his companions with their heads incongruously enclosed in thickly knitted balaclava helmets, with just their eyes showing, like a muffler-wrapped Oliver in cold weather. Whenever Penelope had a breather from her tapestry, she obviously leaped upon her knitting needles and set them rattling. The men's hearts would sink as another heavy parcel arrived, and they dutifully drew on another layer of helmet just to please their leader. Sweat dripped down and darkened the wool in the hot Greek sunshine. What daft things to wear. Unless they were a sort of disguise to confuse the hazards that beset them in their epic voyagings . . .

Frankie put his keen, analytical brain to work, keen to clarify this enigma of the balaclavas.

Eureka.

Acropolis.

Amphora.

Halvah.

Balaclava.

He listened hungrily to the words, hoping for a glimpse of wine-dark sea, gods and goddesses come to earth amidst them.

Bradley – with an eagerness that suggested he'd waited long for this perfect moment – produced the copy of the Reverend Henry Belcher's *Greek for Christians* that he'd brought in to show to Dr. Crowninshield. He was not shy in soliciting favorable comment. Always quick to sense when he was being summoned to a higher calling, he had been – he made it perfectly clear – drawn to the Hellenic promise of heaven in that title, and quick to purchase a copy when he'd noticed it. The alphabet, he had to admit, was going to prove something of a problem – like the Chinese and the Japs, like the Arabs and the Indians, the Greeks, for some reason, had not chosen to express themselves (it was clearly some sort of code) in a *proper* alphabet – but the road to salvation was beset about with difficulties. They would make victory all the sweeter, a *Pilgrim's Progress* of a journey to eternal salvation.

"*Alpha,*" he pronounced ostentatiously, making sure that everyone could read the title. He held it in the way that Mabel Peartree held her sheet music, propped up in front of him for instant access. *Alpha.* You might as well begin at the beginning. He'd heard of *alpha.* His brother Edward was in Year Two (*alpha*) at Otsego Lake Academy. *Alpha* sounded real, almost convincing as a language. "*Beta, gamma, delta* . . ." He'd also vaguely heard of these before, but found it hard to be persuaded that some of the purported later letters of the Greek alphabet were really authentic. *Omicron? Sigma? Upsilon? Psi?* He wasn't really convinced by these (*Psi?*) though just saying some of the letters to himself several times, somehow created an atmosphere of exclusivity, the high thin air of rarefied academic distinction. ". . . *epsilon, zeta, eta, theta* . . ." (These three rhyming alleged letters in a row was pushing credulity a little too far, he felt. He didn't believe in them one *iota*.)

"Greek is the language in which, *before all others*, God chose to reveal His . . ." – he made quite sure that they were all fully aware that he had utilized a capital letter at this point – ". . . will to us," Bradley informed them all piously, rather giving the impression that God had informed him of this fact personally, popping in for a little chat before he released the information for the consumption of the general public. He inserted his irritating wheedling tone into his voice in the hope that they'd lose control and thump him and make him feel martyred.

"Gosh!" they muttered politely, at appropriate moments, sounding impressed, rather putting paid to his visions of unparalleled self-sacrifice. Dr. Crowninshield laid great store in their being kind to each other, and they tried hard to remember this. They sometimes felt at their most Christian when Bradley held forth, some minion of Satan sent forth to test their faith. Bradley would not have been encouraged by this analogy.

"It is the language of the New Testament. No other language will ever express the meaning of God's Spirit . . ."

("*Gosh!*")

("*Gosh!*")

". . . as it may be seen to be expressed and known by those who read the New Testament in its original Greek."

(People like *me*.

(That was the unspoken – but unmistakable – emphasis. *He* was the one who'd be reading the New Testament in its original Greek. He would soar to Homeric heights, far beyond *Eureka, acropolis, amphora, halvah*, and *baklava*. *Baklava* was undoubtedly a useful word, but – however much you liked nuts and honey – of limited

259

usefulness when it came to discussing the mysteries of Faith. Admittedly, he'd still got quite some way to go – *kappa, lambda, mu, nu, xi* – but in no time at all he'd be whipping into *The book of the generation of Jesus Christ, the son of David, the son of Abraham. Abraham begat Isaac; and Isaac begat Jacob* . . . – whatever that might be in Greek – with as much gusto as if he was launching himself into the latest issue of *St. Nicholas.*)

"The English tongue *totally fails* to express God's Spirit."

(Time for another "*Gosh!*" at this point. Bradley would wait for it, rather pointedly, and they'd *Gosh!* away, hoping that Dr. Crowninshield was taking note of their saintly forbearance.)

Bradley and God would be chattering away to each other with the unselfconscious ease of two old chums, heads inclining close together as the anise-flavored liqueur flowed freely. The Reverend Goodchild would be gnawing his knuckles with jealousy.

Half a dozen of the boys – others with older brothers at Otsego Lake Academy – had flourished copies of *Latin for Schoolboys,* another of the books written by the Reverend Henry Belcher, attempting to trump Bradley's ace. It wasn't quite the right language for Homer, but showed willing. This did not impress Bradley, who could quite easily have brought in Edward's copy of the book. ("It's Latin!" he'd exclaimed, a rather redundant observation in view of the book's title.)

The same boys – more successful the second time – produced the books again with triumphant flourishes on the Monday morning after the introduction of Latin. Linnaeus' silver dollar, Ben's coat of arms, and six copies of *Latin for Schoolboys.* That Monday had been a day of Latinate luxuriating. Greek was for Christians, and Latin was for Schoolboys. An interesting distinction. You gained the impression that the Reverend Henry Belcher had struggled to make himself heard as he attempted to achieve a modicum of good behavior from his charges during Sunday-school.

"Dr. Crowninshield's choice of reading-matter is *eclectic.*" This had been Oliver's comment after *The Adventures of Tom Sawyer* followed *The Odyssey,* and there'd been a distinct *click* as "eclectic" entered Ben's memory. He'd looked it up in his *Griswold's Discovery Dictionary (Discover How To Increase Your Vocabulary!)*, and it had taken ages for him to find it because he thought that it was spelled "eklectic." It sounded stirring and modern, something vaguely connected with electricity (and far, *far* safer than "cir-cum-cise," "fore-skin," and "pe-nis"). This was one of the surprisingly few occasions when he could remember a new word first registering, though these occasions tended to be *click*, Oliver!, *click*, Oliver! sorts of occasions. It was odd that you could rarely remember the first time you heard certain words, words such as "lackadaisical," "tatterdemalion," or "humdrum," words that entered your memory and stayed there. You'd think that this would be the sort of thing that you'd remember.

They weren't sure whether Dr. Crowninshield was following some profound philosophy of Literature (*definitely* a capital "L" here) in his choice of texts, nurturing a race of child geniuses, or whether they were reading the only books he happened to possess in sets. Oliver had insisted (with his usual air of having received reliable prior information) that *Julius Cæsar* (place your bets now, he'd urged them) would be followed by one of the following: *Sanskrit For Beginners*, *Diseases of Live Stock*, *Elsie Dinsmore*, or *Poor Boys Who Became Famous*. "What a challenge to us chaps!" he'd declared, sounding quite keen. Personally, he rather favored the Sanskrit, though Brinkman sneered that *Elsie Dinsmore* was probably the *very* sort of book that Comstock read all the time. Frank Bradstone was really keen on the idea of *Diseases of Live Stock*. Here was *real* Literature! You could forget that *Odyssey* rubbish! Cows before classics. That was the Bradstone philosophy. No wonder his uncle's bulls were frou-froued about with red rosettes. Horned long-lashed faces emerged flirtatiously above the decorations with moo-moo moues, like those of provocative can-canning coquettes, flourishing their luridly colored underwear on enthusiastic public display.

Julius Cæsar had, in fact — by popular request — been followed by *Coriolanus*, when Dr. Crowninshield informed them that

Shakespeare had written *other* plays swarming with Ancient Romans. They'd so enjoyed killing their headmaster the first time that they wanted to do it all over again. Dr. Crowninshield was able to find only about a dozen copies of the play, and they had to share them between them, but that was a mere detail when they were being offered the enticing prospect of bloody murder (though their enjoyment was a little tempered when they were informed that – this time – it would not be their headmaster that they would be murdering), and a few more words of Latin. They'd be sharpening all their rulers in readiness, the nearest thing to a Woodcraft lesson that Crowninshield's had to offer. There, in the very first scene, as if they'd never gone away, was the same unstable, mutinous Roman mob – "Barabbas! Barabbas!" (muted, in the distance, different words in a different language) – that had appeared in the first scene of *Julius Cæsar*. You could see Frank Bradstone – rather dashed at the lost opportunity of studying *Diseases of Live Stock* – working himself up to asking the important question that haunted all farm-boys faced with *Coriolanus*: "Are there any cows in it?"

It was such a shame that they'd never read as far as Act Three, because (Oliver had pointed out) it contained good news for Frank Bradstone. There – at long last – amidst all the mentions of horses, dogs, sheep, camels, crows, eagles, wolves, and tigers (Shakespeare rather gave the impression that Ancient Rome was a Noah's Ark heaving with animals, the Colosseum crammed for a spectacular day of sport), Frank would have found the word "calved," and the word "herd." (*Twice.*) "*Calved!*" he'd have been repeating delight-edly to Frankie Alloway, on his left, besotted by calf love, prodding it with his stubby finger just to make certain that it was there. "*Herd!*" Frankie – always pleased by the pleasure of others – would have beamed encouragingly. It wasn't much, but it would have been better than nothing. It improved things no end when you had a calf to cling to.

Mabel Peartree and lashings.

Lashings and lacerations, then lashing down.

They'd need plenty of ropes.

They might have to utilize all the rigging from the ship, cutting it all down to leave the masts bare.

Their ship would be left at the mercy of the elements, buffeted by the winds and the tides, drawn into dangers, all its mariners lashed to the mast (they'd be crammed in several bodies deep) and helpless, all the oars abandoned, hanging uselessly in midair, swaying like storm-lashed saplings. Dr. Crowninshield, ears crammed with candles – it would have taken them far too long to melt the candles, so they'd just shoved a candle into each ear so that he looked like an elaborate Renaissance candelabra – was deaf to their warning cries, far too busy in leering at the seductive vision of Mabel Peartree erotically arranged on the rocks ahead of them, her nose a come-hither lighthouse luring them to a watery grave. He nodded his head from time to time, faintly hearing her *Cooee-Big-Boy!* blandishments, and the ends of the candles wobbled.

Did they face Charybdis and Scylla before or after they'd faced the sirens?

Not much chance of surviving either of those two if the candles and the lashings remained firmly in position.

There was never a dull moment with Odysseus, once you'd got past that first section.

"I'll supply the ropes, sir."

(Frank Bradstone. The ropes would smell of cows.)

"Miss Peartree wouldn't take much persuading, sir."

"She'd be over like a shot, sir."

(A shot was sometimes the very thing you longed for, once Mabel Peartree started up, and escape was impossible. All decent-minded members of the public deplored the sight of dumb animals in obvious pain.)

"What song *did* Miss Peartree sing?" Dr. Crowninshield asked Oliver, apparently starting to weaken, tempted by the idea of lashing them to the mast *really* hard with the hairy cow-stained cords. If he sprinted up the road to All Saints' – he could be there and back in no time – he could scoop up a good supply of candles for the purpose of deafening . . .

(Was he calling their bluff?

(Slight signs of unease in some of the more delicate members of the class. What if they really *did* have to listen to Mabel Peartree in front of them, *close up*, all the Roman columns tugging at their thumbtacks as she hit the high notes? Sometimes you could see her back teeth, the gold glinting like ore secreted in a deep mine, dangly bright ropes of wet spit, and you got *sprayed*. It was nearly as bad as it was on a Sunday, when the Reverend Goodchild got going on the sinners. It would be *awful*. Unease began to build up to panic.)

"It was an aria from Bellarossallini's *Il Idioti di Brinkmani*, Sybili's lament at the death of Alberti. It is extremely moving. Handkerchiefs may be required." He began to sing complete gibberish, with utter conviction, as Brinkman — totally missing the *Brinkmani* reference because it had been pronounced with such assurance — rolled his eyes in a what-did-I-tell-you? meaningful manner. Ben recognized the melody. Dubious though the words were — and you could guarantee that some of the words would have set his mama's fan fluttering if she'd heard them clearly — Oliver was undoubtedly singing the same aria (Italian, not Latin, this word) that Mabel Peartree had recently chosen. It had been something to do with sleep, Ben vaguely remembered, not that there was any possibility of sleep when *she* got started. Most of the class seemed fairly convinced of its authenticity — gibberish, Latin, Italian: it was a fine distinction, as far as most of them were concerned, they were all as bad as each other — and John Drinkwater looked gloomy. If only he'd had the nerve to leap right in like Olly Comstock, and not think about what Brinkman might say. That elusive gold star could have been within his grasp. Dr. Crowninshield, a great lover of music, listened like one rapt, occasionally joining in. Most of the class — as if it were the most natural thing in the world, and with perfect politeness — firmly pressed their fingers into their ears and looked apprehensive. It was what they always did when Mabel Peartree let rip. You cleared your throat, you blew your nose, you braced yourself against something substantial, and you took precautions to block out all sound.

264

"One of my favorites!" he declared, when Oliver had finished. "And so well sung!" (Snigger from Brinkman.) "The *ne plus ultra* (Latin) of singing. Thank you for clarifying the matter, Olly." Dr. Crowninshield turned to John Drinkwater. "Just as I suspected, John. It's *Italian*, and not Latin. Sadly, we cannot add that to our list of Latin. Miss Peartree will not be performing for our delectation, much as we'd like to hear her."

(Phew!

(That had been close!)

"Unless you all insisted, in your ceaseless quest for culture? I could always contact Miss Peartree, and I'm sure that . . ."

No!

(The first panicky refusals employed italics.)

No.

(A more dignified response followed shortly.)

No *thank you*, Dr. C.

They did *not* insist.

It was then that he taught them the one Latin verb he knew. He'd researched it especially for their educational benefit, he informed them, and chalk scratched once more across the blackboard. They'd have to raise the fees before much longer, the amount of chalk he got through in a week.

He soon had them chanting, and feeling clever.

"*Amo!*"

"*Amas!*"

"*Amat!*"

"*Amamus!*"

"*Amatis!*"

"*Amant!*"

Latin verbs!

"I love! I am loving! I do love!" they chorused, keen to demonstrate their emotional generosity, their capabilities for affection. *Amo* meant all three of these declarations! Some of them stressed the "do" quite defiantly, as if someone had doubted their abilities for loving.

"Thou lovest! Thou art loving! Thou dost love!" That was *amas.*

"He, she, or it loves! He, she, or it is loving! He, she, or it does love!" His, her, or its love-embracing all-inclusiveness was loudly declaimed.

"We love! We are loving!"

"Ye love! Ye are loving! . . ."

It was as satisfying as reaching twelve-twelves-are-a-hundred-and-forty-four without making a single mistake. The conjugation — the word had something arithmetical about the sound of it — made flamboyant use of "thou" and "dost" and "ye," to stress its Shakespearean respectability, its close approximation to the language spoken by the *real* Julius Cæsar, the multi-stabbed *Et-tu-Brute?* Julius Cæsar. You could guarantee that the *Brute?* — though Frankie Alloway was under the impression that the murdered statesman (and quite right, too) was denouncing Brutus as a brute because he'd stabbed him — instead of *Brutus?* would be something to do with grammar. Grammar always did daunting things to foreign languages (grammar was daunting enough with *English*); they'd already grasped this much.

Then it was time to reveal more of their discoveries in their search for the Latin that lay everywhere about them. *Delirium tremens* (rather worrying, this) from Chas Swartwout. (They'd heard some of the comments about his papa. Chas also contributed *in flagrante delicto*, and you couldn't help worrying about his home-life. He was clearly *in medias res* when it came to family drama.) *Noli me tangere, Gloria in Excelsis Deo*, and *Consummatum est* were three of the phrases that Charles Bradley had remembered from the Bible. There had been no searching through the Bible to find them — he had made this quite clear to them — these were words that had always been at the forefront of his consciousness, up there with "Good morning," "Hello," and "A second helping, please." Miss Augusteena would have been proud of her star pupil's ever-more-rapid ascension to the star-spangled skies. *Ex libris. Pax. Carpe diem. Non compos mentis.* (Brinkman, accompanied by a leer at Frankie Alloway. "I thought you'd know that one, Sid!" Dr.

Crowninshield had said briskly, in his usual encouraging way, but his tone of voice hadn't quite suited Brinkman. It had made him sound *persona non grata*. Latin!) *Urbi et orbi*. (Frank Stoddard.) *Et in Arcadia ego. Magna est veritas. Cogito, ergo sum.* (Philosophy slotted in smoothly between Geography and Arithmetic at Crowninshield's.) *Amor vincit omnia. Vade mecum. O tempora! O mores!* (There was a great deal of *O! O! O!*) *Reductio ad absurdum. Bona fide. Sui generis.* (This from Frankie Alloway. "It means 'one of a kind,'" he'd added, his gold star conferring strange powers upon him. "My mama says that I'm *sui generis*," he'd added, rather proudly, and Brinkman – busy brooding over *non compos mentis* – had missed an excellent sneering opportunity.) *In vino veritas.* This was one of Oliver's. "How decidedly verging-on-the-controversial of you, Olly. I do hope it's not an insight drawn from personal experience," Dr. Crowninshield commented, writing it on the blackboard with the translation. *In wine is truth.* Censorious little hiss from Charles Bradley. He just couldn't stop himself. "'Be not drunk with wine.' Ephesians, Chapter V, Verse xviii." "Proverbs, Chapter XXXI, Verse vi," Oliver retorted instantly. He could almost always cap one of Bradley's quotations, giving rise to much unChristian fuming. *Veni, vidi, vici.* They came, they saw, they conquered, and Latin fell helpless before them. *Deo volente.* The blackboard filled, clouds of white dust rose, enveloping the front row. Hugh Petteys, John Drinkwater, Tom Akenside, and William French needed to be dusted down after a hard day's teaching, like carpets slung over a clothesline.

Finally – *tempus*, as it tended to do, *fugit*ing – they'd had to hurry through their discoveries from All Saints' graveyard, the words that they could speak in the language of the dead. Damp from drizzle, they'd wandered amidst the Pinkertons and the Comstocks and the Finches of the past, all the families who'd lived in Longfellow Park before them. They hadn't shirked their search of the gravestones, even though it had been a raw day. They were words that they were reluctant to say out loud, in case the dead heard them – they hadn't forgotten *momento mori* – and it took Dr.

Crowninshield considerable prompting before their findings began to spread across the blackboard like another – class-sized – tombstone. In a florist's shop sort of kinship, the names of the flowers in Frankie Alloway's list were followed by the results of his graveyard gleanings, but – sadly reducing his final total somewhat – they turned out to consist mostly of some of the more unusual names borne by past residents of Longfellow Park. If he didn't know the word, it was probably Latin. This had been the grand plan (*one* of his grand plans) to make his list longer.

R.I.P.

He'd got that one right, however.

(The Ancient Romans' fondness for abbreviations even extended to tombstones. Breath was short in death, and it was a way to say much in little. That was their theory.)

Requiescat in pace.

(That was what it was short for.)

May he rest in peace.

(That was what it meant.

(That was an easy one. *Rest In Peace*. The Latin abbreviation precisely suited the English words, though *peace* wasn't the word that came to mind amidst the dark, rain-soaked stones. Nor was *rest*. Fifteen years later, the graves would all be dug up, and the bodies disinterred, as All Saints' was sold and demolished.)

The Romans had lined the roads out of Rome with the tombstones of their dead, that was what Dr. Crowninshield told them, and they pictured columns, urns, huge monuments like triumphal arches, all of them inscribed across with words in Latin, words that the dead could understand, with travelers moving to and fro between them. To enter the heart of the living, you had to penetrate the resting-places of the dead.

In memoriam.

There'd been a lot of this one, comfortingly familiar from memories of a book of poetry.

Mamas – it had usually been mamas – would take down the book, with its frontispiece engraving of (you might have guessed!)

a man with a beard, and start to read aloud, whenever an impulse to improve the cultural opportunities offered to their families seized them.

"... Ring out, wild bells, to the wild sky ..."

– they'd begin (this passage was a popular choice; you heard the voices in chorus) –

"... The flying cloud, the frosty light:
The year is dying in the night;
Ring out, wild bells, and let him die ..."

You couldn't get very far away from dying if you came across the words *In memoriam*, that much was clear.

In perpetuo.

Not so many of this one.

Hic iacet.

This one was *everywhere.*

"Here lies."

("Just like you, Dr. C.!")

("My brave boys! Jesting in the face of death!")

They weren't very keen on the thoughts inspired by this one, despite Olly's joke. They'd been *very* careful not to step on the graves with this inscription.

Most worrying ...

Most worrying of all ...

There had been ...

Resurgam.

I shall rise again.

This was the grave that they had treated with *especial* caution.

This was the only legible word on a weather-beaten gravestone – all other words weathered completely away into crumbling – in a dark corner of the graveyard, under a yew tree. On a gloomy February day it had been enough to send them scurrying home to warmth and light, feeling that they were being pursued by something to which they could not give a name. They didn't rest entirely in peace that day.

I shall rise again.

("Euch!" from Olly.)

Another blackboard full of Latin. Another frenzy of cleaning, and Hugh Petteys, John Drinkwater, Tom Akenside, and William French vanishing in clouds of white dust, so that they themselves looked like Roman monuments amidst the graves and all their inscriptions.

Dr. Crowninshield couldn't get enough of Latin, once he'd got it started.

It filled a real need, one that he'd never realized had been there all the time. As usual, he became competitive with them, trying to beat their totals by bringing in new examples of Latin that he'd discovered. You imagined a family confabulation each evening – Dr. C., Mrs. C., and Allie C. (carefully propped up) sitting around the table like generals making a battle-plan – and Dr. C. informing Mrs. C. and Allie that Frankie Alloway's mama had been assiduously searching in her gardening books again. There was no holding Frankie when a gold star was on offer. "Twenty-three new phrases today!" he'd be informing them. "That's the total to beat! Any suggestions? You first, Allie." Dr. C. clearly had his heart set on a Friday afternoon when Mrs. C. would come into the classroom, and pin the gold star to *his* chest. "My clever husband!" she'd exclaim proudly.

Whenever his mind went blank – a regular occurrence, he cheerfully admitted – he would screw up his eyes, a man in prayer or pain, and (in the spirit of an invocation) chant *"Auxilium ab alto!"* It meant "Help from on high!" and Dr. Crowninshield invested it with all the agony of a desperate appeal to hostile gods.

"Auxilium ab alto!" they started to repeat out loud to themselves, as they labored over some task – if it was good enough for Dr. Crowninshield, it was good enough for them – and their parents would be baffled. This was a further reason why the expression

recommended itself to them. They felt quite wise when they saw the *alto* part of this written on the blackboard. *High* voices were *alto* voices. They recognized the linguistic link. (*Click!*) Their alto voices linked them with the skies, where the gods lived. They competed with each other to sing the sentence in the highest possible voice. "*Auxilium ab alto!*" they'd shriek, Frankie Alloway threatening the windows, and setting dogs howling three streets away. "*Auxilium ab alto!*" Oliver's mama didn't like the sound of it *at all*. *Latin!* Nearly as bad as *French!* Even worse – the beginnings of panic – when you considered the *religious* implications! Oliver used Latin a lot in the vicinity of his mama, considerably more than was strictly necessary. You wouldn't put it past him to invent words that sounded vaguely like Latin, just for the pleasure of increasing his mama's pulse-rate to a pounding *patter-patter-patter*, and seeing her go purple.

On dark, unilluminated days Dr. C. tended to exclaim "*Fiat lux!*" ("Let there be light!") or "*Spero meliora!*" This last was his response to an especially dreadful piece of work from someone.

"I hope for better things!" the class would translate, for the benefit of monolingual passers-by in the street outside.

"Much, *much* better things!"

Sometimes, when they surpassed themselves for dimness – no *lux* whatsoever, the entire planet dark and lightless – he'd mutter encouragingly to himself, "*Dum spiro, spero!*" (The *dum* part was a bit cutting for the more sensitive amongst them, and lips trembled.)

"While I breathe, I hope!"

"Very little breath! Even less hope at the moment!"

It was at one such moment – it was one of the days on which they were toga-clad – he'd paused with an expression of beaming pleasure. It was a day on which "*Spero meliora!*," "*Fiat lux!*" and "*Auxilium ab alto!*" had been flying about with particular fluency.

"How *on earth* did we ever manage before we learned Latin?" he mused, and it didn't sound like a rhetorical question. Then he added, "*Docendo discimus!*" helpfully translating, as he wrote it on the blackboard. "We learn by teaching!"

"We learn by teaching!" the class chorused, well drilled in its response.

"*I'm* the one doing the teaching around here!" Dr. C. corrected them firmly. He then added, not quite so firmly, "Unless I'm the one doing the *learning*. I know it's one or the other. It's *definitely* one or the other. Er . . ."

They tried to comfort him.

"*Errare humanum es*, Dr. C.!" they chorused. "To err is human!"

"Er . . ."

"Er . . ."

"Er . . ."

3

Now here they were at Otsego Lake Academy.

(Latin and Greek at Crowninshield's! Otsego Lake Academy should hold few fears for them.

(But it did.)

To err was human, but all that they could think about was erring.

"Er . . ."

"Er . . ."

"Er . . ."

That would be them at Otsego Lake Academy, struck dumb because they were guilty of being human, and all lined up for vigorous chastisement.

Beware! Beware!

That was what Oliver had been chanting back down the icy corridor that stretched emptily away in front of them. Down that way they'd walked.

The satchel had spun round and round on the end of its strap as Oliver pranced balletically around them, demonstrating – as he expressed it – his natural sylph-like grace.

"Do you think we'll know enough Latin?" Linnaeus asked. This was clearly one of his chief anxieties about what would be expected of them at their new school. Could they speak the language? Did they have it in them to become men? He'd brought his lucky silver dollar with him, the one that had pleased Dr. Crowninshield so much. It had accompanied him to all his new schools, and he was planning to show it to his Latin teacher, hoping that *E PLURIBUS UNUM* might forge a linguistic link between them. Ben didn't think that Mr. Rappaport would respond to such overtures. He *knew* that Mr. Rappaport would most definitely *not* respond, but he didn't like to say so.

It was nearly time to go inside, and join the others.

"'It fills me with grief and misery to think what weak and nervous children go through at school – how their health and character for life are destroyed by rough and brutal treatment,'" Oliver quoted zestfully from *Tom Brown's Schooldays* with crisp patrician precision.

"Oh!" dolefully from Linnaeus, not encouraged.

"Every medical man knows the fatal effects of terror, or agitation, or excitement, to nerves that are over-sensitive." By now, the quotation marks had disappeared. This usually happened with Oliver, as the words from books became the words he himself spoke, seemingly for the first time. It became impossible to tell the difference after a while.

("Oh!" again from Linnaeus. "That really, *really* helps, Olly!"

(Terror.

(Agitation.

(Excitement.

(It was not a night-before-Christmas sort of excitement, even with the presence of new-fallen snow.)

Oliver had his eyes set on the position of George Arthur for himself, lying – saintly and fragile – beside an open window, with the rays of the sun stealing in gently and lighting up his white face and golden hair. Thomas Hughes had showed remarkable restraint in allowing George Arthur to survive the fever. He was more tender-spirited than most novelists, whose flinty little Dickensian bosoms were usually made ruthless by the irresistible appeal of a dying child. This was a surprise, considering his get-up-and-whack-'em leanings, his biceps-pulsing position as one of those muscular Christians all lined up like a rugby team going into the attack. Oliver had read the description of his chosen rôle aloud to Ben. "'A slight pale boy, with large blue eyes and light fair hair, who seemed ready to shrink through the floor.' The resemblance to me is positively uncanny! I don't recollect ever being introduced to a Thomas Hughes (he may have been at one of Mama's "At Homes"), but he has captured me here to the *life!*" Hmm. Oliver was a boy who would – you could guarantee – *never* be ready to sink through the floor. He'd rip up the floor, and beat you about the head with it first, singing something sprightly as he did so.

"I'm a bit worried about the Latin," Linnaeus admitted again. "Latin and Sport." This was not the sort of thing he would have said in the hearing of Brinkman. He'd looked carefully behind him before he'd said it. It was as well that Linnaeus was unaware that Mr. Rappaport was to be their teacher for both these subjects. Linnaeus was *completely* unaware of Mr. Rappaport, and Ben hadn't had the heart to warn him of what was lying in wait for him. *Tom Brown's Schooldays* – Oliver had given a thrilling account of the novel to Linnaeus after their tour of the school two weeks earlier – conjured up a picture of swarming crowds of schoolboys battling to the death with sports equipment. The last thing cricket-bats were for was playing cricket, it appeared. In the hands of Rugby boys – the very name of their school a defiant assertion of aggressive sportsmanship – cricket bats, wickets, fives balls, the entire contents of stripped-bare gymnasia, were potential weapons waiting to be zestfully employed in pitched blood-spurting battles. This was not the sort of thing designed to appeal to Linnaeus. It must have been the illustration of the aftermath of the football match in Chapter V that had given him cause for concern, Tom slumping down unconscious as white-clad figures crowded in around him. Perhaps it was this very *crowding* that most disturbed him. It was just the sort of thing that made him become anxious.

"*Cricket,*" he said, closing in on a specific concern. Not football, after all. (This mention of football was a little confusing. You'd have thought that they'd have called it *rugby* at Rugby.) Linnaeus was very worried about *cricket*, a new language as daunting as Latin, and one never spoken by Dr. Crowninshield, who was more of a baseball and lawn tennis sort of a chap. He'd somehow formed the impression – his attention must have lapsed at a vital moment during Oliver's account of boarding school life – that cricket was a compulsory activity at Otsego Lake Academy, even though it wasn't a boarding school.

Oliver, whose depths of research were astounding, explained cricket to Linnaeus.

"It's sort of like baseball," he said. "But not *very* much like it."

This didn't appear to comfort Linnaeus very much. He'd formed the opinion that it had sounded more like fencing.

"Not *very* much like it," he repeated, committing it to memory in preparation for a test.

"You wear white. You stand about in white, a bit like Druids, though you worship willow instead of oak. *Willow, titwillow, titwillow! . . ."* – he sang this last bit – ". . . You hit a ball with a bat. You run."

"Oh," said Linnaeus, doubtfully. The mention of Druids hadn't inspired confidence, though the part about running probably appealed. *Willow, titwillow, titwillow?* Brinkman would have sniggered at the "tit" bit. Tits always had him tittering.

"That more or less sums it up. Wouldn't you agree, Pink?"

"Couldn't be clearer," Ben agreed, completely baffled.

"I doubt *very* much that cricket will feature on the agenda. Did you notice any mention of cricket equipment on your list?"

(Otsego Lake Academy had supplied each boy's parents with a dauntingly long list of *Essential Clothing and Equipment for New Scholars*. The cash registers at Oldermann & Oldermann must have been red-hot. No wonder Mr. Oldermann & Mr. Oldermann looked so sleek and prosperous, and Mrs. Oldermann & Mrs. Oldermann were so weighed down with jewelry.

(*Scholars!*

(As Oliver had said, thinking of some of the pupils from the academy, you had to laugh.)

"No."

Linnaeus brightened a little.

"Any mention of *one cricket bat*?"

"No."

"Any mention of *one cricket ball*?"

"No."

"Any mention of *one brightly colored cap with peak and tassel*?"

"No."

"A pity. I quite liked the sound of that." The illustration of George Arthur sitting cross-legged (*Turkish fashion* was the phrase employed) on the grass at the edge of the cricket ground during the cricket match in Chapter VIII of Part II of the novel ("Tom Brown's Last Match") showed him transformed into a Slavic-featured youth dressed in rather exotic Russian-looking clothing – you felt that he should have been grasping a *balalaika* instead of a cricket bat – though the cap that he was wearing notably failed to feature a dangling tassel. Tom Brown, sitting on a bench in front of him on his last day as a schoolboy, was resting his arms on his knees, his bat clasped horizontally in front of him, his fingers curled around its edge, gazing down at it in a worshipful sort of way, investing it with a sacerdotal significance. Cricket was really serious, that was quite clear. Though he was playing cricket rather than boating, he was wearing a boater, not a cap. Perhaps Oliver had read about the tassels somewhere else, or perhaps he just liked the idea of having one. He'd toss his head, and the strands would flare up like a horse's mane. It would add a pleasing emphasis to the utilization of italics. In two or three of the illustrations some of the schoolboys – it was clearly a particularly aristocratic sort of a school, almost the equal of Otsego Lake Academy – were wearing tall silk hats, young gentlemen on the point of stepping from a cab outside an opera house or approaching the venue for a fashionable *soirée*. You'd have thought that these might have appealed to Oliver. You could just imagine him languidly strolling into a classroom wearing the tallest of silk hats. "Any mention of *very, very white trousers*, and *very, very white shirts*?"

"No. Not really."

"Well, then . . ."

Another worry.

Linnaeus always seemed to need a worry.

"That Latin lesson."

(Ben.)

They were all rather worried by the description in the novel of the Doctor's behavior on examination day.

A boy – a boy *connected* to the Doctor – had read out eight or ten lines of Latin, and then had been asked to construe it. When he made a mistake, the Doctor – the saintly, great-hearted *Doctor* – had taken three steps up to the boy (they imagined him running full-pelt, his arms swiveling like a windmill's sail, the wind positively *whistling*, rather in the way that Oliver had sprinted to hurl himself upon his sword when he'd been Brutus) and boxed him on the ear, so that the boy fell backward onto the floor!

This was Latin for you!

This was what Latin lessons would be like!

Proper Latin lessons!

The most worrying feature of this scene was that the boy's mistake – he had translated *triste lupus* as "the sorrowful wolf" – seemed perfectly correct to them, an impeccable rendition of the Latin. They'd discussed it at great length, but had been unable to think of what it ought to have been. Even Oliver hadn't known. This one hadn't turned up at Crowninshield's.

Latin – they had decided – was going to present them with very particular problems. How right they were.

At the far end of the ice corridor, they could see Bradley beginning to run toward them, slithering on the hard-packed snow.

"Wait . . .!" he was calling to them faintly. "Wait . . .!"

"*And* they're pretty beastly to chaps who pray in public," Oliver added, his mind still on *Tom Brown's Schooldays*, his vocabulary as impeccably researched as if he'd polished up his French phrases for a holiday in Paris. "Big brutal fellows throw slippers at you, and call you a sniveling young shaver." It was a struggle to picture Oliver praying in public. He indicated the schoolboy panting nearer. "We shall have to haul Bradley upright if he ever starts to go down on his knees, even if he resists. He's *bound* to resist." (How on earth would Bradley be *able* to spurn the opportunity of a martyrdom so conveniently on offer?) "We Crowninshield's boys must demonstrate our mutual support, to help us gain strength and survive the ordeal that lies ahead of us!"

"All for one!"

(Ben.)

"One for all!"

(Linnaeus.)

"*Tous pour un, un pour tous!*"

(Oliver – in uninhibitedly bilingual form – keen, as ever, to go that little bit further. It was a pity that his mama was not within hearing. He utilized the French language as a convenient and economical method of agitating her into appalled wobblings, discordant disapproving squawks.)

"*E PLURIBUS UNUM!*"

(Linnaeus again, ensuring that he said it in capital letters, to make it stronger. He held his lucky silver dollar out in the palm of his hand, and they all removed their wet gloves and touched Liberty's well-worn coiffure, young warriors swearing an oath of loyalty before they went into battle.

("Olly!"

("Pink!"

("Linn!"

(This was another *All for one, one for all* ritual, each in turn repeating his name, proudly defying the malignity of the gods. Liberty would protect them! There they stood, high in the air above Bedloe's Island, godlike, looking out across the sea through Liberty's eyes, the uplifted torch illuminating all that was around them.

(*Fiat lux!*

(*Fiat lux!*

(*Fiat lux!*)

They checked their pocket-watches. It was time to go inside.

Linn began to recite to himself, invoking some protective presence with rosary-snapping insistence. It was like Frank Stoddard discreetly crossing himself each time he entered Crowninshield's, passing into the domain of Brinkman.

"*Amo, amas, amat . . .*"

". . . *amamus, amatis, amant,*" Oliver and Ben added, all-foroneing.

Liberty and Latin.

Those two should be a help.

They sounded like boys standing before the door of an examination room, convincing themselves that they knew what they ought to know.

"*Tempus fugit.*"

"Doesn't it, just?"

"*Horas non numero nisi serenas.*"

"If only!"

Oliver offered some final words of advice to Linnaeus.

"A great deal depends on how a fellow cuts up at first. If he's got nothing odd about him, and answers straightforward and holds his head up, he gets on."

"'Nothing *odd* about him'?" Linnaeus repeated mischievously, tapping Oliver in the chest with the rim of his dollar, and looking interrogative.

"You impudent young blackguard!" Oliver replied blithely, getting in another quotation, pushing open one of the double-doors, peering in like a dubious salesman. (Not much chance of a sale in this place!)

Linnaeus, *teasing*!

He was beginning to show signs of developing a whimsical sense of humor, and they were keen to encourage this. He had named Charlotte's two recently acquired kittens for her. One he named Douglas Robert after their veterinarian, D. R. Falkirk D. R.

Falkirk — judging by the initials of his Christian names, his parents had nurtured hopes of raising a physician in the family — had declared himself honored and delighted by this mark of favor.

"Douglas Robert has peed in Linnaeus's hallway again," Oliver grew fond of announcing to his mama, and a visible *frisson* would vibrate around the outer layers of her bulk as her imagination (an ambitious choice of noun in this context) raced to embrace the concept of this spectacularly misbehaving professional. (She wouldn't let him anywhere *near* her Chinky-Winky, a man whose manners demonstrably verged on the seriously unsatisfactory.)

This appealed to Oliver so much, that — you could tell — he wouldn't be content to draw the line at a Douglas Robert. He'd be acquiring pets — cats, dogs, any moving thing beneath the sun — and naming them after people in the neighborhood, just for the pleasure of announcing, "All the dogs have been sniffing Mabel Peartree's bottom again. I'll have to have her seen to. She bit Dr. Twemlow again yesterday," "Mrs. Goodchild is very constipated," "Mrs. Alexander Diddecott has worms," or, "I'm thinking of taking the Reverend Goodchild to Mr. Falkirk, to have him castrated." He'd be saying this last one a *lot*, and his mama would vibrate spectacularly.

The other kitten was named Fido, a satisfyingly canine choice of name for a feline, and also a choice that provided further evidence that Linnaeus was one of the select band of Crowninshield's boys, *all* of whom could speak Latin. "*Fido*" meant "to trust," "*Fido*" meant "to believe." It wasn't really the most appropriate name for a kitten that chose to join Douglas Robert in uninhibited peeing in hallways. Fido never displayed any signs of being worthy of the exemplary qualities embodied in his name, and would wander promiscuously after anyone who proffered a tempting tidbit.

"Wait . . .!" Bradley was panting, a little more loudly as he drew nearer. "Wait . . .!"

But they didn't wait.

One for all.

All for one.

But it *was* only Bradley, after all.

"*Exeunt omnes,*" Oliver said.

He paused dramatically at the entrance.

Another appropriate Latin expression had just occurred to him.

"*Ave, Cæsar, nos morituri te salutamus!*"

Small gladiators, men doomed to die, they saluted Cæsar.

It wasn't a terribly encouraging choice of expression, and Linnaeus groaned. ("Oh!" he'd soon be saying again. "That really, *really* helps, Olly!")

"*Ave, Cæsar, nos morituri te salutamus!*" was another of the expressions that had passed into common parlance at Crowninshield's, that lost paper-drawn quarter of Rome where Latin still lingered. Oliver had come across it again the previous week, kept indoors as the storm raged, when – risking brain-damage – he was rereading *The Curse of the Colosseum*, one of the Reverend Goodchild's more incompetent historical sagas. Whenever he felt a little depressed, and in need of an unsophisti-cated hearty laugh – you felt the urge to exclaim, "*You! Unsophisticated!*" to Oliver at this point – Oliver opened a volume from the Reverend Goodchild's *œuvre*. (You just *knew* that Oliver would insist on the employment of a ligature: *œuvre*, and not *oeuvre*; *oeuvre* would *not* have been acceptable to Olly.) It never failed to have the desired effect, usually within seconds, especially as the misprints (there were always numerous misprints) were unusually unfortunate in this novel. First *Tom Brown's Schooldays*, then *The Curse of the Colosseum*. This had been Oliver's technique for riding out the storm in a house crammed with Big Mama and Big Sis Myrtle, both of whom seemed to have expanded to fill the space left by Big Papa.

"*Dum spiro, spero!*"

(Ben, attempting to be positive.)

"I'm not sure that I *am* breathing," Linnaeus replied. "I'm *defi-nitely* not hoping much."

"*Post tenebras lux.*"

(Oliver.)

"After darkness, light."

(And Linnaeus seemed equally unconvinced by this.)

"*Auxilium ab alto!*"

Would there be – *mirabile dictu* (wonderful to relate) – help from on high?

In they went.

4

Their eyes took a little while to become accustomed to the gloom, and they began to make out the shapes of the Crowninshield's boys, grouped like stray sacrificial steers, lassoed and corralled by the headmaster's minions. They were rather disconsolately gathered together in one corner, fearful of attack, wary of venturing out into the cavernous central space. They were *huddled* – that was the word – waiting to find out what was going to happen to them. Ben, Oliver, and Linnaeus went to join them, and Bradley – gasping for breath – came in after them. They'd nearly all arrived by now. There was no sign of Frankie Alloway, but he was always late for everything.

The entrance hall at Crowninshield's had been smaller than the one in many of the boys' homes, but the one at Otsego Lake Academy was designed on a suitably intimidating scale. It was a scornfully look-on-my-works-ye-puny-and-despair sort of place, its general gloom making it seem even larger, but Oliver showed few signs of despairing. The whole of the echoing hollowness was deserted, with only the wet footprints of melting snow – leading left and right down corridors on either side of the double entrance doors – remaining to show that anyone had ever been there.

Intermittently, unexplained bells rang in the distance – they rang throughout the morning, throughout the day, their purpose never explained, signaling intelligence to some higher race of beings – and each time the bells rang, the boys froze a little, expecting that *this* time they might mean something, something would happen, someone would appear, and something unpleasant would inevitably follow. They half-felt that they should be genuflecting, displaying some appropriately reverent obeisance to all that the bells symbolized. Frank Stoddard, with his Corpus Christi years of training, must have forced himself to remain upright by sheer effort of will. All the walls were bare. It was like the antechamber to some austere ballroom in which music was never played, or a waiting room in a sanatorium high in the cool air of the mountains. Faintly, in the distance, there'd be the hollow sound of consumptive coughs, and there'd be white-clad figures lying on iron-framed beds in rooms with tall windows. They hadn't been counting on sumptuous feasts, and laughing crowds, bearing gifts, hurrying forward to embrace them warmly, but – still – it wasn't much of a welcome.

(*Beware! Beware!*

(These words came to mind again.

(Dr. Crowninshield had warned them about strangers, especially Greek strangers, bearing gifts. "*Timeo Danaos et dona ferentes,*" Oliver would mutter learnedly at this point. "Probably something to do with the Trojan horse. It *was* a Greek horse, after all, not a Trojan one.")

"We'll see a great many cruel blackguard things done, and hear a deal of foul bad talk," Oliver told them. "I'm *really* looking forward to it."

The linoleum floor was polished to a fearful shine, and the air was very cold. You'd have thought that the corridors, like the ice-cut corridors across the park, had been shaped out of packed snow, designed to lead them deeper into coldness. They were mirrored in such clear detail by this floor that they felt that they were being watched by their own reflections. This inhibited conversation, and what was said was whispered.

"I can *see* my breath!" Brinkman commented, slightly above a whisper to demonstrate what a big, tough man he was. His voice echoed, swallowed up and muted by the emptiness around them. Otsego Lake Academy went in for (voice deepens) *men*, not boys, and Brinkman was demonstrating that this held no fears for him. It wasn't surprising that he could see his breath. The way he munched on raw onions you could positively *see* his breath at all times, as you reeled away, choking. He'd guffaw, or make a crude comment, and he seemed to assume that the expression of agony on the recipient's face, the pale-faced choking, was a testament to the power of his biting wit.

Charlie Whitefoord gave them a wave, but didn't say anything. This was not a place in which you shouted.

They waited for a man with a list of names to come marching toward them, a bearded man with his papers rustling importantly, a man who – rather ominously – would call them out one by one, a man with withering comments. From beyond the double-doors at the far end of the entrance hall, opposite the entrance itself, there was the sound of other – more distant – doors opening, orders being given. They knew what was behind those double-doors. It was the main hall of the school, with its painted cupola beneath what Oliver had sardonically described as the "stately pleasure-dome," the most striking architectural feature of the building. It was two weeks since their tour of the school. The plan had been that they would have this, and then – one week later – they would begin at the school, easing their way in by attending it for the last two weeks of the Spring Term. One week later had, however, been the day that the blizzard had swept down, and all thoughts of school had had to be abandoned.

(They would have been abandoned, anyway, as far as Ben was concerned.

(It hadn't only been the week of the blizzard.

(It had also been the week . . .

(The week . . .

(The week . . .

(The week of Papa's death.)

It looked no different now from how it had looked on the day of the tour, the time when Papa had still been alive.

(You would imagine that the whole world would look different. But it was just the same, still as oppressive, as empty, as echoing.)

They'd been trailed around like tourists visiting Mount Vernon or the White House, and no attempt had been made – perhaps it was a commendable honesty, though it hadn't felt like that – to make them feel that what they would be coming to would be anything other than rigorous. It had been a Sunday – first the service in All Saints', then lunch, then Otsego Lake Academy – and there had been no pupils there. All the schoolmasters had been there however, loitering about, making no attempt to hide the fact that they were feeling distinctly peevish at being hauled in on a Sunday. They were what Ben had heard Alice and Charlotte referring to as The Bearded Ones, generally accompanying this expression with strange mocking hand-movements, as if casting a curse. The Bearded Ones gathered in groups on the fringes of the larger rooms, followed them in the corridors, looking, whispering comments to one another.

They weren't *quite* all bearded – there were one or two younger men amongst the staff (Mr. Rappaport was one of them; Ben had soon become aware of Mr. Rappaport's presence) – but the majority had the look of something out of the illustrated edition of *Idylls of the Kings* that he would be looking through again at Grandpapa and Grandmama Brouwer's house the following weekend, when he went to stay there with Mama, Allegra, and Edith. He'd liked the thought of being there for that weekend, the weekend before he started at Otsego Lake Academy, though he hadn't – in the end – started until a week after that.

Because of the blizzard.

Because of the other reason.

He always felt a sense of sinful disobedience as he read books – as he read *poetry* – at his grandparents' house, away from Papa, who seemed to avoid going there, and he *knew* that it was something of which he would scornfully disapprove. This was, most of the time, a part of the pleasure of reading. The four parts of the poem – "Enid," "Vivien," "Elaine," and "Guinevere" – all bore the names of women, but, in amongst the pictures of large-eyed damsels with flowing garments and flowing hair, there were the knights with their swords and their beards, both aggressively angled, both weapons with which to attack and defend. Not much chance of

Geraints, Arthurs, or Merlins at Otsego Lake Academy (and no chance whatsoever of lots and lots of Lancelots with this lot), though Mr. Rappaport – despite the lack of a beard – had obviously modeled himself upon Earl Doorm in his general demeanor.

Mr. Rappaport had been coming to their house for most of the previous week, to be given his instructions – this was Ben's interpretation – and to be told what to say, how best to mold an – er – unpleasing son into a more acceptable shape. Karin would answer the door, and Mr. Rappaport would be there, looking eager, waiting to be led into Papa's study to the right of the front door as he entered. You imagined him putting up his hand to answer Papa's questions. He had that sort of look about him. There'd be whispering behind the closed door for long periods, the sound of laughter. You couldn't help hearing, with the big gap between the floor and the bottom of the door. You could smell the cigar smoke. You could *see* the cigar smoke, see it uncurling in the colored beams of light shining through the glass panels around the front door. Ben had read James Fenimore Cooper, curled up in a chair in the front parlor, his fingers pressed into his ears. After a while, without realizing he was doing it, he removed his fingers as he became aware of nothing but the words he was reading, though he was not aware of reading words. The trackless forest was all around him. For miles and miles around him there was no one there.

Papa called Ben into his study, and the two of them were there.

"This is Mr. Rappaport, Franklin. He'll be keeping an eye on you at your new school."

This had not been said in an encouraging sort of way. It had been more like a warning.

Mr. Rappaport had looked down on Ben from his height, and had not seemed impressed. He looked like one of those tall young men who'd push past you on a city street, hardly seeing you, thrusting you impatiently to one side because you delayed his progress.

"*Both* eyes," Mr. Rappaport had said, and he and Papa had laughed.

Ben – oh hell, oh hell, *oh hell* – had blushed. He wasn't given to swearing – even within his own head – and the blush might have been partly caused by the oh hell-oh hell-*oh hell*, fearful that the two men could sense the words that he was thinking, though, seeing them as a promising sign of latent manliness, they would probably have been encouraged by them.

("Say 'hell' again, Franklin."

(*Rattle, rattle!*

("Say 'hell' again. Say it!"

(*Rattle, rattle!*

(The cigars prodded through the bars of the cage.

(There was a hiss as they caught at the feathers.

("Hell!" he said again.

("Say it again, Franklin!"

(This was Papa.

("Hell!"

("Say it again, Pinkerton!"

(This was Mr. Rappaport, taunting the parrot parrot-fashion. He looked at Papa for permission before the first time he did it, and then he didn't look for permission anymore. He'd look at Papa after he'd done it, to bask in Papa's approval, to share a smile.

("Did I do it properly?"

(That was the unspoken question.

("Was that good enough?"

("Will that do?"

("Do you approve?"

(Yes.

(Yes.

(Yes.

(That was the answer to all the questions.

(He did it properly.

(It was good enough.

(It did.

(Papa approved.

(It made Ben feel strange, to be called "Pinkerton" like that in front of his father.

("Hell!"

("Pretty Pinkie!"

(Papa.

(*Rattle, rattle!*

("Pretty Pinkie!"

(Mr. Rappaport.

(*Rattle, rattle!*

("Now for some other words for you to learn."

(Papa.

(*Rattle, rattle!*

("Stand up straight!"

(Mr. Rappaport, his Otsego Lake Academy training coming into action.

("Arms by your sides!" he'd be ordering.

("Keep right!" he'd be ordering.

("Follow me!" he'd be ordering.

(He wouldn't be saying "No talking!" because he wanted Ben to talk.

(*Rattle, rattle!*

("The first word is . . .")

Ben blushed deeper as the word occurred to him.

("Say it!"

(*Rattle, rattle!*

("Say it!"

(*Rattle, rattle!*

(Papa and Mr. Rappaport bared their teeth, and hissed out foul cigar-smelling breath between the gaps as they demonstrated the "f" sound with which the word began.

("F! Say it!"

("F! F! F!"

("F! Say it!"

("F! F! F!"

("F" was not for "Franklin."

(It was like a grotesque parody of *Baby's First Word*, one of Mrs. Alexander Diddecott's sentimental paintings, the father and mother – their arms linked around each other – bending over the cradle where their angelic-faced infant pouted out its lips to utter a word that was highly unlikely to have been the one so enthusiastically recommended to Ben to speak.

The thought made Ben's blush deepen even further.

(Coriolanus had blushed.

(The great Roman warrior was a man who blushed.

(This was a fact from which Ben sought to derive comfort.

(He'd have blushed even more if he'd been at school with Brinkman. Brinkman was a boy particularly blessed in spotting possibilities.

("Coriol*anus*!" he'd sniggered, as soon as the books had been handed round to the class – once more toga-clad in anticipatory relish – "Coriol*anus*!" Ben was glad that he hadn't been sharing his copy of the play with Brinkman, even gladder – for a whole variety of reasons – that it was Oliver playing the part of Coriolanus, and not himself.

("Brink*man*! Brink*man*!" That's what Brinkman could call himself, keen to demonstrate the proof of his impeccably masculine credentials. Coriolanus was Coriol*anus*, and Pinkerton was Pink*erton*, but Brinkman was ever and always – assume deepest, toughest voice for the last syllable – Brink*man*.

(Brink*men* were strong.

(Brink*men* were fearless.

(Brink*men* were manly.

("*Anus*!" he'd sniggered – strong, fearless, manly – as Oliver declaimed. "*Anus*!"

(Coriolanus' real name had been Caius Marcius, and when he'd returned from the field of battle after capturing the city of Corioli, the general had named him "Coriolanus" in memory of his triumph. "I will go wash," Coriolanus had said, "And when my face is fair, you shall perceive / Whether I blush, or no."

("*Anus! Anus!*"

(Well might Coriolanus blush.

(They had read no further than Act Two, Scene Two in

289

Coriolanus. A vague feeling that this should be written Act II, Scene ii, like one of Bradley's morally improving Chapter II, Verse ii sort of references, linking Shakespearean – it seemed entirely appropriate – with biblical usage, the shared "thees" and "thous" drawing them together in literary kinship. Menenius and the two tribunes of the people – confusingly, one of them was another Brutus, a Brutus stripped of all his nobility – were attempting to persuade Coriolanus to put on the gown of humility, and entreat the people to give him their vote.

("It is a part / That I shall blush in acting."

(That was what Coriolanus had said.

(Another reminder that here was a great and brave man who *blushed*.

(They'd reached this far in the play when Crowninshield's had suddenly closed. Their last day at the school hadn't even been at the end of a week, and they hadn't known, throughout that day, that it was their last one there. Somehow, it would have been nicer to have known that, to have been able to experience each thing for the last time knowingly, to have said their goodbyes.

(They all knew that Coriolanus was going to die, but they didn't know how it was going to happen. Oliver had told him how the play ended.)

He looked at Mr. Rappaport, saw Mr. Rappaport's meaningful look toward Papa.

(Coriolanus' little boy would rather see the swords and hear a drum than look upon his schoolmaster. He ran after a gilded butterfly; and when he caught it, he let it go again; and after it again; and over and over he came, and up again; caught it again, set his teeth, and tore it to pieces.

(That was one of his father's moods.

(He was a noble child.

(Ben had gained the impression that the little boy had ripped the butterfly between his teeth, feeling the tug of the wings tearing. If butterfly dust could blind you, could it turn you dumb if it entered your mouth, making you unable to speak as the dust – become a bitter gritty sediment as it mixed with your spit – gathered beneath your tongue? First the silence, the fighting to speak, and then – as you swallowed its poison down – death, the longer silence.

(Almost at the end of the play, and it had certainly spelled the end for Coriolanus, the little boy – with his mother and grand-mother – had been sent to plead with Coriolanus to spare Rome, his own city, the city he was determined to destroy with all its people, including his own family. Oliver had shown him this bit in his *Illustrated Complete Works of Shakespeare*. His family had kneeled before Coriolanus to beg for mercy, but the little boy had been defiant. His father was *not* going to tread on him!

("I'll run away till I am bigger, but then I'll fight."

(That's what the little boy had sworn.

(Marcius.

(That was the little boy's name.

(The same name as his father.

(He wanted to be more like Marcius, setting his teeth, tearing the butterfly to pieces.)

Papa and Mr. Rappaport were looking at him.

(*Then* I'll fight.)

His blush deepened further.

"See what I mean," Papa had said, speaking as if Ben wasn't there. He often did this. Ben felt that Papa would have *preferred* it if he hadn't been there. Papa had wanted a son – three girls in a row had been a depressing experience – but he'd wanted a *proper* son.

He wasn't a proper son.

"Quite a challenge!" Mr. Rappaport agreed.

"Look at this!" Papa said, a joke just that moment occurring to him, a spontaneous pleasantry to put a guest at ease, and pulled a brightly colored box from the top of the bookcase beside the fire-place. Ben recognized what it was.

"Please don't, Papa," he said, though he knew that it was too late, that his father was going to show it to Mr. Rappaport, that his plea would add to Papa's pleasure.

It was the box that had once contained his "My Brave Boy"

Mechanical Walking Sailor Boy, the one toy that his father had bought for him, though bought to entertain the father and not the son. The box, and what was written on it, was the source of the most entertainment, a cause of far more hilarity than the toy itself had ever been capable of producing.

"*Please*, Papa."

"Look at this!"

Papa leaned in against Mr. Rappaport, nudging him conspiratorially, in the manner of an intimate offering a surreptitious peep at something spicy, a recommended page – thoroughly satisfactory – in one of his dirty books.

("Page one hundred and sixty-three!"

("Page one hundred and eleven!"

("Page eighty-nine!"

("Page seven!")

Papa had tried and tested all the words of wounding upon Ben, and those that had worked best – blushes, tears (if especially effective) – were about to be passed on with enthusiastic recommendations. Mr. Rappaport took notes. He'd be making a list, with discreet little stars beside the comments to grade their efficacy.

I have a son who is prettier than any of my daughters.

(Five stars.

(*****)

Having girlie thoughts, Franklin?

(*****)

Overcome by girlie modesty, Franklin?

(*****)

What on earth can you be thinking, to cause that attractive *blush, Franklin?*

(*****)

Don't forget the smelling salts!

(*****)

And the others.

All the others.

Papa's pointing forefinger, moving as if he were attempting to scratch off some crusted stain with the edge of his nail, emphatically slid back and forth beneath a favored phrase. He tapped – wishing to ensure complete attention – and the sound was loud and hollow on the empty box.

My Brave Boy.

That was probably the first phrase he'd chosen.

(*****)

"My brave boy."

That was what Coriolanus had said to his son.

"Just look at *this*!"

(Papa, snorting with amusement.)

Tap, tap, tap.

He tapped his finger beneath the words he'd chosen, and then – flicking up that same finger – indicated Ben as he stood in front of them, his hands behind his back, his head a little lowered, like a boy called into his headmaster's study for reprimand.

My Brave Boy!

Franklin!

(Ben.

(It was *Ben*.

(It was *not* Franklin.)

Papa's face had the expression of a man who had just spoken the last line of a favorite joke to a sycophantic underling.

Laughter from Mr. Rappaport. He knew what it was that he had to do, what he was there for.

"I see what you mean!"

That went down in Mr. Rappaport's notebook in his neatest handwriting.

Another ***** phrase.

Tap, tap, tap.

Flick.

Laughter.

"How very apt!"

Another ***** phrase.

Tap, tap, tap.

Flick.

"That's a good one!"

Appreciative chortle.

(As he scratched the little rows of stars, he sounded like a lover scrawling a row of kiss-kiss-kiss-kiss-kiss crosses beneath his name on a sloppy love-letter, his lips all pursed and pulsating for slobbery kissy action as he concentrated on the killer phrases.)

"Look at *this*!"

Almost Six Inches in Height.

(*****)

Tap, tap, tap.

"Spot on!"

"Look at *this*!"

Guaranteed to Delight Any Boy.

(*****)

Tap, tap, tap.

"Most amusing!"

There were several phrases from which to choose, a generous selection of phrases Guaranteed to Cause a Blush, the starry-starry five-star favorites.

*****

*****

*****

*****

*****

"Look at *this*!"

A Particularly Handsome Article.

(*****)

Tap, tap, tap.

"I *really* like this one!"

"Look at *this*!"

As Much Like a Real Boy as it is Possible to Make It Appear.

(*****)

Tap, tap, tap.

Snigger.

There it was.

The laughter had now become a snigger.

Mr. Rappaport had already perfected the Otsego Lake Academy snigger, and this must have been one of the very first occasions on which Ben had heard it. Mr. Rappaport would have practiced it repeatedly, listening to it echoing around the gaslight in the evening, as he sniggered for hour after hour to get it just right.

He'd got it just right.

Papa tended not to let his standards slip much below a four-star comment, honing his skills to an impressive level of – *Zip! Zip! Zip!* – bull's-eye accuracy as the darts were unleashed on their target. (Papa's arrows would not make a *swisssh-swisssh-swisssh* sound; they'd opt for the reassuringly masculine zippiness of *ʒip-ʒip-ʒip*.) Practice made just about perfect. That was clearly one of Papa's mottoes, one of his kissy-kiss-the-boy-and-make-him-blush platitudes as the arrows winged vibratingly home. Ben thought of the extinguished stars in the ceiling at All Saints' Church, all the recommended insults studding the sky as he kneeled, as he prayed, as he sang hymns of praise each Sunday. There was a darkness, and not a light, above the Reverend Goodchild's head as he flaunted his teeth in the pulpit. The Reverend Goodchild had started to insinuate his way into the pulpit at All Saints', preparing his way for the *coup* when he would leap in to displace the Reverend Calbraith.

All the boys at his new school would know that he was a girlie.

(He'd be a four-star, five-star kissy-kiss blusher from the very first day.

(They'd all be pointing at him.

(*That's him!*

(*That's him!*

(*That's pucker-up Pinkie!*)

Mr. Rappaport would see to that, with Papa's help.

It would do him good.

It would make him a man.

(*Go to the inner room.*

(He said the words to himself repeatedly, as he felt his agitation beginning to increase.

(*Go to the inner room.*

(*Go to the inner room.*

(He repeated his formula for calmness, the words he used to try and make himself acceptable, to drive away the troubling emotions.)

*****

*****

*****

*****

*****

So many stars.

So little light.

It was always dark in the inner room.

More tapping.

More flicking.

More sniggering.

It all came down to sniggering in the end.

More amused and approving comments.

Mr. Rappaport was *very* keen to make a good impression.

Ben stood there.

"He's *very* – ahem – '*friendly.*'"

(*****)

Snigger.

(Now that he'd started sniggering, Mr. Rappaport didn't seem to want to stop, eager to demonstrate that he'd got the snigger just right. "Listen to me sniggering": that's what the sniggers seemed to demand.)

"He's *very* – ahem – '*musical.*'"

(*****)

Snigger.

Ben stood there.

He *wasn't* "musical."

He'd stopped playing the piano.

He'd stopped singing.

He didn't do either of those things anymore.

He didn't.

He *didn't*.

Mr. Rappaport was being offered a first glimpse of his script, and was determined to pass the audition. This was the part that he was longing to play. He'd be a brilliant improviser, once the part was his, a man unrestrained by the need for a script.

More baring of teeth.

More cigars prodding through the bars of the cage.

More hissing, foul cigar-smelling breath.

Perhaps – for the benefit of Mr. Rappaport – Papa might make him smoke a cigar again, might make him drink brandy. He'd made him drunk once, and Ben had vomited in his bed. He'd vomited, and he'd wet himself. Papa had laughed hugely, and thought it very funny. Ben had tried to wash the sheets himself, though he wasn't sure how to go about it. He hadn't wanted Karin to see them. He hadn't wanted *anyone* to see them. Mr. Rappaport would enjoy seeing him vomiting, seeing him wet himself. Ben knew this already. Side by side, Papa and Mr. Rappaport would sit down in the study, conspiratorially cozying up together for the afternoon's entertainment. He somehow thought of what Brinkman had told them went on in his father's club. Tits, inevitably, came into it. Tits and garters and feathers, and the delectation of the baying crowd of men was complete.

Things were simpler here. Here there was no need for tits and garters and feathers, even though Papa probably believed that garters and feathers were the very things for Franklin. All that was needed was vomit and pee.

"Vomit again!"

"Vomit again!"

"Pee again!"

"Pee again!"

They'd lean forward for a good, close look.

("Pretty Pinkie!"

(Papa.

(*Rattle, rattle!*

("Pretty Pinkie!"

(Mr. Rappaport.

(*Rattle, rattle!*

(If he was a parrot in a cage, the parrot he wanted to be like was Hilderbrandt, Oliver's parrot. Hilderbrandt did exactly what *he* wished to do, and what he wished to do involved intemperate streams of filthy language, and biting huge chunks out of anyone who ventured too close to his stand. Myrtle would have been halved in size in no time if she'd veered in Hilderbrandt's direction, flesh ripped away as if she'd been strips of jerky. Oliver often said rude things to his sister when he stood near Hilderbrandt, hopeful that she'd lose control and trundle into the attack, lurching absent-mindedly into gouging range as she raised an arm to strike.

(Hilderbrandt.

(That was the parrot to emulate, if a parrot were what he had become.

(Filthy language.

(Biting.

(Ben had been taught – "Say it again, Franklin! Say it again, Franklin!" – the filthy language; now all that he needed to learn was the biting.

(He'd run away till he was bigger.

(But then he'd fight.

(He'd bite.

(Teeth ripping butterfly wings.

(One of his father's moods.

(A noble child.)

"Say it again, Franklin!"

Franklin.

His father had chosen his Christian names, and – with Benjamin Franklin – long-nurtured ambitions were placed upon Ben at his baptism, imposed at the font by Dr. Vaniah Odom as the light glowed red through the stained-glass window of the murdered teacher.

These ambitions had not been realized. Papa had been disappointed by the sex of his first three children, and then – he made this perfectly clear – soon disappointed by the qualities of his first son and final child.

Three girls and a girlie.

Some men populated *the earth*, and all he'd managed had been three girls and a girlie.

That had been his pitiful legacy, scarcely something to set posterity panting!

The one toy his father had ever bought for him had been the "My Brave Boy" Mechanical Walking Sailor Boy.

The one book had been Benjamin Franklin's *Autobiography*.

When he was about five or six – perhaps he had been even younger, perhaps it had been as soon as he had learned to read his first few words (*Jack, Jack, look at the rab-bit!*, whispering, shadows on the wall) – Papa had given him the *Autobiography*, a book bearing his own names as the title, as if his were a life that had already been lived, and he would spend the years ahead of him doing nothing but reenacting movements that had already been made – *tap, tap, tap* – and speaking words that had already been spoken. Perhaps his father really did hope that he would take the pattern of his life from what was written in that book: he had no use for imaginative literature, and probably regarded the book as an instruction manual for something that was difficult to operate. Of course, Ben had not read the book when he was so young – he was a diligent and well-behaved pupil, anxious (overanxious) to do well, but he was not precocious – but he came to believe that the book actually was an account of his own life and no one realized this, only Alice, when he eventually told her, when the fear became too great. His father did not explain to him that he had been named after someone else, someone who had lived before he was born, and Ben had been terrified to open the *Autobiography* in case he discovered, in the final pages, the hour of his own death, and the manner of his own dying. That seemed to him to be the most terrible thing to know, to spend your life counting down the days to a known date, a known time, and to know that on that date, at that time, you would cease to be.

The last year.

The last month.

The last week.

The last day.

The last hour.

The last minute.

Time hurtling him onto damnation.

Years later, when he'd seen a performance of *Doctor Faustus*, he hadn't known why the final scene had affected him so deeply, the scene in which Faustus knew that he was facing the last hour of his life. It was an unrecognized memory of that childhood terror, and had given him nightmares. More taunting from Papa at his unmanliness.

> *Stand still, you ever-moving spheres of heaven,*
> *That time may cease, and midnight never come;*
> *Fair nature's eye, rise, rise again, and make*
> *Perpetual day; or let this hour be but*
> *A year, a month, a week, a natural day . . .*

A year.

A month.

A week.

A natural day.

(*Looks as Natural as Life.*

(*****

(*Looks as Much Like a Real Boy as it is Possible to Make It Appear.*

(*****

(Stars.

(Ever-moving.

(Time.

(Ceasing.

(Midnight.

300

(Never coming.)

Virtually the last words Faustus spoke – as he was dragged down to perpetual torment – were "I'll burn my books!" and Ben had longed to burn that one particular book, but hadn't dared.

He'd lain awake, thinking of the words that were hidden in that book. If he accidentally read them, they would enter inside him, and stay there. That's what words did when you read them. You couldn't forget them. He had hidden it away, barricaded as the years went by, behind his secret store of novels (bought for him by Alice or Mama), the heroes of his childhood protecting him from the fact of his mortality, the Pathfinder finding him a path that led him away from death.

When he did read the book – his father had written no inscription in it – at an age when he was well aware of the reality of another Benjamin Franklin, who had died in 1790 – he held it open in front of him as he read – even though it made his wrists ache – so that his father could see him reading it, rather in the way that he had tried to make his father realize when he was playing with "My Brave Boy."

Look at me, Papa.

Look what I'm doing.

(From his drawings, a tiny, tiny Linnaeus waved out. You could see that he was there only if you knew that he was there.)

He followed all the instructions.

He was very good at following instructions.

He Wound Up the Concealed Spring.

He Placed the Mechanical Boy Upright on a Smooth, Level Surface.

He Ensured that it was Pointed in the Direction in Which He Wanted it to Walk.

He Let Go.

That was how he played with the toy that was Guaranteed to Delight Any Boy.

The book was a book to be read like any other book. He opened it up and exposed the pages, and read the words so that they would enter inside him.

He found that he had been named after a man who possessed all qualities except a sense of the poetic, the unfathomable, or the beautiful . . .

("*Bee-oo-tiful! Bee-oo-tiful!*"

(Exaggeratedly high-pitched voices mocked the presence of a forbidden word.

("Oo!"

("Oo!"

("*Oo!*")

. . . a man for whom everything was real and scientific, and could be explained, dissected, and labeled in a brightly illuminated interior; a man who could cure smoking chimneys; a man who chopped down trees to clear America of woods and destroy the wilderness, and cut the gods down to size; a man who decided he would arrive at moral perfection, and live without committing any fault at any time; a man who would conquer all that either natural inclination, custom, or company might lead him into; a man for whom there were no mysteries; a man without imagination.

This was the man that Ben ought to become like.

This was what was expected of him.

The engraving opposite the title page showed a man with cold eyes and thin, tightly compressed lips, a smug face that could be studied on bank notes, a face like the face of God – a jealous God – in Whom we trusted.

It seemed quite unlike his father that he had not marked certain lines for particular attention, like passages of instruction. He'd expected double lines drawn in the margin with the gray fountain pen, neatly inscribed in red ink, the gold nib sliding firmly down the side of a ruler. *Why increase the sons of Africa by planting them in America, where we have so fair an opportunity, by excluding all blacks and tawnies, of increasing the lovely white and red?* That would have awoken a response, and not only in Papa, that would have set the pen nib scratching. ("That is Mama's favorite sentence," Oliver had told him, when Ben had shown him it because of something Brinkman had said about Gabriel, a black boy who painted walls for

Mr. Hennebelle. "She has it embroidered on her drawers so that she can feel those comforting words across her bottom whenever she sits down." You'd be utterly convinced that he was being serious when he said such things. He'd look straight at you, matter-of-fact and wide-eyed. You hardly liked to disbelieve him.) If not this, then the list of the thirteen virtues might have been an appropriate section to mark for particular study; for study and for acting upon.

In such fashion, Ben would arrive at moral perfection, and live without committing any fault at any time, the necessary requisite for anyone who bore the name of Benjamin Franklin Pinkerton and wished to please his papa.

1. *Temperance.*
2. *Silence. (Speak not but what may benefit others or yourself; avoid trifling conversation.)*
3. *Order.*
4. *Resolution.*
5. *Frugality.*
6. *Industry.*
7. *Sincerity. (Use no hurtful deceit; think innocently and justly; and, if you speak, speak accordingly.)*
8. *Justice.*
9. *Moderation.*
10. *Cleanliness.*
11. *Tranquility.*
12. *Chastity. (Rarely use venery but for health or offspring, never to dullness, weakness, or the injury of your own or another's peace or reputation.)*

Ben had blushed at *Chastity*. He'd looked up *venery* in the family dictionary, on the alert for witnesses, in case he was caught, and blushed even more. It had been bad enough when he'd been set searching by *circumcision*. He'd been very careful to replace the dictionary *exactly* as he'd found it. Well, that one should be easy enough to follow, he'd thought. He'd never want to do *that* sort of thing, that *sex-u-al in-ter-course* sort of thing.

13. Humility. (Imitate Jesus and Socrates.)

In silence, and with humility, he would strive to become what was ordered in the words that were now within him. He'd think innocently and justly. He'd imitate Jesus. (He didn't know much about Socrates, though he knew that he'd killed himself. He'd been given poison, and he'd drunk it.)

The list of thirteen virtues looked like the answers to a test.

How would he be graded?

Would he pass?

Would he be accepted as a Real Boy?

From time to time, in childhood, he added up his total out of thirteen.

Thirteen was a worrying number to choose for the list of virtues. Were they like the Ten Commandments, broken forever if you broke them just once, even if accidentally, doomed to damnation forever like Faustus, with no chance of salvation? This was the general impression you gained from the Reverend Goodchild when he was in one of his Up-God-And-Get-'Em! moods, the sort of mood that – he'd heard – had been the unchanging mood, the perpetual scowl, of Dr. Vaniah Odom, the man who'd baptized him into the faith. He'd already failed with Temperance. (Vomit. Pee.) Tranquility was going to be a problem. (Of all the thirteen, this was the one that seemed the nearest to being impossible for him to achieve.) He confused Humility with Humiliation, and thought that at least Papa was proving immensely helpful with this one, even if he'd ruined Temperance. Silence would not be a problem. There'd be no difficulty with Order. Everything in his room was neatly – almost obsessively – ordered, the contents of every drawer. Even the things that were never seen were neatly ordered.

Benjamin Franklin's use for a cross made of two light strips of wood was not to see it as a symbol of faith, but to tie the four corners of a large thin silk handkerchief to the extremities to make the body of a kite, and fly it with twine into a thunderstorm, a key fastened to the twine by a silk ribbon close to the hand.

Years later, years and years later it seemed — though they were not so many years — Ben stood on a hill in Nagasaki with a small figure in a kimono beside him during a storm, flying a kite made of elaborately decorated silk, like fragments of paintings floating in the air, calling down fire from heaven with the front door key from the house of his dead father in New York. The rain plastered their clothes to them, and they were both laughing.

You didn't know such things when you were young.

You didn't know that things could become different, that time would pass.

You thought that things would always be the same.

Time ceased.

Daylight never came.

5

On the Sunday afternoon tour, for the first time, he saw Mr. Rappaport *inside* Otsego Lake Academy. He hardly heard the words that Mr. Scrivener, the headmaster, was speaking as (shadowed by hovering Bearded Ones) he led them around; he was too conscious of the nearness of Mr. Rappaport. He saw him, unspeaking — but observing — on the outer edges of the groups of schoolmasters.

Soon, he'd be drawing nearer.

Soon, he'd be speaking.

Every weekday, from now on, he'd be seeing him there, the days stretching out for six years, seven years, eight years, a folk-tale term of bondage.

Oliver had treated the whole of the Sunday afternoon like one of Dr. Crowninshield's nature rambles. Whenever the weather had been particularly good, Dr. Crowninshield would announce, "Nature ramble!" and they'd set off in just such a ragged group, wandering along behind him as they scoured the fringes of the lake (the dome of the academy rising above the far side like a reminder of what was to come), or explored Heneacher Woods, on the alert for what were learnedly described as "specimens" as they botanized or set alarmed birds winging upward.

Now *they* had become the specimens.

(The speci*men*.

(They had ceased to be boys once they were through the portals of Otsego Lake Academy.)

That was what it had felt like, as The Bearded Ones peered and pointed (they'd probably end up pinned out on a Nature Table, like the short-lived wilting twigs and flowers that were the fruits of their expeditions), but Oliver had been undaunted.

"Note the curious facial features of the male members of the scavengers," he'd been commenting to Ben, Linnaeus, and Charlie Whitefoord when they first noticed that they were being observed.

"Male *members*!" Brinkman – overhearing – had started to snigger, demonstrating his superior knowledge of smut, his forthright filthiness, his I-really-feel-at-home-here Otsego Lake Academy sniggering. "You might have known that Comstock would be looking out for *male members*!" The italics were like a nudge. Swartwout – although he clearly hadn't a clue what Brinkman was talking about – had sniggered along. He was never one to be left out when muckiness was in the offing. He didn't understand the words, but he'd no trouble whatsoever in understanding the tone of voice.

Snigger Required!

That was the mucky message, and he was activated into automatic sniggering.

Time for a grubby guffaw!

It was a sound that was easy to make, even if you didn't know why you were doing it, with no activity required – this helped a lot – on the part of the brain, if a brain were present.

Mr. Scrivener – this was one of the few Bearded Ones whose name they knew (though Ben knew the name of one of the few Unbearded Ones) – threw open the double-doors with an impressive crash (you could tell he'd practiced doing this, several times, to get the correct level of impressiveness into the crash) and led them into the main hall. The doors must have been generously oiled in preparation. Mr. Scrivener was so frail and flimsy, so tottery and ancient, that any slight resistance from the doors would have bounced him back into the entrance hall, demolishing new boys in heaps. In the main hall, The Bearded Ones were lingering, utilized as decorative features to add a little visual interest to an otherwise deserted interior. A group of three or four – all with whitened beards like winter pelts (with their keen animal instincts they had sensed the nearness of snow) – were whispering together, grouped in a pack. They held their hands in front of their mouths, for discretion, but the hands only served to draw all the more attention to what they were doing.

("I want *that* one for my collection," one of them was probably saying. "I'm very short of redheads," and Frankie Alloway – he'd arrived late – would be picked off.

("I'll have that tall one. He can reach things down until the library ladder's been repaired." Charlie Whitefoord would be picked off.

(So it would continue.

(Howling for blood, you sensed, would not be much longer delayed.)

"The Beards – this is the technical term we choose to employ – are probably designed to enable them to blend in with the background, so that they can draw near without being noticed. Note how they lope and linger hungrily, preparing to pounce."

(Brinkman would have pounced on "pounce." If you could snigger at "members," you could – *Snigger, snigger, snigger!* – snigger at "pounce," but he didn't hear what Oliver had said. Oliver –

sensing an air-sniffing restlessness on the part of one of the nearer Beards, an ear-twitching alertness – had lowered his voice to be on the safe side. Best not to be attacked by howling packs of peda-gogues before he'd even started at the school. That was probably Oliver's reasoning.)

It had been exactly as it was later on their first *real* day there – as cold, and echoing – and all that was missing was the sound of the distant bells in unseen corridors. It seemed curious, a Sunday with-out the sound of bells.

On that oddly silent Sunday, the Crowninshield's boys had gath-ered right in the center of the hall, looking upward at the interior of the dome, painted with scenes from James Fenimore Cooper novels, trying to assume the correct expressions of impressed awe, wide-eyed agoshment.

You dropped your jaw.

You pointed.

You looked oddly vacuous.

That was what was expected.

"I can see a tit," Brinkman – a boy who could be relied upon to go right to the heart of a subject's significance – sniggered, leering up at Cora Munro's heaving bosom. He was a tip-top tit-spotter. This had been about the level of his observations during nature rambles. He'd found a pair of drawers once in some bushes in the park – they'd been the subject of much puzzled speculation – and pulled them over Linnaeus's head. They had not been allowed a place on the Nature Table, despite much urging. Dr. Crowninshield had been quite firm about this. He'd probably been scared that Allie might start eating them, the well-chewed border of a frilly leg hanging down from the corner of his mouth in mute accusation.

"The scavengers gather on the outskirts of the herd," Oliver was continuing. "They seek out the weaker members – the young, the frail – to drag them down, to kill and eat them."

"This is *really* helping," Linnaeus was saying, looking pale. "This is *really* helping." He was struggling to get the hang of teas-ing, even gentle teasing rather worrying him. "Gentle" and "teasing" were two words that – you felt – had rarely appeared in the same sentence, in his experience. The Bearded Ones did not look like men who went in for anything that could be described as "gentle."

They whispered.

They pointed.

They prepared to pick off.

And now – two weeks later – they'd be meeting The Bearded Ones again, who'd march them off down long dim corridors into regions which they had not been allowed to see on the Sunday. The prospect failed to elicit joyful cries.

There they'd be now, The Bearded Ones, gathered together in the hall, and all the pupils would be there with them, waiting and watching, and they – also – would be whispering, pointing, preparing to pick off the pupils from whom they had been so carefully shielded.

Oliver, unable to resist the ice-like surface, began to slide out across the middle of the hall toward the closed doors, taking a run up to achieve a good sliding distance. This did not seem like a good idea.

Swisssh!

Swisssh!

Swisssh!

Bells rang again, alerting the unseen authorities of such unsanctioned pranksomeness.

Everyone froze, and gazed away in other directions, disassociating themselves from these illicit cavortings, but Oliver ignored the bells completely.

He pressed his ear against one of the doors, near the keyhole.

"Muffled voices," he said. "Scraping chairs. They are gathering together. All very sinister. Devil worship is probably involved. Right up your street, Brinkman. Black robes. Chanting."

("I *want* the blanket-tossing!" he was probably on the point of shouting – it was all a little disappointing so far – attempting to encourage a coordinated chant.

("I *want* the roasting!"

("I *want* Brinkman barbecued!"

(That would have received a good response.)

Then he noticed someone down one of the side corridors.

He had read *Tom Brown's Schooldays*.

He knew the right sort of thing to say in the circumstances.

"I say, you fellow!" he called.

A boy, three or four years older than they were, appeared from the corridor on their right.

"Oh, it's you, Comstock," he said, not unfriendly. "So you're here."

(Brinkman was not best pleased to discover that Oliver knew at least one of the older boys, and one who seemed favorably disposed toward him. His face went all Neanderthal. He'd have had lots of his favorite insults for Oliver – a wide selection was available – all ready to use to impress, to demonstrate his chappish credentials, to ingratiate himself with the more raucous elements of his new *alma mater*. Oliver wasn't too keen on anything that involved a *mater*.

(Oh.

(*Alma mater*.

(Latin!

(You just couldn't stop yourself thinking in Latin once you'd entered the rarefied intellectual air of Otsego Lake Academy.)

Oliver considered the boy's last comment for a moment.

"So I am," he eventually conceded. "Hello, Vellacott."

"Welcome to Dotheboys Hall."

They'd received their welcome at last, though it was not a very encouraging one. They weren't quite sure what it meant, but what it meant could not be good.

"Where's Squeers?"

Brinkman didn't understand this interchange, but didn't like the sound of it. Why was Comstock asking for something queer? Not that this was any surprise, from *him*.

"That's Scrivener's real name," Vellacott said. "Didn't you know?" He'd quickly checked that there was no one else within hearing before he said this, and whispered dramatically.

"And is your real name Brooke?" Oliver asked, assuming a hero-worship simper, reaching up to breathe on one of Vellacott's coat-of-armed brass buttons (coats of arms were clearly destined to add an air of aristocratic refinement to their schooldays) and polishing it with his cuff as if it were an apple for the teacher. Oliver had told Ben about Brooke. He was the cock of the school in *Tom Brown's Schooldays*, head of the School-house side, and the best kick and charger in Rugby. Ben wasn't *quite* sure what all this meant, but it sounded impressive. Brooke was clearly the sort of chap who'd be right at home at Otsego Lake Academy. There was going to be a great deal of kicking and charging (probably with added gouging and biting). This much they'd sensed already.

"Vellacott," said Vellacott. "I'm Vellacott. Do the next button."

He indicated his preferred choice from a frontage armor-plated with gleaming buttons. He clearly had favorites amongst them.

Oliver breathed again.

"I can *see* my breath!" he commented, in an inane voice.

Brinkman stirred restlessly.

"Is there anyone named Flashman in this place?" Oliver asked, as he polished. "*He*'s the chap one has to be careful about, or so I gather."

(A month or so earlier, Oliver had had one of his learned literary discussions with Alice — those discussions that Ben could follow only haltingly — in which he had compared the character of Steerforth in *David Copperfield* with that of Flashman in *Tom Brown's Schooldays*.)

"No. No Flashmans."

"I confess to a feeling of disappointment, a sense of being rather cheated. I thought every decent boarding school worthy of the name had a Flashman."

Breath.

Polish.

"This is *not* a boarding school, as you well know." Vellacott had obviously survived many of Mrs. Albert Comstock's "At Homes" by talking to Oliver. His reply had winged straight back.

"You mean I've got to *go back* to Mama's tonight!" Oliver said, in a tone of unutterable horror. "I'm going to be seeing her *again* today?"

"Afraid so." Vellacott smiled, assuming an expression of evil gloating.

"You fill me with dismay. I'd *far* rather be roasted by Flashman, especially on a day as cold as today."

Breath.

Polish.

"I'm not surprised! Who *wouldn't* be dismayed?"

This was Brinkman, seizing the chance to impress one of the older boys with what he thought of as being his well-honed vicious wit. It was not one of his better efforts. He still labored under the delusion that the worst thing you could say to a boy was to express some lurid insult to his mother, completely ignoring the clear evidence of Oliver's feelings about *his* mother. The more you insulted her, the more you were recognized as a friend. That was Oliver's attitude.

"Thank you for your support, Brinkman," Oliver said, in the voice of one deeply touched. "I value your sympathetic solidarity."

"Next button, you miserable little milksop, before I beat you to a pulp," Vellacott said cheerfully.

"*Thank you*, Vellacott." Oliver sounded delighted. "That's *exactly* the way I expect to be spoken to in a reputable private school. I feel much more at home now that you've said that. That's the sort of thing our parents pay for. Foul bad talk. *Already!* I'm greatly encouraged."

Extra strong breath.

Extra vigorous polish.

He turned to Vellacott, indicating Brinkman. "We've brought a *Brink*man with us," he said. "If you haven't got a Flashman, then you ought to have a Brinkman. It's in full working order. Did you enjoy the free demonstration?"

Breath.

Polish.

"Can it do lots of things?"

"*Oodles* of things, though not what you'd describe as clean with his personal habits. I wouldn't advise standing too close. There's always a certain amount of unpleasantness vis-à-vis Stinkman's drawers. Strong men keel over in mid-sentence, fighting to remain conscious. His breath fair makes your eyes water, and he can be careless about his socks. Isn't that so, Sidder-knee?"

This was not going down well with Brinkman.

("Is it weakness of intellect, birdie?" Oliver tended to ask him whenever that same expression of suspicious incomprehension came across his face. It was an expression that you saw often when Oliver was in his vicinity, and it frequently developed into one of baffled outrage. Brinkman couldn't quite follow what was going on, but he didn't like the sound of it. This was what the expression conveyed.)

Brinkman hated being addressed by his first name – presumably it was not manly enough – particularly when it was pronounced "Sidder-knee."

"Shall I clean your boots when I've finished the buttons?" Oliver continued. "I don't mind getting close to *your* socks, Vellacott. I doubt that I'll be facing unhygienic hell with *your* footwear."

(Sidder-knee was looking fit to be tied.

(And when he was tied, Oliver would produce the branding-irons.

(*Hiss! Hiss!*

(The name would be sizzlingly emblazoned across all areas of exposed flesh.

(*Hiss! Hiss!*)

Oliver kneeled down in front of Vellacott, with an entranced, worshipful expression, prior to cleaning his boots. At the exact moment that he kneeled, the bells rang again somewhere down a distant corridor – trust Oliver to have the unseen gods in his power – and this lent an unexpectedly religious significance to his action. You thought of Tom Brown, and the significant, reverential manner in which he held his cricket bat. Frank Stoddard must have been straining at the leash to join in. He was one of the choirboys at Corpus Christi, his sad, spotty face emerging from above an impressive Elizabethan-looking ruff. They'd seen him in a procession once, and you couldn't help giving thanks that Oliver had never been entrusted with a censer. The repercussions would have had half the city choking, engulfed in impenetrable fogs, and ships would have been colliding all round Manhattan with ear-splitting smashes. Oliver raised his arms high into the air, and groveled with comprehensive abasement, tight-locking his arms around Vellacott's ankles in an ardent gesture. He looked on the point of licking the boots clean, or polishing them adoringly with his long fair hair. When Oliver set out to impress, he believed in doing the job thoroughly.

Brinkman was about to launch into the attack – if verbal didn't work (it never did with Oliver), then physical might be called for – when a man with a beard as big as his board clip came into the entrance hall from the other direction, his heels click-click-clicking. He probably walked about in the dark for hours at night, when the school was all locked up, when no one else was there, enjoying the important sound he made.

There had been no bells to signal his entrance, and this – somehow – unsettled them. They'd have expected bells. They froze even further into frosty oblivion. The last thing they needed to do in that cold wasteland was to think of freezing.

"Vellacott," The Beard said. "Take up your position."

A talking beard.

Oliver unclasped his arms and looked up at Vellacott from his kneeling position, expecting some balletic pose, some straining of hams and graceful attitude, but Vellacott only said, "Certainly, sir," and walked back the way he had come. He was clearly a boy with impeccable manners, managing a discreet nod of acknowledgment to Oliver as he left.

"No talking!" The Beard called after him. You'd have thought that Vellacott were given to talking to himself. "Keep right!" he added.

The Beard made no comment about Oliver's servile posture. He obviously regarded it as perfectly normal, and, indeed, commendable, seeing in it an all-too-understandable sign of deference to himself. He made an upward jerking on-to-your-feet-boy gesture with the edge of his polished wooden board clip. It was like a clergyman indicating "You may rise" after prayers. Oliver rose.

The man with the list of names had at last come marching toward them, the papers fluttering on his boardclip.

He was the bearded man with his papers rustling importantly.

The Crowninshield's boys all assumed expressions of alertness. Brinkman, overdoing it as usual, almost went cross-eyed. They wouldn't let Dr. Crowninshield down! Their old school had bred boys with tone and intelligence. This was what they sought to convey.

He was the man who called them out one by one.

"Adams?" he read from his list.

"Here!" Adams said, sounding pleased as anything, apparently under the impression that he'd been chosen for other than alphabetical reasons.

This was how they had replied to Dr. Crowninshield in such circumstances.

"You say, 'Present, sir' here," The Beard corrected, rather tetchily.

"Present."

"'Present, *sir*.'"

"Sorry."

"You say, 'I apologize, *sir*' here," The Beard said.

"I apologize."

"I apologize, *sir*. *Get it right!*"

"I . . ."

"Don't forget the 'sir.' Are they all fools like you from your school?"

He was the man with withering comments.

They were being welcomed.

They were being made to feel at home.

They were being shown what to expect.

Say what you like about Mr. Scrivener – and Vellacott had conveyed a distinct lack of enthusiasm about the man – he was a man as good as his word.

"I apologize, sir."

"And are you present, Adams?"

Adams thought furiously.

Was he present?

He appeared to check himself, all his buttons bobbling.

"Present, *sir*," he managed eventually.

"About time."

Adams didn't look pleased anymore.

The Beard removed a single sheet from a sheaf of foolscap – was worrying Symbolism involved here? – papers that was attached to the board clip, sliding it out carefully from beneath the brass spring.

"Take this – er . . ."

He consulted his list, to remind himself of Adams's name. Individuals, it was being made clear to them, were not to be regarded as memorable at Otsego Lake Academy.

". . . Adams."

Adams took the proffered sheet of paper.

"Thank you, sir," he remembered to say, and bowed his head to read what was written upon it. Judging by the expression on his face, it was something deeply depressing. The roster for blanket-tossing and roasting – the roaster-roster – had been drawn up, and Adams was first. Something like that. They were going to be blanket-tossed and roasted in alphabetical order. The Otsegoan arms would be tired by the time that they got to Pinkerton, the fires would be beginning to die down. That was Ben's hope for survival.

"Do *not* lose it."

"No, sir."

Next name on the list.

(The choice of names did not appear to please The Beard.)

"Akenside?"

"Present, sir."

Akenside had always been one to learn quickly. He had watched and listened to what had happened with Adams, and the benefits of paying close attention were impressively demonstrated. He knew what the right thing to say was, the right thing to do. The Beard had no withering comments to offer Akenside. You could tell that this disappointed The Beard slightly.

"Take this — er — Akenside."

"Thank you, sir."

Another sheet of paper.

Another depressed expression.

"Do *not* lose it."

"No, sir."

Those blankets would be shooting up and down in the air like a scene from drying-day in a Lower East Side laundry. If they had them there. Mrs. Albert Comstock thought it *most* unlikely. There'd be enough roasting for a Thanksgiving Day feast of thousands.

"Alloway?"

Silence.

"Alloway?"

Silence.

"He's not here yet, sir."

Brinkman was seizing an opportunity to make a good impression, and had stressed the "sir" with Uriah Heep-like umbleness.

"You say, 'Absent, sir' here," The Beard said. He was obviously the sort of teacher who marked his attendance register with alternating strokes morning and afternoon to make a herring-bone pattern, and took out another fountain pen with different-colored ink solely to mark absences with *red* circles. Brinkman's attempt at making a good impression had come to naught! His bottom lip began to stick out. He looked about him with you-be-careful withering glances. A bad mood was building up.

"Bradley?"

"Present, sir."

"Take this — er — Bradley."

"Thank you, sir."

Paper.

Depression.

"Do *not* lose it."

"No, sir."

There was a crash as one of the entrance doors was flung open. Frankie Alloway burst through like a winner breasting the tape at the end of a sprint. He was covered in snow from head to foot, and only recognizable by the racy yellow muffler that had been knitted by his grandmother. It was about twelve feet long, and he kept entangling his legs in it and falling over.

"Oh," Frankie said, seeing the expression on The Beard's face. He carefully tiptoed back the way he had come, and quietly closed the door behind him. It was like someone saying "Drat!" when he'd just accidentally wiped out his entire family. He walked back again, still tiptoeing, to stand at the back of the group, trying to look casual. Snow fell from him, and he left a trail behind him. The expression on his face settled for ingenuous helpfulness.

He beamed at The Beard in a feel-free-to-continue sort of way.

The bells rang again.

Freeze.

Frankie's beam increased.

Bells ringing, especially to welcome him!

"What do you say?" The Beard snapped.

Frankie thought about this.

Beam.

This was a good question.

Beam. Beam.

He'd work out the answer sooner or later.

Beam. Beam. Beam.

"My beamish boy!"

It was Oliver, standing just behind Ben, who said this.

Displaying an uncharacteristic sensitivity to the sensibilities of

The Beard, he'd lowered his voice and whispered into Ben's right ear.

"Come to my arms!" he added.

Frankie was a boy prone to beaming, and this encouraging comment was one that Oliver had often said to him at Crowninshield's.

Come to my arms, my beamish boy!

(Trainee Lake Otsego Academy sniggers from Brinkman.

(*Come to my arms!*

(It was just the sort of thing you expected to hear spoken by Comstock to another boy.)

Oliver propped his chin over Ben's right shoulder.

"O frabjous day!"

(Whisper.)

Sometimes he hooked his chin there and lifted his feet completely off the ground, swaying slowly from side to side. Ben very much hoped that he wouldn't choose to do this now. Even when he'd been warned — hardly ever: Oliver liked to spring surprises — Ben was almost invariably overbalanced by the sudden weight, and was pulled off his feet, collapsing back on top of Oliver in a heap. According to Brinkman — *snigger, snigger* — this was Comstock's sole motivation in the first place.

Snigger, snigger.

It was an odd sort of feeling, to be made embarrassed and uncomfortable by something that you did not really understand. Ben did not think that that briefly swinging silent pendulum, that tangle of arms and legs crashing to the floor, was the sort of thing that would recommend itself to a tetchy Beard.

Silent.

Oliver was rarely silent for long.

He'd probably copied this pouncing maneuver from his parrot, a bird given to disconcerting tactics in the music room long before he'd gone too far — *much* too far — and been banished perpetually from public hearing. Hilderbrandt would attach himself to visitors — upside down on worryingly unsuitable perches was the favored posture — and make himself comfy before making a start (it

319

was the bit he enjoyed most) on the unstoppable torrent of defecating and filthy language. It was always unsettling when Oliver locked his chin in the pre-pounce posture, as you never knew quite how far his pursuit of authenticity would take him. Once he was in the grip of a Good Idea he became completely uninhibited, and forgot all questions of taste. It was best to pretend you hadn't noticed that he was there.

"Callooh! Callay!"

(Whisper.)

"*What* do you say?"

Eyes of flame from The Beard.

Beam. Beam. Beam.

Frankie stood awhile in thought.

Give him a bit of time.

Beam. Be . . .

"*What* do you say?"

Realization dawned.

Beam faltered.

"I'm sorry I'm a bit late."

He was so out-of-breath that he could scarcely speak.

"You say, 'I apologize for my lateness, *sir*' here."

The "sir" was clearly the most important part of any sentence to The Beard, and every sentence contained a "sir." Verbs and periods didn't get a look-in when "sirs" were clamoring for attention. His children obviously failed to respect him, and servants sneered behind his back.

"*I* say . . .?"

Frankie's brain and mouth were not yet coordinated, as he labored to breathe.

"What *you* say is, 'I apologize for my lateness, *sir*.' They clearly *are* all fools from your school. What a bunch of imbeciles! They should be clearing the wards at the North River Lunatic Asylum!"

The jaws that bite, the claws that catch!

Ben lowered his head slightly, so as not to see the reactions of those around him, pressed in damp-clothed closeness, thinking of his sister Alice, and wondering if that was what they were thinking also, the things that had been said, the things that had *not* been said, the sudden silences from the likes of Mrs. Albert Comstock, Myrtle Comstock, and Mrs. Goodchild if he happened to be within hearing. He felt the beginnings of a blush, like a wave of heat in the cold hall. But it was Oliver they were thinking of, not of him, most of them.

Those nearest to Oliver discreetly began to edge a little further away from him. It was at this stage in a conversation that Oliver tended to make a bright remark. He did not, however, say anything. He tended to be biding his time when this happened, and this was even more dangerous. They edged even further away, just to be on the safe side. Just like – though for different reasons – Mrs Albert Comstock, Myrtle Comstock, and Mrs. Goodchild did if Alice happened to sit near them.

The Beard said his last sentence again, clearly pleased by his choice of words from the wide selection available.

"They should be clearing the wards at the North River Lunatic Asylum!"

He chortled in his joy.

(Welcome, thrice welcome, little strangers!)

Again he looked at Frankie, his board clip held at a threatening angle to jog his memory a little.

Frankie caught on.

Beam faded.

"I apologize for my lateness, sir. What happened was that . . ."

"I don't want to know. And, in any case, you're rather more than 'a bit late,' as you chose to express it."

He drew out his pocket-watch from somewhere within his beard. There was probably a salami sandwich in there, somewhere (careful forward planning helped to keep the worst pangs of hunger at bay), next to his bicycle.

"Twenty minutes before the hour. You're ten minutes late. Ten minutes is not 'a *bit*.' Ten minutes is *very* late. *On your first day here.*"

Brinkman clearly thought about emitting a loud gasp of horror at this information. It was the sort of thing that might predispose The Beard in his favor. It might go down well. He began to take a deep breath.

Too late.

There'd been too long a pause.

It would have lost any sense of spontaneity by now.

The Beard looked Frankie up and down, and referred to his list, as if it gave useful clues as to each of the new pupils' personal characteristics. (*Yellow muffler. Tends to be late. Disconcerting beam. Verging on idiocy.*)

"Who are you?"

Frankie had to think about this one, also.

This was a tough one.

Who *was* he?

Was it a trick question?

"Who *are* you, you idiot?"

Realization dawned again.

"Frankie," he said, with a certain you-can-call-me-Frankie informality of manner, smiling in his friendliest way.

Beam tentatively reappeared.

He saw the expression on The Beard's face, and thought for a while. This was clearly not the right answer.

Beam vanished completely.

"Frankie, *sir*," he eventually offered as a more pleasing alternative version, an upward, questioning inflexion of his voice revealing that he was still uncertain of its acceptability.

His uncertainty was well founded. "Frankie, *sir*" was *not* pleasing to The Beard.

"Not the name your *mama* calls you by," he snapped, with withering sarcasm. "Your *man's* name." Tone of apoplectic impatience. Frankie Alloway's mama, in fact — she was a great fan of *The Mikado* — addressed him as Franki-poo. The Beard, you felt, would have feasted for weeks upon this information. He'd have reduced Frankie to a thing of shreds and patches in no time.

322

"You use your *man's* name here." He repeated the phrase, to stress its utmost importance.

They were *men* now, not boys anymore.

This was never to be forgotten.

The uniforms from Oldermann & Oldermann – the very name of the firm a ringing twofold declaration of muscular maturity – had given them the outward appearance of trainee manliness. Now it was time for the Ceremony of Confirmation, the Blessing of the Beards, or whatever it was they'd call it. There'd probably be some humiliating . . .

(*23. Humility.*

(*Imitate Jesus.*

(*Imitate Socrates.*)

. . . some humiliating – vaguely medical, vaguely Masonic – ceremony in front of the whole school to hurry them *men*ward and remove the last lingering traces of unwelcome and untoward boyishness from these newly apprenticed beard-growers. That was what was going to happen to them beneath the dome, in the hall, through the double-doors. It was why they were going to be marched in last, why they'd been asked to arrive half-an-hour later than everyone else. Thank heaven he was wearing clean underwear and a new pair of socks. There'd be a table set up, all ready for a public dissection, and Mr. Scrivener would hold his shiny sharp-pointed instruments (something geometric or – if this involved instruments, he wasn't sure – logarithmic) high into the air, like an Aztec priest preparing for human sacrifice, eager to hold up the ripped-out palpitating hearts of the Crowninshield's sacrifices as offerings for the sun god whilst the whole school chanted. They would not – you could guarantee – be chanting *amo, amas, amat.* This, most certainly, would not have been an appropriate choice of verb. Back the sun would come in full force, and all the snow would be melted. It would be one of the highlights of the year for The Bearded Ones, the treat that kept them going through the more boring parts of schoolmastering, where there wasn't much to look forward to apart from the occasional vicious beating.

"Frankie Alloway, sir." Still the upward inflexion of his voice. With good reason. He looked at The Beard's face, and tried again.

A total absence of beam.

"Frankie," it had dawned upon him, was the unacceptable part of what he had said. He was no longer "Frankie." "Frankie" had ceased to exist. He was now . . .

He was now . . .

"Alloway," he said.

Another look at The Beard's face.

Not pleased.

Another attempt.

"Alloway, *sir*."

This was not one of Alloway's better days.

Alloway.

No more Frankie.

No more Oliver.

(Olly was *completely* out of the question.)

No more Linnaeus.

(And there'd certainly be no mention of Linn.)

No more Ben.

(There wouldn't even be a Benjamin or – here was some consolation – a Franklin.)

That was what it sounded like.

The Beard looked at Alloway for a long time, and then – a little grudgingly, a shopkeeper not entirely happy with the goods he had just accepted for delivery – made a tick next to Alloway's name on the list. All his ticks were exactly the same size, and at exactly the same angle. This must have come from years of practice. Thank goodness The Beard hadn't specially taken out his other fountain pen, specially unscrewed the cap, and specially drawn a red circle for absence.

He removed another sheet of paper from beneath the brass spring.

"Take this, Alloway."

He hadn't needed to say "er," or to look at his list to remind himself of what Alloway's name was. By now, he *knew* what Alloway's name was. This was not necessarily a good thing for Alloway.

"Thank you, sir."

He'd remembered to say "thank you," even without witnessing the good examples of Adams, Akenside, and Bradley. *And* he had remembered the "sir." Perhaps, after all, there was hope for Frankie Alloway's survival.

"Do *not* lose it."

"No, sir."

(*Another* "sir"!)

The Beard moved his pen down past Bradley's name, and onto Bradstone's. Before "Bradstone?", however, he had one more thing to say to Alloway, who was – a little prematurely – starting to relax.

"And Alloway . . .?"

Alloway had barely started to lower his head to examine what was written on the foolscap sheet of paper, and the first saggings of depression had not yet started to drag down his facial features and his shoulders. He still had his usual ever-hopeful playful puppy – "Throw me a stick! Throw me a stick!" – expression on his face. It wouldn't last for long in the Empire of The Beards.

"Yes, sir?" Alloway – though he'd remembered the "sir" (he was *definitely* showing signs of improvement) – asked his question rather hesitatingly, rather uncertainly. He was half-bracing himself to be told, "You do *not* say, 'Yes, sir?' here. You say, 'Would you do me the honor of clarifying your query, sir?' here," or, "You say, 'What is it you wish me to do, sir?' here." ("For God's sake, take that sour expression off your face, and give me a saucy smile," was not amongst the acceptable alternatives available for Frankie to press into usage.)

"Remove that yellow muffler."

That was what The Beard said.

(Sour expression.

(Not the remotest hint of a saucy smile.

(No chance whatsoever of a saucy smile.)

Alloway began to unwind the muffler from around his neck. It seemed to take about ten minutes. The boys nearest to him tried not to flinch as an indoor blizzard showered down upon them, fearless carol-singers defying nature's worst excesses. Alloway was removing from himself the sign of infectious disease – and was now out of quarantine, and harmless – but the nearest boys began to edge away from him, as they had edged away from Oliver, still fearful of contamination. He pulled it over his head, and his disheveled red hair was further disarranged.

"What color do you call that hair?"

"Auburn, sir."

Alloway was as touchy about his hair color as Mrs. Twemlow was.

"*Auburn!* It's the first time I've ever heard of an *auburn* light being used as a warning signal! It'll keep people away for miles around, if they've got any sense."

Some sort of elaborate pun was being unleashed here. Brinkman could have endeared himself to The Beard with an appreciative snigger if he had understood it. Another opportunity recklessly squandered. Alloway could sense that what was being said was supposed to be witty, but he couldn't really follow it, and didn't quite know what to say. He hesitated between saying, "Yes, sir" and saying, "No, sir," and finally opted for, "Will it, sir?" as probably being the safest response.

"*Am* I being given a warning signal . . ." – there was a slight pause as The Beard tipped the board clip at an angle to see the list, and remind himself of what Alloway's name was, so short was memory when it came to things of no importance – ". . . Alloway?"

"No, sir." Alloway felt on safer ground this time.

"I should hope not. If I see that muffler again I shall confiscate it, Alloway. It is not a part of the uniform of Otsego Lake Academy. It will be destroyed."

"Yes, sir. I understand, sir." Alloway tried two different formulæ of response, in case one of them was wrong, and both of them contained a "sir." The improvement was continuing unabated. He could have looked more pleased about what had just happened with the muffler. The chances of his falling head over heels and breaking a limb had just been significantly reduced, though – come to think of it – his grandmother would probably unleash her fury upon him. A grandson swathed in hand-knitting was a sign of a stable and loving household. That was one of the basic precepts in her philosophy of life. He didn't have a father, so she'd knitted him a muffler. No visible hand-knitting, and the very foundations of domesticity were threatened. Knitting needles would start rattling indignantly as soon as Frankie arrived back home – assuming, that is, he survived the day – and, row by row, plained and purled, new yellow garments would emerge, cast off and completed, to enclose him securely within the necessary winter warmth.

He'd agreed with The Beard. He'd understood. He'd spoken two sirred sentences, two unslurred sirs, fastidiously enunciated.

One of Alloway's sentences must have been right. The Beard turned back to his list.

Alloway let out a sigh of relief, a little too loudly, and The Beard looked up again.

"What was that, Alloway?"

"Nothing, sir. I unintentionally breathed, sir."

"What a relief it will be for all of us on the day that you finally stop."

The Beard turned his attention back to the board clip, with its nicely polished brass spring.

After he'd breathed on all The Beard's buttons (though the schoolmasters' garments possessed far fewer buttons than the boys' willfully eccentric uniforms), Brinkman – always quick to steal promising-looking ideas from other boys – could breathe on the brass spring as his method of ingratiating himself with one of the sources of power, polishing away like an overambitious Aladdin. The Beard would be beating him off with the sharpest corner of his board clip, almost overcome by the fumes as Brinkman breathed out his most ambitious oniony exhalations. If they were fortunate, The Beard would be rendered semiconscious, and they could all make their escape, scampering back down the tunneled iceway to Crowninshield's, leaving a trail of ripped-off brass buttons behind them as the sign that they had rejected Otsego Lake Academy. In the dusty hollow rooms where Crowninshield's had once been — the furniture sold, a few words still legible on the blackboard (they'd gaze upon them, trying to remember the day on which they were written, attempting to hear a long-forgotten voice again) — they could fence with their wooden rulers up and down all the bare, echoing stairs, and be little boys again.

Dr. Crowninshield might still be there, roped tightly to the one overlooked unsold chair, reenacting the memory of the day on which they'd said their good-byes to Joe Rasmusson when — feather-clad, war-painted, and with wooden tomahawks (more for show than scalping) — they'd danced around him as he recited from *The Song of Hiawatha*.

"Boys!" he'd exclaim with delight, as they thundered back into the classroom. "Boys!"

Again, they'd whoop and circle.

Again, he'd chant.

> ". . . Swift of foot was Hiawatha,
> He could shoot an arrow from him,
> And run forward with such fleetness,
> That the arrow fell behind him!
> Strong of arm was Hiawatha;
> He could shoot ten arrows upward,
> Shoot them with such strength and swiftness,
> That the tenth had left the bow-string
> Ere the first to earth had fallen! . . ."

They shaded their eyes, and gazed up into an arrow-darkened sky.

Alloway's head had lowered during The Beard's sally, as a way of hiding the expression on his face, and he tried to make it look as if he had done this solely in order to be able to read the thank-you-sir sheet of paper he had been handed *gratis* (Latin! You just couldn't stop yourself!) by the generous Beard, the sheet of paper he must *not* – no, sir – lose. The tail had ceased to wag. The puppy didn't feel like chasing after the stick at the moment, thank you very much, because the stick would be used to beat him. This was what he now realized. This was his first lesson at his new school. He had been told that he had to put all his efforts into learning to stop breathing. That was the way to gain approval at Otsego Lake Academy. That was the way to please his mama. That was the way to hear her say, "Well done, Franki-poo!" That was the way to set Grandmama – who had bought all his new schoolbooks for him – smiling proudly. Whatever was written on The Beard's paper, it was quick acting in its effects, and probably lethal. Depression – already incipient during the attentions of The Beard – leaped into full-blown, cold-breathed maturity. Everything saggable sagged. Frankie Alloway sighed again, not a sigh of relief this time – anything but – and then agonized when he realized what he'd done. His head remained bowed, an attempt at invisibility, but all visible parts agonized. Fortunately, The Beard was too busy concentrating on his next name-take-this-er-do-*not*-lose-it to have heard him.

"Bradstone?"

"Present, sir."

With every name on his list there was the ritual with the sheet of paper.

"Brinkman?"

"Present, sir."

"Comstock?"

"Present, *sir*!"

Such was the volume of Oliver's "sir" that the board clip was almost blasted out of The Beard's hand. You expected a salute, clicking heels, a call to arms. The Beard gave Oliver a long, thoughtful look – Oliver smiled winningly, demonstrating that here was a Beard he liked and trusted (he appeared to be on the point of crawling deep inside it, and hibernating in guileless sleepiness within its deepest depths; if only Brinkman had thought of this!) – and appeared to make a little note beside Oliver's name. Oliver was probably going to be the first in line for roasting. Adams had lost his place at the head of the line. No chance of an answering smile for Oliver from The Beard. No glint of teeth from within the shaggy undergrowth, though – judging by the state of his suit – his were probably teeth that were in no fit condition to glint. It seemed to be the first time he'd seen a smile (an uninhibitedly, teeth-displaying, fully activated, really nice smile) in ages (Frankie's smiles went right across his face from side to side, but failed to feature teeth), and it clearly worried him.

"You don't smile here."

That's what The Beard would be snapping, as yet another basic rule of etiquette was discourteously flouted.

You wouldn't *feel* like smiling.

("I say, you fellow," Oliver would be saying, rotating at quite a lick. "Don't forget the chestnuts. Who's brought the mustard?")

"Darville?"

"Dibbo?"

"Drinkwater?"

The roll call continued, moving on from Comstock in its alphabetical-order journey down all the Crowninshield's boys toward Whitefoord, and everyone remembered to say "Present, sir," "Thank you, sir," and "No, sir," though no one else attempted to emulate Oliver's rather commendable enthusiasm, carefully avoiding any hint of italics or exclamation points.

The bells kept on ringing.

And they kept on freezing, tensed to carry out the rapped-out orders that they expected to hear at any moment.

("Present, sir," Ben practiced inside his head.

("Present, sir."

("Present, sir."

("Thank you, sir."

("No, sir."

(It was as if it was he who was liable to stuttering, rather than his sister.)

But it was Linnaeus who stuttered.

"Finch?"

"P-P-P . . ." he began.

(*P-P-P.*

(He heard Alice trying to pronounce "Papa" as her father fired a question at her, one of his give-me-the-answer-*now* questions.

("P-P-P," she would begin.

(And "P-P-P," Papa would repeat mockingly, because she couldn't say his name.

(Papa was dead, but he still wasn't buried.

(*Resurgam.*

(That was the word of warning, a *Beware*, a *Danger*, a *Keep Clear* sort of a word.)

"P-P-P . . ." Linnaeus said again.

(Papa wasn't buried because of the snow, the frozen condition of the Arctic ground. He was lying somewhere in Highland Kinsolvin's premises – a scene that Ben shrank from picturing – waiting for a thaw so that he could then be laid into the ground in the churchyard at All Saints'.

(*Laid into the ground.*

(That was the sort of phrase that came to mind.

(Not "at rest."

(Papa would never be "at rest."

(He had never been at rest when he was alive, and he would never be at rest in death.

(*R.I.P.* would not be what was engraved on the gravestone, when there was a gravestone.

(*Resurgam.*

(That would be the word, the only legible word, all the others worn away. This was as it should be. Papa had always detested words when they were written down. That was what it had felt like.

(The dark corner.

(The yew tree.

(Cold water dripping down from the low-drooping branches.

(The one word.

(The angry, threatening word.)

"My father died during the blizzard."

He'd practiced saying that, just as he was now practicing saying, "Present, sir," trying to sound calm and dignified, a young son proud of a brave father's desperate fight for life in appalling conditions.

"My father died during the blizzard."

This was what he would say if boys questioned him.

His friends hadn't asked him anything about what had happened, but he knew that the boys of Otsego Lake Academy would. They'd keep on and on at him, eager for details, hoping for tears, lured toward him by the helpful identifying mark of the black band. It was the sort of thing that they looked forward to. He knew this, though he didn't know that some of the masters would show an even stronger thirst for the refreshing flow that gushed out with sobbing, despite its salty flavor. Perhaps they were men who had fed on grief for years, driven insane by their saltwater drinking, like shipwrecked sailors marooned in their rotting boats, posed as a better-dressed companion-piece to *The Raft of the "Medusa"*, signaling frantically for more victims.

"My father died during the blizzard."

It had the sound of something tragic and heroic about it, a solitary figure battling through the storm in bleak wastelands far from anywhere. Howling winds deafened him, snow blinded him as he trudged doggedly on, drawn by the thought of a light in a window, a glowing red fire, an anxious family waiting, sleepless with worrying.

It conveyed nothing of the truth.

The messy suicide in the study, the knife he had used for opening his letters now opening his throat and letting life out. The blood on the snow, the snow that had blown into the room through the open window. Ben hadn't seen it, but he'd heard about it, listening at closed doors. They thought he didn't know. They still used the word "accident," some of them — not Alice — sounding as if they believed it, but Ben knew that his papa had killed himself. It was what he *wanted* to believe.

They had all been at Grandpapa and Grandmama's when it had happened, all of them except for Alice. It was Alice who had found the body, Alice who had been alone in the house with it for several days, trapped by the snow as the blizzard raged.

"My father died during the blizzard."

If he said it often enough, then Papa really would be dead, and he wouldn't hear his voice again, even though he wasn't buried.

Perhaps he'd feel differently once Papa *was* buried, once he'd seen him laid in the ground and the earth piled on top of the coffin.

Perhaps it would be different then.

He didn't think it would be.

He *knew* it wouldn't be different.

Papa would never be dead as long as he himself continued to be alive.

"P-P-P."

Linnaeus's third attempt.

"P-P-P," Brinkman said, very softly.

He probably didn't even know he'd said it. It was just a habit with him, this taunting. The Beard did not appear to notice.

"Having trouble speaking English, are we?" The Beard asked Linnaeus.

"No, sir."

"It *sounded* like it! Do you think you'll manage to say, 'Thank you, sir,' and, 'No, sir'?"

"Yes, sir."

Linnaeus managed the "Yes, sir" without a stutter, closing his eyes, and leaping out into space, not looking down at what lay beneath him.

Bells.

Freeze.

He managed the "Thank you, sir," and the "No, sir," floating himself out into the silence, hovering there by force of will.

"French?"

("Present, sir," from William French.

("Thank you, sir."

("No, sir."

"Henderson?"

("Present, sir," from 'Arry 'Enderson.

("Thank you, sir."

("No, sir.")

After Hugh Petteys had said "No, sir" — and it was his turn — Ben managed to say "Present, sir" without drawing attention to himself. The Beard hadn't even looked at him, and had held the sheet of paper blindly out to one side. His eyes had already been searching for the next name on the list — Frank Stoddard, ever since Joe Rasmusson had left Crowninshield's — and Ben, time now for his "Thank you, sir," and "No, sir" (no problems with either of these), had had to reach out toward where the foolscap was being impatiently shaken with a clearly audible rattling sound. The Beard's fountain pen, held in the same hand as the sheet of paper, gushed blue ink on the back of Ben's hand — and the nib almost stabbed him — as it shook from side to side. The always-acquiescent schoolboys of Otsego Lake Academy were only too deferentially honored to be employed as pen-wipers. Ben should have felt proud to have been the chosen one. Confused — not wishing to drop the paper, and unable to wipe the ink away with his neatly folded just-ironed white handkerchief, awkwardly inaccessible in his high-angled trouser-pocket — he found himself brushing the back of his ink-stained hand against his lips. He'd have blue lips all day. He began to suck frantically at his lips, attempting to be discreet about it, wincing at the metallic taste.

("Why are you making that kissing sound, Pinkerton?"

("Please don't . . ."

("Why the kissy-kissy-kiss slurping, Pinkerton?"

("*Please* don't . . ."

("Getting yourself in position, Pinkerton?"

("*Please* don't . . ."

("Who's the lucky chap you've chosen, Pinkerton?"

("*Please* don't . . ."

("Anyone fancy a peck from Pinkie?"

("*Please* . . ."

("Comstock looks quite keen."

("*Please* . . ."

("Come on, Comstock, pucker up for Pinkie."

("*Please* . . ."

(He knew, already, exactly what Mr. Rappaport was going to be like. He'd be please-*please*-pleasing Mr. Rappaport for as long as he was within his power.)

The ink seemed infected by all the metal nibs that had been thrust into the bottle, all the sharpness of the sentences that they had written, the sentences he had sucked down inside himself, staining himself indelibly blue inside with blue-blood academy remonstrances.

Are they all fools like you from your school?

They should be clearing the wards at the North River Lunatic Asylum.

(And the other sentences.

(The sentences dictated by Papa to Mr. Rappaport, whispering, whispering, pursing his wet lips to enunciate clearly, so that no mistakes would be made.

(Sentences were what were made of the words you spoke or wrote.

(Sentences were the days and months and years that you spent in imprisonment, unable to move from the place in which you had been placed, unable to see beyond the walls that enclosed you.

(Sometimes a sentence was so complete a summary of all that you were that it became a life sentence.

(He heard Papa speaking the life sentences to Mr. Rappaport.

(He heard Mr. Rappaport speaking the life sentences like words that he had thought of all by himself, words that expressed what he really felt, words that he enjoyed speaking.)

As Ben sucked his lips, with a slight slurpy sound, he began to

335

study the piece of paper that induced instant depression, and a sagging of all visible features.

It was the timetable for their lessons.

Sag.

Sag.

Sag.

Long ruler-straight lines stretched from side to side and from top to bottom of the paper, and every space was filled – in firm no-nonsense-from-*you* printing – with the name of a subject and the name of its teacher and the number of the room in which they would be taught, and there was no time remaining to them that was not unaccounted for, and there was no place in which they would be that was not known at all times. The thick black lines drew themselves around him, enclosed him securely. Every subject occupied a big square box, strong-drawn boxes with no gaps to allow escape, and recesses and lunchtimes (if it was a map of time drawn to scale) seemed to occupy no more than minutes, than *seconds*, would. It appeared advisable to be absolutely certain to visit the lavatory before you set out for school in the morning, to avoid swallowing any liquids, and to cultivate a rapid gulp-down-without-chewing method of eating. It was an austere pile of boxes, with no attempt made to suggest any possibilities of frivolous enjoyment. That was *not* what they were there for. The school supplied lunch, and there'd be no more midday dawdlings to and from home, no talks about what you'd done that morning, what you were going to do that afternoon. (You wouldn't *want* to talk about what you'd done, and you certainly wouldn't want to think about what you'd be doing.)

Meals would be eaten in silence (they'd be trapped in stern Trappist noiselessness, and when they weren't not talking, not talking, they'd be keeping right, keeping right), with synchronized hands and mouths, the alert observing Beards ensuring that the correct angles were employed for all movements. They were about to become illustrations – *Fig. (a)*, *Fig. (b)*, *Fig. (c)*, *Fig. (d)* (all those figs, and no leaves with which to hide their stared-upon nakedness) – in a book of arithmetical problems.

Chemistry.

Arithmetic.

Grammar.

Geography.

Room 4.

Room 9.

Room 16.

Room 29.

He saw dim corridors lined with these mysterious austerely numbered rooms (no letters allowed, nothing but numbers), all of them with their doors closed, and all of them in no particular order. Order would make things *far* too straightforward.

Go to the inner room.

Go to the inner room.

This was a room with no number upon its door.

This was a room he would never find, a room somewhere deep inside him.

Draftsmanship.

Biology.

Sport.

A momentary raising of the spirits for the hearties amongst them when they grasped at *Sport*, those for whom ignorance allowed a brief-lasting bliss, those who did not possess the knowledge to realize what would lie ahead of them when the name *Mr. Rappaport* was printed beneath *Sport*. It was always *Mr. Rappaport* whether or not *Sport* was followed by *Gymnasium* or *Field*. Not much chance of sprinting, or hopping, stepping, and jumping with the snow the way it was. They'd be reduced to supervised sledding or synchronized drilled snowballing.

(*Hit him in the face, you idiot!*

(*Harder!*

(*Why isn't there a brick inside your snowball, you fool?*)

Latin.

Mr. Rappaport — Ben also knew — was to be their Latin teacher, and there his name was — printed in the boxes below *Latin* — to prove it.

Room 37.

And there was the room number.

A sense of a silent corridor, a firmly closed door.

Dr. Crowninshield had encouraged the first tentative shoots in the new growth of Latin; soon, it might be time to snip-snap with the pruning shears. You reduced the garden to a desert and claimed that you were encouraging new growth. Latin had become an unpromising subject (considering the teacher), but Ben *liked* Sport.

Had liked Sport.

Would have liked Sport.

Could have liked Sport.

Clad in their Sport clothing, they marched and countermarched as they were drilled, chanting the words they had to learn by heart.

Sport should be liked.

Sport wilt be liked.

(You could guarantee that wilting would be involved.)

Sport should have been liked.

Sport wilt have been liked.

Sport will have been liked.

Sport might be liked.

Sport may have been liked.

Sport should have been liked.

It was his first day at Otsego Lake Academy, and – already – his knowledge of different tenses was improving in leaps and bounds.

Present tense.

Future tense.

Tension everywhere you looked.

"Leap *higher!*" Mr. Rappaport snarled, hurling sharp-edged Latin textbooks with unerring skill at the backs of people's heads to demonstrate his skills as a Sport teacher. "Bound *further!*"

Two lessons with Mr. Rappaport on their first day.

They'd be having Sport that afternoon.

They'd be having Latin that morning.

They'd be having Latin as their very first lesson in their new school.

They'd be leaping higher and higher.

They'd be bounding further and further.

Ben could see what was going to happen, what it was going to be like.

Every Monday they'd be beginning the week with an hour and a half of Latin with Mr. Rappaport.

That would be something to look forward to all weekend, something to send you skipping back to school each Monday morning with a song in your heart, and a spring in your step. After the school had done with them what the school was about to do with them beneath the forested dome this first morning, they'd be released – the few survivors, limping slightly after their adjustments – to enter a new thralldom in the cold classical Room 37 domain of Mr. Rappaport and his completely inflexible verbs, his vocabulary lists of words that were the only words to be spoken, the only words to be held within the head. No other words would be permitted.

Ben had been given his orders in the shape of a timetable.

He would *not* lose it.

(No, sir.)

He would carry it about with him everywhere, reverentially folded, memorizing it, whispering the words upon it to himself in the still, quiet hours of the early morning darkness, his prayer of strength from his little *Book of Hours* – long, long, endless hours – to see him through the day ahead.

Depression.

Deep, deep depression at the thought of what lay ahead of him, the path down which he was directed, and the only way there was for him to walk: cold, closed-in, shutting out all views of what lay beyond.

Sag.

Sag.

Sag.

He'd nothing left to sag – as well as being small, he was quite skinny – but he still felt he hadn't done with sagging.

And he'd said, "Thank you."

At Otsego Lake Academy, you had to say "Thank you" to Mr. Scrivener after he had beaten you, and he'd beat you often if you gave rise to dissatisfaction. That's what they'd heard. It was one of the attractions he had on offer, and it appealed no end to parents. *You Pay Me And I Beat Them. Both Sides Benefit!* This, impressively translated into Latin by Mr. Rappaport, or one of his more senior colleagues, was probably the school motto.

The Beard made some snide comment to Frank Stoddard about his spots, little comments about several of the boys, remarks about the way that they spoke, or the way that they stood, or the way that they were dressed and the way that they looked (none of these was favorable), but his heart clearly wasn't in it. He had a job to do, and lacked the time in which to enjoy himself. Ticking came first, and the fountain pen was inclined from left to right, left to right, left to right. The little tussles with Adams and Alloway were small indulgences that he'd allowed himself, and now he'd reached the end of the list. Ben continued to study the timetable. Latin lessons were on Mondays, Wednesdays, and Fridays, and each of them lasted for one and a half hours. He'd thought no further sagging was possible, and yet he sagged further. Then there was *Sport* to speculate over. Even further sagging. He found within himself the powers for more sagging than he would have ever thought possible, an inexhaustible supply of saggability.

The Beard reached the end of his list.

"Whitefoord?"

"Present, sir."

"Thank you, sir."

"No, sir."

Another Beard appeared from the opposite direction from which the first Beard had appeared, from the corridor down which Vellacott had walked to take up his position. This time, he was someone whose appearance did coincide with the sound of bells, and they regarded him with heightened respect. A man whose every appearance was heralded by ring-out-wild-bells significance.

Oliver failed to display heightened respect. He began to whisper quietly, with gloomy theatricality.

> "Hear the sledges with the bells —
>> Silver bells!
> What a world of merriment their melody foretells! . . ."

("I wouldn't count on much merriment!" That was what he was intoning.

("The bells! The bells!" That was what he was thinking, the sound a harbinger of doom.)

Second Beard looked at First Beard, with an interrogative angle to his head.

"All present," First Beard said.

"What do you think?" Second Beard asked, indicating the Crowninshield's boys with a flick of his hand like a dismissive gesture.

"Not impressed."

They spoke as if the boys weren't there.

> ". . . How they tinkle, tinkle, tinkle,
>> In the icy air of night! . . ."

("*Ante* bell*um!*" A whisper from Charlie Whitefoord.

("I'm definitely *anti* these *bellums*." Oliver's reply. "Ring out, wild bells, and let him die!"

("I can't claim to be *wild* about the bells, but I like the dying.")

"No talking!"

The two Beards turned toward them with coordinated scowls.

"No talking!"

They turned back to their discussion.

They were like two customs officials checking a cargo. They'd probably be examining them for signs of possible damage in a minute — that stutter of Finch's might merit a claim from their insurance agent's, and Alloway should definitely be returned for a refund – holding them up at different angles, just to check the condition that they were in. They were kidnappers who had received the ransom they had demanded. The parents had paid up, and now they could do whatever they liked with their child hostages.

First Beard said, "All you men . . ."

(They weren't boys anymore, now.

(They were *men*.

(That's what pupils were – or were made to be – at Otsego Lake Academy.

(The first – er – *adjustments* were about to be undertaken to ensure that a full growth of beard could – in the fullness of time – be harvested from the unpromising chins that had been gathered together.

(In the central hall, beneath the painted ceiling, the necessary alterations would be carried out to guarantee the athletic excellence – and not only *athletic* excellence – for which their academy was so noted.

(Sound minds.

(Sound bodies.

(*Mens sana in corpore sano.*

(Latin!

(Juvenal in brackets.)

". . . follow us!"

"No talking!"

(Second Beard.)

"Keep right!"

(First Beard.)

First Beard and Second Beard led them across the center of the entrance hall, and to the closed double-doors that led into the main hall. They did not talk. They tried to keep right, unsure though they were of where right began and ended They gathered in a little group, not quite sure what they were supposed to do. The two Beards seemed to expect them to *know* what to do.

What *was* the correct etiquette for potential human sacrifices?

Pause.

How *were* you expected to comport yourself, as the last seconds of life ticked away?

Pause.

Sighs of impatience from both Beards.

"Get in line, in order of size, starting at the doors!" First Beard said.

(That's what you do *here*.)

"The tallest at the back!"

(Second Beard.)

Ben realized what was going to happen.

He *hated* what was going to happen.

Order of size.

This was something they had never done at Crowninshield's.

They could have formed up in alphabetical order *instantly*, with hardly any need for thought, and each boy could have named who should have been in front of him, and who should have been behind him. This had been Dr. Crowninshield's method of taking a roll call.

6

"Roll call!" Dr. Crowninshield shouted as he came in through the door, and they instantly formed the alphabetical-order line, all in position before Dr. Crowninshield reached the front of the room. He ran down the line, patting them on the heads, ruffling their hair (an extra-vigorous ruffle for Frankie Alloway because of the redness).

"One!" from Tom Adams.

(Adams was Tom at Crowninshield's.)

"Two!" from Tom Akenside.

(And Akenside was Tom.)

"Three! *Ouch!*" from Frankie Alloway.

(*Frankie.*)

"Who's missing?" he asked, noticing a gap in the numbering, and they all told him in chorus, as if he hadn't realized whom it was.

Dr. Crowninshield did not wish to waste his time on boring mundane tasks.

He wanted to get on with twelve-inch ruler sword-fights, drawers-discovering nature rambles, really important things like that. The more Ben thought of Dr. Crowninshield, the more he realized how much he'd liked him. This was probably the first lesson he would learn at Otsego Lake Academy, that a fraud could be a person you liked, even when you *knew* he was a fraud.

Dr. Crowninshield hadn't *meant* to be a fraud.

Ben was sure about that.

(Though he *must* have been a fraud. He must have persuaded his papa that he was something that he was not, otherwise Papa would not have been interested in sending his son to his school, even if it did possess a coat of arms with a crown and a shield and a lion and a unicorn. He must have persuaded his papa that he would be a strong, demanding, unyielding pedagogue, with the ability to reduce any boy to whimpering by the merciless whiplash of his mocking tongue.

("Excellent!"

(*Snigger.*

("Most amusing!"

(*Snigger.*

(Dr. Crowninshield must have lied.

("I have a confession to make. I've just told you all a lie!")

Dr. Crowninshield hadn't *meant* to be a fraud.

He was just a young man who had wanted to have a coat of arms and play at being a boy for a little while longer, a young man who had somehow accidentally got his sums wrong.

Dr. Crowninshield had never been very good at sums.

"Ahem, sir."

That had been Oliver's not-so-very-secret message to Dr. Crowninshield whenever he made a mistake with his calculations on the blackboard during

Arithmetic. (His mother made frequent use of "Ahem," and

Oliver had appropriated it for a different purpose, though it still made reference to what was unspeakable.)

"Whereabouts this time, Olly?" Dr. Crowninshield would ask humbly, and Oliver would tell him.

"The second line down, sir. Nine sevens are traditionally accepted as being sixty-three. You seem to have opted imaginatively for fifty-four."

Dr. Crowninshield would rub out the mistake, and chalk in the correct answer.

"How very humiliating. Thank you, Olly. What would I do without you?"

"Glad to be of service, sir."

"Ahem, sir."

"Whereabouts this time, Olly?"

Sometimes – especially if there was more noise than usual – Dr. Crowninshield's pretty young wife (she was the age of their older sisters, not the age of their mothers) would come downstairs from the four rooms in which they lived at the top of the house.

"Are the boys being too rough with you, Edward?" she'd ask him. She'd turn and face the class. "Are you boys being rough with my poor husband?"

"*Yes!*" they'd say, pleased to be thought naughty, bullying their teacher.

(They were always *boys* at Crowninshield's. Even the owner of the school was a boy.)

They all liked Mrs. Crowninshield. For the last lesson of the week on Friday afternoon, she'd bring down a cake she'd baked, and they'd all – including Dr. Crowninshield – sit and eat a slice as she read from *The Adventures of Tom Sawyer* to them. Tom Sawyer's was more Ben's sort of school than Tom Brown's. He'd read Mark Twain's novel again in the days after Papa's death, thinking of Dr. and Mrs. Crowninshield, and wondering where they were, what had happened to them, how they were managing without Oliver to help them with their sums. When he read the description of Tom Sawyer being made to sit with the *girls* in class

345

(Chapter VII coming up next: Tom trying to put his arm about Becky Thatcher, Tom trying to tell her that he cared for her, the strange feelings this created in Ben), the classroom he was in was the one at Crowninshield's, the room in which he'd never be again.

"Roll call!"

"One!" from Tom Adams.

(Tom.)

"Two!" from Tom Akenside.

(Tom.)

"Three! *Ouch!*" from Frankie Alloway.

(Frankie.)

Ben had been number eighteen, with Hugh Petteys in front of him, and Joe Rasmusson behind him, Joe who had the loudest laugh of anyone Ben had ever known – "Batten down the hatches!" Dr. Crowninshield would say. "Brace yourselves against the mast!" (you'd have thought that Mabel Peartree had turned up after all, clearing her throat, and wielding her sheet music) – Joe who had gone to live in Hiawatha, Kansas, with his widowed sister after his mother remarried. He hadn't been laughing so much since that had happened.

"I'm sorry we're losing you, Joe," Dr. Crowninshield said. "I hope Kansas has been warned about that laugh, a full alert in all areas. The inhabitants will be fleeing to their cyclone cellars. Remember our Geography lesson last Tuesday." A gesture indicated the luridly colored drawings of wheat fields – every yellow pencil in the class sharpened away into nothingness – and swirling, giddiness-inducing cyclones that were affixed to the wall with thumbtacks (Linnaeus's meticulous drawing of a group of farm buildings given pride of place), flapping slightly at their lower edges in the breeze from the open windows. Wheat and cyclones. That was Kansas. It did not seem like a sensible combination. Would Joe be safe? Dr. Crowninshield had anticipated that question. "Hiawatha is the best possible place to be for a boy who comes from a place named Longfellow Park."

They'd all put war paint on for Joe's last day – Injun Joe they called him — and dressed up as Red Indians, doing a war dance round Dr. Crowninshield's desk. He was tied to his chair, and not loosely, waiting to be rescued by Mrs. Crowninshield.

"Out of childhood into manhood
Now had grown my Hiawatha . . ."

— Dr. Crowninshield chanted, as they whooped around him with their feathers wobbling (Bradstone's uncle had a farm that included chickens amongst its animals, as well as the imagination-worrying bulls) —

". . . Skilled in all the craft of hunters,
Learned in all the lore of old men,
In all youthful sports and pastimes,
In all manly arts and labors . . ."

They'd thought of Tom Sawyer, Huck Finn, and Joe — another Joe! — Harper escaped to Jackson's Island, striped with black mud like zebras to be Indian chiefs, ambushing each other with dreadful war whoops, and killing and scalping each other.

"Four!" from Charles Bradley.

"Five!" from Frank Bradstone.

"Six!" from Sidney Brinkman.

"Seven!" from Oliver.

(Charles, Frank, Sidney, Olly.)

Occasionally, if he wished to convey the impression of a quietly impressive scholastic atmosphere for the benefit of a visitor, Dr. Crowninshield would institute a more formal method, reading out their names — "Thomas Adams, Thomas Akenside, Frank Alloway, Charles Bradley, Frank Bradstone . . ." — and they'd be answering "Here!" as they sat at their desks. Most usually it was the one-two-three-*ouch* method. He called Thomas Adams and Thomas Akenside "the Tom-Toms." They were two of the three Thomases in the class (the Crowninshield's parents tending to go in for Tom,

347

Dick, and Harry names): three Thomases, four Franks, and — as Alice described it — "enough Charleses to populate the Complete Works of Jane Austen." It was "the Tom-Toms" — Dr. Crowninshield could be a demon for a pun — who had played the tom-toms at the farewell war dance for Joe Rasmusson.

7

"The tallest at the back!"

Thoughts of Crowninshield's faded.

Adams and Akenside replaced "the Tom-Toms." Frankie faded as Alloway took his place. Charles . . .

"The tallest at the back!"

Charlie Whitefoord immediately walked out several yards back into the entrance hall, knowing that he'd be the one at the back of the line. Brinkman, with a certain see-how-tall-I-am swagger, followed close behind him. Most of the boys weren't too sure about how they fitted into an order-of-tallness line, and there was something of a scrimmage in the center. There was a confident grouping starting to form at the back of the line for the tallest.

"The smallest at the front!" First Beard said, unnecessarily, to emphasize the humiliation of what was about to happen.

"At the *front!*" Second Beard seconded, not to be outdone when the opportunity to mortify someone was on offer.

There was an embarrassed, reluctant lingering, and three or four of the boys started to move toward the front of the line — nearest those closed doors with the murmurings behind them, the scraping chairs, the (in all probability) devil worship and human sacrifice — knowing that they were going to be openly revealed as being amongst the smallest boys in the class, in the *school*.

Ben was one of these boys.

He could feel his heart starting to beat more rapidly, knowing how Linnaeus must have felt if he had been made to read in front of them all, a poetry book trembling in his hand as he came forward to

348

read out his favorite poem. This was something they'd done each week at Crowninshield's, each boy preparing a poem for the time when his turn came to read. Most boys tended to choose poetry with a martial or a patriotic subject, though Oliver would have them all believe that he was a devotee of Mrs. Alexander Diddecott's most outrageously sentimental effusions – when that woman wasn't being maudlin with a paintbrush, she was simpering over a pen – and he'd read them out with a sensational loss of emotional control, and wildly dramatic posturings. "I recited one of your poems in class this week," he'd inform Mrs. Alexander Diddecott when she came to call on his mama, though he neglected to let her know that his renditions always made Dr. Crowninshield weep with laughter. "There were *tears*," Oliver would whisper thrillingly – he could be disconcertingly, if misleadingly, honest at times – and Mrs. Alexander Diddecott would feel gratified. (The tears were entirely appropriate and, just as things ought to be, a true confirmation of her status as a practiced wringer of withers.) That boy had a highly developed sense of culture, she felt. Quite remarkable when you considered what his parents were like. That woman! That *man*!

Ben knew the sort of poem that Linnaeus would be likely to read – more ammunition for Brinkman – something like "Oft in the Stilly Night," something rather sad and gentle, something – indeed – that hovered on the verge of being a little too like one of Mrs. Alexander Diddecott's mawkish efforts. Linnaeus did tend to make things difficult for himself. He always found it difficult to speak in front of a large group – you'd see him change color, hear him start to struggle with his breathing, see his fingers beginning to shake – and Dr. Crowninshield had never asked him to read aloud to the whole class. Sometimes Linn insisted on being allowed to read, feeling self-conscious at being left out. "Oft in the Silly Shite!" Brinkman would jeer buffoonishly. "Just like you, Finch!" Linnaeus wouldn't even be able to pronounce the title. "Oft in the St-St-St . . ." he would begin, fiercely concentrating, the whole weight of his being pinned down to the sound of the word, balancing precariously upon it. Ben could see Oliver and Charlie Whitefoord mouthing the words for Linnaeus, trying to speak them for him, to make it easier, and his own lips made the same movements.

(Oft in the stilly night
Ere slumber's chain has bound me . . .)

Ben's friends had moved away from him, and he felt alone all of a sudden. Oliver and Linnaeus would be somewhere in the middle. Linnaeus would not start to shoot up suddenly until he was fourteen. They were part of the milling central throng, unwilling to be condemned to smallness, silently – they'd remembered that "No talking!" from Second Beard – mouthing their claims to superior tallness, and struggling with each other.

"Hurry up!" First Beard hissed impatiently.

"Hurry up!" Second Beard seconded.

The Beards suddenly lost patience, and started grabbing the Crowninshield's boys, thrusting them in twos back to back, attempting to find matching pairs, shoving them forward or backward as the comparative heights were gradually established. They probably had twelve-inch rulers in specially tailored inside pockets, all ready to whip them out so that they could check and adjust their judgments precisely. The rulers would have markings for eighths of an inch, sixteenths of an inch, *thirty-secondths* – (was there such a word, hard to pronounce, and rather splashy?) – of an inch in all likelihood. It was horribly like when teams were being selected for a game, the gradual picking off of boys one by one from the group, the slowly lessening numbers. This was worse than this, this was worse than being the last boy chosen, not that Ben had ever been in that position. He was quite sporty, quick and agile, good in a team, even if – that condemnatory word again – rather *small*. They were about to be marched through into a hall packed with a schoolful of boys, and the smallest boy would be the first boy through the doors. It was slaughterhouse day on the farm, and the animals were about to be forced up the ramp into the wagon.

It was a procedure that appeared designed to make him blush.

Linnaeus was liable to tears, and Ben was liable to blushes, and both crying and blushing were fatal at Otsego Lake Academy.

It was between him and Petteys.

One of the two of them was the smallest boy in the class.

Hugh Petteys – they all called him Huge Petteys – had long been recognized as an unusually tiny boy, and Ben had been comforted by the thought that there would always be someone smaller than himself in the class. In recent months – it seemed like an overnight mushroom growth – Huge (though their name for him could not yet be considered adjectivally accurate) had ceased to be tiny, and had grown so much that Ben had become alarmed.

He'd stood immediately behind Petteys often enough when "Roll call!" was shouted to know that they were now almost exactly the same height. The same *lowth*. "Height" seemed too ambitious a word for someone his size.

(He heard Papa from behind him, leaning down to whisper into his ear.

(*Almost Six Inches in Height*.

(That was what Papa was saying.

(*****)

Slowly, on opposite sides of the central line, he and Petteys began to walk toward the front of it, the division between the two doors. To Ben's right, to Petteys's left, the line of boys was forming up, all positioned in readiness for the battering ram with which they would force their way through the doors and on into the hall beyond, plunging through with jubilant, victorious cries.

They weren't looking very jubilant.

They weren't *feeling* very jubilant.

Bradley was at the front of the struggling line, only a foot or so away from the doors, confident in his superior tallness to Ben and Petteys. Either Ben or Petteys would be pushing himself up against Bradley, standing on top of Bradley's feet, allowing no space into which the other might insert himself to escape the humiliation of being judged the runt of the litter.

*(. . . Fond memory brings the light
Of other days around me . . .)*

First Beard grabbed Ben.

Second Beard grabbed Petteys.

They were thrust together so violently that the backs of their heads collided, and Ben bit his tongue. It was what they no doubt expected in the main hall – the hushed, eager throngs lined up in readiness for the entry of the tiniest of gladiators – the trickle of bright blood spilling from the corner of his mouth and down his chin. The taste of blood mingled with the earlier taste of ink, one seeming to lead unavoidably to the other.

"*Ave, Cæsar, nos morituri te salutamus!*"

That's what Oliver had said, just before they'd walked into the school that morning, those Corinthian columns the opening to a gladiatorial arena.

Hail, Cæsar, we who are about to die salute you!

You imagined the gladiators practicing their salutes in the gloomy labyrinths of rooms beneath the sand-strewn circle. Christians practiced their hymns, and gladiators practiced their salutes. It helped to stop them thinking of what was to follow.

Bloody but unbowed, that's what he'd be, walking into the arena with his head held high.

Well, not *very* high.

That was the problem.

(And – the worrying realization occurred to him – he'd been sag, sag, sagging, ever since he'd been given his thank-you-*sir* timetable, ever since he'd walked through the entrance doors, and making himself even smaller. He could not afford to diminish himself by the tiniest of measurements, not by a thirty-secondth of an inch, not by a sixty-fourth. *The smallest at the front.* Had he left it too late?)

He strained himself up as high as possible, defying gravity with a resolve that would have had Newton worried. Going up on tiptoe would have been a little too risky – The Beards were clearly trained observers, on the alert for dubious practices – but he allowed his heels to rise a little from the polished linoleum.

First Beard suddenly thrust him back against Bradley. Another collision with the back of his head, and a hiss of pain from Bradley.

(Bradley was so taken by surprise that he even missed the opportunity for an agonized, "I forgive thee!" This was *most* unlike Bradley. He tended to stress the agony as much as possible, in order to make the forgiveness all the more inspirational. He liked to give the impression that he could hardly talk for the unbearable pain.)

Then the back of Petteys's head hit Ben in the nose, and it was time for *him* to hiss. Battered from in front, battered from behind! The former Crowninshield's boys would be staggering home with broken noses and split skulls, dark with dried blood and humiliated blushes. "Did you have a nice first day at your new school?" unobservant mothers would be automatically asking, their thoughts on other things, as they glanced up from their novels at their battered progeny.

But . . .

Agony was irrelevant!

Petteys had been placed in front of him!

Petteys had been officially recognized as the smallest boy in the class!

The smallest boy in the *school*, possibly, though there might be some poor malnourished mite in Year One or Year Two (frightful to contemplate if he were a member of any class higher than these) even smaller than he was.

Ben was safe!

Safe for a little while longer!

That was the thing to hang onto, as he grunted, and closed his eyes, and concentrated all his efforts into making himself grow taller.

If nothing else good came from this day – and he was fairly

confident that it wouldn't – then at least this had been established. He'd often wondered, me or Petteys? as Petteys's inexorable growth continued. Petteys or me? But he'd never been too keen on finding out the answer, orbiting Petteys like some minor satellite planet, but not drawing near enough to know, keeping his eyes lowered so that he wouldn't see where the top of his head was when he was pressed up against him in roll call. Now he knew. There had been a clue in Petteys's name all the time, a clue that should not have gone unnoticed by a Pinkerton.

Petteys was petty.

Petteys was diminutive.

Petteys was negligible.

Petteys looked like *petite*.

Petteys sounded like *pretties*.

Petteys was *smaller than he was*.

They were so near in height – thank goodness that he hadn't had his hair cut as Mama had suggested: that might have made a slight but vital difference – that the back of Petteys's head was exactly opposite his face, in the very same position that was so familiar from Crowninshield's. He sometimes felt that he knew the back of Petteys's head better than he knew his face. (You weren't missing much if you couldn't see Petteys's face.) If he trod very closely behind Petteys, then Petteys's head would obstruct his face like a mask, and no one would see him, though there was the danger that some of the less observant in the hall might gain the impression that his body was topped with Petteys's head. He'd have to coordinate his steps very carefully with Petteys's . . .

"Arms by your sides!"

(First Beard.)

"Stand up straight!"

(Second Beard.)

"Follow me!"

(First Beard.)

"I shall bring up the rear!"

(Second Beard.)

"No talking!"

(Combined effort.

(But no one *was* talking.)

"Keep right!"

(Combined effort.)

First Beard grasped the handle of the left-hand door.

Second Beard – briefly abandoning his rear-guard position – grasped the handle of the right-hand door.

A discreet peep into the hall from First Beard, opening the door two or three inches to check that the time was right. He nodded, in response to some signal.

He nodded again to Second Beard.

Resurgam.

(Papa was there, standing behind him instead of Bradley, shrunk down to Bradley's size so that his beard scratched the back of Ben's neck. There was now a Third Beard.

(Papa was marching in behind him on his first day at his new school, to keep an eye on him, to keep *both* eyes on him, to make sure that he said and did all the right things, the things that ought to come to him naturally but did not. Mr. Rappaport would be watching, and Papa would be watching with him. Sniggers would be involved at some stage. He just knew that sniggers would be involved.

(Papa was whispering, his voice low, so low that only Ben could hear it, the voice coming from inside his head and not from the figure behind him, the words it was speaking words from within his own mind.

(But he could still feel the breath – cold, not warm – against the back of his right ear. Something was leaning a little closer, to ensure that it would be heard.

(*P-P-P.*

(Stuttering, shivering with the cold.

(P-P-P for Papa.

(P-P-P for Pinkerton.

(P-P-P for Pinkie.

(P-P-P for Pink.

(P-P-P for *prettier*.

(*P-P-P*.

(The figure behind him was not speaking in English.

(It was dead.

(It was speaking in Latin, the language of the dead.

(*Go to the inner room*.

(*Go to the inner room*.

(*P-P-P* for *Post mortem*.

(That's what it was saying.

(*Memento mori*.

(*Novus ordo seclorum*.

(This was whispered like a threat.

(A new order of the ages.

(It didn't say *Requiescat in pace*.

(That wouldn't be a sentence that it would *ever* speak.

(*Hic iacet*.

(It said this.

(*Resurgam*.

(And this.

(It whispered this repeatedly.

(*Resurgam*.

("I shall rise again."

(*He shall rise up* . . .

(*Snigger*.

(*Guffaw*.

(*All the daughters of musick shall be brought low* . . .

(*Snigger*.

(*Guffaw*.

(*Amo, amas, amat* . . .

(These words were the most insistent words of all.

(. . . *amamus, amatis, amant* . . .

(It loved.

(It was loving.

(It did love.

(It *did*.

(It *did*.

(With truculent persistence it insisted that it *did*.

(It loved, and it would rise again.

(*Snigger.*

(*Guffaw.*)

The two Beards briskly pressed the handles down with one hand, and pushed the two doors forcefully inward with their other hand, coordinating their choice of hands and their movements so that each was a mirror-image of the other.

Bells.

This time the bells *did* mean something, that something would happen. *They* were to be the someones who would appear.

The doors crashed back as if a battering ram had – after all – been employed to effect an entrance, and the Crowninshield's boys were marched into the main hall to meet their new chums.

(. . . The smiles, the tears Of boyhood's years,
The words of love then spoken . . .)

357

FIVE

Out of childhood into manhood.

("Right leg!" First Beard should have been barking.

("Left leg!" Second Beard should have been barking.

("Swing the left arm!"

("Swing the right arm!"

("No talking!"

("Keep right!"

(But nothing was said.)

In silence, the miniature gladiators marched in, led toward the very center of the hall, beneath the cupola, First Beard in front of Petteys, Second Beard behind Charlie Whitefoord. It gave a sense of all possible avenues of escape being closed against them, trained dogs salivatingly unleashed into the deep-cut trenches in the snow. The hall was dimly lit, but all Ben was aware of seeing was the back of Petteys's head, the brushmarks in the dark hair where he'd been carefully prepared for his first day at the school. He was walking so closely behind him that occasionally he had to perform a clumsy little marching-on-the-spot maneuver, a double-shuffle with his feet, to avoid a collision. Behind him, Papa was doing the same thing, struggling to avoid colliding into *him*. An awful picture of imminent disaster came into Ben's mind. At the very end of the line, Second Beard would slam into Charlie Whitefoord, Charlie Whitefoord would topple into Brinkman, and — with a dreadful compulsive inevitability — the whole line of Crowninshield's boys would slowly topple over into a struggling mass, like a line of roped-together mountaineers sliding toward a chasm, hacking vainly at the ice with their axes as they slithered to their doom.

"No talking!" First Beard would bark as they opened their mouths to scream for help.

"No talking!" Second Beard would bark as they glided in silence to their deaths in the frozen deeps.

"Keep right!" First Beard would bark as they fought for breath, attempting to free themselves from the heaving mass.

"Keep right!" Second Beard would bark.

He and Petteys would be right at the bottom of the pile, and he'd be crushed by Papa, his cigar-smoke-smelling beard pressed against and around his head in an attempt at suffocation. The rest of the school in which they had once been happy piled upon Papa, their weight crushing down.

Like hockey-stick-struck pucks they'd glide across the ice, and The Beards would be holding their hands in front of their mouths, sniggering at the avalanche of doomed mountaineers as they slid across the ice toward them, arms and legs flailing frantically, not talking, struggling to keep right . . .

They'd be sniggering . . .

Then Ben became aware of what he was hearing all around him.

There *was* sniggering, and the sniggering was not coming from The Bearded Ones.

"No talking!"

That's what The Bearded Ones were exclaiming, at regular intervals.

"No talking!"

What he was hearing was the characteristic sound of Otsego Lake Academy, the sound of the (not very) suppressed snigger, and *they* were the cause of the sniggers. If it wasn't the sound of bells, it was the sound of sniggers. He'd heard the sound demonstrated in Papa's study by Mr. Rappaport, and now it was multiplied all around him.

"No talking!" The Beards exclaimed again, but the gathered

schoolboys of Otsego Lake Academy were sniggering, not talking, and sniggering was not being forbidden.

Snigger.

Snigger.

Snigger.

"No talking!"

They were beneath the central dome.

> . . . *I feel like one*
> *Who treads alone*
> *Some banquet-hall deserted,*
> *Whose lights are fled,*
> *Whose garlands dead,*
> *And all but he departed!* . . .

(When he was nervous, as Ben was nervous now, Linnaeus would never have reached as far as the second verse of a poem without stammering. There'd have been an abrupt stop, as if he had suddenly run into a barrier that was too high for him to jump. He'd pause, and begin to take deep breaths, working himself up for the leap that had to be taken.)

First Beard stopped suddenly, and braced his hand against Petteys's chest, a custodian denying him access to a guarded place. Ben almost ran into Petteys, and — behind him — he felt Bradley put his two hands flat against his back to steady himself, pushing him forward slightly.

Snigger!

Snigger!

Snigger!

(The sniggers were louder now, and the snigger, snigger, snigger made him want to sag, sag, sag all over again.)

Bells.

Freeze.

Ben looked down as he struggled to remain upright, to try and prevent himself from standing on the backs of Petteys's boots, and noticed that the whole group of them had been positioned in line across a chalk mark drawn on the shiny blackboard of the floor. There was a thick line for where the front of the line was to be – it was at this that First Beard had stopped Petteys – and, at right-angles to this, another line was drawn across the floor from beneath the cupola out across to the doors, and it was on this line that they were standing, balanced like tightrope walkers across a drop, their wet boots starting to rub it out into invisibility so that they would drop into the void beneath. A line of chopped carrots, trodden upon, partially mushed – the débris of some weeks-ago meal – was strewn at right-angles across this line, probably in an attempt to lure an unsuspecting rabbit toward the kitchen casserole.

(That's what it looked like to Ben.

("Here, little bunny!" Mrs. Economou cooed seductively, with unconvincing friendliness – sounding just like Olly trying to lure the Comstocks' parrot back into his cage as Hilderbrandt eyed him suspiciously – the cleaver clutched firmly behind her back. One rabbit should be enough meat to keep the school going for most of the week.

("Jack, Jack, look at the rab-bit!"

(It was quite a long line of carrots, and disappeared away to his left. He didn't raise his head to see how far it went, because he didn't want to see Year One (*A*) sniggering at him.

(Mama's hands came together, as if in prayer, and shadows were cast across the wall of his bedroom.

(The rab-bit wiggled its ears.

(The rab-bit twitched its nose.

(There was no warmth of fur or blood.

(There was only paper.

("Oh dear! Oh dear! I shall be too late!"

(All the time, Ben was thinking this.

(He was starting to breathe more quickly, like Frankie, still not recovered from his frantic slithering sprint through the snow tunnels.

(*What a relief it will be for all of us on the day that you finally stop.*

(That's what First Beard had said to Frankie about his breathing.)

There were, Ben realized, chalked lines everywhere across the floor, radiating out from the center of the hall like the markings of a clock, or of a giant points-of-the-compass, a full thirty-two-point compass, like the one on the map in *Treasure Island*, one with all the in-between naval subtleties of direction, not just north, south, east, and west.

(*Cape of ye Woods*, he was thinking, *Skeleton Island, Strong tide here, Ye Spye-glass Hill.*)

Down all these lines boys were arranged – year by year, class by class – in order of size, the smallest at the center.

Because the Crowninshield's boys were an extra class, slotted in a year earlier than was usual, they were not Year One.

They were Year Naught.

That was what they had been told on the Sunday of the tour. It was as if they did not exist. They were certainly of no account. That had been made perfectly clear to them.

It is naught, it is naught, saith the buyer: but when he is gone his way, then he boasteth.

That sentence came into his mind, but he did not recognize where it came from. It had all the signs of something said in All Saints', something said with the voice of the Reverend Goodchild.

Not much about which to boasteth here.

On their left was Year One (*A*) – the source of much of the sniggering. The *relief* it must have been to them when they were presented with a whole group of boys who were of even less account than they were, even smaller, a richer source of sniggering! He wished to move his head, and look to his left, just to check if there were any smaller boys in Year One (*A*), but he didn't dare. The sniggering would not be suppressed once they were outside the confines of the hall. You just *knew* that.

And it wouldn't just be sniggers.

You knew that, also.

Loud and uninhibited, the sniggers would echo in every direction around them, the titters and the giggles and the guffaws and the heehaws and the her-her-hers.

(Would *they* become a Year One when the next school year started — one of three Year Ones, presumably — or would they continue their way through the school always as Year Naught, never becoming anything, never being of any account, never changing?)

On the left of Year One (*A*) was Year One (*alpha*), and on the left of Year One (*alpha*) was Year One (*aleph*). On the left of Year One (*aleph*) was Year Two, with its own *A* and *alpha* and *aleph*. Like the spokes of a wheel, each *A* and each *alpha* and each *aleph* radiated out from the center — order of age, order of size — until the oldest and biggest of all the boys in the school (cruelly emphasizing the nothingness of Year Naught, their puniness, their teeny-tiny worthlessness, their naughty-naughty naughtness) were ranged to the right of Year Naught, towering above them. Some of them had already entered the ranks of The Bearded Ones (the word "boys" was one you would hesitate to use in order to describe them), and others — with effortful fuzziness of feature — were striving to join them. They were not sniggering. They were above even noticing the likes of Year Naught — down below eye level, unworthy of observation — and stared straight ahead, to the circular raised platform that had been positioned beneath the exact center of the hall beneath the cupola, arms down by their sides in manly comportment, faces expressionless.

Their arms were by their sides.

They were standing up straight.

They were not talking.

They were — you somehow *knew* it — keeping right.

This is the way to do it.

That was what they were demonstrating, positioned like an explanatory diagram in a textbook.

This is what seven years at Otsego Lake Academy will do for you, if you obey your orders.

Straight arms.

Upright posture.

Silence.

Rightness.

Beards.

It was like a diagram of the effects of time.

As you moved around the clock-face in the direction of the hands of the clock, you became older. Year by year, you'd be moved a few degrees in a clockwise direction, and each time you moved you'd be a year older – a year clockwiser – as time ticktocked past. Year Naught were noon – that was how Ben thought of it – and the big boys were midnight, licensed for darkness and freedom, with no set bedtime. Vellacott, Ben supposed – thinking of the boy who had talked to Oliver, the boy instructed to take up his position, not talk, and keep right – would be in line somewhere between five and six o'clock, opposite them.

They were part of a diagram in a classroom, placed within a pre-arranged problem awaiting solving. They'd be solved, and then they'd be erased, and new problems would be drawn on the blackboard that filled the whole hall, the blackboard on which the whole school was assembled. At the back of the line – Ben didn't look behind him to check, he was too occupied in attempting to efface himself with Petteys – Second Beard would be hauling back at one of Charlie Whitefoord's shoulders, to stop him from moving any further forward. For what seemed like several minutes, the line tottered and trembled before it became still.

Snigger!

Snigger!

Snigger!

Bells.

Freeze.

"No talking!"

Bells.

Freeze.

There seemed to be even more bells than there had been earlier, their ringing closer together, louder, more insistent.

"No talking!"

An extra-authoritative command from Second Beard, unseen behind them.

This time, the snicker of suppressed sniggering really did seem to fade, and Mr. Scrivener tottered into the hall through the same double-doors by which they had entered, stumbling past the in-order-of-size line of Crowninshield's boys, like a head of state too unobservant to inspect a conspicuously unarmed corps of under-sized elite troops.

Creak.

Pause.

Click.

Pause.

Creak.

Pause.

Click.

Pause.

The pauses were considerably longer than the creaks and clicks.

He hadn't improved much in the two weeks since they'd last seen him.

He still looked about three hundred years old, and could scarcely remain upright. He had the blinking, overwhelmed look of a tortoise yanked out of its protective shell. The edges of pieces of paper projecting from the book he was carrying under his arm rustled like a paper windmill. He headed for the raised platform, and it took him a long time to reach it. He had to lift his head from time to time, to remind himself where it was, so that he wouldn't wander off his course, and collide with massed schoolboys, sending them rolling like bowling pins. It sounded – by his breathing – as if he was coming to the end of a marathon he had run (this was a decidedly overambitious choice of verb) all the way from the tip of Manhattan, beginning his run the previous Thursday, crunching through the snow.

He seemed to be wearing new boots, and you weren't sure whether the audible creaking sound was from them, or from Mr. Scrivener's ancient limbs. You could also hear – clear as a blacksmith beating out a horseshoe – the metallic click of his cleats.

The two-feet-high wooden circle, upon which the lectern was

positioned, was an obstacle too far on his obstacle course through the hall. He made several attempts to lift his right leg high enough to clamber upon it, almost falling over the last time. For a moment there was the attractive possibility that he was about to go down on his hands and knees and crawl his way forward. First Beard hurried over to help him, making no attempt to be discreet about it, making his thrust quite vigorous. You gained the impression that he was only just preventing himself from hoisting Mr. Scrivener over his shoulders like a sack of coal, prior to dumping him down the coal chute of the lectern.

"Look who's the real power here!"

That was what his assertive shove proclaimed.

"Look who's the man who *ought* to be headmaster!"

Last Thursday had been the Ides of March.

First Beard bore all the signs of a lean and hungry man.

Such men were dangerous.

"Ye gods!" he was all but shouting, elbowing Mr. Scrivener aside – with a quavery shriek the headmaster would have obliterated the smallest boys in Year Two (*alpha*) – "It doth amaze me, / A man of such a feeble temper should / So get the start of the majestic world, / And bear the palm alone."

He made his feelings *perfectly* clear.

Put a palm leaf into Scrivener's hand, and he'd keel over.

That was the message.

Mr. Scrivener, swaying slightly, was eventually positioned in front of his lectern, clutching firmly at its edges to remain upright. That was the impression he gave. The lectern was aligned so that Mr. Scrivener was facing straight down the line of Year Naught, and so that each of the Crowninshield's boys would feel that he was looking straight at him for a particular reason that he was not prepared to divulge. The Bearded Ones, freed from the tyranny of time, hovered in the dimness around the outer circumference of the hall, or roamed up and down in the spaces between the lines. If they'd thought to supply themselves with bullwhips – it was probably just an oversight on their part – they could have lashed out with satisfying thwacks at boys whose arms were not by their sides, who were not standing up straight enough, talking, not keeping right, or were in other ways displaying disturbing symptoms of wanton defiance.

(It was just like the scenes in the Roman slave-galley in *Ben-Hur*, with added thwacking. To keep the slaves in order it was necessary to thwack them on a regular basis.

(*Franklin Pinkerton. Presented For Meritorious Attendance. All Saints', Longfellow Park, Sunday-school. December 19th, 1886.*

(Ben had been mortified when Miss Augusteena had presented the book to him, a copy of the same book to him and to Oliver and to Bradley, smiling encouragingly in front of the assembled, applauding – most of them – Sunday-school as she shook their hands. It had felt quite grown-up to have their hands shaken by Miss Augusteena. Oliver, quite the gentleman, had bowed in response, but – in unusually restrained mood – he had refrained from kissing the back of her hand. Inside, the decorative page had the inscription in her careful copperplate, but it was the gold-embossed title, glinting in the gaslight, that had horrified him.

("*Ben-Hur!*" he had thought, alert – as ever – for the taunting potential lying dormant within his name. "*Ben-Hur!*" Ben wasn't hearing *Hur*; he was hearing *Her*.

(He heard Brinkman's voice – Monday morning at Crowninshield's, as they formed in line for one-two-three-*ouch!* roll call – insinuatingly hissing, "Ben-*Her!* Ben-*Her!*" It had been bad enough already with the numerous opportunities offered by Pinkerton and Pinkie – not to mention Benjamin Franklin – but now he'd have Ben-*Her* to contend with as well. That had been his first thought.

(*Her! Her! Her!*

He heard the new sound of sniggering, the onomatopoeia of mockery. Brinkman would be practicing all Sunday afternoon, to get it just right for Monday.

(Miss Augusteena thought that the blush that spread across Ben's face – it was inevitable that he should have blushed – was a commendable demonstration of quiet modesty. "Well done!" she had murmured encouragingly, looking pleased for him.

("Ben-*Her*! Ben-*Her*!"

(That would be his new name.

(He wouldn't be a he; he'd be a her.

(*Her! Her! Her!*

(It would open up attractive new prospects of taunting to Papa.)

Mr. Scrivener was not another Arrius, the tribune, who would look with partiality upon one of the slaves under his control, and neglect to have his leg-irons locked. Mr. Scrivener had no time or talent for the slaves, and was quite keen on tight-locked leg-irons. All slaves could remain rigorously chained as far as he was concerned, the metal biting deep into their flesh, and rubbing against their anklebones. It was the parents upon whom his special skills were expended, the parents who commented favorably to each other about him, this man who was so firm and impressive, so decisive with their sons. He did not actually *teach* their sons, but was the figurehead – Ben had a brief, sacrilegious, nauseating glimpse of Mr. Scrivener as one of the brazen big-busted bare-breasted ships' figureheads that lined the street across from Grandpapa Brouwer's office (Cora Munro, the hussy, had much to answer for in her shamelessly corrupting example) – high above the foam that guided the ship of the school through stormy seas to a safe anchorage.

Brinkman looked up into the cupola, seeking comfort in Cora Munro's right tit as it trembled tantalizingly above him. They'd imported a sniggerer into the very heart of the Otsego Lake Academy sniggerers, one – echo-like – fully capable of integrating titters, giggles, guffaws, heehaws, and her-her-hers into his repertoire of taunting. He'd be so eager to ingratiate himself that he'd leap a superhuman height right up into the dome, and grab Cora Munro's right tit. "I am a *titter*!" he would announce triumphantly, if it was titters that were required. He'd be a giggle. He'd be a guffaw and a heehaw and a her-her-her, if giggles, guffaws, heehaws, and her-her-hers were the necessary requisites for

368

acceptance. He'd *Her! Her! Her!* with hectoring, meaningfully stressed sniggerdomness. He'd soon feel right at home there, sniggering away with the best of them, full of little hints and secrets to increase the volume of sniggering from its so-far somewhat subdued level. He had favored information after his years at Crowninshield's. He'd be able to inform all Otsegoans of every embarrassing fact about the new boys in Year Naught, the little victims newly brought to sacrifice, listing them in full detail, demonstrating his superior snotty sniggers.

("Did you know . . .?" he'd be asking Otsego Lake Academy boys, all cozying up for his chosen rôle of popular new boy.

("Did you know . . .?"

(He'd be pointing. Brinkman was capable of pointing and sniggering at the same time. He wasn't quite as stupid as he looked. This would have taken quite some doing.

("*That* one!" he'd be saying, giving the boy's name, the embarrassing fact.

("*That* one!"

("*That* one!"

(Alloway's mama calls him Franki-poo . . .

(Finch stutters and weeps . . .

(P-P-Pinkerton, the one with the loony sister, is a blusher – and, he'd probably be adding with considerable enthusiasm, P-P-Pinkerton's p-p-papa had killed himself, and P-P-Pinkerton's p-p-papa had thought his son *prettier* – no stuttering on this word, just to emphasize its importance – than any of his sisters . . .

(Akenside wets the bed . . .

(Stoddard even has spots on his backside *and* is a Roman Catholic . . .

(Comstock . . .

(Comstock . . .

(Well, they *all* knew about Comstock.

(You hardly knew where to *start* with Comstock.

(They'd soon know all sorts of things about all the Crowninshield's boys.)

No one in the hall was seated.

They all faced their leader, though the six o'clock area – life's race half-run – would be seeing nothing but the back of his head. Lucky devils. Perhaps the wooden circle revolved slowly as he spoke. Small sweaty slaves would strain in the darkness beneath Mr. Scrivener's feet, their leg-irons chinking like loot being counted – it was probably a traditional punishment at Otsego Lake Academy for some appalling infringement of the rules (forgetting to say "sir," insufficient servility, not standing up straight, talking, not keeping right, breathing) – turning an elaborate system of levers. The headmaster – thus set in motion – would jerkily circle the very center of the hall like a planet in orbit (though he surely regarded himself as the sun, around which all the lesser planets revolved, those tiniest nameless pieces of rock in the darkness), or – in the center of this chalked-out clock-face – like a mechanical figure on a town hall timepiece, spreading his beneficence on each year in turn as he moved from noon to one o'clock, two o'clock, on and on into the dark bearded hours of midnight. Even in the hours of darkness he would bring his light unto them. For a brief, welcome respite – between the hours of four and eight – those who were Naught would be seeing little beyond the back of his head, though they'd continue to hear his voice, echoing around within the interior of the cupola like a single thought within an otherwise empty head.

Mr. Scrivener strove for an impressive pause as he slowly undertook the ritual of unfolding his spectacles and placing them upon his nose. It took him three attempts to do this. He almost poked out his right eye on his second attempt. It was like some ritualistic moment in a church service: the Elevation of the Host or chalice. He had an enormous white beard that would have smothered an entire church choir, snuffing them out in mid-*Hallelujah!* like provocatively Roman Catholic-like candles being righteously extinguished. Here was a Santa Claus who brought no gifts. It was even bigger than Papa's beard had been, even bigger than Great-Grandpapa Brouwer's beard had been. Ben had seen the oil-painting in the Occidental & Eastern Shipping Company offices. Papa was probably hiding inside Mr. Scrivener's beard, staring out at him, seeing what he was doing, how he was behaving, on the alert for untoward unmanliness. At the same time, ubiquitous Papa (immortal, invisible, Papa only wise, in light inaccessible hid from our eyes) was behind him, pressing up against him – he didn't like it when his papa touched him – and whispering in his ear in the place where Bradley should have been.

"P-P-P!" he said.

"Resurgam!" he said.

This was one he said repeatedly.

(Most blesséd, most glorious, the ancient of days, almighty, victorious, his great name be praised.)

Resurgam.

And graves have yawned, and yielded up their dead.

And ghosts did shriek and squeal about the streets.

Like God, he was everywhere at once.

Like God, he saw everything.

Unresting, unhasting, and silent as light, nor wanting, nor wasting, he rulest in might, his justice like mountains high soaring above, his clouds which are fountains of goodness and love.

> *We blossom and flourish as leaves on the tree,*
> *And wither and perish; but naught changeth thee.*

This Naught would certainly not change him.

Ben did not altogether approve of God, despite his Sunday-school prize For Meritorious Attendance. For a moment – Ben's head leaning back in order to see the headmaster's face – it was like being in All Saints' Church on Sunday, watching as the Reverend Calbraith began his sermon, resting his head back against the pew so that he could see up into the pulpit. Mr. Scrivener took one of the sheets of paper out of the book he had lain open upon the lectern, and held it up, looking like First Beard had looked with his list and board clip.

"The newcomers are now amongst us," he declared, as if he'd

just noticed. Some of the boys at Otsego Lake Academy were not very observant. That instantly became clear.

He sounded like God – there He was again (embosomed deep in His dear love, held in His law, Ben stood) – creating man in His image. God saw that it was good. Beards and potential Beards stretched out around him like tall-grassed prairies vanishing into the horizon. James Fenimore Cooper would have felt right at home.

"Adams," Mr. Scrivener read from his list – he had to hold the list right up against his eyes, and peer really closely – looking down the line in front of him, and pausing.

Like the first man after him – a man, a man, a *man*, not a boy – God gave names to all cattle, and to the fowl of the air, and to every beast of the field, and the first-named of His creations (appropriately enough) was named Adams.

Mr. Scrivener probably didn't have a clue as to which of the boys lined up in front of him was Adams – helpful alphabetical order had yielded to unhelpful height – but he appeared to scan their faces, searching for evidence of Adams-like leanings. You could tell his eyes weren't properly focused, and that – in fact – he wasn't really seeing them. He was performing all the actions of a pre-planned series of movements. Judging by the expression on his face, he regarded the boys in front of him as being about on a level with the beasts of the field, particularly beastly beasts, and the field not well tended.

(It *was* the same list as the one that First Beard had held. It was the list of all their names.

(There was an awkward, uncertain silence, and Ben could imagine Adams agonizing. How was he supposed to respond? *Was* he supposed to respond?

(Ben was glad that his name was eighteenth on the list, and not first.

(Were you supposed to say, "Present, sir" again?

(*You say, 'Present, sir' here.*

(Was the little scene in the entrance hall with First Beard a rehearsal for what was happening now?

(It was very confusing.

(Adams would be about two-thirds of the way down the line. It would seem incorrect to be responding in alphabetical order, dispersed as they were for tallness. There'd be no problems for Charlie Whitefoord. He was last in line both alphabetically and by reasons of height. No wonder he had the air of a natural leader about him. No crisis of confidence with Charlie.

(A horrible thought occurred to Ben.

(A really horrible thought.

(Were they supposed to *walk forward to the headmaster* as their names were read out, drawn toward him by an implacable summons in front of the whole school, enveloped in a rising roar of soon not-at-all-suppressed sniggering? Were they supposed to stand there, one at a time, as the sniggers rose to titters, as the titters rose to giggles, as the giggles rose to guffaws and heehaws and her-her-hers?

(Was it time for the human sacrifice?

(Was it time — at the very least — for the *adjustments*?

(Was Adams going to be the first amongst them to be *adjusted*, set right like a clock bad at timekeeping?

(One by one they'd be spread-eagled beneath the tits, arms and legs bound, limbs staked out like a doomed prisoner about to be rent asunder by galloping horses.

(It would be time.

(Time to grow out of childhood into manhood.

(Time to become skilled in all the craft of hunters.

(Time to become learned in all the lore of old men.

(*Chemistry*.

(*Arithmetic*.

(*Grammar*.

(*Geography*.

(Dr. Crowninshield was straining at his bonds in the long-abandoned schoolroom. They had been fastened far too tightly, and he would never escape from being a prisoner.

(Time to forget all youthful sports and pastimes.

(Time for all *manly* arts and labors.

373

(*Manly* would be stressed like an imperative.

(Time for the tom-toms.

(Time for the chanting.)

There was no reaction at all from Mr. Scrivener when Adams failed to respond.

(No response, clearly, was the response expected.

(Not even a "Present, sir."

(No "Thank you, sir."

(No "No, sir."

(What a relief this was!

(He nearly let out his breath in an Alloway-like gasp of relief, but didn't, in case the too-close First Beard heard him.

("You don't unintentionally breathe here."

(That was what was being said.

(Each breath was to be intentional, an act of will, knowing all the time that if you stopped you would be dead.)

He did breathe out – a cautious, silent exhalation – in courageous defiance of all the exhortations of The Beards.

(An accusing shriek from The Head Beard.

("That boy *breathed!*"

(Consternation.

(Increased, frantic thwacking.

(Loud rattlings of chains.)

Brinkman had been perfectly correct.

You *could* see your breath.

After the pause – it seemed like a counted pause, Mr. Scrivener possessing a very precise notion of how long it should last – he looked down again at the list in his hand.

Again Mr. Scrivener read.

"Akenside."

Again he looked down the line.

Again he paused.

"Alloway."

Look down line.

Pause.

"Here!" Frankie replied, loud and clear, sounding as pleased as if he'd remembered something important.

Audible I-might-have-known-it hiss of annoyance from First Beard. Ben could see it spreading out like a dampening tidal wave down the length of his beard, and almost felt the outer reaches of the spray. It was just as well that he didn't wear spectacles.

You could always rely on Alloway.

(He hadn't even said, "Present, sir." He could at least have got it wrong in a right sort of way.)

"Here!" echoed several times around the interior of the cupola.

(*I'm called Alloway!*

(*Here I am!*

(*Here!*

(*Here!*

(*Here!*

(*I've got red hair!*

(*I've got a yellow scarf!*

(*I'm always late for everything!*

(*I'm not very bright!*

(*My mama calls me Franki-poo!*)

The sniggers – not any longer sniggers that might have been described as "suppressed" – started on the left of Year Naught, and swept around the hall in a clockwise wave of ridicule.

(*Snigger!*

(*Snigger!*

(*Snigger!*)

(Ben found himself hoping that Alloway would be blushing, a deep, painful, long-lasting blush that would precisely match the color of his vivid hair, an allover head-to-toe fire of humiliation. He hoped that the blush would become as *permanent* as his hair color. Then Alloway would become known as the boy who blushed. It wouldn't be Ben.

("That's *him!*" the Otsegoans would be saying.

("That's *him!*"

(And they wouldn't be pointing at Ben.)

Mr. Scrivener didn't react directly to this, but he did seem to look down the line with increased attention, as if he really was seeing them this time.

(*That one!*

(*That one!*

(*That one!*

(*The one with red hair!*

(*The one with the agonizing permanent blush!*

(That was what Ben was thinking.

(Ben *liked* Frankie Alloway.)

The pause was precisely the same length of time as the previous pause. Mr. Scrivener was definitely counting out the seconds. Ben concentrated, head back, looking at his lips really closely for signs of movement. He might not be very good at arithmetic – like Dr. Crowninshield – and his lips might have to move on the higher numbers, like a poor reader struggling with a long word in a text.

"Bradley."

Look down line.

Pause.

Ben heard Bradley swallow behind him, a distinct gulp.

Mr. Scrivener spoke the name into the sniggers, not in the least perturbed. Mr. Scrivener would read his list even if the rotunda collapsed upon him, even if half-stunned by a whack from Cora Munro's abruptly descended aggressive right tit. Right hooks had nothing on right tits when it came to unexpected stunning blows.

"Bradstone."

Look down line.

Pause.

There were no more "Heres!" and no "Present, sirs!"

"Brinkman."

Look down line.

Pause.

It was worryingly like the ceremony that was performed in the churchyard at All Saints' every year on April 14th – the anniversary of President Lincoln's assassination – when parishioners gathered at the Civil War memorial, and the Sunday-school's star pupil would read out the names of the dead who had been from the Longfellow Park neighborhood.

"Brouwer, E. T. L . . ." the reader – it was almost always Bradley (even the keenest girls failed to get a look in when Bradley got going) – would begin.

Brouwer, E. T. L. was Ben's Uncle Teddy. He knew his face from photographs, and the image of his face always came into Ben's mind as he heard the name. He was wearing his uniform, and standing up at attention, with the look of a participant in some parade-ground ceremony, drawn up in line with other soldiers as they were now, within the hall of Otsego Lake Academy. Arms by their sides, standing up straight, not talking, keeping right, they adhered to all the rules of well-behaved schoolboys as they marched off to their deaths. In the Sunday-school room at All Saints', there was a photograph of the unveiling of the memorial with crowds around the bright and new-looking stone. The monument had been erected in a spirit of reconciliation – this sounded *nothing* like Dr. Vaniah Odom, the man who had been the minister at the time of its unveiling – and small boys were lined up in rows dressed in miniature homemade Union and Confederate uniforms, an infant infantry. Some of the uniforms might very well have been genuine uniforms – bullet holes carefully sewn closed, blood washed away – so small had been some of the soldiers. If the ceremony *had* been Dr. Vaniah Odom's idea, you could guarantee that it would have ended with a battle to the death between the miniature soldiers, with heaps of massacred rebel boys stretching to the horizon like a blue-tinged hilly Virginia landscape. It would be a battle with only one sure end.

> *Alas, regardless of their doom,*
> *The little victims play!*
> *No sense have they of ills to come,*
> *Nor care beyond today.*

377

He heard Oliver's voice.

He saw the distant figures cavorting in the snow.

Years and years ago when that happened, it seemed.

In the background behind the memorial, some distance from the other participants, and the furthest away from the camera, was a group of black-clad women, like an enclosed order of nuns.

These were the bereaved: the widows, the mothers, and the sisters. You'd have thought that only women could mourn.

Brouwer, E. T. L. didn't have a widow.

He'd been too young to have been married.

Without the guidance of chalked lines, the soldiers would be marching and countermarching, and only watchers in the skies would be able to discern the patterns into which they formed. Ben couldn't have named all the dead, but the list began with Brouwer, E. T. L. and it ended with Winterfield, Q. He'd often speculated about that "Q," and he often wondered what had happened to the Winterfields. There was no longer any family of that name in Longfellow Park, the line seemingly wiped out with the death of Winterfield, Q.

Mr. Scrivener was reading out the names of the dead, and it was they who were the dead. They were, after all, now in the place in which Latin was spoken, and it was the dead who spoke in a dead language.

"Comstock."

Look down line.

Pause.

(A distinct ripple of recognition on "Comstock."

(A sense of heads turning, feet edging up to tiptoe.

("Olly Comstock!"

("The Little Lord Fauntleroy suit and the long, blond curly hair!"

("Comstock's Comestibles!"

("The son of Mrs. Albert Comstock!"

("*Her!*"

("Euch!"

("*Her!*")

("The awful sister!")

("The farting dog!")

("Olly Comstock!")

("*Him!*")

("*Him!*")

(That's what the schoolboys were thinking.

(That's what the schoolboys were whispering.

(You could see the heads turning.

(Oliver was probably waving at them in acknowledgment, an aristocratic curve to his raised hand. "Hello, you chaps!"

(You could hear the *buzz-buzz* of news being shared, the glad tidings of teasing potential.

("Look at all the new pupils we have in the school!"

(That's what this list-of-the-dead was saying.

("It's not even September!"

("Make sure you tell your parents what a successful school this is!"

(This was the message that mattered.

("Let them know how lucky you are to be here!"

("They're *fighting* to get in!")

They're fighting as soon as they *get* in.

That was the fear, the supposition.

First it was *snigger*.

Then, slowly, inevitably – there was a whole series of inch-by-inch gradations (guffaws would be involved, titters, giggles, heehaws, her-her-hers, name-calling, spitting, in all probability) – the arms-by-your-sides would be raised, and they'd be bearing fists on the ends of them, though they'd still be sniggering, as if that with which they had begun had been there with them all the time. The sniggering made it far worse.

He wished his eyes were capable of casually scanning the by-the-sides arms of the Otsegoans – they were one of the lesser-known, more primitive tribes – to check for bunchiness about the knuckles, aggressive angling to tight-curled fingers.

Sticks.

Stones.

Words.

Words above all.

Words and sniggering.

Ben had been pleased that he was eighteenth on the list, but now he was not so sure. Now he wished that his name had already been read out, and he could relax, if only temporarily.

Soon it would be time for "Pinkerton."

Look down line.

Pause.

Into that pause would come the second wave of – now irrepressible – sniggers. They would rise and fill the hollowness above Mr. Scrivener, far louder and far more uncontrollable than those caused by that puny little "Here!" had ever been. Mr. Rappaport would step forward and – like a choirmaster teaching his charges a new song (he was in the choir at All Saints' and would know *exactly* what to do) – he would lead them in the chorus of their new sing-along favorite, his arms gesticulating to keep them to the correct rhythm, his voice the deepest and loudest of anyone's. "All together, boys!" he'd be shouting encouragingly to all those massed beneath him. "Sing! Sing!" (This coded reference to the Westchester county prison would not be accidental.) "Louder! *Louder!*"

"*Pinkerton!*"

"*That* one!"

"*That* one!"

"*Her! Her! Her!*"

The words came in waves, surging in, *Resurgam!*-style, and Papa joined in enthusiastically.

They'd soon be able to identify which one was Pinkerton. They'd soon forget any signs of a blush from the pale-faced red-head – Alloway, in fact, *was* fairly liable to easy flushing with his coloring – when they witnessed the spectacular sunset of one of Ben's more out-of-control displays.

It wasn't just Pinkie when he got going.

It was Reddie.

It was Crimsonie.

It was Scarletti.

He was sure that there was composer with a name like this last, someone wigged and eighteenth-century and bent over a harpsichord. This was the kind of information Papa did not like him to possess – *Moonshine!* – but he had seen some battered old sheet music by this composer on the music rack at the Comstocks', not the place in which you expected to come across such a rarity. Ben had never heard of him before, had never seen any music by him on display in Columbarian & Horowitz. The music clearly belonged to Oliver, and was handwritten, not printed, with little comments in Oliver's italic script written between the staves. He might have written it himself, inventing the composer as a mask for his hidden, redheaded Frankie Alloway side, effortlessly essaying an eighteenth-century personality. The Reverend Goodchild *had* once informed Oliver that he was in the wrong century. Ben wasn't quite sure what was meant by the comment. It clearly wasn't meant to be taken as a compliment, but Oliver had perversely chosen to interpret it as if it were. Bounding to the keyboard – the very image of a young Mozart – Oliver would launch himself upon several hundred of the Scarletti sonatas simultaneously, all fingers ablur.

Women tended to exclaim sentimentally whenever Oliver chose to play something touching or pretty. (Such pieces were always popular choices.) "He's nearly in tears, the little lamb," they'd whisper to each other, briskly positioning their handkerchiefs for an enjoyable sniff, and ensuring full value from the emotion. "You can tell he's really moved!"

Oliver told Ben that – on such occasions ("Nearly in tears!" "Really moved!") – he was usually concentrating on little else but thinking ahead to a part in the music where he knew that there was a one bar pause for the left hand, one that would allow him to scratch an agonizing itch on his nose. He was – he claimed –

planning to publish a book of carefully selected pieces of music for pianists afflicted with performance-devastating itching, arranged in order of the lengths of time they allowed for ever-more ambitious scratchings: a nose, a knee, an ankle. The chosen pieces in the final pages of the album – catering for a compre-hensiveness of itching not usually encouraged outside an isolation ward (squelchy Reverend Goodchildian probings, advanced gymnastic grapplings): rolled-up sleeves and well-cut fingernails were definitely a necessity – could not be recommended to those with delicate constitutions. He'd had advanced discussions about *Pieces for Itchy Pianists* with Emmerson Columbarian. Columbarian & Horowitz were keen to place a large order. There'd be a special display in one of the windows, next to the sheet music, and – throughout the shop – there'd be enormous piles (not the most sensitive choice of phrase in this context) of the album, artistically positioned. He'd make a fortune.

Ben did not play the piano anymore. When he watched Oliver playing – Oliver loved music of all kinds – he wondered if the ability was still there inside himself, like the ability to ride a bicycle or swim. Papa had not thought piano-playing suitable; it was not a manly thing to do, so Ben no longer played, and he no longer sang, though he had once enjoyed both.

It was something to do with "musical" and "musicality."

These were the words Papa had employed, he, Dr. Wolcott Ascharm Webster, and the Reverend Goodchild, and the words were always accompanied by silent "ahems" just before they said them, and the words were always in quotation marks. They were words that meant something else, like words in a foreign language.

"Oliver is very musical," Mrs. Albert Comstock would announce after one of Oliver's performances in the music room at an "At Home." (This was when she was not announcing – rather wearily, and rather more frequently – "Oliver is very satirical," "Oliver is very humorous," or "Oliver is very provoking.")

And . . .

"Oh, *yes* . . ."

– Papa, or Dr. Wolcott Ascharm Webster, or the Reverend Goodchild would instantly agree –

". . . he's certainly *very* . . ."

(ahem)

". . . '*musical*.'"

And Papa, and Dr. Wolcott Ascharm Webster, and the Reverend Goodchild would struggle not to snigger – all of them, you felt, and not just Papa, clearly Old Otsegoans, trained in all the arts of sniggering – and would avoid catching each other's eyes. Like Mr. Rappaport, some years later, they'd got the tittering off to a T. You wouldn't have been surprised if they'd nudged each other matily in the ribs in the way that Mrs. Albert Comstock and Mrs. Goodchild did when they recognized something new to mock, a sort of pleasurable anticipatory shudder. The sniggers were firmly contained within soundproof brackets, suppressed by strictly employed punctuation.

"He's very musical."

"Oh, *yes*, he's certainly *very* . . ."

(ahem)

". . . '*musical*.'"

You could *hear* the quotation marks.

(*Snigger*.

(*Snigger*.

(*Snigger*.)

Their mouths twitched.

Their eyes danced.

Their hands crept up to cover their mouths.

They whimpered slightly.

They looked and sounded – for all the world – like the agonized small boys, red-faced and struggling to keep control, desperate not to burst into howls of laughter, as Chinky-Winky farted like a steamboat whistle and set the clock vibrating. They hid behind their beards as their shoulders heaved.

Ben had to keep careful control. He had to be on full alert so that he would not display any signs of

(ahem)

"musicality."

A liking for music was not something of which to be proud. It was a shameful predilection, suppressed and unacknowledged, something fit only for girlies. He had learned to keep his body absolutely still if he heard any (ahem) music in his vicinity, and not display – by the tapping of a single foot or finger, by a low half-heard hum, however discreet or muted – that he recognized a rhythm. Papa touched him on the shoulder, warningly, if he caught him doing this, pinched him like a schoolroom tormentor, and his beard leaned in toward him. The strong smell of cigar smoke was connected with a firm rejection of music's alluring siren song. Even though he wasn't using words, Ben had been caught speaking a language that was forbidden, and he should remain silent. It was girlie. It was *swisssh-swisssh-swisssh*, the sound of silk and simper-ing, the nice new dress with the right sort of flounces, Franklin (flouncing would certainly be involved), the *really thick* rouge on the cheeks, Franklin. It was as bad as showing signs of being friendly with Oliver, and "friendly" was another word that set The Beards vibrating with amusement. He'd heard the three of them whispering together – and not always whispering – about certain young men, sometimes one of the young men playing the piano, or his violin, or flute at an "At Home." "He looks very . . ." (ahem) ". . . '*friendly*.'" That's what one or other of them would say, a private joke in a public place that always produced shoulder-vibrat-ing sniggers, seemingly unmindful of the fact that Sobriety Goodchild – the Reverend Goodchild's son (the Brinkman of his day, Alice had told Ben) – had, as a small boy, trilled out sentimen-tal songs whenever cultured society was gathered together. You couldn't escape him, wherever you sought to flee. This took some believing, when you looked at Sobriety Goodchild today – difficult to believe he'd ever been "musical," *impossible* to believe that he'd ever been "friendly," that he'd ever been a small boy – though you could still easily see him as a Sidney Brinkman.

(In a few years' time Dr. Wolcott Ascharm Webster's younger

son, Max, still a baby at this time, would develop into the new Infant Phenomenon of Longfellow Park, squeakier and more persistent than even Sobriety Goodchild had ever been at the height of his fame as a soprano-voiced celebrity, and quite capable of clearing your sinuses or loosening your ear wax when he hit a top note. You developed a sense of irony very early in Longfellow Park.)

If it wasn't being very (ahem) *"musical"* that you had to guard yourself against, it was being very (ahem) *"friendly,"* but (ahem) *"musical"* was worse. Much worse. Papa always snorted when one of the smart young men from the neighborhood approached the piano, bearing his sheet music and — with varying degrees of success — attempting to smile modestly.

It was bad enough if they played a musical instrument.

Discussing the latest pretty little waltzes with the girlies so that you can learn to play them on the piano, Franklin?

It was even worse — louder snort — if they *sang.*

Oliver played the piano, *and* the mandolin.

The *mandolin.*

You might have known it.

To help him to play the mandolin when he was standing up, Oliver attached a ribbon around the neck of the mandolin and fastened the other end to one of the buttons of his jacket.

Much nudging at the sight of the ribbon.

Much nudging accompanied by much sniggering.

Ribbons came as no surprise *whatsoever* to the manly voiced upholders of certain standards.

(It was as if they knew what was going to happen.

(As if nothing could have stopped it from happening.)

"Now, what *color* do you imagine might be the most appropriate one for him to choose for his *ribbon?*" This was the Reverend Goodchild to Papa and Dr. Wolcott Ascharm Webster. He spoke in a tone of teasing, at ease with his chuckly chums.

"Now let me think . . ." This was Papa to the Reverend Goodchild. An approximation of deep and searching thought, hands pressed to furrowed forehead, histrionic agonizings.

"Might it be . . .?" This was Dr. Wolcott Ascharm Webster. No stranger to fine-honed repartee. This was the effect at which he aimed. Ever a quip on the tip of his tongue.

"Might it *possibly* be . . .?" Papa.

> *(I think it's pink.*
> *(I think it's pink.)*

"Pink?" Dr. Wolcott Ascharm Webster.

"*Pink*?" The Reverend Goodchild.

"Might it possibly be *pink*?" All three simultaneously. A little more rehearsal time, and the vaudeville theatres of the nation would be beckoning eagerly, ambitious managers flourishing wads of cash. *Pinkerton, Goodchild & Webster!* the garish posters would be screaming as the crowds poured in. *Learn How to Mock Girlies! Sniggers Supplied! Guffaws Guaranteed! Terrific Titters!*

They shrieked, they minced, they fluttered their hands. All in a very manly sort of way. It wouldn't do to be too good at that sort of thing. It wouldn't do *at all*.

"*Pink!*"

"The very color!"

"He could have matching ribbons fastened around his neck!"

"In his hair!"

"Big, bulging pink bows."

"It would take lots of bows for all that hair."

"Yards and yards . . ."

"He could have matching ribbons fastened round his ears!"

"His wrists!"

"His ankles!"

"He could have matching ribbons tied around his . . ."

Snigger.

"Tied around his . . ."

Snigger.

"Tied around his . . ."

Whisper.

386

Guffaw.

"If he's got one."

Guffaw.

"If he's got one!"

They tended to repeat – in encore-like approval – particularly telling aphoristic thrusts made by each other. Oscar Wilde would have been rendered speechless, inarticulately inadequate, in the face of such exquisitely jewel-bright, rapier-like wit. "I wish I'd said that!" he'd be muttering to himself, jealous and sulky. "I *wish* I'd said that!" He'd stamp his foot in a little pet, quite put out and pouting. He'd stamp his foot *on* a little pet, he'd be so comprehensively peeved, squashing a Chihuahua in pique.

They wouldn't have been the slightest bit surprised if Oliver had played a *harp*, elbowing in on Mabel Peartree's territory, carefully steering his body well clear of her enormous nose as he insinuated his fingers across the strings with – you shuddered at the very thought of it – effortlessly girlie grace.

Oliver *sang*.

Oliver was in All Saints' choir.

Oliver was *very* – ahem – *"musical,"* and Oliver was *very* – ahem – *"friendly."*

The quotation marks rested around the words, touched the words, like cold hands resting against the upper part of his leg, just a little too high up.

Snigger.

Snigger.

Snigger.

Mr. Rappaport was in All Saints' choir.

Mr. Rappaport did not appear to be the *slightest* bit friendly, with or without the ahem and quotation marks.

Pink!

The very color!

*Pink*erton.

The very name!

The last time Ben had sung, sung a solo seriously – singing in church didn't count, particularly if you took care to be not very good – was a time his father had come in and heard him. Come in and *caught* him. That was what it had felt like, as if he had been captured in some shameful covert activity.

He'd caught him singing as Alice played the piano, and it was the last time he'd sung. He'd been too embarrassed to do it again. It was something they had been working on for a little while, a piece by Handel. They'd thought that Papa would be at the Occidental & Eastern Shipping Company office all afternoon. Mama, Edith, and Allegra had all been listening as they worked at their cross-stitch, their little patterns of flowers and letters. Cross-stitching or reading novels. It would have been one or the other. Allegra, the prettiest of his sisters – the only one of his sisters who *was* pretty, and she was much, *much* prettier than he was – harmonized as he sang, decorative flourishes at the end of each line as he sang it. (*She* had been in the church choir, though not at the same time as Oliver or Mr. Rappaport. She'd met Bayard Guilfoyle, the man she'd married, in the church choir.) It hadn't been religious music that Ben had been singing, though it somehow seemed religious. Part of him thought, rather unconvincingly, that Papa would have found it a little more acceptable if it had been religious music, something Ben would have sung in church on Sunday with the rest of the congregation. Handel might have had good, manly names – George Frederick (Papa wouldn't have recognized "Frideric" as a name) – but Handel had *not* been acceptable. Ben had wondered if perhaps Papa had been made to think uneasily of Oliver Comstock and his "musicality" because his mama's chiming clock played a tune by Handel, and had disapproved for that reason, but Papa would never have recognized that the same composer wrote it. "The Star-Spangled Banner," "O Columbia!," a few mucky songs sung exclusively in smoking rooms (*very* mucky songs, *very* smoky rooms) and that was about it as far as Papa and music were concerned.

"... Where'er you walk ..."

— Ben sang —

"... cool gales shall fan the glade ..."

— They hadn't heard Karin open the front door, hadn't heard Papa (who was not a particularly quiet man) coming into the hall, and turn left into the front parlor — where they were — instead of right into his study. It was as if he'd deliberately crept up on them, pouncing to catch them doing something that they should not have been doing. They *were* — it turned out — doing something that they should not have been doing -

"... Trees, where you sit, shall crowd into a shade,
Where'er you tread, the blushing flow'rs shall rise,
And all things flourish where'er you turn your eyes.
Where'er ..."

All things did *not* flourish where'er Papa turned his eyes.

"What a pretty little voice. Shouldn't you be wearing a pretty little dress so that you'll look even more like one of your sisters, or would that make them feel jealous? You certainly *sound* like one of them. So shrill. So dainty. Did you say '*blushing*,' Franklin?"

This was the first thing he said, the first thing that made them realize that he was there, behind them, and Edith and Allegra — still holding their cross-stitch in little wooden frames — had stood up guiltily, detected in some unforgivable infringement of strict etiquette. Alice had stopped playing the piano.

(*Go for his eyes with the needles.*)

(*Go for his eyes with the needles.*)

(These were the words that had come into Ben's head, words that stabbed like weapons.

(*Pull the frames down over his head, and go for his eyes with the needles.*)

They waited.

"'*Blushing* flowers?'"

They waited.

"Now, who on earth would want to write a song about *you*, Franklin? Is the pretty little flower with the pretty little voice *blushing*?"

The pretty little flower *was*.

They waited.

"This is how you spend your afternoons, is it, the blushing flower and the weeds?"

"Papa!"

(Allegra.)

He had started, and he was away.

He often began with a list of questions, but he did not expect answers, did not *allow* answers.

They let him enjoy himself.

(*I'll run away till I am bigger, but then I'll fight.*

("That's my brave boy!"

(Coriolanus had said these words to his son, as his son kneeled to plead before him, commending his small son's vow to resist him. They were the same words that Papa sometimes said to Ben, but Coriolanus – as Oliver read the words in the music room, explaining how the play ended – had said them as if he meant them. Coriolanus' son – like Hamlet – had the same name as his father, but no one seemed to call him by his name. He was just *Boy* when he spoke his few defiant words to a father who was a god, a man whose followers killed with the confidence of boys pursuing summer butterflies.)

"Lincoln . . ." Mama began, once or twice, but that was all she managed to say.

"Do you often demonstrate your 'musicality' . . ." – not even an "ahem" this time – ". . . when I'm not around, Franklin?"

Ben didn't sing anymore.

He didn't play the piano or read music, though he once could. (He'd fall off any bicycle; he'd drown in any water.)

He'd look at the sheet music, and try to will it into Arabic or Japanese, a language that he was totally unable to understand, another dead language. He hadn't realized that you could *forget* a language that you once knew. It wasn't like this at all for Oliver. He was astounded by the faultless way Oliver appeared able to perform, even when reading the music for the first time. Reading the words from a book must – he supposed – appear equally magical to those incapable of understanding the printed symbols on the page.

He had to be careful to avoid any possibility of being accused of "musicality" again, accused of being very (ahem) "musical." He didn't really have that many friends, so perhaps he was safe from being accused of being "friendly," though – admittedly – one of the friends he did have *was* Oliver Comstock.

Silent and friendless.

That was the ideal at which to aim, your beard wrapped about you in solitary manly glory as you smoked your cigar and spat and swore, the only words you ever spoke beginning with the letters "f" or "c" or "b" or "p," standing in a proud and lonely attitude like Napoleon on Saint Helena.

"Darville."

Look down line.

Pause.

"Dibbo."

Look down line.

Pause.

Above him, Cora Munro shrieked as a Huron plunged a knife into her all-too-freely displayed breast, and Magua – grinning with evil pleasure – was killing Uncas, the Last of the Mohicans: no better start to the day for growing boys than scenes like these. It was a high, dim, echoing interior space, like the inside of a building in Rome.

"Drinkwater."

Look down line.

Pause.

"Finch."

Look down line.

Pause.

(At that moment, more than anything else, he hoped that Linnaeus would emulate Alloway, and say "Here!" or – even better – "H-H-Here!" or – better still – "P-P-P-Present, sir!" Alloway would be revealed to the whole school as the blusher, and Linnaeus as the stutterer. Best of all, Linnaeus might stutter, and then burst into sobs, and become known as the sobber. No one would notice P-P-Pinkerton then as a blusher, as a boy possessing a name rich with potential for teasing.

(Linnaeus was his *friend*.

(One of his *best* friends.

(Linnaeus said nothing.)

He began to study the paintings on the cupola in more detail, trying to shut out the sound of Mr. Scrivener's voice, the sense of the watching eyes, the latent sniggers. On the Sunday of their tour Mr. Scrivener had claimed that the paintings were completed by Constantino Brumidi (an Italian name always produced confidence where painting and sculpture were concerned, as Carlo Fiorelli well knew) in the late 1850s, before he had gone to work on the dome of the Capitol in Washington D.C. Ben thought of *The Apotheosis of George Washington*, the naked and half-naked figures, the flowing robes like a complicated story from the Old Testament or Greek mythology. Here was patriotism to inspire the masses. The murals, judging by the amount of flesh wantonly on display (surely it would have been far too chilly, deep within those dark shadowed James Fenimore Cooper woods, out on those exposed wind-swept prairies, for such carefree casting-off of corsets?), were far more likely to have been apprentice work by Dickinson Prud'homme. That had been Oliver's comment. He'd assumed a prim, disapproving voice, a disturbingly good approximation of his mama's when she was in full flow, and the nearest boys around them had flinched. Dickinson Prud'homme's well-endowed fleshy classical nudes were spreading all across Longfellow Park, in commercial premises and more uninhibited private houses, and you saw them everywhere you went, as if some enterprising decorator had managed to offload cheap surplus supplies of the same shade of pink paint to every property in the neighborhood. If Dickinson Prud'homme hadn't painted Cora Munro's saucily exposed (right) breast (there were promising fields of research here for the ambitious art historian), then a glimpse of it high above him must have inspired him to a life of zestfully painting big-breasted matrons, in the way that the sight of a rare bird might lead to a lifelong devotion to the joys of ornithology. One of Oliver's nightmares about his mother (he had a wide selection) was that she would enthusiastically agree to pose for one of Dickinson Prud'homme's paintings. (*Mrs. Albert Comstock as the Spirit of Niceness Goes into Battle against the Filthy French.* Something like that.) This would lead to a worldwide shortage of pink paint, and the collapse of the arts of portrait- and figure-painting.

"French."

Look down line.

Pause.

(You might have guessed that the word "French" would time its entrance to coincide with the appearance of mucky pictures. All things French were unflinchingly filthy in the eyes of Mrs. Albert Comstock, the grim-faced guardian of goodness.)

In the historical scenes in which Dickinson Prud'homme specialized, large-sized ladies did not remain in possession of all their clothing for very long. As soon as he appeared, paintbrush firmly clasped, stays were unloosened, and all caution thrown to the wind, though there couldn't have been too much wind. The weather had clearly been a lot warmer in those days of Corinthian columns, olive groves, and bare legs. In twenty years' time, Sidney Brinkman – made sensitive to art by his gentle nurturing at Otsego Lake Academy – would be penning his acclaimed seminal work *Dickinson Prud'homme: In Pursuit of the Tit.* The enormous paintings – on walls, on ceilings, on most stationary surfaces – contributed in no small way to the rising tide of sniggering that threatened to engulf the entire community, the titters (especially the titters), the giggles, the guffaws, the hechaws, the her-her-hers.

"*That* one!" the sniggering Otsego Lake Academy schoolboy would be saying, pointing out a particularly impressive breast to his sniggering friends.

"*That* one!"

Perhaps – concealed, snug and warm, beneath his all-embracing beard – Mr. Scrivener had a little surprise (a rather *large* surprise, *two* rather large surprises) tucked away with which to astonish them all. This was Oliver's theory. Rather shyly, Ben's thoughts returned to the picture of Mr. Scrivener as a vast-breasted ship's figurehead, undulating his body, sashaying his beard from side to side to afford provocative glimpses of what lay beneath, with a sultry twist to his large, purply lips. This was Ben's understanding of the art of erotic dancing. Brinkman claimed to have seen such a display, peering through an imperfectly closed door at his papa's club, and gave them every detail as proof of his superior manliness. The story changed a little at each telling, but the one fact that never changed was that Brinkman had *definitely* seen a tit. Tits gathered all about Brinkman – this was the impression he liked to convey – like wild birds waiting for breadcrumbs to be scattered, though he seemed to see them solely in the singular.

"Tits generally come in matching sets of *two*, Sidder-knee."

(Oliver.

(Though his mama had somehow contrived to consolidate her matching set of two into one gigantic, awe-inspiring eminence.)

"*Huh!*"

(Brinkman. Sidder-knee was not gifted at repartee. He specialized more in threatening gestures and dark, meaningful looks.)

"*Huh!*"

(When he knew that something he had said had failed to be suitably impressive – this was most times he said something – Brinkman, rather illogically, rather like the Reverend Goodchild, tended to say it a second time for emphasis.)

Mr. Scrivener, ogling his audience saucily, began to sway his beard from side to side, building up an erotic rhythm.

("*No*, sir!" That's what the gathered schoolboys would be

chorusing, as panic seized their ranks, realizing what it was that was about to be unleashed upon them as the beard was whipped aside. "*No! No! Definitely* not, sir!" They'd been well trained by First Beard and Second Beard and wouldn't forget to say "sir," even as uncontrollable nausea overcame them.)

If you looked closely, you could just discern two telltale humps breasting up – no other verb would suffice – beneath the upper portion of Mr. Scrivener's beard. Oliver had quite convinced them of this on their Sunday afternoon tour. "Cora Munro has *exactly* the same eyes as Scrivener. Hadn't you noticed?" He, Linnaeus, and Charlie had scrutinized Mr. Scrivener with a concentration that he must have found gratifying, if a little disconcerting. They gazed at him, holding their hands up so that they shut out the sight of his beard, and compared the two sets of eyes, their own eyes moving between the threatened maiden in the cupola, and the man standing upon his wooden platform being impressive in front of them. You could tell that he enjoyed standing on his platform, and gaining two feet in height. He was the tallest man in the hall, *and* the one with the biggest beard, a being of godlike stature. That was why all those Crowninshield's boys were – *Ha! Ha!* – *shielding* their eyes as they gazed awestruck upon him, dazzled by his radiance. He probably refused to part from his much-cherished circular dais (the most prized symbol of his office), and was at all times wheeled around the school on it, like a Cæsar in his chariot. You'd hear it trundling down the corridor, and you'd stand more erect, discreetly smoothing your hair as you awaited the entrance of your beloved leader – with a tremendous *crash!* – bursting into your classroom to the deafening sound of bells. *What a world of merriment their melody foretells!* You'd hear him – for that matter – being trundled through the park on his way to and from his home, put-out pedestrians leaping to safety as the juggernaut hurtled toward them. He'd be really annoyed that the snow had temporarily put paid to his triumphal progress. He'd probably have a sedan chair in readiness for just such an emergency, sag-sag-sagging youths chained to its poles. That would teach them to say "*No*, sir" and reject the generous offer of his freely tendered carnal cavortings with such offensive ingratitude.

Oliver was right.

Exactly the same eyes.

Crikey!

"Spot the tits."

That was what Oliver had called it – he'd developed his theory after Brinkman's trainee sniggering about Cora Munro – and Ben felt greatly daring just thinking the phrase. Oliver regularly used rude words when he spoke to his mama's visitors, using such a matter-of-fact tone of voice that most of them didn't notice, or assumed that they must have misheard him. Sometimes they'd ask him to repeat what he'd just said, and he'd say it again, smiling politely. They still couldn't quite believe he'd said what they thought he'd said. The more innocent believed that here was a little boy repeating words he had overheard but did not understand. (It certainly made them look at Mrs. Albert Comstock with renewed interest.) The more knowing just thought, "Oliver Comstock." (They, also, tended to look at Mrs. Albert Comstock with certain thoughts in their minds.)

A quotation from a James Fenimore Cooper novel – unpunctuated, endless, an ouroboros of a sentence – ran around the base of the cupola. It was not one Ben recognized, or could have completed. The section he could read from where he was, the words circling Mr. Scrivener's head like a halo round a saint's, was: *AND + UNFINISHED + STEPS + OF + EARLY + CIVILIZATION* (this was not a word you expected to find at Otsego Lake Academy) + *DISAPPEARED* (conversely, *CIVILIZATION DISAPPEARED* was the *very* phrase you'd expect to find) + *AND*. All Saints' had *When they saw the star, they rejoiced with exceeding great joy* above the chancel arch; Otsego Lake Academy had *AND + UNFINISHED + STEPS + OF + EARLY + CIVILIZATION + DISAPPEARED + AND.*

UNFINISHED and *DISAPPEARED* were oddly dispiriting words to have in gigantic letters high above you, like a call to silence and nothingness, a pledge to dedicate the rest of your life in a search of that which was incomplete and unapproachable. Perhaps *this* was the school motto. It may not have been in Latin, but it would require an impressively large badge to bear all the words of the complete sentence — whatever that was — upon it.

(Faintly he saw, faintly he heard, Dr. Crowninshield standing in front of them on a Friday afternoon, and the words he was declaiming were undoubtedly — though they hadn't realized it at the time — an attempt to warn them of what the motto of Otsego Lake Academy was going to be.

(*Keep Us All In Servile Fearfulness.*

(That was a motto that would have commended itself to all potential parents. He'd tried to alert them, and they'd ignored him, and now it was too late to *exeunt.*)

If Oliver was also trying to make the time pass — now here was a dilemma for Ben: the faster he made this time pass, the sooner he would be having Mr. Rappaport for Latin — he would be employing it intellectually in making anagrams out of the letters in those words. He was very good at anagrams, though not as good as Alice.

Alice would probably be capable of making a complete coherent sentence, one that employed every single letter, with not one remaining. Ben tended to find just small words here and there, with numerous letters left over, like an incompetent pocket-watch repairer, unused parts scattered across the surface of his workbench as he clicked the back of the watch once more into place, and wondered why it would not tick. Time would have come to a stop completely if he attempted to repair a watch in the random way he went about searching for anagrams.

PAPA was there.

You just knew that Papa would have been there, high above him in large lettering.

Papa was everywhere.

(And *LINCOLN*, Papa's first name. Would you call it a Christian name, when it wasn't a name from the Bible? Would you call it a Christian name, when it was a name borne by *Papa*? He felt slightly nervous, thinking of his papa by his first name, and thinking such thoughts, a child guilty of disgracefully unfilial impertinence.

(He had heard *LINCOLN* spoken many times by his mama. It was the only voice in which he had ever heard the name spoken. This had only just occurred to him. He had never heard Grandmama or Grandpapa Brouwer refer to Papa by his first name, that Christian or unChristian *LINCOLN* of a name.

("Yes, *LINCOLN.*"

(Mama. Eyes lowered. Humble, respectful.

("No, *LINCOLN.*"

(A woman who knew her place.)

PAPAS SUICIDE.

That was there, for all to see.

Not one part of Ben's name was there.

No *BENJAMIN*. Not even a *BEN*. No *FRANKLIN*. No *PINKERTON*. He had ceased to exist – *DISAPPEARED* – driven out by *RAPPAPORT* and *PAPA*. Perhaps this was a good sign, an omen to show that he really did not *belong* there, though he'd realized that already.

MAMA wasn't there, although *LUCINDA*, her first (her Christian?) name was there. He'd never heard Papa address Mama as "Lucinda." This, also, was a recent realization. He felt even more uncomfortable holding the name *LUCINDA* in his head than he had holding *LINCOLN*. Papa – he well knew – would never have approved of his thinking *LUCINDA*. He felt that he was intruding into private places, areas where he did not belong, and should not be, areas within his own mind as much as within the house.

It was the same sort of feeling he had when – alone in the house except for the servants – he had daringly gone into Papa and Mama's bedrooms. He had done this a few times – driven by a need to find something – and stood there in the semidarkness of the chambers with their half-drawn drapes, not quite sure what had made him want to be there. He'd turned slowly round, seeking to find something that he knew was hidden there, something he could not find.

Sometimes, when he knew that Papa and Mama were out of the house (seldom together, seldom at the same place at the same time), he'd find himself starting to walk up the first flight of stairs. He didn't know that he was going to do it. He'd just find himself being drawn there. At the top of the stairs, he'd lean over the banister, and listen to the sounds of the servants from below. He knew their routines, knew when they were likely to be in the upper rooms.

Then, once he was confident that it was safe, he'd turn to his left, and go down the dark corridor to the end. Through the first door – going through this door was easy – there was an inner passage, and the two doors side by side. Going through one of these was not so easy. There were photographs and prints on the walls of the passage, hidden away on these inner walls, things (you'd have imagined) that could not be displayed in the hall or in any of the rooms downstairs that were visible to visitors. He did not examine them in detail in case he might discover what it was that made them somehow unsuitable. He did not wish to enter his father's room blushing, even if his father was not there to see him. They were, he could recognize, scenes connected with the Occidental & Eastern Shipping Company. Some were of ships, or of low, fragile-looking, wooden houses; some were of trees in blossom, hills, harbors, and mountains. Some of them were pictures of pretty Japanese girls with whitened faces, as if they were attempting to disguise what it was about themselves that made them Eastern, though they had been unable to disguise the shape of their eyes. They appeared shy, many of them, their faces slightly averted, or half-hidden by fans or slightly curved hands. He glanced at them with his face askance, equally shy, trying not to let his eyes linger, though the light was too dim for him to be able to distinguish much. All the pictures were Papa's, that was easy to recognize – nothing was here that was his mama's, Papa staking his claim to this whole area as exclusively his – and there were no pictures of his family.

There were two chairs standing against the wall, facing the opposite one, the one with the two doors, like chairs in a gallery. They seemed to be positioned ready for Papa to sit there – in the indistinctness, in the room that was not a room, in the room with no natural light – studying what it was that made these pictures things to hide.

Slowly, he pushed open Papa's door.

The chairs, a discarded shoe lying on its side, the dressing-table . . .

He stood so that the mirror would not reflect him, to make himself feel that he was not really in the room, was not in the place he should not have entered. From downstairs he heard doors closing, faint voices, water in the pipes as a faucet was turned on. You could never really feel alone when there were servants. That sense of movement in the house around you, a silence that was not a full silence, words you couldn't quite hear. He tried to be alert for the sound of the front door, the return of members of his family (he thought of them as *members* of a family, but not as a family), but – at the same time – he tried to lose himself completely in a sense of the dimness of that room.

The door that led into Papa's dressing room . . .

(*Go to the inner room.*

(*Go to the inner room.*)

Some days he didn't dare to go into that windowless room beyond. There'd have been an oppressive feeling of suffocation, he knew that. He'd be pressed in against fur-edged pockets and dark wool, caught in a crowd of adults, all of them far taller than he was. He couldn't see any of their faces, read their expressions. He'd become many years younger, a tiny child lost in the streets full of hurrying strangers. All he would be aware of was their clothes, moving about him with a life of their own, scurrying cast-off garments.

He could smell the leather of Papa's new gloves and boots. He saw the fingers of the gloves, stiff and unlined, shiny with newness, the polished unscuffed surfaces of the boots that looked as if they had never stepped out of the soft, carpeted enclosure of that room.

The smell of him was everywhere.

The smell of him was everywhere in the house.

Papa did not just smoke his cigars in his study.

He smoked them when and where he wanted, and the whole house seemed tinged with a dark, yellowish stain, all materials impregnated with his odor.

The door that led through into Mama's room . . .

The dividing door . . .

There was no key in the lock.

You could tell, by the marks in the paint, the different shade, that bolts had been removed from the door. There was an indentation in the dark wallpaper, a whitish raw edge of damage, where the door had repeatedly been swung back against the wall so that the handle had dug in. You felt that it must have been banged back, that it must have made a sound that would have awoken the whole household.

He seemed to melt through the door, without knowing that he had opened it – there was no resistance, no tugging creak from an unoiled hinge, no scraping against the carpet – in the way that you move through doors in dreams.

He was in Mama's room . . .

The smell of Papa was in there, too . . .

It would be in Mama's dressing room, on all her nice coats and hats and dresses.

Amo.

Amas.

Amat.

Amamus.

Amatis.

Amant.

You recited the verb over and over again, to convince yourself that you knew it off by heart.

He couldn't walk more than a step or so into the room.

He avoided looking at the bed . . .

It felt as if . . .

As if . . .

He had a sensation as of infringing some biblical prohibition. Was he dishonoring his father and his mother? Would his days not be long upon the land which the LORD his God had given him? Was he – this was even worse – seeing his father's nakedness, like Ham had done with Noah? It made him feel small and faint when he read this. It served him right for seeking out – with Oliver – the passages that Miss Augusteena tactfully avoided reading in Sunday-school. Oliver was of a curious disposition, and didn't like to miss anything. Fearlessness without a conscience was a combination that invited experimentation. Noah drank of the wine, and was drunken, like Papa often was, and was uncovered within his tent. And Ham the father of Canaan, saw the nakedness of his father.

"*Euch!*"

Discreetly, squirming with revulsion, they had expressed their distaste at the very *idea* of this with an appropriately Hebrew-sounding exclamation. ("Well that puts paid to all thoughts of sleep for *me* tonight!" That had been Oliver's comment.) Shem and Japheth took a garment, and laid it upon both their shoulders and went backward, and covered the nakedness of their father; and their faces were backward and they saw not their father's naked-ness. He saw himself and Oliver laying one of Papa's hairy cigar-smelling dressing-gowns upon their shoulders and going backward into the bedroom to cover up Papa. It was far too late for Oliver to attempt to cover up *his* father's nakedness. He saw it every time he went into the park and caught sight of *The Curse of Constipation*, Carlo Fiorelli's inadequately clad statue of Albert Comstock as a (particularly) Ancient Roman. It was a statue that made it all too clear why Oliver chose to refer to his papa as Bertie Buttocks. The wind whistled around its gigantic unclad nether regions, jutting out from beneath the flimsy valance of the tunic, one that did little to conceal its fixtures. When the winds blew from certain directions – you visualized winds from the unpeopled polar districts, winds with the smell of snow upon them – they seemed to whistle saucily, channeled between the buttocks as if through a pair of poutily pursed fleshy lips. The high-pitched shrieks thus produced made your blood run cold. Nervous promenaders, on Sunday afternoon strolls in wintertime, chose long, complicated detours to avoid approaching that part of The Forum (the more circumspect eschewed The Forum completely), to escape seeing something that seemed to invite sensational speculation, quite spoiling the virtuous pleasures of the day. And Noah awoke from his wine, and knew what his younger son had done unto him. And he said, Cursed be Canaan. It seemed all too typical of the Bible that a son should be cursed for something that his father had done. Ham's face – you couldn't help thinking – was pink and glistening, it, also, possessing something fleshy and naked about it, a face that assumed a misleading air of quiet rectitude, as safe and domestic as the boiled potatoes amongst which it lay, neatly arranged in symmetrical folds.

It felt as if . . .

As if . . .

As if Mama and Papa were lying there – watching him – lying fully dressed in all their street clothes, side by side on their backs, their arms down by their sides and clutching their umbrellas.

"Yes, Lincoln," Mama was whispering.

"No, Lincoln."

"Yes, Lincoln."

"Yes, Lincoln."

They were not looking at each other, but at him.

(Bedtime.

(Dim lighting.

(A shadow cast upon the wall.

(*Jack, Jack, look at the rab-bit!*

(The shadow was that of a rabbit, cast from the shape of Mama's hands, her fingers held so that they produced the form of what she said.

(Its ears wiggled.

(Its nose twitched.

(The smell of just-extinguished candle.

(A light in the corridor.

(*pe-nis, n. the male organ of copulation [L]* . . .

(*cop-u-la-tion, n. sexual intercourse, coition* . . .

(*co-i-tion* . . .
(Mama . . .
(Mama . . .)

Mama was fading away, like a word being rubbed away on the blackboard when a lesson was over, and Papa was becoming more and more distinct, absorbing her into him, the two become one flesh. It had always disturbed him, this marriage-service countenancing of cannibalism, Papa yum-yum-yumming as he munched away at Mama.

Papa liked his food.

Mama faded away.

LUCINDA faded to *UCINDA*.

UCINDA faded to *UCIND*.

You sinned.

He was the *you* exposed to public accusation, the one to whom all faces turned with expressions of accusatory revulsion.

He was the *you* revealed to all as a not-so-secret sinner.

You.

You.

You.

And all the fingers pointing.

They *all* knew.

All.

UCIN.

You sin.

He.

He.

They knew what he'd been doing.

He was the *you*, and the he-he-he was the sound of sniggering.

CIN.

IN.

I.

Sin in I.

You sin!

You sin!

And soon the only "I" that remained was Papa.

"Franklin . . ."

Papa's voice.

"Franklin . . ."

Papa's voice, stronger than it had been before.

"F-F-F . . ."

A taunting invitation to say the forbidden word in that room.

Noah lived after the flood three hundred and fifty years. And all the days of Noah were nine hundred and fifty years: and he died.

He *died*.

(Though he lived for nearly a thousand years.)

"F-F-F . . ."

He looked again at the hidden words above him.

OLIVER.

He found this quickly, and his eyes lingered on the letters.

LINNAEUS.

CHARLIE.

They were there, also.

He felt a little better when he found these, made stronger by words.

BRINKMAN was *not* there!

Sometimes, with Brinkman, he felt that he wouldn't mind sticks and stones, wouldn't mind broken bones. With Brinkman it would be the *words* he didn't want to hear, and Brinkman would speak those words – chant those words, pointing – the words that could most certainly hurt him. With Brinkman, words were almost always the weapons of choice. Papa had supplied the words to Mr. Rappaport and Mr. Rappaport – with a relay race sweaty eagerness, damp hand firmly grasping the baton – would pass them on to all the Crowninshield's boys, to all the Otsegoans (the whole crammed and sniggering hall) in the spirit of someone educationally writing a new vocabulary list on the blackboard during a Latin lesson, words to be chanted in unison, over and over. This was not a language that could be called dead. It would grow into vigorous life as Mr. Rappaport breathed into it, like God breathing the breath of life into Adam's nostrils.

(*A verbis ad verbera!*

(Another of Dr. Crowninshield's zestfully acquired Latin phrases.

(He heard the voices chanting in chorus, as faint and faraway as if he were listening to the words from a long way down Indian Woods Road, cold in the shadow of All Saints', Crowninshield's completely out of sight.

("From words to blows!"

("When blows have made me stay, I fled from words." That was what Coriolanus had said. He hung onto the thought of being like a Roman hero in at least one respect, even if the hero *had* been killed at the end.

(Coriolanus hadn't minded sticks.

(Coriolanus hadn't minded stones.

(It had been words that he could not endure.)

"Pinkerton!"

"The great detective!"

"Ben-Her!"

"Benjamin!"

(Benjamin was beloved, his father's favorite. It said so in the Bible.)

Ben abruptly became aware that . . .

("Stoddard."

(Look down line.

(Pause.

("Swartwout."

(Look down line.

(Pause.)

. . . the Head Beard had read out "Pinkerton," and that he hadn't even noticed. A small feeling of an unprepared-for blessing, like awakening and discovering that something bad had happened only in a dream. (Not that "only" was quite the qualifying word you felt like applying after *some* dreams.) Surely, if there had been any loud sniggers at his name – the name that so invited sniggers – he'd have noticed, and been drawn out of his musings.

Perhaps he didn't exist, after all.

Good.

If that *was* good.

Mr. Scrivener began to approach the final names in his list of Crowninshield's boys. One of the older Otsegoan boys began to move forward down the aisle between Year Five (*aleph*) and Year Six (*A*) on Ben's right, heading toward the headmaster from the direction of nine o'clock, holding a Bible-sized book open in front of him, all ready for reading. Ben recognized Edgar Blennerhasset. Though Miss Winterflood had died long ago – the old elocution teacher had been dead long before Ben had been born – her vowels lived on in the mouths of the Blennerhassets, the family that had produced her star pupils. The Blennerhasset mantelpieces groaned with cups and rosettes.

(He shouldn't have thought about rosettes.

(They had brought thoughts of Bradstone's bulls to mind again.)

Listening to Edgar Blennerhasset was like listening to the voice of someone long dead, the voice of Reynolds Templeton Seabright, the aged actor brought back to life and made youthful once again.

Mr. Scrivener had reached the end of his list.

He paused an extra long time, giving the impression that Charlie Whitefoord was lucky to be included, as if – at that very moment – he was reconsidering whether or not to admit him. This was all part of his paraphernalia of impressiveness, but Ben was glad that his had not been the last name on the list.

"Whitefoord."

Look down line.

Pause.

(*Impressive* pause.

(This was the effect aimed for.)

Mr. Scrivener repeated his opening ritual in reverse, removing his spectacles, and slowly folding them. You could hear the click in the cold silence of the snigger-free hall. He slowly – there was a lot of slowness involved; it was another part of the impressiveness –

looked all the way from three o'clock to nine o'clock (straight over the head of Edgar Blennerhasset, standing three feet from his left elbow) and back again from nine o'clock to three o'clock, a gesture also reminiscent of Reynolds Templeton Seabright in full actorly mode. The Pretenders to his throne – the lesser Beards – swarmed opportunistically around him, First Beard to the fore, all their weaponry of assassination secreted within their whiskers. The term "Pretenders" had always puzzled Ben.

"I don't *really* want to kill him!" First Beard pretended.

"I don't *really* wish he was dead!" Second Beard pretended.

"I don't *really* want to be the new headmaster!" First Beard. (Pretending.)

"Neither do I!" Second Beard. (Ditto.)

"May The Head Beard live forever!" they chorused fervently, rummaging about in their beards, reaching for their daggers.

"Hail Head Beard!" all The Beards pretended.

A messy assassination would be just the thing to liven things up.

Mr. Scrivener nodded at Edgar Blennerhasset – even the nod was slow and impressive – and Edgar Blennerhasset, aiming right at Mr. Scrivener's left ear, began to read. For a moment, Ben thought that he was going to hear something from the Bible; one of the more obscure passages, that was what Otsego Lake Academy would favor.

The Blennerhasset vowels were in good form.

"From this time to the close of April . . ."

Not the Bible, but a piece well chosen for the place in which it was being read.

What they were hearing was a reading from the works of James Fenimore Cooper, Ben realized. Here was their God. His imperfectly clad angels were suspended in the air above them, and here were his words upon earth. Ben had been, when a very little boy, eager to become a pupil at Otsego Lake Academy, eager to enter the world he stepped into every time he opened one of the novels, the novels he read whenever Papa was not around to witness him.

". . . 'Awake! awake! my lady fair! the gulls are hovering over the lake already, and the heavens are alive with the pigeons . . .'"

Perhaps (here was another, more attractive, thought) Edgar Blennerhasset's reading of the slaughter of the birds (he'd recognized the passage from *The Pioneers*) was the long-awaited signal for the assassination of Mr. Scrivener, the coordinated daggers descending on some designated word. You gained the distinct impression that this was a passage that would often be read at the academy, the prescribed text to put its scholars into the correct sort of manly mood, a Lord's Prayer of Slaying.

Beyond Petteys, First Beard had started to lean forward as the reading continued, on the alert to hear the signal, some suitable word that would set the blood spurting: *release, thraldom, awake, pigeon-shooting, fire-arms, dead, wounded, death, attacks*. There was any number of appropriate words.

SCRIVENER DEAD.

That was written above them.

All the sway of earth shook like a thing infirm.

The prowling Beards were about to be seized by an ambitious impulse, and a *coup d'état* would no longer be delayed.

Birds began to tumble from the sky, the birds that were so numerous and so vulnerable that even long poles, in the hands of those on the sides of the mountain, were enough to strike them to the earth.

After all their preparatory work, they'd acted out *Julius Cæsar* at Crowninshield's, stabbing Dr. Crowninshield with their twelve-inch rulers so that he fell to his death like a porcupine with all its quills quivering. Oliver – as predicted – had been a splendid Brutus, and Charlie Whitefoord – by his casting proscribed from assassinating his teacher (comforting murmurs from his classmates) – had been a commanding Mark Antony. Ben had been Octavius, and Linnaeus had been minor characters on the fringes of the action, voices in crowds with no long speeches: senators, citizens, servants, friends.

Linnaeus had started with the one-line part of one of the

Commoners in the first scene. All the Commoners were clutching their rulers as swords. Although Dr. Crowninshield had carefully pointed out that Commoners would not have had swords, they had somehow contrived to form the impression that all male characters in Shakespeare plays carried swords about with them at all times, like middle-class men in wet weather with their umbrellas. Perhaps it was just that they liked the sense of getting the feel of their implements of assassination. Dr. Crowninshield had *promised* them they were going to be allowed to assassinate him. Ben doubted that Otsego Lake Academy would offer such opportunity to its schoolboys.

"Why, sir, a carpenter," Linnaeus had to say, explaining what his trade was.

"Why, sir, a c-c-c . . ." he had started, his stuttering flaring up, his ruler drooping.

"A c-c-c . . . I'm sorry, sir."

"That's perfectly all right, Linn. Just say 'a sawyer.' You managed the 's' just fine." You felt breathless with admiration at this masterly transition from *The Adventures of Tom Sawyer* to *Julius Cæsar*. Few were capable of achieving this so smoothly. *And* Tom Sawyer had said, "Great Cæsar's ghost!" in Chapter XXIX, when he described how he'd nearly stepped on Injun Joe's hand in the tavern. (It had become the vogue to say, "Great Cæsar's ghost!" at Crowninshield's, a curse usefully sanctioned by Literature.) Dr. Crowninshield was a genius!

"Just say 'a sawyer.'"

"Why, sir, a sawyer."

"Splendid."

Linnaeus's sword perked up again.

("C . . ."

("C . . ."

("C . . ."

(Papa's voice prompted him. The words he had to learn. The words he had to say.

("He loves no plays."

("He hears no music."

("Seldom he smiles."

("Such men as he be never at heart's ease."

(Papa had walked out at him from within the ink-spattered pages of the red-bound Swan edition of Shakespeare that Dr. Crowninshield had bought cheaply from a failed – another failed – school.

(Papa was one of the murderers, and not the one who was murdered.

(The one who was murdered fell down in the market place, and foamed at mouth, and was speechless.)

"'I loved to see them come into the woods . . .'" the Leatherstocking was lamenting, "'. . . for they were company to a body; hurting nothing . . .'"

("For who so firm," First Beard was asking, with the confident air of a man who knew the answer to his question, "that cannot be seduced?"

(The Beards drew closer on the word "seduced." Here was a word they liked to listen to.)

". . . the work we have in hand, / Most bloody, fiery, and most terrible."

(They liked "bloody" also.

(They liked "fiery."

(They liked "terrible."

(They *particularly* liked "terrible."

("It must be by his death."

(Yes.

(Yes, please.

(There was but one mind in all these men, and it was bent against Cæsar.)

"One day," Dr. Crowninshield said, "you might stand in the Forum in Rome, and see the place where these things happened, and remember today."

Charlie Whitefoord had just made his oration over Cæsar's assassinated corpse, and Dr. Crowninshield was still lying flat on his back in front of the blackboard, surrounded by friends, Romans, and countrymen.

The sunlight was coming in from the windows on his right-hand side, and the rulers – they were reluctant to leave go of their upraised ready-for-action rulers – cast long shadows down the uncertain perspectives of columns and porticoes in colored pencil. The small white-clad figures grouped together, manifestations in a ghost-haunted schoolroom.

Blennerhasset drew to the end of his reading. You could tell he was on the point of finishing, because he read more and more slowly, stressing the words significantly. *This is the important bit!* That was what he was saying. (Italics *and* underlining.) He stood very still, his voice vibrating, every vowel stretched out and twanging in the true Blennerhasset manner, the young orator posing for his portrait. He kept looking up from the page, gazing into the near-distance, straight through Mr. Scrivener's left ear, out through his right ear, and focusing somewhere amongst the medium-sized boys of Year Two (*alpha*).

Mr. Scrivener, recognizing the signs, seemed to awaken from his refreshing doze.

"'. . . the field is *covered* with them; and, like the Leatherstocking, I see nothing but *eyes* in every direction . . .'"

He could really *see* what he was describing, you could tell, and four-feet-eleven-inch schoolboys were lost from sight in heaps of dead and dying pigeons. There were feathers and emphatic italics everywhere. You wondered how as sensitive a soul as Edgar Blennerhasset was revealing himself to be had managed to survive for so many years at Otsego Lake Academy. He did look a bit bruised on the parts of his skin that you could see emerging from his uniform.

"'. . . as the *innocent* sufferers turn their heads, in *terror* . . .'"

(He knew *all* about innocence and terror. That was the secret message to his teachers, the audacious cry for help in the midst of his enemies, as carefully hidden as the anagrams within the words above Mr. Scrivener's head. The teachers didn't seem the slightest bit interested. There may well have been – of course – a possibility that it was *they* who were the tormentors. A *strong* possibility.)

"'. . . to examine my movements. Full one half of those that have fallen are *yet alive*: and I think it is time to end the sport . . .'"

(Long, long, meaningful pause. Mr. Scrivener almost started speaking, thinking that Blennerhasset had finished, spoiling his big climax, even though Blennerhasset's voice had held a wait-a-minute upward inflexion on the word "sport.")

". . . *if sport it be.*'"

The big climax.

Rather daring stuff.

Most of the boys in the hall were undoubtedly embryonic Uncle Eugenes, all agog to get killing and shooting. Most of them had probably chewed on gun barrels as teething rings, picking off the odd misbehaving servant for target practice, gurgling with infant pleasure as the unsatisfactory retainers expired at the foot of their cots.

("*Naughty* baby! *Naughty* baby!"

(But you couldn't scold them for long when they smiled at you with such gummy impishness.)

Blennerhasset paused for a moment, holding his pose with his open book before him, gazing – rapt – into the middle distance, clearly enthralled by the magic of his own voice reading.

If sport it be echoed round and round within the rotunda like a ball in a Monte Carlo roulette wheel, clattering, clattering, slowing down . . .

Which letter would be the winning letter?

F-F-F?

C-C-C?

B-B-B?

P-P-P?

Say it! Say it!

Then Blennerhasset snapped his book to with a surprisingly resonant gunshot sound (even *this* was not the signal for assault) that made Mr. Scrivener leap half-an-inch into the air. It drew a startled

"Whoop!" from Dr. Brown, standing between Year Three (*alpha*) and Year Three (*aleph*, more of an *aaagh!-leph*, you couldn't help thinking, if Dr. Brown had chosen to address them at that moment). You could tell that this was the most enjoyable part of the reading as far as Otsego Lake Academy was concerned.

Even more pigeons fell dead at the sound, and the rest of Year Two (*alpha*) disappeared completely from sight in an avalanche of white feathers. Who dare accuse the manly chaps of the academy of such comprehensive cowardice?

Blennerhasset had employed all the arts of oratory — all that was lacking was a large sign around his neck helpfully pointing out *This bit is really sad, Mr. Scrivener!* — but Mr. Scrivener still completely missed the point of the James Fenimore Cooper passage.

"Wasn't that *splendid*, men?" he inquired of them all, recklessly taking it upon himself to improvise a response — he was someone, Ben already felt, who was much better when restricted to a script with large print and very short words — distinctly under the impression that what they'd all just been hearing (a passage he'd heard repeatedly, year after year) was an enthusiastic celebration of all that was best in sport. He'd rather have liked to have been there and joined in with the killing himself, he told them, as he was sure that they all would. After the birds, the Red Indians. (A liquescent gulp from Uncle Eugene .) *Splendid!* It had sounded *admirable*. He himself possessed an excellent rifle — distinct intake of breath at the prospect of Mr. Scrivener in charge of a loaded rifle — and in the last week of the winter vacation he had shot a stag with antlers *this* big. Mr. Scrivener stood with his hands outstretched, fisherman-like (this one had *not* got away), an expression of justifiable pride recognizable above his beard. A look of anguish spread across the face of one of The Beards, standing behind Mr. Scrivener in the aisle between Year Four (*aleph*) and Year Five (*A*). He was probably a Literature teacher, though it seemed highly unlikely that the staff of Otsego Lake Academy would include such peripheral figures, overlooked, scorned, doomed to languish unpromoted for years, dusty as unread books.

Things were drawing to a close, and now it was time for the school song.

Then it would be Latin, their introduction to the intellectual delights freely – well, not quite freely – on offer to them, the brain-expanding rigors of the groves of academe. These groves would not be cultivated groves, but groves that had grown wild and uncultivated. *Cultivation* – like *CIVILIZATION (DISAPPEARED)* – would be anathema to the powers-that-were. These groves would be deep and dark, would close in around complex mazes that were as narrow and well walled as the paths through the ice that had led them there.

And Latin would mean Mr. Rappaport.

They'd been told that Otsego Lake Academy had a school song during their Sunday afternoon tour, second only to the more celebrated patriotic songs of the nation in its stirring ability to set blood racing through the veins of all right-minded men. From Mr. Scrivener's tone of voice, it had been made quite clear that a song – *singing* – was a daring concession to modern requirements, a controversial concession to parental pleading. Exclamations of "Ooh, good!" had clearly been expected, but even Oliver hadn't obliged.

A uniform, a coat of arms on their buttons, beatings, a school song.

What more could they ask for?

Their parents certainly got what they paid for when they eagerly enrolled their sons at this fount of knowledge, scarcely able to write their names – in this they were like so many of their offspring – in the excitement of scrawling their acceptance of the offer of a place.

"In the steps of the Pathfinder
We walk through the wood . . ."

This was a song that singularly lacked the jaunty rhythm of one of Harry Hollander's compositions. That immediately became clear.

The Beards – all thoughts of assassination temporarily scuppered – resumed their wanderings up and down the aisles. They were sorely missing their bullwhips, you could tell, and their fingers flexed and unflexed convulsively, as if rehearsing a strangulation. Mr. Scrivener had better not relax prematurely.

"Sing louder!" The Beards were ordering the assembled academy. These were the words they were speaking, though other thoughts were within the secret places of their hearts.

(They'd moved on a bit from "No talking! No talking!"

(Now it was "Sing louder!"

("Sing *louder!*")

Thwack!

The phantom bullwhips snaked up and down the whole length of the slave galley as the groaning slaves bent over their oars, speeding them away from pursuing dangers.

Thwack!

Thwack!

The song sounded even worse when sung more loudly. Blood did not race through the veins, though they could have done with a little racing blood in that cold interior.

"Sing *louder!*"

The schoolboys sang louder.

> ". . . Searching for a light in darkness,
> Searching for a source of good . . ."

– they'd be searching for *ages* at Otsego Lake Academy, playing a parlor game with a moral dimension –

> ". . . In the emptiness of silence,
> Staring out across the plain . . ."

The words – the rather disheartening words, as soul-sinking as *UNFINISHED* and *DISAPPEARED* in the air above them – made the academy into a school for apprentice explorers, sending its schoolboys out into an unmapped vastness, and not bothering too much whether or not they returned. Would they *want* to return? They would stand like tiny figures in a Thomas Cole landscape (Charlie Whitefoord lived on Thomas Cole Street in the Hudson River district of Longfellow Park), their shadows long behind them, staring out across primeval forests, unconquered peaks. Tentatively, feeling their way, the escaped schoolboys pushed through the undergrowth listening for sounds of pursuit, the buttons on their uniforms gleaming in the half-light, marking them out as targets, lost in the wilderness.

"Sing *louder*!"

"Sing *louder*!"

The Beards urged louder singing, though The Beards did not sing. Singing — you felt — would have outraged one of their most firmly held beliefs, like a priest breaking his vow of celibacy. (Priests were *always* doing this. Another firmly held belief, this, one of Mrs. Albert Comstock's. She held it so firmly that she almost crushed it.)

The Crowninshield's boys did not know the words of the song, but "*Louder! Louder!*" The Beards were demanding, flexing their invisible means of causing pain. Ben — wondering if Petteys, in front of him, and all the boys behind him, were doing the same thing (he leaned his head back a little, and detected some movement in Bradley's jaw with his hair) — began to mime. Papa seemed to have disappeared for a moment (there'd been no springy mattressy beard pressing against the back of his head), but he'd return. He'd never be away from him for very long. He wasn't buried yet, and even when he was buried, there was always that threat of the single word on the crumbling tombstone, the one beneath the dark tree on which the other words could not be read.

He opened and closed his mouth to form shapes that roughly accommodated the words he should have been singing, each movement slightly late, made after the word had just been sung — *Louder! Louder!* — by the boys on either side of him (deep voices on his right, shrill voices on his left). He would have been among the shrill voices if he had sung, like all the Crowninshield's boys. They'd sung regularly at Crowninshield's. It was where he had learned "Where'ere you walk." He had a *pretty* little voice, and should be wearing a pretty little dress. Where'ere he walked, cool gales – the last thing he needed at that moment was more coolness – would fan the glade, trees, where he sat, would crowd into a shade.

He was another of the Pretenders in the school of Pretenders.

He was miming.

He was only pretending to sing.

He was not demonstrating his "musicality."

He was not sounding like his sisters.

He was not blushing.

He opened and closed his mouth, opened and closed his mouth, but he said nothing. Slightly later than the words had first been spoken, he mouthed the pre-learned words of others, but was silent.

It was a better and more accurate summing-up of what his life was going to be like at Otsego Lake Academy than anything else could have been.

When the school song came to an end – it was *Louder!*, distinctly *Louder!* at its conclusion than it had been at the beginning, a certain relief at almost having finished detectably improved the volume of the final verse – there was a slight hiatus, and Mr. Scrivener looked around, waiting to be told what it was he had to do next.

There was a distinct wait-a-minute!, wait-a-minute! tension in the air, a ready-steady sense of waiting . . .

Then . . .

Bells.

> *What a world of solemn thought their monody compels!*
> *In the silence of the night,*
> *How we shiver with affright . . .*

Freeze.

"Take up your positions!"

(First Beard.)

"Take up your positions!"

(Second Beard.)

(What was the position for Year Naught?

(What was the position for Year Naught?

(That was the question that occurred to Year Naught, the boys who had once been known as Crowninshield's.

"Take up your positions!"

(Both Beards.)

The embryonic Beards on their right stepped left and right of their original position – some complicated patterning was involved, but they were too close to see its shape – and wheeled forward and backward from where they had been standing. Some circled around the central platform and began to move up the aisles in the wake of the retreating Beards, and others fanned out around the outer circumference of the hall.

Clearly, no one was going to be given the opportunity to make an attempt at escaping.

By now, you really *felt* like escaping.

Ben hadn't been aware of the eyes upon him them when they'd first entered. He'd been too preoccupied with keeping as close behind Petteys as possible, matching his movements step-for-step, pressing up against the marks of the comb. Now he became aware that every head in the hall was turned in their direction.

As slowly and discreetly as possible, Ben began to edge forward, attempting to hide himself in Petteys, lowering his head slightly.

Like the Leatherstocking, I see nothing but eyes *in every direction . . .*

("I'm not really here."

(That was what Ben was saying to them.)

The innocent *sufferers turn their heads, in* terror . . .

"No talking!" from First Beard.

"No talking!" from Second Beard.

And . . .

"No talking!" from the Beards-to-be, in perfectly mimicked Beard-like voices.

They'd been at the school enough years by now, and knew what to say in the circumstances, and the right tone of voice to adopt. They had learned the lesson of their masters. It was an end to "Sing *louder*! Sing *louder*!" and a return to "No talking! No talking!" Singing was at an end, both the audible, and the silent.

"No talking!"

The only talking you could hear was voices saying, "No talking!"

Bells.

Freeze.

Simultaneously, all three sets of double-doors were flung open, the ones behind them — through which they had entered — and the two others, at three o'clock and nine o'clock, on either side of them.

Mr. Scrivener — with the air of someone launching himself out into a big adventure — released his grip on the lectern, and moved slowly toward the edge of his platform. He stood there, a high-diver about to *boing* his way off a twangily vibrating board. Far below him, he could barely see the glint of the frozen water in the distant swimming pool.

Here was another opportunity for First Beard to hurry forward to demonstrate his suitability for successful succession, treading schoolboys underfoot as he leaped lithely onto the platform to demonstrate his athletic prowess. (*So* unlike senile Scrivener.)

He'd set Mr. Scrivener going.

Mr. Scrivener had become the clockwork toy that Ben had had as a small boy (an *even smaller* boy).

Become the toy, just as Ben had.

Another "My Brave Boy" Mechanical Walking Sailor Boy.

(*Made of Iron and Handsomely Painted in Bright Colors.*

(*Almost Six Inches in Height.*

(*A Toy That is Guaranteed to Delight Any Boy.*

(*Price $2.00.*

(*Packed One in a Box.*

(*A Particularly Handsome Article That Walks in a Manner That Looks as Natural as Life.*

(*It Looks as Much Like a Real Boy as it is Possible to Make It Appear.*)

(One toy, and one book: that was what his father had bought for him. Perhaps they had been in the nature of experiments.)

It described itself as a *Toy* with emphatic firmness. It was making it absolutely clear that the "My Brave Boy" Mechanical Walking Sailor Boy was *not* a doll. It was never called a doll because dolls were something that girls had.

Papa had watched Ben's reactions closely as he removed the brown paper in which the shop had wrapped the cardboard box containing it, and – following the instructions closely – Ben did his best to look *Delighted*, conscientiously attempting to achieve *a Manner That Looked as Natural as Life*. This, after all, had been *Guaranteed*, and it *had* cost Papa two dollars. Part of him believed that Papa wished to see him look *Delighted*, but part of him – the greater part of him – believed that Papa was amusing himself by watching him attempting to convey a pleasure that he could not really feel, that Papa *knew* he could not really feel.

That was the whole point of why Papa was doing what he was doing.

Ben (*Franklin*) – he felt – was himself the toy with which Papa was being amused for an hour or so, and not "My Brave Boy."

(*"My Brave Boy!"*

(*Snigger.*)

Papa did not say anything. As usual, he had just watched, and – as usual – Ben hadn't really known what it *was* he was supposed to be doing, and the not-knowing made him awkward and self-conscious. It didn't take much to make him awkward and self-conscious. There were right things to do and say, and there were wrong things to do and say, and there were right and wrong *ways* of doing and saying, and Papa would want to have the right things, and the right ways. The right ways did not involve blushing and stuttering.

Papa did not react as if his *Delight* had been worth two dollars. He had looked on the verge of removing the "Brave Boy" from Ben – it had been a strain to look *Delighted* for the long while the Sailor Boy took to walk all the way to the wall, swaying from side to side in a manner that might have been intended to look nautical, but ended up appearing extremely intoxicated – and taking it back to the shop for a refund. The instructions gave you full details of how to work the "Brave Boy," but were vague about how you were to set the apparatus of *Delight* in convincing motion. *Any Boy* – the words on the box had claimed – would be *Delight*ed (this had been, after all, *Guaranteed*), but it hadn't worked for Ben (for *Franklin*), as if Ben were really not a boy at all. After all, Ben was not Ben when Papa was in the room.

The instructions for the "My Brave Boy" Mechanical Walking Sailor Boy were perfectly clear.

You Wound Up the Concealed Spring.

There was some ambiguous wrestling with the back of Mr. Scrivener's jacket as First Beard stepped up beside him on the wooden platform.

You Placed it Upright on a Smooth, Level Surface.

First Beard assisted Mr. Scrivener to step down onto the floor, taking particular care to ensure that he was Upright. A slight sense of grappling.

You Ensured That it was Pointed in the Direction in Which You Wanted it to Walk.

First Beard aligned Mr. Scrivener so that he was facing back the way he had entered, so that he would once more pass by on their right-hand side.

You (this was the risky part, with Mr. Scrivener) Let Go.

First Beard hovered for a moment, in case The Head Beard should not be equal to the challenge of unaided walking, and then – he was clearly a man who relished a sense of danger – left Mr. Scrivener, and stepped back in front of Petteys.

The "My Brave Boy" – though not, admittedly, a Particularly Handsome Article – Began to Walk in a Manner That Looked as Natural as Life. (Advertising had a tendency to excessive enthusiasm in its descriptions.)

Mr. Scrivener lifted his head to remind himself of where the double-doors were.

And off he went, a Toy That was Guaranteed to Delight Any Boy.

He seemed even slower than when he entered, exhausted by his superhuman efforts on the platform. The new-boots creak, and the click of the cleats, echoed around *UNFINISHED* and *CIVILIZA-TION*, and, eventually, *DISAPPEARED*. He slid his left foot – flat against the Smooth, Level Surface – forward a bit, just like the "My Brave Boy" Mechanical Walking Sailor Boy, and then slid his right foot forward a bit. He even managed a good approximation of the rolling nautical gait.

He remembered to keep lifting his head.

He passed First Beard. No dagger appeared from beneath the beard, though Ben held his breath for a moment, just in case.

A slight sense of disappointment.

He passed – creaking and pausing and clicking and pausing – Petteys, and Ben, and Bradley. He passed out of Ben's field of vision – it would not have occurred to Ben to turn his head – and passed, creaking and pausing and clicking and pausing, right down the in-order-of-size line of the boys who had once been Crowninshield's boys, and when he'd passed Charlie Whitefoord and Second Beard, he'd have been on his way out through the double-doors behind them.

Ben couldn't help hoping that he might wander off course, and walk into the wall. Ben wouldn't see what happened next, but he would hear it, and – it was something he had seen often enough – he would be able to picture precisely what was going on behind him, causing the loudest wave of *snigger, snigger, sniggers* yet from all the schoolboys facing in the right direction, those fortunate lines from nine o'clock to three o'clock with a good view, though some of the adjoining hours would be able to see at least some of what was occurring by a slight turn of their heads. When the "My Brave Boy" Mechanical Walking Sailor Boy ran into an obstruction, it would press itself right up against it, whilst its feet continued to slide forward — right foot, left foot — and its body to sway from side to side. After a while, it would, with a distinct *click*, tip forward, and — its feet still making their regular little to-and-fro movements — slide slowly down the obstacle with its nose pressed up against it, to end up facedown, making a tinny whirring sound like a trapped and annoyed bluebottle, jerking from side to side, the "My Brave Boy" quite undaunted by this considerable inconvenience, gamely laboring to keep going. The paint on the Handsomely Painted Mechanical Walking Sailor Boy's nose had been the first to go.

Mr. Scrivener did not wander off course.

The creaks and the clicks faded, and Mr. Scrivener left the hall. His next challenge was to align himself — entirely unaided — in the direction of his study door, and reach that successfully. The Concealed Spring retained its power for quite some time, if it had been wound up tightly enough.

All around them, the hall began to empty, as lines of boys — amidst cries of "No talking! No talking! Keep right! Keep right!" — were wheeled about and marched out, their boots thumping.

They'd been welcomed.

That was what had just happened.

Now what were they going to do with them?

A feeling of nervousness.

" *'My Brave Boy.'* "

He heard Papa whispering behind him.

He made absolutely sure that Ben could hear the quotation marks, sending out a shower of spit on the "B" of "Brave," the "B" of "Boy."

There was "F-F-F."

There was "C-C-C."

There was "B-B-B."

There was "P-P-P."

They all seemed to involve spit.

Papa made absolutely sure that Ben knew that the quotation marks were as much for the word "Boy" as they were for the word "Brave." It was awful when the spit landed on his lips. He didn't like to wipe it away in front of Papa, and tried to keep his lips absolutely still so that he didn't accidentally suck it inside his mouth and swallow it. This made it difficult to speak.

"*A Particularly Handsome Article That Walks in a Manner That Looks as Natural as Life.*"

He heard this, also.

After Papa had said this to him in a meaningfully lingering way, he'd found it impossible – for a while – to walk naturally when his father was looking at him. He wasn't walking in a way that a boy ought to walk.

He'd . . .

He'd actually . . .

He'd actually fallen over once.

He'd been on Chestnut Street, walking across to the house from Chestnut Hill, and he'd noticed Papa watching him from the schoolroom window. It was as if he'd chosen the schoolroom so that Ben wouldn't expect to see him there, wouldn't be looking at that window. As soon as he became aware of his papa's eyes upon him – he'd made no effort to conceal himself once Ben had seen him – Ben couldn't think of the right way he ought to be walking. He froze for a while, trying to decide upon an acceptable way of continuing up toward the front door, and – when he attempted to make a start – his legs had given way, and he'd fallen over into the gutter. He'd nearly made it right across the street. He lay there, blushing, attempting to work out how to get to his feet, the "My Brave Boy" Mechanical Walking Sailor Boy, still spasmodically twitching its legs. It hadn't been Cæsar, it hadn't been Papa, who'd fallen down in the market place, and foamed at the mouth, and was speechless. It had been him.

"*It Looks as Much Like a Real Boy as it is Possible to Make It Appear.*"

425

That was something else Papa had said.

"*'Like a Real Boy.'*"

(That was what Papa had whispered significantly to him, stressing the word "*'Like.'*"

"*'As it is Possible.'*"

Here the significantly stressed word had been "*'Possible.'*"

The toy itself might have been something of a disappointment, but you couldn't deny that Papa had derived full value from the words that had been written upon the box. Those words had been *well* worth two dollars, and he'd shared his pleasure so zestfully with Mr. Rappaport several months after he'd bought it. You might say that it had given him a new lease of life, but as he'd killed himself a week later, perhaps it was best not to.

Almost Six Inches.

A Particularly Handsome Article.

Walks In a Manner That Looks as Natural as Life.

As Much Like a Real Boy.

As it is Possible to Make It Appear.

For about a month, these seemed to be the only words that Papa ever spoke to him, and Ben saw them in the air, flourishingly inscribed in their elaborately whorled and brightly colored lettering. Inside the dimness of the box, wrapped in rustling tissue paper, smelling of the bright new paint, he waited in silence to be unwrapped, to be taken out, to be played with, a toy for a lonely rich boy, Dorian Gray in his schoolboy's schoolroom.

Not long after he'd bought him the "My Brave Boy" Mechanical Walking Sailor Boy, Made of Iron and Handsomely Painted in Bright Colors, Almost Six Inches in Height, Papa destroyed it in front of Ben. Like a small child, Papa had derived far more pleasure from the box in which the toy had been packed – the *words* upon the box in which the toy had been packed – than he had from the actual toy. The toy had served its purpose, and could now be destroyed.

He'd keep the box.

Oh yes, he'd keep the box.

(He'd *share* the treasures of the box.

(As Mr. Rappaport had discovered.)

If you were a man not much given to "book learning" – unless the books were dirty books, where not much actual learning was involved – a cardboard box might very well become your favorite reading. There weren't too many words (some of those novels were *far* too long), and every word was a source of fun.

He hadn't said anything when he'd destroyed "My Brave Boy." Part of his method was the casualness with which he had done it.

He had walked across the hall from his study, and into the front parlor. Ben, hearing his footsteps on the tiles, had guiltily thrust *The Water-Witch* beneath the cushions of the chair in which he'd been seated. He didn't really understand everything in the James Fenimore Cooper novels, but the words (not all of which he knew) took him somewhere else for a little while when he read them. For a time – like an obsessive collector anxious to complete a set of something – he'd felt a compulsion to seek out and read every single one of the novels. It had seemed important that he should do that, though he couldn't understand why. He wasn't entirely sure that he *enjoyed* reading them. "Which ones haven't you read?" Alice or Mama would ask him, always willing to buy him another, and he would tell them. Sharing this with them had been a part of its significance.

He remembered himself in the front parlor, breathlessly silent, tensed for the sound of a snapping twig, lost in the forest that had grown up around him, and in which he could hide.

He pressed himself back against the hidden book. When Papa came into the cool parlor Ben was sitting stiffly upright in the chair, staring in front of him at the fire (all set ready for lighting), his arms rigidly by his sides, and his legs extended out in front of him, looking like he'd been sitting in that position for hours. He'd not been quite sure to do with his arms and legs. He felt as if he had been propped up in the chair, like a ventriloquist's dummy awaiting manipulation, the silent mouthing of the words that he was not really speaking, or like one of Edith's old stiff-limbed dolls, something silent that had been placed there to be scolded. Edith did a lot of scolding.

Papa had barely glanced at him.

He was quite irrelevant to what Papa had decided to do.

"*Looks as Natural as Life.*"

That had been all he said.

He never tired of this one, and sometimes shared it with other men as they bent to light their cigars, or refill their glasses. Ben had heard him say it at Mrs. Albert Comstock's "At Homes" to the Reverend Goodchild, Dr. Twemlow, or Dr. Wolcott Ascharm Webster, indicating him with a just-look-at-that! gesture. Perhaps Papa thought he needed to be examined by Dr. Twemlow, to discover what it was that was wrong with him, why he wasn't working properly, even though he'd been Guaranteed to Delight. There'd be a lot of sniggering about his – ahem – Gentleman's (*man's!*) District, you could be sure about that. There was definitely some important part missing, despite the Handsomely Painted Bright Colors. Perhaps Papa thought he'd be more suitable as a case for Dr. Wolcott Ascharm Webster – that would be Guaranteed to Delight Brinkman – and it was time for him to be walked across to his consulting room on Park Place, delivered to him like an article sent to be repaired. It was where all the loonies went. There he'd discover what was missing from the inside of his head, bright parts spilled out across the deep-cut workbench. He'd be walked through the park, and across The Forum, watched by the white marble statues of Reynolds Templeton Seabright (recoiling in horror) and John Randel Jr. (pointing warningly), out through the gates, across the road, and up the steps to number 11, Papa holding him firmly by the hand. All the while, he'd be concentrating fiercely, and attempting to walk in a manner that looked as natural as life. Somehow, the thought of this firm grasp, this *touching*, his hand completely covered by Papa's – with its tobacco stains and dirty nails – was what disturbed him most of all. He thought of flowers that flinched, that withered at a touch. (There! He'd just likened himself to a flower. Could anything be *clearer* than that?) Dr.

428

Wolcott Ascharm Webster might think it necessary for him to be sent away to the Webster Nervine Asylum to be mended, in the way that Linnaeus had been sent away to schools in Massachusetts and New Hampshire and Maine. There might be reduced terms for children. This would certainly appeal to Papa.

There'd been the hint of a snigger when Papa spoke, a thoughtful touch – so typical of him – to nurture Ben into an awareness of what to expect in the years to come at Otsego Lake Academy.

(*Much Like a Real Boy*.

(That was what Ben had thought to himself, as Papa began to rummage about in the built-in mahogany cupboard to one side of the fireplace.)

Matter-of-factly – making sure by a sidelong glance that Ben was watching what he was doing – Papa lifted out the "My Brave Boy" box, and, with a Christmas Day rustle of soft paper, took out the sailor boy. It was still handsome, its colors still bright, though Ben had dutifully played with it whenever he knew that Papa was in the house. He sometimes played in the hall. "Played" seemed the wrong word for something that was carried out with such seriousness, such unsmiling concentration, though he intermittently assumed every appropriate expression. Over and over he repeated those grave, solemn-faced, conscientious actions, kneeling on the cool tulip patterned tiles in the hall.

He played there so that Papa could hear him from his study, and know what he was doing. He was obeying all instructions. He was trying to Look as Natural as Life, as Much Like a Real Boy as it was Possible to Make It Appear. He was trying to be Delighted.

He Wound Up the Concealed Spring.

He Placed the Mechanical Boy Upright on a Smooth, Level Surface.

He Ensured that it was Pointed in the Direction in Which He Wanted it to Walk.

He Let Go.

He watched the Mechanical Walking Sailor Boy lurch, with an echoey rattling sound, across the tiles toward the front door. He'd opened the glass-paneled inner door, so that it could walk all the way across from the bottom of the stairs to beneath the mail-slot. Briefly, as it effortfully whirred forward, it was tinted red from the light shining in through the colored glass. He did this with no sensation of enjoyment, winding up the spring repeatedly, listening for a sign that Papa knew what he was doing, an awareness of his listening. He'd watch it for a while at the end of each of its journeys, as it lay on its face with its head pressed against the . . .

— he couldn't think of the word for it —

. . . the *threshold* (this seemed too portentous and biblical a word for what it described), its legs uselessly toiling. It lay expiring on the very point of escaping, still attempting to battle onward, even though its efforts were doomed to failure, an insect at the onset of winter.

My Brave Boy.

He didn't go across to pick it up again until it had finally stopped moving, and there was silence in the hall. Feeling as Mechanical as the Walking Sailor Boy itself, Ben assumed a smile as he bent forward to pick up the toy, just in case Papa might be able to see his face.

Then he Wound Up the Concealed Spring, and did the same thing all over again, all the time that Papa was in his study, just through the wall. He imagined him listening, though he did not imagine the expression on his face.

Perhaps he'd been attempting to weaken the Concealed Spring within the toy by repeatedly using it, weakening, and then destroying.

Perhaps he'd been attempting to destroy the Concealed Spring within himself.

(The Concealed Spring . . .

(The hidden parts . . .

(*Go to the inner room.*

(*Go to the inner room.*)

Papa placed the Mechanical Walking Sailor Boy face up on the hearth (you could tell that he preferred face up, that he really wanted to see that jauntily intrepid red and pink blue-eyed face as he destroyed it), and placed his heel upon it, grinding down with his full weight. It was the way he sometimes crushed empty tin cans on the back step before they were thrown out. It was done almost casually, with nothing dramatic about it, in three separate actions. First the legs were crushed, then the body, then the head. He saved the head until last, in the way that – at mealtimes – he always hoarded his favorite bits of food on the plate until last, eating them with loud open-mouthed relish.

"After all . . ." he said, like someone responding to a question, ". . . you don't play with it, do you?"

That was all he said. He usually didn't say much. Language wasn't really needed when Papa made his feelings known. It was an irrelevance.

How was he to reply?

Should he say, "I *do!*" and sound upset and tearful, throwing himself – sobbing inconsolably – upon the broken fragments of his toy?

That would please Papa.

Perhaps he should say that.

Should he shrug his shoulders indifferently, demonstrating that – as far as he was concerned – nothing was of any importance?

Was that Much Like a Real Boy?

As Much Like a Real Boy as it was *Possible* to Make It Appear?

Would that please Papa more?

By the time he'd thought these things through, the moment had passed, and it was too late.

As usual.

Papa watched him, doll-like in the chair, his arms stiffly by his sides, his legs extended – just as stiff, just as straight – in front of him, heels against the rug, toes up.

He paused for a moment, savoring the possibility of repeating the action he had just carried out with the Mechanical Walking Sailor Boy.

He'd pick Ben – *Franklin* – up, his arms and legs all dangly like

431

a ventriloquist's dummy ("F-F-F . . ." said the ventriloquist, and "F" wasn't for Franklin), and place him face up on the hearth, his hair fanned out in the ashes. Then he'd place his heel upon him, grinding down.

He'd come to heel.

He'd beg.

He'd roll over.

He'd play dead.

Papa's full weight would crush down.

First the legs would be crushed.

Then the body.

Then the head.

He'd save the head until last.

Papa spoke again.

"*'As Natural as Life.'*"

He said the same words he'd said when he first entered —

Snigger.

— and then went out, and back across the hall to his study.

After he had gone, it was intensely quiet in the front parlor, unnaturally quiet. Karin, he realized for the first time, must have forgotten to wind the clock. He hadn't noticed until then. The hands were still, the gleaming pendulum hung unmoving behind the patterned glass. The hands were set at one of those positions in which one hand was completely hidden by the other, and you thought that they had become jammed together, or that one had fallen down, hidden by the lower edge of the case.

For a moment, Ben had wondered if Papa was standing just out-side the parlor door, hoping for tears, but decided not to oblige. They'd both know that he didn't really mean it, and there'd be no pleasure for Papa in feigned weeping. He kneeled down on the hearthrug, and began to collect together the pieces of "My Brave Boy." The rosy-cheeked face — with its silvery-shiny, slightly bat-tered nose — was still complete, if a little flattened. It had a somewhat vacuous heroic expression, with a get-up-and-go-get-'em-boys! brainlessness about it, an Uncle Eugene sort of expression. He'd never really liked it, just as he'd never really liked Uncle Eugene. You didn't pretend to weep for something you never really liked. He'd discover that later, at Papa's funeral. Fragments of flaked-off paint – mainly blue and white – led in a trail across the carpet to the door, Papa playing hare and hounds with the littered debris of a hero. There'd be paint embedded in the deep ridges on the soles of his boots.

He began to pick up the broken pieces.

Perhaps Papa – thoughtful Papa – had created a new game for him, an *Assemble Your Own Brave Boy* sort of game. When he'd read a little more of *The Water-Witch* he could attempt to put the pieces of the puzzle together, and create the shape of a handsome article. This would point the way, demonstrating the method he should employ to assemble himself into something acceptable. If he couldn't do it with himself, he'd do it with this simulacrum that was Made of Iron and Handsomely Painted in Bright Colors.

Papa had taken the empty box out of the room with him. He'd kept it – it was sturdy, a useful size – in his study, and used it for keeping loose papers in order. His study – its interior sometimes glimpsed briefly when the door was opened – was full of scattered documents, spilling from every surface. From time to time, he'd pick up the box and read the words printed upon it, smiling, like someone turning for comfort to a favorite passage in a novel.

As Ben then did.

. . . *Lounging in the belvedere lately, at night, we saw torches gleaming in a distant lane. Presently the sounds of the funeral chant reached us; these gradually deepened, until . . .*

He had not spoken a word the whole time that Papa had been in the parlor.

When he'd finished reading he'd take the key from the top of the clock case – he'd have to stand on a chair to be able to reach – and wind up the clock. He'd set the hands to the correct position – he'd have to go into the hall to look at the clock there, he didn't have his pocket-watch with him – and then he'd wind it up. He liked doing this, setting time going, spinning the hands round so that time moved more quickly.

"No talking!"

"No talking!"

"Keep right!"

"Keep right!"

They said, "No talking!" even when people weren't talking, and "Keep right!" when they were keeping right.

The last few boys had been marched out of the hall, and "No talking! No talking! Keep right! Keep right!" echoed faintly back from unseen speakers down the corridors. The hall seemed bigger and emptier than ever.

They waited, as they had waited in the entrance hall.

The chalked pattern of lines on the blackboard floor had been blurred and partially erased by the wet-soled boots of all the boys. The ashed and muddied footprints, like a chart of movement, seemed to crowd and gather in most profusion around the doors.

After a while, First Beard reappeared from the three o'clock door on their left, still clutching his board clip like a proud symbol of office.

"Arms by your sides!" he said.

"Stand up straight!" he said.

"No talking!" he said.

"Keep right!" he said.

"Follow me!" he said.

Arms by their sides, standing up straight, not talking, keeping right, they followed him round the central platform in a clockwise direction. They were about to move in the direction of the three o'clock door, when First Beard seemed to remember something. He might have been unable to function without the accompaniment of Second Beard, who had disappeared through the nine o'clock door, or he might have been waiting for the necessary sound of bells as a signal to move. He paused, and they paused behind him, waiting to be told what to do.

Ben looked behind him and upward.

Some of the words he had been reading around the inner rim of the cupola were now no longer visible, and new words had come into view, an earlier part of the sentence from which he had been working out anagrams.

FORESTS + WERE + AGAIN + RESTORED + THE + FIRST + RUDE + AND + UNFINISHED

There was also the greater part of a new painting, in which Cora Munro was still shrieking. Magua, with the identical evil smile he'd employed when he'd been killing Uncas, was hurling his toma-hawk at Cora's sister, Alice, slicing off swathes of blonde hair, as Duncan Heyward – with white-manly courage – struggled to free himself from the ropes tying him to a tree. Cora, this time, was dis-playing her left tit, offering Brinkman the opportunity of completing his sighting of a full set, for which there'd probably be bonus points available, whilst Alice had selected her right tit for dis-play. *RUDE*, indeed. Duncan Heyward – not to be outdone by their more substantial female bosoms – had ensured that his entire chest (poised on the very verge of titness), all muscles bulging, was visible through his ripped shirt. What beasts these Hurons were! Tits and tomahawks, and they were in their element.

Were the schoolboys – as he had supposed – moved around the clock-face in the direction of the hands of the clock, as they became older? Year by year they would be moved a few degrees in a clockwise direction, so that the words they could read, the paintings they could see, were slightly altered each year, and their voices would echo differently from their new positions. At the end of eight years at the school (Year Naught would be there for *eight* years, not seven, a punishment for some trans-gression) they would have performed a complete circuit of the area beneath the dome, ending up facing in almost exactly the same direction as on the day on which they first entered the school. You couldn't help feeling that there'd be something deeply symbolic about this.

PAPA wasn't there above him anymore, but this was an absence that would not last long. He knew this. There'd be other words, new words, but he couldn't bear to search.

435

He lowered his eyes, and turned round to face in the direction of three o'clock.

Papa was directly in front of him.

Resurgam.

Just that one word.

In the dark corner.

Under the yew tree.

Cold water dripped down from the low branches and on to the back of his neck.

Ben saw Papa's name, suddenly leaping out from a board mounted on the wall to the left of the open double-doors. It sprang at him, like his name whispered in a crowded room, though this was more of a shout.

("Brouwer, E. T. L . . ."

(He heard Charles Bradley's voice beginning to read the list of the dead.

(He saw the names on the Civil War memorial, All Saints' churchyard hazy with morning mist.

(Small soldiers in gray, small soldiers in blue, grasping unconvincing homemade painted wooden guns. "Bang! Bang!" they were intoning as they peered down the barrels and squeezed their fingers on non-existent triggers. "Bang! Bang!" They said the sound so quietly that the differently clad boy who was their chosen target could not have heard it, but it was powerful enough to kill at a distance, even if only they could hear the sound within their heads. He couldn't see the faces of the distant women, hovering on the verge of the battlefield already dressed in black, their uniforms for keening and wailing and sobbing out the names of their husbands, or their sons, or their brothers. They would not be saying, "Bang! Bang!")

Resurgam.

It was a name amongst a list of names, inscribed in gold letters, like the Ten Commandments displayed at the front of All Saints' Church. He was in a church, a Baroque church with the swirling figures in clouds crowded across the interior of the dome. It was a service in an unfamiliar church, an unfamiliar religion, and he was uncertain of when to bow, when to remain upright, when to remain silent, when to speak, the very language in which he ought to speak unknown to him.

PINKERTON, L. J. T. (1851–1854)

It made it seem as if his father had died as a very small boy.

Not speaking much, not walking far unaided, the tiny figure toddled to its death.

None of the dates that followed each name covered a period of more than seven years, and he realized that what he was seeing was a list of the boys who had been the very first schoolboys there when Otsego Lake Academy had opened in 1851, and the dates when they had been there. The list was like the names of those who had died in some Children's Crusade, the names of tiny lost victims on a monument, dead in a long-ago war.

Papa — he knew — had entered the academy at the age of fifteen. People had been telling him that his papa had died young.

(*Died*.

(That was the word they used.

(You'd have thought that it had been something that had happened to him, something outside his control, like the weather . . .

(*My father died in the blizzard*.

(. . . or heart attacks.)

If Papa was fifteen in 1851, that meant that he had been . . .

— After the spelling, came the arithmetic —

. . . fifty-two when he died — *killed himself* — last week.

Quite old.

Not young at all.

He placed his hand around the black band on his arm, pressing against some source of pain.

Bells.

Freeze.

First Beard lurched back into action.

"Arms by your sides!" he said.

"Stand up straight!" he said.

"No talking!" he said.

"Keep right!" he said.

"Follow me!" he said.

This more expensive "My Brave Boy" was provided with a beard and the ability to talk, though the clipped and mechanical method of speaking did not sound very lifelike. Like all such toys, it possessed a small vocabulary, but these were all the words that were necessary to express everything that it needed to say. It said the same few things, and it said them many times.

They followed him through the doors and down a bare, dimly illuminated corridor, not talking, keeping right, standing up straight, their arms by their sides. There was no sign of the other boys who had been marched through the doors before them. Even their footprints could not be seen in the poor light. The only sound was the stamping sound that they were making. This sounded like the sort of sound that some people would get to like, people who liked large bands playing recognizable tunes very loudly. Brinkman, with every appearance of enjoyment, was already starting to grunt each time he brought one of his boots down as loudly as possible.

Their legs moved right and left, though their bodies kept right. Brinkman was enjoying the grunts so much that he would soon be grunting even when he wasn't stamping.

They – losing their sense of direction, not sure where they were in relation to the main entrance, all the corridors appeared to be inner corridors, components of another ice-corridored maze – were led into a dark room, with windows so high that they could not see out of them. They felt that their eyes needed a little time to adjust, that they were attempting to see out across a great distance.

Room 37.

"Wait here," First Beard told them. "No talking."

There were twenty-four desks set out in rows, the same number as there had been in the schoolroom at Crowninshield's, set out in the same pattern: six rows of desks along the width of the room, and four rows of desks from front to back. Seeking familiarity in something that was bewildering, they sat at the desks in the order in which they had once sat at Crowninshield's. Petteys, Drinkwater, Akenside, and French (no longer were they Hugh, John, Tom, and William) positioned themselves beneath the blackboard, as if nostalgic for clouds of chalk dust, the deep rising drifts of whiteness, the sound of coughing. They were like refugees attempting to create a home in an unfamiliar landscape, seeking domesticity in a prettily patterned piece of cloth, and a single small picture of something nice torn from an old magazine. It felt odd not to have windows on their right-hand side, just a dark, bare wall. It made them feel shut in, that sense again of all avenues of escape being closed.

They waited. They didn't talk. They'd been struck dumb, unable to speak any words, either of English or of Latin, lost in the silence between languages.

Bells.

Freeze.

They heard metal cleats clicking toward them down the corridor.

They were inside the dark-lined first box of the week.

It was time for Latin.

It was time for Mr. Rappaport to demonstrate how well he'd been trained.

SIX

I

The door had barely shut to after First Beard, when it was flung open again, and Mr. Rappaport strode into the room. With no further preamble, he scrawled *Subject, Object, Predicate* on the blackboard, and began. The first lesson was going to be a shortened one, because of their later arrival, and the ceremony that they had just attended in their honor (though *honor*, somehow, was not the word that came to mind), and he was not going to waste a moment of it. He entered the room with a piece of chalk in his hand, so as not to interrupt his flow. Indeed, he entered the room with his right arm already upraised – chalk poised for action – giving him the appearance (the most appropriate appearance) of being a Cæsar entering the Forum at a triumphant homecoming after victory in battle, rose petals falling from the skies, acknowledging the acclaim of a cheering multitude.

Mr. Rappaport did not explain that Latin had once been a living language – he did not even think to explain that what they were beginning to study was, in fact, called Latin – and if it hadn't been for Dr. Crowninshield's pioneering linguistic coaching, a number of the boys would have spent the first few weeks with the distinct impression that what they were learning was an arbitrary invention, like the uniform, something designed to be an outward demonstration that they were students at Otsego Lake Academy, dressed in their distinctive clothing, speaking their secret language, like

440

clever men using long words that only they could understand. They knew that some of the older established private schools in New England, where the ivy grew so thickly on the walls that the original brickwork could not be seen, had developed esoteric rituals and vocabularies of their own, like tribes living in isolation from the rest of the world (some of them were, after all, in Vermont), and they would have accepted it, like the many-buttoned uniform, as an eccentricity designed to demonstrate apartness. Wearing its clothes, speaking its language, they were defined as belonging to a particular place, a race of beings whose parents could afford to pay handsomely for their education.

Mr. Rappaport turned to face them for the first time – he didn't say what his name was, or what he was there for; in a black gown he stood before them, in mourning for a whole dead language – and tapped on the word *Subject*, with the side of the chalk and not just its tip, to make more noise, and said, "Subject!" He was a dapper young man with an air of arrogant superiority, and his hair was precisely parted. He looked at them all, and tapped once more. The expression on his face – even though it was an unbearded face – was the face of Papa facing a whole room full of girlies, avid to scorn. It was as if that first chalked word, that *Subject*, was there to define what each boy was, each boy's inferior position within that room; every one of them subjected by him, and he become their Cæsar. There was an air of suppressed excitement about him. You felt that he'd been waiting years for this moment.

Subject! meant bow down and cower.

Hail, Rappaport!

Subject! meant worship and adore.

Hail, Rappaport!

Peace, ho! Mr. Rappaport speaks.

When Mr. Rappaport says "Do this," it is performed.

Dr. Crowninshield was dead.

Once more, the daggers descended.

Long live Mr. Rappaport.

In no time at all the class would be dividing itself into two factions, Ben knew this. One faction (the majority) would be whispering (careful not to be overheard), "This Rappaport is a tyrant!" and another faction (a select and self-selected aristocracy, with Brinkman at their head) would be declaiming Barabbas-like acclamations (in their loudest voices), "O noble Rappaport!"

After the long emptiness of waiting – how his voice must have boomed out with particular emphasis during those words in the school song, "In the emptiness of silence, / Staring out across the plain . . ." – it was Mr. Rappaport's time for pleasure once more.

A whole week without schoolboys to torment because of all that sodding snow!

A whole week without stuttering and blushes and tears!

A whole week!

He could hardly wait.

No more emptiness.

No more staring into nothingness.

Now he could see and hear things really close up once more.

Stuttering!

Blushes!

Tears!

"Subject!" he repeated.

(The subject would be stuttering.)

Tap.

"Say it again," he said.

"Subject!" the class dutifully chorused.

(The subject would be blushes.)

(The subject would be tears.)

It was their first lesson, after all, and they were keen to make a good impression. Most of them didn't have a clue what he was talking about, but they were willing to show the right attitude. The more competitive boys – Tom Akenside and Frankie Alloway amongst them – cultivated an air of edge-of-seat alertness. They'd spend their lessons with Mr. Rappaport in chanting the words he gave them to speak, and this church-like worshipful antiphony began with the very first lesson. They couldn't claim that they weren't being taught what to expect.

Tap.

"Object."

Tap.

"Say it again."

"Object!"

He whirled round on William French, at the front, and corrected him angrily, as if he had been insolent to him.

"*Ob*ject, not Ob*ject*!" he said. "It's a noun, not a verb, you fool."

There was a perceptible ripple through the rows of boys, as they realized – those who did not know already – the sort of man who was in charge of them. Some of the edge-of-seat alertness began to seep away a little, as bodies sought refuge in hastily improvised invisibility. Frankie Alloway slid down in his seat. This didn't seem like a gold-star sort of a place.

Mr. Rappaport grasped William French's upper arm.

Squeeze.

"Say it again."

"*Ob*ject!"

Harder squeeze.

"*Ob*ject, *sir*!"

Squeeze.

"Say it again."

"*Ob*ject, *sir*!"

He released William French's arm, casting him aside like a spurned lover, and turned back to the blackboard.

Tap.

"Predicate!"

Tap.

"Say it again."

"Predicate!"

(What on earth was a capital-lettered *Predicate*?)

Tap.

He turned back to the blackboard.

Beneath the word *Subject* he wrote *Pater*; beneath *Object* he wrote *filium*; beneath *Predicate* he wrote *amat*.

(There was a ripple of hopeful recognition on *amat*, a sense of hands reaching out to grasp something familiar, a long-lost friend returning to greet them.

("*Amo!*" they'd once chanted.

("*Amas!*"

("*Amat!*"

(And here was *amat* in front of them.

("He, she, or it loves!" they felt like chanting, to impress their new teacher – whatever his name was – to make him like them, and be nice. "He, she, or it is loving! He, she, or it does love!"

("Sir . . ." someone – probably Brinkman eager to seek his place in heaven on his first day at the academy – almost broke in.

("Sir, I *know* that!"

(He'd have been planning to say, "I know that," not, "We know that." You just knew that this would be what Brinkman almost said.

(Sir ignored this totally, if he'd even noticed it.

(All he was interested in was tapping with the side of his piece of chalk. That was what he'd planned to do.

(*Tap*.

(*Tap*.

(*Tap*.

("We *tap*, here."

(That's what he'd be saying, with First Beard's voice.

(*Tap*.

(*Tap*.

(*Tap*.)

Tap.

"*Pater!*"

Tap.

"Say it again."

"*Pater!*"

Tap.

"*Filium!*"

Tap.

"Say it again."

"*Filium!*"

Tap.

"*Amat!*"

Tap.

"Say it again."

"*Amat!*"

Tap. Tap. Tap.

"*Pater filium amat!*"

Tap. Tap. Tap.

"Say it again!"

"*Pater filium amat!*"

Beneath the word *Pater* he wrote *The father*; beneath *filium* he wrote *(his) son*; beneath *amat* he wrote *loves*.

The father (his) son loves.

Circles and arrows in both directions went round the last two sets of words, and beneath this – vaguely arithmetical, vaguely scientific – diagram he wrote *The father loves (his) son*.

Latin puts words in a funny Mrs. Webster order.

That was what he was showing them.

Werbs at the end of sentences put were.

(If you were one of the few people to have heard Mrs. Webster speak, you'd have known that, with her accent – rarely had Austria seemed so remote and far away – "werbs" was her chosen pronunciation of "verbs." "Mrs. Vebster." That's what Oliver's sister called her. When Myrtle Comstock began to demonstrate her delightful sense of fun, you had little difficulty in understanding why Olly couldn't stand the sight of her.)

Tap.

"The father!"

Tap.

"Say it again."

"The father!"

445

Tap.

"Loves!"

Tap.

"Say it again."

"Loves!"

Tap.

"His son!"

Tap.

"Say it again."

"His son!"

Tap. Tap. Tap.

"The father loves his son!"

(You didn't hear the brackets around *his*.)

Tap. Tap. Tap.

"Say it again."

"The father loves his son!"

(No brackets.)

Ben's right hand slid up the side of his left arm, and rested on the black band, covering it.

He knew what was going to happen.

As soon as he saw *The father (his) son loves* he knew what was going to happen. The brackets around *his* suddenly appeared to be the most important part of everything that was written on the blackboard, and he stared at them, as if he could draw them protectingly around himself, and feel safe inside them.

Mr. Rappaport lived up to expectations.

(*Quite a challenge.*

(That's what he'd been thinking, looking at Ben, looking at Ben with *both* eyes.

(That's what he'd be *saying*.

(*I see what you mean.*

(*How very apt!*

(*That's a good one!*

(*Spot on!*

(*Snigger.*

446

Tap. Tap. Tap.

(The *tap, tap, tap* echoed hollowly upon the brackets, demanding entrance, Papa wishing to see his blushes again, to enter his head, though he had never *left* his head. He was always there, the guardian to the inner room, though Ben sometimes – but not for very long – forgot that he was there.)

"*Pater filium amat.*"

Tap. Tap. Tap.

(Already, the brackets began to crumble, too fragile to withstand the tapping.)

"Say it again."

"*Pater filium amat .*"

Tap. Tap. Tap.

(The brackets collapsed completely.)

"The father loves his son."

Tap. Tap. Tap.

(Were no longer there.)

"Say it again."

(Had vanished completely.)

"The father loves his son."

Mr. Rappaport looked around the room, as if idly.

"Year Naught," he muttered to himself, though they were meant to hear it. The fact – clearly – did not impress him. He stressed the word "Naught" with emphatic descriptiveness.

His eyes appeared to alight on Oliver, quite by chance.

"Stand up. Name?"

(As if he didn't *know* the name.)

"Oliver."

(As if Oliver didn't *know* that Mr. Rappaport meant his surname.

(As if Oliver didn't know that the reply should have been followed by a "sir."

(Any sentence to an adult at Otsego Lake Academy ended with the word "sir" – there were a few women about, but they were not the sort of people to whom you were expected to speak – and the "sir" was as essential a part of the grammatical correctness as the period full-stopping the sentence was of the punctuation.)

Mr. Rappaport repeated exactly the same words that First Beard had used to Frankie Alloway in the entrance hall, in the same tone of withering sarcasm.

"Not the name your *mama* calls you by. Your *man's* name." He added, as his important little personal touch, "If you've *got* one."

(*Pink!*

(The very color!

(He could have matching ribbons fastened around his neck!

(In his hair.

(His wrists.

(His ankles.

(Tied around his . . .

(Tied around his . . .

(If he's got one.)

A slight snigger from Brinkman. As early as now did a disciple announce himself. Mr. Rappaport did not look particularly gratified by the snigger; neither did he rebuke Brinkman.

Oliver knew what he meant.

"Comstock."

(Still no "sir."

(You knew that accident played no part in this omission.)

"Oh yes. I've heard all about *you*, Comstock."

(Of course he had. He'd been singing with him in All Saints' choir for several months, even if segregated two rows from him by virtue – hardly the right choice of word, this one, you felt – of his deeper voice, and the hirsute embellishments of manliness, even if he had chosen the path of beardlessness. Oliver had expressed a powerful desire to join the choir in the very same weekend that his mama had left All Saints' to attend a church elsewhere, one where her hats might receive more discerning attention, and where a clergy-man less wishy-washy than the Reverend Calbraith would launch himself upon sinners with an aggressive enthusiasm that recalled Dr. Vaniah Odom letting rip in the I-see-hell! good old days.)

448

"And I've heard all about you too, sir."

The first appearance of a "sir," but – somehow – the sentence sounded less satisfactory because of it. There was no heavy sarcasm, no sneering – Oliver was far too clever to lay himself open to charges of sarcasm, and he was certainly not sneery – but there was something not quite right about that "sir." "Sir" was not the name Mr. Rappaport's mama called him by; it was his man's name, the name upon which all The Beards – First Beard nearly lashing out with his board clip when it had been withheld – strenuously insisted. It had *not* sounded like a proud proof of manhood, the way that Oliver said it.

It was said in a polite, friendly sort of way – bright-eyed and beaming – as were most things that Oliver said, but there was a slight rise in the pressure of the room. The rest of the class knew Oliver well. A bright remark would soon be on the way. Those seated nearest to him assumed expressions in which keen anticipation grappled with nervousness, sliding along in their seats until they were as far away from him as possible. He'd managed – by a superhuman effort – to avoid a bright remark to First Beard in the entrance hall, and a corker would be due any moment now to compensate.

"Comstock!" Mr. Rappaport snorted, in the tone of someone who'd suddenly developed an aversion to something. He said it again, barely able to believe what he had heard the first time. (That was the intended effect.) "*Comstock!* What a name! . . ." – what would he make of Pinkerton? – ". . . I don't like your name, *Comstock*. You ought to change it."

Oliver's response – thrilled excitement – was instant.

"Ooh, *sir*! Is that a *proposal* of marriage?"

Short pause.

"And me so young! Flutter, flutter goes my heart! I'm all confused, conflicting emotions battling within me for supremacy. Pride, nervousness . . ."

(*Nausea*.

(He didn't say this one.)

449

Longer pause.

Frankie Alloway slid so far over in his seat that he fell off into the next aisle, but Mr. Rappaport didn't even notice.

Very long pause indeed.

Eventually — there was a distinct sense of Mr. Rappaport pulling himself together — their teacher elected to ignore this. Various possibilities had been considered and reluctantly discarded. Oliver had known just the right sort of thing to say.

Time for Mr. Rappaport to reestablish supremacy.

He grasped the top of Oliver's left arm.

Squeeze.

He did it with the ease of a man given to much practicing. The cushions in his house would be all squeezed out of shape, lumpishly misshapen, and cast about the floor. The nap on the arms of his chairs would be as rough as unpicked rope-knots, as if a life-sentenced prisoner had been perpetually unloosing oakum.

"'Comstock, *sir*,' is what you say here if I ask you your name!"

(He'd spotted that pointed omission.)

Squeeze.

"Say it again, Comstock."

"*Sir!*"

Harder squeeze.

"Comstock, *sir*!"

Squeeze.

"Say it again, Comstock."

"Comstock, *sir*!"

Squeeze.

"*Pater filium amat.* The father loves his son."

Squeeze.

"Say it again, Comstock."

"*Pater filium amat.* The father loves his son."

Harder squeeze.

"The father loves his son, *sir*."

Squeeze.

"Say it again, Comstock."

"The father loves his son, *sir*."

(Oliver's friendly smile never wavered, and he managed to convey the impression that he was thoroughly enjoying this little game with the nice man.

("Faster!" he'd be ordering, any moment now. "Faster!"

(He'd be a small boy shrieking with excitement as his papa pushed him on the swing.

("Higher! Higher!")

His left arm had a line of chalky white handprints all the way up.

"Sit down, Comstock."

"Yes, sir."

Oliver – suspiciously – was uncharacteristically subdued after his first response.

The gaze wandered about the room again. Ben's hand remained over the black band, trying to hide it. His head was bowed. He *knew* what was going to happen.

"Stand up."

Ben knew that it was his turn now.

Mr. Rappaport had chosen the two boys in the room who had recently lost their fathers.

"Put your arms down straight, boy. Name?"

(As if he didn't *know*.)

"Pinkerton, sir."

(*Pink!*

(The very color!)

He hoped he wouldn't be made to blush. He felt about his blushing, as people must feel about uncontrollable incontinence.

(*Pink!*

(And becoming even pinker.)

Mr. Rappaport was keeping *both* eyes on him.

(*Laughter.*

(It was going to be quite a challenge.

(*Laughter.*)

An inspiring example to his pupils, he would have spent hours on his homework the night before, his *fiancée* testing his memory of the four and five star phrases that guaranteed blushing, a man as surrounded by chanting as a monk in a monastery. To learn something by heart, all you needed to know were the words and phrases that prompted whole sentences, drawing them out from within the memory. Perhaps teachers could be as ambitious for gold stars as the children they taught could.

(Blushing would be good.

(*****

(Tears would be even better.

(*****)

Perhaps it was upon his *fiancée* that he also practiced his squeezing, achieving his enviable technique by repeatedly compressing areas of her arms and legs for hour after hour – he'd tire of unresponding cushions and chairs (gasps of pain were an essential part of the pleasure) – to achieve rock-hard biceps by patiently unremitting exercise. Men were expected to squeeze women. You came to a certain age, and you'd start your squeezing with a carefully selected girl. It was one of the duties that the approach of manhood brought with it. This had come from Brinkman, as he'd smirkingly revealed the mysteries of tits and garters and feathers to them beneath the lime tree. This squeezing was something that they'd be expected to do on a regular basis. You didn't need any special equipment, but you had to wash your hands – *both* hands were involved, apparently – carefully. You blushed to think about it. They'd stared at their hands, aghast, essaying a few experimental graspings and ungraspings against the empty air like a group of Macbeths attempting to clutch the air-drawn dagger. "You don't know?" Brinkman repeated, incredulously. "You don't *know?*" They'd felt ashamed that they didn't *know*. Those grasping, unknowing hands would always be closing upon emptiness. No girl would ever volunteer any portion of her anatomy for squeezing to *them*.

(If he thought the words, Mr. Rappaport wouldn't *say* the words. (*My Brave Boy.*

(*****

452

(*Almost Six Inches in Height.*

(*****

(*Guaranteed to Delight Any Boy.*

(*****

(*A Particularly Handsome Article.*

(*****

(*Walks in a Manner That Looks as Natural as Life.*

(*****

(*Much Like a Real Boy.*

(*****

(*As it is Possible to Make It Appear.*

(*****

(You made a wish when stars fell from the sky.

(He was Handsomely Painted in Bright Colors.

(He was Made of Iron.)

"Pinkerton!" Mr. Rappaport ruminated over the name as though it was one he hadn't come across before, one that amused him mightily with its many entertaining possibilities. "And I've heard all about *you*, Pinkerton. You're not a *defective* detective are you, *Pinkerton*?" Ben had been teased often enough before because of "Pinkerton," because of that shared name with the founder of the detective agency. "'We Never Sleep'!" they'd sometimes called after him, chanting the firm's motto, and he'd been rather pleased, seeing it as a mark of distinction. This was a motto without clouds and sunshine. He'd drawn neat versions of the ever-open Pinkerton's eye, the eye that never slept (it would have been blinded by sunshine) on his books as his personal shorthand. It was an eye that belonged more to clouds. It seemed appropriate that his father's name should be somehow commemorated in this way, watching remorselessly, ever-vigilant, ever on the alert, unblinking, missing nothing. He hadn't really minded the joshing at all (up to now), and certainly preferred it to "Pinkie." He would – he knew – be called "Pinkie" *a lot* at Otsego Lake Academy, and he also knew that he wouldn't think of this as "joshing."

"*Are* you defective in any way?"

Brinkman sniggered more loudly than he had the first time, recognizing that the boundaries were being drawn. He knew which side of the line he would stand.

"No, sir."

"*Are* all your parts in full, working order?"

"Yes, sir."

"*All* parts?" (A suggestion of salacious surprise.)

"Yes, sir." A little more uncertain.

Even louder snigger from Brinkman. How your heart warmed to that boy, the way his hand reached shyly out in tentative friendship toward his new master.

"*Really?*"

It somehow seemed the wrong answer to have given, although "No, sir" would have been even worse.

(Wouldn't it?)

"Defective detectives must be *corrected*, Pinkerton, mustn't they?"

Another Brinkman snigger, verging on a guffaw. No reaction from Mr. Rappaport, though Ben thought he saw a slight, pleased smile, quickly suppressed, the sort of unpleasant smile you tended to see on an evil-minded *child's* face, when he asked his teacher an embarrassing question. Mr. Rappaport was clearly a man who encouraged followers. They'd march in line – tramping their feet very hard, coordinating their grunts – and they'd have special salutes and slogans as signs of their chummy exclusivity.

"Yes, sir."

Squeeze.

"Say it, Pinkerton."

"Defective detectives must be corrected, sir."

Harder squeeze.

"Defective detectives must be *corrected*, sir."

Ben's "corrected" had been incorrect. Ben's "corrected" had failed to make use of italics, and "corrected" must be stressed, though there was a not-quite-spoken sense that the word that *really*

454

ought to have been stressed was "defective." Ben knew that the full details of his defects would be laid out for the delectation of the class in time, and that that time would not be long in coming. Mr. Rappaport was the sort of man who liked to pace his pleasures, and he'd plan a day of indulgence in the not very distant future.

(Ben's would be the naked body spread out across the table, there to be indicated and prodded and dissected, as the lecturer warmed to his subject.

(He disliked being undressed in the presence of others, disliked others seeing him removing his clothes. *Sport*, he was thinking, *Sport*, Mr. Rappaport seeing his thin arms and legs, the rich taunting potential of his uncovered body.

("Note!" Mr. Rappaport hectored his audience, prodding with his pointer, and all the students would strain to see from their tiered seats.

("Note!"

("Note!"

(*Nota bene.*

(Latin.)

"Defective detectives must be *corrected*, sir."

Mr. Rappaport dug in the ends of his hard fingers so that it really hurt, choosing the best place carefully. Perhaps he sometimes assisted Mr. Caswell with muscular demonstrations in Biology lessons. As the Sport teacher, he'd know all about where all the groupings of muscles were, or where they ought to be if they had existed. He'd know the most effective positions into which to insert digits to ensure the maximum amount of pain. It would be a part of his training by The Beards, a part of his vocational pleasure.

("To really hurt someone with the end of your fingers, you dig them in the tops of their arms just . . ."

(He'd pause, luxuriating in the suspense of the pause, as the class gathered around in watchful silence, his fingers starting to close in around Ben's upper arm.

(". . . just . . ."

(He'd make the pause last as long as possible.

(Sudden pounce, sudden tightening, *pain*.

("... just *here*.")

His *fiancée* would be allover black and blue, a painted warlike heathen ready for the attack. (Quite a good description of the woman in question, this – you'd agree – once you'd met her, glaring out from beneath her bonnet.)

Harder squeeze.

Ben winced, and struggled not to cry out.

"*Pater filium amat.* The father loves his son."

(Just over a week ago, Mr. Rappaport had been standing next to Papa in his study, and looking down at him from his amused height.

("See what I mean," Papa said.

(Mr. Rappaport, an ambitious man listening to his patron's joke, demonstrated huge mirth.

("Quite a challenge."

(Ben had watched Harry Hollander walking past outside the study window, and tried to imagine the music he would be hearing in his head as he composed a new song.)

Squeeze.

"Say it again, Pinkerton."

"*Pater filium amat.* The father loves his son, sir."

He stood in silence, and studied Ben for a moment, throwing the piece of chalk casually from hand to hand like an athletic showoff with a ball. You imagined him practicing this at home as he waited restlessly for the holidays to be over, so that the fun could begin again. His collars were very high and very white, and his studs gleamed in the light. His face was pale. His colorless eyes seemed to draw the color out of whatever it was that he was watching, and now he was watching Ben.

"Another one with blond hair and blue eyes," he commented musingly, the voice of an enthusiast pinning a specimen into its position in his collection.

(Blue eyes.

(The time he'd made a reference to the color of Oliver's eyes.

(Papa had soon put him right.

(Boys did *not* notice the color of other boys' eyes.

(Blue.

(Blue was not permissible.

(Black and blue was more the sort of thing for chaps.)

"Blond hair and blue eyes. A matching pair. Are you in any way related to Comstock?"

"No, sir."

"Hmm. Are you *quite* sure no relations are involved? Two pretty blond boys like you two, quite the beauties of the class?"

This time Brinkman did guffaw. One or two others – Adams, Swartwout – joined in a little uncertainly, still on the lower slopes of slight sniggers. The numbers in that group would grow.

"Virgil is alive!" Mr. Rappaport announced. No one knew what he meant, but it sounded dirty. (The tone of voice was in itself enough to nudge all salaciously inclined listeners into activating their snigger muscles, and the fact that "Virgil" sounded a little like "virgin" was a bonus.) "The second eck log lives and breathes before me!" (It *sounded* like "eck log." *What* the 'eck was an 'eck log'? It didn't sound like something to boast about.) "*Surely* you're the beautiful Alexis, Pinkerton, and Comstock is Corydon, all on fire for love?"

(Sniggers.)

Mr. Rappaport pranced about a bit, declaiming simperingly, hand on heart, fluttering his eyelashes.

He spoke a few words that they couldn't understand, and – although they couldn't understand them – they knew that they were – after *Pater filium amat* – the first words of Latin that they had heard spoken in Otsego Lake Academy, though they were not *mea culpa* words (they were already beginning to realize that *culpa* would be playing a large part in Latin lessons), not *post meridiem* or *nota bene* or *Deo volente* words (*Deo* was highly unlikely to be involved). No one had ever heard of Corydon and Alexis before, but they soon realized the sort of names that they were, Romeo and Juliet sorts of names. Romeo and *Benvolio* sorts of names. (*Snigger*.) Realizing that his Latin was being met with complete

457

incomprehension (though he probably enjoyed demonstrating his prowess as an intellectual giant) Mr. Rappaport helpfully began to translate what he was saying into English. More chance of sniggers with English, a greater possibility of guffaws.

"'Lovely white-skinned youth!'"

To make doubly sure that they realized he was quoting someone else's words — it was vital to him that they were aware of this ("This isn't really *me* speaking, you know, chaps!") — he not only employed the special this-is-a-well-known-quotation tone of voice, he also (for the benefit of the less academically gifted) lifted his hands and fluttered little punctuation marks in the air. He armored himself with quotation marks and brackets, flourishing them like shields, and — safe behind his well-punctuated protection — he unleashed his barbs of wit.

"" fluttered the first two fingers of his right hand.

"" simultaneously fluttered the first two fingers of his left hand.

Flutter-flutter fingers.

Flutter-flutter eyelashes.

("Flutter, flutter goes my heart." That's what Oliver, prescient as ever, had said a little while earlier, and now the flutter, fluttering was all around them, a cool breeze of coyness strengthening in the air.)

Mr. Rappaport fluttered his fingers and eyelashes throughout the whole of the sentence, rising up slightly with his heels off the floor. He had the demeanor of one of those small child angels in a painting, with tiny feather-like embryonic wings too fragile to lift him more than an inch or so into the air. Eyelashes batted vigorously to increase the skyward tilt, to tug him — arch-eyed — heavenward. He hovered around Ben, a bird of prey with feathers that were decorative rather than functional. The sound of unfurled whirring wings; Hilderbrandt, the Comstocks' foul-tempered parrot, stirring restlessly on his perch, fluffing up his feathers and shaking himself vigorously from side to side like an enraged swan with carnage on his mind.

"'Lovely . . .'"

(Not one of the words that Hilderbrandt chose to squawk with high-pitched beak-snapping insistence.)

Flutter-flutter fingers.

Flutter-flutter eyelashes.

("Shit!" was more a Hilderbrandt sort of word.

("Fuck!"

(One of his favorites, this one.

("Botheration!"

(Oliver – disconcertingly – did have a tendency to lose interest in something after the initial enthusiasm had worn off. "Botheration!" – you had to admit – failed to live up to the heady excitement of "Shit!" and "Fuck!" and all the other words that Oliver had patiently taught the parrot, planting them inside him like exploding booby traps with malfunctioning timer devices, but it was another word that featured regularly in Hilderbrandt's vocabulary of vehemence. The parrot chose the sounds to suit his mood, and his mood was never a good one.

(The high moral tone of Mrs. Albert Comstock's "At Homes" had – you had to admit – taken a dive, a doomed parrot plunge, ever since Oliver – bright-eyed and eager – had started to take a keen interest in Hilderbrandt's educational development. He rehearsed the parrot like the most demanding of elocution teachers, insistent that the pronunciation be worthy of his high professional standards.

("Could you enunciate the 'sh' more sharply?" he'd be asking Hilderbrandt, as the parrot eyed him dubiously. "'Sh!' 'Sh!' 'Sh!' Like that?"

(These shushes were not shushes for silence.

(Anything but.

(The louder the better.

(That's what these shushes were saying.

(Sniggers.

(Sniggers for "Shit!"

(Sniggers for "Fuck!"

(Sniggers – different sorts of sniggers – for "Botheration!"

Sniggers — like most things — had carefully graded levels of meaningfulness, and once you'd learned to interpret the levels, the periodic law of laughter, Society hastened to welcome you as one of its own, clutching you — not too closely — to its chill and perfumed bosom.

(Sniggers — extra-special high-pitched sniggers — for "Lovely."

(Little difference — it seemed — between Hilderbrandt's lexicon of lewdness, and Mr. Rappaport's.

(*Lovely!*)

"'. . . white-skinned . . .'"

Flutter-flutter fingers.

Flutter-flutter eyelashes.

Sniggers.

"'. . . youth!'"

Fluttering fingers.

Fluttering eyelashes.

Sniggering.

This went down so well that he fluttered further.

" "

(Right hand.)

" "

(Left hand.)

"'Corydon, Corydon, alas!'" Pause. "I'm not surprised that they think he's a lass, the way he behaves!"

(Puns as well as punctuation.)

Another success.

" "

(Right hand.)

" "

(Left hand.)

"'Cruel Alexis! Must I die for love?'"

This went down even better.

" "

(Right hand.)

" "

(Left hand.)

460

"'Come to me, my beautiful boy!'"
The most successful sally yet.
("Bee-oo-tiful!" from Brinkman.
(Sniggers edging into guffaws.)
""

(Right hand.)
""

(Left hand.
"'Lured by a peculiar joy!'"
A *great* success, this.
("Perc-oo-liar!" from Brinkman.
(Bee-*oo*-tiful!
(Perc-*oo*-liar!
(Guffaws overwhelming the last vestiges of sniggering.)
("Oo!" from Brinkman.
("Oo!" simultaneously from Adams and Swartwout.
("*Oo!*" from all three.)
""

(Right hand.)
""

(Left hand.
(Fingers.
(Eyelashes.
(*Frantic* flutterings.)
"'Come to my longing arms!'"
(Punctuation *very* firmly clicked into position for this one.
("Oo!"
("Oo!"
("*Oo!*")
"Steady on, sir!" from Oliver.
Come to me, my beautiful boy!
Come to my longing arms!
The Oo! Oo! *Oo!* eck log words were the same as the
"Jabberwocky" words, the words reflected in a mirror and seen
the wrong way round.

Come to my arms, my beamish boy!

("My beamish boy!"

(Oliver, earlier, standing just behind Ben in the gloom of the entrance hall, whispering.

("Come to my arms!"

(His chin propped over Ben's right shoulder.

("Oh frabjous day!"

(All the exclamation points.

(Ben thought of this, hung onto this, to make himself feel stronger. Oliver's voice, the amused, unafraid edge to the words, chortling in his joy.

("Callooh! Callay!"

(Ben had no vorpal sword with which to snicker-snack.

(But he had Oliver.

("Jabberwocky" words, he thought. "Jabberwocky" words. He tried to feel stronger.)

After his success with the eck log, Mr. Rappaport – emboldened by "Go on, sir!" guffawing – went on to make some deeply meaningful remarks about George 'Icks. Brinkman, Adams, and Swartwout – guffawing fit to bust – strove to give the impression that they knew what it meant. *George 'Icks?* They 'ad an 'Arry 'Enderson, present and (on rare occasions) correct, but George 'Icks was an unencountered stranger.

(" 'Ic!" 'iccupped 'Icks. " 'Ic!"

(*'Ic jacet 'Icks.*

("Guffaw!" from Brinkman.

("Guffaw!" simultaneously from Adams and Swartwout.

("Guffaw!" from all three.

(It would be a few years before they'd encounter *The Eclogues* and *The Georgics*, and Ben would be caught out by the words as he read them, blushing, ten years old again, hearing a taunting voice.)

A jolly atmosphere had now been expertly established, a milieu of fluttery fun set fair to beat the best efforts of an overheated "At Home" when all fans sprang simultaneously into wrist-wrenching action. Hilderbrandt had met his match in Mr. Rappaport when it came to activating snotty sniggers.

("Oo!"

("Oo!"

("*Oo!*")

Mr. Rappaport suddenly seemed to notice something for the first time. He came a little closer to Ben, and began to lean forward.

(Still the sensation of "*Oo!*" in the air.

(*Pater filium amat.*

(The father loves his son, sir.)

"Why are your lips all covered in blue ink?"

He'd forgotten about First Beard splashing him with his pen.

He put his fingers to his mouth, as if the ink might still be wet, and he could rub it all away. First he'd rubbed his ink-splashed hand on his lips, and now he rubbed his inky lips against the sides of his fingers. He avoided the still-stained back of his hand. He remembered the feeling he'd had, the sense of words being written deep inside him, their bitter taste.

He looked at his fingers.

No ink.

He hadn't removed *any* of it.

Mr. Rappaport came to stand right up against him. He took hold of Ben's head in both hands, and bent it back, leaning in toward him, like a bold lover moving in for an enforced kiss.

("Oo!"

("Oo!"

("*Oo!*")

Ben didn't know what he was going to do, didn't know what was going to happen, didn't know what to do with his hands. He thought he was going to fall backward, and flailed his arms in the air, slowly, awkwardly, trying to achieve a sense of balancing. He did not want to clasp hold of Mr. Rappaport. He'd rather fall to the floor than do that.

"Open your mouth," Mr. Rappaport said.

He did as he was told.

"Say 'Aah.'"

He said, "Aah."

It was like being examined by Dr. Twemlow, though without any of the doctor's usual shrinking self-consciousness. You could sense Dr. Twemlow bracing himself to touch you. Mr. Rappaport had no problems with touching.

Mr. Rappaport peered closely into his mouth for a moment, holding his head quite firmly – Ben avoided looking into his eyes as he did this – and then straightened up.

"Well, well," he said. "Blue lips. Blue tongue. You're probably blue all the way down inside. A drinker of ink." He suddenly assumed a poetic voice, the voice of someone mocking the very idea of poetry. "O, for a draught of vintage! The true, the blush-ful . . ." – Ben tensed at this word, a word Mr. Rappaport seemed to stress, it had been more *"blushful"* than "blushful" – ". . . Hippocrates."

"Hippocrene."

(Oliver, in bluntest "Ahem, sir" mode – though neglecting the "sir" – realizing that any attempt at the subtlety of eyebrow-signaling would be wasted on Mr. Rappaport, making it clear that "Hippocrates" was *wrong*.

(Keats.

(Ben recognized it as Keats, because of Oliver.

("Is the blushful Hippocrene in residence?"

(The same words, but they hadn't sounded the same at all when Oliver had said them to him.)

Mr. Rappaport ignored Oliver. More appropriate words from Keats had just occurred to him. Only a manly chap like Mr. Rappaport could get away with quoting from *poetry*. That was the message.

"Beaded bubbles winking at the brim, / And purple-stained mouth!" he added, sneering to make quite sure that they would be left under no misapprehension about what he thought of poetry.

"The viewless wings of Poesy," Oliver said, quite clearly, in a sentimental voice.

It was the kind of baffling comment that Oliver tended to make, but Mr. Rappaport ignored this, also. Something amusing to say had occurred to him.

Ben could see it in his face.

He said it, leaning up close again, as if whispering something confidential, though the whole class could hear it. They could probably hear it in the corridor outside. Ben could smell his tooth powder. His face was pink and scrubbed and clean.

(Purple-stained mouth.)

"Blue lips. Blue tongue. Have you been sucking Comstock's *pen*, Pinkerton?"

Mr. Rappaport made this sound absolutely *filthy*, and several boys gasped, and were surprised into sniggering, not just Brinkman.

("Oo!")

("Oo!")

("*Oo!*")

Swartwout – who liked dirty things (perhaps he was just living up to the "swart" part of his name) – sniggered even more loudly than Brinkman. Otsego Lake Academy was a very sniggery sort of school. They'd soon realized that. Latin vocabulary was not the only thing that they were being taught.

"No, sir."

Voice steady.

(*Made of Iron.*)

Oliver's hand shot up eagerly. He'd been biding his time. He'd probably said "Hippocrene" and "The viewless wings of Poesy" without thinking. Now it was time for another bright remark.

"No questions, Comstock."

"Oh, but, sir . . ."

(And he wasn't above inserting a "sir" when it served his purposes.)

"No questions, Comstock."

Ben was starting to blush, though he wasn't quite sure why. It was more the tone of voice than the words that were being used.

"Are you blushing, Pinkerton?"

"No, sir."

"Are you *blushing*, Pinkerton?"

"*No*, sir."

(He was blushing.

(Coriolanus blushed.

(*Coriolanus* blushed.

(His sword was death's stamp, and where it did mark, it took. From face to foot he was a thing of blood, and his every motion was timed with dying cries. He ran reeking over the lives of men, as if it were a perpetual spoil.

(This was the last speech he could remember Dr. Crowninshield speaking.

(He had played the general, Cominius, and this was how he'd described Coriolanus as he struck Corioli like a planet.

(Oliver had been Coriolanus.)

"Oh, you are! You are! Lift your head up, Pinkerton. Turn round so that everyone can see. Why are you blushing? He *is* blushing, isn't he, everyone? Prettier than ever!"

"Yes!" (Brinkman. Distinct enthusiasm. Here was a boy who learned quickly.)

(They'd been disappointed that Dr. Crowninshield hadn't cast himself in the rôle of Coriolanus. They'd really been looking forward to killing their headmaster again, hacking him down like another Julius Cæsar, but he'd insisted that Oliver would be much better in the part than he could be.

(*Kill, kill, kill, kill, kill him!*

(That's what the Conspirators — at the very end of the play — had chanted as they'd murdered Coriolanus. They were clearly men who believed in expressing their requirements in as succinct and unambiguous a manner as possible. Aufidius called him "Insolent villain!" and then, after they'd kill, kill, kill, kill, killed him, Aufidius *stood* upon his body. There'd have been tremendous competition for the part of Aufidius if Dr. Crowninshield had been playing Coriolanus.

You got to call him "Insolent villain!"

You got to kill, kill, kill, kill, kill him.

You got to *stand* upon him, wobbling slightly as you tried to keep your balance, brandishing your ruler, and saying, "My noble masters, hear me speak."

It would have been even better than killing Julius Cæsar!

(*Kill, kill, kill, kill, kill him!*)

"Why are you blushing? Do you feel *guilty* about something, Pinkerton, the lickspittle *pen*-sucker?"

("Oo!"

("Oo!"

("*Oo!*"

(*Guffaw.*)

"No, sir."

Oliver's hand was still in the air, waving frantically from side to side, signaling a vital message across a vast distance, the keenest boy in the class all out to please teacher.

"*Sir!*"

Mr. Rappaport looked at Ben, and suddenly seemed to lose interest in him.

"Sit down, Pinkerton."

Ben sat down suddenly, as if his legs had given way, and began to stroke at the chalk marks on the black band, like someone caressing a cat (though tenderness played no part in the gesture), and there was silence. He bowed his head.

Mr. Rappaport leaned up close again.

The same piercing whisper.

"Head raised, Pinkerton."

(A slight hint of a stress on the "Pink" part of his name.

(*Pink!*

(The very color!)

Ben raised his head.

Mr. Rappaport leaned in closer, but his whisper became louder, not softer.

He seemed full of energy.

"I'm not surprised your father died, with a son like you."

It was said matter-of-factly, like an incidental observation.

Ben could feel his heart pounding, his lips starting to work at the onset of a stutter.

Mr. Rappaport seemed about to say something.

Oliver's whole arm was still sawing the air.

(He was a sawyer.

(Ben thought of *The Adventures of Tom Sawyer*.

(He thought of Friday afternoons and chocolate cake.

(He thought . . .

(He tried to think . . .

(*I'm not surprised your father died, with a son like you.*)

" *Sir!*"

"No questions, Comstock."

"Oh, but, sir . . ."

"No questions, Comstock."

He'd said it four times now, never raising his voice, just speaking casually and automatically, the way you brushed off an insect without even looking at it. In just such a way, Uncle Eugene — or so he liked to suggest — would have effortlessly shrugged off the corpses of butterflies, birds, leaping tigers, and (especially) Red Indians with threateningly upraised tomahawks, his smoking gun gripped in his fearless fingers. Perhaps Mr. Rappaport had received lessons in how to do this from Papa. Papa had been good at that sort of thing.

He'd said it four times, but Oliver wasn't hearing him.

" *Sir!*"

Mr. Rappaport turned to face Oliver, a new thought just occurring to him. He was wearing gleaming new shoes — all of his clothes seemed new and freshly brushed (when you went out to enjoy yourself, you dressed with special care) — and he spun silently round, the soles still slippery and never-before-walked-upon.

"Could it be that you have a *confession* to make, Comstock? Could it be that you, also, have a sense of guilt like your pretty friend?"

(*Guffaw.*)

"No, sir. It's not that, though thank you for the compliments about my personal charms, sir. It's usually women who say that sort of thing, sir. They coo in the way that they coo at baby's fingers, the tiny daintiness. *Men* all too rarely make such comments, sir."

Oliver seemed to have employed the word "sir" several dozen times, but this seemed – somehow – to make what he had to say (impeccably polite though his tone might have been) sound curiously (you sought for the sort of word that a schoolmaster might choose to employ) *unsatisfactory*.

(Slight increase in the intensity of the silence.)

Oliver continued.

"My papa died recently, hence my mark of mourning, but I'll be sure to let my mama know your generous assessment. No, sir. I just wanted to ask, sir, whether you'd just made that up. 'Defective detectives must be corrected.' Frightfully funny, sir."

(*Frightfully funny!*)

He looked at Mr. Rappaport in his most guileless Little Lord Fauntleroy manner. Now that he was in school he was no longer dressed in the velvet and lace that his mama insisted upon swathing him in – the male equivalent of cruelly constricting corsets – but the hair and the manner remained. He was a plainclothes Lord Fauntleroy, that was what Mr. Rappaport was thinking, a disguised Pinkerton of prettiness. Trapped in a mask of his mother's making, he could play no other part.

"Did you just make that up, sir, or did you have it already prepared, sir? Have you got one prepared for my name, sir? I could give you some ideas if you haven't, sir. There are numerous humorous possibilities . . ."

Mr. Rappaport strode right up to Oliver.

"*No questions, Comstock*," he hissed, without raising his voice.

Oliver stood up.

"If you squeeze my arm, I'll say it again, sir." Mr. Rappaport reacted as if Oliver had made a clumsy and unwelcome attempt at seduction, a disgustingly blatant bribe flaunted before a not-to-be-corrupted manly chap. "If you wish, sir. 'Are you *quite* sure no

469

relations are involved?' 'Quite the beauties of the class.' Frightfully funny, sir. Brinkman, who is fabled far and wide for the sophistication of his taste . . ."

(A look of suspicious bafflement from Brinkman. No guffaw.)

". . . is positively convulsed. I'll be *sure* to tell Mama, sir. She'll . . ."

"*Sit down, Comstock.*"

Oliver saw the expression in Mr. Rappaport's eyes, and sat down. He had already calculated precisely how far he could go with Mr. Rappaport, and Mr. Rappaport was well aware of who Oliver's mother was. There was another short silence, as of equilibrium being reestablished, and then – as if nothing had happened – Mr. Rappaport scanned the faces in the class. Most people tried to avoid catching his eyes, staring – apparently fascinated – at the words on the blackboard, or at their own hands. Frankie – he'd resumed his seat inch by inch, barely moving, hardly breathing, never taking his eyes off their teacher – was very still.

Mr. Rappaport walked up to Linnaeus.

"Stand up. Name?"

Linnaeus was trembling.

("*Amo*," he'd be saying to himself, "*amas, amat* . . .")

(His left hand kept straying to the hidden pocket over his heart, the one in the shirt beneath his jacket, the one in which he kept his lucky silver dollar.

(". . . *amamus, amatis, amant.*")

"Finch, sir."

"*Ah!*"

A note of delighted discovery.

He reached over to his desk, and picked up a list, glancing at it.

"Vorhees-Finch. Vorhees *hyphen* Finch. We have a *hyphenated* fellow in the class to raise the tone, chaps. Jolly good!"

This last was an attempt at a strangulated aristocratic accent.

He spoke as if the boys in front of him didn't already know each other, strangers who had been gathered together for the first time in that room.

"I don't *have* a h-h-h . . ."

Linnaeus's stutter started. It was not as bad as Alice's was, but bad once it got going.

You could tell, by the gleam in his eye, that this was even better than Mr. Rappaport had hoped. Perhaps some intelligence system had been activated, some capital-lettered communication upon a staff noticeboard thumbtacked there by First Beard after Linnaeus's "P-P-P" in the entrance hall. *STUTTERING NOTIFICATION! BOY TO MOCK IN YEAR NAUGHT! POTENTIAL TEARS AND BLUSHING ALSO SIGHTED! ENJOY YOURSELVES, MEN!*

"*H-h-h?*" Mr. Rappaport repeated, making it seem like the most stupid sound in the world — "Huh?" — a gawking country bumpkin, vacant, uncomprehending, scratching his straw-strewn poll, his mouth lolling open.

"*H-h-h?*"

He said it again, as it had gone down so well with Brinkman the first time.

(Ben heard his Papa mocking Alice's stutter.

("*P-P-P!*"

(Alice couldn't say "Papa."

("P-P-P . . ."

(She tried to say it, but couldn't.)

"I don't *have* a h-hyphen in my name, sir."

Mr. Rappaport thrust the list into Linnaeus's face, too close to his eyes for him to be able to read it.

"Well, the list with which I have been supplied *definitely* has you down as Vorhees *hyphen* Finch. I was quite thrilled. A *hyphen!* A much-needed fillip to the generally plebeian tone of this class."

(Brinkman wasn't too sure about this use of "plebeian" — impeccable though its usage might have been in a Latin lesson — and forbore from guffawing. They knew all about plebeians from *Julius Cæsar* and *Coriolanus*, and they hadn't been impressed by them.)

471

Mr. Rappaport must have spent *hours* working on his script over the weekend.

"It's a mistake, sir."

"What is? My list, or your name?"

"Your list, sir. I do *not* have a h-h-hyphen."

"*H-h-h?*"

(*Guffaw!*

(Brinkman didn't waste time shilly-shallying around with sniggers now.

(He went straight for the guffaw.

(It saved time.

("H-h-h" was for "Ha-ha-ha!"

("H-h-h" was for "He-he-he!" and "Ho-ho-ho!" and "Her-her-her!"

("H-h-h" was the promptest of prompts for guffawing.)

"A *mistake*, sir."

(There was a note of desperation in Linnaeus's voice.

(You began to suspect the sort of life that he had led in the mysteriously unnamed school in New Hampshire, the sort of things he had experienced.

(You began to wonder about the nervousness, the quietness, the lack of confidence. Not that Ben himself was one who could claim to ooze a quietly confident air. He entirely lacked Oliver's breezy assurance.

(You began to wonder if the school had, indeed, closed down, or if Linnaeus had just *had* to come home. It might have been something to do with the precarious state of his father's health – Colonel Finch had been unwell for years; things were whispered – or it might have been something very different. Mr. Rappaport, an unexpected lapse in his intelligence sources, had failed to bait Linnaeus with passages about the love between fathers and sons as he had done with Oliver and Ben. Perhaps he preferred to wait until the fathers were dead, spurred into action by the black bands around the arms of his selected pupils, the bands of mourning helpfully indicating that here might be a good choice of victim if it was tears you were after. Mr. Rappaport had missed a really good opportunity with Linnaeus. Anyone who knew the difficulties that Linnaeus experienced with his father would have known that this was a perfect choice of subject to induce sobbing. As they were to discover — as they were already beginning to discover — Mr. Rappaport was a man who was very keen on tears, and did everything in his power to encourage them. He wouldn't let boys cover their faces once he got the tears flowing, and he was quite prepared to go to considerable pains to achieve this. He liked watching the tears emerge, standing up close so that he could have a good view, peering, sniffing, longing for a taste.)

"I do *not* have a h-h-hyphen, sir."

"H-h-h."

(Brinkman, back in confident control of his guffawing.)

"I heard you perfectly clearly the first time you said it, Finch."

(Rappaport.)

"There is a mistake on your list, sir."

"Hmm. Not the only mistake around here, I suspect. What a disappointment! I was so honored to have a hyphen in my class, a personified piece of patrician punctuation. I thought you might be wearing purple when I noticed the hyphen, a glimpse of shapely ankle from beneath a spotless toga."

The list — if it was a list — was crumpled in his hand. It was probably a blank piece of paper, or a list on which a hyphen had been inserted in differently colored ink.

"*Linnaeus . . .*" — he stressed "Linnaeus" just enough to make clear that he thought the name hilarious (it was the only time he ever spoke Linn's first name in all the years he taught them) — ". . . Vorhees Finch. No hyphen. I admit to a feeling of disappointment."

He looked again at the list, smoothing it out, pretending to read. "*Ah!*"

Again that note of delight, the pretense that something had just occurred to him that moment

"*Vorhees!* There might be a sad absence of hyphen, but perhaps

473

we might have a 'jolly good' . . ." – again the bastardized attempt at aristocratic pronunciation – ". . . sort of fellow after all!"

Linnaeus could see what was coming, and an expression of patient humbleness came across his face. He lowered his head. His left hand, all his thin fingers trembling, was touching the hidden pocket over his heart, for the feel of Liberty, the touch of her hair pressing against the bitten edges of his nails for reassurance.

"Hands by your sides, *Vorhees*."

Linnaeus pressed his hands by his sides. He lowered his head, and his hair fell down to hide his eyes.

"Head raised, *Vorhees*."

Linnaeus raised his head. His throat was working, struggling to say something.

With his hands by his sides, and his head raised, it was as if he were being left undefended, prepared for a blow that was about to fall. He flinched, sensing this, seeing something approaching. Mr. Rappaport noticed this.

"Did you *flinch*, Finch?" he inquired. He was clearly keen on wordplay, a good man to have on your side in a game of Charades. They *all* knew what was coming. Brinkman, slightly prematurely – urging Mr. Rappaport into action – began to hum the appropriate tune.

Activated by this, Mr. Rappaport was off and away.

"*Vorhees* a jolly good fellow!" – Mr. Rappaport pranced around Linnaeus, manly chap fashion (it was what they'd all been waiting for) – "*Vorhees* a jolly good fellow! *Vorhees* a jolly good fellow!" Each time, he stressed his pun, for the benefit of the dimmer members of the class, to ensure as wide a spread of merriment as possible amongst those present.

"And so say all of us!"

(This last from Brinkman, who had found his rôle in life now that Mr. Rappaport was around.)

(They were going to be new best chums.)

(They'd be exchanging tokens as a symbol of their undying fidelity.)

(Fido.

(That was a good name for a dog, even if Linnaeus had appropriated it for one of the Finches' cats.

(Begging posture.

(Cold shiny nose.

(Glossy coat.

(Bright eyes.

(Woof, woof.)

Mr. Rappaport ignored this.

"Not *all* of us, sir."

(Oliver.)

Mr. Rappaport did not ignore this.

"What was that, Comstock?"

"I was merely correcting Brinkman's last comment, sir. I can see already how you like to get things right. He said . . ."

"I *heard* what he said, Comstock. And I heard what you said. What you *merely* said."

"The 'merely' was natural reticence on my part, sir, and as you heard what I said, you'll understand what I was saying, sir." There was never a shortage of "sir" when Oliver was speaking to Mr. Rappaport. Unwary listeners might have gained the impression that Oliver rather respected him. "We don't *all* say, 'Vorhees a jolly good fellow,' sir. *I* don't for a start, sir. It's a rather puerile sort of comment to make, don't you think, sir? Not something you'd describe as sophisticated . . ."

"And you regard yourself as *sophisticated* do you, Comstock?"

"You flatter me, sir."

"That day will be a long time dawning, Comstock."

"But I still maintain that we don't *all* say, 'Vorhees a jolly good fellow,' sir."

Mr. Rappaport returned to the front of the class, and stood before the blackboard, his head blocking out the central section of it. The top line of chalked words – *Subject, Object, Predicate* – was on a level with his ears, *Subj* running into his right ear, and *icate* emerging from his left ear.

(*Subjicate.*

(Wasn't that what conquerors did to a country they'd defeated?

(It was something to do with making people your *subjects*, subjects not for discussion, but for conquest and humiliation.

(Unless it was something to do with *subdue*. It sounded a bit like *subdue*. You'd make them submissive and quiet, not much given to contributing to conversation.

(They'd kill all the soldiers in battle, and then they'd subjicate the countryside. They'd heard a lot about subjicating from Dr. Crowninshield, probably in History, but he couldn't remember exactly when. Cities and crops were burned, cattle slaughtered, women and children sold into slavery.

(That was subjication.)

Mr. Rappaport addressed the whole class.

"Who *doesn't* say, 'Vorhees a jolly good fellow'?"

Oliver's hand shot instantly into the air, the keenest pupil in the school, desperate to be chosen to answer. Charlie Whitefoord's hand rose simultaneously. After a pause, Frankie Alloway – *Frankie!* – copied them, though his arm was wobbling a little, his head was bowed and his eyes were closed. (If he kept his eyes closed, Mr. Rappaport wouldn't see him.)

Ben lowered his head, and began to arrange his right hand carefully around the top of his left arm, neatly covering the black band without crumpling it up. This was the most important thing in the world at that moment, a concentration that eliminated the need for all further thought.

"*Merely* you, Comstock, you, that lanky one, and Ginger here."

(Little whimper from Frankie, eyes screwed up more tightly.)

"Then my comment is perfectly correct, sir. We don't *all* say what Brinkman says, sir. Three of us, at least, do not."

If Ben closed his fingers up neatly together on top of the black band, so that there were no gaps . . .

Mr. Rappaport suddenly lost interest in the conversation. He often seemed to do this – they began to realize – at the moment when you braced yourself for his going in for the kill. He turned

476

back to Linnaeus, still patiently standing, arms by his sides, head raised, and again the tapping and the chanting began.

Tap.

"*Pater filium amat.*"

Tap.

"The father loves his son."

Tap.

"Say it again, Finch."

"*Pater filium amat.* The father loves his son, sir."

Tap.

"*Pater* is therefore the Subject," Mr. Rappaport added.

With considerable force, he threw the piece of chalk he was holding as if he were aiming at a target, and Linnaeus caught it in his left hand. There'd have been more amusing comments if Linnaeus had dropped it, Mr. Rappaport dutifully carrying out his pedagogic responsibilities as Sport coach.

"Write that last sentence on the blackboard, Hyphenless Finch."

Mr. Rappaport watched, as Linnaeus carefully printed out *Pater is therefore the Subject.* He was shaking so much that the chalk dithered on the first letter when he started to write, *P-P-P*, his stutter conveyed into the very movements of his body, infecting every part of him. He paused for a moment, took a deep breath (the sort of thing he'd done before forcing himself to recite in class), and then wrote out the sentence with firm strokes. When he had finished, Mr. Rappaport stared at him for a while, until Linnaeus flushed. (Should he have written, *Pater is therefore the Subject, sir?* That was probably what Linnaeus was thinking.)

"Why did you use your left hand?"

"I'm left-handed, sir."

"Not in my lessons."

"I don't understand, sir."

"It's perfectly clear. You will not use your left hand in my lessons."

"Sir . . ."

"No questions, Hyphenless Finch. Sit down."

477

He stared at Linnaeus in silence after he'd sat down, and Linnaeus flushed again.

(Part of Ben was hoping that Linnaeus would blush more and more, his whole face infused with redness.

(Part of him was hoping that Rappaport would pick on Linnaeus all the time for blushing, and leave him alone.

(He was ashamed that he felt this, but he felt it.)

When Mr. Rappaport spoke again, it sounded as though what he said was the result of deep thought, a question asked in a spirit of disinterested scientific inquiry.

"Did it *hurt* when you had your hyphen removed, Finch?"

("Oo!"

("Oo!"

("*Oo!*"

(Mr. Rappaport had taught them that The father loves his son, sir; Mr. Rappaport had taught them that *Pater is therefore the Subject, sir*; and Mr. Rappaport had taught them "Oo! Oo! *Oo!*" You didn't need a "sir" for "Oo! Oo! *Oo!*")

Linnaeus had obviously thought that Mr. Rappaport had finished with him when he had told him to sit down. He tensed, and pressed his thumbs against the top surface of his desk, to hold himself firmly in place, his fingers hanging down loosely over the edges. The little finger of his right hand, the hand that Ben could see, was shaking. Once more, he began to lower his head.

Again, as in his earlier comment to Ben, Mr. Rappaport managed to make what he said sound really dirty. Again, some startled sniggers that he should speak in this sort of way.

"I understand that it's quite a delicate operation, having your *hyphen* removed . . ."

(*cir-cum-ci-sion, n. the act of circumcising [O.F. circuncisiun]* . . .

(*cir-cum-cise, v.t. to cut off the foreskin as a religious rite* . . .

(*fore-skin, n. the fold of skin covering* . . .

("Jack, Jack, look at the rab-bit!"

(Shadows on the bedroom wall.)

". . . In fact, come to think of it, I should never have imagined that you possessed a hyphen in the first place. You were quite right, Hyphenless Finch. There *is* a mistake on my list. I do apologize for doubting you."

Rarely did an apology sound so like an insult.

"It's perfectly obvious by the way that you walk . . .

(*Walks in a Manner That Looks as Natural as Life.*)

". . . that you had your hyphen removed a *long* time ago. I doubt, in fact, that you have *ever* possessed a hyphen."

("Oo!"

("Oo!"

("*Oo!*"

(*Guffaw.*)

"I have been wrong on several counts. I freely admit to it. Again, Hyphenless Finch, I apologize."

(Linnaeus's face was invisible, he'd lowered his head so far.)

"Don't hide your face in that rather rude manner. When I'm talking to you, I expect to see your face."

(Mr. Rappaport was hoping that there might be tears starting to emerge.)

Linnaeus looked up. His face was burning.

(Perhaps Mr. Rappaport would pick on Linnaeus in future when he had a taste for blushing.

(Perhaps Mr. Rappaport would leave Ben alone in future.

(Ben hoped so.)

"Yes, I was *wrong.*"

He made it sound like a handsome concession.

"You're not a jolly good fellow after all. You're not jolly. Pretty miserable looking, come to think of it. You're not good. In fact, let's face it, as you're lacking a hyphen, you're not really a *fellow,* either. Vorhees not a jolly good *fellow!*" – again, the manly chap prancing – "Vorhees not a jolly good *fellow!* Vorhees not a jolly good *fellow!*"

"And so say all of us."

(Once he'd hit on an idea, Brinkman just kept on repeating it.)

"Not *all* of us."

(And Oliver was not one to be outdone.)

Mr. Rappaport ignored them both.

Linnaeus did not produce his lucky silver dollar to show to his teacher, to point out the words in Latin.

Frankie was still bent over in his desk with his arm in the air, his eyes closed, clenched into invisibility.

Bells.

This time, the sound of the bells was welcome, though not to Mr. Rappaport. There was an ill-disguised hiss of annoyance from him that the shortened lesson was already over. He'd just been getting into his stride, and he'd been waiting for *so* long. He'd really been enjoying himself. He should have had an hour and a half!

He made them all stand up.

For one final time that lesson they chanted what he had written on the blackboard. They'd be spending much of their time in chanting the words he wrote down.

He chose the words.

They memorized them.

They chanted them.

"Subject!" they chorused. "Object! Predicate! *Pater filium amat!* The father loves his son!"

("The father loves his son, *sir!*" from Oliver, with an expression of eager willingness, keen to correct an omission by the rest of the class, a child clearly anxious to impress.)

"*Pater* is therefore the subject!"

("*Pater* is therefore the subject, *sir!*" from Oliver.)

"Comstock?"

"Yes, sir?"

"Lessen the excessive sirring."

"What do you mean, sir?"

"Sir! Sir! *Sir!* That's what I mean."

"Surely we can never be *excessive* in our expressions of understandable deference, sir? To one such as yourself, sir? Children as mere as we, sir? Sir? A sign of our deep respect, our servile fearfulness, sir?"

(Though he quoted the same words that he'd once quoted for Dr. Crowninshield, and even though he'd used an identical tone of voice, the words somehow sounded very different when spoken this time.)

Mr. Rappaport – as he had done before – chose to ignore this, and change the subject completely.

"I also teach Sport, as well as Latin," he said, with meaningful emphasis. "I'm *very* keen on Sport."

"*Goody*, sir!" Oliver said gamely, just beating Brinkman with an expression of enthusiasm, though Brinkman would not have opted for *Goody!*

"I'll be seeing you all again today for your first Sport lesson with me," he added, pausing, as if to hear another "*Goody*, sir!" but even Oliver seemed to have recognized that this *would* have been bordering on the excessive. "This afternoon, two o'clock."

Doors were opening in distant corridors. The sounds of subdued voices, echoing footsteps.

He paused, and smiled.

"We shall seize the opportunity to inspect Hyphenless Finch closely in order to check for evidence. Something to look forward to. We shall inspect Finch for signs of a hyphen at two o'clock," he announced. "Bring your magnifying glasses. I'm sure that we'll need them. Dr. Brown will be able to arrange the loan of all the necessary equipment."

("Oo!"

("Oo!"

("*Oo!*"

(*Guffaw*.

(Mr. Rappaport had taken against excessive sirring, but – it had already become clear – he couldn't get enough of ooing and guffawing.

(Brinkman was settling in nicely at his new school. A friendly child soon finds himself courted for companionship.)

"The next Latin lesson is on Wednesday. Do *not* enter the room. Wait outside in the corridor. I shall be placing you in your *proper* places before the lesson begins. Today's free-for-all was not the way in which things are going to be organized in future. Things are going to be *properly* organized from now on."

(This came as no surprise.)

He looked to his right.

"Class dismissed. Row by the window first. No talking. Keep to the right."

Row by row, the class began to leave the room, not quite sure what they were to do next, where they were supposed to go. It was recess. Smiling Otsegoans would be waiting in groups to welcome them and make them feel at home. (Were they supposed to *chant* the Latin as they left? If someone had started to do so, they would all have joined in, swinging their arms and legs in unison. No one had said, "No chanting!")

"That was most enjoyable," Oliver announced, in his clear, carrying voice, as he filed past Mr. Rappaport. "My interest has certainly been awoken. Who would have guessed that Latin could be so much fun?" He beamed appreciatively at Mr. Rappaport as he walked past him, his beam outdoing even Frankie's best efforts in the entrance hall, clearly fighting the urge to embrace him in manly comradeship.

Beam.

Beam.

Beam.

Mr. Rappaport neglected to say, "*No talking!*"

(Ben wanted to look at Mr. Rappaport's face, to see how he reacted to this – the alertest of listeners would not have detected the slightest note of irony, though irony weighed down every letter of every word and all the spaces in between – but he did not dare, in case he caught his eye.

(*Sag, sag, sag.*)

As Linnaeus walked alongside Mr. Rappaport, head down, Mr. Rappaport made him stop so that he could use him to clean the chalk-dust from his hands. First of all – he made the action some-how heavy with significance – he clapped his hands together (this was *not* applause) so that Linnaeus's head was enveloped in a white cloud, and then he wiped his hands down Linnaeus's arms, both sides. There was something oddly intimate about the way in which – without saying a word – he drew Linnaeus in against him, and briskly ran his hands up and down several times, like a customs officer frisking him for contraband. They wouldn't have been surprised if he'd picked him up with both hands – he wouldn't have weighed much – and used him to clean the blackboard, a good vigorous polishing front and back. Linnaeus remained silent, his head drooping further, not quite sure what to do with his arms.

"Two o'clock," he said when he'd finished, as if arranging a *rendezvous*, giving Linnaeus a little push in his back.

For some of them he had a little comment to make as they walked past him – he ensured (a sort of inside-out running the gauntlet) that they all had to walk past him in rows on their way out of the classroom – to let them know that he was not impressed by what he knew about them, and would not forget what it was that he knew. He didn't spell out what it was that he knew about them – most of the time – he just *implied* things, things that were whispered, inaudible to others, things that he could tell the rest of the class when he was in the mood.

(They'd outdo anything that Brinkman had to contribute. They'd beat blushing and bed-wetting and spotty bottoms. You knew this as a certainty.)

Whatever it was that he said to Frankie Alloway, it made him go red, and tears came to his eyes. You thought of tears as creeping up on you slowly, but Frankie's appeared instantly, fully formed, and rolled down his cheeks.

He said four things to Ben, detaining him by grasping one of the buttons of his uniform, one on his chest. Ben – swaying forward and backward, suspended, as Mr. Rappaport tugged or pushed at him – felt as if he were being activated, set into motion or stillness by the choice of the right button, as if he were, as if he were . . .

("*Almost Six Inches in Height.*"

(That was the first thing that Mr. Rappaport said to him.

("*Guaranteed to Delight Any Boy.*"

(There was no *tap, tap, tap*, but he flicked his forefinger in the direction of Oliver as he disappeared out of the room.

("I use the word 'boy' in an imaginative sort of way," he explained. He paused, awaiting an "*Oo!*" or a guffaw, even a snigger would have sufficed, but — alas! — Brinkman had passed out of hearing.)

. . . as if he were a Mechanical Walking Sailor Boy.

My Brave Boy.

Mr. Rappaport had learned his lines well. No chance of any more gold stars for Frankie Alloway, or for any of them. The teacher had commandeered them all for himself, usurped all the stars so that he would blaze like the bravest of all generals, weighed down by his decorations for gallantry, glittering like a night sky in wintertime.

*****

*****

*****

*****

*****

Van Gogh's starry, starry nights were fog-shrouded and funereal, quite incapable of rivaling the pulsating brilliance of a Mr. Rappaport constellation.

He expected to see Papa standing behind Mr. Rappaport, whispering into his ear in the way that he had been whispering into Ben's, giving him all the right answers so that he would do well in his tests, all the tests to come. Mr. Rappaport's mouth opened and closed, but the voice that came out of it was Papa's. "This is what you need to say," Papa was whispering. "Blushes! Tears! Stutters!" These latter were spoken enticingly, the rewards that beckoned for the teacher who passed his tests.

All manner of delight.

The lever in the back of the toy that was not a doll was pulled out firmly, and — like a musical box with words — it uttered the same phrases repeatedly, for as long as some tension remained in the clockwork. Then all you had to do was to wind it up again, and again it would whirringly repeat those same few phrases. The tension created the words that were spoken.

("*Walks in a Manner That Looks as Natural as Life*."

(He said this, also.

("*As Much Like a Real Boy as it is Possible to Make It Appear*."

(And this.)

Mr. Rappaport was reminding Ben of what he knew, and everyone could hear what he was saying.

Not *very* much Like a Real Boy.

It wasn't really *Possible* to Make It Appear like one, struggle as you might to achieve it.

These weren't the words that he was actually speaking, but these were the words that were heard.

Quite a challenge.

Some challenges would be beyond even the labors of a Hercules.

You saw what he meant.

It was very apt.

Spot on.

Tap, tap, tap.

Flick.

Laughter.

My Brave Boy.

Ben heard the hollow tapping of the fingernail on the empty box with all its lettering in elaborate script.

He saw the heel descending on the face with a vigorous, dismissive twist.

Outside the classroom, Vellacott was walking down the corridor toward them.

"Any survivors?" he asked.

"The *twattiest* Roman of them all."

That was all that Oliver said.

"He's more of a Spartan when it comes to Sport."

"Go, tell the Spartans!"

That was their first lesson with Mr. Rappaport, and their first official sentence in Latin.

Their first Latin verb had been *amo, amas, amat, amamus, amatis, amant.*

"I love!"

That's what they'd chanted.

"I am loving! I do love!"

Their first Latin sentence had been *Pater filium amat.*

"The father loves his son."

That's what they'd chanted repeatedly in Room 37 with Mr. Rappaport.

"The father loves his son."

"The father loves his son."

"The father loves his son, *sir*."

A shortened lesson.

On Wednesday they would have another Latin lesson. That would be a full one and a half hours with Mr. Rappaport.

And on Friday they would have this again.

And that afternoon they would have Sport with Mr. Rappaport. (Or Mr. Rappaport would have Sport with them.)

Something to look forward to.

2

In their second Latin lesson, on the Wednesday afternoon, Mr. Rappaport began to throw the Reverend Henry Belcher across the room. As became habitual with him, he somehow contrived to combine Latin with Sport, and copies of *Latin for Schoolboys*, pages whirring like wings in flight, were flung in all directions. The rather subdued schoolboys hurled themselves – up, down, sideways – at the Latin in order to grab it, like baseball players achieving spectacular catches (or, more usually, misses), as Mr. Rappaport made withering comments about their feeble techniques. ("Hopeless! Just like a girl!" was a typical shrewd scientific assessment from their drillmaster.) Frankie Alloway's Reverend Henry Belcher – wouldn't you just know it? – split in two down the spine when it hit the metal frame of his desk, and Frankie (surpassing any feat he ever achieved on the playing field) managed to catch half a Belcher in each hand. Not quite sure what to do, they looked back at Mr. Rappaport for a while, and then – it seemed the right sort of thing to do – they began to examine the contents of the book, the book they'd last seen produced at Crowninshield's as evidence that Latin really did exist. They pointed at the title meaningfully. The pleasure that book had brought to the brothers of some of them! (That seemed to be the sort of reaction that was expected. Cries of delight, they couldn't help suspecting, would have been found perfectly acceptable, though no one managed any.) They flicked through the pages, hoping to find words or phrases that they recognized, like exiles hungering to hear a voice speaking in a familiar but long-silenced language.

Mr. Rappaport informed them that the words that they'd be using for the first year would be adapted from the words of Julius Cæsar. That was the basis of the Reverend Henry Belcher's educational philosophy: Julius Cæsar was the perfect choice of man to create a hunger for knowledge in the modern schoolboy. In no time at all they'd be chattering away in Latin like a Forumful of tunic-clad Junior Romans. They'd thought about this for a little while, imagining Mr. Rappaport speaking the words that they'd last heard spoken by Dr. Crowninshield, before they assassinated him.

"Cowards die many times before their deaths;
The valiant never taste of death but once . . ."

That's what Mr. Rappaport would be saying, as they – the ghost-clad Ancient Romans (feeling very much more Ancient these days) – stood around him with their rulers poised for action. The memories of sheets of paper covered in fragile pencilled columns and architraves would flutter on the empty walls around them as they moved in for the kill. (Perhaps Latin was going to contain a certain element of pleasure, after all.)

Or he'd be saying:

"The Ides of March are come."

Or:

". . . I am constant as the Northern Star . . ."

(Rather worrying this one.)
Or:

". . . We are two lions littered in one day,
And I the elder and more terrible . . ."

("Terrible" sounded like a particularly appropriate word for Mr. Rappaport to speak.)

For the first time in that place – Monday hadn't gone too well, and Tuesday had been worse – they might begin to feel at home, buoyed up by the memories of Crowninshield's.

But he spoke none of these words in the weeks and months that followed.

The words Mr. Rappaport wrote on the blackboard, the words they labored to translate into Latin, the words purportedly from the mouth of Julius Cæsar, didn't sound much like the Julius Cæsar that they'd come across at Crowninshield's.

The sailors of Galba wound the sailors of Titus with arrows.
The Gauls wound the lieutenant with swords.
The workman inflicts wounds on the children of the Cimbri.
Fire lays waste the cities.
Rivers hinder the march of the army.
The ramparts have been very strong.

This was the sort of thing that was spoken by the Reverend Henry Belcher's Julius Cæsar, Mr. Rappaport's Julius Cæsar, a Julius Cæsar who sounded *nothing* like the Julius Cæsar that they'd come across in Shakespeare, *and* he wasn't dead.

This Julius Cæsar spoke exclusively in very *manly* sentences, dwelling long on campaigns and killing, sentences that seemed to cry out for the employment of the Vocative Case and vigorously brandished weapons of destruction. *O arrows!* they should be chorusing enthusiastically, invoking the things that they worshiped. *O swords! O wounds! O fire!* On every page, there was Julius Cæsar – the sort of man who saw himself in the third person – laying waste, wounding, frightening, thoroughly enjoying himself, attacking diagonal assaulting (this was the puzzling phrase spoken by Mr. Rappaport). Every time it came to any discussion of the verb *oppugno*, Mr. Rappaport would chalk *to attack/assault* on the blackboard, and then he'd say those confusing words "attack diagonal assault." It might have been something to do with the way that Julius Cæsar held his sword, the unexpected diagonally angled weapon rendering his every stroke lethal, the unique Julian technique that ensured success against baffled and outclassed attackers. Brutus wouldn't get much of a look in when he was attacking diagonal assaulting, and the Gauls would flee in hairy Gallic disarray, with all their bucklers buckled!

O famous leader, be thou loved by all the soldiers!
O Cæsar, be thou praised!
The hostages fear Cæsar.
Cæsar fortifies the citadel with high towers.
Ye must fortify the town, lest Cæsar may come.

These were the sort of sentences that received Julius Cæsar's seal of approval. For a change – and not at all like the Julius Cæsar that they'd come across at Crowninshield's – *this* Julius Cæsar was the one in the forefront of the stabbing, *doing* all the stabbing, and not being stabbed. *This* Julius Cæsar would ensure that he had a monopoly – one of the prerequisites of being a tyrant – on any attacking diagonal assaulting that was going on in the Roman Empire.

Cæsar destroys the enemies of Rome.
No wonder!
Attacking diagonal assaulting, he'd make them fall helpless before him!
(Brutus, Cassius, Casca, Trebonius, *all* the conspirators were

lopped away to Bru, to Cas, to Casc, to Tre; to B, to C, to C, to T –
Butchery! Chaos! Carnage! Treachery! – to nothing at all, as Julius
Cæsar laid waste.

(*Huh!*

(*He'd* soon put paid to Shakespeare!)

All who were captured within the walls were slain by Cæsar.

(You imagined Julius Cæsar as being the only one who possessed a sword, the man enthusiastically slaying whole cities, as all
the soldiers watched him closely, picking up tips on the diagonal
technique. "You lop the head off, so!" he'd explain casually. "The
best way to disembowel in my experience . . ." He'd sound just like
Mr. Rappaport yelling at a team. Encouraging chats – they knew
this instinctively, without needing to be told – would not be a
method that he'd be likely to employ before a vital match.)

Cæsar lays waste the citadel with fire.

Cæsar destroys the high towers with great stones.

(Tireless, unrelenting, that was Cæsar. Who would have guessed
that killing could be so much fun?)

Cæsar attacks with swift ships.

Cæsar will wage war, that he may frighten the Cimbri.

(The Cimbri had a tough time whenever Julius Cæsar was in the
vicinity and assuming the diagonal posture for slaying, all the folds
in his toga settling into symmetry.)

A very fierce battle was fought by Cæsar.

Cæsar ordered them to be killed.

Cæsar will be feared.

(This last seemed to be an order, rather than a translation exercise, a barked command that specified the emotion that was
considered appropriate before the pen was grasped in the hand.
Just holding a copy of *Latin for Schoolboys* was enough to produce
the desired effect.)

Julius Cæsar – *lays waste, destroys the high towers* – had been a
great one for subjicating. He ordered them to be killed. He was
feared. *That* was probably where he'd first heard the word from
Dr. Crowninshield, when he was telling them all about him before

they'd read the play. "Subjicating" did sound like one of those words that you came across in Shakespeare, words you tended not to use very much in your everyday life when you spoke, "proscription" and "conspirators" sorts of words.

The very first words that Ben had read in *Latin for Schoolboys* – an accurate enough taste of what was to follow – formed part of a list of well-chosen verbs.

I lay waste, I wound, I attack/assault, I frighten, I teach (this verb somehow slotted in effortlessly with all the others around it), *I surround, I break, I conquer, I punish, I guard, I fight, I command, I kill* . . .

"*Vasto!*" they'd be chanting with great relish, when they reached page forty-four. "I lay waste!"

"*Vulnero!* I wound!"

"*Oppugno!* I attack diagonal assault!"

"*Terreo!*"

"*Doceo!*"

"*Cingo!*"

These were verbs to set the pulses of all right-minded schoolboys racing excitedly. You could see the swords glinting, hear the lopping and gouging sounds as the blood sprayed into the dust and the heads bounced. "*Bella, horrida bella!*" (Virgil) might have lamented from his brackets, letting everyone know – *Wars, horrid wars!* – how horrid wars were, but Julius Cæsar wasn't listening, his ears enjoyably deafened by all the sounds of slaughter.

"*Frango!*"

"*Vinco!*"

"*Punio!*"

"*Custodio!*"

"*Pugno!*"

"*Jubeo!*"

"*Occido!*"

("*O! O! O!*" That was how all the verbs ended, and "O! O! O!" was how they were expected to respond, squeals of unsuppressed excitement. If it wasn't "Oo! Oo! *Oo!*" it tended to be "O! O! O!"

(Stabbing Mr. Rappaport to death was not, they soon realized, an option offered by Otsego Lake Academy — enthusiasm did rather wane at this realization — so they had to channel all their aggression into nouns and verbs. *Amo, amas, amat* faltered and faded, the chanting becoming a whispering, the whispering becoming inaudible, cowed in the face of such assertiveness. The Reverend Henry Belcher — here was a muscular Christian, bulging with Belchily out-of-proportion muscles, all sinews straining like tug-of-war ropes — was an author unafraid to meet the most insistent demands of the most belligerent of audiences.)

More laying waste!

More wounding!

More attacking diagonal assaulting!

This was what his readers tended to demand, and the Reverend Henry Belcher was more than happy to oblige, as assiduous in meeting the requirements of his audience as Dickinson Prud'homme when he painted his gigantically bare-breasted women. He was a man who believed in making learning fun.

As early as page ten he had them declining the word for "war," keen to maintain the interest of schoolboys in Latin. It was a word you *needed* to learn early on if you were dealing with the deeds of Julius Cæsar. It wasn't just a matter of Latin for schoolboys; the Reverend Henry Belcher also intended to ensure that schoolboys should be *for* Latin, fervently in favor of militaristic verbs and nouns. *Second Declension (O-Nouns), Neuter Nouns in "-um"* was chalked across the blackboard as they chanted, and *"Bellum!"* they chorused, threatened into all the outward manifestations of enthusiasm, lining the streets to cheer armies marching away into battle, waving flags with patriotic fervor.

"Bellum!"

"Bellum!"

"Belli!"

"Bello!"

"Bello!"

War!

O war! (Worshipful posturing.)

War!

Of war!

To or for war!

With, from, or by war!

"*Again!*" Mr. Rappaport would order, and they'd chant it again. "*Again!*"

If it wasn't "*Again!*" it was "*Louder!*"

"Drilling" he called it, and they were drilled for every word, until every word was drilled into them. Like soldiers – suitably martial miniature men for Julius Cæsar as they launched themselves into attack on verbs and adjectives, trained to obey every order issued by their commander – they were drilled in every lesson, wheeling and turning, sharpening their swords on vowels and consonants as they marched and countermarched, marching in line on the long journeys that led nowhere in the chalk-dusted Roman roads of Room 37. They were no longer the ones waving the flags; they had become the armies marching away into perpetual battle.

They began to see Latin in terms of *Useful Foreign Phrases* for tourists, and they were the tourists. "Tell me, O men of Rome," they'd be asking tentatively, consulting their phrase book word by word, as baffled natives listened, "where are your weapons?"

"I require to purchase a toga for the festival."

"Rufus eats a lettuce at the baths."

"Why do you not move your camp from the riverside to the mountain?"

"I forgive the man who damaged my chariot."

"Be wary of my catapult, O man of Gaul."

Useful phrases like those.

They moved through the pages of the book, lesson by lesson, and the sentences grew in complexity about them. First the unadorned statements, then the adjectives, then the comparisons, the phrases and clauses multiplying and expanding as if to block a path that led onward.

Sometimes – even if they were supposedly adapted from Cæsar's writings – the words seemed to possess a particular resonance adapted to the needs of Mr. Rappaport.

O boys, be ye taught by the master.

That would be written on the blackboard, with – you couldn't help feeling – an extra meaningful twist to the chalk as it scratched across the surface.

The voice of the master must be heard by the boys.

As if they needed to be reminded!

Bad boys must be punished.

That certainly struck a chord.

The boys love the master.

How triumphantly the words of a classical language expanded the possibilities of the imagination!

Beware! You will be punished.

Be ye advised, lest ye may be punished.

(Subjunctive constructions were slipped in to catch them out, and keep them on their feet.)

The happy boy has received a most beautiful book from the master.

The timid boy fears, lest he may be punished by the master.

(Another subjunctive booby trap. Another booby lured to destruction.)

The boy, who loves the master, is good.

(*Tap. Tap. Tap.*

("Say it again!")

The boy, whom the master loves, is good.

(*Tap. Tap. Tap.*

("Say it again!")

Good boys are happy boys.

(*Tap. Tap. Tap.*

("Say it again!"

("And *again!*"

("And *again!*")

These were the sorts of words – in English, and in Latin – that were written on the blackboard, every Monday, Wednesday, and

Friday in that first year, and on different days in the different years that followed, so that no day remained unspoiled, but the words that Ben continued to see on the dark, imperfectly cleaned surface — the loops and whorls of old lettering showing through like the memories of old correspondence on blotting paper — were words that were no longer there, the first sentence in Latin that Mr. Rappaport had written. The words were wiped away, but remained fully visible inside his head.

Pater filium amat.
The father loves (his) son.

3

It was a black gown for Latin, and white shorts and a whistle for Sport.

Beneath his crisp white shorts — almost the equal of Dr. Wolcott Ascharm Webster's in their pristine magnificence — Mr. Rappaport's athletic knees flaunted their manly hairiness. His knees were the sort of thing that you rather wished you hadn't seen. They were up there — *down* there — with Mabel Peartree's tonsils, Oliver's mama bending over (pause for deep breaths, slight sense of faintness), and the Reverend Goodchild's teeth or the Reverend Goodchild's beard or — indeed — virtually *all* of the Reverend Goodchild. To compensate for the lack of a beard on his face, his legs were startlingly hairy. Beards appeared to be nestling beneath his shorts, thrusting out and straining against the neatly ironed creases, hanging down from the cavernous tent-like structure, neatly secured in position and entirely enclosing the upper parts of his legs like hand-knitted combinations. The hairs were the exact color and texture of the coconut matting in the gymnasium — so it was grandly termed — the painfully sharp-bristled matting that made their knees and elbows (and — if they were especially unlucky or ungraceful — their cheeks and foreheads) bleed as they hurtled into it from a height, awkwardly spread-eagled in a thudding fall from the vaulting-horse or the buck. The thought that you were landing on combings from Mr. Rappaport's body did not add to the æsthetic appeal of this, quite apart from the torn skin and the blood loss. Mr. Rappaport harvested his spare body hair twice a week, and utilized it to weave (a Penelope with not many suitors) the coconut matting himself. It was a useful source of extra income, and – as a further bonus – another method of inflicting pain on his charges. Chunks of him lay all around the gymnasium for them to hurl themselves upon with gladsome schoolboy shrieks, giving rise to the traumas that would later emerge to keep Dr. Wolcott Ascharm Webster gainfully employed for many years into the future.

"You did *what*?" Dr. Wolcott Ascharm Webster would be gaping, almost forgetting to scribble, scribble, scribble, aghast at these promiscuous pubic cavortings. (Aghast, but delighted. This could take *years* to cure, if – indeed – a cure proved possible.)

The gymnasium was the same hall as the one in which the school ate its lunch. Once they'd pulled their white shorts on, it magically transformed itself into a gymnasium, even though it still looked exactly the same as before. It was the same hall as the one in which the school assembled each morning, the impressive hall beneath the painted dome that was high on the list of places that were guaranteed to get impressionable potential parents panting. The pupils – panting for different reasons – would be sitting prodding glumly at Mrs. Economou's unidentifiable grayish-green concoctions, steering them about the plate a bit, in an atmosphere of sweat and embrocation. This singularly failed to whet the appetite, and the appetite needed all the help it could get once Mrs. Economou started stirring her ladle in a brisk clockwise direction. Appetites were uniquely challenged on Thursdays, when lunch followed immediately after an hour and a half of the oldest boys in the school hurling themselves about the place in pools of perspiration that was so potent that it could take the shine off a leather boot or wither a geranium. Dr. Brown could have bottled it for his laboratory, and shakily labeled it

Hydrochloric Acid. The tables and chairs, the very plates and cutlery, were dimmed to dubious dullness, and the whole hall stank like a marathon runner's armpit. Mothers often commented that their sons tended to be listless and off their food when it came to Thursday evening dinners, with a worrying tendency to vomiting.

This was the place in which they were to become skilled in all the craft of hunters, learned in all the lore of old men, in all youthful sports and pastimes, in all manly arts and labors.

As soon as they arrived for Sport — Gymnastics was a part of the all-embracing term of "Sport" (and this was not the only embracing you'd see going on once Mr. Rappaport was unleashed, this was the impression) — they'd undress around the out-of-action piano (so neatly encapsulating Otsego Lake Academy's emphatic rejection of the dubious allure of music), trying to keep clear of Brinkman, self-consciously aware of Alice and Cora Munro — shrieking and half-naked, they just couldn't *help* seeing tits — staring down at them with no sense of shame from the dome (the biggest tit of all) above them, as the diffident schoolboys falteringly tugged their undershirts into public gaze. (Cor! Cora was a corker, and no mistake! That was the thing to say, and they mustn't forget to snigger.) The school had no special room for changing. Some of the boys developed favorite areas of the piano (Bradley could always be found unlacing his boots somewhere near the hard and soft pedals) and contrived little bowers for themselves with their clothing, like shipwrecked mariners hanging onto a vision of domesticity.

When they were ready, they'd pull out the equipment for the lesson, and position the coconut matting in the areas where people were most likely to fall. This left little of the floor uncovered. People would rather have fallen on the wooden floor (well littered with debris from the meals eaten earlier in the week: a popped-in cold potato could revitalize a flagging gymnast and improve a forward roll no end) than on the coconut matting, but the coconut matting had to be positioned. Scattered vegetables were a constant hazard. One skid on a lump of cauliflower, and you'd end up with your head jammed in the wall-bars.

Conversely, gymnasium equipment could be a hazard during lunch.

4

Years later.

They were in Year Five (*aleph*).

The ropes became unknotted from around the top of the wall-bars, and whistled lethally down the aisle between the rows of tables. The metal bit at the end of one of them, the hook used for piratical grappling, whacked into Brinkman's groin at about fifty miles an hour. Brinkman grunted, and fell face forward onto the floor, his head landing with a squelch in the bowl he'd been carrying, piled high with the stewed apples he'd just filched from Linnaeus and several other boys. After a while, Brinkman – partially muffled by the stewed apples – started shrieking, the most uninhibitedly high-pitched shrieks they'd ever heard from him. No one did much to help, and the shrieks went on for quite some time. It was immensely satisfying, one of those moments you wished to see happening over and over. Stewed apples *and* entertainment. The puzzling claim in the school prospectus – *Few schools can offer facilities to equal those at Otsego Lake Academy* – at long last rang with a sound not far from truth.

They had waited for years for it to happen, and it had been worth the waiting.

They had already been in saucy mood. They'd just had Latin with Mr. Rappaport, and this always made Oliver playful. Then they'd seen what was on offer for lunch. The first course had been – just about identifiable as such after Mrs. Economou had launched herself upon it, bellowing (this was how they imagined it) – *liver*, and it had awoken memories of long ago in the minds of the Crowninshield's boys. (They still imagined themselves as such, most of them.)

"Lodged into his liver! Lodged into his liver!" they'd started chanting – automatically reenacting the death of Eurymachus (doomed, like Prometheus, to perpetual liver-tampering) – baffling boys at other tables.

The chanting then became "*Oliver! Oliver!*"

Dr. Brown, the master on duty, concentrated very hard on cutting his liver into small, neat pieces, not easy with a blunt knife and a liver cooked by Mrs. Economou. You'd have thought that he taught Biology instead of Chemistry, so rapt was his dissection, so neat his slicings. He cut *really* straight segments.

Ben, Oliver, and Linnaeus had – between them (it was one of their long-running private jokes) – created a rich inner life for Dr. Brown, quite convincing themselves that it was uncannily accurate.

They knew what he'd be thinking, though he wasn't saying much.

Throughout his lunch duties – though they'd been lured away by liver on this occasion – they made each other laugh by saying out loud what they thought Dr. Brown was thinking, fitting the words to the expression (depressed, most of the time) on his face. It was something secret between the three of them, and they took it in turns.

(*Object.*

(*To eat liver and survive lunch duty.*)

(These two aims were not necessarily mutually compatible.

(*Equipment.*

(*Really sharp-edged knife.*)

(*Really sharp-pronged fork.*)

(*Really strong plate.*)

(*Really, really strong teeth.*)

(You had to use "really" a lot when it came to Mrs. Economou's liver.)

These were the sort of things that they'd be saying to each other. Linnaeus surprised them both by revealing an unsuspected gift for mimicry, producing an instantly recognizable version of Dr. Brown's pedantic, flatly unstressed way of speaking.

(*Materials.*

(*Piece of liver.*

(*Gravy.*

(*Mashed potatoes.*

(*Diagram* would have to wait for a while.

(*Method.*

(*The knife and fork were introduced to the liver, which was dissected, with the use of the knife, into pieces approximately half an inch square.*

(He was concentrating really – *another* "really"! – hard. He had two hours with Year Four (*alpha*) next, and was not feeling strong. There would be major explosions. This might very well be the last meal he ever ate.

(Mrs. Economou's liver!

(The last meal he ever ate!

(Boys at his table – those not distracted by the growing tumult from Oliver's table – edged away a little as Dr. Brown started to whimper. This happened quite regularly, and was not conducive to a good appetite, and appetites needed all the help they could get once Mrs. Economou got cracking.

(*The fork was used to convey the liver, piece by piece, toward the mouth.*

(Another whimper.

(There seemed to be some sort of coordinated chanting going on, something in – of all things – praise of Mrs. Economou's liver, possibly a popular demand for second helpings.

(Extraordinary.

(Quite extraordinary.

(Personally, he thought it was absolutely foul.

(*Really, really strong teeth.*

(Indeed!

(Revolting taste in his mouth, as of something dead crammed in to silence him.

(He could do with a glass of water.

(H_2O.)

"*Oliver! Oliver!*"

Bradley looked scandalized as Oliver began to unbutton the front of his jacket – this took quite some time – and pull up one side of his shirt to expose part of his chest. Charlie poised his knife and fork above the exposed nipple (his right, the same as the one favored by Cora Munro, an artistic symmetry typical of Oliver), an epicure about to luxuriate on some culinary delight, one of those small expensive specialties from an exclusive restaurant: larks' tongues, lambs' brains, peacocks' hearts (possibly). They'd crunch briefly, and then melt into the mouth.

"Into his chest, beside his nipple," he commented.

"And lodged into his liver."

They paused, hearing some faint, distant sound.

("Lodged into his liver!"

("Lodged into his liver!"

(A misty glimpse of the protective railings that shielded them from the attacks of the optician and the chiropodist.

(The edges of invisible twelve-inch rulers dug into the palms of their hands as they grasped them firmly.)

"Would you like some gravy to accompany that? I've got a spare lump of it here." Linn. It was always nice when Linn joined in.

"And some mashed potatoes?" Ben.

Laden knives and forks lunged toward Oliver's chest from all directions. Some of the boys were standing up. Some of them were practically kneeling on the table. Dr. Crowninshield had certainly nurtured a keen zest for killing in his charges.

(*As the liver approached, the mouth was opened, and the liver was introduced to the mouth.*

("Hello, mouth!"

("Hello, liver!")

Leonard Merrill, who rarely spoke, was overcome by the excitement of the moment. Sometimes you felt like treating Merrill in the way that the March Hare and the Hatter treated the Dormouse in

Alice's Adventures in Wonderland – using him as a cushion as he slept, resting your elbows upon him, and talking over his head. They still tended to greet him with the words, "My gracious silence, hail!," words they'd seized upon when they'd come across them in *Coriolanus*. Words and phrases – "Lodged into his liver!" was one of many – lingered from Crowninshield's, some of them almost unrecognized as such any longer. Merrill's invisible Dormouse existence might have continued indefinitely if it hadn't been for W. S. Gilbert. Merrill had been at the academy for less than a year when W. S. Gilbert – the power wielded by the pen! – had named a character Leonard Meryll in *The Yeomen of the Guard* (the variation in spelling was scarcely noticed, another – er – momento of their years of Dr. Crowninshield's training), and brought a little unwelcome notoriety to disturb his Dormousy slumberings.

> "Leonard Merrill!
> Leonard Merrill!
> Dauntless he in time of peril!
> Man of power,
> Knighthood's flower . . ."

That had become the regular greeting, and Merrill sighed mightily.

Now the Dormouse – dauntless he in time of peril! – spoke, and he did not speak about everything that begins with an M, mousetraps, and the moon, and memory, and muchness. He spoke about breasts.

Breasts!

And he wasn't indicating Alice or – Cor! – Cora with a meaningful leer, and a lubricious cant to his cutlery.

> "Thy two breasts are like two young roes that are twins,
> Which feed among the lilies."

This was what he chose to say, as he held his knife and fork six inches from Oliver's proffered chest.

(*Breasts!*)

Something of a sensation all around the liver-laden table. It was the sort of thing that gave rise to a "Gosh!" when Mr. Rappaport said it. It was the sort of thing that Mr. Rappaport said rather often.

It was a Monday.

Yesterday they'd had rather an erotic morning in Sunday-school, browsing through The Song of Solomon, and it was The Song of Solomon that Merrill had been unable to resist quoting. Miss Augusteena had gamely struggled through the last chapter of Ecclesiastes as the sniggers multiplied. As they were now in Year Five at Otsego Lake Academy, their sniggers had come on a treat. The weekend was a convenient time in which to demonstrate what they'd been learning at school all week.

"Remember now thy Creator in the days of thy youth, while the evil days come not, nor the years draw nigh, when thou shalt say, I have no pleasure in them . . ."

(Dogged, determined. That was Miss Augusteena, braced so that all sniggers would bounce right off her.)

The Song of Solomon was conveniently positioned right next to Ecclesiastes.

All around her were excited whisperings as *great* pleasure was experienced.

"Thy cheeks are comely with rows of jewels . . ."

That's the sort of thing that they'd been whispering to each other with exaggerated leers.

"He shall lie all night betwixt my breasts . . ."

(*Betwixt!* There he was, precariously balanced, struggling not to fall off, trying to keep still. It would be awful if he developed a cough. He'd have to sort of *brace* himself, wedging himself in with a breast on each side of him. Did breasts part conveniently to allow this sort of positioning? Anxious speculation.)

"And my bowels were moved for him . . ."

Distinct surge in sniggering for the moving bowels.

"Therefore do the virgins love thee . . ."

Miss Augusteena – there'd been an even more distinct surge in sniggering on "virgins," more of a tidal wave – had raised her voice competitively. She was equal to any challenge. Whether it was bowels or virgins, she was a woman who knew how to fight back.

". . . when the sound of the grinding is low, and he shall rise up at the voice of the bird, and all the daughters of musick shall be brought low . . ."

If anything, the sound of the sniggering – not low, like the grinding – increased.

Grinding!

Rise up!

(Sniggers metamorphosed into guffaws at "rise up.")

Daughters!

Brought low!

They'd reached the stage where even "the" or "and" or "he" throbbed with filthy hidden meanings.

Miss Augusteena magisterially rose above such petty-minded muckiness, and raised her voice even further. She wouldn't be handing out many colored pictures of saints today to this lot!

Breasts!

Merrill had just said "breasts."

Monday!

Monday *lunchtime!*

And he'd said "*breasts!*"

Breasts!

Thy two breasts are like two young roes that are twins, / Which feed among the lilies.

That's what he'd said, and he'd said it to Comstock!

Breasts!

Chaps had chests, not breasts! They might have been lumbered with nipples, but they were chappy, chesty sort of nipples, with nothing whatsoever breasty about them, unless they were as fat as Bak in Year Four (*alpha*).

(Bak's breasts – breasty, not chesty, that was Bak – wobbled!)

But this was Comstock!

Two breasts!

The fact that he'd obviously counted them – a sense of leaning closer, just to check – somehow made it far worse. There was something disturbing and calculating about that "two." They pictured the breasts, companionably rooting side by side, like two pale well-nourished porkers, crunching and snuffling as they laid waste to the lilies. It would be like the time when Mr. Hennebelle's pigs had broken through the fence into Mrs. Alexander Diddecott's and vandalized her garden, a garden as neat and formal as a diagram in a geometry book devastated! Breasts on the rampage, devouring all that lay before them!

Euch!

It was clear that Merrill had not yet recovered from the excitement of the day before, The Song of Solomon sauciness. He had been corrupted in the days of his youth. The sun and the light and the moon and the stars would be darkened!

"*Merrill!*"

Delighted outrage.

"*Breasts!*"

Oliver on the very cusp of goshing.

(There'd already been a "*Gosh* sir!" in Latin, just before lunch. Mr. Rappaport had virtually lost control of himself. "Yet my love lives, although no hope have I!" That's what he'd been *singing* to Olly. *Gosh!*)

Oliver looked down critically at his chest, pressing his chin in, and trying to focus his eyes, in an attempt to glimpse the two young roes – shy, wild creatures – feeding among the lilies, before they scampered off out of sight, startled by a snapping twig. After a pause, he brought his right hand up and primly covered his nipple. "The almond tree shall flourish, and the grasshopper shall be a burden, and desire shall fail," he observed, somewhat obscurely. "Vanity of vanities; all is vanity."

"How true." Charlie.

Oliver turned to Merrill.

"I thought it was bad enough with Rappaport, without *you* starting," Oliver commented, nipple securely guarded, in the tone of one greatly disappointed by a person in whom he had had the utmost faith. He'd opted for joshing, rather than goshing.

Merrill's knife and fork drooped.

"Not much sign of desire failing when Rappaport's salivating." This was Swartwout, a boy with a gift for finding the right words for the occasion.

"Thank you, Swartwout. As ever, you're a great source of comfort. Does Brinkman give out gold stars, casting his bread upon the waters?"

Mr. Rappaport had been in rapt form that morning.

It was the Monday after he'd been to see *Patience*, the Monday on which he'd started to serenade Oliver with "Twenty love-sick maidens we." He'd virtually launched himself upon Oliver from the light-fittings. Thank heavens he hadn't. Brinkman, Adams, Bradstone, and Swartwout had followed Oliver all the way down the corridor to the hall for lunch, bellowing out the song.

> "All our love is all for one,
> Yet that love he heedeth not.
> He is coy and cares for none,
> Sad and sorry is our lot!"

They were troubadours in the presence of their beloved.

"Still brooding on their mad infatuation!" That had been Olly's only comment.

The Song of Solomon had been in their minds even before Merrill had galvanized them all by his unguarded licentiousness. It was rather enjoyable to act all prudish and appalled, to rear back and drop your jaw, and look shocked.

> (*The voice of my beloved! behold, he cometh*
> *Leaping upon the mountains, skipping upon the hills.*)

You could just imagine Oliver skipping upon the hills. All that was lacking was the lutes.

(My beloved is like a roe or a young hart:
Behold, he standeth behind our wall,
He looketh forth at the windows,
Shewing himself through the lattice.)

Brinkman – always a careless, hasty reader – had been under the impression that this last line was "Shewing himself through the lettuce," and, not the slightest bit surprised, had snorted contemptuously. This was *exactly* the sort of thing you could imagine Comstock doing, coyly waggling the lettuce leaves like a fan dancer getting into her stride as he shewed rather too much of himself with considerable enthusiasm, a salad days sissy *sans* tits. Feathers never hovered far from sinfulness when they featured in Brinkman's mind. Tits and garters and feathers. The things he'd seen through the imperfectly closed door at his father's club! (A judiciously jammed ice hockey stick – carefully angled – and a slew of pucks generally did the trick. Papa's club, after all, did foster a sporty sort of image.) The things he'd seen had broadened his horizons in the mucky thoughts department, and he was quick to pass on these thoughts to others in a disinterestedly generous desire to share his knowledge with the less experienced. He wouldn't have been at all surprised to discover that Comstock wore red frilly garters – stretched to the point of twanging – to hold up his socks. They were just the sort of thing he *would* choose to wear.

"Sunday-school," Merrill began, trying to make it perfectly clear that the source of his erotic utterance was an impeccable and well-documented one, and that the words were not the result of an unfortunate lapse of concentration on his part, one of those all-too-human moments of unguarded weakness to which politicians – in particular – appeared to be all too prone.

"The Song of Solomon."

The more he tried to explain, the worse it sounded.

"Miss Augusteena."

He cast around for further words from The Song of Solomon

with which to convince them. They were trying to look unconvinced, to make Merrill struggle for a little longer.

"'Stay me with flagons, comfort me with apples . . .'"

It was Charlie who'd rescued him. He had no apples, but his words brought comfort.

"For sweet is thy voice, and thy countenance is comely . . ."

As Charlie said this, he moved his knife and fork back into liver-lodging position. First you pierced beside the nipple, and then you went down to lodge into the liver. You had to get the angle just right.

Merrill's cutlery perked up once more.

"'Thy *speech* is comely," Oliver said, starting to sound as though he might be prepared to be won round. "Honey and milk are under thy tongue." He rummaged about a bit on his chest with his left hand, muttering, "Two young roes. Twins. Feed among the lilies." He thought for a moment, and then removed his right hand from his nipple, with an air of firm resolve – burst of applause – and – all around the table – knives and forks assumed about-to-feast positions, following the lead set by Charlie.

Sunday morning Song of Solomon memories were stirred.

"Thy lips are like a thread of scarlet . . ."

"Thy temples are like a piece of pomegranate . . ."

"Thou hast doves' eyes within thy locks . . ."

"The smell of thy garments is like the smell of Lebanon . . ."

"Thy hair is as a flock of goats . . ."

(You'd think that some of those Old Testament compliments might have been rather more thoughtfully expressed. Some of those Old Testament compliments sounded like the very thing to get crockery flying across the room when those of a more sensitive disposition were being thus addressed. "Thy nose is as the tower of Lebanon / Which looketh toward Damascus" would have had Mabel Peartree foaming and bunching her fists. Neither would she have expressed much enthusiasm for "thy breasts shall be as clusters of the vine, / And the smell of thy nose like apples." It was no-no to noses with Mabel Peartree, the woman with the biggest nose known to all seekers-out of sensational snouts.)

"How much better is thy love than wine!
And the smell of thine ointments than all spices!"

This was Merrill, emboldened again, though not choosing his quotation well. Oliver had sprained his ankle on Sunday afternoon when attempting to pole-vault with a window pole over Chinky-Winky onto the sofa (a quick method of reaching an orange), and – an uncharacteristic smell – he reeked of carbolized petroleum. You'd have chosen spices – nutmeg, cumin, ginger, cayenne, *anything* – rather than his ointments any day. (Dead flies cause the ointment of the apothecary to send forth a stinking savor. That's what it said in Ecclesiastes, and Ecclesiastes clearly had carbolized petroleum in mind.) The smell of his garments wasn't much like the smell of Lebanon either, not unless there'd been an epidemic of cuts and bruises along the shores of the Mediterranean, collapsing cedar trees bringing chaos to an embattled populace.

"Man of power!"
(Charlie.)
"Knighthood's flower!"
(Oliver, sounding pleased.)
Things rapidly deteriorated from then on, as a controversial spirit of competitiveness set in.
"My beloved is white and ruddy . . ."
"His head is as the most fine gold . . ."
"His cheeks are as a bed of spices . . ."
"His lips like lilies . . ."
"His belly is as bright ivory overlaid with sapphires . . ."
"Steady on, chaps!" Oliver. "I shall inform Mama of these unseemly blandishments!"
He heedeth not.
He was coy.
He cared for none.

509

Sad and sorry was their lot.

It was at this point that Bradley felt he should step in, before it got completely out of control. *Belly!* He saw himself as the spiritual guardian of Year Five (*aleph*), not that the rest of the class showed much gratitude for his soul-saving tactics. They'd be telling Oliver that his legs were as pillars of marble, set upon sockets of fine gold. They'd be telling him that his mouth was most sweet: yea, he was altogether lovely.

There wasn't a moment to lose!

"God shall bring every work into judgment, with every secret thing, whether it be good, or whether it be evil." Bradley got this in quick, panting slightly. He seized his moments whenever he could. "Ecclesiastes, Chapter XII, Verse xiv."

As usual, most of them clearly hadn't a clue what he meant.

Though . . .

You could see that *some of them* were thinking about what he'd said, that he'd pricked the conscience of one or two of them.

(*Every secret thing.*

(That's what some of them were thinking about, and it had nothing whatsoever to do with conscience.

(*Every secret thing.*

(That sounded promising.

(*That's* what they were thinking.)

Oliver looked speculatively down at the floor, debating whether to take his jacket off completely, and go the whole hog for nostalgia. Hog would certainly have been an improvement on the liver.

He'd be beating his head against the jacket-cushioned floor.

He'd be shrieking piercingly. (Though not as piercing, these days, as he'd once been.)

He'd be drumming his heels.

Oliver!

Oliver!

Concentric circles of gravy and mashed potatoes would guide the cutlery to its intended target. "Cast thy potatoes upon the breasts!" That's what Oliver would be encouraging, as he assumed a Christian martyr position. "If the potato fall toward the south or toward the north, in the place where the potato falleth, there shall it be." (How very, *very* true that was.) Lunchtimes could be really messy when Dr. Brown was on duty, and it was hell in Gymnastics afterwards. Shrieking gymnasts hurtled in all directions, skidding like skaters who'd totally lost control.

Lodged into the wall-bars!

Lodged into the wall-bars!

Sensing that one nipple couldn't cope with so much weaponry, Oliver hoisted up the other side of his shirt with an heroic thus-I-go-to-my-death sort of gesture. Bradley averted his gaze, crossing his knife and fork protectively in front of him in an attempt to keep sinfulness at bay. People began to come across with their knives and forks from other tables, with the feeling that they were missing something. Even Julius Cæsar hadn't mustered so many zealously knife-wielding assassins lining up for a stab.

Bradley's mouth went prim and pursed, and he averted his gaze, hoping that God saw his shudder. What a sacrilegious affront this was to the sufferings of St. Sebastian! He'd gone right off his liver, having to witness such unsavory scenes. (He hadn't fancied eating it in the first place, but it was so much more satisfying to be able to reject his food with what he could claim as a virtuous impulse.)

It was at this point that the metal hook on the end of the rope (some of the lucky nearer spectators claimed to have heard a distinct squelch as it made contact) *whistled* into Brinkman like some mediæval siege-breaking machine. Even Miss Stammers' dogs (enormous in size, with claws that could gouge holes in brick walls) had never caused such spectacular sounds of agony when they launched themselves upon a convenient crotch with thrilled cries of doggy delight.

"Ooh, look!" Charlie said, in his best Mrs. Albert Comstock manner, and — knives and forks still held in midair — they watched (and listened: they might have missed the squelch, but they heard every shriek) with rapt attention as Brinkman howled.

"Lodged into his balls!"

That became the new chant.

"Lodged into his balls!"

Faintly, Dr. Brown was aware of his fork beginning to tap on his plate, as some half-heard primitive rhythm began to take possession of him.

Faintly, Dr. Brown was aware of a distant agonized screaming. Was it coming from him?

He did, after all, have to face Year Four (*alpha*) after lunch.

Two hours with Year Four (*alpha*).

He could still smell that awful stink from Bak's jacket – igniting Bak's jacket with Bunsen burners was a popular activity with Year Four (*alpha*) – from the last time that they set fire to him, that nostril-hair-shriveling stench of barbecued sheep herds. Mind you, he could hardly blame them. Bak was such an irritating little twit that he felt like joining in with them half the time. Let's face it, Bak was such an irritating little twit that he felt like pouring several gallons of some highly inflammable substance across the back of his jacket to intensify the ferocity of the blaze. He had a wide selection of suitable substances from which to choose. Now, which of them would guarantee the most spectacular results? The fat would certainly be in the fire once Bak started sizzling.

He mused.

(Ben, Oliver, and Linnaeus convinced themselves that they knew *exactly* what it was that he'd be thinking.)

Year Four (*alpha*) had long ago driven him into the – quite enjoyable, to be honest – thrall of spirituous liquors. "Spirituous liquors": this was the expression he favored for the various bottles not-all-that-discreetly secreted about his bachelor's rooms. He far preferred spirituous liquors to the product of ammoniacal liquors, a man with no need for smelling salts. He embraced unconsciousness – not alertness – when things were bad, and as things were often bad, the spirituous liquors played a vital rôle in achieving the wished-for condition of obliviousness. The expression "spirituous liquors" added, he felt, an air of refinement to drunkenness and vomiting. If any tightly corseted lady began rummaging helpfully in her reticule for smelling salts, he'd kick the smelling salts across the room and vomit into the invitingly gaping interior. He'd soon show the lily-livered fainter what he thought of smelling salts.

Lily-livered.

Liver! Liver!

He kept hearing the word in the distance, and he could have sworn that he'd heard the word "lily" earlier. It was worrying when they started to hear your thoughts, and there was nowhere safe left for dark-souled pondering.

Cocoa had long lost its efficacious powers when confronted with Year Four (*alpha*). They'd been bad enough when they'd been Year Three (*alpha*), and they were even worse now that they were larger. There'd be something symbolic and cleansing, perhaps, about drenching Bak's jacket thoroughly with an entire bottle of spirituous liquor – soaking him ("marinating him": was this the correct terminology?) for some sinfully alcoholic dessert – and watching from behind the shielding barrier of his well-guarded bench as Bunsen burners went to work and Bak blazed with an eyebrow-threatening intensity. There might even be screaming. It would be much more fun if there was screaming. "Silence!" he could shout, with an air of authority that would impress Caswell in the adjoining laboratory. "You're making *far* too much noise! Silence *at once!*" He'd show Bak who was boss. This was the sort of thing that might very well add an element of genuine pleasure to teaching, even when the lesson involved was one with Year Four (*alpha*).

Wodka.

(Wodka had first appeared during one of Oliver's monologues.)

He might try wodka. Vodka was spelt *wodka* on the label of the cheap brand he bought, and he pronounced it thus, as if this spelling was an authentic guide to pronunciation, particularly after a heavy night's drinking. He'd developed quite a taste for wodka recently, swigging it back – it helped no end in creating an appropriate atmosphere – as he worked his way through the novels of

Dostoyevsky, laughing uproariously of an evening at the fun-filled antics of Raskolnikov and the Karamazovs. He'd be no Brother to Bak. Blazing like a beacon, Bak – reeking of wodka – began to dance, big black boots shooting out like a Cossack can-can dancer. "Yip!" he kept emitting shrilly, whistling. "Yip!" He sounded like one of those squeaky little dogs being given a kick up the backside, Mrs. Albert Comstock's awful Pekinese hurtling twelve feet into the air. When Dr. Brown needed cheering up, he always found solace in Dostoyevsky. His characters seemed to derive far more *enjoyment* out of life than he'd ever managed, zestful and giggling, whatever life threw at them, always game for jokes and juggling. Wodka certainly made you see the events in novels in a whole new light.

(Dostoyevsky, also, had been one of Oliver's ideas.)

Wodka.

Alcohol . . .

C_2H_5OH . . .

He often lingered long over formulæ and equations, and sometimes conducted whole conversations in his head – chattering away to himself for hours – with nothing but equations. Why bother with words, when equations said so much more in far less time? Sometimes, all that he saw were the formulæ that were hidden inside words, and not the words themselves. *Words* got in the way; words were a bar to understanding. Give him the elegant lucidity of logically arranged letters and numbers any day. The first time he'd realized that two twos were four was the time when he'd sensed that this new language was the only way of speaking for him from now on. He'd progressed a little beyond two twos are four by now, but twos and fours still featured regularly in his thoughts, along with more advanced sixes and nines and twelves.

"$C_6H_{12}O_6 + 6O_2 = 6CO_2 + 6H_2O$ . . ." he'd repeat in a respiratory sort of way to himself, in the swooning manner of someone reciting a particularly euphonious line of poetry.

"$CaCO_3 + 2HCl = CaCl_2 + H_2O + CO_2\uparrow$ . . ."

He'd feel himself dissolving.

"NaOH + HCl = NaCl + H₂O . . ."

This was the one to which he returned the most often.

Time and time again, he'd return to $NaOH + HCl = NaCl + H_2O$.

When things were really bad you couldn't beat $NaOH + HCl = NaCl + H_2O$.

Though there was always C_2H_5OH.

He was all in favor of extracting alcohol from water.

C_2H_5OH (bpt. 173°F)–H_2O (bpt. 212° F) = an afternoon of guaranteed undiluted pleasure.

You could forget a dozen red roses, a casket of chocolates, candlelight, and music . . .

What he had in mind possessed a chocolate-box prettiness that far surpassed these.

Object.

To incinerate Bak.

Equipment . . .

Materials . . .

Wodka.

Box of matches.

Bak.

That was all it would take.

$C_2H_5OH + 3O_2 = 2CO_2 + 3H_2O$.

He mused.

Hmm.

This was a self-interrogating, thoughtfully considering sort of "Hmm," an upwardly inflected sort of "Hmm."

Hmm.

But it was followed, shortly afterward, by a more dubious, head-starting-to-shake sort of "Hmm." A downward inflection for this sort of "Hmm."

Hmm.

It would –

however enjoyable;

especially the *Observations;*

it would be *very* enjoyable, and that pale blue flickering alcoholic flame would add an attractive coloring to Bak's demise; why on earth did some people assume that Science masters were entirely deficient in æsthetic sensibilities? -

be somewhat wasteful to lavish an entire bottle of wodka on Bak's jacket.

Wery wasteful of wodka.

"Wodka's weally wonderful!" he'd slur to Dr. Twemlow as they began their regular morning run up to Hudson Heights. He'd started losing his way, and falling over — once landing on that dopey dog of Twemlow's with quite a crunch — and Dr. Twemlow was becoming distinctly petulant about it. You'd have thought that he'd done it on purpose. He'd called him a tosspot once. Dr. Brown wasn't quite sure what this meant, but you could guarantee that it wasn't complimentary.

Twemlow could talk!

Dr. Brown might be in not-so-secret thrall to the allure of C_2H_5OH — using the formula added a bracingly scientific air of respectability to alcohol — but Twemlow.

— ahem —

was not above dabbling

— rather more than dabbling, shoveling it in like Mrs. Albert Comstock unleashed on a sugar-bowl, that was more like it, that's what he'd heard —

with cocaine.

Cocaine!

$C_{17}H_{21}NO_4$.

Just by looking at it —

C_{17}!

Seventeen!

H_{21}!

Twenty-one, for God's sake! —

you could see that cocaine was a far more dubious proposition, chemically, than alcohol was. Alcohol was positively *restrained* in comparison to cocaine.

And Twemlow had the nerve to call *him* a tosspot!

No.

Not wodka.

Not spirituous liquor of any description, despite the undoubted attractions of Symbolism.

Being a Science master did not altogether rule out the lure of the cultural.

Methylated spirits?

He'd sniffed at bottles of this, on occasion, when wodka was wanting, when Year Four (*alpha*) were waxing – waxing wroth, that's what he was doing – feeling the first stirrings of temptation.

No, not methylated spirits. The flames would be too insipid, a weedy pale yellow-tipped candle-flames-in-daylight sort of flickering, and Bak demanded something dramatic and – preferably – apocalyptic. If you did something, you might as well do it properly. That was his philosophy. He was not unlike Oliver in this.

He'd a distinct hankering after coal-tar naphtha, a plentiful supply of which he had in his fume cupboard. Carefully applied, this could incinerate Bak better than Elizabeth I barbecuing a whole monastery full of good Catholics. There'd be lurid yellow light, thick smoke – all the accoutrements of a well-attended Viking funeral – with added screams and the smell of the gasworks, the rituals of the past chummily integrated with the sterner demands of modern science.

He mused.

Coal-tar naphtha.

$$2C_8H_{10} + 21O_2 = 16CO_2 + 10H_2O.$$

He liked that C_8.

He *really* liked that H_{10}.

Though he liked the idea of screams most of all.

Why did he keep thinking of screaming?

And . . .

And if he waited until the Fourth of July, he could ensure that Bak's jacket was well packed with firecrackers to ensure him a really sensational sizzling demise. There wouldn't just be sodium yellow flames, there wouldn't only be the sound of crackling flames. There'd be exploding stars, intensely flaring barium greens, copper and cesium blues and calcium reds, strontium crimsons, whistling and hissing, camera flash white magnesium (he'd *certainly* be taking photographs) sending long shadows leaping. You could construct whole paragraphs from the formulæ for this lot. He saw them in front of him, agitatedly scrawled across his blackboard — all those firecracker bangs! — and began constructing anagrams.

NaCl.

BaCl$_2$.

Well, there was Bak — more or less — straightaway, all dose-of-salts green before the blackening.

CsCl.

CaCl$_2$.

$2Mg + O_2 = 2MgO$ . . .

"Do it again, sir!" Year Four (*alpha*) would be demanding. "Do it again!" Long had he dreamed of cries of acclaim from Year Four (*alpha*).

Only a few months to go.

Only a few months until the Fourth of July was celebrated with unprecedented gusto.

You needed something ahead of you to which you could look forward when you were a teacher.

There wasn't much pleasure in the present, as far as Dr. Brown was concerned.

He mused, not unenjoyably.

Coal-tar naphtha.

Hmm.

$2C_8H_{10} + 21O_2 = 16CO_2 + 10H_2O.$

Hmm.

Bak would have been engulfed by air.

Bak would have been engulfed by fire.

Bak would have been engulfed by water.

No.

Not water.

That element might have saved him.

All that remained would be earth.

That would be the blackened wreck of Bak being buried.

Hic iacet Bak's jacket.

That would be the moving inscription upon the gravestone.

Elemental, my dear Brown.

Hmm.

The Fourth of July.

Hmm.

Fourth . . .

Four . . .

Year Four (*alpha*).

Sense of enjoyment faded.

Year Four (*alpha*).

Sense of panic intensified.

Whimper.

Alpha.

That reminded him of something.

Alpha.

(That screaming was definitely becoming louder.)

Alpha.

It was from some poem-sort-of-thing that Mrs. Scrivener, the headmaster's wife, had intoned to him – with soulful mournfulness – when he had found himself sitting opposite her at dinner at the Outcaults'. Mrs. Scrivener was always quoting poetry with great intensity, like that Ancient Greek prophetess – Gladys, Ethel, whatever her name was – and like Gladys, Ethel, whatever, or so he'd once read, her poetry tended toward the sonorous and gloomy. She came across some lines that spoke to her soul – this was how she worded it – and lost no time whatsoever in sharing her soul with whomsoever happened to be in the vicinity. On this occasion – it may very well have been a pioneering attempt to bring a rare glimpse of culture into the hitherto brutish mind of a Science master – she'd leaned right between the candlesticks, looking meaningful, earrings glittering, eyes rapt, aiming the words at him. She'd clearly formed the impression that they'd speak directly to his soul, also.

Poetry for Science masters.

It was a natural progression from her missionary work, she felt. Coleridge.

That was the choice of text for this week.

Mrs. Scrivener did her best.

> "In Xanadu did Kubla Khan
> A stately pleasure-dome decree . . ."

she informed Dr. Brown, conversationally, as if he'd really like to know.

"*Really?*" he responded politely, thinking she'd said all that she wanted to say, wondering what on earth she was talking about. He hadn't had time to read the newspaper that morning, and was not feeling fully *au fait* with the latest news. He was about to elaborate upon his "*Really?*" – not quite knowing *how* he was to do this, but struggling to create an impression of geographical awareness – when she kept right on going. She hadn't finished, after all.

> " . . . Where Alf, the sacred river, ran
> Through caverns measureless to man . . ."

Alf!

That was what she said.

What a stupid name for a river!

You'd have thought that explorers would take a little more care as they scribbled away on the blank bits of their maps, thinking up names to fill all those disturbing immensities of emptiness.

Alf!

He'd rather liked the next bit, though, whatever it was about.

Caverns measureless to man.

He felt himself being drawn far, far away, into a peaceful and quieter world, floating away into a dark and vaulted stalactite-encrusted interior, faintly gleaming, and still. It was an unpeopled, unmeasured, place of silence, and it was everywhere around him.

Drip.

Drip.

Drip.

That was the only sound, the sound of time, the unutterable slowness of the growth of the rocks. Outside, rocks were weathered and worn away into dust, scattered to nothingness as the rains fell, as the winds blew. Here the rocks grew, the slow accretion of the centuries upon centuries.

Drip.

Drip.

Drip.

No.

He couldn't fool himself.

This *wasn't* the only sound that he could hear.

"Balls!"

"Balls!"

That was the sound that he was hearing, faintly – not all *that* faintly – in the background. *"Balls!"* and screaming. This was not a combination that fostered an atmosphere conducive to a healthy digestion at lunchtime. A vague sense of liver and mashed potato and – in even bigger lumps than the mashed potatos – gravy flying about around him.

Screams.

Extremely high-pitched screams.

His thoughts returned to Alf, the sacred river.

He couldn't help himself from picturing the sacred river as sporting a large and unbecoming moustache because of that name. It floated there, bang in the middle of a wide stretch of water, like an accumulation of rotting driftwood. He knew an Alf with just such an excrescence, flaunting the emblem by which each Alf recognized his fellows.

Alf.

He saw it as a river running deep into the peacefulness of an inner sea, deep, deep inside the measureless caverns inside himself. Its banks were straight and parallel, like those of a canal, an equals sign that led to peace.

Alf + boat + caverns = peace.

"Equals . . ."

The word was whispered.

"Equals . . ."

"Equals . . ."

=

=

=

(The underground secret river, the measureless caverns, the equals signs: all these were from Linnaeus, a part of his contribution to the inner life of Dr. Brown. Oliver's chanting about the sunny dome, the caves of ice, on their way to their first day at Otsego Lake Academy would not have baffled Linnaeus as it had baffled Ben. Linnaeus knew all about Coleridge and *Kubla Khan*, and Ben and Oliver listened open-mouthed as he talked and talked, his voice low, taking them with him into the place where he went.)

He thought for a while of his favorite symbol, drawing him away into the parallel line infinity of a better place, lulled by this central symbol of his chemical mantra. An equals sign always gave him comfort, a sense of equilibrium, of things being exactly as they ought to be. Nothing could equal an equals sign. It was his secret source of serenity. His little bridge would lead him away from the hurly-burly life of a teacher – some of Year Four (*alpha*) were alarmingly burly, and far too fond of hurling – to a safer and serener place, a place mercifully free of "*Balls!*" and screaming.

"*Balls!*"

"*Balls!*"

Screaming.

Louder than ever.

Time to seek safety in equations.

Time to begin his chemical mantra, his slow slide into the solace of silence.

It always gave him comfort, even when cocoa failed him. Even when *wodka* failed him. This happened sometimes.

Cesium.

Rubidium.

Potassium.

Sodium.

Lithium . . .

That was how it began, and it was always in this order, as he mentally tested the reactivity series of metals, beginning with noise, and – gradually, soothingly – shifting ever closer to soundlessness.

Cesium first.

$2Cs + 2H_2O = 2CsOH + H_2 \uparrow.$

The loudest possible sound first.

On really bad days he began with nitroglycerine.

$4C_3H_5(NO_3)_3 = 12CO_2 + 10H_2O + 6N_2 + O_2$ (+ whatever else he could pile on, really, shoveling away with a generous hand).

There'd been a lot of really bad days recently.

The school exploding into nothingness.

Three dollars fifty size eight running shoes.

Faster, faster, faster!

Impending *KER-BOOM!!!*

Faster, faster, faster!

His blurred figure hurtling across the park, his piston-pumping arms in their mathematically correct $45°$ position, mirroring that of his knees – *Faster, faster, faster!* – miraculously sprouting angel-like, dove-like wings to lift him away to a far, far, far better place, far away, far away – *Faster, faster, faster!* – where, in the wilderness, he would build him a nest . . .

He'd remain there for ever at rest.

Drip.

Drip.

Drip.

The caverns were deep and dark and safe, and no man could measure them.

(It had been Linnaeus saying all this, his eyes seeing what he said, and they listened raptly.)

Diminuendo.

Then rubidium.

$2Rb + 2H_2O = 2RbOH + H_2\uparrow.$

Another explosion, but not as catastrophic an explosion.

Gradually . . ..

Slowly . . .

Soothingly . . .

Diminuendo . . .

Diminuendo . . .

Potassium.

$2K + 2H_2O = 2KOH + H_2\uparrow.$

Distinctly quieter.

An æsthetically lingering moment of Mauve Madness – thoughts of William Henry Perkin – in the flicker of the lilac and purple flames.

Diminuendo.

Sodium.

$2Na + 2H_2O = 2NaOH + H_2\uparrow.$

Diminuendo.

Lithium.

$2Li + 2H_2O = 2LiOH + H_2\uparrow.$

Slower . . .

More soothing . . .

Scarcely a bang with lithium . . .

A fizz, just a fizz, like a carbonated drink, a drink for coolness in the heat of a summer's day, a drink to refresh and revive . . .

Dr. Brown repeated his mantra of equations in his quest for perfect peace.

The less reactive they were, the happier he was.

After lithium, there would be . . .

There would be . . .

In this mood (he felt the beginnings of perfect peace) he traveled in search of an equation in which nothing whatsoever happened — a neutralization of an acid and an alkali, a neutralization of all explosions and bangs and *Balls!* and screams — and his travels always followed the same route. It was a journey he was following increasingly. He was drawn deeper into the soothing *drip, drip, drip* darkness of measureless caverns. He was lying on his back in the rowboat, but he was not rowing. The current was drawing him silently along, silently drawn into an ever-deeper silence, down into the sunless sea.

It was always the same equation.

Diminuendo . . .

NaOH . . .

Diminuendo . . .

. . . plus HCl . . .

Diminuendo . . .

. . . equals . . .

It equaled peace.

It equaled silence.

It equaled soothing sunlessness, a sunlessness with warmth.

. . . equals NaCl . . .

Diminuendo . . .

. . . plus H_2O.

Always *diminuendo* . . .

Even the H_2O *drip, drip, drip* faded away.

Equals . . .

Equals . . .

Equals . . .

The sunless sea.

The silent sea.

The lap, lap, lap of water.

That was the place for which he longed.

(All this was a part of one of Linnaeus's monologues, the longest speech they ever heard him make, and it had flowed from him like something he'd long thought about, like something he knew.)

NaOH + HCl = NaCl + H_2O.

His favorite equation.

The *irony* of that NaOH! The same formula that played a part in laboratory-threatening experiments when Dr. Brown — breaking free of all the constraints of civilized behavior — liberated hydrogen by dropping a gigantic chunk of sodium into a sink full of water!

This time there was no danger of *SIZZLE!!!* and *CRACK!!!* and screaming.

Diminuendo . . .

Diminuendo . . .

Always *diminuendo* . . .

There was no danger whatsoever of a *KER-BOOM!!* with sodium hydroxide and hydrochloric acid. The neutralization of an alkali and an acid was the neutralization of all that was threatening, all that was *KER-BOOM!!* and chaotic, all that was schoolboys and shrieking.

Two colorless solutions produced a colorless solution.

Dr. Brown — despite the autumnal shading of his surname — definitely preferred things colorless.

A colorless solution to all his problems.

No color . . .

No sound . . .

Nothing you could see or hear . . .

This was safe.

This was soothing.

This was *There, there!* and a gently encouraging caress.

This was the equation for peace and forgetfulness.

NaOH + HCl = NaCl + H_2O.

He repeated this equation to himself sometimes, his prayer in moments of stress.

To him, it possessed the poetic perfection of one of the more celebrated lines from Keats. There was truth and there was beauty in

$NaOH + HCl = NaCl + H_2O$. It was all you needed to know on earth. That was his opinion.

$NaOH + HCl = NaCl + H_2O$ . . .

$NaOH + HCl = NaCl + H_2O$ . . .

"Equals . . ." he breathed to himself.

"Equals . . ."

=

=

=

There were no explosions whatsoever.

Not even a scarcely audible carbonated drink fizzing.

All that happened was that — silently — the colorless solution grew warm. A gentle, soothing warmth spread throughout the contents of the test-tube as the sodium hydroxide combined with the hydrochloric acid to form sodium chloride, a sea-salt solution.

That was it.

You sort of wondered why you'd bothered, but that was $NaOH + HCl = NaCl + H_2O$.

If only all Chemistry experiments could be like this one. It wasn't one that would have given rise to much enthusiasm in any of his classes at Otsego Lake Academy — a distinct lack of bangs and smells — but it was a result for which he longed as pants the hart — Dr. Brown always saw this word as "heart," and it was *his* heart, *his* — for cooling streams when heated in the chase.

Dr. Brown pressed the length of the warm test-tube against his cheek, with the nurturing gesture of a mother inserting her elbow into her baby's bathwater to test that it was the correct temperature, not too hot, not too cold, just . . .

Just . . .

Just warm in a way that lapped and lulled.

That hushed . . .

That pacified . . .

He rocked slowly from side to side with a lullaby rhythm, cuddling his beloved test-tube, whispering its name, crooning a little . . .

"NaOH + HCl = NaCl + H$_2$O . . ."
"NaOH + HCl = NaCl + H$_2$O . . ."

("Hush little equation, don't say a word,
Papa's going to buy you a mockingbird . . .")

"Don't say a word!" Dr. Brown whispered soothingly. "Shh! Shh!"
And then he said it again. "Shh! Shh!"

Boys nudged each other meaningfully, as Dr. Brown – with a
beatific expression on his face, a mother embracing her beloved
baby – leaned a large piece of lukewarm liver against his face and
patted it gently. You didn't know where to look! Too much to take
in at once! Brinkman catastrophically castrated to right of them,
Dr. Brown gone totally loony (again) to left of them, liver totally
surrounding them, the pupils of Otsego Lake Academy volley'd
and thunder'd.

"There, there," Dr. Brown whispered to the favored lump of
liver. "There, there!"

There! There! boys signaled to each other eagerly, *There! There!*,
pointing at Dr. Brown as he nuzzled his nose caressingly into his
liver. *There! There! He's doing it again!*

"Shh!" again from Dr. Brown. "Shh!" He was saying it to himself rather than anyone else – he certainly wasn't shushing the
screaming or the "Lodged into his *balls*!," he was scarcely aware of
them – lulling himself further within the caverns where serenity
was to be sought.

"NaOH + HCl = NaCl + H$_2$O . . ."
"NaOH + HCl = NaCl + H$_2$O . . ."
"*Equals* . . ."
"*Equals* . . ."
=
=
=

Caverns measureless to man.
(Linn's voice.

(Linn's voice saying the words.)

A sea-salt solution.

That was all that there was to it.

Object he'd chalk on the blackboard.

To find peace.

To find peace.

To find dove-winged peace.

Equipment.

Materials.

Diagram.

Method.

Observations.

He'd chalk all these things on the blackboard and all that would happen would be that he would have created . . .

"The salt of the sea . . ."

These were the next words he whispered, nostalgic as a mariner banished to a lifetime of land.

"The salt of the sea . . ."

There seemed to be something Godlike in creating the salt of the sea. Dr. Brown — with a Sistine Chapel impressiveness (the beard helped) — moved upon the face of the waters, and Dr. Brown saw that it was good.

He could hear the sound of the warm tropical sea, the waves rising and toppling, rising and toppling, the soothing unchanged rhythm of eternity sweeping out and thinning on the glittering wetness of the sea-darkened sands. He pressed the test-tube against his right ear, as if pressing a hollow shell there in order to hear the waves the better, the waves that were the sound of the rhythm of his heart's blood beating within him, the swisssh-swisssh sound of the waves.

There! There!

The signaling around him increased dramatically, as Dr. Brown pressed his lump of liver tenderly against his ear.

"Shh!" shifted into "Swisssh!" though it was spoken with a "Shh!"-like sibilance.

"Swisssh!" he was saying raptly, lingering lovingly over the "s" sounds. "Swisssh!"

There! There! There!

Boys stood up, pointing

There! There! There!

Another agonized high-pitched scream from Brinkman. The screams seemed to come in waves.

Where to look?

Where to look?

Why couldn't exciting things space themselves out sensibly? You hated to miss a moment. You wanted feast-feast-feast in perpetuity, not the Lent-like stinginess of famine elbowing its way forward. (It was not often that the word "feast" came to mind during the rigors of one of Mrs. Economou's meals.)

Boys from Year Four (*alpha*), a little disheartened by the complete inedibility of the meal, brightened perceptibly. Whenever this happened with Dr. Brown in lunch (it was happening increasingly with Dr. Brown in lunch), it always meant an unusually enjoyable afternoon would follow in the Chemistry laboratory.

There'd be no windows left unbroken!

The doors would be dangling from their hinges!

There'd be a corpse-strewn wasteland of rubble and broken glass!

Brinkman castrated, and anarchy unleashed in the Chemistry laboratory. The best Monday afternoon for ages was shaping up all around them.

"Swisssh! . . ."

Alf, he'd decided, was a sea-salt river, a tidal-surge river . . .

"Swisssh! . . ."

The salt of the sea glinted in the white-sand dunes undulating in Sahara Desert vastnesses all around him. He began to salivate, imagining the taste of the grains upon his tongue.

"Swisssh! . . ."

Slight gurgle, this time, with the saliva.

Alf!

He couldn't get over that "Alf"!

It was like naming the Pacific Ocean "Percy," or the Himalayas "Jeremy."

Alf!

Stupid name for a stupid river.

The same name as his cousin in New Glarus, Wisconsin.

The Alf with the unbecoming moustache.

Stupid name for a stupid cousin.

Last time he'd seen him, he'd been dressed as a Swiss cuckoo clock and singing "I'm a cuckoo clock, I'm a cuckoo clock" to the accompaniment of the *William Tell* Overture played by his wife on a saxophone. This was the kind of thing they did to pass the time in New Glarus, Wisconsin. It suited Cousin Alf just fine.

Alf!

Whimper.

"... Down to a sunless sea.

So twice five miles of fertile ground ..."

Mrs. Scrivener went on for *ages*.

("The salt of the sunless sea," he was thinking to himself. "The salt of the sunless sea."

(This was what he thought, but what he said was "*Really?*")

"*Really?*"

Nod, nod.

"*Really?*"

Nod, nod.

That's what he'd said, that's what he'd done, right the way down to:

"... For he on honey-dew hath fed,

And drunk the milk of Paradise."

His neck was really aching when she'd finished. He'd paused a while, just to check that she really *had* finished, and then — when the signs were good: lengthy silence, breathy exhalations – he'd nod, nodded one last time, though he hadn't managed another "*Really?*" He was right out of "*Really?*" by the end.

On honey-dew hath fed.

Honey-dew . . .

The liver didn't taste anything *like* honey-dew.

(*With the aid of the really, really strong teeth, the liver, piece by piece, was thoroughly masticated, employing the Mrs. Amelia Manager Hygienic Digestion method, chewing every mouthful thirty-two times. Thirty-two is good for you! See, especially, Fig. 24(d) on page sixty-three of her most instructive manual.*)

Twenty-eight . . .

Twenty-nine . . .

Thirty . . .

Thirty-one . . .

Even thirty-two chews, somehow, were not enough chews when you were faced with chewing liver. You began to develop a sneaking compassion for the poor, tormented eagle doomed to 30,000 years of chewing on Prometheus' liver. You just knew that a man who had stolen fire from heaven, and steadfastly rejected the allure of Pandora's seductively proffered box (flourished like a fresh three-pound box of violet creams; "Go on, have a root around!"), would possess a liver with the rock-hard consistency of one of Mrs. Economou's jaw-challenging efforts. Forget Prometheus! All your concern centered on the eagle, and you prayed for Hercules to arrive on the scene, and put paid to its misery with a merciful dispatch.

"Lodged into his balls!"

The words kept breaking through, pursuing him into his secret place and echoing around the measureless caverns, winging like graceful gulls across the surface of the sunless sea.

"Lodged into his balls!"

The word "balls" was starting to become louder and louder, as excitement rose. Some of the younger pupils – the Crowninshield's boys could no longer be regarded as amongst the younger pupils –

were on the verge of hysteria. (*Balls!*) Brinkman, as if in response, screamed ever more agonizingly, spurring on the shriekers to ever-shriekier heights. A certain competitive element had crept in.

(*Observations.*

(*An immediate sensation of revulsion spread throughout my entire body, accompanied by a powerful desire to vomit. I attempted to control this almost irresistible urge by the hasty ingestion of large quantities of mashed potato, utilizing the aforementioned knife and fork, in an attempt to . . .*)

Dr. Brown's *Observations* weren't the only *Observations* that were going on.

Mr. Caswell was peering eagerly in at one of the windows. He always hovered in the vicinity when Dr. Brown was on lunch duty, hopeful of major catastrophes. This was even better than last time! You couldn't help feeling sorry for Dr. Brown sometimes.

(*Observations.*

(Mr. Caswell was observing *everything*.

(He was *writing things down*.

(Scribble, scribble.

(He didn't need a beaker to press against the wall *this* time. It wasn't Dr. Brown doing the talking, but what was being said was spoken – chanted, chorused, *howled* – loud and clear. *Very* loud, and *very* clear.

(Scribble – pause for snigger – scribble.

(The Scriveners were in for a treat this Friday. Extra large slices of lemon cake – Mr. Scrivener had still not got around to telling his wife how much he disliked lemon cake – and second and third cups of tea. *Lodged into his balls!* might imperil a precariously balanced china plate on Mrs. Scrivener's knees. Such language was a rude intrusion into the ineffable world of poesy. Some of those crumbs took ages to brush out of the carpet.)

Knives and forks were utilized as batons to ensure a good rhythm, and Eury was quite forgotten. This was a *far* more enjoyable (they could hope) death.

(Scribble, scribble.

(Brinkman, lying on floor, clutching crotch – Mr. Caswell paused awhile to repeat this phrase to himself several times; he, too, possessed a sense of poetry – *most vulgar, vulgar chanting left unreprimanded, Dr. Brown quite oblivious, chewing his liver. I observed several portions of mashed potatoe –* Mr. Caswell never could spell "potato" – *scattered beneath the tables in different areas of the dining hall, together with veritable pools of gravy, not condusive –* nor could he spell "conducive"; Mrs. Scrivener was going to have her work cut out with Science masters – *to civilized demeanor at the dining-table. I observed that Comstock appeared to be only partially clad, with a knife and fork in his hand. The vulgar, vulgar chanting became loud and offensive . . .)*

"Lodged into his *balls!*"

Bradley nearly choked.

"Lodged into his *balls!*"

"Not so much black-balled as black-and-blue-balled," Oliver commented, starting to tuck his shirt back in. This was even more entertaining than the Euchiest of Eurys. He rebuttoned his jacket, ungravied, unmashed potatoed, as smart as ever. He'd recently scandalized them all by indicating the sensational word *black-balled* in his smuggled-in copy of *The Picture of Dorian Gray*. "Well, it's good to see that the Mystic Malison of Linnaeus is still in full working order."

"Unlike various important parts of Brinkman," Charlie added.

"Can we refer to him as Brink*man* ever again?" Ben, pleased to get this in.

"How did you manage to arrange the angle of that hook so that it was just right to cause the maximum pain?"

Linn tried to look mysterious and knowing.

"Could you do it again, please?"

"And again."

"And again."

"I vote that it becomes a regular feature."

"It might whet our appetites."

"They could do with all the whetting they can get."

"And Brinkman might wet his trousers."

"Well, at least we won't need to take him to Mr. Falkirk, after all," Linn decided. "That'll save us some money."

"The day just keeps getting better and better."

A long-standing private joke – developing from one of Oliver's ideas – was that one day they'd drag Brinkman along to their local veterinarian to have his balls snipped off, thus raising the tone of Year Five (*aleph*) no end. With luck, D. R. Falkirk might be persuaded to dispense with the anaesthetic.

"Though we still need to take Rappaport," Oliver added. "The sooner the better. He's becoming decidedly *too* frisky of late. Our innocence besmirched on a daily basis. No one's safe."

"Rape-a-pope."

"Not even the pope's safe."

"Though he's a bit on the old side for Rappaport, wouldn't you say?"

"I can just imagine Leo XIII lashing out with his crosier, his tiara all askew."

"Looking thoroughly disapproving."

"Red in the face."

"You do tend to become a little short-tempered after the fourth or fifth time it happens."

No anaesthetic for Rappaport either.

They'd long ago decided upon that.

They settled down to listen to the continuing screams of agony. You had to seize your pleasures when you could. *Carpe diem*. (Latin.) That's what Dr. Crowninshield had told them. You could rely on Dr. Crowninshield.

5

At the exact moment that the last piece of Sport equipment had been positioned in the gymnasium – Oliver could be quite pernickety in getting the angles just right – Mr. Rappaport (you felt that he'd been watching through some secret spyhole) marched in toward them to flaunt his knees, his whistle glinting on the end of its ribbon. No dubious bright colors for Mr. Rappaport. This ribbon was an unadorned manly black. They dreaded the day that Mr. Rappaport became confused, and turned up for Latin in shorts, blasting away on his whistle, and clogging the air in Room 37 with molted hairs. (All seasons were molting seasons for the Rappaport breed.) They'd be running on the spot as they chanted, deafened by the shrillness of the whistle in the far smaller room. Mr. Rappaport really enjoyed using his whistle. He could be high-pitched without any untoward aspersions being cast upon his manliness.

> "Sports prepare, the laurel bring,
> Songs of triumph to him sing . . ."

Oliver tended to sing this as Mr. Rappaport advanced toward them, squeak-squeak-squeaking on his rubber-soled shoes, their conquering hero coming, as if he'd brought his mama's clock from the music room with him to feel at home. (The *last* place Oliver felt at home was when he was at home.) Their conquering hero had no need of trumpets and drums. Those noble knees were flaunted in an impressed silence. He'd stand there for a while, soliciting favorable comment. "Look at the hairs on these!" was the unspoken invitation, and you felt that some sort of polite response was required.

"Very erotic," Oliver commented loudly on their first appearance.

The silence intensified.

Mr. Rappaport had given Oliver a long, thoughtful look and Oliver had utilized his really nice smile.

It was a silence on the point of something being said.

But nothing was said.

The lesson began.

"*Higher! Higher!*"

Boys — high in the air, and attempting to climb higher, palely angled against the painted scenes from the works of James

Fenimore Cooper as they were lured titward – fell from the ropes like picked-off pigeons, impaled on the Reverend Henry Belcher's *Latin for Schoolboys*. That would teach them to laugh at the name Belcher, when they thought he wasn't listening!

"*Further! Further!*"

Extra vigorous hurl of the Reverend Henry Belcher, and Alloway fell screaming from the top of the wall-bars. That would teach him to demonstrate his belching prowess at the side of the lake, frightening a passing group of swans, and setting their wings flapping defensively. Alloway was a boy who found delight in simple pleasures.

Otsego Lake Academy was justifiably proud of its ability to nurture academic excellence.

6

Pater filium amat.

The father loves (his) son.

It was a sentence he saw in front of him written in other rooms, on other blackboards, on the bare walls, everywhere around him.

He saw it on the blackboard – still fresh-chalked and vivid – when he walked into a Year Naught Arithmetic lesson, as if Mr. Rappaport was one of those teachers who did not clear up, leaving his thoughts behind him like an emblazoned message in the sky to inspire those who followed after in all the rooms he entered. The Arithmetic teacher set the blackboard monitor (Brinkman, again seizing an opportunity to impress) to work, clearing away the alarmingly complicated-looking calculations from the previous lesson. It was of a difficulty that suggested that the brains of the near-bearded "No talking!" giants had been tested to their utmost limits. *One day, this too, will be within your grasp.* Perhaps that was the unspoken message for the yet-to-be-bearded, the flag flapping on the peak of the mountain toward whose base they struggled, breathless and fearful. It did rather put you off.

Brinkman – with the air of a connoisseur of cleaning, buffing away as he polished an heirloom – cleared everything away, every line and letter of the daunting brain-damaging diagrams, but Ben still saw the Latin sentence, together with *Subject, Object,* and *Predicate. The father loves (his) son* and the other words were wiped away with a damp cloth, but *Subjicate* and *Pater filium amat* remained, like the sum of all learning. Ben studied these words as a triangle took shape beneath it, hearing the chanting voices repeating the words, just as they now repeated, "The theorem of Pythagoras states that in a right-angled triangle the square on the hypotenuse is equal to the sum of the squares on the other two sides." After Latin, Pythagoras: Otsego Lake Academy took pains to ensure that its pupils were worthy of wandering amidst the white-pillared classical architecture that characterized the larger public buildings that were emerging all around them. They'd been expecting "One one is one, two ones are two, three ones are three," a chanting advance through twoness and threeness to twelve twelves are a hundred and forty-four (this was the grossness of arithmetic that had ever marked the furthest frontiers of knowledge), but Mr. Stolley, clearly, had more ambitious plans for them.

"The theorem of Pythagoras states that in a right-angled triangle the square on the hypotenuse is equal to the sum of the squares on the other two sides."

("What a wealth of knowledge is unfolding before our awed eyes!" Oliver remarked, sharpening his pencil to an assassin's sharpness. Perhaps he harbored hopes of Mr. Rappaport embracing the fate of St. Cassian of Imola, struck down by his vengeful pupils. It was the kind of thing that kept you going. Every child needed a laudable ambition to spur him onto greater effort.

(Oliver did not, in fact, make use of pencil for his assassination when the time eventually came. He chose to make use of chalk, even more appropriately symbolic for the destruction of a teacher.

(Pedagogicide?

(Would that be the word? It certainly filled a need where Mr. Rappaport was concerned.)

As Mr. Stolley (big-bearded, but quite nice, the first teacher who'd bothered to tell them what his name was) chalked *A*, *B*, and *C* at the three corners of the triangle, with *C* at the right-angled corner ("*A*, *B*, *C*," Oliver hissed, impressed, pointing. "It's virtually *algebra*!") and added *HYPOTENUSE* and *RIGHT ANGLE* *90°*, Ben studied *Pater filium amat*, though – vaguely, at the back of his mind – *HYPOTENUSE* was starting to worry him a little, one of those not-to-be-spoken-most-of-the-time Shakespeare sort of words. The immense lumbering creature disported itself in the muddy shallows at the edge of an African waterhole, its challenging bellowings booming out across the long sunset shadows of the swamps. With the metallic taste of the ink on his lips and tongue, he examined the indelible blue Latin words that were written deep inside him, and not the words on the blackboard in front of him.

He'd already known *pater*.

He had vague memories of Alice playing the schoolmistress when he'd been a very small boy, and saying "*pater*" and "*mater*" when she pointed at framed photographs from the top of the piano, though she hadn't known the word for "sister." It was "*sœur*" in French, she'd said, so it would be something like "*sœur*." "Sororicide" was the murder of a sister, she'd informed him darkly, as if she'd looked it up with a particular purpose in mind. Allegra had been annoying her again. "Paternal" meant father-like. "*Amat*" was like "*amour*," love, one of the French words most likely to get Mrs. Albert Comstock quivering agitatedly, though the nearness of *amour* to *armor* had always disheartened him. Love was threatening and dangerous; you needed to be protected against the threats posed by love. When Dr. Crowninshield had proudly produced "*amas*" and they'd chanted all the words of loving, Ben had – *Click!* – thought of "*amour*." He wished he'd said this to Dr. Crowninshield. It was just the sort of observation that would have given him pleasure. He often thought of things he wished he'd said after a conversation was over.

"*AB* squared equals *AC* squared plus *BC* squared!" chanted Year Naught at the urging of Mr. Stolley. They weren't quite sure what it meant, but chanting it somehow boosted confidence, creating a feeling of uncontroversial unanimity, a four-fours-are-sixteen sense of certainty.

Pater filium amat.

The father loves his son.

An idea began to take shape in Ben's head during that Arithmetic lesson, and it was not just a grasp of the theorem of Pythagoras, appropriately classical though this concept was. In the lessons with Mr. Rappaport that followed – particularly when they moved away from the words of Julius Cæsar after their first year – this idea began to develop further, as more evidence was revealed with each turn of the page in his Latin textbooks.

He began to realize something that had never occurred to him before.

Latin grammar could be – he had the sense of venturing out into a new vocabulary, tentatively trying out a new word for pronunciation – insidiously *psychological*, far more so than any of the so-called sciences. *Pater filium amat* had spoken to something private deep inside him, a sentence waiting to speak just to him. It was true of both the words in Latin, and the words of explaining, words that seemed to explain far more than the meaning of the Latin.

Psychological.

The words in the grammar book began to speak directly to him, both the Latin and the English.

He had always imagined that grammar would be austere and immutable, like the temperature at which water froze or boiled, the capital of Pennsylvania, the height of Mount Washington, or the price of thirty-nine pocket inkstands (their arithmetic books certainly believed in making the subject relevant) costing twelve cents each, but – as the weeks and months and years went by – and the lists and sentences grew down the blackboard, and in his exercise book (scrawled on the blackboard, neat and meticulous in the exercise book), Ben found, more and more, that – ignore it as he tried – emotion crept into the grammar, as he worked his way through the ink-stained textbooks with which they had by then been issued.

Half-consciously, his right hand would creep up the outside of his left arm, and rest upon the black band, trying to hide his symbol of mourning. Even when the time came that he no longer wore the band – it was removed on a calculated day: grief (like pregnancy) had a set period of time in which to come to a natural end (the facts of pregnancy were a recent discovery, bringing about blushes as Brinkman sniggeringly pontificated) – he still found himself automatically performing this gesture, half-forgetting why he did it, his nervousness gone to his hands, as it had with Linnaeus.

Other lessons, other voices.

Year One, Year Two, Year Three, Year Four, Year Five; the same careful, rounded handwriting in his book.

He felt that – with the unchanging handwriting – though he himself changed, grew taller (though he failed to grow tall), his true self, his inner self, was expressed in the way he wrote, and this inner self was changeless, still a boy of ten. This was, perhaps, as it should be, something that would have given rise to a rare nod of approval from Papa. There was always something a little *worrying* about a man with beautiful handwriting, or perfect spelling. This had been Papa's belief. Ben was a poor speller and punctuator. He found a comforting illusion of strength in his frequent misspellings, sought solace in mistakes, as if *"momento"* was a *memento* of manliness. He worried about the little-boy gap between his front teeth, his little-boy looks, his little-boy handwriting, his unbroken voice, the younger brother surrounded and spoiled by sisters. Mr. Rappaport seemed to know this; he seemed to sense the causes of unease, and pounced upon them, loudly proclaiming his discoveries like an explorer unearthing treasure.

(*What have we here?*

(*What's this? What's this?*)

Words came and went on the blackboard, written and then wiped away, written and then wiped away, words that were chanted and chanted again, echoing away into silence day by day, words that remained lodged in the brain like fragments of grapeshot.

Brinkman leaped and leaped with the duster like a Dr. Brown

beset by discordant booms, enveloped in a snowstorm of chalk-dust, but the chalked words were out of reach, and remained there at the top of the blackboard. Other words from other subjects, words and diagrams, came and went, came and went, beneath them: a map of the Holy Land, the bones of the hand, an isosceles triangle (Mr. Stolley – whose wife had her eye on Washington Thoroughgood – was *obsessed* with triangles), seven column grammatical analysis, many subjects came and went, but those words stubbornly remained.

Pater filium amat.

(Of course. That was *always* there.)

Gladius was a sword.

That one was there forever.

Amo, amas, amat.

The words for love incongruously lingered, also.

Dolor.

Disto.

Formosus.

Laetus.

Laevus, Facilis descensus Averno.

Puella, puella, puellam, puellae, puellae, puella.

These words had long been paused over and thought about, particularly the tentative brackets in the translation.

A girl, O girl, a (the) girl, of a (the) girl, to or for a (the) girl, by, with, or *from a (the) girl.*

A girl somehow became *(the) girl* when he was about fourteen, embarrassing though it was to find yourself thinking of girls, whether the girl was *a* or *(the)*. The brackets helped a bit when it came to *(the)* girl, and he tried, sometimes (even in the crowded classroom, *especially* in the crowded classroom sometimes, shutting out all that was around him), to think about *(the) girl*, though it would be some years before he saw Kate Calbraith. Before, that is, he saw Kate Calbraith as being potentially *(the) girl*. He'd seen her many times over many years before she somehow became – potentially (he guarded his feelings carefully) – *(the) girl.*

O girl merged with *(the) girl* when he began to think of Kate Calbraith.

Kate Calbraith.

He'd watch her in All Saints', shutting out the voice of the Reverend Goodchild as he shut out the voice of Mr. Rappaport. He'd watch her particularly when it was her father – not yet totally elbowed out of the church by Sobriety's push-pushing Papa – preaching. It was the way she tried to convey her support to her father, the way she leaned forward, so that the Reverend Calbraith could see that here was someone who loved and supported and believed in him. Her father sometimes seemed to catch her eye, and to be given renewed confidence – his confidence sometimes faltered (not a weakness ever ascribed to the Reverend Goodchild) – his voice growing stronger, more certain, as a result of seeing her there. She was only a little girl then, but it somehow remained in his mind. He wasn't sure whether it was her, or the love she showed for her father, but he didn't forget it.

Kate Calbraith.

Was she *(the) girl?*

The words crowded in around him, the words that were written on the blackboard, and then wiped away. You wondered sometimes why teachers bothered to write words on the blackboard when they were always wiped away.

You wondered how your brain coped.

The words were wiped away and wiped away and wiped away, but the words remained inside you, like metal-tasting swallowed ink.

Defective detective.

Pretty blond boys.

Beauties of the class.

Why are you blushing?

Prettier than ever.

A sense of guilt.

Your pretty friend.

Popular.

These, also – and many more like them – were useful words and phrases for expressing yourself in a foreign language. These, also, were vocabulary lists to be learned and chanted, put into regular use.

7

As they entered the Summer Term, as they moved on into the fall and began their first full year at the academy (still as Year Naught), as they eventually became Year One (*aleph*) – not destined, as they had feared, to be a perpetual Year Naught, after all – and then Year Two, Year Three, Year Four, Year Five, as they stood, as they answered questions, as they chanted, as the chalk dust was wiped down their bodies, as they moved from the Subject on to the Object – *Quem amat? Filium. Who does he love? (His) son* – and on to the Predicate – *Quid agit pater? Amat filium? What is it the father does? He loves his son* – and on into all the complexity of expression held by language, Ben could feel – overpowering in its unexpectedness – the emotion coming over him, as, in the words of a dead language, they spoke of love between a father and his son, the exercises in a Latin grammar book moving him to the edge of tears.

It was always this subject, it seemed, this the subject he always sensed.

What is it the father does?

He loves his son.

Water freezes at 32° Fahrenheit and boils at 212° Fahrenheit.

The capital of Pennsylvania is Harrisburg.

The height of Mount Washington is 6288 feet.

The price of thirty-nine pocket inkstands costing twelve cents each is $4.68.

Go to the inner room.

Go to the inner room.

Go to the inner room.

The inner room was a place without tears, whether of grief or of joy, without any expression of emotion. He'd be safe in the inner room, protectively armored against *amour*. He bowed his head, and the writing in his exercise book became blurred. He was scared that tears would run down his face, and people would see him crying.

The inner room.

The inner room.

The inner room.

Here was a place where he would be safe.

It was very quiet there, a place to which no sound penetrated, and restful on the eyes because there was little light.

He was scared that his tears would fall onto the page, make a mess of his handwriting, and make Mr. Rappaport angry, even though Mr. Rappaport enjoyed seeing tears. He had perfected a technique that never failed to produce them in certain boys, particularly Linnaeus. He went right up to them as they wept, drawn by a delicious scent, the promise of a delicious taste. Perhaps he longed to lean forward, cozy up close, and lick away the tears — shuddering ecstatically — with a long, wet tongue.

A particular memory.

A lesson on a cold day, a lesson like any other, though a part of it had stayed in his mind.

Year Five (*aleph*).

All those years and months and days and hours in Room 37 with Mr. Rappaport.

More a 32° Fahrenheit day than a 212° Fahrenheit day.

Pages rustled quietly in the room as the boys around him consulted the dictionary at the back of the book. They'd had the questioning, and everyone was now seated. Soon, there'd be more questioning, questioning and chanting.

("Why has *proficiscor* no Gerundive Participle?"

(Mr. Rappaport.

("The hours I've spent *agonizing* over that very question."

(Oliver, a muttered aside.)

Random words and phrases leaped out at him as he turned the

pages, seeking to remind himself of the Latin word for "obey." His mind sometimes went blank when Mr. Rappaport demanded an answer now, now, *now*.

When I think how I love you I can hardly believe you are so far away.

That sentence, fortuitous as all such things, seemed to be waiting for him to notice it.

(Mrs. Alexander Diddecott opened the Bible at random to seek for guidance when she was troubled, to find the words that would tell her what to do, the words to ponder.)

He looked at the Latin words above the English translation, grasping rather aimlessly – as he always did – at the words that he thought he recognized, trying to understand the way in which the emotion was being expressed. It was like trying to listen to someone when you couldn't understand what it was that they were trying to say. Oliver dissected as if in Biology; Ben grasped randomly.

Amem.

There was "love."

Credere.

There was "believe," like "credit," like "creed."

Longe . . .

What was *possum* doing in that sentence? He'd suddenly noticed *possum*.

He struggled to make sense of the words.

When I think how I love you I can hardly believe you are so far away.

Oliver's bowed head, the words above him on the blackboard.

Blue.

Blue.

The color of his eyes was everywhere.

When I think how I love you I can hardly believe you are so far away.

Sometimes, the English seemed as remote from understanding as the Latin.

Psychological.

Perhaps it would be better if he didn't look at the words on the pages as he turned them, oppressed by too much to take in at once, but he couldn't stop looking.

O amici, quando ad forum Romanum venietis et monumenta Romae antiquae videbitis?

O friends, when will you come to the Roman forum and see the monuments of ancient Rome?

That wasn't too bad, though it brought to mind words that had been spoken in the schoolroom at Crowninshield's.

The next page was more troubling.

DOUBLE ACCUSATIVE.

Certain words of asking, teaching, concealing, take a Double Accusative.

1. My father taught me letters.

Double Accusative.

2. My mother would have taught me music.

Double Accusative.

3. We have concealed our crimes from our fathers.

Double Accusative.

4. It is very difficult to conceal (one's) faults from a friend.

Double Accusative.

5. We should have called you our father on account of your kindness.

Double Accusative.

In many of the sentences in English, words or groups of words were printed in italics. His lips moved as he whispered these words.

Me letters.

Me music.

Our crimes from our fathers.

Faults from a friend.

You our father.

Double Accusative.

Verbs of asking.

Verbs of teaching.

Verbs of concealing.

Especially verbs of concealing.

(The sense of shame, of eagerly accusing digits, confirmed his belief that Latin Grammar was somehow psychological, saw inside him, knew the way to the inner room, knew the things he'd hidden inside himself, certain words of concealing.

(His father . . .

(His recent feelings . . .

(The things that he was starting to feel . . .

(The things that he'd been feeling for a long time before he realized what it was that he was feeling . . .

(The things that he'd been doing . . .

(For weeks now . . .

(For months . . .

(Winter . . .

(Spring . . .

(Early summer . . .

(Fridays, after school.

("Yes?"

(The question.

("Yes."

(The answer.

(The inner room.

(The inner room.

(The inner room.

("*That* one!" they were saying, doubly accusative, pointing with the index fingers of both hands, like gun dogs in attitudes of alertness sensing game.

("*That* one!"

("*That* one!")

Faintly, he heard Mr. Rappaport's voice – "Are you acquainted with any other form for the Present Subjunctive, Comstock?" – and Oliver's reply: "Well, we haven't actually been formally introduced yet, sir." Comstock, meet Present Subjunctive. Present Subjunctive, meet Comstock.

Somewhere in his exercise book, in his neatest – if still childish – handwriting, spread across a double-page, was a list in three columns. In the first column was the Latin (*miseret me, piget me, pudet me, poenitet me, taedet me*); in the middle column were the literal translations (*it distresses me, it disgusts me, it shames me, it repents me, it offends me*); and in the last column were the final versions (*I am sorry, I am disgusted at, I am ashamed of/I am ashamed at, I regret/I repent, I am wearied at*).

I am sorry.

I am disgusted at.

(His feelings . . .

(His recent feelings . . .

(The things he was doing . . .)

I am ashamed of diagonal I am ashamed at.

I regret diagonal I repent.

The diagonals were there again, the thrusting actions of wounding and killing, the Julius Cæsar technique for ensuring annihilating victories.

First the diagonals, then the subjicating could begin.

I am wearied at.

He began to scan through the dictionary.

Ancient (what has ceased to exist): antiquus . . .

Ancient (what still exists): vetus . . .

The word for which he was seeking was *pareo*.

How could he have forgotten the word for "obey" in Room 37?

He turned back to the *SENTENCES TO BE DONE INTO LATIN*. His back to them, Mr. Rappaport was copying the same twenty sentences onto the blackboard. Every head around him was bowed, no faces visible.

They were studying the Genitive case.

(Oliver's head bowed, his hair hiding the side of his face. He was writing furiously. He was a few desks in front of him, but seemed far away.

(His feelings . . .

(His recent feelings . . .

(November the tenth, last year, Oliver's sixteenth birthday. Was that when he had first started to realize what he ought to have known a long time before then?)

Mr. Rappaport turned around, and caught Ben's eye.

"Stand up, Pinkerton. Read the first two sentences."

"It is the duty of a father to do good to his children," he read. "It is the duty of good children to obey their parents."

This subject.

Always this subject.

Again, words in some of the sentences were printed in italics, and he thought that this meant that these words had to be whispered when the sentences were read aloud. (Whispers for italics; shouts for capitals: that was the rule for reading in class. Ben wanted to do it properly.)

"*The duty of a father*," he whispered, "*the duty of good children.*"

"Is there something wrong with your voice, Pinkerton?"

"No, sir."

"Speak up then, boy. No need to be shy just because your voice hasn't broken *yet*. Don't mumble."

Mr. Rappaport was always commenting on Ben's unbroken voice, the voice that was still unbroken in the very last lesson that he had with him. Not only was he keen on getting his charges chanting, he was himself a chanter, chanting along with Papa in chummy harmony.

Mr. Rappaport had tried to make Ben sing to the class once, to make them laugh.

The words and phrases they chanted, the ones he'd heard so many times.

His voice had become one that whispered. Because of Mr. Rappaport he fell into the habit of always talking quietly, so that his easily mockable small boy's voice (small boy's handwriting, small boy's face and body, small boy's voice) was not so apparent. He never grew out of this habit. People kept having to ask him to repeat what he had just said, because they had not heard him the first time. It was as if he'd been made into someone whose utterances were never heard, or were instantly forgettable, someone perpetually reduced to being a Naught, carrying nothingness about within him. That was what it felt like. Long after Mr. Rappaport had gone, this legacy remained, Ben patiently repeating what he had only just said, as if the Say-it-again, Say-it-*again* chanting had become a habit that would never be broken.

Another lesson.

"Stand up, Pinkerton. Read the next sentence."

"What can be pleasanter than to have a son of beautiful countenance and admirable disposition?" he read, lowering his voice for *of beautiful countenance and admirable disposition* because they were in italics, as if these particular phrases were a cause of coyness.

"'Of beautiful countenance!' 'Admirable disposition!'" Mr. Rappaport shouted, in the same voice he used when coaching from the sideline. "Say it again, Pinkerton."

Squeeze.

"Louder this time."

("*Tackle harder*, boy!" you heard him saying. "You've got a voice like a *girl*, and you're *playing* like a girl!")

Squeeze.

"'Of beautiful countenance.' 'Admirable disposition.'"

"'Of beautiful countenance.' Now, who on earth does that remind me of? Blond hair, blue eyes?"

(*Guffaws.*)

"Could this be a reference to you, Pinkerton, or to your pretty friend?"

(*Guffaws.*)

"I don't know, sir."

"'Admirable disposition.' Ah, no. I've made a mistake. 'Beautiful countenance': a definite yes. 'Admirable disposition': sadly, no. This couldn't possibly be a reference to you after all, could it, Pinkerton, the defective detective, and *certainly* not to your pretty friend?"

Squeeze.

"No, sir."

"Louder, boy."

Squeeze.

"No, sir."

"Why are you grabbing at your arm like that?" Ben still found himself reaching for the top of his left arm, to cover the black band that had not been there for years, to hide a reason for mourning. "Can't you keep your hands off yourself? Like someone else I might mention?"

(*Guaranteed to Delight Any Boy.*)

(It was as if he knew.)

"I don't know, sir."

"Sit down, Pinkerton."

"Yes, sir."

It distresses me.

It disgusts me.

It shames me.

It repents me.

It offends me.

Another lesson.

There was always another lesson.

A Recapitulatory lesson.

"Turn to the exercises at the end of the section. You are to write out in full the declensions . . ."

"I decline," said Oliver, loud and clear.

"What did you just say, Comstock?"

"I do apologize, sir," said Oliver, all sincerity, blond curls wobbling with innocent enthusiasm. No one could be politer than Oliver was when it came to addressing Mr. Rappaport. "I must have been overcome by excitement at your persistent references to my physical charms. It was what is known as a pun. A moment of childishness on my part, an aberration."

"Rather like yourself, Comstock."

"Oh, sir," Oliver replied instantly. "What a saucy thing to say! I've gone all pink."

Mr. Rappaport, as Oliver very well knew, never knew quite how to cope with this sort of comment, and usually chose to ignore it. He quite ignored the taunting possibilities of "gone all pink." A definite aberration this.

"As you're so keen, Comstock, you may decline for us."

"I *accept*! A chance to shine! You won't regret it, sir."

Mr. Rappaport, seeing an opportunity for wit, told Oliver to decline the noun *puella*, the word for "girl."

"You look the sort to decline a girl, Comstock."

(*Guffaws.*)

As Oliver began, with perfect accuracy (this was, after all, Year Naught stuff), to decline *puella*, Ben turned back the pages of his exercise book. *To help the poor and miserable is the mark of a good man.* Oliver was a demon for declensions and conjugations. When Frankie Alloway had still been at the academy, he'd used the second hand of his pocket-watch to time exactly how long it took Oliver – who'd come a long way from *amo, amas, amat* – to rattle through every possible conjugated form of *amo*, all the way from the Present Indicative to the Supine. Ben had forgotten what the record had been. Oliver seemed to do it all on one breath, every word precisely pronounced, not even appearing to flag as he roared into the final straight with – somewhere there, in amongst all the others – *amans* and *amatus* and *amandum* and *amandus* and *amatum*.

"I should be loved," he was saying, "thou wilt be loved, thou wilt have been loved, he will have been loved, I might be loved, I may have been loved, I should have been loved . . ."

Ben hadn't known that love could take so many forms.

("To love" had been the very first verb he'd learned in Latin, and yet what it meant seemed to be perpetually beyond his comprehension, always out of reach in the distance.

(That's what he'd thought.)

Soon, they'd all be chanting the declensions for *puella*.

"*Puella!*" they'd be chorusing.

"*Puella!*"

"*Puellam!*"

"*Puellae!*"

"Puellae!"

"Puella!"

A girl!

The exclamation point somehow seemed more significant when you thought of the word in translation.

O girl!

A (the) girl!

Of a (the) girl!

To or *for a (the) girl!*

By, with, or *from a (the) girl!*

His thoughts returned to *puellam.*

(The) girl.

He tried to think of *(the) girl.*

He tried to think of Kate Calbraith.

He could see her, across the aisle in All Saints', if he leaned forward slightly, shielding his face with the opened pages of his hymnbook. It was as if the church was the only place in which he ever saw her. She was there ahead of him, out of reach, like Oliver in Room 37.

"The summer days are come again . . ."

– the congregation was chanting dolorously, as if they, also, were reciting *puella, puella, puellam* -

". . . Once more the glad earth yields
Her golden wealth of ripening grain . . ."

– puellae, puellae, puella –

". . . And breath of clover fields . . ."

She was too young (much too young) for him to think of her as *(the) girl,* even though he was so young himself, but he began to think of her.

554

He began to think of *(the) girl.*

It wasn't something he could talk about.

It wasn't something he could talk about with *anyone.*

He was walking out on the edge of thin-iced feelings, not pressing down with his full weight.

It was a sunny Sunday morning, and her profile was dark against Elphinstone Dalhousie Barton's bird-crowded stained-glass window of St. Francis of Assisi, as sharp as a cameo.

Deepening shade of summer woods . . .

Glow of summer air . . .

Winging thoughts, and happy moods . . .

He remembered thinking how incongruous it was, to be thinking of summertime, so he must have been having these thoughts in winter. It was difficult to distinguish the seasons in Room 37, a room that was almost perpetually in semidarkness, the windows too high up to be able to see any views of the world outside.

The only views in Room 37 were of the words – the words that were perpetually wiped away – upon the blackboard.

Perhaps it was a memory of the first time that he'd noticed Kate.

Really noticed Kate, the girl becoming *(the) girl.*

Strange feelings . . .

The Use of the Future Perfect in Adverbial Clauses, Phrases Expressing Time, Consonant Stems, Ablative of Instrument and Ablative of Cause – they all had initial capital letters, like the titles of Harry Hollander's songs (in the hushed music room, eyes filled with tears as the haunting words rose into the candlelit dimness, "All things are closed against me, the windows and the doors, / The ablative of instrument and the ablative of cause . . .," and handkerchiefs dabbed discreetly as the tender-hearted fought for control) – Third Declension Nouns, Neuter i-stems, The Verb Sum, Demonstrative Pronouns, Phrases of Motion and Position, Pronominal Declension, Third Conjunction in -io, Ablative Absolute – Mr. Rappaport was absolute for the Ablative – Uses of the Supine, Subjunctive Mood – "I'm in rather a Subjunctive Mood today," Oliver would warn – Adverbial Clause of Purpose,

Imperfect and Pluperfect Subjunctive Active, Interjections, Phrases of Distance and Dimension, Passive, Passive, Passive (these were the regular reminders of the attitude that they were compelled to adopt as Mr. Rappaport zestfully dissected them: they were the Subjects of the Verbs, they were the ones affected by the action of the Verbs), Deponent Verbs, Adverbial Clauses of Result, Indirect Command and Petition, Peculiarities in Nouns, Peculiarities in Verbs — "You'd know all about peculiarities, Comstock, wouldn't you?" "Jolly funny, sir" — Uses of the Infinitive — here was a philosophical speculation to set the imagination soaring, you would have imagined, wrongly — Adverbial Clauses of Concession, Causal and Concessive Adjectival Clauses, The Four Conjunctions, Recapitulatory (this turned up most lessons), Conditional Sentences in Indirect Statement, Copulative Verbs (Mr. Rappaport looked challengingly around the class whenever he wrote this expression on the blackboard, sniffing the air for unauthorized sniggering; in just such a way would Mr. Caswell look as he labeled dubious areas of an animal's anatomy on the blackboard in a Biology lesson, the ends of his arrows tactfully never quite making contact), Constructions Involving the Superlative, Defective Verbs ("You, of all people, will need to pay *particular* attention to these, Pinkerton!"), The Passive of Intransitive Verbs, Expressions of Doubt — plenty of these — Verbs of Fearing — and plenty of these — Verbs of Hindering, Preventing and Forbidding — and even more of these . . .

The words were wiped away and wiped away and wiped away, but the words remained inside you.

The taste of ink.

Blue lips.

Blue tongue.

A drinker of ink.

Have you been sucking Comstock's pen, Pinkerton?

No, sir.

(It was as if he'd known.)

Are you blushing, Pinkerton?

No, sir.

(It was as if he'd known what was going to happen, six years later.)

He couldn't see Kate's face, just its outline. It made her, somehow, seem far away and unattainable, someone he didn't know at all.

(The) girl.

He needed to keep those brackets.

For a little while longer.

(Strange feelings . . .)

Then, what would he do?

It was toward the end of the lesson now, and his left arm was covered in chalk dust. He began to pat at it gently, trying not to make a noise, beginning with the place where the black band had once been. The dust rose around him, caught in a stream of pale light. He tried to remove every last particle from the blackness of his uniform, the traces of Mr. Rappaport, flicking with the tips of his fingers, the fine white powder settling on his shoulder, on his hair.

I should be loved.

Thou wilt be loved.

Thou wilt have been loved.

He will have been loved.

I might be loved.

I may have been loved.

I should have been loved.

He heard the words inside himself, whispering with Oliver's voice.

8

Their first lesson with Mr. Rappaport was on Monday, March 19th, 1888.

Their last lesson with Mr. Rappaport was on Friday, June 15th, 1894.

The sort of thing that had happened in the first lesson happened in the last lesson, and happened in all the lessons in between, sometimes repeatedly.

It was what Latin lessons were like.

Sometimes it was not so bad.

Other times — as in the last lesson — it was far, far worse.

It went on for all the years in which they were aged ten to sixteen. It was what they were there for.

Some things changed.

Frankie Alloway and Hugh Petteys soon left Otsego Lake Academy, vanishing, with no official reasons given for their departures. With Hugh Petteys gone, Ben was now unquestionably the smallest boy in the class, failing to outgrow Charles Bradley. New boys moved in to replace them. But some things remained the same, Latin lessons amongst them. They stopped only when Oliver destroyed Mr. Rappaport on June 15th, 1894, and Ben alone knew how he had done this.

Latin lessons assumed a routine that soon seemed natural, the way things ought to be.

They began with questions, and they ended with chanting.

After the chanting, Mr. Rappaport would use one of them to clean his hands (a contemptuous cleansing of a class that was unworthy of his notice, far, far beneath him), and then — row by row — they'd leave the room.

As soon as they arrived at Room 37 for a lesson, they'd enter — even if Mr. Rappaport was not there — and take up their positions in the places that had been appointed in the second lesson, the positions that were not the same as those they'd had at Crowninshield's.

As promised, they had been placed in their *proper* places.

As promised, things were *properly* organized.

They had to stand, in silence, until he arrived. Sometimes he was late — "Probably disemboweling a twelve-year-old somewhere," was Oliver's explanation after a particularly long wait — but they were not supposed to speak, not allowed to sit. They had to be standing, all ready for questioning. This standing was not just a "Good morning, Mr. Rappaport," or "Good afternoon, Mr.

Rappaport" courtesy, but an essential part of his pleasure in what was to follow. As soon as you had answered a question or command correctly you were allowed to sit down. Sometimes – he was unpredictable in this – it took a number of correct responses before he would indicate that you were allowed to sit.

"To what Declension do U-nouns belong?"

"What is the Declension and Gender of *leo*?"

"Repeat the whole of the Active Voice of the Four Conjugations."

"Decline *vulnus*."

(There was a well-planned trap in this one.)

"Decline *nauta*."

That sort of thing.

At the end of the lesson – and throughout the course of the lesson – there'd be the chanting, the repetitive sound of rote learning, the by-heart memorizing, though *heart* didn't come into it. *Heart* was rigorously avoided.

"Substantives are declined by Number and Case!"

"Adjectives are declined by Gender, Number, and Case!"

"There are three Genders: Masculine, Feminine, and Neuter!"

("You will have considerable problems if you become confused about Gender. As you may have noticed, Comstock."

(*Snigger.*

("Now which one might you be, Comstock? Any suggestions, anyone? Masculine?"

(*Snigger.*

("Feminine?"

(*Snigger.*

("Neuter?"

(*Guffaw.*

("A Clipt Stem is a Stem without its Vowel Character!"

("You'd know all about Clipt Stems, wouldn't you, Finch?"

(*Snigger.*

("What's it like, not having a Vowel Character?"

(*Snigger.*

("What's it like, not having a *Stem*?"

(*Guffaw.*

(Always these comments.

(Always these sniggers and guffaws.

("You'd know all about Anomalous Verbs, wouldn't you, Comstock?"

("*Fero, ferre, tuli,*" Oliver replied cheerfully. "I bear, sir. I endure, sir.")

"There are two Numbers: Singular and Plural!"

(The thought of a future in which there would only ever be two numbers.)

"There are six Cases!"

"There are three Moods!"

(The mood he began to feel in Latin lessons was not Indicative, Subjunctive, or Imperative, though Imperatives featured largely in Mr. Rappaport's teaching methods. Depression was the most usual mood, either that or apprehension.)

These questions, these chants, were from one of the earliest lessons.

There was no time for the niceties of "Tell me," or "Give me." All Mr. Rappaport had time for was the bare bones of demanding, with no time allowed for thinking. If you paused, you were wrong, and you remained standing as the next boy was asked something new. Mr. Rappaport had no time for this "men" business with his pupils. They were *boys* – he used the word with a contempt that almost equaled Papa's pronunciation of *girls* – and mere boys did not impress an undoubted man amongst men. He was the giant in the Lindstrom & Larsson catalogue, positioned in manly posture, and they the prancing puny pygmies beneath his notice, scampering about down at knee-level. He might not have had a beard, but he was coconut-matted with manliness over every square inch of his body. You averted your thoughts from dwelling for too long on the pictures that this brought into your mind. If they lingered in your brain they'd be left deep inside your memory, like a disease-bearing germ introduced into the bloodstream. Mr. Rappaport flexed his square inches as he bent his knees or blew his whistle, and the coconut matting was activated into he-man rustlings. In Sport lessons (in *Latin* lessons, half the time) you expected him to grab a passing boy by the hair on the back of his head – a great handful grasped to give good purchase – and ram his face up into his sweaty, glistening armpit, rubbing it from side to side. "That's what a *man* smells like!" he'd announce triumphantly. Year Two, Year Three, Year Four, Year Five, and they were all still boys, with boys' looks, and boys' handwriting, those of them – that is – who weren't more like *girls*, with Oliver Comstock the girliest of all the girlies. Papa might have traveled beyond this earthly bourne, but he had left his disciple upon earth behind him, and this disciple had been taught well.

"Sit down!" Mr. Rappaport would snap, when he had decided that the right number of questions had been answered correctly – he was no believer in praise (praise, clearly, was a girlie sort of thing) – and the relieved pupil would begin to sit, the next question already being rattled off at the next boy before he'd reached his seat. Up and down he prowled the aisles between the desks, spinning round on his slippery soft soles as he chose the next boy, his finger aimed at him like a loaded weapon. So the lesson continued, boys falling from the sky, fewer and fewer on their feet, until the last person standing - there was always a long, long pause as Mr. Rappaport walked toward him, beginning to take a deep breath - was comprehensively eviscerated for his stupidity. This was the treat Mr. Rappaport designed for himself, the tidbit toward which he roared in hunger. He probably needed a brief lie-down, a period of recuperation before his next lesson, when the same process would start all over again with the next class.

Usually, this part of the lesson might be over within a quarter of an hour or so, and then they would open their textbooks, those of them still in a condition to do so. Sometimes, however, he timed things so that some boys spent the entire lesson on their feet in a state of continual nervousness, to the delight of Brinkman and his lieutenants. There were several lieutenants within weeks, within *days*. Tom Adams, Frank Bradstone - it was a shame about Frank –

and Chas Swartwout soon lined themselves up alongside him. They quickly realized what it was that Mr. Rappaport liked to see and hear. Disappointingly, Brinkman, though not particularly clever – his imbecilic sniggerings demonstrated him for what he was – possessed a reasonably good memory (memory, more than intelligence, took you a long way at Otsego Lake Academy) and was always one of the favored few to be sitting down within the first five minutes, lolling back and vastly entertained by the agonies of the sweating standers. Mr. Rappaport (a living testament to the power of well-chosen words) had made several boys burst into tears, with Linnaeus – always Linnaeus – the preferred choice.

He made Linnaeus wear an apparatus of something like a partial straitjacket – as if he were half mad – tying his left arm across his chest with the extended sleeve, to prevent him from attempting to use his left hand for writing. Mr. Rappaport had probably made it himself in the evening, happy and fulfilled, sewing busily away by the light of an oil lamp, singing "Stitch! Stitch! Stitch!" as his needle glinted, thinking longingly of the day ahead. Mr. Rappaport strapped it onto Linnaeus at the beginning of each lesson – salivating held at bay, you found yourself thinking, solely by the exercise of enormous willpower – and unknotted him at the end.

He tied it tightly.

Knotting, questions, chanting, unknotting.

This was his ritual of control.

Year after year, Linnaeus was made to undergo this ritual, half-bound in every lesson to make him right-handed. It didn't work, of course, but was the source of much pleasure to their teacher. It brought the tears ever closer, an enjoyable by-product of a necessary and beneficial taming. At the end of each lesson, trying not to cry, Linnaeus would rub his left arm, to get the feeling back into it, and Mr. Rappaport would laugh at him. He submitted silently to all that was done to him. It was quite a surprise that Mr. Rappaport hadn't tied down Linnaeus's left arm and – you might as well do a job properly – left leg for the Sport lessons as well. He'd certainly missed a tempting opportunity there.

(Oliver: "If Finch has his arm tied, shouldn't I have a gag, sir? You do say that I talk too much, sir. Wouldn't that be fairer, sir? To *me*, I mean, sir, so that I don't feel overlooked, sir." Pause. "I think there were too many 'sirs' in that last sentence, sir. I've just counted, sir.' Pause. By now, Oliver had worked out that he could say more or less anything to Mr. Rappaport, and get away with it. "You could fasten the knot on the gag quite tightly, sir. If you liked. As tight as a squeeze. I wouldn't mind, sir. Honestly." He made it sound like an enticing treat, which is what it clearly was. You could tell that the prospect appealed to Mr. Rappaport, especially that possibility of fastening a really tight knot. He liked his knots to be tight. You needed long fingernails to be able to untie them, make that first vital tug. If you bit your nails through nervousness – like Linnaeus – you'd remain trapped and tight-knotted in perpetuity, a permanent prisoner of Mr. Rappaport.)

He'd soon given up trying to make Oliver cry – he'd succeeded with Ben, occasions that Ben did not like to recall – even when Oliver's self-proclaimed emergence as an æsthete encouraged him to enthusiastic excesses of taunting. Mr. Rappaport was fascinated by Oliver, couldn't leave him alone, particularly by the time they were in Year Four. He chose his victims lingeringly, with the seductively luxurious leisureliness of a sultan choosing a favorite for the night from his harem.

When they were in Year Five, Mr. Rappaport had been to see a revival of a Gilbert and Sullivan operetta – *Patience* – performed by a traveling company from Chicago. The portrayal of the swoony æsthete Bunthorne – a caricature of Oscar Wilde – had supplied Mr. Rappaport with material that kept him going for ages. (*The Yeoman of the Guard* for Merrill; *Patience* for Comstock.) He'd gone with his *fiancée*, a sniffy-looking brunette in a big bonnet who looked at pupils in the street with undisguised aversion, clearly regarding them as potential rivals in their claims upon the valuable time of her beloved. Big Bonnet clutched her *fiancé* closer to her as schoolboys drew near, alerted by the light catching on the buttons of their uniforms, and scowled. Her bonnet hid most of her face (no bad thing, you felt, capturing glimpses of what lay within) – she stalked about like someone in disguise – but the scowl was fully visible. "Don't talk to him!" was the unmistakable message in the glare, suspecting that eager pupils would besiege their schoolmaster whenever they came across him, desperate for urgent guidance.

"Sir! Sir! What is the rule for determining Nouns of the Masculine Gender of the Third Declension?"

"Sir! Sir! What is the meaning of the terms Causal, Concessive, Final, Temporal, and Dubitative, as applied to Conjunctions?"

(The Reverend Henry Belcher, to stress the importance of Latin, tended to be very free in his use of capital letters. This, in conjunction with the controversially positioned verbs, gave Latin an unexpected – and decidedly confusing – kinship to German. No wonder all those Germanic tribes had jostled to invade Rome. It would have been just like coming home, a place where they could feel free to unloosen their sentences, and plunk their verbs down any old how. You could only do this sort of thing when you felt really relaxed somewhere.)

Big Bonnet's fingers – bony fingers, bony body – clutched tighter at the sound of such racily uninhibited interrogation.

"He's *mine!*" said the glare. "I saw him first! Conjugate elsewhere! Clear off!"

It was as if she knew what was going to happen, long before it did: the acrimoniously ended engagement, the suppressed scandal, and Mr. Rappaport's midterm removal from the school.

This time Oliver had been the one pointing his finger, the one moving more and more slowly as he approached the standing figure beside his desk.

On the Monday morning after he had seen *Patience* – the top of his right arm still aching from Big Bonnet's long-nailed nips (*she'd* soon escape if he ever tried to lash her down, *she'd* get her revenge for all those limb-numbing squeeze-sessions) – Mr. Rappaport entered the classroom humming "Twenty love-sick maidens we." This was when this particular song had entered his repertoire of derision, and they heard it often. As a member of the choir at All Saints' Church — this was where he had met Big Bonnet, catching her eyes during a rehearsal of "Angel of Peace, Thou Hast Wandered Too Long" — he was quite accustomed to singing, and had started to sing songs with satirical intent, when he humorously felt that certain words (particularly of popular songs) held applications to certain pupils. Oliver was a favorite choice for these attentions, and was so again on this Monday morning.

> "Twenty love-sick maidens we,
> Love-sick all against our will . . ."

— he began (not even a "What are the Imperative and Infinitive Moods of *punio?*," not even a "Conjugate the Passive of *terreo*"), looking across at Oliver as he stood at his desk with his usual air of keen politeness, third in from the window on the front row. This had always been his position since Mr. Rappaport had assigned them their places in their second Latin lesson. Oliver was *always* placed on the front row; you felt that Mr. Rappaport liked to position him within reach —

> ". . . Twenty years hence we shall be
> Twenty love-sick maidens still.
> Twenty love-sick maidens we,
> And we die for love of thee . . ."

— Brinkman and his lieutenants got their guffaws in early, though most of the class stood poised to decline or conjugate. They were used to this sort of thing by now from Mr. Rappaport —

> ". . . Love feeds on hope, they say, or love will die —
> Ah, miserie!
> Yet my love lives, although no hope have I!
> Ah, miserie! . . ."

Mr. Rappaport was — you could tell — conscious of feeling greatly daring at singing these words, expressing such sentiments. It required — he no doubt felt — a certain manly confidence to carry it off without risk of misunderstanding, and he employed his most athletic gymnasium poses and deepest voice. You had to do it in this manner to prevent potential embarrassment or misinterpretation.

He was not altogether successful in achieving this.

("*Gosh* sir!" from Oliver. "You've brought a blush to the cheek of the Young Person.")

(Slight pause from Mr. Rappaport.)

(Then the performance continued. The poses were more virile and muscle-straining than ever, the voice even deeper. It was his "Hit-him-harder!" voice, his "Aim-for-his-chin!" voice, his "Kick-him-where-it-hurts!" voice. Sportsmanship took second place to winning where Mr. Rappaport was concerned. He would willingly have equipped the school football team with shotguns if it had helped with scoring. Desperate measures were required for a team as poor as they were.)

Whissssh!

Mr. Rappaport spun on his silent soles.

His finger pointed at Oliver, as if about to demand, "Decline *tres pueri.*"

"Who is the gentleman with the long hair?"

That, in fact, was what he inquired.

Brinkman, who had been taken to *Patience* by his cousin Euphemia's parents (though he wouldn't have admitted it to anyone), knew what to say. He recognized the question that had been spoken by the Duke of Dunstable. So, for that matter, did Oliver, who had gone with his mama and his sister Myrtle. He knew exactly what was going to happen.

"I don't know," Brinkman said, quoting the next line, Colonel Calverley's reply.

(Not even a "sir"!

(The majority of the class were baffled by Brinkman's answer, and by its dangerously unceremonious form.)

"He seems popular!" Mr. Rappaport continued, delighted to have found fertile ground.

"He *does* seem popular!" Brinkman added, his useful memory leading him onward to yet another triumph, one unconnected — this time — with the world of conjugations and declensions. Brinkman's star ascended ever upward, and Adams, Bradstone, and Swartwout (Three Unwise Men, but following the star) — though they didn't understand a word of what had just been said — sensed what was required, and guffawed appreciatively. Uncomprehending repetition was one of the skills that they had been taught in Latin.

Baffling though this exchange was to the rest of the class, Mr. Rappaport worked assiduously to create a usage, loading every rift of "popular" with smutty innuendo. (First it had been "musical," then it had been "friendly," and now it was "popular." Papa had shown him the way, and now he was perfecting the technique that had been demonstrated to him.)

"Blond, curly hair . . ." he'd begin — at least Ben had been spared curls (part of him was glad that Oliver had curls) — ". . . and those pretty blue, blue eyes. Comstock must be the most *popular* boy in the class."

(And part of him was glad that it was Oliver who was picked on most. Ben was about third in the picking-on order because Mr. Rappaport liked to see a blush at regular intervals. Linnaeus was second favorite. Pertness, then sobs, then blushes: this was the order of preference when Mr. Rappaport was amusing himself after a fierce translation session.

(Translations between English and Latin were not the only translations that were required if you were studying Mr. Rappaport's behavior.

(Oliver had soon sensed that.)

Mr. Rappaport drew closer to Oliver, pausing before him with the air of a bashful suitor.

"They all prefer this melancholy literary man," he commented, adding, "Do you despise female clay, Comstock?"

Mr. Rappaport leaned in across the front of Oliver's desk, resting his hands on either side of it. Oliver looked back at him, all polite attention. Their faces were about six inches apart.

"You're uncharacteristically subdued," Mr. Rappaport remarked to Oliver, rather sulky and disappointed, drawing the attention of the class to a failing.

"I'm demonstrating my *Patience*, sir."

"Most amusing."

"There is a strange magic in this love of ours," Oliver continued, the really nice smile at full power. Mr. Rappaport's knowing smile tightened slightly. "I, the very cynosure of your eyes and heart, remain icy insensible. Do you droop despairingly, sir? Are you soulfully intense, sir? Are you limp . . ."

There was enough of a considered pause here – unusual for Oliver to hint coyly at unspeakable mucky things (he usually came right out with them, finding them perfectly speakable, *relishing* the speaking of them) – for Swartwout to snigger dirtily. All he'd recognized was the possibility of a filthy meaning – *limp!* – quite missing the point that it was Oliver who had said it, and not Rappaport. Brinkman would have words with Swartwout later. Sniggers and guffaws – the louder the better – were to be strictly restricted as reactions to things that were spoken by *Rappaport*, especially things that were said to mock Comstock, Finch, or Pinkerton.

". . . and do you cling, sir?"

Mr. Rappaport attempted an amused chuckle.

"You're really *precious*, aren't you, Comstock?"

"Oh, sir. What a sweet thing to say. Amongst us chaps you're widely regarded as something of a pearl of great price yourself. I think that was the expression employed. 'Pearl' definitely came into it. I *think* 'pearl' came into it, some nuanced hint of a pearly gleam."

"'Precious' is a word with more than one meaning, Comstock, and not all of them are complimentary."

Oliver contrived to give the impression that this came as a revelation to him.

"*Really*, sir?"

Another spasm of effortful amusement.

"I presume that your poetic effusions are the words of Gilbert and Sullivan?"

"Of Gilbert actually, sir. Sullivan tended to concentrate on the musical side of things, as I assumed you'd have known. An agreeable blend of two complementary talents. Finch's sister is a tremendous enthusiast for the works of Mr. W. S. Gilbert and Sir Arthur Sullivan, sir. She's just like Bradley with the Bible, sir. Many a time we've sung along together. Quite harmonious. Much favorable comment."

"*Most* amusing."

A strange expression came across Mr. Rappaport's face, even as he spoke those words. He'd attempted to sniff at the same time as he'd said the word "amusing," and the sniff rather disintegrated his pronunciation. After he'd finally managed "amusing," he sniffed again, more comprehensively.

"I don't think much of your new perfume, Comstock."

"Alas, sir, it's carbolized petroleum, a treatment for a rather . . ." — he lowered his voice, but kept it loud enough so that everyone could hear him — ". . . *personal* complaint."

You wouldn't have realized that what he was referring to was a sprained ankle. This was the very sort of thing that soon had Mr. Rappaport grunting, off and away in pursuit of gleeful guffaws. This was just what he liked.

(Oo!

(Oo!

(*Oo!*)

"Could there be hidden horrors lurking beneath your clothing, a hideousness to rival Stoddard's spotty botty?" he inquired of the class, hopeful of graphic details. "What fun we'll have!"

Encouraging guffaw from Brinkman.

"Are your peach-like contours marred by unpleasant carbuncles, Comstock?"

Swartwout joined in quickly with the guffawing, eager to

demonstrate that his response to "limp" had been a momentary lapse in concentration. Too much laughing at "limp," and he'd be limping when Brinkman got hold of him, limping along with Comstock. Comstock had been the one limping when he'd come into the academy that morning, he'd been the one clinging to the wall to remain upright. No one had offered to help him, chummily supporting him, arms around each other's shoulders, synchronizing their steps. Who on earth would risk doing that with *Comstock?*

"Shall we be rearing back with revulsion when you expose your pustuled personage in Sport? Not very *sporting* of you to have us all recoiling, is it? Not much of an advertisement for Griswold's Discovery, are you, Comstock, bearing Unseemly Imperfections Of The Skin upon your body?"

Mr. Rappaport seemed to use "Comstock" a lot when he spoke to Oliver, almost as often as Oliver used "sir" when he spoke to him. Mr. Rappaport was like a lover repeating the name of his beloved to himself when they were far apart, so that he could feel closer.

"But there is nothing unseemly upon my body, sir. My body is perfection, sir, as I'm sure you've noticed on numerous occasions. I've not been unaware of those shy, lingering glances in my direction when I've cast my garments from me, clad in naught but Nature's garb. My right elbow has a fascination that few can resist. That was a quotation from *The Mikado*, as I'm sure you will appreciate, sir. Miss Finch greatly prefers *The Mikado* to *Patience*, and I am at one with her on this."

(*Squeeze.*

(That was what Ben found himself thinking.

(*Harder squeeze.*)

Oliver raised his left leg up toward Mr. Rappaport, and indicated his ankle. There was a distinct air of seductiveness. He had grown quite tall by now, and his leg extended right across the aisle to Adams's desk. "I was once known as Oliver of the slim ankles, in the vanished days of my youth. My left ankle, in particular, was —

and still is — held in high regard. People come miles to see it. It is a miracle of loveliness (more *Mikado* here, you'll have noticed, sir), though — I regret to say — a little damaged at the moment. I'd wiggle it about a bit to illustrate its appeal, but I fear I'd swoon with the agony. *Here* is the source of the displeasing aroma that sullies your sniffing nostrils, sir. A dramatic domestic accident shattered the Sunday afternoon quietude in Hampshire Square. I damaged my slim left ankle in kicking an unsatisfactory servant. Dr. Twemlow was hastily summoned. By sheer effort of will, I survived."

He tugged his trouser leg up slowly, with the air of one of the shameless hussy dancing girls at Papa Brinkman's club smolderingly inching off her first glove.

(Tits.

(Garters.

(Feathers.

(Ankles.

(You shouldn't forget the allure of ankles.

(Socks.

(After ankles, it was socks.)

Oliver began to peel down his sock. He'd be lingeringly unwinding the bandage next, an Egyptologist discovering the erotic excitement of releasing a mummy from bondage.

"Would you like a closer sniff, sir? Carbolized petroleum. Very arousing."

Oliver placed the heel of his boot on the edge of Adams's desk. There was a certain sense of Mr. Rappaport being prevented from leaving, an escape route down the aisle blocked. A sense of a model posing for a life class, an unclothed body stretching out languorously across a *chaise longue*.

(The man's hand pressed down on the face of the boy, covering his features completely.

(Only his naked body could be seen, and Ben averted his eyes.)

"Feel free to inhale, sir. You can bend as close as you like."

Adams assumed an expression of manly disgust, and edged away to a slightly safer distance, as Oliver – thumbs and index fingers neatly extended – grasped the loose ends of the bow that fastened the bandage.

Ben began to wonder if Oliver had been drinking again. He'd been slightly drunk in lessons several times before.

"Twenty love-sick maidens we,
Love-sick all against our will . . ."

Mr. Rappaport again began to sing the song with which he'd begun the lesson, eager to encourage an unwinding, but – like one fighting a powerful urge to temptation – Oliver (*No! I mustn't do this! I mustn't! I mustn't!*) slowly released the bandage, reluctantly (or so it appeared) rolled his sock back up, and replaced his leg beneath the desk.

"Go, breaking heart . . ."

– Oliver sang –

". . . Go, dream of love requited . . ."

"But who is the gentleman with the long hair?" Brinkman repeated, thinking that Oliver had hogged the limelight for long enough.

"I don't know." Swartwout. (It had seemed to go down well when Brinkman said it to Rappaport. It seemed to go down well all over again. This was something that would bear repetition.)

"He seems popular!" Adams.

"He *does* seem popular!" Bradstone. Through frequent practice, they'd developed a barbershop quartet closeness in their responses.

Brinkman and his lieutenants soon got the message. They'd been given their lines, and now they used them. They'd been loaded, and now they fired.

"But who is the gentleman with the long hair?" one would call out in a voice full of meaning.

"I don't know," another of them would add.

"He seems popular!"

"He *does* seem popular!"

"*Popular!*" they'd call after Oliver. "Comstock, the most *popular* boy in the class! *Popular, popular* Comstock!"

"Oo!"

"Oo!"

"*Oo!*"

Oliver contrived to look gratified.

"It's very kind of you to say so, Brinkman. That's something that no one would *ever* say about you."

Brinkman claimed to be delighted by this latter fact, but Oliver resolutely failed to recognize any meaning for the word "popular" but the usual one. He would allow Mr. Rappaport no definitions in *his* dictionary.

Most of the time it wasn't Brinkman, Adams, Bradstone, and Swartwout that you had to be most wary of.

Most of the time it was Mr. Rappaport.

There were undoubtedly dangers involved in being an æsthete, quite apart from the effect upon Mr. Rappaport. Oliver had pointed out an alarming detail in Chapter XI of *The Picture of Dorian Gray* after he had first read it, with the air of someone spotting an intriguing possibility. He tended to refer to the novel as *The Portrait of Dorian Gray*, claiming to be confused by a Henry James novel with a similar title, and no one knew what on earth he was talking about. "Listen to this, chaps!" he'd said, sounding undaunted, and they'd gathered – rather keen – to see what he'd found in the dirty book (they'd all *heard* about Dorian Gray; the Reverend Goodchild had nearly fallen down all eighteen steps out of his pulpit, he'd been so emphatic in his denunciation), as he read from it with thrilling emphasis. It made a pleasant change, and made them feel rather daring and chap-like. It was usually Brinkman who produced all the dirty books. "*He* – that's Dorian Gray – *was very nearly black-balled at a West End club.*" This Fearful Fate (far more Fearful even than the Fate for foul-mouthed teachers) – announced not long before Brinkman, even more Fearfully (you couldn't help laughing, her-her-her), was black-and-blue-balled – shocked them agreeably, and they paused a while in shuddering silence to contemplate the thought of what was clearly some particularly humiliating initiation ceremony that had to be undergone by trainee æsthetes, the sort of thing that happened to some young apprentices – coopers, for instance (he'd some vague memory about coopers: no wonder James Fenimore Cooper had sought solace in literature, and fled into those trackless forests) – to mark their emergence as one of those at long-last recognized as fully trained, one of those finally conversant with all the mysteries of his craft. To become fully qualified for sunflowers and lilies and dados and peacock feathers and blue and white china you had to submit yourself to something *really* embarrassing that involved boot polish.

In a club.

With everyone staring.

(That thought of having his nakedness exposed to others, that thought that had long tormented Ben. He didn't like to imagine this inner-room fearfulness, afraid to work out why this thought so preyed upon his mind.)

This West End club sounded remarkably like the club of which Brinkman's papa was a member (if you could believe half the stories that he told about it), with a virtually identical choice of entertainment on offer for its baying hordes of well-soused cigar-sucking men. There wasn't much that was tender about this area of the Tenderloin. Boot-polish – even though the very thought of it made them shudder – seemed an appropriate choice of material for a profession that placed such store on immaculate personal grooming.

They shifted uncomfortably, visualizing the sort of thing that would be involved. It was even worse than becoming a Mason! Brinkman, Adams, Bradstone, and Swartwout would be there at the beginning of a Sport lesson, tugging at buttons, whooping, stripping their squirming chosen victim into Sport lesson *déshabillé*, thrusting their knees into his chest with a forcefulness that stifled shouts, several Number 2 large size cans of *Le Sans Rival* French blacking ($1.40 per dozen) – lids already removed in readiness, contents gleaming darkly – positioned conveniently to hand across the closed lid of the broken piano. Gleefully – *Snigger! Snigger! Snigger!* – they'd have invested $2.80 in this unrivalled feast of fun. (*Sans Rival*: no language but French would suffice to plumb the depths of depravity when Dorian Gray and black-balling were involved.) Two dozen cans would guarantee complete satisfaction. All the areas gently nurtured beneath vests and drawers would be transformed to a minstrel show blackness. There Brinkman and his chums would be, scooping up huge dollops in their fingers like Frank Stoddard applying spot cream. "This blacking, of superior quality, is recommended to all our customers desirous of preserving the strength and elegance of their boots and shoes and balls," they'd chant with Latin lesson irregular verb vigorousness, dragging down drawers and getting busily to work. Dorian wouldn't be Gray for much longer, as the blacking was generously applied to the not-so-private parts from squelchily well-filled palms. Their victim's head would be jammed up against the hard and soft pedals, implements carefully positioned to be a refinement of the torture. Bradley's boots – with their neatly balled socks – would be kicked to one side, and his folded shirt and jacket would be strewn down and crumpled beneath the writhing body. Why lament the quite deplorable lack of organized bounce-against-the-ceiling blanket-tossing, or the cozy glow, the appetizing smell, of fellow pupils being slowly roasted in front of roaring fires when this sort of activity was readily available? (Otsego Lake Academy had failed to supply the delights that were on offer in *Tom Brown's Schooldays*. You felt like demanding a reduction in fees: that was Oliver's opinion. Otsego Lake Academy didn't even *possess* any roaring fires. Pneumonia was good for them, and toughened them up.) This was *much* more enjoyable. This was to be a minstrel show for the most sniggersome of private audiences, a minstrel show of the sort that would certainly receive a standing (or as near as they could manage) ovation at Papa Brinkman's club when tits and feathers and garters palled. It certainly went down well when auditioned in front of Mr. Rappaport. "You've missed a bit, there," he helpfully indicated, between manly chortles at the healthy chappishness of his young chums. They really enjoyed it when they did this sort of thing to Linnaeus. They were certainly *sans rival* when it came to humiliation and unhappiness, these minstrel-show molesters singing "Old Black Joe."

There'd they be, rubbing in the blacking gleefully, like four demented Aladdins getting to work on the lamp as their wishes were granted. It was after one such occasion – the day of the love-sick serenading – that the metal-tipped rope had shot across the room during lunch and nearly emasculated Brinkman, and it had given Oliver *particular* pleasure to be able to comment that he'd been well and truly black-and-blue-balled.

You'd have expected Oliver's æsthetically indicating, well-manicured forefinger to have been trembling at the horrors to come revealed in *The Picture of Dorian Gray*, but – just as fearless as he had been at the prospect of being tossed up to the ceiling in blankets or being roasted in front of well-stoked fires (and what a disappointment *they'd* turned out to be!) – he seemed distinctly enthusiastic to embrace whatever experiences life chose to offer him. It must have been at this time – it was toward the end of October – that he had pointed out to them that he had the same birthday as Dorian Gray, November the tenth. You might have thought that he'd said this to refresh their memories, nudging them into an awareness of the acceptability of gifts in two weeks' time – something æsthetically parceled, the color of the string contrasting nicely with the chosen paper – but his main motivation had been to claim a pleasurable kinship with the intriguingly corrupt and sinful Dorian.

Some dissections took place with Mr. Caswell in the Biology laboratory; other, messier dissections, took place during Latin, with words instead of scalpels.

Juvenal had nothing on Mr. Rappaport, once Mr. Rappaport was in the mood, and he was always in the mood. Enthusiasm was ever the attribute of the outstanding schoolmaster. Oliver regularly gave incorrect answers deliberately so that he could continue his verbal clashes with Mr. Rappaport – Oliver was always impeccably polite – for as long as possible. Time and time again Mr. Rappaport seemed to court this outcome. He had even been known to claim that Oliver had answered a question incorrectly when he had not done so. A burst of sobbing from Linnaeus, a spirited spat with Oliver, and Mr. Rappaport was as near as he'd ever be to being a fulfilled and happy man.

Once, when Linnaeus had yet again been reduced to weeping, Oliver's hand had risen with its unfailing air of excited eagerness.

"*Sir!*"

Mr. Rappaport had moved past the stage of "No questions, Comstock," and now he almost always responded when Oliver did this, with a casual air that did not disguise his eagerness.

"*Sir!*"

There were generally two or three *Sir!*s before Mr. Rappaport deigned to come across the room. He was probably pausing a moment to organize the witty ripostes he'd been practicing the night before. He always stood alongside a boy as he questioned him, sniffing the whiff of fear like a connoisseur at a wine-tasting. (That was what Oliver said, though – surrounded by an atmosphere of *Eau de Cologne* – he remained resolutely whiffless. The interlude with the carbolized petroleum had been uncharacteristic of him.)

"What is it, Comstock?"

"Sir, I hope the rest of the class is as impressed as I am by your imaginative attempts to bring your subject alive for us by re-creating the thrilling atmosphere of the Roman amphitheatre in your lessons. Do you think Mr. Caswell would allow us to carry the tiger through from his lab to add to the authenticity? I know that it's stuffed, sir, but judiciously positioned pupils could activate it into movement. Mama would be perfectly happy to supply bunches of grapes for Brinkman to nibble on during the gladiatorial combats."

"Very amusing, Comstock."

"It was a perfectly serious suggestion, sir. I myself will volunteer to play the part of a *retiarius* in the arena. I have already armed myself with a trident and one of Mama's hairnets in readiness."

"Are you positive that it's not one of your *own* hairnets, Comstock?"

(This was about the level.)

For a while, Brinkman and his friends amused themselves by adding the word "hairnet" to their vocabulary of taunting. Many of the words were short, and there was not a lot of them (they included "Little Lord Fauntleroy," "Dorian Gray," "Olivia," and "Oscar Wilde," as well as "popular": Mr. Rappaport was not a man overtroubled by imagination), but they were taught as conscientiously as — and with considerably more enthusiasm than — the Latin was taught. Mr. Caswell listened. Mr. Caswell made notes. Mr. Caswell remembered. Perhaps the use of "Olivia" showed that Oliver's ambitions to become George Arthur in *Tom Brown's Schooldays* had been achieved at last, as — the very thing Tom Brown feared would happen with George Arthur — he was always getting laughed at, and called by some derogatory female nickname. The words hurtled like weapons down the echoing corridors, interspersed with the occasional chants of "Vorhees a jolly good fellow!" and "And so say all of us!" (particularly after a lesson in which Linnaeus had been crying), or — Ben heard these a lot — "Defective detective" and (especially: it contained unspecified dubious undertones) "Pinkie!" He had always imagined that he would be mocked because of his first names, but it was his surname — Pinkerton — that was seized upon, and this hurt more because it was not just his name, but also the name of his mother and his sisters. "Pinkie! Pinkie! Beautiful! Beautiful! *Bee-oo-tiful!* Oo! Oo! *Oo!* "

They thrust their hands down the front of their trousers, and pushed their little fingers out between the buttons, wiggling them like a new obscene gesture, the tiny writhing member held against the groin.

9

Double Accusative.

My father taught me letters.

My mother would have taught me music.

We have concealed our crimes from our fathers.

It is very difficult to conceal (one's) faults from a friend.

Verbs of asking.

Verbs of teaching.

Verbs of concealing.

I am sorry.

I am disgusted at.

I am ashamed of diagonal I am ashamed at.

I regret diagonal I repent.

I am wearied at.

What can be pleasanter than to have a son of beautiful countenance and admirable disposition?

Have you been sucking Comstock's pen, Pinkerton?

Are you blushing, Pinkerton?

Perhaps it was just as well that Papa had died . . .

(Had killed himself.)

. . . because if Papa hadn't killed himself, then Ben could have been the one who'd been the killer. He could have killed him without the need to touch him (he'd always shrunk from this, whether his hands were arid or sweating), without the need to employ any instruments of harming. All that it would have taken would have been words, if the right words had been chosen to speak to him, his father's own weapons deployed against him. Ben could have experienced his own brief taste of godlike power.

Not sticks being used for beating.

Not stones being cast, though he was not without sin.

(He did not allow his mind to dwell on the thought of his sinfulness.)

Words.

"Papa . . ."

(The words were difficult to think, *impossible* to speak.)

"Papa, I think that I'm in love with Oliver Comstock."

Those words.

For a time, he'd thought that they were true.

For a time, he'd thought that what had happened in those weeks and months (that winter, that spring, that early summer) had meant something.

He'd wanted to know what love felt like.

He'd wanted to experience that feeling.

They'd be enough to do it, the shock sending Papa – purple-faced and choking – plunging to the floor with a crash. If Papa had lived for six more years, Ben could have chosen the day on which to kill him with words.

I think I'm in love.

Ben had tried to work out how this had happened, this unlooked-for thing, the moment when he'd realized.

He often did this, lying in bed at night, hearing the words he'd heard, seeing what he'd seen, moving on a little further each time, making it happen again. It was like recalling the stages of a journey, picking out the landmarks as a way of remembering how he'd found his way there.

November 10th, 1893.

Oliver's sixteenth birthday party.

It had seemed like a beginning, but the final stages of the journey had started then.

The Picture of Dorian Gray.

The Three Shocking Sentences.

The only way to get rid of a temptation is to yield to it.

(A lie.

(He knew that now.

(Yielding to a temptation made that temptation stronger.)

What is it that one was taught to say in one's boyhood?

Lead us not into temptation.

Forgive us our sins.

Wash away our iniquities.

Oliver, singing in the music room, surrounded by a crowd of Dorian Grays – the boarding school boys, that's how he'd thought of them – endless reflections of a mirror facing a mirror.

> *But youth, of course, must have its fling,*
>> *So pardon us,*
>> *So pardon us,*
> *And don't, in girlhood's happy spring,*
>> *Be hard on us,*
>> *Be hard on us,*
> *If we're inclined to dance and sing.*
>> *Tra la la, tra la la . . .*

A drape drawn partially across a window-seat.

> *Then buy of your Butterfly – dear Little Butterfly;*
> *Sailors should never be shy . . .*

Sss! Sss!
   (Flare-of-a-match sound.)
   Flutter, flutter.
   Come on, Butterfly.
   Fly for the flame.
   This way.
   This way.
   Shall I light some more matches?
   The laws against flirting are excessively severe.
   Come to my arms, my beamish boy!
   But we are quite alone, and nobody can see us.
   I'm not being too subtle for you, am I?
   (A little further along the way.)
   A voice calling out to him on a day of snow.
   A figure on the edge of the cast light.
   Fare thee well, attractive stranger.
   Call me, and I'll come to thee!

Would you like me to help?
I'm a devil with irregular verbs.
Yes?
Yes?
Shall we tackle Tacitus?
I'm inclined to dance and sing.

A figure dancing down into the darkness at the edge of a frozen lake, singing.

The swooping, circling figure on the ice, the what-do-you-think? display of skill.

Swisssh!
Swisssh!
Swisssh!
Come on, Hans Brinker!

A hidden face.

Voices echoing across the ice.

Oliver had skated across the frozen lake, dragging Ben along behind him using his muffler as a towrope. Ben had crouched down, his eyes closed, feeling the spray of the shaved ice freezing his face and the whole of the front of his body, enclosing him in a frozen carapace.

He had tried not to think of what might follow when they reached Oliver's house.

It was what he wished for, and it was what he feared.

(He cried sometimes when he was alone at home, completely alone: no mother, no sisters, no servants. These times were few; the opportunities for weeping had to be seized and made use of, and he planned them carefully, hiding himself away in Papa's dressing room, the inner room, where the clothing of the dead man still hung around him, swaying on its hangers, brushing against his face and shoulders. Even though he was alone, he never cried aloud, suppressing the sounds of sobbing so that it became like something unacknowledged even to himself. He huddled in, nursing his hurt, his hands pressed to his eyes in an attempt to stem the flow of water that seeped between his shaking fingers. The whole of him shook, though he struggled to be still.

(*Thou boy of tears.*

(That was what Tullus Aufidius had called Coriolanus, and the words had enraged him more than anything else that was ever said to him.

(Oliver had shown him the words on the page when he'd asked him how Coriolanus had died.

(*Name not the god, thou boy of tears!*

(Tullus Aufidius had said this, just before he'd killed him, just before *Kill, kill, kill, kill, kill him!*, just before he'd stood on top of him when he'd fallen.

(When Ben thought of *Coriolanus*, he sometimes thought of the words *I will go wash: / And when my face is fair, you shall perceive / Whether I blush, or no*; sometimes he thought of the words *When blows have made me stay, I fled from words*; or *It is a part / That I shall blush in acting*; or *I'll run away till I am bigger, but then I'll fight*, and all these words brought him comfort. At the age of sixteen Coriolanus had fought like a hero in the battle against Tarquin, and was the best man in the field, this boy who blushed.

(There was no comfort at all in *Name not the god, thou boy of tears!*

(At the age of sixteen Ben wept like a girl, alone in his dead father's dressing room.

("Name not the god!" he whispered to himself sometimes when he tried to pray, when he tried to seek for guidance in the way his mama had shown him. "Name not the god!" It was shameful to bring God into such things, such thoughts. That was what he felt.

(*Boy of tears.*

(Shameful.

(Much of the crying was because of his father, things said and things unsaid, and much – a more secret much – was because of other things, things he did not like to think about or name . . .

(Things about himself . . .

(Things that he wished were otherwise . . .

(More as they ought to be . . .

(That vague sense of wrongness, like his tendency to fainting . . .

(If he didn't smile much, if he rarely spoke, he could hide it, just like he hid the little-boy gap between his top two teeth by the very same methods. Not speaking was an important part of the rôle he found himself playing. If he kept silent no one would hear his little-boy voice, the still unbroken embarrassing fluting.)

Swisssh!

Swisssh!

Swisssh!

He lost all feeling in his hands and face, dragged along in the darkness.

A little further, and they'd be there.

A little further.

(A little further.)

Springtime . . .

The residents' garden in Hampshire Square.

The other things that had happened.

Can't you spell "kisses"? Is it a word you don't see very often?

Yes?

Yes?

Yes?

(Oliver, amused, teasing, insistent.)

Yes.

(Ben speaking the words that would kill.)

I'm rather hoping that one thing might lead to another.

(Oliver.)

He stopped himself from thinking much beyond this point.

(*I am disgusted at.*

(*I am ashamed of diagonal I am ashamed at.*

(*I regret diagonal I repent.*)

He stopped himself from remembering what happened next, though he'd said yes.

The Latin lessons.

The kissing lessons.

The . . .

The "irregular verbs."

The whole journey was no more than that from the winter to the early summer in a single year, though it had started years earlier. The actual setting out on a journey is often more of an end to something than a beginning, he had realized that.

("I've met a girl . . ."

(That was what it had been like for Charlie Whitefoord.

("I've met a girl . . ."

(He had been glowing, his eyes bright.

(You could sense it around him, like an aura, and that was what had made Ben scared for a while, the thought that it would show, that people would look at him and know.

(That people would be able to tell)

Had you noticed?

(that he was in love.)

Amo.

That was what he was thinking.

Amo.

Amo.

I love.

I love.

I love.

Page six.

Latin for Schoolboys.

Papa would have noticed.

Papa would have been watching.

Papa was always there and was always watching, and everything that Ben did was witnessed, even if he couldn't see the watcher.

"Papa, I think . . ."

The diffidence, the use of that "think" was nothing at all to do with Oliver. He was, for a time, absolutely certain that he felt something strongly. His diffidence lay in the word "love." That was the word in which he had no confidence, the word he felt he had no right to use, to identify as something experienced by himself. Falling in love was the moment of realizing something that you'd known all the time: was that what it was? The words were words he could never have brought himself to speak to his Papa, even if a death had been assured. That death – he had to acknowledge – might very well have been his own. He would have died if those words had been spoken, and overheard, burning away with disgust and self-loathing at having made such a humiliating confession. He knew that it was something that he would never be able to talk about. Even to think about it, to hold it within himself, was painful. He couldn't even have spoken the words to Oliver. They expressed the most secret thing about himself, the most hidden and shame-ful – the thought of pointing fingers, sniggering whispered words, terrified him – unless the most shameful thing of all about himself was that his father hadn't loved him, had found nothing in him about which he might be proud. Papa had pointed his finger, and Papa had sniggered, but he hadn't whispered the words that he'd spoken. He'd spoken them loudly and clearly – and repeatedly – so that no one would miss them.

Everyone knew what Papa had thought about him.

Perhaps he'd already known, known before he'd known himself.

It was the thought of being held.

It was the thought of someone else's arms around him, someone touching him.

That was why he'd said yes.

What would love feel like?

He'd thought that it was love.

10

It was their last lesson with Mr. Rappaport, though none of them – including Mr. Rappaport – knew this. It was the day on which Oliver destroyed him, the day on which Oliver had been the one pointing his finger, the one moving more and more slowly as he approached the standing figure beside his desk, a living embodiment of the Accusative Singular.

It was Friday, June 15th, 1894.

Their last lesson with Mr. Rappaport, their last lesson of the day.

It was a day on which Mr. Rappaport had reduced Linnaeus to helpless sobbing on an unprecedented scale. He'd already been on at him in Sport earlier in the day, the lesson just before lunch. Now it was the smell of their sweat that lingered in the air throughout lunch, and that hung around them throughout the hour and a half of Latin in the afternoon. As they waited for the bells to ring and release them, free from Latin and Sport, free from another week of Otsego Lake Academy, they felt — breathless, sweating — that they were reaching the final stages of a race.

Linnaeus fell to the floor in Latin, unable to right himself again with his bound arm. Perhaps six years and more of Mr. Rappaport had just become more than he could bear. He had so wanted to do well at the school; he had worked so hard.

"The Present Infinitive Active of *audio?*"

The questions were snapped out at the beginning of the lesson. One by one, they sat down as they gave satisfactory answers.

"Decline *puella pulchra* in the Plural."

"The Third Person Singular and Plural of *credo?*"

"Conjugate the Imperfect Indicative Active of *oppugno.*"

They were all seated now, and Linnaeus — the last one to be left standing — was still sniffing, trying to do it quietly, dabbing at his eyes with his handkerchief.

Mr. Rappaport had already grilled him mercilessly.

"What interjection would you use for joy?" he had asked him when he was one of the three or four boys still standing.

"*Io!*" Linnaeus said nervously, the fingers of his right hand (the only one he could use) — pale against the dark uniform — starting to flutter up toward his heart, pressing his palm hard in against himself, the better to feel the faint imprint of his lucky silver dollar through the wool.

587

Hard, hard.

In God we trust.

These would be the words if the reverse faced forward in his shirt pocket.

E PLURIBUS UNUM.

Or these, if Liberty faced forward, the worn lips and hair, the shiny abraded lettering.

Hard, hard, imprinting the words into his skin in reversed mirror writing.

"Say it as though you *mean* it, Finch!"

Pause.

"As though you *mean* it."

"*Io!*"

Linnaeus tried to sound joyful.

"*Again!*"

"*Io!*"

"*Again!*"

"*Io!*"

"You'll have to give us all a translation, Finch. It's so difficult to make out what the emotion is intended to *be*, the way you say it."

"Oh, joy!"

(Very quietly, almost whispered.)

"*Very* convincing! *Again!*"

"Oh, joy!"

"*Again!*"

"Oh, joy!"

"*Louder!*"

"Oh, joy!"

"*Louder!*"

"Oh, joy!"

"Say it as though you *mean* it!"

"Oh, *joy!*"

The guffaws had started by the time of the first repetition. He made Linnaeus say it again and again, in Latin and in English, and — each time he said it — it sounded sillier and sillier. Linnaeus was clutching at one of the brass buttons on his jacket, his clenched hand opening and closing. This was a button he'd torn off several times.

"Hand by your side, Finch."

Linnaeus pressed his hand by his side.

"Head raised, Finch."

Linnaeus raised his head.

"Now the interjection for sorrow."

"*Vae!*"

(This time, the guffaws started immediately.)

You could tell that Linnaeus was trying to sound sorrowful, trying to put the correct expression into his voice, but Mr. Rappaport was not satisfied.

"*Mean* it!"

"*Vae!*"

"*Again!*"

"*Vae!*"

"*Again!*"

"*Vae!*"

"Now give us the translation."

"Woe!"

"*Again!*"

"Woe!"

"*Again!*"

"Woe!"

"Whoa! . . ," – Mr. Rappaport demonstrated his ready wit by the employment of a pun – ". . . That's far too quiet! *Louder! Louder!*"

Even though Linnaeus had already answered two questions correctly, Mr. Rappaport had still not finished with him. He wouldn't be finished with him for quite some time.

"Now a subtle blend of the two, if it's not beyond your capabilities. What interjection would you use for 'Alas, alas, woe is me!'? You know the one I mean, the slightly *comical* one."

"*Eheu!*" Linnaeus answered awkwardly.

(Guffaws. Instantly.)

"*Again!*"

"*Eheu!*"

(Guffaws.)

"*Again!*"

"*Eheu!*"

(Guffaws.)

"Translation!"

"Alas, alas!"

(Guffaws. Mocking cries of "Alas, alas!")

"Don't forget 'Woe is me!' Finch."

"Woe is me!"

(Guffaws. "Woe is me!"s.)

"'Alas, alas, woe is me!' Finch. Do it *properly*!"

"Alas, alas, woe is me!"

(Loud, shrieking, banging-on-the-desks-helplessly guffaws.)

Linnaeus was really struggling, almost starting to stutter. He seemed completely resigned to what was happening to him, as though it were something for which he was responsible, something he'd brought upon himself, a deserved punishment.

"*Again!*"

"Alas, alas, woe is me!"

(And again the guffaws.)

"*Again!*"

"Alas, alas, woe is me!"

(And again.)

"Well, well, well. That was truly *woeful*. I said *slightly* comic, and you were absolutely hilarious."

(Fists thundered on desks.)

Linnaeus kept lowering his head, and Mr. Rappaport kept making him raise it.

Mr. Rappaport made Linnaeus repeat interjection after interjection, demanding the appropriate emotion for each. Even though it no longer clutched at buttons, his clenched hand – down by his side – opened and closed, opened and closed, with no coat of arms against which to force it. Sometimes he'd spread it, clutching onto himself with his middle finger pointing down the seam of his trousers, pressing in hard as if in an attempt to stop the trembling. Then it would be opening and closing again, opening and closing.

"*Heus!*" Linnaeus was exclaiming, trying to say the word in the right way. If you were an Ancient Roman and you experienced an emotion, there was the correct interjection to be spoken, the correct expression to employ. You made the sound, and then people knew what you were feeling.

"*Ecce!*"

"*Ei!*"

"*Ah!*"

"*Pro!*"

"*O!*"

("Oo!"

("Oo!"

("*Oo!*")

"Hello, there!" he was saying.

"Behold!"

"Alas!"

"Ah!"

"Forbid it!"

"Oh!"

("Oo!"

("Oo!"

("*Oo!*")

He made Linnaeus say them all, and for all of them he had to say them as if he *meant* them. He had to say "*Ah!*" the Latin way, and "Ah!" again a different way for the English. "*O!*" could be said in lots of different ways. "*O!*" could be a cry of amazement, delight, mockery, or pain, and he had to differentiate between them all. He had to sound amazed, delighted, mocking, in pain. He had to do appropriate gestures, and stand in certain appropriate positions. Mr. Rappaport took his arm, and pushed and pulled it so that it was arranged as it should be.

He had to sound joyful.

He had to sound sorrowful.

He had to sound surprised, delighted, encouraging, angry, show all the emotions that Mr. Rappaport demanded he show.

He had to say them again and again and *again*, until Mr. Rappaport was satisfied, and he had to say them *loudly*.

Ben could see the expression on Oliver's face, the way that he was holding his ruler. Oliver was experiencing little difficulty in expressing "angry." There was a city made of paper rustling all around him on the walls, and sheet-clad little boys were moving in for the kill.

He was Casca now, the first one to stab Cæsar.

He was no longer Brutus.

"Speak, hands, for me!"

That's what he'd say, as the first ruler slid deep into Mr. Rappaport, past — *well* past — thirty-secondths of an inch, past sixteenths of an inch, eighths of an inch, past three inches, four inches, *this* deep, and blood spurted everywhere from the many gashes.

Oliver's hands *did* speak for him.

Not then.

But that same day.

Soon.

There would be liberty.

Her hair and face and lettering would be bright as a coin new-minted, her untouched features sharply defined.

There would be freedom.

Tyranny would be dead.

Run hence, proclaim, cry it about the streets.

He'd not just be Casca.

He'd not just be Brutus and Cassius and Trebonius, all the conspirators.

He'd be the capital-lettered Conspirators from *Coriolanus*.

He'd be Aufidius.

Kill, kill, kill, kill, kill him!

He'd kill him, and he'd stand on him.

"My noble masters, hear me speak," he'd say.

He would not say, "My rage is gone, / And I am struck with sorrow."

Kill, kill, kill, kill, kill him!

That's what he'd say.

That's what he'd do.

His rage would not be gone, and he would feel no sorrow.

That week's homework was written up on the blackboard. It was already there when they entered the room. It was something that Mr. Rappaport had started to do that year, hopeful – you couldn't help thinking – of intensifying the gloom to create an appropriate mood for what was to follow, encouraging a mood of despondency even though the weekend was so close.

June 15th, 1894.

The Expulsion of the Tyrant.

(Page XCVII, Exercise IX.

("Chapter, verse," he thought.

("Act, scene," he thought.)

There it was, their translation exercise from Latin into English, with the page reference for their textbooks.

Perhaps this title had given Oliver the idea.

Perhaps he'd already translated the passage, and known what to do, how to do it.

Ben, of course, knew nothing of what was to follow.

All he was thinking was that – at the end of the lesson, when they were outside – there would be the regular little ritual.

Oliver would walk behind him down the corridor at the end of school and signal in his usual way, the little private gesture between them that had become habitual, twisting his fingers in the small of Ben's back like someone turning a key. He always did it after Latin on Friday, reminding Ben that they'd be going to his house after school to work on the Latin together, the extra coaching that had started at the beginning of the year after they'd gone across the lake on the ice.

The Death of Britannicus.

That had been the first translation that they'd done together.

("Yes?"

(Twisting his fingers.

("Yes?")

First the Latin lesson.

Then . . .

Then the kissing lesson.

Then the "irregular verbs."

That was what Oliver called what they did.

He tried not to think about it.

Half of the lesson had gone by.

Now Mr. Rappaport stood in front of the blackboard, partially blocking the chalked words of *1. They gave gifts to Cæsar: a helmet, a shield, and two spears.*

T ran into his right ear, and *ears* emerged from his left ear, like *Subj* and *icate*, years earlier, like many other words in all the time between; surrounded by *tears* he was a man who was in the place where he most wanted to be.

SENTENCES TO BE DONE INTO LATIN was the heading — the usual heading — above the twenty sentences that followed.

Three-quarters of the lesson had gone by.

Now Mr. Rappaport had moved away from the blackboard to stand over Linnaeus, who was lying on the floor.

2. Cæsar, to whom they had given these things, had set out for Marseilles.

3. Give me back my legions, Varus, which thou hast lost.

"'*To whom* they had given these things,' Hyphenless Finch. *To whom*. We know that you're not a jolly good fellow, Finch, so are you a jolly *thick* fellow, suspect though that "fellow" is? Vorhees a jolly *thick* fellow, wouldn't you agree? Wouldn't you agree, Finch? Vorhees a jolly *thick* fellow. And so say all of us. And so say all of us. *Virtually* all of us."

But Linnaeus — a tall boy of fifteen at this time, nearly as tall as Mr. Rappaport — was beyond saying anything.

Brinkman said it for him.

"Vorhees a jolly *thick* fellow!" Brinkman — spotting his cue — chanted it quietly but insistently. "Vorhees a jolly *thick* fellow."

Brinkman was himself the thick one, too thick to sense that a boundary had been overstepped, too dense to realize the quality of the silence that had descended upon the class as Linnaeus broke down. He was alone now – alone with Mr. Rappaport – and the guffaws had once more become a Singular guffaw.

Singular spoke of one.

Adams, Bradstone, and Swartwout had all fallen silent.

"And so say all of us."

Mr. Rappaport appeared fascinated by Linnaeus's collapse, peering closely at the writhing boy on the floor, hopeful of spotting a telltale darkening at the front of his trousers, this connoisseur of humiliation hopeful of achieving a longed-for objective. According to Oliver, Mr. Rappaport's ambition was to make a boy wet himself in class, so that he could finally unleash a five-minute tirade about babies and diapers that he had been eagerly rehearsing for weeks. It was surprising that Brinkman hadn't gone up to Mr. Rappaport, and – as one more way of ingratiating himself – whispered the name of Tom Akenside into his ear as a particularly promising candidate for supplying the longed-for wet trousers. Oliver's ambition lay in other directions, however.

"I may very well be *just* the person to make his dream come true," Oliver added darkly, "when I'm in the mood. Stand well clear. Wear your galoshes. Climb on top of your desk."

One day – when he was in the mood, he'd choose his moment well – Oliver would answer all his questions incorrectly, and be the last boy standing, waiting with his bladder primed for action as Mr. Rappaport moved in eagerly for the kill. That would be the day when a boy wet himself, and Mr. Rappaport would soggily regret that prayers were sometimes answered. Before the lesson, Oliver would have spent the early hours of the morning in draining every bottle in the Hudson Row branch of Comstock's Comestibles so as to encourage the natural flow, and ensure a spectacular tidal wave. He had developed a taste for alcohol early. The stuffed animals in their glass cases, just down the corridor in the Biology laboratory, would float out like luxurious individual Noah's Arks for the more

selective I-prefer-to-travel-solo-don't-push-me-into-a-pair creatures, heading out toward the lake. There was Mr. Rappaport in his
striped swimsuit, hairy bits on all visible flesh, coconut matting
floating in search of its tropical island homeland, frantically
demonstrating the backstroke again, and dodging the crocodiles.
"Keep – *glug!* – your arm straight, you – *glug!* – *stupid* boy!"

"I'll wait until he's squeezing my arm, and ruin those well-
brushed trousers. It won't do his boots much good, either." That
thought was something to hang on to in the dark days. Oliver made
his plans thoughtfully. "I can always claim that the squeeze did it.
He does enjoy his squeezes, doesn't he?"

(Perhaps Mr. Rappaport had Ben in mind as the potential
trouser-wetter, reliving the happy manly moments of camaraderie
when Papa had told him about the bed-wetting and the vomiting.

(There wouldn't just be the agonizing squeezing on the upper
parts of the arm. There'd be the squeezing, the harder squeezing,
with the armpit across the face, the sweaty, slippery, farty-sound-
ing, eye-stinging squeezing that would make vomiting more certain
as the armpit-secreted beards – there was much secreting from
these secretions – invaded your eyes and mouth.

(The vomiting would be a valuable bonus.

("Vomit again!"

("Pee again!"

(Though he wouldn't say "pee."

(Brinkman would be laughing so loudly that it would be something of a surprise that he wasn't the one who'd wet himself, a
soggy Sidder-knee demonstrating his uncontrollable pleasure.)

Brinkman was now laughing at Linnaeus, loud laughter well
beyond the muted restraint of sniggering, well beyond even the
more uninhibited guffawing, laughter roaring up toward trouser-
wetting hysterics.

Mr. Rappaport stared and stared at Linnaeus, but did nothing, his
face expressionless. He was probably trying to decide the best point
at which to apply a squeeze.

A harder squeeze.

He leaned in really close.

Perhaps this was the lesson in which at last the long, wet worm-like tongue would emerge, seeking out urine instead of tears, licking away, slurping with delicious shuddering. The upper part of Linnaeus's body and the dark jacket – as they were at the end of every Latin lesson – were covered in white chalk handprints from where Mr. Rappaport had grasped him, and there were scraps of torn white paper adhering to his hair, and across his shoulders. It was like the scene of a messy crime.

The paper was the remains of some of Linnaeus's sketches, torn up by Mr. Rappaport. He had been busy that lesson. Few people shared his gift for packing so much pleasure into a limited space of time. He clearly learned from the subject he taught, and when he decided to *carpe diem* then that day was well and truly plucked, left naked and shivering like a dimpled-flesh chicken as feathers flew in all directions.

Linnaeus loved art, the works of others, and his own drawing and painting, though art was not taught at Otsego Lake Academy. Indeed, the surface of every wall (painted brown, olive, dark green, drab institutional colors) was left pointedly bare of works of art, in emphatic rejection of such unnecessarily girlie embellishments. The only paintings visible in any part of the building were those beneath the cupola in the main hall, that decadent glimpse of distant breast to set a young chap's pulse racing, as damning proof of the austere correctness of the fearful warnings thundered forth by Anthony Comstock and the New York Society for the Suppression of Vice.

Linnaeus had brought in his sketches to show to Ben and Oliver. It was something he'd done before. They didn't often go up to his house. Looking at the sketches was something to be done in private, and they – Linnaeus, together with Ben and Oliver, and sometimes Charlie Whitefoord – would go down to the side of the lake beneath a tree, drawn together secretly, like Brinkman showing his dirty books to his little gang, or Oliver revealing the ordeal facing potential æsthetes in *The Picture of Dorian Gray*. Brinkman's dirty books would probably have gone down better with Mr. Rappaport than the sketches. He'd probably *loaned* the dirty books to Brinkman in the first place — he was one of the most promising sportsmen in the class (bested only by Charlie), a chap with well-developed chappishness, poised on the brink of the beard — with helpful bookmarks in all the best bits to avoid having to waste time in wading through to find them.

Linnaeus had just started to copy *1. They gave gifts to Cæsar: a helmet, a shield, and two spears* neatly (or as neatly as he could manage) into his exercise book, and was pausing for a moment before going on. He'd waited for a while before he'd started writing, waiting for the trembling to stop, like a runner after a race waiting for his breathing to return to normal. He was quite an able boy, but he seemed to fumble even with straightforward exercises in Mr. Rappaport's class, visibly braced for "Hyphenless Finch" or "H-h-h" or "jolly *thick* fellow" even before he entered the room. Briefly, he'd opened his grandfather's atlas to glance at the sketches he'd stored inside it for safekeeping, a sight of them for encouragement in the lesson ahead of him. The questionings were over, and he was just starting to breathe normally again, the little shudder in his breath starting to ease. He'd put his handkerchief back into his shallow pocket, wriggling to force it in. They'd only just started to write — the twenty SENTENCES TO BE DONE INTO LATIN had already been chalked on the blackboard when they had entered — and there were still forty-five minutes of Mr. Rappaport to get through. Across the aisle, Oliver had his head down, and his blond curls — he still had blond curls — were wobbling.

Linnaeus hadn't been attempting to emend his sketches — he had a pen in his hand, not a pencil — but Mr. Rappaport had seen what he was doing. It was difficult for Linnaeus not to be clumsy, when he had only one hand he could use, and that — for him — the wrong one. His handwriting in his Latin exercise book was atrocious as he struggled to learn to write with his right hand, and Mr. Rappaport berated him for this. In all subjects he had always labored to present his work as neatly as possible, taking ages to copy it all out. He actually made rough copies first. You could see him almost weeping as he gazed at the lurching blotted lines of writing in Latin or in English translations. What he saw on the page was not what he saw in his head, what he wished to achieve. This was not work that he could recognize as his own.

Someone else had written this.

Someone else was struggling to express himself in a dead language.

He wrote the date — *June 15th, 1894* — and then, after a pause, *1.* on the next line. Ben saw all that he did because he was watching him, aware that Mr. Rappaport — his head angled to one side — was also observing Linnaeus closely. Perhaps it was time for his next thirsty infusion of tears, the salty blood-like taste of grief. He was an addict, and needed a regular supply, an *increasing* supply, just like — so it was rumored — Dr. Twemlow and his drugs. Mr. Rappaport would probably enjoy injecting more than slurping: the searching for a dark vein beneath the skin, the rapid beat of the excited pulse, the intake of breath just before the thrust.

Linnaeus paused for a moment. Then — rather wearily, rather hopelessly — he fumbled his right hand, still holding its pen, to one side, and eased open his atlas, lying on the desk beside him alongside his scholar's companion with its neatly-aligned pens and pencils. Linnaeus always liked everything just-so. His left arm was unusable, bound across the front of his body, and he had to press one corner of the atlas against his stomach to give himself the leverage to open it. He opened it two inches, three inches, leaned forward to peer inside . . .

And Mr. Rappaport pounced.

The atlas whirled across the room, and landed upside down and open in the aisle between Ben and Charlie Whitefoord. Linnaeus's pen spun round, landed on its nib, and ink flooded across the open pages of his exercise book.

"What have we here?" Mr. Rappaport was demanding triumphantly. "What have we here?"

(Manly little dance of victory. He sensed the nearness of tears, the longed-for gushing.

(*Parents and teachers must keep watch for these traps. Evil things may be found lurking in pocket, desk, and private box of the child; they cannot bear the light of day.*

(*The hideous appearance at first shocks the pure mind, and the poor victim would fain put it out of existence. But the tempter says, 'It can't hurt you; you are strong. Look it over and see what it is. Don't be afraid.' Thus beguiled, a second look, and then a mighty force from within is let loose. Passions that had slumbered or lain dormant are awakened, and the boy is forced over a precipice, and death and destruction are sure, except the grace of God saves him.*)

Mr. Rappaport was holding foolscap sheets high above his head, waving them from side to side, anxious to attract the attention of an auctioneer. Ben knew what they were. He and Oliver had been looking at them in the recess after lunch in their usual place, pale sunshine casting dappled patterns through the branches on to the penciled faces. Linnaeus was still upset after the Sport lesson, and was looking at the portraits, attempting to find a calmness in the memory of the music.

(With Ben it was words rather than music, ever since Papa had spoiled music for him. He repeated words to himself – the words of songs or poems, short prose paragraphs, that he had learned by heart – to make himself feel calm. Alice had told him that it was something that she sometimes did, and that it helped.)

"They're *really* good, Linn," Oliver had been saying. Linnaeus seemed to need encouragement constantly. "They're the best you've ever done."

(This was true.)

Linnaeus lowered his head, staring at the glistening pool of ink as if attempting to find shapes and meanings in its meanderings. He began to dab at it with a sheet of blotting paper. The trembling had started again. The desk tops sloped downward, and the blue pool would be seeping through the previous day's Recapitulatory exercises, through *June 14th, 1894*, through *Time and Numbers*, through

Give your own age in Latin, also the day of the month, the number of days in the year (a great shame it wasn't a leap year; Mr. Rappaport could have experienced a triumphant day of scorning with all those who had forgotten), *the number of days since your last birthday, and the number of the year* (vague, almost vanished, memories of characters scrawled on a long-ago blackboard, *MCCMLXXXVII, MDCCCLXXXVII*), through *Express in Latin: thirty ships, two hundred and seventy men, fifty-five horses, ninety-nine boys, and the odd numbers between 27 and 54.*

"What have we here?"

He fanned out the sheets in front of his chest, himself become the auctioneer, displaying what it was he had to offer to the assembled bargain hunters.

"Pictures! *Pretty* pictures!"

They were portraits of Ben and Oliver.

They had sat for them in the front parlor at Ben's house, Oliver playing the piano as Linnaeus made rough sketches. He drew in secret, not wanting his father to know what he did. He wanted to show his father, but his father – like Papa with Alice's writing – was the sort of man who would – again like Papa – probably exclaim "Moonshine!"

Linnaeus wanted to please his father, to be a good son.

He was very like Ben.

They'd heard the music again as they'd looked at the pictures, some Louis Moreau Gottschalk, the music of Ben's mother that had happened to be on the music rack.

Ben knew what was going to happen next.

"*Very* pretty pictures!"

Mr Rappaport walked up and down the aisles, so that every boy in the class could get a good look, assuming a mincing sort of gait, parading his beauties before a panel of judges. There was a "Moonshine!" sort of expression on *his* face, and something else besides.

There was always something else with Mr. Rappaport.

Faintly, in the distance, "The Dying Poet, Meditation" – Oliver's lips set in a firm line of concentration, his body swaying a little from side to side as he played the piano – "*O! Ma Charmante*" and "*Célèbre Tarantelle*," as Linnaeus – equally far away in what he was doing – sketched in a few lines, rubbed them out, began again, staring as precisely as if focusing his gaze through a microscope.

(Ben was sitting on the piano stool beside Oliver, looking at the patterns of the printed music as he played, beginning to realize . . .)

"The two luscious lovelies!"

(Guffaws.

(At this stage, Brinkman's apprentices – there were more than three of them now; their voices were deeper, and they made more noise – had been guffawing happily along with him. Sniggers had long since been superseded.)

Mr. Rappaport sounded like a barker at a carnival, luring the rubes into his tent to leer at the yawningly unluscious hootchy-kootchy girls. Rather shyly, Ben's thoughts sometimes wandered in such directions, though not now.

Oliver was not watching Mr. Rappaport.

He was leaning a little across the aisle, watching Linnaeus's face closely. Linnaeus was still dabbing with his blotting paper, giving all his attention to doing this, with the same concentration with which he approached all his tasks. His shaking fingers were stained blue.

A memory of blue lips, a blue tongue.

Mr. Rappaport taking hold of him, and leaning him back, pressing up against him.

He was opening his mouth.

A memory of the first lesson in what was to be the last lesson.

The true, the blushful Hippocrene.

Purple-stained mouth.

A smell of tooth powder.

Purple tooth powder.

Blue lips.

Blue tongue.

"Have you been sucking . . .?"

Words being written deep inside him.

Their bitter taste.

Sniggers.

Write the Latin for: ten, ten apiece, twenty at a time, twenty-fifth, two hundred at a time, thirty times, a half, three thousand.

"Aren't they just *enchanting*, positively the most *irresistible* things you've ever seen?"

"They're very good, sir."

This was Charlie Whitefoord.

He cleared his throat as he said it, but he said it, and said it as though he meant it, quite taking Mr. Rappaport by surprise. Charlie rarely volunteered comments.

Mr. Rappaport stopped in the aisle between Ben and Charlie, standing on Linnaeus's open atlas, pressing one of the pages diagonally across with a firm fold. There'd be a permanent line, like the results of some new diplomatic representations, across *Nipan, and Corea.*

"Well, you *would* think so, wouldn't you, Whitefoord? You're very chummy with the winsome threesome, aren't you? With our *popular* pretties? Cutie Comstock over there . . ."

(No response from Oliver.)

". . . and the hyphenless wonder. You even sit yourself within easy *reach* of Pinkie here, defective though he is."

(A blush starting.

(Pinkie becoming pinker.

(Ben looked down at the polished boot swiveling from side to side on top of *Kiousioui*, almost obliterating the whole island.)

Charlie looked back at him, levelly.

"Correct me if I'm mistaken, sir, but I have a distinct impression that you *assigned* our places in your class. We had no choice of where to sit. Is my recollection at fault in this? . . ."

He spoke in his captain-of-the-team voice. He was the one boy in the class who was taller than Mr. Rappaport. His voice had broken really early. Ben envied him this, as Mr. Rappaport once more taunted him into blushing about his voice. After one particularly bad lesson — one of the lessons in which he'd wept — Ben had walked down to the Hudson, and yelled over and over across the river, trying to hurt his throat, trying to damage his voice into deepness.

It hadn't worked.

He'd started shouting the words as soon as he entered the tile-lined tunnel that ran under the railroad to the boat landing. When a train from New York City had passed overhead, filling the tunnel with a tremendous sound, he'd started to scream the words, trying to make himself drown out the sound of that thunder. Then he'd walked through the echoing tunnel and down onto the landing.

(It was the same journey — this thought had come to him, years later — as the last journey that Linnaeus had ever made in his life.)

It must have been a fall or winter day because darkness had fallen, and his voice had gone out across dark water and he had not been able to see the farther shore.

"... Where'er you tread, the blushing flow'rs shall rise,
And all things flourish where'er you turn your eyes ..."

Those were the words he'd been shouting.

(They were *not* amongst the words that he repeated to himself for calmness.)

Those *had* to be the words.

He'd *screamed* out "blushing."

It was this word he'd said the most, the word he'd stressed the most, wiping it away and wiping it away and wiping it away. He hadn't been singing the words, and yet he'd still braced himself, in case he heard the voice of his dead father mocking him.

There'd be the sound of oars from the darkness in front of him, water dripping down.

A muffled figure would be moving slowly across the water toward him.

Resurgam.

"Franklin . . .," it would begin. "Franklin . . ."

Ben was waiting for the day that Charlie went berserk in a Sport lesson and rammed the football down Mr. Rappaport's throat, closely followed by the goalposts from both sides of the playing field, but Charlie never lost his temper. It was, Ben felt at times, his worst fault.

". . . Not that I'd object in any way to sitting next to Pinkerton, sir. He is, after all, a friend of mine . . ."

(Thank you, Charlie.)

". . . as are Comstock and Finch."

"No comments, Whitefoord."

(Annoyed. He'd been interrupted in full flow.)

A spin round on *Corea*, ripping the peninsula into an island, and he went back to stand over Linnaeus.

Write down the signs for the numbers from 1 to 20 inclusive.

Write down the signs for 97, 34, 793, 812, 555, 1776, 1492, 387, 99, 64.

Explain: XC, CX, CCCC, DC, L, LX, LXI, M, MD.

Write down in Latin: May 10th, December 25th, July 1st, August 26th, the dates of all the Fridays of the present month . . .

"Did you get your pretty friends to *pose* for you, Hyphenless? Did you *enjoy* getting them to *pose?* . . ."

(Guffaws.)

". . . Do you have any other, more *private*, drawings that you might care to show to us? After all, the warmer weather's starting, and there's less need for clothes these days. Some of the chummiest of chaps might prefer no clothes at all . . ."

(Guffaws.

(Mr. Rappaport didn't usually spell things out as overtly as this. He was buoyed up, driven to enjoyable excess, by the *bravo-bravo* sound of the guffawers, the chief chap flaunting his *bona fide* chappishness to his followers.)

"There might be one of Whitefoord amongst them. You'd have enjoyed drawing that one. Whitefoord always seems keen to show us all what a *big* chap he is. That would have needed *several* pencils . . ."

(This sort of remark always embarrassed Charlie.)

(Guffaws.)

"Now we're all fellows together, *most* of us . . ."

(Guffaws.)

". . . and so we won't be too shocked at seeing hyphens, particularly — or so I am given to understand — when we won't need to have our magnifying glasses with us *this* time . . ."

(Guffaws.

(The mention of hyphens and magnifying glasses had long brought Linnaeus easily to tears, after what had happened to him in his first Latin lesson.

(Mr. Rappaport went on and on and *on*.)

". . . Do you enjoy looking at other people's hyphens, seeing as you don't have one yourself? I'm sure that Comstock and Pinkerton were quite enthusiastic . . ."

(Guffaws.

(Brinkman and his gang were going to be *exhausted*.

(Was Mr. Rappaport somehow activating them into action, with the employment of a discreet electrical shock, or some such device?)

". . . when you . . ."

"Sir?"

(Oliver.

(He hadn't raised his hand into the air.)

"Sir?"

"*No questions*, Comstock."

He'd already been interrupted once. He didn't want to forget his lines. He and his *fiancée* must have gone through them together on Sunday evening after choir rehearsal. They had little else to talk about with each other. The repeated words might have opened her eyes a little, drawn them closer together, revealing to her that here was her sort of chap: strong, manly, masterful, fearless.

. . . *June 9th, May 24th, March 13th, September 21st, September 29th, January 1st* . . .

". . . *sharpened your pencil* for them."

606

(There was nothing particularly new about any of this.

(They'd had this sort of thing many and many a time before.

(They'd had this sort of thing in most lessons.

(They'd had this sort of thing in *all* lessons.

(But this time it was just too much for Linnaeus.)

Mr. Rappaport held the sketch of Oliver – side view, head slightly bowed, eyes half-closed – over Linnaeus's head.

(Ben . . .

(Ben was glad . . .

(Glad that Mr. Rappaport had cast the sketch that portrayed him onto his desk, skimming it across with the mocking little flick he usually reserved for returning unsatisfactory test papers. It seemed to be as much for the very thought of a chap *drawing*, as for the subject matter.

(A respite, though it might just be for a short time.

(Make *Linnaeus* blush.

(Make *Linnaeus* sob.

(Not me.)

"*Ooh!*" Mr. Rappaport said, ogling the portrait, with pushed-out kissy lips. "Those eyes! Those lips! That hair!"

("Oo!"

("Oo!"

("*Oo!*"

(He spoke as if everyone would think he didn't really mean this.)

He was off again, in a by-popular-demand tone of voice.

"Mystic poet, hear our prayer,
Twenty love-sick maidens we –
Young and wealthy, dark and fair,
All of country family.
And we die for love of thee . . ."

(Guffaws.

(Brinkman and company.)

"*County*, sir."

(Oliver.)

"It's 'All of *county* family,' sir."

Mr. Rappaport sighed sentimentally, and crushed Oliver's portrait to his bosom.

"Ah!" he sighed. "If those lips could only speak!"

"Those lips *could* speak, sir, if you'd let them. Sir?"

"No questions, Comstock. I've already told you."

Mr. Rappaport had been temporarily diverted by an old enthusiasm, and now turned his attention fully back to Linnaeus, once more holding the picture of Oliver over his head. He began to fold it over, and for a moment it looked as though he was going to form it into the shape of a cone, a fool's cap made out of foolscap – this was something he had done before – and place it upon Linnaeus's head.

You couldn't see Linnaeus's face. He was still dabbing with the blotting paper, like someone desperately attempting to soak up all his tears before they betrayed him by bursting from his eyes. He was hunched down, rather awkwardly, like most of the taller boys in the class – Charlie Whitefoord and Brinkman amongst them – because the desk and seat, their metal frame formed all in one unit, left far too little space for their legs. They had to slide in sideways, and then lean at an angle. They were like young adults forced into the postures of children.

You could see that he was bracing himself, his arms and shoulders stiffening prior to lifting a great weight. He was starting to shake, struggling to shift the heaviness of what had been placed upon him.

This was exactly how he'd looked, six and more years earlier, when he'd forced himself to volunteer to recite a poem at Crowninshield's.

> Oft in the stilly night,
> Ere slumber's chain has bound me,
> Fond memory brings the light
> Of other days around me:

> The smiles, the tears
> Of boyhood's years,
> The words of love then spoken . . .

Mr. Rappaport was not forming a fool's cap.

Slowly, lingeringly, he began to rip across the sketch of Oliver.

(This was a surprise.

(You'd have thought he'd have wanted to keep it, to gaze longingly at it alone in his room, his hidden place to which his *fiancée* would never be admitted, one of his little love tokens, another one to add to his collection, the secret shrine at which he worshiped.

(Those eyes would be his.

(Those lips.

(That hair.

(You'd see the blurred bits of the pencil lines, where his lips had moistly lingered. The portrait would be framed on the wall like a relic of a saint positioned for reverence, alongside the sock of Oliver's that had gone missing after a match – Mr. Rappaport would sniff at its faint scent with blissful writhing – and the lock of hair he had cut off, claiming – with much sneery laughing – that he was going to ask Dr. Brown to test it for hair dye.

("Ooh, that picture!" he'd be saying. Unlike Dorian Gray's, this was a picture that would always remain youthful, more to Mr. Rappaport's taste, and taste it he would, his saliva darkening the thick paper.

("Ooh, that sock!"

("Ooh, that curl!"

("Oo!"

("Oo!"

("*Oo!*")

Linnaeus looked up at the sound of the first downward rip. Mr. Rappaport leaned forward, daring Linnaeus to outstare him.

"I . . ."

Rip.

Mr. Rappaport spoke slowly and emphatically, each word

accompanied by a tear. Each time he tore the paper in half, he placed the pieces neatly together, tearing through a thicker and thicker pile each time, always through the longer side of the papers, like a spurned suitor destroying his love letters. It was as if he sought to impress them with how muscular he was, his strongman posturings demonstrating that here was a real man in front of them, the focus of their envious emulating. It was surprising that he hadn't whipped off his shirt and trousers and stood revealed before them in his Sport lesson clothing — his shorts and athletic jersey and well-polished whistle — flaunting the coconut matting that flourished solely on Samson, a he-man of hairiness.

(Look on my hairs, ye girlies, and despair!

(They'd smell his sweat, those girlies.

(They'd despair.)

". . . will . . ."

Rip.

". . . *not* . . ."

Rip.

". . . allow . . ."

Rip.

". . . attention . . ."

Rip.

". . . to . . ."

Rip.

(He was starting to struggle now with the ripping. It was always a challenge to get much beyond six doublings-up.)

". . . wander . . ."

Rip.

(*R.I.P.*)

(He managed this with a little judicious shuffling.)

". . . during *my* lessons!"

(He thought for a moment, and then wisely decided not to attempt a further tearing.)

He agitated the fragments in his cupped hands, an official about to draw out the winning number in a raffle. So might a gambler shake his dice.

There'd be sixty-four pieces.

Ben had worked this out.

It was something to think about.

Something to occupy the mind and prevent thought.

Sixty-four.

LXIV.

The sign for 64.

Mr. Rappaport cupped the pieces in his left hand, and then – a few at a time – he carefully picked them out with the tips of the fingers of his right hand, and slowly cast them upon Linnaeus.

"Here comes the bride," he started to sing.

He was in fine voice that day.

It was then that Linnaeus seemed to try to stand up. He began to straighten as he slid himself off the tip-up seat – it caught on the back of his legs, and fell down with a bang – and then, as if the sudden bang had been that of a shot, he fell to the floor sobbing. He covered his face, ashamed.

"Don't cover your face."

Mr. Rappaport liked to see the tears emerging. Linnaeus should have known this by now. There was a wounded note of rebuke in Mr. Rappaport's voice.

He took up a position for a good view.

(Ben had a sense of a face at a high window.

(A face looking down from a schoolroom.

(A fallen figure lying in the gutter.

(Legs, unable to walk, struggling.

(Hands pressing against the sharp edge of the stone curb.

(The stain and smell of dried horse urine, dark shore-line-like patterns across the road, the crumbling manure brushed into a pile close beside his head, dirty straw, the sense of lying in a flooded ill-kept farmyard.

(*I do smell all horse piss.*

(He heard the words in Oliver's Shakespearean voice.

(*Dog piss.*

(*Horse piss.*

(You could say *anything*, if you employed a Shakespearean voice.

(*My nose is in great indignation.*

(*Do you hear, monster?*

(*If I should take a displeasure against you . . .*

(*Like a Real Boy.*)

Mr. Rappaport leaned over to his right a little, and began to sprinkle some of his improvised confetti over Oliver also, torn fragments of his face.

All the time, Linnaeus sobbed loudly, almost hysterically. He sat up, drew his knees up into his chest, and leaned his head down over the upraised knees, his hand going back across his face.

"*Don't cover your face.*"

He watched Linnaeus's face, as he scattered the other face, the ripped-up face, upon Oliver, beginning to sing. His rehearsals in All Saints' with Big Bonnet had certainly given him a taste for melody.

> "Here comes the bride,
> Blond-haired and blue-eyed . . ."

Mr. Rappaport must have had these words all ready and waiting for a suitable occasion, an occasion that would not have been his marriage to Big Bonnet. "Blonde-haired . . ." – that extra "e" on "blonde" was vital – ". . . and blue-eyed" were not words that would have come to mind to describe Mr. Rappaport's *fiancée*. Faintly, from long ago, he heard Oliver's voice. *Did you just make that up, sir, or did you have it already prepared, sir?* There was no doubt of the answer to that question this time, sir. The words he was chanting – chanting was a prerequisite for most words spoken in that room – were not words that were the spontaneous impulse of the moment. *No one* knew the words of that song beyond that first "Here comes the bride." It was one of those apocryphal songs that everyone thought that they knew, but which didn't really exist, except in one or two parodic versions, and all anyone ever did was sing the first line over and over before lapsing into awkward silence, like those called upon to sing some obscure national anthem on a day of patriotic rejoicing. He'd certainly never heard the words that Mr. Rappaport was now singing. The real words were in German – Oliver had told him that once – and were words from an opera. The real words were not "Here comes the bride," even though the music was the music of a wedding march.

"...Isn't she delightful?
Standing by his side..."

They'd have been practicing their specially written words, Rappaport and Big Bonnet, planning the occasion beforehand, so that he could cause the tears he so craved to see. First they rehearsed the hymns, and then they got onto the good stuff. "Sing it as though you *mean* it!" Big Bonnet would have been urging him on Sunday evening.

He was a man who learned well, ever eager to impress.

He sounded as if he *meant* it.

It was very quiet in the class.

Even Brinkman somehow forgot to guffaw.

"The *blushing* bride, Comstock."

"Oh, but I'm not blushing, sir."

It was said very quietly, but was perfectly audible.

"You make a *lovely* couple."

He kept on doing this until there was no more paper left, singing the same lines, making comments – "The pretty little bride," "The hyphenless husband" – and all the time Linnaeus was sobbing.

Eventually, Mr. Rappaport ran out of paper.

He chose his final line, and leaned right down to say it.

"Vorhees a jolly *thick* fellow. *Ha!*"

He spoke it like the victor in a duel dishonoring the loser's corpse.

He rubbed his hands together, in a gloating sort of movement, in order to remove the last few pieces of paper that adhered to his sweaty palms. People always tended to sweat when they were unusually excited. The last few fragments of Oliver's face fell on to Linnaeus. Perhaps Mr. Rappaport liked picture puzzles. Perhaps that was it. He'd remove the torn pieces from Linnaeus's prone body, as he lay there, curled up, sobbing. This would be pleasurable in itself, feeling the shuddering inhalation of breath as he peeled away the dampened, rough-edged fragments from the skin, tugging them slightly as they adhered. Then – in the privacy of his room, the curtains drawn – he'd piece together the portrait he'd apparently destroyed earlier. He'd lick at the torn edges, the faintly salty taste of sobbing and sweat, all senses a source of pleasure. Again he'd see the eyes (eyes that would be soft, submissive, eyes that would not look back at him coolly), the lips (soft, unspeaking), the hair . . .

The ravaged condition of the portrait would be a symbol of the transient nature of all things sublunary.

Unlike in *The Picture of Dorian Gray*, the destroyed picture was that of someone youthful and (Ben flinched away from the word) good-looking. (He tried to avoid thinking of the forbidden word, the oo-oo-*oo* word, "beautiful," tried to keep that word completely out of his head.)

("Yes?"

(Oliver asking him.

("Yes?"

("Yes?"

("Yes."

(Ben's answer, the answer he always gave.)

Unlike in *The Picture of Dorian Gray*, the destroyer of the picture was not himself destroyed.

Not immediately.

"Sir?"

(Oliver.)

Mr. Rappaport was so lost in reverie that he didn't hear. He'd pursed his lips out again, planning the location for a big wet kiss.

"Sir?"

(Oliver.)

"*Sir?*"

(Each time, it was Oliver.)

Mr. Rappaport began to wipe the chalk from his hands on Linnaeus's bowed shoulders, finding a part of his body that was free of chalky markings. It must have been handy for him, Linnaeus lying there like that.

"No questions, Comstock," he said absently, checking the palms of his hands to ensure that they were completely clean, seeming satisfied by what he saw there.

"No Questions Comstock," Oliver repeated quietly, as if just to himself. "He always calls me that. I sound like an outlaw. I hope there's a big reward offered for me. THIS MAN IS DANGEROUS." He was seething.

Linnaeus lay there, covered in handprints and fragments of paper, both created by the hands of Mr. Rappaport, still sobbing. How could he ever get up off the floor again? How could he ever face the other boys in the class?

(Ben had wanted it to be Linnaeus.)

(Ben had not been able to face the thought of it being himself who was the one chosen this time.)

Bells.

They seemed to come from a long way away, another place, another time.

The whole hour and a half had gone by.

Mr. Rappaport had been enjoying himself so much that they'd — most of them — completed only the first one or two sentences of the twenty on the blackboard. Linnaeus had completed none at all.

The same SENTENCES TO BE DONE INTO LATIN would be there for the next lesson, on Tuesday.

Next week they'd be giving gifts to Cæsar: a helmet, a shield, and two spears.

Cæsar would be setting out for Marseilles.

They'd be asking Varus to give them back their legions that he'd lost.

They'd be trying not to look at Linnaeus.

It would be as if the lesson on Friday, June 15th, 1894 had never happened, though it was a lesson that would never leave Linnaeus.

"Class dismissed. Row by the window first. No talking. Keep right."

Everyone stood up beside his desk, and, row by row, the class filed out, trying to make it appear that they couldn't see Linnaeus. School was over for the week.

"Next row."

Silently, the classroom began to empty.

"Next row."

The row on Ben's left filed out.

Charlie Whitefoord remained standing in his place.

Oliver remained standing in his place.

"Go now, Comstock."

"I'm waiting for Finch, sir."

"I said, 'Go now.'"

"I'm waiting for Finch."

The lack of a "sir" was all the more pointed when Oliver omitted it.

Pause.

"Go now. You do as I say, Comstock. I'm not going to let you ignore what I say. Do you take me for a complete idiot?"

Longer pause.

"Is that a *rhetorical* question, sir?"

Very long pause indeed.

The remaining rows waited to see what would happen.

They stood up straight, looking ahead of them at the words on the blackboard, as Oliver waited politely for an answer. You couldn't beat Oliver when it came to politeness.

Then Mr. Rappaport decided to ignore this. It was the last time he ignored something that Oliver said.

"Your row has gone, Whitefoord."

"I'm also waiting for Finch, sir."

"Next row."

Not even a pause, this time.

Ben was the one who paused.

He paused — just for a moment — and thought of Frankie Alloway, long vanished from Room 37. He could see him, quite distinctly — it seemed like a memory from long, long ago — remaining standing in his place like Charlie and Oliver, with all the other places in the dark room empty around them. Frankie's eyes were closed, his head bowed, rigid and unmoving as a child expecting a blow. Tears were running silently down his face as they had at the end of their first Latin lesson, when Mr. Rappaport had whispered something to him.

The room grew darker, darker.

No one moved.

Ben paused — just for a moment — but then he moved out after Darville. He was the last in his row to move, but he did as he was told, and he went.

II

Outside, down the central corridor, chanting of "Vorhees a jolly *thick* fellow!" from Brinkman, Adams, Bradstone, Swartwout, and the others. There were enough of them now to form a fully manned gauntlet. Mr. Rappaport's followers had multiplied until he could have formed his own personal football team, an imperial guard of carefully selected, trusted men, clanking in their armor as they sprinted into the attack, the sort of guards with which Roman emperors had surrounded themselves protectively.

("*In* the Pink!"

("*In* the Pink!"

("*In* the Pink!")

Another chant, a final chorus for Friday.

He flushed at this one, and pretended he hadn't heard, assuming the attitude of someone absorbed in his Latin book, a first glance at the work set for the weekend.

They were too keen to be out of the building and on their way home to linger long for taunting.

Odd, to be on his own in the way that he was.

He kept expecting to feel Oliver's fingers twisting in the small of his back, the invisible key.

("Yes?")

June 15th, 1894.

<u>*The Expulsion of the Tyrant.*</u>

(*Page XCVII, Exercise IX.*)

A sudden feeling of abandonment, the thought of attempting the translation without Oliver's coaching. It was always Oliver who did most of the work.

He remembered <u>*The Death of Britannicus.*</u>

Innoxia adhuc ac praecalida et libata gustu potio traditur Britannico . . .

He was walking down that same corridor in winter darkness, struggling to read what it was he had to translate, feeling the huge burden of all that he did not know weighing down upon him. *The Cloud of Unknowing.* That was what it felt like. He'd seen a book with this title at Miss Ericsson's, small and prettily bound like a book of poetry.

("What language is that supposed to be again, Pinkerton? Just remind me."

("Latin, sir."

("*Really?* You do surprise me.")

He couldn't bring himself to look at the first lines of the Latin for tonight.

What to do?

What to do?

Your main difficulties are with verbs.

He heard Oliver's voice saying this. He felt awkward about not staying behind in Latin to wait for Linnaeus in the way that Oliver and Charlie had done.

He lingered, as the crowds in the corridor gradually thinned out, the voices dying away into silence. He tried to hide himself in the shadows. Mr. Rappaport had emerged from Room 37 immediately after the last boys to leave. These did not include Oliver, Linnaeus, or Charlie, but Mr. Rappaport had not stayed to say anything to them. After a while, Charlie came out with Linnaeus. It was like watching someone accompanying an invalid, feeling his way falteringly along, trying to support him. Charlie had his arm round Linnaeus's shoulders — this was not advisable at Otsego Lake Academy, even for Charlie, but there was no one there to witness it — and they walked in the direction away from Ben, into the gloom at the far end. It was gloomy there even on a summer's afternoon.

There was something about the attitude . . .

(*I keep thinking of the illustrations in* Tom Brown's Schooldays . . .

(*Two of Tom and Arthur, the one where Tom's comforting him . . .*

(*"Why, young 'un! what's the matter?" he was asking . . .*

(*There are just the two of them in the room. They're sitting side by side at a table in front of a bookcase, and the chair beside the table is drawn so beautifully . . .*

(*They make you think that . . .*

(*They make you think . . .*)

. . . something familiar about the attitude.

But he couldn't bring to mind what it was.

Oliver did not emerge from Room 37.

Ben began to retrace his steps to the classroom.

("Yes?"

(Twisting his fingers.

("Yes?")

First the Latin lesson . . .

The Expulsion of the Tyrant.

It was the white chalk handprints that were Mr. Rappaport's undoing.

All the corridors were empty with an after-school stillness.

He watched Oliver in the otherwise deserted classroom, saw what he was doing through the glass panel of the door from outside in the corridor, standing to one side so that he couldn't be seen. He almost walked straight into the room, but something made him pause. Oliver stood on a chair – though he was quite tall by then, he still couldn't quite reach the very top of the blackboard – and began to rub both his hands across the chalked words written across the width of the board. When he obliterated all the words on one section, he stepped down and moved the chair a little further along, hooking it by his wrists so that he would not rub off any of the chalk on the palms of his hands.

June 15th, 1894 was obliterated.

TWENTY SENTENCES TO BE DONE INTO LATIN disappeared from sight, gathered onto his skin.

They gave gifts to Cæsar: a helmet, a shield, and two spears.

Cæsar, to whom they had given . . .

He placed the flats of his palms in the center of each sentence, and swept his hands from side to side. Mr. Rappaport had been revisiting some of the scenes of his earlier triumphs, subconsciously (modern psychological terms seemed appropriate for what had been happening) made nostalgic by the nearness of his going.

Quem amat? had been at the bottom of the board below the twenty sentences, and *Filium.*

Whom does he love? (His) son.

That was there, together with *Quid agit pater? Amat filium? What is it the father does? He loves his son,* and all these words were drawn into dust on the flat of Oliver's hands. Oliver was obliterating every last trace that showed Mr. Rappaport had ever been in that room.

He worked with quiet, but controlled anger.

Father was in his hands, *son* was in his hands, *love.*

When he had finished, the entire blackboard was bare of chalk, and his hands were white with thick dust. Still avoiding rubbing off any of the accumulated chalk, he dragged at the cloth of his trousers with the front of his forearms to loosen it away from his knees, and then squatted down beneath the blackboard. For a moment Ben had the awful but exciting thought that Oliver was about to exercise his well-developed sense of Symbolism by demonstrating his feelings for Mr. Rappaport in a spectacularly unhygienic manner. This would be far more dramatic than just wetting himself. "Phew!" the next class into the room would be saying, reeling, the room exploding in rottenness around them after a weekend of oppressive thundery weather. "Phew!" They'd had one of Mrs. Economou's more assertive bean concoctions for lunch. Everyone dreaded afternoon school after one of these. You could hear the sound of windows being opened all over the school – whatever the weather – as window pole monitors were hastily sent into action like a first wave of attack from halberd bearers. Oliver's long training with the succession of Chinky-Winkies had rendered him fearless in the face of farts, but it was hell in Chemistry for everyone else. Dr. Brown would have been whooping with a loudness almost worthy of cesium.

He nearly opened the door.

He nearly shouted, "Don't forget to lower your trousers, Oliver!" (When Oliver was in the grip of a Big Idea he sometimes forgot basic precautions.)

But Oliver had another plan entirely.

As Ben watched, uncomprehendingly, Oliver grasped himself firmly – several times – in the groin, and around the buttocks, wriggling his hands around in order to make the prints seem larger. He did this slowly and methodically. The science of crime-detection was in its infancy, and Oliver was counting on this. He repeated his actions several times, inspecting the results with cool critical detachment, like an artist stepping back from his canvas, a woman inspecting her just-applied makeup in her mirror. When he eventually seemed satisfied with this, he began – equally slowly, equally methodically – to slap himself across the face, quite expressionlessly, several times. He did it until there were red marks across his cheeks, and his eyes were brightened with tears.

("His glittering eye!" he heard Oliver chanting, years ago, seeing snowdrifts in June.

(A banner with the strange device.

(High voices echoing down an icy outdoor corridor.

The tears were not as a result of emotion – Oliver was absolutely calm and controlled – but just the natural response of the eyes to the blows across his face. He caught the corner of his mouth with a fingernail, and a little flow of blood was smeared across his chin. Ben remembered walking, bleeding, into the main hall of the school on his first day as a pupil, all the sniggering watchers. Oliver ran his hands through his hair, disheveling it, making it stand on end, pulling it down to obscure his eyes. His fair hair was very bright in the dim classroom, vivid against the blackboard. He ripped off buttons from the bottom of his jacket and the front of his trousers, and pulled out the lower part of his shirt so that it emerged from his flies.

It was very frightening to watch.

O boys, be ye taught by the master.

The voice of the master must be heard by the boys.

Bad boys must be punished.

The boys love the master.

Beware! You will be punished.

Be ye advised, lest ye may be punished.

The happy boy has received a most beautiful book from the master.

The timid boy fears, lest he may be punished by the master.

The boy, who loves the master, is good.

The boy, whom the master loves, is good.

Good boys are happy boys.

You could hear the voices chanting the lessons that must be learned by heart.

It was a dark afternoon, rain clouds building, not like a June day at all.

"Oliver!" Ben wanted to say. "Oliver!"

Whatever Oliver was doing to himself, Ben wished to stop it.

He never told Oliver what he had seen him doing.

He never told anyone else.

Oliver returned the chair neatly to its place at Mr. Rappaport's desk, and began to take deep breaths, panting after a while so that it sounded as if he had been running, fleeing from something terrifying.

Then he was ready.

Ben slipped into the next classroom along, leaving the door slightly ajar, knowing that he must not be seen.

He'd be invisible in the gloomy interior.

The door to Mr. Rappaport's classroom slammed open, and Oliver began to run down the corridor.

"Mr. Scrivener!" he was shouting, sounding out of breath and frightened. "Mr. Scrivener!"

All the way down the corridor he was shouting "Mr. Scrivener!"

Even when he was out of sight, Ben could still hear him shouting.

12

June 15th, 1894
<u>*The Expulsion of the Tyrant.*</u>
(*Page XCVII, Exercise IX.*)

No one saw Mr. Rappaport go, but Mr. Rappaport went.

Some days Ben had not felt that he was on his way to school; he had felt that he was on his way into the hands of Mr. Rappaport, thoughts of him obscuring all thoughts of anything else. You'd have imagined that there would have been more of a sense of a space once he'd gone.

It was on Saturday morning that Ben had first heard what had happened, what was believed to have happened. Mrs. Goodchild had got to them first, breathless either with excitement, or because she'd been running.

Alone, all Friday evening, he'd struggled with the Latin translation, not realizing that he needn't have bothered, trying to take particular care with the verbs. It had seemed odd to be doing it by himself. He had the feeling that something had come to an end, though it was not what he had thought it was.

("Rappaport needed to be stopped," Oliver would say calmly, as if he'd fired a gun, the patient but unrepentant murderer waiting for the police to arrest him, to be quietly taken away.

(But Oliver never said anything.

(Mr. Rappaport had been poised to pounce for years.

(Oliver had hurried things along a little.

(As he often did.

(That was what had happened.

(Ben would have preferred assassination, something messy and prolonged, with lots of screaming, but at least Mr. Rappaport had gone. The method by which he had been eliminated was a secondary consideration.)

This was how Oliver destroyed Mr. Rappaport.

In doing so, he had also damaged himself, but he had not been thinking about himself when he had done what he had done.

Mr. Rappaport might have gone, but his words lingered behind him like a long-delayed echo. An echo of an echo, as Mr. Rappaport's words had been an echo of Papa's. Anyone seen talking to Comstock soon found that out.

SEVEN

I

"They make me think of other things," Oliver was saying. "The illustrations . . ."

The illustrations that Oliver could remember from *Tom Brown's Schooldays* were not the same ones that Ben could remember. Ben remembered the one of Tom's last cricket match; a slightly unsettling one of a long empty shadowy corridor (it had probably grown in length in his imagination, shadows deepening, but it seemed to be a place he knew); and – balancing the one he could remember of Tom's last cricket match – the one of Tom's first game of football on the day of his arrival at Rugby. The half-conscious black-clad figure – surrounded by much taller boys dressed all in white, gathered all around him in heroic statuary-like frozen postures – was being lifted to his feet by Brooke. "Well, he is a plucky youngster," Brooke was saying, Brooke, the cock of the School, the head of the School-house side, the best kick and charger in Rugby.

Ben was aware of the three women walking through the snow toward them, dark clothing against whiteness, the central figure being supported, like the illustration in his mind. On either side of Charlotte, Alice and Kate had linked an arm in hers. The cemetery stretched away all around. There were no other living figures visible, though cemeteries tended to be busy places. There was never an end to burying.

"What I wanted to happen," Oliver said, lowering his voice,

not wanting what he said to be overheard by anyone else, "what I *really* wanted to happen, was for Rappaport to die like that Roman emperor. I can't remember his name. I've been trying to remember it for weeks, and I can't find it in any of my schoolbooks. I still have all my schoolbooks. This emperor was so rotten — so eaten up by disease — that in the end he just burst open, sort of exploded. He was splattered right across the floor and down the walls, and worms from inside him were writhing everywhere."

He paused for a moment, to visualize this the better.

Then he looked at Ben, one of his very intent looks.

"That was what I wanted to happen to Rappaport. I wanted it to happen slowly. I've been trying to remember the name of the emperor who died like that. We must have read it in a lesson some-time, though it sounds too entertaining to have been a lesson. Perhaps I've remembered it wrongly, and it wasn't an emperor. Perhaps it wasn't in Latin at all."

"Nero?" Ben suggested.

The name might have occurred to him because Oliver had men-tioned him just before he'd started talking about the *Tom Brown's Schooldays* illustrations. "Petronius Arbiter," he'd said, "Nero's personal arbiter of elegance," and other words came back into Ben's mind, the description of the death of a murdered boy.

(*He lost his voice, and he lost his breath . . .*

(*He simultaneously lost his voice and his breath . . .*

(*Their eyes were fixed upon Nero . . .*

(*The prince's sister . . .*

(*She had learned to hide her sorrows, her affections, every one of her emotions . . .*)

The women were close. Ben and Oliver moved a little apart to flank the step up into the carriage.

Worms from inside him were writhing everywhere.

It seemed a suitably Nero-like way to die, after the excesses of his life. With Sunday-school primness, only carefully selected passages about him were made available for translation in Latin textbooks. Oliver — driven by his untiring spirit of intellectual challenge (that was his story) – had obtained rather fuller accounts. They beat the allegedly mucky French books of his by a long way. Well might his mama have looked almost as nervous about Latin as she did about French.

(Tacitus.

(*The Death of Britannicus.*

(*A harmless drink, extremely hot, and already tasted to check for poison, was handed to Britannicus, and when he refused it because it was too hot, cold water was poured in to cool it, and in with it went the poison; this ran so rapidly through his whole body that he simultaneously lost his voice and his breath. There was consternation in the people seated around, and the less intelligent began to leave; those who were more perceptive sat absolutely still, their eyes fixed upon Nero . . .*

(There were just the two of them in the room. They were sitting side-by-side at a table in front of a bookcase.

(Other thoughts.)

"Nero?"

"No," Oliver said decisively. "It wasn't Nero. I wish that I could remember who it was."

Ben couldn't think who it was who had died in the way described by Oliver, the man who had died in the way that Rappaport should die. If Oliver couldn't think of the name, then Ben certainly wouldn't be capable of thinking of the name, but – for a little while – he tried. He thought of himself going to Hampshire Square to tell Oliver that he had remembered the name. He wouldn't telephone. He'd go and tell him face-to-face, let him know that he'd spent time finding out. Discovering this detail would – somehow – be doing something for Linnaeus.

Perhaps it wasn't in Latin at all.

Oliver could be correct in this.

It might – the thought came to him – have been a biblical character who had died in this way (this was a vague memory of something at the back of his mind) rather than a character from Roman history. The Old Testament specialized in spectacular deaths, particularly, it seemed to him – rightly or wrongly – if the deaths were those of women.

Jezebel.

The name came to him.

He remembered Jezebel, in particular, her very Old Testament end.

She painted her face and looked out at a window. Jehu lifted up his face to the window, said, "Who is on my side? who?" and ordered two or three eunuchs to throw her down. They threw her down, and some of her blood was sprinkled on the wall and on the horses; and he trod her under foot. This was not a passage that had been read out by Miss Augusteena (she'd have been made uneasy by the mention of eunuchs, never a word she felt able to explain with a convincing enough air of matter-of-factness), though it was a passage that no doubt would have recommended itself to Oliver's mama, particularly the part about the painted face. You could imagine her quoting it – as her Christian duty – with zestful insinuations to the young women from The House of the Magdalenes, Jezebels every one of them, whatever they might choose to call themselves, all lined up at their windows with licentious "Cooee, boys!" expressions upon their painted faces, making come-hither gestures with every available digit. On the wall of the Sunday-school room there was an old map of Palestine, and there also were the brightly colored scenes of the Holy Land, the creaking dark wooden chairs, and Jezebel – rouged and powdered – lying in the dust, still and broken. Ben had seen her quite distinctly. When Jehu had entered the house, he ate and drank, and said, "Go, see now this cursed woman, and bury her: for she is a king's daughter." And they went to bury her, but they found no more of her than her skull, her feet, and the palms of her hands, because the dogs had eaten her. The carcass of Jezebel should be as dung upon the face of the field. This was the word of the LORD. (This sort of word from the LORD was quite an incentive when you were attempting to follow Benjamin Franklin's thirteen-step pathway to virtue, though it wasn't much of a help with achieving Tranquility. It was hardly an encouraging example of Moderation. It was *certainly* not an example of Cleanliness.)

Worms.

Writhing.

It seemed the sort of thing to be hidden away in the solid chunks of small print in one of the more obscure passages in the Bible, something in one of those books that you were hard put to recognize as being from the Bible at all. The Old Testament was rather daunting. You found yourself on an unfamiliar page, and you felt that you'd lost your way, finding a street name you'd never seen before in a neighborhood that you thought you knew well. *Dorabella Street*, *Almaviva Street*, *Elvira Street*, and *Cherubino Street* were some of the more recent street names to have appeared nearby in Longfellow Park since he'd last been home, and each time he came home things had changed more. These last street names were just that: the names of roads with houses not yet built. You gained the impression that a street was something that had houses on it, and these particular houseless streets seemed inappropriately named. He'd look out from the window of his room at the back of the house, and see emptiness stretching up from behind where they lived on Chestnut Street, up toward the lower slopes beneath Hudson Heights, the places where the apple and cherry orchards had once been. He remembered wandering through Heneacher Woods with the other Crowninshield's boys – listening for birdsong (they did this even though the only bird that Dr. Crowninshield could recognize was a cuckoo), looking for specimens, and feeling botanical and learned – and now the woods were being cleared away for more new areas of housing, chopped down like the orchards had been.

What can you see?

What can you see?

What can you see?

There was *nothing* to see, just the emptiness of where there would be places in the future, places where people would be living, but looking now like places where no one had ever been, or would ever be.

Herod?

That was the name that had come into his mind, a name that had something Old Testament about it, and yet was to be found in the more manageable New Testament.

Perhaps it was Herod.

Herod sounded just the sort of man to have been rotten in every part of him, a man so eaten up by disease that he'd explode into a mass of writhing well-nourished worms, across the floor and down the walls. The Bible was *full* of men for whom this would have been a suitable way in which to die, or men you'd hoped might have died in this way, even if they hadn't.

Herod the Great.

"Herod?"

He leaned across the space between them to whisper the word to Oliver, and Oliver leaned closer to listen. Charlotte, Alice and Kate were almost as close to them as they were to each other, and they could hear what Charlotte was saying.

"I remember . . ." she was saying. "I remember . . ."

When someone died you spent your time in remembering, hanging on to him or her for a little while longer.

"Herod?" Oliver repeated, and then, again, "Herod." He didn't say "No" this time. Ben thought of other possible names all the way back to Longfellow Park – it had been very quiet in the carriage – all the way back to *Welcome to the 20th Century!* and the Finches' house on Hudson Heights.

Silence in the carriage.

Silence as they arrived at Delft Place.

(How could Charlotte bring herself go alone through that door?)

Silence in the entrance hall.

Silence in front of Linnaeus's paintings.

Silence at first, and then the low-voiced talking started.

He and Oliver stood in front of one of Linnaeus's unpeopled canvases – the three women whispering closely together in front of another painting on the other side of the room – and Oliver repeated the name again.

As he had done in the cemetery, he leaned closer in toward Ben to whisper.

"Herod . . ."

The smell of his cologne was more noticeable inside.

(Friday afternoon after school . . .

(Just the two of them . . .

(Waltzing around the empty music room . . .

(One, two, three . . .

(One, two, three . . .

("La-di-*da*! . . ."

("La-di-*da*! . . ."

("La-di-*da*! . . ."

("You dance divinely, Mr. Pinkerton . . ."

("As do you, Mr. Comstock . . ."

("Your cologne lends a pleasing fragrance to the sophisticated *ambience*, Mr. Comstock . . ."

("I recommend Forty-Seven Eleven cologne for its agreeable and long-lasting bouquet. Connoisseurs clamor to sniff my armpits . . ."

("Might I make so bold as to grab a whiff? . . ."

("I recommend the left armpit. Apply your nostrils here-abouts . . ."

("Mnun! Enchanting! . . ."

(One, two, three . . .

(One, two, three . . .

(*Slender elegant youth soaked in scent* . . .

(The private language . . .

(The Concealed Spring . . .

(You Wound Up . . .

(You Let Go . . .)

"Herod?"

"Yes," Oliver said. "There *was* something about Herod, and it *was* in Latin."

631

"I don't remember Herod being mentioned in Room 37."

They sometimes said "Room 37" to avoid saying "Rappaport."

"No. It wasn't something we ever did in Latin, though it was in Latin. I remember reading it, and translating it. Parts of it *were* translated, and I translated the rest."

"Taking notes."

"Copious notes."

Oliver thought for a while, and then shook his head. "I can't remember the writer's name. Toward the end, Herod had a sickness that spread throughout his whole body . . ."

Oliver screwed his eyes up, trying to read the words that were written on something far away.

". . . He had many agonizing symptoms. Fever. His entire body itched unendurably, and his bowels were racked with pain. His feet and his abdomen swelled up grossly, he found it almost impossible to breathe unless he was placed upright, and all his limbs shook. His private parts festered, and worms came out." Oliver rather lingered in this last sentence. The words were clearly favorites with him, the chorus of a much-loved familiar song. "The translation described what was festering as his 'privy member,' but I didn't like that much. Distinct lavatorial overtones. That's what I thought."

"Quite appropriate."

"It was a punishment."

(*Worms*.

(*Writhing*.

(These were the words Ben remembered from the cemetery.)

"He was in such agony, that when he was cutting up an apple to eat, he tried to kill himself with the knife. He had his son put to death, and then died five days later." He paused, and thought awhile. "Do you think *we* ought to have offered an apple to Rappaport? A sort of suggestion, testing his Latinate awareness?"

"With a knife?"

"A well-polished apple and a well-sharpened knife. I'd smile at the apple of my eye, all apple-cheeked and cheeky . . ." – Oliver was rather too pale-skinned for this description to be entirely accurate – ". . . hypnotizing him with the dazzle of the blade. 'Stab yourself, you bastard.' That's what I'd be saying, in honeyed tones. 'Go on. Stab yourself.' I'd wiggle the blade about a bit. I'd be the queen with the poisoned apple, and he'd be Snowdrop."

"Not the most obvious comparison to bring to mind."

Oliver didn't even hear Ben.

He was far away, musing.

"'You silly girl!' he quoted. "'What are you afraid of? Do you think it is poisoned? Come! Do you eat one part and I will eat the other.' I'd be the fairest of all the fair, all because of an apple. 'The smell of thy nose like apples.'" He thought a little longer, and added, "'The Apples of Sodom.'" Ben didn't know what this meant, but it seemed a very Dorian Gray sort of comment, a very French sort of comment.

"*Worms*," Ben repeated, stressing the significant, the image of maggot-infested apples momentarily intruding.

"Yes."

"But he didn't *burst open?*"

(The apples writhed and rotted, the flesh brown and liquescent, quite inedible.)

Oliver shook his head.

"No. I'm sure I read about the bursting somewhere else."

"Another death?"

"Yes. Back to one of the Roman emperors. I *wish* I could remember."

"The bursting is absolutely essential?"

"Oh, yes. The bursting open, the exploding, the splattering across the floor and down the walls. *Splatter! Splatter! Splatter! Drip! Drip! Drip!* Essential."

"Worms. Writhing."

"Worms from inside him – lots of well-fed juicy ones from the private parts – writhing *everywhere*."

That was what Oliver wanted to happen to Rappaport.

He wanted it to happen slowly.

Kill, kill, kill, kill, kill him!
A cry heard . . .
A crash . . .
A cry horrible in its agony . . .
Knocking on a door . . .
Calling out . . .
Everything still . . .

Hanging upon the wall was a splendid portrait of their master as they had last seen him, in all the wonder of his exquisite youth and beauty, writhing with the worms that were consuming it.

Lying on the floor was a dead man, in evening dress, with a knife in his heart.

It was from this burst-open body that the worms had exploded.

When he'd returned home after they'd been to Delft Place – Alice had remained behind a little longer with Charlotte – he'd gone to look in the New Testament. He spent a long time looking. It was as good a way in which to keep out thought as any other.

Rappaport was still alive, and prospering.

This had not escaped Oliver's notice.

If Rappaport escaped the worms and the writhing – the imagination rather dwelt on "writhing" – then perhaps the swords through the private parts might prove an acceptable substitute. Something nasty involving private parts was quite the thing in Ancient Rome. He might mention this to Oliver, Oliver with his fencing lessons, his swisss-swisssh-swisssh expertise, his athletic leaping, his brightly shining *épée*, and he would hurl his *épée* – too thin, too fragile, too domestic with its darning needle daintiness – to the other side of the room, and seize upon a machete. It would be large and blunt and stained with much usage.

"*Touché!*"

That's what Oliver would be shouting as he lopped away, trimming an overgrown hedge. He'd enjoyed his little exploratory skirmish with the Reverend Goodchild, and now it was time for some serious lopping, time for screams and spurting blood.

Louder and louder grew the chanting and the applause.

Louder and louder the whimpering, the screams.

The machete would hack a pathway through the coconut matting, private parts shooting off to left and right as salivating dogs pounced. *Oliver* wouldn't be the slightest bit embarrassed at the very thought of a eunuch.

It would — at long last — be time to reenact the death of Melanthius, to restore the unjustly suppressed pages of *The Odyssey*.

(Eurymachus had been fun, but you became bored with nipples and livers after a time.)

Melanthius offered a far richer experience if you hungered for the hideous.

Dragged through the court.

Nose and ears lopped away.

Privates ripped off.

(Unidentifiable giblets-like gobbets flopping out, veins dangling loose, messy spurty gushings.)

Privates fed to the dogs.

Raw.

"Here, doggy, doggy!" Oliver would be calling, distributing the dismembered members with a free and bountiful hand. "Feeding time!"

(Barking, salivating doggies slobbering and crunching.

(*Crunch!*

(*Crunch!*

(*Crunch!*

(Barking, salivating doggies howling for more.

(Oliver generously obliging.

(Doggies cramming their mouths and chomping enthusiastically, rear quarters flailing with tail-wagging bliss.)

Swords through private parts.

Then worms and writhing.

Kill, kill, kill, kill, kill him!

You didn't wish to stint things when it came to planning suitable deaths. It seemed so grudging and housekeeperly, somehow.

635

On the morning of the Sunday that was his last day at home, immediately after the last-ever service in All Saints', Ben went upstairs to his room, where his clothes were laid out neatly — all ready — on the top of his bed, aligned precisely with the edges.

On top of the dresser — its oval mirror tilted back so that it reflected the ceiling — his smaller, personal items were set out in rows, all (like his folded clothes) ordered so that they were exactly parallel with the edge, and all (like his different items of clothing) not touching each other. He didn't like it when things touched. He'd done this the night before, slowly and methodically, when he'd returned from the theater, thinking about Kate, trying to organize his thoughts.

He'd emptied his pockets, and all his loose change was lined up in little carefully positioned columns — silvers and coppers, different values of coin in each column — with all the heads on top, all positioned to face in the same direction. He didn't look at them, didn't want to think about the eagles and the Liberties, the words and the faces.

White handkerchiefs.

Pocket book.

Cigarette case.

Pocket-watch with its Roman numerals.

Leather traveling case.

He sat down on the edge of his bed, and touched the traveling case, bought for him by the Calbraiths when he made his first voyage. He liked all the little separate compartments it had, the neat way the contents fitted together: the hairbrush, the comb, the scissors, the nail (*nail!*) brush, the soap box, the razor, the toothbrush, the little mirror . . .

The interior of All Saints' Church . . .

The Reverend and Mrs. Calbraith . . .

Kate . . .

Camera.

Bottle of quinine pills.

Combination knife.

Bible.

He touched the items, one by one, and lifted up his Bible to place it on the bed in front of him.

Was Mrs. Alexander Diddecott correct?

Would there be words to give him guidance if he opened it at random and read the first words that he saw, words that would speak to him at a time when he needed help? He'd found himself experimenting sometimes, attempting to make the Bible fall open at passages he knew, so that he'd read the words he wanted to read and be comforted by their familiarity.

He opened it at the first page.

For my beloved son, from Mama.

These words wouldn't count.

He paused for a while, and then opened it one-handedly, his fingers swissshing across the thin paper. Another, longer pause, and then he snapped it shut without reading the pages he had exposed.

No.

He wouldn't do that.

Seeing words would make him attempt to make them happen. He was too accustomed to obeying orders, and not yet skilled at giving them.

On the floor beside the bed was another book, the book he had been studying the night before in the moments before sleep. He'd come across it accidentally, not realizing that he still had it, that little children's book (small for small fingers), that worn book containing the first words that he had ever been able to read.

Jack, Jack, look at the rab-bit!

(Whispered words.

(Bedtime.

(Dim lighting.

(A shadow cast upon the wall.

(The shadow of a rabbit, cast from the shape of Mama's hands, her fingers held so that they produced the shape of what she said.

637

(Ears wiggling.

(Nose twitching.

(The smell of just-extinguished candle.

(A light in the corridor.)

He reached across to replace the Bible, and as he did so he caught the columns of coins with his arm, sweeping them all off the dresser, spilling them out across the dark floorboards between the rug and the wall, crashing and jingling.

That sound.

That contemptuous scattered-handful sound of the coins.

That mocking sound to drive an inadequate performer from the stage.

Some coins spun, or rolled right across the room – *Whirr! Whirr!* – but the sound that he was hearing was that initial crash as they hit the floor, that sound, and what it brought to mind, setting his heart jumping.

The inner room.

The inner room.

That sound.

That sound craved for by beggars; the sound that they degraded themselves to hear; the sound that had them scrabbling in the dust, fawning and whining, at the feet of those who'd carelessly flung down their small change in front of them.

A quarter spun at his feet, the persistent high-pitched vibration setting his teeth on edge, entering him.

He trod on it to silence it, and realized that he was trembling.

Heads or tails?

He did not allow himself to think of what this brought to mind, but squatted down – child-playing-in-sand posture – and began to collect up the coins, patiently reforming the neat unstable columns that he had knocked over. He had to concentrate, because of the trembling.

Kate . . .

His thoughts returned to Kate.

Kate had taken some photographs.

It was this, more than anything else, which made it seem like some sort of final farewell, a keepsake being created in order to keep memory alive. She'd taken them in the open air, despite the cold weather, and not in the house. Shivering, wreathed in the white mist of breathing, they'd stood in the snow for a while, assuming the positions that she requested. It made him think of a summer's day five years earlier when she'd also taken photographs of them all in the garden, the one occasion when Joseph had come to stay.

Linnaeus in the photographs.

Joseph.

("My friend, Joseph."

(That's what he'd kept saying.

(It was in letters home, to Mama and to Alice, and they were the words he spoke when he saw them.

("My friend, Joseph."

(They were words that he'd liked saying, this proof that some-one was his friend, and — this was somehow more important — that someone had chosen him to be a friend.

("My friend, Joseph," just like the times when he had said, "My friend, Linnaeus," or "My friend, Oliver.")

Everyone who had been there apart from Kate herself, had had a place in the photographs, though Alice — as usual — had turned her face to one side, hiding from the camera. Kate had an old-fashioned camera, one that involved glass negatives, and he understood little beyond this vague fact. He was more of a Kodak person himself, but Kate developed her own photographs. She chanted snatches of poetry during exposures, her method of ensuring the correct length of time that was required.

He'd promised to bring back something pretty for her, he remembered that (the same promise he'd made to Mama, to Alice, and to Charlotte) — but he imagined Kate thinking of what he'd said, repeating his words to herself. That's what he liked to imagine might happen. He always found it easier to say things to her when he knew that he was going away, even though he knew that he would be coming back. Words spoken on the point of leave-taking: these were the words that came most readily to him, the words that he felt he could speak best. He couldn't imagine himself speaking the day-to-day words, the commonplace utterances of living. These he had always found difficult. He didn't feel that he could know someone like that, living through the unheightened moments of the everyday. He could say things when he was leaving – when he knew that there would soon be no more words to say, and that the person to whom he was speaking would soon be left behind – that he could not otherwise have brought himself to speak, and would always be saying goodbye when he spoke of emotions. He spoke words of love, never seeing again the person to whom he was speaking, never having to prove the truth of those words. The point of leaving was the time when he spoke the best. Returns – after the first moments – were more difficult.

On the journey to Nagasaki he would think of his mother and of Kate, and of the city toward which he was traveling, the words in the book he was reading going ahead of him, drawing it closer, but – most of all – he would think of himself at the age of fourteen, reading *Madame Chrysanthème* at Grandpapa and Grandmama's house in Great Neck, a name he liked because it sounded somehow Red Indian and exotic. It was this book, Pierre Loti's book, which had created Nagasaki for him; this book, and Grandpapa's Japanese prints. The city was already there, in his mind, before he ever read Lafcadio Hearn.

At first he thought more about his younger self – a boy of fourteen – than of the book and the prints, his younger self lying waiting in the words and images of eleven years earlier, called into being by a return to the memories of that time, searching for guidance, a path to follow in the years ahead of him, the words to speak and the actions to perform. When a book was returned to after a long absence, it was not only the book that was found again: so was the person you had been when you last read that book, lying between the pages like grains of sand from a summer beach, or faded springtime leaves.

He had read *Madame Chrysanthème* secretly as he lay in bed in Grandpapa's study during his illness. He felt that it was a book of which his mama would not approve, that there was something erotic and immoral about it, as much as there was in any of the novels with which Oliver took pains to agitate his mother. The existence of a copy in *French* – Grandpapa spoke three languages – kept on the top shelf of the tallest bookcase, behind the English translation he had lifted down one day (a feeling that the original language possessed a licentiousness that could not be conveyed in English) – seemed to support this feeling, a feeling that added to the excitement of reading the book. He hadn't told Oliver about the book, because he felt a little embarrassed about having read it, something he ought not to have done.

Almost shyly, he thought of Madame Chrysanthème – a Madame Chrysanthème of his own – a girl bought and possessed, a girl whose language he could not speak, and who belonged to him. *Chrysanthème*, he thought, *Chrysanthème*, avoiding the word *Madame*, which sounded too like a woman, and a woman was much older than he was, someone the age of his mama.

Again, he wanted to find out what love was like; again, he wanted to experience that feeling. He had felt it only once before; for a few months he had felt it, the few months that had never happened.

Love didn't last for long.

He felt more excited about the voyage to Nagasaki than he had about any other voyage since the one to Italy, as though he were traveling toward an experience that would define who he was, and shape the pattern of the whole of his future life, as had (though he did not fully understand how) his experience in Italy. He thought of white, unnamed areas on maps; the pale blankness of an uncovered body in dim light; unknown areas of his own mind.

He tried not to think about Oliver.

3

Ben looked out through the window of the carriage, out at the falling snow in the darkness.

The words of *Madame Chrysanthème* were still in his mind. He'd been thinking of them on and off throughout most of the afternoon.

Precisely at dawn of day we sighted Japan.

Precisely at the foretold moment Japan arose before us, afar off, like a clear and distinct dot in the vast sea, which for so many days had been but a blank space.

At first we saw nothing in the rising sun, but a series of tiny pink-tipped heights (the fore-most portion of the Fukai Islands). Soon, however, appeared all along the horizon, like a thick cloud, a dark veil over the waters, Japan itself; and little by little out of the dense shadows arose the sharp opaque outlines of the Nagasaki mountains.

The wind was dead against us, and the strong breeze, which steadily increased, seemed as if the country were blowing with all its might against us, in a vain effort to drive us away from its shores . . .

We now entered into a shady kind of channel enclosed between the two high ranges of mountains, curiously symmetrical in shape — like stage scenery, very fine, though unlike nature. It seemed as if Japan opened to our view, through a fairy-tale rent, which thus allowed us to penetrate into her very heart . . .

Into that blank space, behind that dark veil, those dense shadows, he would be traveling; onto that stage he would move: that sensation again of being within a theatre, as if he were moving into a preordained story, within the pages of a book or a play, speaking words which had already been written, performing actions over which he had no control, penetrating her very heart. He was reaching out beyond his dead father, toward his living grandfather, traveling toward the country in which his grandfather had once lived.

The bright page dazzled, and the words could not be read.

"*Amo, amas, amat.*"

That's what he should be saying as he drew closer. He found himself thinking this, thoughts of Linnaeus. This had always been his formula for meeting the unknown, taking a deep breath and jumping as he recited them to himself, the formula taught to them by Dr. Crowninshield.

The Japanese – this was what his grandpapa had told him – did not say what was really in their minds. Much of what they were saying was not said in the words, but in their way of speaking, their looks and gestures. Things were not made explicit, and – to understand the hidden, unspoken meanings in what was being said – you had to translate the silences, find the covert truth behind what was happening.

This was a language he could speak, a language he had spoken – or not spoken – for years.

Perhaps he would find a place in which he belonged.

The snow had increased, and a wind was beginning to whip up the snow that had already fallen. He was traveling through a thick fog that was like low cloud come down to earth. He wiped at the mist upon the window, and peered out, thinking of the three women – almost invisible to him in the darkened room, faintly illuminated by the gaslight from outside the house – waving goodbye. He hadn't been able to see their faces. He thought of Mama. She'd been trying to say something to him. Her mouth had moved, attempting to form the words that she was unable to speak.

Hudson Row, when he was driven down it, seemed very wide and empty with all the awnings hooked away. The windows of the shops were dark, the wind howling down the deserted sidewalks.

After a while, he was being driven down one side of the park, its presence marked by an increase in the darkness outside, the lack of light from windows. There were a few lines of misty globes – very pale, no sense of warmth, little brightness – curving down alongside the paths that ran down to the lake. Even on a bright summer afternoon he wouldn't have been able to see the statue of *The Children's Hour* – his three sisters and Papa – from here. It was positioned too far away, next to the little glass pavilion where the birds would be huddled in the darkness, all song silenced. The figure of the man was supposed to be of Longfellow, but the body was Papa's. Alice had told him this. His sisters, as little girls, had been photographed with Papa when Carlo Fiorelli had been designing the statue. The bearded head of the poet seemed to have been pulled over Papa's features like a mask that didn't quite fit, that failed to hide who it was disguised behind it. The three little girls were positioned upon and around their concealed papa, like children disporting themselves in a sylvan landscape, rapt in the words he was speaking from the book he was holding. The words would be muffled – that's what Ben had thought, as a child – by the stiffness of the mask, the mask that made the face expressionless and unchanging. Edith was balancing on the stool behind the chair, her arms around Papa's neck, leaning over his left shoulder. Alice and Allegra were sitting on his knees, their arms entwined around him, the sides of their faces against the rough hair of his beard, looking up at him.

Ben was not a part of this family, and neither was Mama.

Papa, Alice, Allegra, and Edith: they were the Pinkertons.

This was something else he'd thought as a child, studying the bronze figures near the caged birds, walking around and around the group of which he'd never be a part.

Like the statues of Ancient Romans, like the marble men in The Forum, the man and the three girls were all blind, none of them with pupils to their eyes. Papa's right hand was touching the words on the page so that he could read them that way, drawing them across the tips of his fingers, a Braille-like decoding of the lesson that he was insisting that they learned by heart.

Ben had thought this, also.

"Franklin," Papa was saying. His lips were concealed behind the mask, and you couldn't see them moving.

"Franklin," his sisters were repeating.

(Even Alice.

(That's what he found himself thinking.)

"What a pretty little voice."

(Papa.)

"What a pretty little voice."

(His sisters, in *amo, amas, amat* singsong.)

"Shouldn't you be wearing a pretty little dress so that you'll look even more like one of your sisters . . ."

"Shouldn't you be wearing a pretty little dress so that you'll look even more like one of your sisters . . ."

The lesson.

". . . or would that make them feel jealous?"

". . . or would that make them feel jealous?"

"You certainly *sound* like one of them."

"You certainly *sound* like one of them."

"So shrill . . ."

"So shrill . . ."

(Shrill voices.)

"So dainty . . ."

"So dainty . . ."

(Dainty diction.)

"Did you say '*blushing*,' Franklin? . . ."

Where'er you walk . . .

No one was out there walking in this weather, even though it was a Sunday.

It was just like the view from the back of the house.

. . . cool gales shall fan the glade . . .

He tried to focus on something, straining his eyes to catch a glimpse of figures in the darkness.

. . . Trees, where you sit, shall crowd into a shade,
Where'er you tread, the blushing flow'rs shall rise,
And all things flourish where'er you turn your eyes.
Where'er you walk . . .

A voice from long ago, words distinct as those just spoken.
What could he see?
What could he see?
What could he see?
Emptiness.

ACKNOWLEDGEMENTS

I am grateful to the people who shared their knowledge with me and helped – if only temporarily – to fill some of the many vacancies in my head. They were generous, full of enthusiastic ideas, and helped me enormously. I should like, in particular, to thank Paul Barton, Phil Brown (www.wpbschoolhouse.btinternet.co.uk), Colin and Vivienne Rendall, Eve Hullcoop, Peter Richey, Dave Chapman, Margaret Donaldson, Mike Stainsby, and the North Yorkshire Library Service. The Catullus translations are by Gerard Galloway.

I owe a huge debt to the many writers whose books I consulted during the writing of this novel. I am not conscious of quoting from any copyright texts, but apologize if I have inadvertently done so.